ALMA

By the same author

ALMA

Glen Petrie

WEIDENFELD AND NICOLSON
London

First published in Great Britain in 1989 by
George Weidenfeld and Nicolson Limited
91 Clapham High Street, London SW4 7TA
Copyright © Glen Petrie 1989

Grateful acknowledgement is made to
the following for permission to reprint material:

John Murray Limited, for Alma Mahler,
Gustav Mahler, Memories and Letters,
edited by Donald Mitchell, London:
John Murray, 1973.

Faber and Faber Limited, for Johann Wolfgang von Goethe,
Faust, translated by Louis MacNeice, London:
Faber and Faber, 1953.

04861433

British Library Cataloguing in Publication Data
  Alma.
  I. Title
  823'914[F]
    ISBN 0-297-79527-9

Printed and bound in Great Britain by
Butler & Tanner Ltd, Frome and London

For
ALICE AND STEPHEN
with all love

CONTENTS

The more they praised me,
And the more I was admired –
The more I dreaded life on earth,
The more I longed to come awake.
(Anna Akhmatova, 1955)

PROLOGUE
DREAM CASTLES AND
CRAZY PRINCES: 1889-1892

 ALMA-MARIA WAS sitting on the stone ledge of the bedroom window – one of the many things her mother had told her never to do. She was watching Sophie in the garden, carrying a basket full of pea pods on her arm, and a kitchen bowl. Sophie picked her way round the overgrown edge of the moat pond, and went to sit down on a fallen tree trunk in the woodland shade beyond. There she began shelling the peas, filling the lap of her apron with the empty pods.

Sophie Haas was just turned fifteen. Four years older than Alma-Maria, she was the youngest of the housemaids, the daughter of a laundrywoman from Hernals, the poorest, most disreputable district of Vienna. Alma-Maria's mother objected to her making friends with the maids, but Alma-Maria talked to Sophie more than to anybody else in the castle. Sophie knew a world beyond Plankenburg Castle, a world Alma-Maria remembered only vaguely. It was the world of fashionably dressed ladies and smart, glittering uniforms, of polished carriages, clattering tramcars, of grotesquely ornamented street lamps and colossal, weather-stained statues spattered white and yellow with bird droppings. It was also a world of which Sophie spoke darkly – of lovelorn girls betrayed by gentlemen; where children sometimes starved, or were beaten for not begging enough on the streets; of girls forced to make a living by letting men do nasty things to them.

Alma-Maria jumped down from the ledge. She went down the back stairs. Her mother – Mutti – would be taking her afternoon nap in the

I

drawing room. Fräulein Weyss – *poor* Fräulein Weyss – would be taking
Grete for a walk in the woods. Grete, who was two years younger than
Alma-Maria, was so headstrong and naughty that Fräulein Weyss had
to devote her entire attention and limited energy to her, which suited
Alma-Maria very well. She went out by the garden door, past Pappi's
studio window, through the rose garden and out under the trees where
Sophie was sitting. She joined her on the fallen tree trunk.

Without turning her head to look at her, Sophie said, 'Some lucky
people have nothing to do all day but look for somebody to talk to.'

The smell of starch and carbolic soap about her didn't suggest bad
company and undesirable friendships.

'It's just that I like this spot,' lied Alma-Maria. 'The very first time
Pappi brought me here he said it reminded him of the story of Beauty
and the Beast. He said that this was the Beast's castle, and that when
Beauty came back to save the Beast from dying, she found him here,
lying by the water. He made it sound enchanted.'

'Enchanted!' Sophie snorted. 'Wish it was bloody enchanted. These
peas might shell themselves. The hall floor might scrub itself.'

'I'd be sorry, then.'

'You'd be sorry?'

'Because you wouldn't be here with us. There wouldn't be any work
for you, would there?'

'Huh!' said Sophie. 'There are a lot nicer jobs than this, I can tell
you.'

But Alma-Maria's little compliment had found its intended mark.
Sophie's voice softened.

'I've got a pal's got herself a real nice position – in the Prater. She
works selling tickets for the diorama. Sits in her booth all day – meets
lots of people ...' She giggled. ' ... Lots of handsome young soldiers,
eh? "Kiss your hand, Fräulein!" That's what I call a decent job.'

They sat in silence for a minute or two. Alma-Maria picked a pea pod
from the bowl in Sophie's lap, in the pretence of helping.

'What's all that about Beauty?' asked Sophie. 'And the Beast, when
it's at home?'

Sometimes when they were alone together like this, Alma-Maria retold
stories and legends. Sophie assumed a superior air; but she would tell
Alma-Maria to go on if ever she stopped in the middle of a story. Alma-
Maria told her the story of Beauty and the Beast as she had been told it
by Pappi. When she reached the final scene, and described how Beauty
gave water from the moat for the Beast to drink from her cupped hands,
how she tried to kiss the dying beast back to life, how finally she took
the rosebud from her gown, the perfect rosebud given her by her father,
Sophie let out such a squeal of laughter that she almost tipped the bowl
of peas over.

'I was going to say ...' Alma-Maria said angrily.

'Yes? Go on!'

'... Just that the Beast turned into a handsome prince, and he took her to live with him in his gorgeous palace, as his princess, for the rest of their days.'

'Went off and left her, more like,' said Sophie. 'And never came back to see her, ever again.'

'Why?' Alma-Maria demanded. She was hurt.

'Because that's what men do,' Sophie replied. Then she said, 'Your Pappi! He's a funny fellow.'

'Why?' Alma-Maria asked, rather more fiercely.

'Rosebud!' Sophie laughed again. Then a thought seemed to occur to her.

'Hasn't nobody ever told you what your rosebud is?'

Alma-Maria shook her head. Sophie reached over her disengaged hand and pressed gently with three fingers into the lap of Alma-Maria's pinafore.

'It's the bit in there – right inside.' She bent her face closer to Alma-Maria's ear. 'It's the bit you widdle with. It's the part men stick their things into if you let them get all hot and passionate.'

Alma-Maria went silent. She struggled to ingest this new, fearful interpretation of an old story.

'Sophie?' she asked at last. 'Has a man ever got hot and passionate with you?'

'You mind your business, and I'll mind mine,' Sophie told her, with a tight-lipped little smile.

Pappi was completing an important commission – a portrait in a landscape setting of Mathilde Moser, wife of Sigismund Moser, a wealthy Jewish banker with influence in the Hofburg. Herr Möll, his assistant – a perfect young country *Junker*, in English Norfolk jacket and plus fours – was watching over him, politely keeping him to his task. Herr Möll had his own studio in the castle, but he spent as much time negotiating the commissioning and sale of Pappi's works – at which, according to Pappi, he was wonderfully successful – as he did at his own painting.

Alma-Maria was sitting at the piano by the window overlooking the rose garden. She was playing Schumann's Opus 2 – 'Papillons' – to please Pappi. Schumann was his favourite composer. When she reached the end of the piece, she lifted her hands from the keyboard letting them hover there until the final note died away, as she had seen professional pianists do. On the lid the signed photograph of Liszt, with his long white hair, ascetic cheeks and clerical bands, smirked wickedly at her.

Herr Möll clapped his hands.

'Very good!' he cried. 'Bravo! A beautiful melody played by a beautiful maiden.'

3

She bestowed on him a radiant smile. She knew it was radiant because she had practised it many times in her mirror upstairs. Pappi stood at the easel, slightly stooped, frowning in concentration. From the sunlit rose garden, Grete's voice sounded shrilly querulous. She was telling off Fräulein Weyss, Alma-Maria couldn't hear the words because she was slightly deaf; she flattered old men by her attentiveness to them when they spoke.

Up on the meadow behind Plankenburg, they were cutting the hay; the scent of it was borne on the warm afternoon air. She turned over the music in front of her. She had abandoned her dreams of becoming a piano virtuoso like Clara Schumann after Pappi had taken her into Vienna to hear Hans Richter conduct Schumann's E-minor Symphony, the 'Rhenish', at the Musikverein. The oceanic sound had swept through her brain for weeks afterwards, inspiring in her a dream of becoming Austria's first great woman composer. But it was an ambition she had disclosed neither to Pappi nor to Dr Hübner, her music teacher.

Herr Möll took his leave. Alma-Maria began playing Schumann's Opus 9, number 13 – his nostalgic melody of regret for the lost sweetheart of his adolescence. Pappi said, still concentrating on his brush-strokes, '*Schatzi*, tell me. Do you think it's just possible I might have sold my soul to Carl Möll?'

'To Herr Möll, Pappi?' she stopped playing.

He quoted Goethe: ' "My dog is growing so long, so broad, He puffs himself up so mightily. That is not a dog's anatomy! So what demon have I admitted to my house?" '

'You couldn't have paid off the money you borrowed to buy Plankenburg but for Herr Möll,' she reminded him a little severely. 'You told me so, yourself.'

She loved it when Pappi confided in her as if she were grown up.

Pappi said, 'Perhaps he is of Baron Moser's race, eh? My very own house-Jew; a fellow who has his uses, but whom one is not compelled to like. What do you think?'

He put down his brushes and went and sat down in his armchair, easing his back with a sigh. She went over to him. Putting her hand on his shoulder, she drew his painter's smock from off his trouser legs to seat herself in his lap. As she settled onto him, she drew the long thickness of her blonde hair forward over her shoulder so as not to trap it under her. Pappi ran his fingers through it.

'So beautiful a *liebe Schatz*,' he murmured. 'How did I come to deserve such a beautiful daughter?'

'You chose to be my kindest Pappi,' she told him. 'That's all.'

Mutti would not have approved at all; Mutti said she was too old to sit on gentlemen's knees – even Pappi's. Grete's voice was quite distinct now, through the window. She was saying she wouldn't go in until Fräulein Weyss had found the ball she had lost in the briars.

'Pappi, do you think Herr Möll will ever be appointed a Kaiserlich-Königlich painter, like you?'

Pappi had been commissioned to provide watercolour and pen-and-ink illustrations for the Crown Prince Rudolf's book, *The Austro-Hungarian Empire in Words and Pictures.*

'I'm certain he will, *liebchen.* Carl Möll was made for success.' Now he sounded unhappy. Suddenly he said, 'I can't think what my life would be like without you.'

'Shush, Pappi!' she told him, uneasy at his sadness.

She came across Sophie the next morning, on her hands and knees waxing the boards of a passage upstairs.

'My God! Some people do find time lying heavy on their hands,' said Sophie.

Her round face was shining with sweat.

'Sophie, would you say Herr Möll was handsome?' asked Alma-Maria.

Sophie sat back on her ankles. With the edge of her sleeve, she pushed up a straggling lock of her hair which had stuck to her forehead.

'Put it this way,' she said. 'I expect there'd be quite a few girls'd say yes if Herr Möll asked them to go and see the cherry blossom with him.'

'Would you? Would you say yes if he asked you to go and see the cherry blossom with him?'

Sophie wrinkled her freckled nose. Then she shook her head.

'Handsome is as handsome does,' she said with a great air of wisdom. 'Any road,' she added, kneeling forward again and reaching for the pot of wax and her cloth, 'he'd never ask me.'

'Why not? You're pretty. *I* think you're pretty.'

'He's got quite enough on his plate as it is,' said Sophie.

She returned to rubbing the wax into the floorboards, leaving Alma-Maria to ponder her words as best she could.

For her twelfth birthday, Pappi took Alma-Maria to the Court Opera in Vienna, to see *Tannhäuser.* It was her first visit to the opera. That same night as they drove home through the Vienna Woods in the darkness, she was still dazzled by the glittering crystal lights of the foyer, the great staircases, the gilt, the silver braid and fur pelisses of the guards officers, the furs, white satins, and jewels of the ladies, the *mélange* of perfumes, and the clatter and crush of black varnished carriages in the lamplight of the ramp around the portico. There was the stage and the enchantment beyond the opened curtains: the subterranean luminosity of the Venusberg's craggy walls; the medieval splendour of the Wartburg; and strange Gothic landscapes with crumbling ancient castles glimpsed between forest trees.

But more than all that was the music. There had never been such music; there would never be such music again. Schumann's 'Rhenish'

Symphony was tepid stuff compared to its passion, its religious solemnity, its heart-stopping pathos.

Mutti had been waiting up for her return. Not Pappi's – she ignored him as he took off his coat and then went through to his studio.

'After half past one!' exclaimed Mutti. 'Far too late for a young woman at your time of life. Did anybody say how pretty you looked?'

One or two acquaintances of Pappi's had complimented her on her looks. It happened quite often. She was pretty – people told her so frequently. And she liked being pretty; she was quite sorry for girls who were not. But such considerations were utterly trivial compared to the magnificence of the music which rolled and sounded in her head. She wished she could have shared that experience with Mutti. But Mutti didn't have an ear for the sort of music she and Pappi liked. Mutti liked the music she had sung and danced to when she had been a singer at the Josefstadt Theatre, waltz songs, polkas, czardas, and sentimental ballads – the sort of songs she still sang sometimes in the drawing room to Herr Möll's accompaniment.

'Well, I can't say you look pretty now, *liebchen*,' Mutti told her, but not unkindly. 'you look exhausted.'

They went upstairs together. At the door of the bedroom she now shared with Grete (not because of any shortage of rooms in the castle, but because Mutti said it would be good for Grete to be with her elder sister), Mutti kissed her goodnight.

'Don't wake Gretl,' she whispered.

But Grete was awake. 'I bet it was boring, all that music going on and on and on.'

Alma-Maria managed to swallow her anger. As she undressed in silence, sat down at the mirror and loosened her hair, which was so long it touched the floor, she saw the reflection of Grete's face. There was a sort of greed in it which discomfited her. It was not, after all, her fault that she was prettier than Grete. After she got into bed, she tried to tell Grete the story of *Tannhäuser*. But Grete pretended she had fallen asleep even before she had reached the second act.

She was more successful with Dr Hübner the following morning, and when he came to give her her next lesson, he brought with him piano reductions for four hands of the Overture to *Tannhäuser*, the Venusberg Music and the Prelude to Act Three, so that they could play them together.

Sophie, too, was prepared to listen – at least to Alma-Maria's description of the inside of the Court Opera House, and the clothes, and uniforms and carriages. As a break from her housework, she was even prepared to listen to the story of *Tannhäuser*. However, when Alma-Maria had concluded the tale of how Elizabeth of Thuringia had saved Tannhäuser from spiritual destruction by her exemplary death, she remained unimpressed.

6

'You can't save men like that,' she said. 'Men aren't interested in being saved – not by women, any road. I mean, it's like this pal I had once. She was walking out with this Horse Dragoon – a real cavalryman with a fierce moustache and a proud way with him like he was the only man on earth. Anyway, she didn't like the stink of cigars on his breath and in his hair and on his uniform, and all that. So she said, if he loved her truly he'd stop smoking. And he did. Only he said, in return like, if *she* loved *him*, she'd let him – you know, don't you? – have his wicked way with her. Well – she's now got a baby, he's disappeared like I told her he would. And I bet you a million gold kreutzers the rotten bastard's smoking away like a railway engine.'

It hurt Alma-Maria to think that Sophie couldn't believe in the redemptive power of a woman's love. Next time she was sitting with Pappi in his studio, she asked him whether he believed there could be such a love.

'It is possible,' he said. He was painting, bending close to the canvas, applying tiny brush strokes with a look of utter concentration. 'It is quite possible,' he added. She had not liked to disturb him further. But a few days later, he called her into his studio.

'I have bought you a present, *liebchen*.'

He handed her a wide, flat book with a flamboyantly tooled and decorated cover. FAUST, she deciphered in the whorls of gold on the cover: Goethe's *Faust*. Each of the stiff pages was edged with gilt; every incident of the drama was illustrated in von Kreling's photogravure prints and line drawings. She could not find words to express her feelings.

'This is the most beautiful book in the world,' Pappi said, quietly serious. 'Read it. Keep it always.'

'Yes, Pappi.'

She lifted herself on her toes and kissed him. He took the book from her, turned to one of the final pages and showed it to her.

'This should answer your question,' he told her.

There was a full-page illustration: it showed the Blessed Virgin standing in a billowing ocean of cloud, her entire figure haloed in a blaze of light which split the cloud at her feet; below her was the figure of a naked, dying Faust reaching up toward her through the starry air; beside him was the half-draped figure of Gretchen, supporting his arm, the glow of light about her indicating that, for all her sins, she was already numbered among the Blessed. On the opposite page was the text:

> All that is past of us
> Was but reflected,
> All that was lost in us
> Here is corrected;
> All indescribables
> Here we descry;
> Eternal Womanhead leads us on high.

7

'You see, *kleine Schatz*?' Pappi smiled. He handed the book back to her. 'Let this be our secret, eh?' he said. 'Put it away. Don't tell anybody I gave it to you.'

When Grete had gone out with Fräulein Weyss for a walk down to Tulln, Alma-Maria went up to the bedroom. She hid the book at the bottom of a drawer, under her shifts and bodices and stockings. During the nights which followed, she forced herself to stay awake until Grete was asleep. Then, by the light of a single candle, she took out the book and read. Part One she read easily, voraciously. She was struck in particular by the summerhouse scene, the final stage in Faust's seduction of Gretchen. There was little dialogue and even Alma-Maria could see that it wasn't Goethe's greatest verse. But opposite it was a full-page photogravure of Faust and Gretchen kissing, their lips parted as if to devour one another's mouths, her arms flung tight about his neck, her breasts pressed against his chest, his hands in her back touching the swell of her skirts, drawing the apron lap of her gown between his parted thighs. Alma-Maria had never seen a kiss so graphically portrayed: she was both embarrassed and fascinated, as if she had stumbled upon an encounter at which she had no business to be present.

'You'll have to wear spectacles if you read in that light,' said Grete, her shrill voice coming as a nasty shock. Alma-Maria slid the book under the bed. It chinked against the chamber pot.

'You wouldn't look at all pretty in spectacles, you know,' said Grete.

Then she slumped down on the pillow, turned her back, and pretended that she had dropped off to sleep immediately. Alma-Maria blew out the candle. She intended to hide the book again once she was quite sure Grete really was alseep. But before the moment of certainty had come, she was asleep herself.

After breakfast the following morning, when Grete was in the school-room with Fräulein Weyss, she ran back upstairs.

But the book was gone from under the bed. Foolishly, she searched the drawer, as if she might have replaced it in a fit of abstraction or in her sleep. The limpness of the clean petticoats and stockings mocked the absence of the hard binding of the tooled covers.

As she returned downstairs, Mutti called her into the drawing room. She noticed instantly the gilt-ornamented volume tucked under Mutti's arm. She saw also the open door of the tiled stove in the corner and the blaze of the flames inside.

'No!' she cried. 'You mustn't!'

'I'd have burned it already, I can tell you! Only I thought you should see for yourself.'

'Please Muttichen! No!' Alma-Maria implored.

'You needn't "Muttichen" me, my girl,' Mutti told her. 'This is filth!

Where did you get it – as if I didn't know?'

'Pappi says it's the most beautiful book in the world!'

' "Pappi says"!' Mutti mocked her so vehemently that Alma-Maria wondered whether her mind had become unhinged. 'You and your father! Don't I have any say in your upbringing any more? Have I ceased to exist, only nobody's bothered to tell me?'

It was all such nonsense that Alma-Maria couldn't find anything to say except to murmur, 'Oh Muttichen!'

She wanted to cry out – I want to be as beautiful as you, to wear smart clothes the way you do, I want you to tell me you're proud of me and you love me! But there was no way she could make the words come. Instead she stood and watched dumbly as Mutti threw Goethe's *Faust* into the stove. The gold-edged pages buckled, curled, burned and turned to blackened rags. The photogravure portraits of Faust, Gretchen, and Mephistopheles became martyrs consumed on their individual pyres, while through her tears, she saw the yellow flame tips turn to stars.

She was going one afternoon to Pappi's studio, her music clutched to her breast, when she heard an extraordinary noise coming from the room. It was somebody thumping at the piano as if he wished to demolish the keyboard, and shouting in a shrill falsetto that kept lapsing into hoarseness under the strain. One of the housemaids was pretending to be sweeping the floor in the passage outside. She was grinning all over her broad peasant face.

'Your Pappi has a friend in there.' She nodded her head towards the door.

She turned away to whisk an imaginary speck of dust out of the corner with the edge of the broom.

'Do you know who he is?' asked Alma-Maria.

'They say it's a Herr Wolf,' the maid told her. She shrugged her shoulders. Then she said, 'Maybe he'll eat you if you go in,' and laughed, so that Alma-Maria wondered if the visitor's name really was Wolf.

The voice inside cracked at the climax of a screech. Alma-Maria plucked up courage and went in.

Pappi was standing at his shrouded easel. She noticed how his fingers clutched at the sheet covering it. Seated at the piano was a little man whose black hair was *en brosse*, and whose face was prematurely wizened. She noticed how his shabby suit hung from his frame, as if he had suddenly lost weight through illness. He was not looking at her; he showed no sign of being aware of her having come in. His eyes glared past her with a red, vulpine intensity she had never seen before. He was sweating with the effort he was putting into his dreadful, half-strangulated shouting.

9

He stopped, gulping for breath, the ponderous beads of sweat bumping over the deep lines of his black-stubbled jowls.

'What was that you were playing?' Pappi asked.

He sounded nervous. The little man leered.

He shouted suddenly – '*Aida*!' – so that Alma-Maria jumped. '*Aida*,' he repeated. 'I wrote it in a fit of aberration.'

He looked down at his outspread fingers.

'Music for market porters to howl in the street,' he said gloomily. 'I wrote it – or didn't I write it? A metaphysical problem.'

A smile came over his features like that of a child when it sees something which pleases it.

'Perhaps I did!' he declared. 'Am I not part of that great cosmological whole – that vast entity – which composed *Aida*?'

He noticed Alma-Maria standing at the door. He pointed one finger at her and lifted himself from the piano stool.

'What's that?' he shouted. 'What's it doing? Is it a lightning conductor, or what?'

Alma-Maria caught Pappi's eye. Pappi shook his head slightly. She slipped back out of the door into the passage. The maid was still pretending to sweep. She didn't look up as Alma-Maria went past, but she was still smiling to herself.

'What was the matter with him?' Alma-Maria asked Pappi after Herr Wolf had taken his leave. They were walking in the woods together.

Pappi sighed. 'Poor fellow,' he said. 'I knew him quite well in the old days – before he started behaving like that. They say he was a fine composer – still is, for all I know. Bruckner thought highly of him, and I believe Humperdinck insisted Schott's should publish his scores. But he earns nothing – nothing! And his family won't help to support him. They regard him as a wastrel. Perhaps it's hunger that's turned his brain – that, and self-neglect. He's convinced that Brahms and what he calls the Brahmins are stealing his work and pretending it's composed by Wagner or Verdi . . . He isn't always like that, of course. He usually gets these attacks when he's come back to Vienna from Bayreuth. You know, *liebchen*, I do feel Wagner is bad for some people.'

Alma-Maria was convinced that Wagner's influence couldn't be anything but morally and spiritually uplifting. She decided to have a talk with Sophie Haas.

Sophie had no doubt whatever as to what had been the matter with Pappi's visitor. She had been chattering to the gardeners about him when Alma-Maria found her. She was standing in front of a bonfire of swept leaves, her outdoor coat flung over her shoulders against the autumnal chill. Her cheeks were reddened in the glow and smoke of the bonfire.

'It's an illness people get from loving,' she told Alma-Maria.

She examined her carefully in case she was leading her out of her depth.

'They call it the English disease,' she said. 'There's a lot of it about. You'd be surprised.'

With the edge of her boot, she pushed together a small heap of leaves, then prodded it into the bonfire with her toe.

'Gentlemen get it from going with the sort of girls that haven't got any self-respect,' she went on. 'The sort of girls that don't look after themselves properly, don't keep themselves clean and that. So you can say gentlemen only get it when they've been behaving like animals. It's what they deserve, if you ask me.'

There was a gust of wind. The mould-scented smoke from the bonfire eddied, then flattened over the leaves. Listening to Sophie, Alma-Maria thought, was like spotting unexpectedly a dead animal in the undergrowth: your curiosity compelled you to take notice even though you weren't at all sure you wanted a closer look.

'Some do say it's God's punishment for wickedness,' said Sophie. 'Only it isn't all that quick. I mean, it can take years before somebody starts going barmy. But that's the usual reason why men go barmy.'

The sweet scent of the smouldering leaves mingled with the images which Sophie's words had conjured up in her mind. It made her feel sick.

From the end of winter and through early spring, one topic dominated conversation, the death of Crown Prince Rudolf, at his hunting lodge Mayerling, beside the body of his eighteen-year-old mistress, Marie Vetsera. A week after the event, the Crown Prince's first cousin, the Archduke Johann Orth, was dining – informally of course – at Plankenburg. There had been talk in Vienna of the whole thing having been set in motion by agents of Clemenceau and the French government; there were rumours that Marie Vetsera's Levantine uncles, the bankers Baltazzi, had been persuaded by Berlin to push their sexually promiscuous little niece in the direction of the Crown Prince in order to destabilize the Hapsburg hold on Southern Europe.

On one thing everybody around the table agreed: that the new heir, the Archduke Franz Ferdinand, a prematurely ageing martinet who had married a Czech woman – a vulgar *arriviste* – was an unmitigated disaster, and the thousand-year Hapsburg Empire would surely disintegrate with the passing of the Old Man.

The Mayerling affair inspired Alma-Maria to undertake a song-cycle which – like the song-cycles of Schubert and Schumann – dealt with doomed young love. Dr Hübner was most impressed when, during her music lesson, she played over and sang one of these pieces – 'What the Wild Rose Told Me'. She caught him staring at her with a look of wonderful tenderness in his gaunt, ascetic face.

The next time he came out to Plankenburg, he brought with him a four-hand piano reduction of the Prelude and 'Liebestod' from *Tristan and Isolde*. He told her the story of the opera – how Tristan and Isolde found that only in death could their love be truly consummated. They played it through together, Alma-Maria demonstrating her extraordinary facility at sight-reading. When they reached the end, she sighed.

'It is greater music than *Tannhäuser*, isn't it?'

'Wagner was writing from his deepest personal feeling,' Dr Hübner told her.

'I thought so,' she replied.

She was profoundly moved both by the tragic, heroic fatalism of the story, and the music. She looked up into Dr Hübner's face and saw once again the softness directed at her.

'Will you do me a great favour, Herr Doctor Professor?' she asked.

'What is it?'

'More than anything in the world, I think, I would like to have a copy of Goethe's *Faust* – only, my mother says I'm too young, and it's a bad book. Do you think it's a bad book, dear Herr Doctor Professor?'

'No, *liebchen*. I don't. And for someone who has such a feeling for Wagner's *Tristan* ...' He broke off.

'Yes, dear Herr Doctor Professor?' she urged.

'If your noble and well-born mother thinks you shouldn't ...'

'Mutti needn't know about it,' said Alma-Maria. 'I'd never betray you.'

Dr Hübner was quite taken aback. He laughed abruptly.

'My dear child!'

But on his next visit, he took from his music portfolio a copy of *Faust* in the Tauschnitz pocket edition. Alma-Maria slipped it straight into her own portfolio.

'You are kind, dear Herr Doctor Professor,' she told him. 'And I do love you.'

She would have kissed him, but she saw the anxious confusion in his face and thought better of it.

That evening, as she sat at the piano by candlelight, she examined the small volume, holding it inside a copy of Mozart piano sonatas. She was reading the lines:

> Saved, saved now is that precious part
> Of our spirit world from evil:
> Should a man strive with all his heart,
> Heaven can foil the Devil.
> And if woman's love, also from on high,
> Has helped him through his sorrow,
> Hallowed legions of the sky
> Will give him good goodmorrow ...

Woman's love, also from on high ... If she closed her eyes the candles in their brackets on either side of the music rest shone like haloed orbs. Gretchen, she thought; Elizabeth of Thuringia, Isolde, poor Marie Vetsera, and one day, who knows? perhaps even herself, all rising heavenwards, holding the hand of some stricken hero-knight, some man of genius, towards the welcome, reconciling figure of the *Mater Gloriosa*.

Picturing the scene, she felt so close to the Blessed Virgin that tears started in her eyes. Though she had not been to the parish church since midnight Mass at Christmas, she felt a profound sense of pity for all those – Protestants like Muttichen, and Jews, infidels, and atheists – who were denied the consolation of praying to the Mother of God.

She was going upstairs to the room she shared with Grete, the copy of *Faust* only half hidden under her shawl because she didn't expect to meet anyone at that hour, when the door of Mutti's room opened, and Herr Möll came out. There was nothing very wrong about his appearance – an unaccustomed ruffledness about his shirt at his waist, and slight folds on the shoulders and back of his smoking jacket where he hadn't pulled it straight. There was also his look of discomposure as he said, 'Good evening, Fräulein Almschi,' just a little too loudly.

He didn't think to ask what was the little book she had, pressed tight between her sleeve and her skirt, under her shawl.

For Alma-Maria, the symbol of her growing up, the before-and-after of the end of childhood, was not the onset of her periods, uncomfortable though they were, and the development of her figure; it was being allowed to catch the train into Vienna from Tulln unaccompanied, to take lessons in harmony and counterpoint at the Votivkirche from Dr Josef Labor.

Dr Labor was a legendary figure – blind from birth, he was, nonetheless, a distinguished composer of church music, choirmaster of the Votivkirche, and a virtuoso organist. What made him still more awesome was that he had been or still was the friend of every composer anyone cared to mention – Brahms, Bruckner, Liszt, even Wagner. An old man, secure in means and reputation, there was no need for him to accept pupils. But he had been Dr Hübner's master, and both Dr Hübner and Pappi agreed that Alma-Maria should ask to be taken on by him.

She had found him, a white bearded giant, stooped in the semi-darkness of the great church, over the organ console high above choir and chancel. All around were dusty baroque hatchments and tattered Imperial banners. He was like the old centaur couched in the mouth of his Thracian mountain cave, blindness and years conferring upon him a look of stern wisdom. For the first time in several years, she was encountering a man she would be unable to impress with her looks or her radiant smile.

He had fixed his staring, albumen white eyes on her, as if he could see her in his private darkness.

'Julius Hübner tells me you compose,' he said.

The blank eyes searched her. There was no defence she could offer against them.

'Not very well,' she said, her voice trembling slightly.

'Julius Hübner thinks he is justified in sending you to me,' he retorted gruffly.

'I meant, I know I have a great deal to learn, Herr Doctor Composer.'

'Kapellmeister,' he corrected her.

'I'm sorry, Herr Kapellmeister.'

He nodded. 'We must hear some of your pieces – hear how you play them, also. How old are you?'

'Thirteen, Herr Kapellmeister.'

'And you wish to be a composer?'

'If I have the talent.'

'Talent is God-given of course. It isn't like physical beauty, which is inherited, or skill, which I might be able to teach you if you are apt enough. Are you good-looking, by the way?'

'People tell me I'm pretty, Herr Kapellmeister.'

Dr Labor nodded again.

'Clara Schumann wasn't pretty,' he said. 'There's nothing like good looks in a woman to take the edge off artistic endeavour, eh?'

He grunted and pulled himself up from the organ seat. He reached for his stick; she considered handing it to him, then thought better of it.

'We'd better take you to a piano, youngster,' he told her. Unhesitatingly he led her down the steps of the organ loft. She followed him across the nave of the church to a narrow door, then up a narrow spiral staircase to a small turret room whose narrow window overlooked the Schottentor and the side of the University building. There was a grand piano and cupboards filled with sheet music, and little else. The room smelt of damp. The windowpanes were smeared with bird droppings.

Dr Labor stood resting his elbow on the piano lid, his cane dangling between his fingers.

'Who is your favourite composer, youngster?' he asked.

He pointed to the piano stool. She sat down.

'Wagner, Herr Kapellmeister?'

She made it sound like a question because she was feeling increasingly nervous. She wondered whether Dr Hübner had exaggerated her musical ability.

'Wagner, eh?'

Friend of the great master he may have been – but he did not sound altogether approving. She fumbled in her music case.

'Well?' he asked.

There came a moment of inspiration. Instead of pulling out something from one of her two almost completed song-cycles, she chose a modest Andante and Scherzo for solo piano, an exercise prescribed by Dr Hübner some eight weeks previously. Even while she was playing it, she could see by the way that Dr Labor nodded his head and swung his cane like a pendulum that she had chosen correctly.

When she had finished, he said:

'So you wish to be my pupil, Fräulein Schindler?'

'If you please, Herr Kapellmeister.'

'Then you shall be, if your father writes to me to tell me that it is on his authority.'

'Thank you, Herr Kapellmeister.'

She struggled to keep the excitement out of her voice – not altogether successfully.

'I shall expect my first lady pupil to approach her work with the utmost seriousness. You may find me a hard taskmaster,' Dr Labor said.

'I don't want anything else,' she said. Then: 'I don't want anything else in the world!'

'That from a pretty young maiden, eh?' he asked.

'You shall see, Herr Kapellmeister.'

Over the next few weeks she demonstrated her seriousness by the strict attention she paid to his lessons. Dr Labor rewarded her by introducing her more deeply into the works of Wagner – meaning as well as music. Once, to reward her for a well-learnt lesson, he took her up to the organ loft in the church, and allowed her to attempt the Prelude to *Parsifal* on the organ. Being small, her feet could scarcely reach the pedals; he sat beside her and played the pedal clef for her as she, wondering and amazed, heard in response to her light, pianist's touch, the mighty Grail leitmotiv roll round the stone piers and vaulted arches of the huge church.

Her weekly visits to Dr Labor at the Votivkirche became the most important feature of her life, so that when Pappi called her into his studio one bright morning and said, '*Kleine Schatz*, would you like to come with me to Munich?' her immediate response was the thought that it would mean missing several of her precious lessons.

The success of the late Crown Prince Rudolf's book, *The Austro-Hungarian Empire in Words and Pictures*, with Pappi's illustrations, had led to Pappi's being invited by the Regent of Bavaria to go to Munich to discuss the possibility of a book celebrating the architectural extravagances of his predecessor, King Ludwig II. On the one hand, it would mean missing her music lesson: on the other, Bavaria had been Wagner's chosen home, and the castles which Pappi was being invited to paint and draw were castles inspired by Wagner's stories.

Herr Möll was in a painter's smock, varnishing a canvas. Without looking up from his work, he remarked, 'Perhaps our little Almschi is shy of meeting the Prince Regent of Bavaria.'

'Why? Don't you want to come, *liebchen*?' Pappi asked.

Herr Möll had challenged her. Very well, she would have Pappi all to herself – at least some of the time.

'Of course I want to come with you, Pappi,' she said firmly.

Mutti's immediate response was to take Alma-Maria in the carriage to Aldmüller's in the Kärntnerstrasse to buy a wardrobe suitable for a guest of royalty. The day was pleasant. They drove with the carriage open, holding parasols over their shoulders.

They descended from the Vienna Woods through Döbling, and onto the Währingerstrasse.

'Many years ago, when I used to take a drive on the Ring in an open *fiacre*,' said Mutti, 'every other gentleman, at the very least, used to raise his hat and bow to me. I was really quite famous. And young, of course: both the Ring and I were young in those days, and we had our looks.'

'You are still very, very pretty, Muttichen,' Alma-Maria told her.

She was completely sincere. Mutti's style and appearance made her feel gauche.

'Do you really think so, *meine liebchen*?' Mutti asked.

'Truly, Muttichen.'

A slight sadness came over Mutti's face. She turned her head away.

'Do you know? You've never said anything like that to me before. I appreciate it, Almschi. I really do.'

She gave Alma-Maria's hand a little squeeze.

At Aldmüller's Alma-Maria was fitted with a complete wardrobe of evening and day dresses. Afterwards, they walked across the Kärntner-strasse to Demel's for coffee and tortes – Mutti having explained that one could not go shopping in Vienna without going to Demel's. It did not take Alma-Maria long to see why. She had been sitting only a moment or two admiring the swirl around her of silk hats and taffeta matinée gowns, when a stout, middle-aged gentleman approached to greet Mutti:

'My most devout compliments – Frau Schindler, I suppose one *must* call you, though I confess you will always remain Fräulein Anna Bergen to me ... I hope that does not offend you, *liebe* Frau?'

It was clear from Mutti's gracious smile as she extended her small hand to be kissed, that she was not in the least offended.

'You have been too long in exile, *liebe* Frau ... Or rather, it is we, your poor devotees, who have been in exile while you have been absent from our midst ...'

He was the first of a procession of middle-aged or elderly gentlemen, top hats held to their breasts or uniform caps under their arms, who came to the table to unload their flowery compliments to an unwearied Mutti, and to exclaim at Alma-Maria's resemblance to her.

As soon as her new clothes were delivered to the castle, she ran to her room to try them on. As usual, Pappi was in his studio. Over the years, it had become his virtual home, into which he had withdrawn like a snail into his shell. He was sitting on the window shelf overlooking the rose garden, hugging his knees, his empty pipe clenched between his teeth. Sunlight streamed about his head and beard.

'Do you think I'll do my famous Pappi justice?' Alma-Maria asked. She turned around coquettishly.

'The real question, *kleine Schatzi*, is whether your poor, decayed old Pappi could possibly be worthy of you,' he said.

'Don't talk nonsense!' she retorted. 'I want you to look at me properly. Critically. And tell me what you really think.' She plucked at the skirt. 'Mutti helped me choose it, of course.'

'You had an excellent counsellor,' he replied. 'The best. Your Mutti always had perfect taste in clothes. So what I really think is . . . that you look exquisite.'

'Truthfully?'

'Truthfully. On my honour as a true-born *Herr*.'

'Mutti was very kind to me today,' said Alma-Maria.

In fact, she suspected, Mutti was pleased they were going away.

She went over to Pappi with her arms outstretched like a little child longing to be hugged.

'I want to be with you always!' she said.

He gathered her to him.

'Always, *liebling*? Are you sure? You are going to be a very beautiful young woman – quite soon. And there will be many, many beautiful young men who will want you to stay with them always.'

'It's you I want to stay with, *liebe* Pappi!' she told him. 'Always and always!'

Prince Luitpold stood at the carriage step. All about was the heavy scented gloom of the fir tree forest. He lifted his arms to Alma-Maria.

'Come, little princess,' he said to her, raising his voice above the clangor of the River Pollat rushing down its ravine nearby.

She entrusted herself to his arms, old though he was. He smiled at her as he placed her on the ground, then twisted his moustache ends into place. He was not at all the awesome figure she had expected him to be. In fact, they were becoming fast friends. During the first days of their tour, when Prince Luitpold had led them round the Residenz in Munich, and the country palace and hunting lodges of Herrenchiemsee, it became clear that Pappi had to be allowed to take his own time in order to make rapid sketches as *aides-mémoire*, and to scribble notes. So Alma-Maria became the Prince's particular companion. As always with tall gentlemen, and the Prince was very tall and erect, she had to look directly up at him when he spoke, and he inclined to her. Their attitude

to one another when they were talking suggested a confiden-
tiality, sometimes even a conspiracy, between them. He called her his
'little princess', and no sooner had he begun to do so than the equerries
and palace chamberlains who were always in attendance started displaying a flattering deference towards her.

Leaving Pappi a few paces behind, she walked with him up the broken,
unfinished road to the temporary, narrow iron bridge over the ravine.
As they turned the steep bend and stepped out from the forest darkness,
her breath was snatched from her by the spectacle before her. The spray
leaped from the ravine, soaking the planks of the bridge so that they
shone from under a curtain of mist. Above the mist rose a red sandstone
gatehouse with crenellated ramparts and turrets and a high watchtower.
Behind that, looming above both ramparts and watchtower, and dwarfing
them, was a castle – a castle as she had imagined a castle should be when
she was a small child, its ivory turrets and pinnacles thrusting their
spires in competition with one another to touch the sky, with graceful
lancet windows and tiny balconies from which imprisoned princesses
could let down their hair. Behind the castle, high above its topmost
spire, reaching over it as if to frustrate the endeavours of its pinnacles
was a massive Alpine crag, its peaks shrouded in drifting, torn cloud
through whose ragged holes sunlight dazzled from wet rock faces. As
she stood staring, her head as far back as it would reach, Wotan's
triumphant description of Valhalla sang in her head – *Auf Berges Gipfel
die Götterberg* . . .

> On mountain summits stands the citadel of the Gods:
> Gloriously gleams the glittering building
> Designed in my dreams,
> By my will brought to life . . . .

Pappi must have been reading her thoughts. She felt his hand on her
shoulder, his beard touching her neck, as he said in her ear above the
roar of the mountain river under their feet,

'Remember, *Schatzi*, being drawn into other people's dreams can be
dangerous.'

The Prince offered her his arm to lead her across the bridge. She
looked up at Pappi, half expecting him to hold her back. But he had
taken his sketch pad from the rucksack on his shoulder, and was holding
a bunch of pencils in his hand.

'Come in, little princess,' called Prince Luitpold. 'Your father has
better things to do than to keep company with heathens like us. We'll
let Herr Blomberg show us round inside while your father sets about his
work, eh?'

She took the Prince's arm, but glanced back at Pappi just the same.
Pappi, however, was already staring up at the castle towers and was
absorbed in what he saw, so that she wondered if she had only imagined

the words she had heard him say to her.

As they followed Herr Blomberg, the castle superintendent, up to the gateway, and through the gatehouse into the courtyard, more and more she had the sense of being enclosed, of being drawn inwards – separated from the mountains and forest slopes, and Pappi. The courtyard and all else around her was smaller than she had expected from the outside, cramped almost. The ivory white walls were built high to exclude all view of the world outside. A steep flight of marble steps led them to the entrance of the keep – a narrow door. They passed into the minstrels' hall. She recognized immediately what it was supposed to represent – the minstrels' hall in Act One of *Tannhäuser* – even before Herr Blomberg told her. But it was ridiculous. To start with, it was far too small, and the pictures and mock tapestries round the walls – scenes from *Lohengrin* and the Ring Cycle – were ponderously heavy and literal, while the light through the thick stained-glass windows cast lurid colours everywhere and seemed to exclude air as well as view. Herr Blomberg took an age explaining the pictures and tapestries to her, reciting the stories illustrated by them at detailed length, though she probably knew them better than he.

They passed from the minstrels' gallery to the throne room, a blue, porphyry and gold basilica – a Byzantine cathedral in miniature – then through jewel- and gold-encrusted anterooms and spiralling marble staircases. The evidence of madness, thought Alma-Maria, was everywhere – the riotous obsession with Wagner's operas at every corner, the refusal to admit daylight anywhere. It was not difficult to imagine in the jewelled gloom on the turn of a turret staircase the rain-swept June night in 1886, when, as companies of armed police with fixed bayonets rushed the sentries, the drunken King tottered from room to room, staircase to staircase, in a despairing attempt to throw himself from the platform of the high tor down into the courtyard below.

They entered the royal bedchamber. It was a gothic chapel, a forest of perpendicular arches, palm-vaulting, and carved, pointed finials. The King's bed, to one side of a huge stove fireplace, was canopied and enclosed, with narrow lancet windows in three sides like a late medieval tomb. On the other side of the fireplace was a low arched door. Alma-Maria looked up just in time to see Prince Luitpold winking at his two equerries. It was no more than a split second, but it would remain imprinted on her memory.

'His late Majesty's private reading room,' Herr Blomberg announced.

Prince Luitpold gently guided her through the arch from behind, as Herr Blomberg switched on the electric lighting.

The lights were at floor level. The illumination rose up the walls like fountains, revealing one single comprehensive mural consisting of tree-roots winding tendrils round cave mouths, and beyond the cave mouths, ever-receding vistas of subterranean grottoes and lakes. In the foreground, on a rock, sat the lifesize figure of a prettily handsome minstrel knight, his hand resting upon his harp which stood on the ground beside him. It was, of course, Tannhäuser, Alma-Maria realized, and the cavern that under the Horselberg where Venus, the demon-temptress, lured men to destruction by granting them a vision, a hint of a promise, a sensual fulfilment. Venus herself was beside the knight; she was crowned, and was sitting on her own hair which was as long and full as that of Alma-Maria herself; her breasts were bare, but a corner of white satin was draped over the tops of her thighs. Her arm was about Tannhäuser's shoulder. Close beside where Tannhäuser and Venus were sitting stood Venus's handmaids, three well fleshed naked women smiling vacantly, with hard erect nipples, a faint bluish shadow under their bellies suggesting that their pudenda had been shaved, and a slight indentation to hint at the cleft between their thighs. But it was not to these three women that Venus was drawing Tannhäuser's attention. On the wall opposite, in a grotto immediately through one of the cave mouths, another naked attendant was lying sprawled on a satin-draped rock. Her slabby thighs were parted; between them, mounting her groin, was a great white swan, its powerful wings spread, a coronet about its arched neck. On the face of the woman was a wide-eyed, open-mouthed look of surprised, stupid, pleasure.

Alma-Maria turned back to the bedchamber. She felt sick and weak with disgust. She saw the observant grinning of the equerries which they altered as soon as she turned to them, but not quickly enough. She felt very alone.

'If you please, Highness,' she said. 'I want to go back to my father.'

Prince Luitpold hesitated only a moment before saying in his usual kindly and concerned manner,

'Of course you shall, child.' Then he said, 'I'm afraid I don't often visit this place, my dear. I had forgotten ...' He hesitated again ... 'that some of the late King's taste in decoration is hardly suitable for a young lady's gaze.'

He offered her his arm. As he led her down, back through the castle, he was all concern and consideration. Out in the courtyard where at least the air was fresh and clean, he told her,

'Tomorrow we shall go to Linderhof. I'm sure you will like Linderhof – it is a charming place, a civilized place, not at all like Neuschwanstein ... We shall look forward to it, shall we not?'

That night as they dined at the comfortable inn in the little town of Hohenschwangau, Pappi did not notice in the least that she had been upset. He was only delighted at the rapport which seemed to have grown between his daughter and Prince Luitpold.

'I shall take you everywhere I go, *kleine Schatzi*!' he said. 'You shall collect hearts – and patrons for your poor Pappi. The German Kaiser, the Russian Tsar, the Queen of England ... No, perhaps not the Queen of England. They say that fifty years ago she also had a pair of fascinating blue eyes.'

He reached out to take her on his knee. He was so evidently happy to be alone with her, so pleased with her, she hadn't the heart to tell him about what had happened in the castle, that day.

The following morning, she found that Prince Luitpold's promise regarding the Palace of Linderhof did not prove false. It was a miniature Versailles nestling under the shadow of snow-capped mountain peaks. Firstly, with members of the palace staff, they toured the gardens so that Pappi could choose the perspectives from which to prepare studies of the buildings. At the centre was an artificial lake with a fountain which, though it was not playing, was said to have the highest jet in all Europe. All about the lake were terraced lawns, grass banks, and marble steps leading to raised walks of pleached hornbeam punctuated with box-tree pyramids. Flights of steps, balustrades mounting above balustrades, merged into the mountainside at the far end, ornamented with grotesque gargoyle faces from whose jutting lower jaws water would cascade, bronze cherubs thrusting their little manhoods forward in aggressive mischief, prepared for the moment the spigots in the meadow above were turned on.

When Pappi had surveyed as much of the prospect as he thought necessary, to commence making his preliminary studies, Prince Luitpold led Alma-Maria away into the buildings. He seemed anxious to make up for her discomfiture of the previous day. He took her into the Moorish kiosk to see the Peacock Throne, then through into the palace itself, to the delicately patterned and coloured Rose Salon. They passed through into the Mirror Room where a marble statue of Louis XV of France smiled across the huge eighteenth-century French writing table at King Ludwig's vacant chair. To her delight, Prince Luitpold invited her to sit on the chair. The milky, pomaded French King simpered sweetly at her out of the glass wall panels from every direction, and a multitude of her own face responded with amazed pleasure. Prince Luitpold clapped his hands in applause; Baron Lange, superintendent of the palace, and the two equerries, imitated the Prince.

'I don't suppose that chair has ever been occupied by anyone so pretty,' declared Prince Luitpold. 'What do you say, gentlemen?'

'It would be hard to imagine a more charming occupant,' Baron Lange replied dutifully.

They returned to the French gardens to find Pappi sitting on his folding stool up on the steep sloping meadow above the ornamental steps and balustrades. As they approached him, Alma-Maria saw that a series of grassy steps had been cut from the outer walk of the garden up the meadow to a wooden platform close to the forest edge, on which there was a standpipe.

Prince Luitpold took her out onto the meadow. To Baron Lange he said, 'We can't allow our distinguished painter to paint our little palace without letting him see the fountains playing.'

Alma-Maria was standing level with Pappi, though some distance from him. He was sitting on one of the narrow grassy steps, the fifth or sixth from the bottom, wholly absorbed in his drawing. The view was perfect: the formal gardens were spread out below around the lake, their pattern clearly visible, while beyond them, the palace façade shone white and still in the early afternoon sunlight.

'A surprise for your father!' Prince Luitpold called to her. 'Come with us, little princess!'

Two of the palace staff were already approaching the standpipe at the top of the meadow. The Prince, with Baron Lange and the two equerries sweating into the stiff collars of their *Chevau-légers* uniforms, strode on upwards.

'A surprise for your father!' the Prince repeated, looking back at her. He laughed, putting his finger to his lips to enjoin her to silence.

She started on upwards. The incline was so steep, she found she was scrambling, using hands as well as feet. In doing so, she caught the fashionably pointed toe of her patent leather boot in the web of English lace which formed a band a few inches above her petticoat hem. She felt the lace tear, and swore under her breath, using a word she would not have wished either Pappi or Mutti to have heard on her lips. She heard the sound of Prince Luitpold's laughter from the top of the incline and glanced up, afraid that he had seen what had happened and was laughing at her. Then she saw, beyond the Prince and his attendants, the man at the standpipe. She saw the water spewing from its mouth; she saw the glittering satin sheen as it came cascading over the edge of the topmost step. It seemed to stop for a moment as it gathered on the second step before plunging further down the cascade from step to step. Above the noise of the waterfall splash, there was the sound of Prince Luitpold's laughter again, and that of Baron Lange and the two equerries.

'A surprise for your father, little princess!' the Prince called down.

Pappi, sitting with his back to the oncoming torrent, was quite unaware of its approach. Alma-Maria struggled to lift her petticoat hem clear of her foot to run to him and warn him. She cried, 'Pappi! Look out!' Pappi got up from the stool and turned toward her. Then he saw the water pouring down onto him, but too late; it swept about his feet, ankle-deep, carrying away his small folding stool, bouncing it down the final steps and sweeping it into the conduit mouth beneath the garden parapet.

For several seconds, Pappi's face registered a comical look of astonishment. As he struggled to splash out of the torrent, his foot slipped. He fell face forward and was carried by the force of the current, slithering down onto the step below. He lay there writhing and jerking in pain as the water swirled around his head. Alma-Maria ran to him across the slippery grass. She splashed into the stream to go to him, slipped herself, picked herself up, her wet clothes clammed against her legs, the water ice-cold through her stockings. Pappi was trying to lift himself like a broken-backed horse and falling back again into the water. He was groaning and spluttering. 'Oh my God! Sweet Jesus Christ, have mercy!' She snatched at his arm in an attempt to drag him onto dry ground, but she might as well have tried to drag an ash tree from the mountain side. All the time, he kept groaning and crying out, unable to speak to her for pain.

Others came running, men in pale blue uniforms with silver facings, men wearing mountaineers' boots and thick woollen stockings, with massive, rough hands. They dragged her out of the water away from Pappi, ignoring her struggling and her tears. They drowned his groaning with their loud voices. Somewhere through blurred eyes, she saw the fountain down in the garden, its monstrous jet leaping higher and higher into the silver air.

Darkness had fallen before the ambulance, drawn by two horses and a drag, arrived outside the Moorish kiosk where Pappi was lying to take him to the hospital at Garmisch-Partenkirchen, fifteen kilometres away through the mountains. During the hours of waiting, though she had been allowed to sit with him, she had not been allowed to touch him, nor even to hold his hand to comfort him. Prince Luitpold's senior medical adviser, Dr von Grashey, had been summoned, and had arrived on horseback from Hohenschwangau. He diagnosed a grumbling appendix aggravated by Pappi's sudden fall. It was most unfortunate, of course; but the trouble must have been of long standing, and Herr Schindler should not have neglected to seek treatment for it. In the meantime, he must be moved as little as possible until he was safely in the hands of the nursing staff at Garmisch-Partenkirchen lest the appendix rupture and peritonitis ensue.

Dr von Grashey had left Alma-Maria sitting alone with Pappi amidst the blue and gold enamelled arabesques of the kiosk. A premature twilight came with the rain which beat like the drumming of fingers on the star-spangled domed roof. Pappy lay on the divan-settee groaning hour after hour, and she could do nothing. Occasionally he called, 'Almschi? Are you there?' But before she could lean over him to reassure him, he would be gone once more, drifting away from her on his pain. Once she asked, foolishly but bravely, 'Oh Pappi! Does it hurt very badly?' He replied, weeping, 'I didn't know there could be such pain!'

Blue-smocked attendants carried him out to the ambulance on a stretcher draped with a tarpaulin to keep off the rain which, coming off the mountains, was bitter cold. Servants held umbrellas over the stretcher-bearers and Alma-Maria herself as she followed Pappi to the ambulance. Black, dripping oilskins shone in the glare from the flares while drops of naphthalene floated burning on the puddles. Caped postilions were already mounted on the nearside horses. Attendants helped her up the ambulance step. There was no sign of Prince Luitpold or his equerries among the soaked, anxious faces on the drive; no one expressed remorse or regret. Two smocked attendants clambered in behind her, and the doors were immediately shut on them. The ambulance was already on the move, the lantern suspended from the roof swaying backwards and forwards, as the attendants began to remove the heavy tarpaulin from Pappi's body.

Throughout the long drive, as the ambulance toiled over the mountain pass, she sat cramped on a low stool at the foot of the stretcher. Pappi groaned interminably as the stretcher swayed on its leather straps. Cold draughts bit round her legs despite the blanket wrapped about her knees, and did nothing to dispel the reek of disinfectant carbolic in the narrow cabin. She heard herself say aloud, 'Don't leave me Pappi!' The sound of her voice took her by surprise; not only had she not meant to say it, she had not realized she was even thinking it. One of the attendants leant forward to her and said in a not unsympathetic voice,

'Your Papa shouldn't have let it happen, you know. It doesn't do to ignore a grumbling appendix – not now there's anaesthetics for operations.'

At the time, she had been too weary, too bedraggled, too distressed, to question Dr von Grashey's diagnosis. It was only later – much later, after they had returned to Plankenburg, that it occurred to her that neither Pappi nor anybody else had ever previously mentioned a grumbling appendix.

On the advice of Pappi's doctor in Vienna, they rented a house on the North Sea coast of Schleswig-Holstein, on the island of Sylt, where he might convalesce quietly. Mutti was delighted. Sylt was near her native Hamburg; she had spent childhood holidays there. The house, an old, low-built farm dwelling, stood alone among the dunes. The windows of the morning room which had been built onto it faced the sea and the western light; it made a perfect studio for Pappi. In fact, Mutti and Herr Möll displayed a care for his well-being which took Alma-Maria by surprise. They even arranged for a cottage piano to be brought from the seaside resort of Westerland, two kilometres across the dunes, so that Alma-Maria might practise and play to him at the same time.

Alma-Maria loved the North Sea, facing across to Heligoland, with its grey, white-crested turmoil. She fell in love with its bluster, its salt-tasting spray, the screaming of the gulls, the alteration of stillness and beating wind as she walked among the dunes. It was the sea which beat on the Cornish cliffs in *Tristan and Isolde*; it was the sea which had driven the Flying Dutchman to seek shelter in Daland's fiord.

She was sitting with Pappi one grey, windy afternoon, she at the piano, he at the window with his watercolours. He wasn't the strong peasant woodcutter she remembered from early childhood. He was thin –

surprisingly so for one of his large frame – and his broad face had become lean and pallid.

'When I'm feeling stronger – which is another way of saying when your Mutti permits . . .' he smiled. 'You shall take me onto the shore . . . one day when there are really big waves.'

He scratched on his pad with a stick of graphite.

'To catch a wave – to suspend it in motion . . . Leonardo made scores of studies of waves, you know. He spent many years in northern France. He watched the mighty Atlantic beating against the cliffs of Brittany. Ceaseless motion – that was what he wanted to capture. A paradox, eh? Ceaseless motion recorded in an absolute stillness.'

Alma-Maria went to him and put her arm round his neck. She glanced down at the great curling waves he had drawn, covering the page on his lap.

'Are we going to come here again next year?' she asked.

'Why?' He turned his head to look up at her with an expression of comic suspicion. 'Have you met somebody you like?'

'I love the sea,' she said firmly. 'And I love being here with you.'

She felt guilty. It wasn't that she was doing anything she need feel ashamed about – just that there was a sense of betrayal, and she couldn't understand why.

She had met Max Elser on the dunes. The Elser children with their governess were from Berlin. Their father was professor of Hellenic Studies at the University, and he and their mother spent the summer at an archaeological site in Greece while the children stayed with their aunt in Westerland. There was Bert who was eleven, nearly twelve, and Fanny who was ten; and there was Max who was almost seventeen. Fanny Elser's governess was English, and Fräulein Weyss was overjoyed to find somebody with whom she could practise English conversation. Grete, who was young for her age in Alma-Maria's opinion, was happy enough to romp around with Bert and Fanny. Which left Alma-Maria to stroll chatting amongst the dunes with Max.

Max was quite tall, slim, and had cultivated a thin black moustache. Hidden from the others in the dune valleys, he would take a Turkish cigarette from a new leather case. He even offered her one, saying that girls in Berlin often smoked, these days; she backed away from him, giggling at the idea, and feeling foolish because she was giggling.

He told her about his life at home in Berlin. His father and mother were both preoccupied with his father's work, so that he had become very independent. According to him he spent most of his time at home in the Grunewald, riding and swimming and learning to fight with the sabre. He was going to university in the autumn. He spoke of going to dances in cafés – he seemed anxious to give the impression that Berlin was just as exciting a place to live as Vienna. He also spoke darkly of his relations with girls; he told her that he had never been serious about any of the girls he had encountered, and this had been just as well since none of them was as pretty or as charming as she was.

Every afternoon if it was fine, she would go with Grete and Fräulein Weyss for a walk over the dunes. Every day, she found herself hoping they would see the Elsers and their governess. They usually did. She began to take the arm Max offered as they strolled on the shore. They climbed the highest dunes to watch the ships out of Hamburg and Cuxhaven heading up the Danish coast for Bergen and Trondheim. As they scrambled from tuft to tuft, Max reached and held her hand to assist her. Sometimes he was quite slow to let it go when they reached the summit. Once, when it was blustery, and the wind was whipping strands of her hair which had come loose across her face, he put his arm about her waist as if to steady her. When they were down at the bottom once more, he did it again without excuse. As she turned, meaning to remove herself from his embrace, he bent his head and kissed her on the cheek, taking her by surprise. She turned her face sharply from him so that his parted lips brushed her cheek and into her hair.

The episode had disturbed her profoundly so that she had rehearsed it in her mind over and over again, trying to make some sort of sense of her own reaction to it.

After that, when she strolled among the dunes with Max Elser she let him kiss her on the cheek, first one then the other, and put his arm about her waist resting his hand lightly on her hip. She was never able to respond. Sometimes she wondered if even that ungiving consent had sealed an unspoken agreement between them. She did not know whether she dreaded the possibility or hoped for it. Max began to elaborate to her on his plans to go to German East Africa to help in the building of the Kaiser's overseas empire, and to make a fortune for himself and his children in the ivory business. She wondered if she ought to tell him that she could think of nothing more exciting than to go to Africa with him.

The holiday drew to a close. On an overcast afternoon, with only the odd shaft of sunlight from between the low banks of cloud to justify going out, Alma-Maria persuaded Fräulein Weyss to take herself and Grete to the shore for what might prove to be the last time. When they found the Elsers with Fanny's governess already there, she actually trembled with relief.

'They insisted on coming here,' said Fanny's governess, 'in spite of the breeze.'

'So did these two,' said Fräulein Weyss.

'You mean Almschi,' said Grete, but fortunately nobody paid any attention to her.

'I dare say we can find somewhere sheltered to sit,' said Fanny's governess.

Max led Alma-Maria away. She walked with him in silence until they were out of sight and earshot of the others. He stopped and took out his cigarette case. He opened it and held it out to her. 'Try it,' he urged, making it sound almost a command.

'You know I don't want to,' she told him.

'It might be your last chance,' he said. 'Are you sure?'

'Of course I'm sure.'

'It's up to you, I suppose.'

He took a cigarette, lit it, and smoked it, staring out between the dunes at the white crested sea. Was he really upset by her refusal to accept a cigarette? she wondered. And if so, why? When he spoke at last, it was as if with an effort.

'We came down here, this afternoon, because I was afraid of missing you.' He threw the remainder of the cigarette to smoke in the sand. 'They do what I tell them,' he added.

He took her to a low valley between the dunes, removed his jacket and spread it on the sand, over the stiff tufts of grass. It was warm and sheltered there. She sat down, and he reclined beside her.

'You'll write back if I write to you, won't you, Alma?'

He addressed her as Alma *tout court* because that was what she had told him her name was. Even when Grete and Fräulein Weyss had betrayed her by calling her Almschi and Alma-Maria, he had continued to address her as Alma – when he wasn't calling her 'my dear', that is.

'Of course,' she said.

'You promise?'

'I promise – cross my heart.'

He put his arm round her to draw her down beside him. She resisted, but only a little.

'You're so beautiful!' He stared into her face, examining it. 'I want to photograph you in my mind so that I can see you smiling at me whenever I think of you.'

'Don't be so stupid! You mustn't say things like that.'

'I can't help myself.'

'It's no good, though. I mean, I'm too young to be told that sort of thing ...'

She laughed. But she was also telling herself that she now knew exactly how Sophie Haas's friends felt when Horse Dragoon officers from the Hofburg asked them to go to see the cherry blossom with them.

'Anyway, you're in Berlin and I'm in Vienna,' she said.

'There are trains – and telephones.'

'What about your mission, to the colonies in Africa?'

'You could come too – you'd look beautiful in white muslin and a sun-helmet – that's what ladies wear in Tanganyika.'

She didn't want to lose him – not now, when the time for parting was so close. But there was no way she could bring herself to commit herself to him.

'There wouldn't be any music in Tanganyika. I couldn't live in a world without music. Honestly,' she told him.

He drew her face towards his. She realized he was going to kiss her on the mouth. She turned her face away.

'Don't you want me to kiss you?' he asked.

'I don't know . . . Not like that.'

'What a strange girl! I know you like me.'

He was smiling. He was very confident, she thought. Round the corner from the dunes, the waves sounded on the shore; there would be such a stillness if they were to stop. One would be able to hear the chattering inside one's head. Grete was shouting in the distance, as aggressively competitive as ever. Alma-Maria hoped she would not become so disagreeable Fräulein Weyss would insist they go back to the house.

'Don't you like kissing?' Max asked.

Something prevented her from telling him what he knew perfectly well – that she had never been kissed the way he wanted to kiss her.

'There's always a first time, you know,' he said softly, still sounding amused.

She closed her eyes. She felt his lips alive on her mouth. She parted her own slightly, to accept him, because surely that was what she was supposed to do and she did want to please him. She felt his body close against her, his lap against hers – just like the picture of Faust kissing Gretchen in the book which Mutti had thrown into the stove.

He stopped kissing her. With his cheek pressing against hers, he whispered to her how he had fallen in love with her from the first moment he had set eyes on her coming down onto the beach; how bored he had been in the company of his younger brother and sister, and then, suddenly, there she was, the most beautiful thing he had ever seen in his life; how he had been unable to put her out of his mind ever since, how he could think of nothing and nobody else. As he whispered, and she tried to prevent herself from giggling at him, he moved his hand up under her summer coat to feel her breast through her blouse. She felt the tip of his finger stroke her nipple. The sensation aroused by his touch excited and frightened her. She sat up abruptly, wrapping her coat about her.

'What's the matter?' he asked, taken by surprise.

'You shouldn't have done that,' she told him. Her voice, she noticed, sounded like Grete's, sulky rather than indignant.

She stood up and dusted the sand fiercely from her skirt.

'What did I do?' he asked.

He knelt upright.

'*You* know!' she snapped at him. 'You know very well!'

If he didn't know, she couldn't explain to him the feeling of panic he had aroused in her. He tried to pick up his jacket, but because he was still kneeling on it, he pitched forward onto his hands. She glanced down at him; he looked ridiculous, scrabbling about in the sand on his hands and knees – not at all the confident young sophisticate. That made her even more angry. She told him in a cool, grown-up voice, 'I expect it's the sort of thing you try on with the chambermaids!'

She turned her back on him and scrambled away over the dunes, cursing every time her foot slipped in the soft sand. She called down to Fräulein Weyss and Grete that she wanted to go home, but Fräulein Weyss was deep in conversation with her fellow governess, and Grete, for all her ill-temper, was playing with the other children on the beach. Alma-Maria walked a short distance down the sandy track which led across the flat, treeless expanse between the dunes and the house, then sat down on a hillock of coarse grass to quieten, if possible, the turmoil of her mind.

The skeleton timbers of abandoned boats jutted up from the channels in the sea mosses. A small group of men and women were cutting turfs; ponies carrying wicker panniers waited patiently, untethered, as their peasant masters and mistresses stooped to the short soft grass as if yielding themselves to the wind. It was a picture which Pappi would have loved to have painted – the enormous expanse of emerald, white-flecked sea under a vast grey sky, and the small, bent figures toiling in the immensity of the desolation. She would have to describe it to him – he would not be able to come and see it for himself, not this year. She would study the texture of each level – turf, sand, sea, and sky, and then the figures.

She was an artist's child, touched with the longing to be an artist herself. If she were to offer service, companionship, her very self to a man, it would have to be the sort of man whose spirit had visited the borders of sea and sky, who had embraced the mountain tops – the edges of eternity, who had been touched by the knowledge of fearful things.

All that evening and into the night as she listened to the wind buffeting the timbers under the eaves, she tried to come to terms with the feelings Max Elser had aroused in her. She could, quite possibly, be mistaken about him. Perhaps he was truly in love with her. She recalled his long silence when he had been smoking, and the sudden, almost jerky way he had told her that it had been he who had persuaded the governess to bring his brother and sister to the dunes that afternoon. Certainly he should not have touched her the way he did, but she could have said no, should have prevented him from kissing her.

The next morning was overcast, but she persuaded Mutti that she and Grete should go into Westerland to buy souvenirs. They walked with Fräulein Weyss the two kilometres along the wooden causeway, while gulls circled and screeched overhead, driven inland on the blustery, salty air. Grete grumbled and said it would rain. In Alma-Maria's mind was the prayer that she might see Max again.

No sooner had they reached the small town than it did begin to rain, a wind-gusty rain off the sea which drove them to seek shelter in a crowded restaurant on the new promenade. It smelt of cheap cigars and sour, bottled coffee essence. An hour later they were still sitting there, staring out of the window at the rainclouds. Grete whispered, 'The gentleman by the coats over there keeps staring at us!' – when Herr Möll appeared. He stood at a little distance from them, between the tables, the rain streaming from his fedora and his Inverness cape. He beckoned to Fräulein Weyss, as more than one gentleman watched over the top of his newspaper holder. Fräulein Weyss got up and went to him. Alma-Maria saw the look of anxiety on their faces and began to be afraid. She was already on her feet when Fräulein Weyss called across to them in quite an old-fashioned manner.

'Girls, you must come straight away – straight away!'

'But it hasn't stopped raining!' Grete complained, drawing even more attention to the two of them.

'Be quiet! Do as you're told!' said Alma-Maria, giving her a prod in the back.

'Who do you think you are?' snapped Grete.

In the restaurant lobby, Herr Möll turned to them and spread out his arms from under his damp cape.

'Poor things! Such tidings!' said Fräulein Weyss.

'My dear children,' said Herr Möll dramatically. 'You've no father any more.'

It was extraordinary, thought Alma-Maria; he seriously supposed she would let him enfold her in his damp embrace. She felt neither surprise nor pain. But she knew that pain was on the march – that it would take her soon enough. She walked calmly to the hired dog-cart, where it stood at the end of the promenade.

'Christian-Alois found your Pappi just after you'd gone,' Herr Möll announced from under the umbrella he was holding over Fräulein Weyss. 'Your Pappi had finished dressing, but he'd lain down again on his bed . . .'

He broke off. Perhaps the wind and the rain were too much for him.

'Your Mutti will tell you everything,' he said.

Alma-Maria remained calm as they drove back across the dreary flatland. She was aware of the cold and the wet, and the uneasy swaying of the cart. She was aware of raindrops running like tears down her cheeks, and the way it soaked into her clothing. Otherwise, she felt as though she had been sedated, so that she had to remind herself several times that she would not be able to run in to greet Pappi as soon as they arrived.

She went into the house as soon as she jumped down from the cart without waiting for the others.

'Where is he?' she asked. She did not even begin to take off her coat, drenched through though it was.

'You're not allowed to see him, Fräulein Almschi,' the stout, big-bosomed North German maid told her. 'Oh you poor child!' she cried, catching her and forcibly restraining her as she tried to tear herself away to run upstairs.

It was very strange. She didn't feel in the least distraught. Yet she could hear her voice screaming, much worse than Grete in one of her tantrums, 'Let me go to him! Let me! Let me!' Then Herr Möll came up behind her and held her – she could smell his damp cape. She was kicking and struggling, and shouting, 'Let me go! He wants me! I know he wants me!' until she was exhausted, and her screams no more than moaning. Then they led her upstairs, but only to lock her in her room.

Some time later, how much later she did not know but it was dark, Mutti came to her and sat on the end of her bed. She was white-faced, and old about the eyes.

'There is cholera in Hamburg, *liebchen*,' she explained. 'The doctors have sealed the door of his room. Nobody can see him – not until they come back again.'

Mutti's hands were clenched in her lap.

'I know how much you loved each other, *liebchen*,' she said. 'I'm not completely insensitive. I know you've been closer to him than anybody these past few years.'

Suddenly Alma-Maria was in her arms, sobbing and whispering through her tears. 'He wants me to be with him, Muttichen! He'll be so lonely without me!'

'You can go to him, *kleine liebchen*,' Mutti told her, comforting her, 'when the gentlemen have been. When he's been made ready. I promise.'

But the promise was not kept. That evening, the doctor from Westerland returned with a pair of official-looking colleagues from the burgomaster's office. They were accompanied by two policemen, stolid, serious Schleswigers with felt-covered helmets which they clutched under their arms, and short swords at their sides. They stood sentry outside the door of Pappi's room. When the embalmer and the laying-out woman arrived, they were refused admission until the gentlemen had completed their examination. They had to sit, stiff and awkward, in the tiny vestibule.

The gentlemen emerged from Pappi's room. The senior official from the burgomaster's office spoke to Mutti on the landing in a low voice which was heavy with formally assumed sympathy.

'No question of the departed having died of cholera, of course, dear lady ... Cases reported on the mainland, however, and now we are connected by regular ferry to the mainland we are compelled to take the same precautions ... Regrettable, I know, but the body must be sealed into the coffin as soon as possible ... we will send men with the undertaker tomorrow morning ... No question of taking the body back to Vienna, I'm afraid. The late Jakob-Emil Schindler was a Roman Catholic? We'll send for a Roman Catholic priest from Neukirchen to perform the funeral ... My profound condolences, dear lady – and regrets, but strict instructions from the *Landesrat*, you understand ...'

The gentlemen and the two policemen left, and the embalmer and laying-out woman set to their task. Alma-Maria dozed fitfully during the night, between intervals of desolate wakefulness. Grete slept beside her, but the rest of the household seemed to be awake all night. There was whispering outside the door, and a thumping and scuffling as if furniture was being moved. Then, while it was still the middle of the night, Mutti herself came and woke them. She was dressed for travelling in her fur-trimmed tartan coat and osprey-feathered hat; in no way did she appear to be a widow of less than twenty-four hours' standing.

She stood beside the bed, holding the lamp over them.

'Dress quickly, children,' she told them. 'In your ordinary outdoor clothes. We're taking the first morning ferry from the Elbow; we've got to catch the Vienna express from Hamburg at noon, so hurry.'

Alma-Maria stared stupidly at her, her mind clouded with fatigue and misery.

'Come, Almschi,' Mutti told her severely. 'There will be time for tears when we are on the Vienna express.'

'We can't leave Pappi!' Alma-Maria cried.

'Don't be silly. We're not going to leave your Pappi. Now hurry!'

Fräulein Weyss, also dressed in her travelling coat, came in to help Grete to get ready. One of the maids they had brought with them started to pack, pushing the clothes with hurried carelessness into the boxes. Herr Möll's voice called up the stairs.

'Tell them to hurry, Anny! We must go immediately.'

'They're coming, *liebe* Carl,' Mutti called back from the landing.

Shivering and bewildered, Alma-Maria followed Grete and Fräulein Weyss downstairs.

'Have you told them, Anny?' Herr Möll asked. Without waiting for Mutti to answer, he said, 'Girls, you must be steadfast. you mustn't let anybody know who you are until we are safely out of Germany – and you must certainly not let anybody know that we are taking your father with us. Do you understand, girls?'

'Yes, Herr Möll,' replied Grete dully.

The hideous notion occurred to Alma-Maria that they were going to take Pappi back to Austria in the same way the Baltazzi brothers had taken their niece, Mary Vetsera, away from the hunting lodge at Mayerling with her corpse propped up between them as if she was drunk. She felt she was on the verge of laughter – or screaming. Strangely, yet again Mutti seemed to understand her feelings; she put her arm round Alma-Maria's waist and told her,

'You must trust Herr Möll, *liebling*. He has seen to everything. You wouldn't want to leave your Pappi here, would you?'

Alma-Maria shook her head.

'Then you must do what he says. It's the only way.'

Mutti turned to call up the stairs to the maid.

'We'll have to forget the sheets, Lotte! There's no help for it.'

Herr Möll had gone with Christian-Alois, Pappi's valet, and the groom into the morning room. They dragged the cottage piano out of the door. It was wrapped in canvas sheeting, secured with cords. Alma-Maria noticed that it was labelled for Vienna, though she knew it had been rented from Westerland. Glancing into the morning room, she saw by the light of the lamp on the floor the strung frame from inside the piano case propped like a harp against the wall. Clutching onto Mutti's arm, she stepped outside into the darkness and the cold, rain-washed wind from off the sea. Herr Möll was helping the other men to lift the piano up onto a cart. Poor Pappi, she thought; he had been so gaunt he could scarcely have added much weight to it. Although she wasn't actually crying – at least, not sobbing – tears poured down her face. She couldn't help sniffing.

'Sh, *liebchen*,' Mutti told her softly. 'Not yet.'

She led her to the carriage which was waiting with the cart. They climbed in after Grete and Fräulein Weyss. The servants were climbing into the cart, round the piano. Somebody was going about the house extinguishing the lamps one by one. The carriage set off along the eastward road over the fenland to the ferry harbour on the Elbow. Streaks of grey low in the sky spread a dull, dead half-light across the wet sands. As they drove on into it, Alma-Maria felt that it was like a journey into hell, into a punishment from which there would never, ever, be any escape.

By the time the Requiem had been sung over his coffin in St Stephen's Cathedral, her desolation was turned to a fierce indignation. The newspapers wrote of Mutti and Carl Möll's having brought him back to Vienna for burial as if it was some sort of patriotic achievement. Dignitaries drove out in procession to Plankenburg, to kiss Mutti's hand, and to congratulate Herr Möll and both Alma-Maria and Grete on their loyalty and courage. It was almost as if triumph at having rescued Pappi from the bureaucratic efficiency of the North Germans excluded a genuine sense of loss.

In St Stephen's, she sat in the front with Mutti and Grete, close to the catafalque. The steps of the dais were buried in a sea of wreaths and woven flowers. The coffin had been concealed under a pall heavy with stitched gold. At each corner of the dais stood the huge, gold-encrusted candlesticks reserved for the funerals of Vienna's greatest children. Herr Möll was nowhere to be seen; his place, no doubt, was with his fellow artists and men of letters, at the back of the nave or in the Catherine Chapel. Besides Mutti, Grete, and herself, the principal mourners consisted of the ranks of Kaiserlich-Königlich officials in their blue and scarlet uniforms, burnished cuirasses, and ribboned and sashed frock coats. Seated above them all, on a chair set against the huge red marble Kaiser Friedrich Memorial and overlooking altar and catafalque alike, sat the Archduke Franz Ferdinand, representing the Old Man, his *aides-de-camp* and equerries seated around his feet. In his solitary and conspicuous glory, although holding himself stiffly erect, every twitch of his mouth, every slight jerk of his head, proclaimed his boredom.

The Cardinal-Archbishop, supported – almost carried – by the flotilla of altar boys and assistant priests who held the hem of his heavily embroidered purple cope, censed the catafalque in such dense wreaths of scented smoke that it was almost as if he wished to conceal it from view. The voices of the singers concealed in the Winter Choir above the high altar soared upwards into the stone vaulting.

There was nothing to do with her strongly built, gentle, kind Pappi in all this great place. They had taken him from her, people who neither loved him nor knew him, to re-create him in their own frigid image. Only she amongst all these thousands felt a desperate longing to have him with her again, longed to hear his voice, longed to sit at the piano to play to him. And why had he deserted her? Why had he let himself be carried off by all these stiff, stupid, martinet puppets? Why did he have to go to Munich to draw pictures to please the raddled, painted old Prince? And what companionship did he think was left for her in this bleached, empty world, now he was gone?

1 THE GIRL FROM TANAGRA: 1895-1896

ALMA-MARIA WATCHED the man come walking hurriedly out of the dripping obscurity of the trees. He glanced from side to side before crossing the sweep of lamplit gravel between the park bench on which she was sitting and the semicircle of larger than life-size statues in front of her. He was on the stout side, with a small black half-beard: under his stiff-brimmed Homburg hat, his pale face was that of a man the same age as Herr Möll – in his mid to late thirties. The astrakhan collar of his coat gleamed with tiny raindrops. A violet ribbon drooped from inside his coat, disappearing into his breast pocket. At first she took it for an Imperial decoration, of which there were so many; then she saw that it was attached to a pair of steel-rimmed eyeglasses.

His boots and trouser-cuffs were splashed with mud. Otherwise, his dapper smartness was in complete contrast to Pappi, whose stone likeness loomed in front of her just as she remembered him in life. The carved figure lounged carelessly in an armchair of living rock, his hair, as always, ruffled and flamboyantly untidy, his suit crumpled, his tie loose in the way Mutti had often complained of. But Pappi was his own master now, take him or leave him. The dapper figure passed between them and went on toward the street lamps and carriages on the Park Ring. But just as she turned her head to ensure that he was going, he stopped and turned back. She felt frightened: never before had she stayed out so late after her music lesson. She had noticed with a disagreeable thrill the solitary women loitering just outside the aureoles of lamplight, their boas drooping from their forearms like the laurel-chains on classical reliefs. She clutched her battered music portfolio across her lap. The maids at home all knew of such women, talked of their fate incessantly as if it were a disease anybody might catch – though proper young ladies like herself were supposed to be unaware of their existence.

She ought to get up and walk away as briskly as she could. But there was also pride – the shame she would feel at being driven from her place in front of Pappi. The man raised his hat while still a short distance from her. His scalp gleamed in the lamplight and slight rain, despite the thin hanks of black hair which had been pomaded across it. She could not prevent herself from starting.

'Don't be alarmed, my dear young lady,' the man called. 'I'm not mistaken am I?'

He pointed the steel ferule of his stick at Pappi's memorial.

'I am addressing Fräulein Schindler, am I not? Our beloved Jakob-Emil Schindler's daughter?'

She stood up. She nodded, still holding her battered music portfolio.

'I was acquainted with your father,' he told her. 'And we have been introduced. But I'm sure you won't remember. It was the year before your father's passing. At Segantini's studio on the Grünangergasse; there were so many people. My name is Burckhard, Max Burckhard.'

She remembered the occasion: the stuffy, over-furnished, overheated room from under dusty skylights; the strange, tortured painting of women impaled on the branches of wind-racked trees on a desert mountainside; and the fashionable throng which had come to gawp at it. But she couldn't remember him.

'Am I permitted to ask why I find you sitting here at this hour, Fräulein Schindler? At this hour, and in this weather?'

She wondered how much he knew about her family and herself.

'I go to the Votivkirche on Wednesdays,' she replied. 'I study music with Dr Labor there.'

She looked up into his face. It seemed kind, not predatory. She realized that the soft Vienna rain had seeped imperceptibly but insidiously through her clothes. The hair which had slipped from under her woollen Scotch bonnet felt claggy down her cheek.

'Are you a good pupil?'

'For Dr Labor?' she asked. 'Yes. I'm a good musician for my age. Everyone says so, at least.'

'And you come here from the Votivkirche after your lesson because . . .?' He broke off, pointing at the statue once more.

'When I feel I'd like to talk to my father,' she said quietly.

'You feel especially close to him here? You think it's a good likeness?'

She nodded.

'So do I . . . But you know, Fräulein Schindler, it is rather late. Won't your mother be worried about you?'

She shrugged. 'Mother is very busy,' she said. 'We're moving house, you know.'

'Shall we walk?' he suggested. 'We shall get wet here.'

He placed his hand lightly under her arm, and waved his stick in the direction of the Park Ring and the traffic. She allowed him to guide her towards the path. 'I take a stroll here most nights,' he explained. 'Once my staff assure me that the curtain will rise safely at eight, I feel I can permit myself half an hour in the fresh air. However, if you'll forgive me for saying so, the parks are no place for a young lady alone. Not after dark. How do you propose getting home? Out at Tulln, isn't it?'

'I'll take a tram to the station.'

'Not at this time of night. My carriage is over there. Do you have a telephone at home?'

'Yes,' she said.

'Then we may telephone your mother from my office – to reassure her, and to make some arrangement for getting you home.'

Max Burckhard. Dr Max Burckhard. He was the Director of the Kaiserlich-Königlich Burgtheater, the Vienna State Theatre. She recalled one afternoon – two and a half years ago, it must have been, shortly before their ill-fated holiday on Sylt – sitting with Pappi and one or two of his friends in the Café Griensteidl, and Pappi laughing over Dr Burckhard's appointment.

'Max! Max Burckhard! A damned lawyer to run the Burg! It'll be a colonel of Light Cavalry to administer the Court Opera next. Or an army surgeon to manage the Musikverein, eh?'

Chill had penetrated her clothes with the damp. She shuddered.

'All my father's things have been packed away now,' she said. 'It feels so empty at home. So I come here.'

'I don't suppose your mother is going to be entirely pleased at your staying out so late,' Dr Burckhard said.

'No,' she replied. 'I'm sure she won't.'

A closed *fiacre* was standing against the kerb. Dr Burckhard waved his stick to the driver, and it came up the road towards them.

'Supposing I were to telephone your mother,' he said, 'and tell her that I met you as you left your music lesson – at the Votivkirche, was it? – and that I recognized you, and invited you to take coffee with me at the Burg for your dear father's sake? Then she can blame me for keeping you. And I? Well. Forgive me for saying so, but your mother was an actress, Anna Bergen – I remember her very well. I am known for my talent for apologizing to actresses!'

He helped her up into the *fiacre*.

'Anna Bergen,' he repeated. 'Half Vienna was in love with her in those days. Your father had two advantages. He was a damned handsome fellow. And he was bosom friends with Hans Makart.'

He settled down beside her; the *fiacre* moved off.

'I can't claim any very close acquaintanceship with your father,' he went on. 'I met him when he was sharing the great Hans Makart's *atelier* – before he met your mother, of course. I particularly remember an evening with Liszt. Your father played four hands at the piano with Liszt. Liszt said that he had a good touch . . . for a painter. I expect he talked to you about those days.'

She stared out of the rain-streaked window. They were crossing the wet, lamp-shining expanse of the Schubertring. The garishly new yet old-fashioned palaces along the Ring loomed black behind the street lamps.

'My father met my mother at Makart's studio,' she said.

Mutti had been modelling for one of Makart's vast, slovenly, historical tableaux. Every young actress in Vienna, and many society ladies as well, vied to appear on Makart's fashionable canvases; on Varnishing Day at the Künstlerhaus, the whole of Viennese society attended to see which of their friends, or favourite actresses, could be recognized draped, scarcely draped, or not draped at all, in scenes such as 'The Battle of Mohacs – The Aftermath', in which conquering Turkish pashas were shown selecting suitable women captives from whom to breed Janissaries.

'He painted my mother's portrait. It was his wedding present to both of them.'

'It must be quite valuable now,' remarked Dr Burckhard.

'My mother would never part with it,' she replied.

They were passing across the top of Canovastrasse; at the far end, rearing like a huge stage backdrop, was the brilliantly lit façade of the Musikverein, where Pappi had taken her for the first time to hear the Vienna Philharmonic play Schumann's 'Rhenish' Symphony.

'Hans Makart was my godfather. I can only just remember him.'

Makart had been a giant of a man, already affected by the madness which killed him. He had babbled inconsequential nonsense at her, and she had run terrified to Pappi. It had happened so many years before she encountered Hugo Wolf in Pappi's studio that until that moment, she had not thought there was any similarity between the two events.

She was afraid she sounded as if she were boasting. She changed the subject.

'My father used to take me there.' She pointed towards the Musik-verein. 'His favourite composer was Schumann.'

'And is Schumann your favourite composer?'

She shook her head. 'Wagner,' she replied.

'Do you go to the opera?' Dr Burckhard asked.

'My father took me, but there's nobody to take me now. My mother isn't interested.'

'She was a fine musician in her own field,' said Dr Burckhard.

'Waltz songs. Always waltz songs. They all sound the same.'

'Ah, the intolerance of youth!' Dr Burckhard sighed. 'How old are you, if I may ask?'

'I was sixteen, in August.'

'Perhaps we should try to persuade your mother to let you come to the Burg. Did you know we have a painting by your father?'

'No.'

'Opposite the bar on the first promenade. You shall see it sometime.'

The *fiacre* clattered off the Ring and up onto the ramp in front of the Burgtheater. There were carriages drawn up all round them, their lamps dimmed in the flare from the giant electric mantles above the entrance on either side. The *fiacre* drove between them, round the front of the theatre with its massive square columns, to a side door at the end of one of the long galleries which extended like transepts from the main building. As Dr Burckhard helped Alma-Maria down, a porter came out to meet them, carrying an umbrella. He wore an ill-fitting dark suit, quite unlike the scarlet and gold livery and knee breeches of the commissionaires at the front.

He gave Alma-Maria the merest glance before saying to Dr Burckhard, 'I trust the Herr Director had a pleasant walk. I trust the Herr Director did not find the weather too inclement.'

'Not at all,' Dr Burckhard replied briskly.

He took Alma-Maria's arm and led her inside. They ascended in a steel, wire-meshed lift, then walked down a long, bleakly lit gallery which smelt of carbolic disinfectant. Doors gave onto washrooms and sinks, and attic-like rooms full of clothes. There was the sound of water closets flushing. Women in pinafores, or dark dresses with chatelaines and pincushions hanging from their belts scurried from room to room. If they noticed Dr Burckhard they curtsied briefly and murmured, 'Good evening, Herr Doctor Director,' and padded away on slippered feet. A group of younger women at a lamplit workbench glanced up and saw Alma-Maria, and smirked and whispered to one another.

Passing through a more imposing door at the end of the gallery, Dr Burckhard led her into a wide, lofty, panelled room. Carpets hushed their footsteps. High bookshelves stood in ranks into the room. Models of play sets stood gathering dust behind glass windows. From the distance, there came the sound of laughter or applause. Alma-Maria's slight deafness made it sound to her like waves beating on a far-off shore. She shivered. Dr Burckhard noticed it immediately.

'You are cold? The damp has made you cold?' he asked solicitously.

'No,' she said.

In fact, the metallic-smelling warmth from the central heating was beginning to penetrate to her skin.

'Tired?' he asked.

'A little.' Then she said, 'Pappi would have liked that!'

A large canvas was hanging above the double doors at the far end of the room: a simple, natural study of a young girl asleep, her dark hair – as thick and lustrous as Alma-Maria's own – was spread over her tasselled pillow. Behind her, the shadow of a young man in medieval Italian costume loomed over her, framed by the vaulting of a wall. The girl's face was turned away from him, smiling in quiet joy.

'"Juliet in the Tomb",' Dr Burckhard told her.

'Is she supposed to be dead?' asked Alma-Maria.

'Not yet. Do you know the play?'

'No, but I know the story, of course,' she said.

'Have you never read Shakespeare?'

She shook her head. To prevent his expressing disapproval, she said, 'She looks happy. Do you think she prefers dreaming of love to the real thing?'

'My dear young lady!' Dr Burckhard exclaimed. 'You have hit on the key to the story. You are very perceptive!'

'I am sometimes,' she agreed.

The signature in the right hand corner of the canvas was in remarkable contrast to the delicacy of the painting itself; it had been laid on with impasto-like boldness, and underlined with a tadpole-shaped smear.

'My father never mentioned Klimt to me – at least, I can't remember him mentioning him.'

'Probably not. He's "arrived", as they say, quite recently. He is very much in demand as a portrait artist these days – particularly among the wives of the intelligentsia. Ladies of the nobility still prefer the style of Makart, of course.'

Makart's portrait of Mutti was one of the few larger paintings which was being transferred from Plankenburg to the new apartment on the Theresianumgasse. It showed her as she must have been when she was enchanting the men in the audience of the Josefstadt Theatre – devastatingly pretty in ringlets, and wearing the costume of a maid in a late eighteenth-century comedy, with ruched satin skirt over panniers, and a pink rose pinned to the fichu above the bib of her tiny apron. Alma-Maria had come to hate it: it was arch, a pretence; it was everything that Pappi had been moving away from in his work.

'I believe Klimt is an associate of Herr Carl Möll,' said Dr Burckhard. 'If you're interested in his work, you should ask Herr Carl about it.'

He took her through a small side door into another bleak, undecorated passage. The echoing sea sound of the audience's laughter or applause sounded closer. He stopped outside a door.

'The director's *sanctum sanctorum*,' he explained. He called, 'Irma?' and a middle-aged woman in a white pinafore came out of a nearby pantry cupboard. Alma-Maria noticed a large yellowish stain on the skirt of the maid's pinafore. It had been inadequately concealed by rubbing white powder over it.

'Take Fräulein Schindler's coat, will you Irma, and dry it, please.'

They passed through into what would have been a large, comfortably furnished library-study but for the enormous, heavily carved table with its telephones and trays of documents. The maid drew Alma-Maria's coat from her shoulders. Alma-Maria felt ashamed of her shabby, pleated black dress and collar and tie – relics of a brief stay at boarding school.

'And bring us coffee, please, Irma.'

'Yes, Herr Doctor Director.'

As the maid left, he asked Alma-Maria, 'What is your telephone number at Tulln?'

'Thirty-seven. Plankenburg Castle.'

He scribbled it in pencil onto a pad on the big table. Glancing up, he saw her examining the bookshelves.

'So you've never read Shakespeare?' he asked. 'Do you read English?'

'I'm very uneducated,' she told him. 'My mother's always saying how ignorant I am. When I was young, she used to get very angry because I didn't know the simplest things. She locked me in my room once, for a whole day. She said she wouldn't let me out till I'd learnt the names of all the trees from a book.'

'And did you?'

She laughed. 'By evening, she'd forgotten all about me and the trees . . . But after my father died, she sent me away to school – to the Maria Theresia Institute . . .'

She had been about to say, *Herr Möll sent me*; she checked herself just in time. She couldn't tell a stranger the truth about the episode.

Dr Hübner had tried to kiss her during a piano lesson. It had been horrible: after she struggled away from him, he sweated and shivered and wept apologies to her so that she was afraid he was going out of his mind. Because he had always been kind to her, she could not bring herself to complain of his behaviour to Mutti – still less to Herr Möll. Unhappily, one of the maids had seen what happened, through the window, and reported the incident. As a result, Mutti and Herr Möll were convinced that, whether by accident or design, Alma-Maria must have led him on. So they decided that the best place for her while she matured into full womanhood was boarding school, and Herr Möll exploited his rising influence in the world of business and the arts to have her placed in the most prestigious girls' school in the Dual Monarchy.

The memory of her five weeks at the Maria Theresia Institute still caused her nightmares – even after the passage of almost two years. There had been the forty iron bedsteads in rows of twenty in the bare, scrubbed dormitory, with the heavy crucifix suspended at one end and curtained-off cubicles at the other for washing, and the performance of natural functions. There had been the nuns, knotted cords dangling like rosaries from their wool-mittened hands, croaking orders to the girls as if they were Prussian drill-sergeants reincarnated in the bodies of religious women. Alma-Maria had no experience of making friends with girls of her own age. But even if she had, 'particular friendships' were regarded by the nuns – and therefore by some of the girls – as occasions of sin. Worst of all was not having any more music lessons with Dr Hübner and Dr Labor. At the institute, music was reduced to the practice of Czerny's piano exercises and, since it was said His Holiness the Pope disapproved of polyphony in church, the singing of plainchant. She was not permitted to play at her own standard of performance, or to show off her sight-reading and improvisation lest they prove yet another occasion of sin – that of pride; according to the nuns, trying to be a Clara Schumann did not help a young lady to become a Christian wife and mother.

'But you are not there any more,' said Dr Burckhard.

'I ran away,' she replied. 'They only sent me there because they wanted to get married behind my back.'

She stared out of the tall window. Through the wrought-iron balcony railing outside, she could see the trees and bushes of the Volksgarten gleaming in the lamplight, and the empty mock-Hellenic Theseus Temple among its linden trees. The rain was now pouring down.

'But they are not married,' said Burckhard.

'Not yet,' Alma-Maria replied. 'That's because I ran away.'

'Didn't your mother send you back?'

'She knew I'd only run away again. I can be quite determined.'

The maid came in with the coffee. When she had gone away again, Dr Burckhard indicated that Alma-Maria should sit down on the large antique-looking sofa opposite the table. He came and sat beside her.

'I can imagine your being determined,' he told her as he poured the coffee. 'You have a very determined chin.'

Nobody had told her that. It worried her for a moment. Then he said, 'The most perfectly blue eyes, flawless complexion, and a determined chin. You are a very beautiful young woman. Not pretty – pretty girls are five for a florin in Vienna. Beautiful.'

He put down the coffee pot.

'So there your education began and ended, eh?'

He drew a handkerchief from an inside pocket and wiped his fingers. It was amazing, she decided: even in her shabby black dress and mud-stained petticoat and shoes, with her hair damp and falling loose all over the place, he thought she was beautiful.

'My father taught me things – an awful lot, really,' she said. 'About art – what to look for in paintings. He started me loving music above all. And poetry. We were such friends, Pappi and I.'

It was the sympathetic way Dr Burckhard nodded as she spoke, as well as his compliments: it was a trap, but a trap she wanted to fall into.

'After I ran away from the Maria Theresia, Herr Möll tried to teach me about art and literature. I suppose he wanted to prove to himself he could be a father to me.'

Dr Burckhard nodded again. He patted her hand. Now it was resting on her knee.

'He tries to be kind,' she said – it was a grudging admission.

'I know that Wagner is your favourite composer. What about poetry? What poets did your father instruct you in?'

'Goethe. He thought *Faust* the greatest book ever written.'

'Excellent. Though there is Shakespeare, you know ... What about *Egmont*? Early Goethe compared to *Faust*, of course. But, as it happens, we are putting it on shortly, with the great Kainz in the lead. We shall be using the Grillparzer edition with Beethoven's music. You must come to the *répétition générale* – one of our final dress rehearsals. A number of people come as friends and associates of the Burg, or as my personal guests. Would you care to? I should value the comments of so attractive and intelligent a young lady, I assure you.'

'I ... I would like it very much!' she said. 'More than anything.'

'You – and your esteemed mother, of course – will be my personal guests, in the Director's loge ... And now – ' he patted her knee again – 'I must telephone your mother.' He drew his eyeglasses from his breast pocket and perched them on his nose. His polished scalp glowed in the lamplight through its sparse covering of hair. He went round to the far side of his enormous table and fumbled through a heavy, calf-bound appointments book.

'Let us see ... *Répétition générale*. Eleven o'clock, the tenth of November. Not quite a fortnight's time.'

He closed the book. He reached for the telephone; he was about to crank the handle when he asked, 'How do they address you at home, Fräulein Schindler?'

She hesitated only a second before replying,

'Alma.'

'A Latin name, eh? It means, the kind girl, doesn't it? That's nice.'

If only it could have been Pappi he was telephoning. If only she could come here to the Burgtheater for the first time to see a play by Goethe, and to share it with Pappi. That would have been truly wonderful.

'Max Burckhard!' Mutti exclaimed, clasping her fingers together. 'Fancy Max Burckhard taking the trouble to introduce himself to you!'

She had said it the night before, when the hired carriage had brought Alma-Maria home. All reproach had been wiped away by Dr Burckhard's importance.

The great hall was stacked with packing cases and crates. A portly, white-bearded man in a coarse white apron and two tatterdemalion boys were hammering them up with nails which they took from their mouths. Rain was weeping gently down the high windows, smearing the far side

43

of the grime. Watery patterns were reflected onto the stone walls.

'Oh, if only the Director of the Kaiserlich-Königlich Burg had come and introduced himself to me in the old days, when I was walking across the Josefplatz . . . !' said Mutti.

'They don't do operetta at the Burg, do they, Muttichen?' asked Grete, who was loitering between the crates, tugging at the labels to see if they were securely tied on and dropping them surreptitiously onto the floor when they came off.

'Gretchen! What on earth are you up to? Can't you find anything better to do than to get in the way of those men?'

'Why don't you tell Almschi to find something to do?' asked Grete. 'She's been making eyes at them all morning.'

Alma-Maria could only shake her head at the monstrous absurdity of the accusation. Fortunately Mutti didn't believe it either. She sent Grete to her room, and Alma-Maria retreated down the passage past the stairs, to Pappi's old studio. It was stripped bare except for the cushioned window alcove and the baby grand piano.

She was sitting at the piano when Herr Möll came in.

'Please continue playing, Almschi. I didn't mean to disturb you.'

Poor man! There was no denying he made an effort to be kind, just like in the old days.

'I hadn't started,' she told him.

Mutti would have liked her to address him as 'Uncle Carl', but Alma-Maria could not bring herself to do it.

'Do you know a painter by the name of Klimt?' she continued.

'Gustav Klimt? Why yes. Of course. His work is much in demand, particularly with the ladies – for their portraits.'

'Dr Burckhard showed me a painting of his, at the Burg. "Juliet in the Tomb". It is very beautiful.'

'Ah yes. Shakespeare's Juliet on her deathbed. It is very fine.'

'Pappi would have liked it,' said Alma-Maria.

'I believe he would,' Herr Möll agreed.

She began playing softly.

'If I were the widow of a great artist,' she said, 'I could never bring myself to marry again!'

She lifted her hands from the keyboard. She hadn't meant to speak so openly. Scenes were Grete's *métier*, not hers. She found she was trembling slightly.

'You will come to understand in time,' said Herr Möll quietly. 'The way you feel now is quite natural.'

'What will I understand?' she asked.

'Compassion. The need for compassion . . . I've wanted to have a frank little chat with you. You have given me the opportunity, I think.'

She stared through the smear of the window – dust inside, rain outside – to the rose garden.

'Would you mind if I smoked a cigar?'

He wasn't really asking her permission. Already he had the cigar between his fingers, and was about to clip the end with a tiny pair of scissors.

She waited as he lit round the circumference of the cigar's end.

'I'm sure you are old enough – and shrewd enough – to know that your Pappi and Mutti were mismatched,' he told her.

She nodded. She wondered if she would manage to endure what was to come without bursting into tears.

Herr Möll rested his hand in the small of his back, and drew on his cigar.

'I do speak as one who has loved them both, you know. Will you believe that?' he asked.

In so far as she believed him capable of love, she believed it. 'When they met,' he continued, 'your Mutti was sitting for Makart.' He smiled as he remembered. 'Makart painted her in the sort of roles she played on the stage,' he said. 'Please understand, I'm speaking no ill of your Pappi when I say that he was something of a Bohemian – fond of good company and laughter. The world met in Makart's studio. It was his element. For your Mutti – well, it was a place where she worked, that was all. She enjoyed approval and applause. But really she was private and careful.'

And Pappi had fallen in love with the role she played, the pert, flirtatious Viennese lady's maid. It was desperately sad. She stared down at the keyboard. With her right hand only, she picked out the Woodbird's song from *Siegfried*. 'Oh let Siegfried beware of the treacherous dwarf!'

'Almschi,' he said. 'this is what I want to say to you. I believe, in all honesty, that your Mutti has a chance of happiness as my wife.'

He put his hand on her shoulder. His cigar smoke wreathed and unfurled between her eyes and the music on the piano.

'She loves you. Very dearly. She cares about what you think, more than you know. Do you understand what I'm saying?'

She breathed in deeply.

'I don't want Mutti to be unhappy,' she said. 'I don't want anybody to be unhappy.'

'God bless you, Almschi,' he said.

She waited until he was gone. She raised herself up, snatched at the music lying on the piano lid and searched through it until she found 'Valse Brilliante' by Adolf Lambertini. She slapped it open in front of her, then pounded out its trite melody and insistent rhythm – one, two, three, clash, da, da! One, two, three, clash, da, da! Nobody came in to tell her she was making too much noise, not even when she sang out the tune. This was Pappi's wing of the house: an empty carcase, stripped to the bone. One, two, three, clash, da, da! – a fantasy of the Christmas Ball at the Sophiensalle, and the hundreds of couples swirling and circling under the clusters of crystal chandeliers ever more wildly until all dull considerations, all sad thoughts were hurled away into the vastnesses of space. Only when her fingers were tired did she stop playing, to stare once more at the rain-swept garden. The thought – more than a thought, a realization – had dawned on her. Möll was Grete's father. It was so obvious, she wondered she hadn't grasped it before.

Mutti put her down at the entrance to the Burgtheater but would not get down herself. A ragged balloon-seller was crossing the wide cobbled emptiness between the kerb and the glass-panelled entrance. The balloons bobbed and swayed above his head, glistening in the soft drizzle. Alma-Maria glanced across to the lawns of the Volksgarten and back again down the stately canyon of the Bankgasse where they were parked. There was not a child in sight. In any case, the man seemed to have sunk into unawareness of what he was holding in his filthy hand, as if the gaily coloured balloons had become an irrelevance.

Mutti stood half-crouched in the carriage doorway, as if she couldn't quite be bothered to rise from the seat. She intended to drive on to their new apartment, 6 Theresianumgasse, to supervise the unpacking there. A single horse cab swung off the Ring and clattered up the cobbles to the theatre entrance. Its fare jumped down nimbly. As he turned to pay off the driver, Alma-Maria caught a glimpse of an angularly thin man in a Scotch tweed cape. Under a shock of black hair which threatened to displace his weather-stained hat was a high forehead; intense dark eyes were magnified by his wire-rimmed spectacles; he had thin, almost hollow cheeks, a curved beak of a nose, and a thin, tight-lipped mouth over an aggressively jutting chin. For all its gauntness, it was one of the most brilliantly alive faces she had ever seen. Their eyes met across the open forecourt only for a moment. There was no message except her knowledge that he had noticed her. As the cab drove away, he ran up the steps quickly with a strange half-limp which did not seem to impede his progress.

'Fancy coming to the Burg in an *Einspänner*!' said Mutti. 'He must be a journalist. He can't possibly be a gentleman.'

Alma-Maria hoped that she was right. Since he had caught her looking at him, she would be even more embarrassed than she was already if she were to meet him inside.

Mutti pushed her head through the carriage door. The long feathers of her hat brushed the sides.

'Enjoy yourself, *meine liebchen*. I mean it.'

'Thank you, Muttichen.' Alma-Maria climbed up onto the step once more to kiss her.

'And come straight over to the Theresianumgasse, won't you?'

'Yes, Muttichen.'

Alma-Marie set off up over the cobbles. She remembered to hold up her skirt in the correct way so as to show off the lace on her petticoat; she wobbled on her new high-buttoned, high-heeled boots, and hoped that Mutti wasn't watching. She felt relieved when she heard the carriage moving away.

She entered the theatre to find the foyer deserted except for an elderly, silver-haired man in shirtsleeves and apron washing down the marble floor. As she went over to him to explain who she was, she felt dreadfully conspicuous. The man waited for her to come to him, leaning on the handle of his mop. His features were those of an elder statesman who was prepared to receive news of revolution, catastrophe or triumph without betraying personal response. When she asked him where she might find the Herr Director, he nodded wisely, without answering, and stood waiting for her next request.

'Please,' she said. 'Dr Buckhard is expecting me.'

'Ah! Expecting you – yes, Fräulein,' he replied, but did not go to tell anyone she had arrived.

She began to wish she had not come. She was looking back through the glass panels of the main entrance, at the empty kerb beyond, when a voice called, 'Fräulein Alma! My dear Fräulein Alma!' And Dr Burckhard, his morning coat parted to show the gold watch chain and seal looped over his waistcoat, and the morning light from the windows gleaming on the bald head under the carefully placed strands of hair, came tripping youthfully down the steps.

'I do apologize for keeping you, my dear … I kiss your hand … I have other guests, it is true, but I was just about to make arrangements to have you brought immediately to my *loge* upstairs when' – he stretched out his hands ruefully – 'quite unexpectedly, who should arrive to attend our little rehearsal, but the Director of the Hamburg State Opera. Come, come, my dear, we must be in time for the overture.'

He led her up the stairs, talking as they went.

'Herr Mahler travelled overnight, it seems, for the particular purpose of hearing von Mildenburg sing. As we're performing the Grillparzer-Beethoven version, we have given the part of Klarchen to von Mildenburg of the Leipzig Opera. It appears he is thinking of capturing her for Hamburg. It'll be the *Klatsch* of all the coffee houses for weeks to come …'

The lights were already down as she entered the Director's *loge*. Two men rose to greet her in the plush-hung gloom. The first, a plump, clean-shaven man with a soft, damp hand, offered her a chair at the front of the *loge*, overlooking the auditorium.

'Richard Heuberger,' he introduced himself with a slight bow over her hand.

He smelled of stale tobacco and coffee. But that wasn't the only thing that prejudiced her against him. She knew he was music critic for the influential *Neue Freie Presse*, a newspaper almost entirely in the hands of Jews; that he was heir-apparent to the *doyen* of Vienna music critics, Eduard Hanslick, and, like Hanslick, was a fanatical anti-Wagnerian.

A second man loomed behind Heuberger, and reached for her hand before she could take the chair offered to her. She had the impression of a burly giant with strong hands and the frame of a peasant woodcutter, like Pappi.

'This is Gustav Klimt, Fräulein Alma,' Dr Burckhard said in her ear. 'Whose painting of Juliet you so much admired.'

Heuberger moved aside to allow Klimt to bow over her hand. She saw the small red beard and sparse red hair, but it was the eyes which impressed her – confident, unblinking, amused.

'I am honoured to meet the daughter of our great Jakob-Emil Schindler,' he said.

His tone of voice made her wonder if he was making fun of her or, worse still, of Pappi? She felt a tremor of panic. Had she been lured into a nest of the most hateful people she could have imagined? What was she to do?

'Fräulein Alma has expressed great admiration for your Juliet,' Dr Burckhard explained.

'That is true, Herr Klimt,' she confirmed.

Was it her own deafness merely which made her voice seem almost inaudible?

'And I have heard, my dear Fräulein Schindler, that you are one of the loveliest girls in Vienna,' said Klimt. 'From an unimpeachable source, I may say – your future stepfather. But alas, the light . . .'

'I think we had better rescue you, Alma Schindler, from these courtiers.'

The voice, a low contralto, belonged to a lady sitting almost at her elbow, so that she was overcome with embarrassment at not having noticed her.

'Let me introduce myself. Berta Zuckerkandl . . . Max? You should have presented your charming *protégée* to me immediately, then I could have protected her from these ruffians . . . Sit down beside me, my dear.'

She was small – smaller even than Mutti, or herself – with a bird-like face and grey hair cropped short as a boy's.

'My most devout apologies, *liebe* Hofratin,' Dr Burckhard bowed over her.

'You are forgiven, Max.' She waved him off impatiently. 'I can't claim any intimate acquaintance with your father, my dear, though one met him on a number of occasions. My husband, however, has a great admiration for his later work and we have several landscapes by him at home – including a most charming gouache, I think, of the Strudengau with the church of St Nikola in the foreground . . .'

The opening, sustained, sombre chords of Beethoven's overture

48

sounded. Alma-Maria took the chair beside the Hofratin Frau Zuckerkandl. The others settled into the gloom behind them, Dr Burckhard behind her shoulder. She looked out across the auditorium. There was a sprinkling of heads in the velvet and gold horseshoe of the *loge*-circle, and rather more in the orchestra stalls below. Conspicuous by being entirely alone in the third row was the man she had seen getting down from the *Einspänner* outside the theatre. He was leaning forward toward the stage as if wishing to catch every note of the music; the light from the orchestra pit shone on his face, so that she could see clearly the shining pallor of the high forehead and aquiline features under the untidy, wiry mop of black hair. The slovenly performance given by the conductor and theatre band scarcely deserved the attention he was giving to it. It was a relief when the curtain rose.

Once the stage performance was under way, she was drawn further and further into it. Egmont, as played by Josef Kainz, South Germany's most distinguished actor, was a heroic figure, and his downfall, therefore – his entrapment by the Spanish in Brussels because of his love for the *petite bourgeoise*, Klarchen – seemed all the more pitiful. However, when, at her mother's fierce accusation, 'Isn't it bad enough my only daughter should be a fallen woman?' Klarchen replied proudly, 'Fallen woman? Egmont's mistress a fallen woman? There isn't a duchess wouldn't envy Klarchen her place in Egmont's heart!' Alma-Maria knew that here was a heroine different and even more wonderful than Gretchen in *Faust*.

The curtain fell on the first half, with Klarchen cradling the sleeping Count Egmont in her arms and singing her lullaby, and Alma felt a sharp resentment at being jolted back into the real world.

'I see Mahler is leaving us,' Heuberger remarked.

He had half-risen from his chair and was leaning forward. Alma-Maria saw that the man in the third row of the stalls had got up and pulled his cape over his shoulders. Hat and cane in hand, he loped with his curiously rapid, limping gait up the aisle and disappeared under the *loge*-circle.

'Of course,' Heuberger continued, 'von Mildenburg has nothing but death and dumbshow in the second half. And I don't suppose the worthy Director of the State Opera wishes to hear any more of your orchestra, my dear Max.'

'I'd better catch him before he leaves,' said Dr Burckhard. 'Forgive me.'

He nodded around him and left the *loge*. Alma-Maria felt she had been deserted. Frau Zuckerkandl sensed how she felt.

'Not to worry, my dear,' she said. 'He'll be back soon enough.'

'Who is Mahler?' Alma-Maria asked, anxious to show that she wasn't worried.

'We'd better ask our distinguished critic here,' said Frau Zuckerkandl.

'Richard? Are you going to tell Fräulein Schindler who Mahler is?'

'I know he is the Director of the Hamburg Opera,' said Alma-Maria.

'There are some who regard him as the son of God,' replies Heuberger. 'Brahms swears he is the only conductor in the entire world who knows how to interpret Mozart's operas. Tchaikovsky has said that he is the only conductor to whom he can entrust his operas with absolute confidence. When he conducted *Fidelio* at London's Covent Garden, they say the audience gave him a ten-minute standing ovation – though an English audience could hardly be regarded as the most penetrating of critics.

'He also composes – other people's music, mostly. He's edited and "improved" the orchestration of all four of Schumann's symphonies – though he did have the decency to wait for poor Clara to die first. His supreme creative act – one hardly has breath to state it – has been to re-orchestrate the scherzo of Beethoven's Ninth . . .'

Frau Zuckerkandl leaned across to him and rapped his hand with the programme she was holding.

'Enough, Richard,' she laughed. 'Quite enough! You'll be saying he's a Jew next.'

'With pride, dear Frau Hofratin!' Heuberger replied obsequiously.

'How these musicians love one another,' commented Klimt.

He was lounging back in the chair which looked too small and elegant for his large frame, plucking at his short red beard and smiling shrewdly. He winked at Alma-Maria as if to draw her into a private conspiracy.

'Are painters any better behaved, my dear Gustl?' Frau Zuckerkandl asked.

'Thank God, Frau Hofratin, painting is not the Viennese passion,' Klimt replied. 'Even the beggars here are music critics.'

The lights were going down when Dr Burckhard returned to the *loge*.

'Come, dear boy, tell us,' said Heuberger. 'Is Mildenburg to be signed up for Hamburg?'

'The Director of the State Opera said nothing about it,' Dr Burckhard replied. 'He merely thanked me for allowing him a most interesting morning. A taciturn devil, if you ask me.'

'Because he has frustrated your lust for gossip?' asked Frau Zuckerkandl.

Alma-Maria found it a mercy that the action of the stage was beginning. More and more she felt excluded, a shy child on the edges of a party – a party of Jews, she told herself, who regarded themselves as too superior to notice the wonderful things that were happening in the play.

Klarchen had seen from her chamber window the scaffold being prepared for Egmont's execution, and was about to poison herself to the accompaniment of Beethoven's solemn music:

'It is now my time. Premonition of morning leads me to my grave. I don't ask anyone to follow me. Put out the lamp quietly, for I am going to my bed. Creep away softly, close the door quietly....'

Alma-Maria gasped involuntarily; the sound was more like a sob. In her feeling of suspense, she had forgotten to breathe. It seemed impossible that anything could move her more deeply. She prepared to watch Egmont's final scene, in the condemned hold, with no more than passing curiosity. Then, Egmont, having bidden farewell to his friends and foes, settled down, wrapped in his cloak, to sleep, and the light began to glow around him and music to play. Within the radiance of the light, the classical figure of Victory took shape, a laurel wreath about her loosened hair – a Victory in the form and figure of Klarchen transfigured. Egmont stirred, raising himself from his couch, his eyes still closed in sleep. The heavenly Klarchen took the wreath from her head. Holding it aloft, to the accompaniment of Beethoven's triumphant music, she glided to Egmont's side and placed the wreath on his brow. Alma-Maria turned her face away, unable to bear so much glory. Goethe's words closing the final scene of *Faust* echoed in her brain:

> All indescribables
> Here we descry;
> Eternal Womanhead leads us on high.

Frau Zuckerkandl applauded vigorously as Josef Kainz and Anna von Mildenburg took their bow, attempting to reinforce the sparse applause from the rest of the house. When she could do no more, she turned to Alma-Maria.

'It's a wonderful experience to see the performance of a masterpiece for the first time. And I'll tell you something else, *liebchen*. It is a privilege for somebody like myself to be allowed to share that experience with you.'

Alma-Maria wondered if Frau Zuckerkandl, being Jewish, could truly understand the Christian message of intercession and redemption which made the climax of *Egmont* such a glorious experience. But she was grateful, just the same.

'Thank you Frau Hofratin,' she said.

'There's no need for the stupid title, *liebchen*,' Frau Zuckerkandl told her. 'There are altogether too many titles used these days. I'm a simple Frau, and my husband is a practising surgeon; the title *Hofrat* makes him sound like a politician, heaven forbid! So, just Frau Zuckerkandl for the time being. And then, if we grow to like one another, as I'm sure we will, perhaps you may call me Berta.'

Dr Burckhard was at her side.

'Shall I sent out for a *fiacre*, Frau Hofratin?' he asked.

Berta Zuckerkandl smiled at Alma-Maria. To Dr Burckhard she said, 'Thank you, no. My carriage is waiting by the Minoriten Kirche ... Fräulein Alma, you are lovelier than Möll says you are, and your costume is quite perfect. Did you choose it for yourself?'

For a moment, Alma-Maria thought of lying. Instead she replied, 'My mother chose it for me.'

'Well, it goes to show that mothers are not always wrong, doesn't it?'

Alma-Maria wondered if she was referring to Mutti's engagement to Herr Möll. Frau Zuckerkandl held out her hand to her.

'When your mother is settled into your new place, you must both come and visit us. I know that my husband will be quite enchanted by you.'

Dr Burckhard took her arm to escort her from the *loge*. Heuberger followed. Klimt came to Alma-Maria's side.

'You're not running away immediately, Fräulein Alma?' he asked.

She looked up at him.

'No. I don't think so.'

She wasn't certain what she should do.

'Did you know there is a painting by your father hanging in the Upper Promenade?'

There was something Olympian about the way he smiled down at her – his physical powerfulness and confident good looks.

'Dr Burckhard told me,' she said.

'Shall I take you to see it?' he asked.

They had followed the others out onto the landing. Groups of the small audience, mostly men, were descending the stairs, pausing to light cigars or pipes on the way. Dr Burckhard turned from Frau Zuckerkandl's side to look back.

'I should certainly like to see it,' Alma-Maria said.

She noticed the look of disappointment on Dr Burckhard's face, and was surprised by it.

'The Herr Director will have to pay his formal homage to Herr Kainz and Fräulein von Mildenburg,' said Klimt.

For the first time, she detected the rough Naschmarkt accent in his voice. It went with his grin.

'I should like that very much,' she confirmed.

'I shall join you shortly on the Promenade,' Dr Burckhard told them.

He escorted Frau Zuckerkandl and Richard Heuberger down the stairs to the foyer. Alma-Maria wondered if she had misbehaved and, if so, whether Dr Burckhard would forgive her. She was confused by the incident. At the same time, she knew that she had understood what had not been spoken, rather like when Siegfried, walking in the forest, realized he understood the song of the birds.

She went with Herr Klimt up the next flight of stairs, and round the deserted Promenade until they reached the bar. The painting hung on the wall opposite. It was in oils – a long canvas representing the procession on the Ring of the trade and professional guilds to celebrate the Silver Wedding of the Old Man and the Empress Elizabeth. Pappi had often spoken to her about the occasion. It had occurred the year of her birth.

Hans Makart, with Pappi's assistance, had designed the costumes and decorations as a re-creation on a massiva scale of the Entry of the Guilds in Act Three of Wagner's opera, *Die Meistersinger*.

This was not the formal record of the occasion: that had been painted by Makart himself, with the Old Man as the central point of interest. Here, Makart occupied the middle of the canvas, a handsome, bearded giant not unlike the man standing beside Alma-Maria now, his hand resting lightly on her shoulder; except that Makart was on horseback, dressed inappropriately as Rubens, his feet thrust forward, lounging back in the saddle, a tipsy smile on his face, one hand clutching the reins, the other holding an oversize paint palette and brushes. A group of ladies crowded over a balcony throwing flowers and very nearly themselves at his horse's feet. At his horse's head, holding the bridle and gazing up over his shoulder at Makart with an expression of awe-struck admiration, was the unmistakable self-portrait of Pappi himself.

'It's satirical, of course,' said Klimt. 'See, here is poor old von Bülow looking around the crowd for his wife, and here's Wagner dressed as a sweep carrying her off – Cosima's in the sack over his shoulder . . . And here is Franz Liszt on a mule, dressed as a cardinal.'

'I don't like it,' said Alma-Maria.

'Why?' Klimt asked gently.

But she couldn't answer. She felt disgusted.

'I doubt whether your worthy father would count it among his better work,' he said. 'It's only a game. It's even painted as a parody of Makart's style . . . Is it the way he's portrayed himself?'

She nodded.

'Makart was his friend and master, wasn't he?' Klimt went on. 'Your father shared his studio, didn't he, back in the seventies?'

She nodded again.

'Then you must allow him this act of gratitude, eh? Love transmutes all sins to virtue, and I expect your father loved the old rogue.'

He put both hands on her shoulders, and turned her to him.

'I'll tell you this, Alma Schindler. Your father was ten times the painter Hans Makart ever was!'

'Thank you,' she whispered up at him.

'Did you ever sit for him?' he asked. 'Your father?'

She shook her head. He put his fingers under her chin and tilted up her face.

'He probably took your looks for granted,' he said.

She heard the clatter of the lift door at the far end of the Promenade. As Dr Burckhard's voice called out, 'Ah, here you are!' she thought she heard – was sure she heard – Herr Klimt say distinctly, 'Oh, shit!' just like one of the servants caught off guard.

The transient but unmistakable expression of pique she observed on Herr Klimt's face astonished her: it was so inappropriate in one of his strength and stature. It struck her as silly; men such as he were designed to act heroically to music by Wagner – or Beethoven. At the same time, she felt a secret, vertiginous excitement that she should be the cause of such masculine folly. A spirit of contrariness, or perhaps a first, experimental touch on the levers controlling life's course, caused her to offer Dr Burckhard as he joined them her most winning smile, and to reach out her hand to touch his arm.

She returned home late from her music lesson, not for the first time. The move from Plankenburg to their new home at Theresianumgasse 6 had at last been accomplished. The tram-ride from the Schottentor to the Karlplatz was simple and safe. Dr Labor had given her a book to celebrate becoming a true Viennese – Nietzsche's *Also Sprach Zarathustra*. He had told her that reading it would help her to understand better the meaning of Wagner's operas. He had talked about it to her until he had been summoned to play the organ for Benediction in the Votivkirche.

In any case, since they had moved, dinner was always served late because Möll always came in late, and, of course, they weren't allowed to start without him. Now that they were living in an apartment overlooking and overlooked by other apartments, Mutti and Herr Möll had decided between them that it would be improper for him to sleep there until they were married. He came for his evening meal, however – and the evening meal had to wait until he chose to arrive. Alma-Maria threw her portfolio onto the piano in the drawing room – there was no music room in the apartment. The metal rod over the handle which secured the flap clattered across the lid.

'That's a silly thing to do,' said Mutti. 'It'll scrape the polish.'

'Pianos shouldn't be French polished,' replied Alma-Maria; 'it's bad for them.'

'And I keep on asking you to come home before dark,' Mutti went on. 'You never pay any attention.'

'Dr Labor wanted me to teach him some pieces. It was important.'

She kissed Mutti on the cheek. She had come to realize that in the old days Mutti's anger, ostensibly directed at her, had in fact been directed at Pappi.

She went up to her room on the second floor of the apartment. It looked out over the courtyard with its gas lamp and solitary tree. During the day, the maids hung washing from window rail to window rail, taking the opportunity to chatter to one another. There were also other musicians in the block – a Herr Groebler, a violinist with the Volksoper, who practised cadenzas and complicated trills every morning as well as fragments of popular light opera, and a Fräulein Bella Kalman, who played dance music on the piano and was regarded by all the maids as a great virtuoso. At the moment there was silence, broken only by the distant clatter and hiss of the tramcars crossing the points on the Theresianumgasse on the other side of the building.

She took off her day dress and stockings, and sat, half-lying, on the bed in her petticoat, basking in the warmth of the stove. Unknown to Mutti, she had stopped wearing drawers. This was partly as a reaction against the coarse serge garments she had been forced to wear at the Maria Theresia Institute, but also because she liked the flow of silk against her body as she moved about. She opened the book which Dr Labor had given her and which she had brought up with her, and began to read:

> He who creates goals for mankind, thus giving the earth its meaning and its future – he it is who creates the quality of good and evil in things.... The noble man – the true *Herr* – knows that he himself is the determiner of values. He has no need of the approval of others.

It came to her with all the excitement of discovering something which, in her heart, she already knew but which she had been waiting for somebody wiser than herself to put into words. It was what *Faust* was all about, and Egmont and Klarchen defying the law both of Spain and of conventional morality ... And Jesus – of course. '*I* am the Way, the Truth, and the Life.'

'Fräulein Almschi?' Noni–Ilona, the maid from the Hungarian *pusta* who looked after her – was knocking at the door. 'Your Mutti's sent me. She says where have you got to? – the soup is on the table!'

'All right, Noni.'

She rose and went to the door to let the maid in.

'I was reading. I forgot I was supposed to be getting ready. Help me dress, please Noni.'

'It must be nice being able to read like that,' said Noni in her heavy Magyar accent. 'I like a good story – you know, a romance.'

She drew the corset about Alma-Maria's waist and began fastening the hooks.

'My mother used to read,' she said. 'She had five or six books of her own. She'd read them so often the pages were falling out.'

Having her evening corset laced tight always sent a thread of excitement needling through Alma-Maria which conjured fantasies in her brain – Isolde saluting Tristan as she lifted the chalice to drink the potion of love and death, Brunnhilde, her armour golden in the dawn sun, sitting up on the mountain rock to find Siegfried, strong and handsome as an angel, gazing at her in rapture. *Thus from out of myself –* what had Nietzsche written? – *cried and laughed my own wise desire ...*

After they had finished the meal, Herr Möll took out his cigar case as had been his practice at Plankenburg.

'Not in here, darling man,' said Mutti in a tone of sweet affection.

'The dining room at the castle was such a desert, wasn't it? But here the smell will linger.'

Herr Möll obediently put away his case. Alma-Maria caught Grete's wicked smile; it made her feel quite close to her for once.

'Why don't we go through to your study?' suggested Mutti. 'I'll tell Kathe to bring the coffee.'

Your study, Alma-Maria noticed. Herr Möll folded his napkin very precisely.

'I saw Klimt at the Kunsthistorisches Museum this afternoon,' he said casually. 'He's back at work.'

'Gustav Klimt?' asked Mutti. 'So he has recovered. They say the poor thing was like a lost soul after the death of his brother.'

Alma-Maria thought of the red-bearded peasant-giant she had met at the Burgtheater. 'Poor thing' and 'lost soul' were unexpected descriptions of the man she remembered.

'Ernst Klimt has been dead for over two years now,' said Herr Möll. 'Gustav has decided to complete his work on the grand staircase.'

He glanced across the table at Alma-Maria. For no reason that she could think of, she felt a touch of guilt. She looked down at the cloth, but noticed as she did so that he was dabbing his lip with his neatly folded napkin.

'It appears that our Alma-Maria was introduced to him the other day – by Burckhard, at the Burg,' he remarked.

'You didn't tell me you had been presented to Herr Klimt, Almschi!' Mutti said.

'I wasn't *presented* to him, Muttichen. He was in Dr Burckhard's *loge*. That's all.'

Herr Möll moved uneasily.

'My dear Anny,' he said to Mutti. 'He made a request of me. He asked me if I would seek your permission for Almschi to sit for him – for one of the panels between the columns of the Kunsthistorisches Museum stairs ... It would be a fully draped figure, of course.'

Grete stared at Alma-Maria as if seeing her for the first time. Mutti uttered a little gasp.

'*Liebe* Carl!' she said. 'The very idea! You quite surprise me!' She put her own napkin down and pushed back her chair. 'Dear me!' she said. She glanced at Alma-Maria. 'You were never alone with Herr Klimt, were you, *liebchen*?'

Alma-Maria shook her head vehemently and hoped that she would not actually have to speak a lie. To Herr Möll, Mutti said,

'She's still only a child. What would people think?'

'You sat for Hans Makart, Mutti – several times,' said Alma-Maria.

'That was quite different. Makart's atelier was a public place, to all intents and purposes,' Mutti replied. 'Besides Herr Klimt has something of a ...' She paused fractionally ... 'a reputation,' she concluded.

'Lots of women have their portraits painted by him,' Alma-Maria persisted.

'Sitting for a portrait is one thing,' said Mutti sharply. 'Sitting as a model is quite another ... I think you had better leave Uncle Carl and myself to discuss it.'

Herr Möll said, 'Do what your Mutti tells you. Leave the room, if you please. And you, Gretchen.'

'Yes, Uncle Carl,' said Grete with a meekness which was belied by the smirk she gave Alma-Maria.

Alma-Maria followed her out, having said nothing.

As she closed the dining room door behind her, Grete said to her, 'What have you been up to?'

There was a note of respect in her voice, so that Alma-Maria was almost sorry to have to reply, 'Nothing. Not a thing.'

Fortunately, Grete couldn't believe her.

'What is he like?' she whispered.

'Sh!' whispered Alma-Maria.

They stood on the stairs as Mutti's voice came from the dining room: 'Everybody talks about what goes on in the Mariahilferstrasse at the Casa Piccola!'

'Emilie Flöge is his sister-in-law, *liebchen*,' Herr Möll said. 'He designs the fabrics for her costumes.'

'Carl! I'm not deaf and blind. Everybody knows how things stand between them. And between him and one or two of her seamstresses, so I've heard!'

Grete giggled loudly. 'Sh!' Alma-Maria repeated.

'He is my friend, Anny,' Möll was saying. 'There is no question of Almschi being alone with him – she must be chaperoned, naturally ...'

'By whom?' Mutti demanded. 'I haven't the time. Have you? And if Noni or Kathe went with her the world would assume they'd take bribes to keep their mouths shut just like most maids do.'

'I would ask you to think about it, Anny.' said Herr Möll. 'There are young women of good family who would be proud to find themselves portrayed on the walls of the Kunsthistorisches Museum.'

'I'll think about it,' Mutti replied. 'But my answer will be the same. You forget that I have good reason to know about these things – better reason than any man could ever have!'

As they crept up the stairs, Grete whispered to Alma-Maria, 'Almschi? What *is* he like? Is he very handsome?'

'Herr Klimt?'

'Who do you think, stupid?'

'He's very big. Tall.'

'Taller than Dr Burckhard?'

Dr Burckhard had come to dinner – invited as a return for his kindness toward Alma-Maria. Grete had not been impressed. ('Ugh! He's *bald*!')

'Yes. Much.'

'Has he got more hair?'

'I don't know. I couldn't see the top of his head.'

'Be serious, Almschi!'

'Why? There's nothing to be serious about. He just happened to be sitting in the Director's *loge* at the same time as me. So were a lot of other people.'

'But *they* didn't want to paint you, did they?'

Alma-Maria went to her own room and closed the door. She lay down on the bed without undressing, without so much as taking off her shoes. She just wanted to think. Or, rather, she just wanted to rehearse from memory what had happened when she had met Klimt at the Burgtheater, and what he had said to her. She lay back in the darkness, staring out of the window at the lights through the curtains opposite, her hand resting on the book she had left when Noni had disturbed her. Particularly, she remembered how put out Klimt had been when Dr Burckhard had come up in the lift. The recollection sent a pang of excitement through her.

'Dr Burckhard? What exactly is "the Superman"?'

'"The Superman"?' Dr Burckhard asked curiously.

He had been preoccupied with administration all morning. Not that it worried Alma-Maria. She was no longer regarded as a stranger in the Burgtheater. She came and went as she pleased: the statesman-like janitor bowed to her when she crossed the foyer; the cleaning women smiled at her and passed joking comments, which frequently she was unable to hear. If there was no rehearsal, she wandered about examining the paintings on the walls and ceilings of the foyer and grand staircase – particularly the sequence depicting the History of the Stage which Klimt had painted with his brother seven or eight years earlier. If Dr Burckhard was busy, she sat in his office reading from the vellum-bound playbooks which lined the shelves. She read promiscuously, voraciously, entering new worlds for which she had no chart – the war-torn vistas of *Wallenstein's Camp*, the mysterious dread which haunted *Ghosts*. Sometimes scenes lodged in her mind either for their almost unbearable pathos, such as the death of Hannele in Gerhardt Hauptmann's *Hannele's Assumption*, or because of a frightening unease, like the appearance of the Button Moulder in *Peer Gynt*. Sometimes she encountered domestic scenes which, because of their homely charm, pained her for they made her think of what Pappi and Mutti's marriage had been like, or as with *The Father*, made life at Plankenburg rosy by comparison.

'*Behold I teach you the Superman*,' she quoted.

The phrase resounded in her mind. Already she was toying with the idea of setting it to music – a great triumphant statement for choir and full orchestra.

'Nietzsche,' said Dr Burckhard. '*Zarathustra*?'

She nodded.

'Where have you got a copy of *Zarathustra* from?' he asked. 'Or should I say, from whom?'

'Dr Labor,' she replied. 'He told me I would probably understand Wagner better if I read it.'

'Then perhaps you ought to ask him, *liebchen*,' said Dr Burckhard, not quite able to conceal the stiffness in his voice.

'I'm sure you know,' Alma-Maria said, and, suddenly inspired, she added, 'You probably know better than Dr Labor. Musicians never really understand anything except music.'

Dr Burckhard came from behind the table. He was smiling.

'So you've noticed that, have you, *liebchen*?'

It had been one of Pappi's aphorisms, but she wasn't going to tell him so. Not now.

He sat down on the sofa beside her. She hoped he wouldn't put his hand on her knee. She was sure his fingers reeked of stale cigar.

'Very well, I'll try to explain what Nietzsche means,' he said. 'The Superman is he who has made himself master of himself. Right?'

Alma-Maria nodded.

'He is not a slave to laws and conventions imposed by others. On the other hand, he is not a slave to his own passions. Right? He knows himself; he lives by a moral code which is the product of his conscious will. That is what makes a hero a hero ...' He broke off. Then he said, 'I'm afraid I shall never become one of Nietzsche's heroes. I am certainly enslaved ...' He paused again. 'Do you know, *liebchen*? There's not a day goes by when I don't think of you? Does that offend you?'

'No, of course it doesn't,' she replied. 'But it's silly, isn't it?'

'Is it?' he asked. 'You have the most penetrating, perfectly blue eyes I have ever seen. As if one can see the intelligence shining through them, like lamps of the soul.'

She felt apprehensive, but dared not move.

'Maybe I'm watching a scene at rehearsal, or reading a play script. I find myself asking, what would dear little Alma think of this: that sharp little mind and devastating honesty? And I see those blue eyes gazing.'

'Dr Burckhard,' she laughed, though she did not really feel like laughing, 'what do you think my mother would say if she could hear you?'

He looked seriously at her.

'I think she might be pleased – pleased to discover how much I appreciate her daughter's worth,' he said.

She reached behind her for her woollen hat and her gloves. His confidence had given rise to an uneasy suspicion in her mind.

'I must go,' she said. 'We have guests coming tonight.'

She rose.

'I have offended you!' he said.

'Why should you have offended me?' she asked. 'You've said the nicest things.' But she felt she was at the end of her social resources.

He held her shoulders gently, stooped and kissed her cheek.

'I wish you would call me Max,' he said softly.

'I am very young still,' she said, carefully easing herself from his embrace. 'My mother says I'm still a child.'

'It is a great privilege to be allowed to watch so beautiful a girl growing into womanhood,' he told her.

'Thank you, Dr Burckhard.'

'Max. Please?'

It was a false playfulness. Perhaps he was as embarrassed as she was. She tried to smile, and murmured, '*Auf wiedersehen*,' without adding any mode of address. As she ran down the great echoing staircase to the deserted grand foyer, wobbling uncertainly on the high heels she always wore outside so that she should not look smaller and younger than her years, she felt as though she had entered a forest foolishly and unwittingly, where the tracks were becoming ever more confused and labyrinthine.

'Fräulein Almschi, you have to get up!'

Noni was shaking her shoulder.

'There's a Christmas present for you, downstairs.'

Alma-Maria opened her eyes blearily. 'A Christmas present?' she asked.

Drowsiness lay warmly, comfortably enclosing her, enticing her to shut her eyes once more. Last night, they had attended Mass at the Karlskirche as a family, Herr Möll, the maids, even Mutti. Afterwards, there had been mulled wine, pastries, and the exchanging of presents; Mutti had given her a bottle of the same mimosa-scented perfume she herself wore. When finally they had retired, Alma-Maria had allowed Grete to come into her room to look out of her window so that she could see, across the courtyard, all the Christmas trees candlelit in the windows opposite, and below the big Christmas tree which the Kalmans had set up in the yard itself for the enjoyment of the entire block – even though they were not themselves Christians.

She sat up. Noni draped a shawl about her shoulders.

'Who is the present from?' asked Alma-Maria. 'What is it?'

'Who knows?' Noni replied. 'It's a big one. It's taken two men with a barrow to bring it.'

The sky over the rooftops was a leaden grey. Snowflakes hovered uncertainly, drifting to and fro past the window. Alma-Maria got out from under the body-warmth of the quilt. She wrapped the shawl over her nightdress and pinned it across her breast with a heavy brooch, then went with Noni downstairs. Mutti was waiting by the front door of the apartment; like Alma-Maria, she too had a shawl wrapped over her nightdress, and had her hair down, though it did not reach the backs of her legs like Alma-Maria's. There was a smell of freshly ground coffee.

'Alfred is with them, down in the entrance.' Mutti sounded quite excited. Alfred was the janitor. They went down to the arched, cobbled passage which connected the courtyard to the street. A two-wheeled barrow, its contents covered with a canvas sheet, stood against the wall. As Alma-Maria stepped out onto the cobbles, the cold whipped about her ankles and clutched at her throat. The two porters who had brought the barrow were in Alfred's lodge by the gate, warming themselves at the stove. When they saw Alma-Maria and Mutti through the dusty window, they came outside, clutching their caps to their chests and bowing.

'*Grüss Gott, gnädige Frau! Grüss Gott, gnädige Fräulein Schindler!*'

Alma-Maria recognized the porter at the Burgtheater.

'The Herr Doctor Director sends his compliments and wishes for a happy Christmas to both ladies . . .' He pointed to the barrow. 'We shall carry these upstairs, if you please.'

He drew back the canvas sheet. The barrow was heaped with books. Alma-Maria went over to examine them, huddling her shawl about her against the wind which was blowing sharply down the passage. They were sets of classics, calf-bound and gilt-tooled: Schiller, Lessing, Molière, Shakespeare, Goethe, Dante, Racine, Grillparzer, von Kleist. She picked a volume from off the top and opened it.

'See, Muttichen!' she exclaimed.

A bookmark was pasted on the inside cover. Enclosed in an Indian ink design of hanging vines were the words in heavy gothic lettering, *Ex Libris Alma Maria Schindler*. She noticed instantly that there was no hyphen between the 'Alma' and the 'Maria'. She took up another volume and then another. All had bookmarks pasted in them.

'They must have cost him a fortune!' said Mutti.

The porters carried them up to the apartment and stacked them on the hallway floor. Mutti went into the drawing room to fetch her purse from her bureau. Grete sat on the stairs watching. When Mutti had returned and had given a florin to each of the porters, Grete said,

'Almschi is going to have to make up her mind quite soon, isn't she, Mutti?'

'I've not the faintest idea what you mean,' Alma-Maria replied.

'Gretl is right,' Mutti said. 'You're going to have to make an important decision one of these days.'

She sounded arch.

'If you mean about Dr Burckhard,' said Alma-Maria. 'He's just trying to educate me, I'm sure. He thinks I'm a complete ignoramus.'

'What is he educating you for, Almschi?' asked Grete.

'Oh don't be so stupid, Gretchen!' Alma-Maria raised her voice.

'Sh! Don't let the maids hear you,' Mutti told them. 'Gretl, go to your room and get dressed.'

'What about Almschi?' Grete asked.

'Almschi too,' Mutti agreed.

She was being unwontedly patient.

'Dr Burckhard thinks of me as a child,' Alma-Maria told Mutti when Grete was gone. 'I mean, I can tell. Honestly.'

She was anxious, if it were at all possible, to head off Mutti's wishful thinking, or aspirations, on her behalf.

'Can you, *liebchen*?' Mutti asked wisely.

Alma-Maria's heart sank. She busied herself searching for *Faust* among the books. She found it. It was beautiful to look at and to touch, and it smelt of new leather. She carried it up to her room.

> ... if woman's love, also from on high,
> Has helped him through his sorrow,
> Hallowed legions of the sky
> Will give him good goodmorrow.

Poor Dr Burckhard! Had he ever known woman's love, she wondered? Surely he wasn't seriously thinking of her in that way. She hoped and prayed not. It wasn't just that she didn't feel the least in love with him; she couldn't imagine how any woman could. His pallid face and the smell of stale cigar which hung permanently about him made the thought of any form of physical intimacy with him quite repellent. The trouble was that he had appointed himself doorkeeper to what was for her a splendid new world from which she could not contemplate turning back.

She walked the short distance from the Burgtheater to the Votivkirche, across the Rathauspark and behind the University. There weren't many people about in the cold grey January afternoon. Several nursemaids were wheeling cane-sided bassinets, stopping to exchange the time of day on the pavement of the Rathausplatz. A toy-seller set his clockwork soldiers marching along the side of the path, more to alleviate his own boredom than to attract custom. The inevitable balloon-seller had been driven in desperation to stand on the steps of the Rathaus itself, bobbing and nodding his balloons ingratiatingly in the direction of any passing city bureaucrat. As a child, Alma-Maria had longed to see a balloon-seller lifted into the air by his wares, to float away over the statue of the Rathausmann standing with his lance and banner up on the tower of the Rathaus, and off into the sky between the tall spires of the Votivkirche to vanish far above the summits of the Wienerwald beyond. Pappi had told her that it was the great hazard of being a balloon-seller; it had taken her a long time to accept that he had been teasing her.

She buried her chin in her soft angora comforter. Because people said that it was a firm, determined little chin she was sure that it stuck out; she had become self-conscious about it. She had just been to the Burgtheater to thank Dr Burckhard for his present. He had put his arm round her shoulder, only lightly, not enough for her to object to openly and pull away. Now she was certain he was in love with her. It was a shame, really; and she didn't know what to do about it.

It was a relief to go to Dr Labor. She loved him, and he was fond of her. She had grown to feel comfortable when she was with him ever since she read his unmistakable delight when she had returned to take lessons from him after she had run away from the Maria Theresia Institute. But the desolation of the winter afternoon seemed also to have affected him. He was sitting in the choir room, amidst the dusty heaps of scores he couldn't read and shelves of neglected manuscript books, his frail old body wrapped in a bulky overcoat and muffler. She sat down at the piano. She had prepared a passage from Nietzsche which she had been setting as a part of her great Nietzschean cantata for soloists, chorus and symphony orchestra. She had to light the candles in order to read her own manuscript in the ecclesiastical gloom.

'Bad as that, is it?' asked Dr Labor. 'Damned winter!'

In her head, the section on which she had been working was especially magnificent. She believed she had managed to convey something of the splendour onto the pages spread in front of her.

She should have been warned by the grunt which came from behind her. But, after many months during which she had felt no creative urge of any kind, the return of desire to set words to music was both an excitement and a relief.

She chanted out both solo part and chorus as she played. On finishing, she lifted her hands from the keyboard.

'It's my fault,' said Dr Labor. 'I should never have let you loose on the organ. It ruins one's touch for the piano.' He cleared his throat. Then he said, 'You've gone a fair way to spoiling a very pleasant light soprano. I suppose it comes from singing Wagner to yourself. You were never cut out to be a *Heldensoprano*, my dear young girl.'

They sat in silence, Alma-Maria waiting for his verdict on her setting of Nietzsche. He grunted once more, shifted in his chair, then lapsed into silence again. A moment or two later, he pulled himself up.

'Let me play something to you. Let me play something by another disciple of Dr Nietzsche.'

She surrendered the piano stool to him. He began to play and to chant the words in a hoarse *Sprechstimme* which nevertheless perfectly conveyed the vocal melody.

> O Man! Take heed!
> What says the deep midnight?
> 'I slept, I slept –
> From a deep dream I have awoken –

She listened, and as she listened, a sense of awe overcame her resentment. When he was finished, she could not speak at first. Then she said, 'It goes to the very heart of things.'

The suspicion crept into her mind that that was the reason why he had played the piece to her – that instead of criticizing her own work, he was seeking to demonstrate how far she had to go.

'Do you know who wrote it?' he asked.

'No.' The style was unfamiliar to her.

'Our next Director of the Court Opera.'

'Felix Mottl?' she asked.

'Mottl?' Dr Labor laughed. 'Is that the *Klatsch* from the coffee houses? Do you mean the news hasn't leaked out yet? Has Vienna gone deaf all of a sudden? Mahler is coming from Hamburg.'

'Gustav Mahler? But he is a Jew! A Czech.'

'I don't think he could do anything about having been born in Bohemia. But they say he has accepted Christian baptism – "Paris is worth a Mass", you know?'

'And he wrote that?'

'He is very considerable composer.'

There could be no mistake about what she had just heard. It had been heartrendingly beautiful – the sort of music which could drive her to wonder why she ever attempted putting notes to a manuscript stave.

'I am sorry I can't recommend you to Herr Mahler as a pupil,' said Dr Labor. 'He'll be too great a man now, as well as being a very busy one. Besides, your honoured and well-born mother would never forgive me. Mahler has a terrible reputation with the ladies ... Though it is said his preference is for singers. What I will do is to recommend you to one of his best pupils, Alexander von Zemlinsky. He's a young fellow: I should be surprised if he's as much as ten years older than you. But he's highly regarded; he's already got a court of aspiring young composers about him. And it won't do you the least harm to rub shoulders with other composers. You can find out what you're competing against.'

He was telling her that he believed her talent was worth developing, and that she should study under somebody who, unlike himself, was a practising composer. She stood behind him and put her arms about him.

'Thank you, dear, dear Herr Kapellmeister,' she whispered.

She felt she wanted to sing out with relief. As she gathered up her manuscript music and thrust it away into her portfolio, he sat staring past her.

'You will find that von Zemlinsky is a very good teacher of composition,' he said.

She detected the note of regret in his voice, but was too happy to regard it. On leaving him, she went round to the east front of the church to catch a tram home.

'Fräulein Schindler? Alma-Maria Schindler?'

She recognized him immediately as he stepped out from the lamp-light and approached her across the grass. There was his giant stature as well as the red beard, which was not entirely concealed under his scarf.

'Why, Herr Klimt!'

She could feel the beat of her heart. She wondered if he had known she had been with Dr Labor and had been waiting for her. It was the way he had come through the lamplight out of the darkness.

'I'm afraid that your excellent mother has declined my request – that you should be allowed to sit for me.'

'I'm afraid she has, Herr Klimt.'

She felt short of breath.

'Are you going to the tram stop? May I keep you company until your tram comes?'

'If you wish, Herr Klimt.'

He walked beside her, towering over her;

'It is Fräulein Alma-Maria, isn't it?' he asked. 'Or do you prefer to be called Alma?'

'My family call me Almschi. I prefer Alma to Alma-Maria. It sounds more grown-up, doesn't it?'

'I suppose it does. You know, Fräulein Alma, it is a terrible thing to discover I have so little reputation left that well-brought-up young ladies have to be protected from one.'

She gave an involuntary little giggle.

'Actually, I don't think I am terribly well brought up,' she replied.

'Worse and worse!' Herr Klimt exclaimed, clutching his forehead in mock distress. 'Even badly brought up young women have to be pro-tected from me.'

There was a small knot of people standing huddled in their winter coats about the tram stop. Alma-Maria felt the chill feather touch of snowflakes on her cheek. Snowflakes were melting into her hair. She drew her thick angora-wool comforter up over her head. Through the trees along the Ring, she could see the lamps floodlighting the entrance to the Burgtheater, and beyond, row upon row of tiny, square lit windows around the Hofburg.

'I hope that in this family discussion, Möll took my part?' asked Herr Klimt.

'I think so,' she told him. 'I was sent out of the room. But it did sound like it.'

'What about you, Fräulein Alma? If you had your way, would you sit for me?'

'That isn't fair, Herr Klimt.'

Two trams came clanking and hissing, shooting sparks into the night air as they passed under the junctions of overhead wires. Neither were heading for the Theresianum.

'Did Möll tell you anything about the painting I wanted you to sit for?'

'He said it was a wall panel in the Kunsthistorisches Museum.'

'Exactly so.'

'He said something about how many properly-brought-up young ladies would be proud to find themselves so ...' She paused, shy of actually saying it: ' ... immortalized?' she suggested.

Herr Klimt clapped his gloved hands enthusiastically.

'Did he so? Did he indeed?' he cried out so heartily that several people standing in front of them at the tram stop looked round. Alma-Maria smiled up at him.

'He tried to convince my mother that I was to be shown fully draped,' she said.

She burst into a fit of the giggles. Now he was smiling down at her, on the verge of laughter.

'My dear Fräulein Alma!' he declared. 'There could be nothing more respectable, I promise you – nothing to ruffle a mother's feathers in the least.'

This provoked more curious looks from the others at the stop.

'Dear girl – let me take you back to my studio. I wouldn't keep you for long, I promise; just long enough to take five or six photographs of your head and shoulders, that's all.'

She was very tempted, but she said, 'I couldn't do that, Herr Klimt.'

'Do you always obey your mother?' he asked.

'Always,' she replied, because it was the first thing that came into her head.

'My studio is just down the Josefstädterstrasse. Five minutes' walk. I must have a study of you while you still wear your hair down.'

'Really, Herr Klimt!'

The tram for the Karlsplatz and the Theresianum came nosing round the corner and approached down the Ring, its bell clanging. Herr Klimt had seen it too. His face registered that same look of bad-tempered, childish disappointment she had noticed when Dr Burckhard had joined them on the Promenade of the Burgtheater. She too felt disappointed.

'Demel's!' he exclaimed. 'Even your mother couldn't complain if I took you to Demel's.'

There was a tram stop at the top of Kärntnerstrasse. She only had to break the ride.

'You couldn't take photographs of me in Demel's,' she said.

'I could sketch you. There's plenty of light there.'

A couple – clerk from the Rathaus, no doubt, a spare, sallow-faced little man in a grimy wing collar and stained bowler hat, and a portly middle-aged woman in a fur stole which had seen better days, with a soiled satin toque over her sagging grey features – glared their resentment at a youthful freedom they themselves had never experienced.

'I don't know,' said Alma-Maria. 'My mother is bound to ask why I was out so long.'

She wasn't. It would depend, as always, on what and how much Mutti had on her mind. But Alma-Maria didn't want her surrender to appear absolute. She clambered up onto the platform of the tram. He mounted aboard behind her, and said to the conductor,

'Two to the Kärntnerstrasse.'

The conductor saluted and bowed, smiling as he took the fare, happy to play his tiny role in the transportation of a pair of lovers to their presumed coupling. Herr Klimt helped her to a bench, and stood over her. She found herself catching her breath. *What does your conscience say?* she reminded herself of Nietzsche's words. *You must become him – or her – you are.*

They couldn't talk in the rattling, oil-reeking interior. It was the sort of situation which really tried her defective hearing. When, very shortly, the tram clanged to a halt at the top of the Kärntnerstrasse, and Herr Klimt stepped out onto the platform, bending his head under the lintel of the door, she followed him. He got down first onto the street, then turned and lifted her down. She felt his strength in the smooth, effortless way she seemed to float to the pavement.

She had to trot the short distance down the Kärntnerstrasse, clinging to his huge arm, to the dazzlingly lit front of Demel's. Thick snowflakes had begun to fall; they hung on her long eyelashes – as long as Mutti's, and as much envied by other women – and she had to brush them off with her sleeve. The interior of Demel's, under the glare of the clusters of electric lights on their crystal stems, and reflected back by the mirrors which made up the walls, always seemed vast and to contain multitudes – multitudes who, no doubt, recognized her and were acquainted with Mutti. Even if she escaped being recognized singly as she made her way between the tables to the buffet, there was an army of Alma-Marias reflected in the mirror walls, marching in every direction.

She selected a couple of pastries quickly, almost without looking at them, and snatched the numbered tickets from the waitress. She followed Herr Klimt to a small table behind a carved wooden balustrade where she was at least half hidden by a velour curtain. Herr Klimt sat opposite, fully exposed to public view. Even reclining in his chair, his jacket open to display the respectability of a gold watch chain and fob on his sober grey waistcoat (she couldn't help remarking that there was no sign of a paunch under it, unlike poor Dr Burckhard's), his stature made him conspicuous among those sitting around him.

A waitress all in black – Demel's young ladies were not permitted the frivolity of white, laced-edged aprons – glided to the table:

'*Haben schön gewahlt . . .?* Has madam bestowed on us the inestimable favour of having made her choice?'

Alma-Maria felt a sudden pang of regret. Pappi had christened the extraordinary jargon employed by waitresses at Demel's *Demelinerinnen*-speak. He wove entire fantasy conversations using *Demelinerinnen*-speak, encouraging her to improvise with him. She would like to have told Herr Klimt about it, but was held back from doing so by some inhibition she did not understand.

She handed her tickets to the waitress, and asked Herr Klimt if she might have lemonade instead of coffee. When the waitress was gone, he drew a sketch pad from his pocket. He took several pencils from a slim wooden case, and slipped all but one of them into a breast pocket. He stared across the table at her, glanced down at the pad, then stared at her again. He started working rapidly, his pencil point brushing the surface of the pad. She hardly dared move, even when the waitress placed the pastries and lemonade in front of her.

'I watched you in Burckhard's *loge*,' he said quietly, so that she had to strain to catch what he was saying. 'A lovely young Viennese maiden with her hair still down but wearing what I was sure was her first grown-up, fashionable day dress. There was light – just enough light – from off the stage to observe the expression on her face. It was that which convinced me it was her first visit to the theatre; a look of enraptured concentration – eyes wide open in wonder, gleaming in the light, and lips slightly parted ... And all about her there were Max Burckhard's busy, world-weary friends – "I've seen Kainz act better than this in Munich," and "Who is this singer? Why a singer, anyway?" But she was watching, not Kainz, not von Mildenburg, but Goethe's *Egmont*. She alone of everybody in the *loge* – probably everyone in the theatre – was watching a poet's great masterpiece ...'

His voice was hypnotic. When he lowered his pencil and asked her, 'Don't you want your pastries?' she was taken by surprise.

'Can you draw if I move?' she asked.

'I can try ... They say you were very close to your father.'

'I was the person he talked to,' she replied.

He stared at her curiously.

'Do you know what I mean?' she asked uneasily.

'Absolutely,' he assured her. 'Are you reconciled to the thought of Carl Möll taking his place?'

'I can't imagine why my mother wants to marry the pendulum when she has been married to the whole clock,' she told him.

She surprised him – even shocked him. He put his pencil down on the table. 'My dear girl!' he exclaimed.

She shouldn't have said it, of course. Herr Klimt was a friend of Herr Möll's; there was no reason why his judgement of Herr Möll should be similar to her own. She felt herself blush with embarrassment. He began to smile again, however.

'Hasn't it occurred to you that your poor mother might find life a deal more comfortable attached to the pendulum, as you put it, rather than to the whole clock?'

He picked up his pencil again.

'Clocks aren't always the most comfortable things to live with. Not for ladies like your mother, at any rate.'

He was saying the same thing as Herr Möll had done. She wondered if they had talked about Mutti together at the Café Griensteidl or some other painters' café.

He moved from the chair in front of her to the one beside her, and began to sketch her profile. She couldn't see him now except as a distant figure in the mirror on the far wall. Once more, she sat frozen into immobility.

'What I need to catch – ' He returned to his original theme – 'is the expression of wonder – of dedication almost. Perhaps we should have you as a nun. A young novice at the moment of taking her vows.'

She thought back to the Maria Theresia Institute: she had been present at a service of Consecration, and all she could remember was that a lot of the girls had sobbed noisily and ostentatiously, and that it had been very long and boring. Then the thought came to her: would Mutti possibly consider sending her back to the Institute when she found out that she had been with Herr Klimt in Demel's . . .?

That same night, she caught Herr Möll as he was about to leave the apartment to go to his own lodgings. She followed him out onto the public stairway down to the gateway passage.

'Uncle Carl?' There. She had managed to say it for the first time.

He turned back. 'Why, Almschi!' He had already wrapped his muffler over his mouth; a fierce draught carried the bitter cold up from the passage below. Alma-Maria could see the lamplight from the janitor's office gleaming on the snow.

'Can I tell you something?' she asked.

'You'll freeze to death out here,' he replied.

'It'll only take a moment.' She drew the shawl she had flung about her shoulders more closely around her. 'I do need your advice, Uncle Carl.'

Herr Möll tweaked the muffler down from off his mouth. He looked gratified.

'There's something I ought to tell Mutti. Only I don't know how,' she explained.

He glanced at the door behind her. 'What is it, Almschi?' he asked benevolently.

'This afternoon, when I was coming home from my music lesson, I met Herr Klimt.'

'Aha!'

'It was quite by chance. I was just crossing to the tram stop when I met him. He asked me to go to Demel's with him. I'm afraid I accepted.

He said he wanted to do some sketches of me. I said I couldn't go to his studio, so he took me to Demel's and sketched me there.'

'Gustav Klimt in Demel's, eh?' said Herr Möll. 'That must have caused some fluttering in the dovecotes.'

'Doesn't he usually go to Demel's?' she asked anxiously.

'Good heavens no,' Herr Möll laughed. 'It's the bastion of Dr Lueger and his ultra-nationalist cronies. Klimt usually goes with the *Neue Freie Presse* crowd to the Central.'

'The trouble is, there must have been people there who know Mutti and could recognize me. I only agreed to go with him because I didn't think anybody would suspect anything if we were at Demel's. But then I thought, supposing somebody tells Mutti that they saw me with Herr Klimt?'

'You are quite right, Almschi, to take me into your confidence,' Herr Möll told her. He glanced at the apartment door a second time. 'You may find there's no need to tell your Mutti. It's a lottery. Gossip, I mean.' He lowered his voice, stooping to speak into her ear. His breath was lukewarm on the cold air, and smelt of cigar. 'If she does hear of your little escapade, tell her that you told me, eh? You could even say that I had been present. What about that? Tell her I was there, only I was called away to speak to somebody for a few minutes. How's that, eh?'

She gazed solemnly up at him.

'Thank you, Uncle Carl, dear,' she said. 'You really have taken a load off my mind.'

He bent down and kissed her frozen cheek.

'Thank you, *liebchen*, for confiding in me,' he said.

She returned to the apartment. As she reached the bottom of the stairs, Mutti called from the drawing room,

'Is that you, Almschi? What are you doing, tiptoeing about out there?'

'I'm looking for Noni,' Alma-Maria called back. 'I'd like her to draw a bath for me.'

It was partly true; a bath would certainly be the best means of thawing the cold out of her. In fact, the single virtue of the apartment had been the existence of a bathroom with hot and cold running water.

Before she got into the bath, she sat, wrapped in a towel, on a stool beside it, her head bent so that her hair spilled across the water, covering it like seaweed across the Sargasso Sea. Noni had the task of washing it, the steam rising like sweat onto her naturally red face.

'Perhaps I should become a nun and have it all cut off,' Alma-Maria suggested as Noni wound her soaking tresses into a towel.

'You become a nun?' Noni laughed. 'You don't even go to Mass!'

She drew Alma-Maria's face against her apron lap as she pressed the towel to soak up the wetness of her hair. The apron smelled of laundered starched linen and carbolic, just as Sophie Haas's had done.

'You were never the sort to be a nun,' she said. ''Tisn't God's will for you.'

There was a mysterious smile on Noni's broad, damp features.

'What do you think God's will is for me?' asked Alma-Maria.

Noni chuckled. 'Here,' she said, and unwrapped the bath towel from about Alma-Maria's body. As Alma-Maria stepped into the bath, she spread the towel to warm over the stove. Alma-Maria lay back in the hot water. Her breasts and her thick blonde pubic thatch gleamed like islands in the steam on the water's surface. There had been a time when she had wondered nervously whether all women had so much hair below their stomach; paintings and statues, unfortunately, never showed such things, while at the Maria Theresia Institute the girls had had to dress and undress and bathe wearing all-concealing grey tents. More recently, she had come to realize that if there had been anything really unusual about her body, Noni would have commented on it.

'Maybe it's God's will you should be the sweetheart of the Director of the Burgtheater,' Noni suggested.

'Who said anything about the Director of the Burg?' Alma-Maria demanded.

'Everybody!' Noni called back through the rising mist. 'The postman asked Karin downstairs if it was true the Director of the Burgtheater is your sweetheart.'

'That's ridiculous!' Alma-Maria protested. 'Dr Burckhard has been very kind to me. It's because he was a friend of Pappi's. That's all.'

'People are such chatterers here. Everybody at home would be shocked if they knew what chatterers people are in Vienna,' said Noni consolingly.

Alma-Maria wondered what the servants suggested passed between herself and Dr Burckhard. How disappointed they would be, if only they knew how uneventful her relationship with the poor man was.

'I tell them they're envious,' Noni continued self-righteously, 'because he is such an important man, and they would like to have admirers who are important like him.'

She was holding the towel to the stove, her back turned to Alma-Maria. Alma-Maria ran her fingertips through the clinging hair in her lap, teasing it upwards to see how long it had grown. It wasn't just that Herr Klimt was handsome, in spite of his receding hair, and that there was no paunch under the watch chain across his waistcoat; nor was it the scandalized awe in which people whispered about his relationship with his sister-in-law Emilie Flöge, and his goings on in her shop on the Mariahilferstrasse. It was that Dr Burckhard was a mere lawyer, a bureaucrat, whereas she had been excited by Herr Klimt's work even before she knew who he was. There were no princely Egmonts left these days – not, at least, in weary old Vienna since the death of Crown Prince Rudolf at Mayerling. But to be the Klarchen – the handmaid and inspiration – to an Egmont of the Arts, to be the Beatrice to a present-day Dante; to have one's own maiden creativity absorbed into the genius of a Beethoven, a Goethe, a Wagner ... The thought made her shiver with pleasure.

She decided to call on Alexander von Zemlinsky, armed with Dr Labor's letter of commendation, at his lodgings in the Freihaus auf der Weiden – a notorious quarter adjacent to the Naschmarkt but still only a short distance from the Theresianumgasse. She would go there, before taking a tram to the Votivkirche and her usual lesson with Dr Labor. She did not tell Mutti about this diversion from her accustomed route. She set off in the early afternoon, across the gardens of the Theresianum, behind the Favorita Palace. From the path, heavy with grey slush and pools of liquid mud, she could see across the lawn of glistening snow the small stone and glass conservatory which Herr Möll had bought from the authorities for a studio. The balustraded steps up to the terrace on which it stood, the half-columns and scroll-carved architraves, let alone its setting, would make it the most imposing artist's atelier in the whole city. Was he really so successful and important? she wondered. Had she been underestimating him all these years? Was he more important than Herr Klimt?

After her encounter with Herr Klimt she had looked for him in the lamp-lit, misty afternoon gloom, each time she left the Votivkirche, half expecting him to be waiting for her. But he never was. Perhaps he did not wish to see her again.

When she had crossed the Mozartplatz, she left the broad thorough-fares with their squares, monumental buildings, and brightly lit shops, and entered the steep, narrow lanes of the Weiden district. She began to realize that the freedom she was permitted had its snares. Again and again she was accosted by men with the appearance of gentlemen. The first time, she did not understand what the well-dressed *Herr* wanted of her – and she couldn't hear clearly what he was saying. It was the way he touched her that told her what he was after; then the look on his face shocked her to her stomach, and she turned away. As she hurried down the slippery cobbles, another gentleman approached her from round a corner. She saw that he was prosperously dressed, but that his grinning face was hideously pockmarked. She tugged her sleeve from his grip. He shouted abuse after her; she thought she heard the laughter of women, but it sounded thick and confused in her ears. Then a fat man with eyeglasses and greasy black curls showing from under the brim of his polished black top hat stood in her way, forcing her to step into the running kennel in the centre of the narrow street. Cold, dirty water splashed through her stockings and soaked the hem of her petticoat, but she dared not lift her skirts. She managed to dodge past the fat man, but he came after her, calling '*Schatzi*! Come here, *kleine Schatzi*! Not afraid of a little kiss, are you? – a little kiss and a cuddle, eh?'

It was with relief that she stepped out into the Naschmarkt, and began to make her way between the stalls and baskets. She was accustomed to the gross obscenities bawled after her by the padded, quilted market women behind the stalls – they treated anybody who did not stop to buy in the same way. A wide-span arch led under the yellowing, cliff-like walls of a crumbling tenement building. A cobble floor tunnel went through into a yard as dank as the floor of a well. All around, the yellow walls were ridged with open galleries under which ragged washing hung vainly in the damp air, and windows from which broken weatherbeaten shutters hung crazily. There was a heavy cart with a spavined horse, its ribs showing painfully, in the shafts. The wooden *duga* arched over the horse's back indicated that the cart had come from the east – from Galicia in Poland. Families of Jews were unloading pathetic household goods from the cart and carrying them to the nearest staircase: shaven-headed women whose crude wigs were concealed under tightly bound headscarves, ringleted men in greasy fur caps and shiny kaftans and sad, unhealthy children with myopic eyes and hanks of hair like rats' tails dangling from shaven heads. Men, women, and children alike seemed anxious to hide their apprehensions under the guise of the determined business of unpacking.

'Forgive me, Fräulein? Can I be of any assistance?'

She hadn't heard him coming up behind her. She was astonished by what she saw: her first thought was Rumpelstiltskin in a Tirolean hat and jacket, carrying a paper bag of shopping. He was no taller than herself, but he wasn't a child. In fact, it was difficult to judge his age. His hair had receded from his scalp leaving a quiff like the prow of a galley thrusting over his forehead. His face was as angular as the rest of his small frame, with a hooked, beaky nose, and beady, wary eyes. He looked as if he had grown out of his clothes, for stick-like wrists thrust out from soiled shirt cuffs. He smelt of schnapps and tobacco.

He nodded toward the Jews and their cart.

'Court of Miracles,' he said. 'I sometimes think the whole of Vienna is becoming a Court of Miracles.'

'Court of Miracles?' she asked.

'Come on!' he said. 'I can see you're a girl from the educated classes. *Notre Dame de Paris* – Victor Hugo. It's the place of sanctuary where gypsies and vagabonds and thieves – and Jews, I dare say – can live without fear of being hounded by the authorities. All these buildings here in the Weiden are bursting with families seeking sanctuary – Magyars from Rumanians, Croats from Magyars, Slovaks from Czechs, Ruthenians from Poles, and Jews from everybody. They all think they'll be safe if they come here and live under the protection of the Old Man. God alone knows what they think'll happen when he's gone. And there's no work for them here ...'

Children's voices chanted in strident chorus from one of the galleries:

Jews, Jews, go away!
But please come back another day!
Come back when we're ready for you
And then we'll show you what we'll do...!

There was a scuffling above Alma-Maria's head. Pinched, dirty faces looked over. The people round the cart knew better than to take notice of their tormentors; they continued to busy themselves in carrying rolled-up mattresses to the stairs. Only the peaky little children buried their faces in their mothers' aprons.

'Herr von Zemlinsky's got a sweetheart,' a girl's voice called down.

'Ooh, ugh!' another girl shouted down. 'Fancy making love to Herr von Zemlinsky! He's batty, he is!'

'Are you Alexander von Zemlinsky?' Alma-Maria asked.

'I have that very doubtful honour,' the man replied.

Alma-Maria fought against the inclination to leave immediately. Instead she dragged the letter out of the music portfolio she was carrying.

'Dr Labor said I should come to see you,' she explained, giving it to him.

He tore it open. A pair of pince-nez hung about his neck on a twisted blue ribbon. He perched them on the crook of his nose.

'Fräulein Schindler? Fräulein – er – Alma-Maria Schindler?'

'Alma,' she corrected him. 'Alma Schindler.'

He glanced down at the letter.

'If you prefer it,' he said. 'But you are Jakob-Emil Schindler's daughter?'

'Yes.'

'And they let you come to this place by yourself?' he asked.

'*They* don't know I'm here. *They* think I've gone to my lesson with Dr Labor. I do pretty much what I like, Herr von Zemlinsky.'

He smiled, letting the pince-nez fall. The smile irradiated his face so that it was almost attractive.

'Then I had better take you up to my apartment,' he told her. 'It won't do your reputation any more harm than standing out here, I dare say.'

'Herr von Zemlinsky is batty,' the voices called as von Zemlinsky took her arm to guide her to the staircase.

The cold air between the yellow brick walls of the staircase passage smelled of stale urine. There was a scuffling of feet at the top. When they reached the first gallery, Alma-Maria just caught sight of the huddle of dirty, ragged urchins between the drooping banners of faded washing. Von Zemlinsky led her to the second staircase. The scuffling followed them down a passage to the farther side of the building. She went up in front of him and she could hear what sounded to her like loud whispering. A hoarse child's voice called, 'Herr von Zemlinsky's in love with Christa!

Herr von Zemlinsky paid Christa forty hellers to show him her drawers!' An adult woman's voice shouted, 'Wash your mouth out, Anneliese, or I'll take the rod to you – see if I don't!' There was laughter, and the scampering of feet into the distance. Alma-Maria and von Zemlinsky reached the second gallery above the yard. She felt strange as she walked along it with him, ducking under the dripping washing; she wasn't used to being with somebody of the opposite sex who was the same size as herself. It was almost like having a twin brother.

'So the excellent Josef Labor sent you to me,' he said as he opened the door of his apartment and showed her in. 'Why is that, do you suppose? He is not in the habit of referring attractive young ladies to me.'

'He said I should come to study composition with you.'

'Composition is a most unusual pursuit for a woman,' he replied. 'Have you never thought of following your father's profession? There have been women painters, I believe – though I can't think of any in Austria.'

She had never been in a living room as dirty and as untidy as the long attic studio. As he went round lighting the lamps, it looked even worse. The grand piano dominated the space. Its music stand was up but the lid was closed, and on it were five or six unwashed coffee cups, heaps of manuscript, pencils and pencil shavings, and ashtrays heaped with grey cylinders of cigar ash. The floor and the rest of the furniture were covered in discarded clothes, books, ink bottles and music scores. She picked her way through the mess. It was the authentic *vie de Bohème*, she supposed; and if it was, she didn't see anything romantic about it.

'Herr Möll – my future stepfather – says that women shouldn't paint,' she told him. 'They may sketch, and play with watercolours, but oils and powder paint ruin our complexions and our clothes – and of course we have to look nice, don't we? I suppose I could try my hand at verse. That's a proper occupation for a lady, as long as I don't spill the ink over my frock, or write anything that actually means anything.'

He was looking at Dr Labor's letter again.

'There's no need to be angry,' he told her. 'Dr Labor speaks quite highly of you. Play something . . . Go on! Sit down.'

She looked doubtfully at the piano bench. It shone with congealed grease. He took her fur coat from her and she peeled off her gloves. She wondered if the bench would mark her skirt.

There was a rattling at the window. Through the holed lace curtains she could see the small horde of urchins peering in. Von Zemlinsky picked up a stick and went to rap on the pane. Deliberately, she drew her skirts about her, sat down at the piano. She put her gloves carefully by the keyboard, then drew a sheet of manuscript from her portfolio and spread it out on the stand. There were yellow and brown stains on the keys and a burn mark on one of them, where von Zemlinsky had put down his cigar and then forgotten about it. She couldn't understand how any serious musician could treat his instrument like that.

He came and stood over her shoulder.

'Whose is the poem?' he asked.

'Mine,' she replied.

'Really!' He sounded genuinely impressed.

But it didn't stop him from turning away to rap again at the window. Irritated by his distraction, she began to play and sing. When her final notes had died away, von Zemlinsky said,

'I owe you an apology, Fräulein Schindler. That is a very accomplished piece.'

She giggled with pleasure, and felt childish all of a sudden.

'It doesn't sound too much like Schubert?' she asked.

'You can't throw off the influences which have formed you that easily,' he said seriously. 'Do you know Schubert's B-flat Symphony? I wonder how many people have mistaken the opening allegro for Mozart. But it remains a masterwork. Mind you, I'm not saying that this is a masterwork but it's nothing to be ashamed of.'

She moved up the bench to let him sit beside her.

'Let me show you something,' he said, and spread his long twig-like fingers across the keys.

She eased up to the end of the bench to leave him further room.

'Supposing you were to have the opening phrase in the major the first time,' he said, 'then modulate it to the minor, like this ... D minor, you see? Then through the major-minor, G flat, to the B minor ... There! You don't want the whole phrase in the minor – there's no sense of conflict.'

He played the passage through, singing in a strange, gravelly voice which was, nevertheless, absolutely true.

'It's the lesson Wagner teaches us, you see?' he said.

'The voice tells the story. The accompaniment expresses mood, emotion, forewarning.'

He removed his hands from the keyboard.

'There are other devices, of course,' he said. 'It's up to you.'

She felt resentful. It wasn't only because he had made the passage more effectively dramatic, but that in doing so he had perfectly fulfilled her own intention.

'I can't change it now,' she said.

'Why not?'

His eyes stared at her magnified by the thick lenses of his pince-nez. He was ageless. That was what Dr Labor should have warned her about. He was black and ageless like an ossified scarab.

'It wouldn't be mine,' she said. Then she added, staring down at her hands, 'It would be so much better than anything I could do.'

'I presume you came here because you thought you might learn from

76

me?' He looked at her for a moment. She struggled to contain her hurt pride. Then he said more gently, 'I'm presently working on another opera. It's more or less complete – in short score. In one or two places, I've been having trouble with the instrumentation. I'm not ashamed to tell you that last week I travelled all the way to Hamburg to ask Gustav Mahler's advice.'

She continued to look down at her hands.

'A work of art,' he went on, 'has a life of its own. If that life will be enhanced by its creator following the advice of others, it can only be a greater work of art – isn't that true?'

'I suppose so,' she whispered, keeping to herself her own opinion – that a true work of art was uniquely the child of its creator's soul.

'And if any of your other attempts at composition are half as good as this one, I would be honoured to accept you as my pupil,' he told her.

'Would you, Herr von Zemlinsky?'

'Of course, my dear young lady.'

A shadow fell over the winter dullness of the studio. Alma-Maria glanced over her shoulder. The children were back, their noses pressed against the window. When they saw that they were observed, they pulled faces at von Zemlinsky, and began to imitate the motions of a grotesque hunchback. As she rose from the bench, he, recognizing her anger on his behalf, held her arm.

'They're only children,' he said. 'It isn't as if they were critics, eh?'

She must have been looking as fierce as she felt, she decided, because the children ran off.

She arranged for him to come to the Theresianumgasse to give her lessons, at least to start with. She was well aware that Mutti would put her foot down if she found out she was going to lessons with a twenty-four-year-old, unmarried man in the Naschmarkt district. He saw her out to the market. As they descended the stairs, there was the scuffling of children's feet descending the stairs on the other side of the block. Their lamp-shadows came dancing after them down the tunnel leading into the court. As von Zemlinsky led her across the court, past the cart to the gateway arch, she heard the children's voices calling like voices in a nightmare,

> Jews, Jews, go away!
> Come again another day ...'

She braved the obscene shouting of the market women and, clutching her music portfolio to her breast, she ploughed through the grey, trampled slush between the vegetable baskets, and caught a tram from the Karlsplatz to the Votivkirche.

She found Dr Labor sitting in his apartment, and told him about her encounter with von Zemlinsky.

77

'That's good. You'll need a new teacher,' he told her when she had finished. 'I'm leaving Vienna.'

'What do you mean, you're leaving Vienna?'

'Only as far as Grinzing. No distance at all on the new tram. I have a widowed sister in Grinzing. She's going to look after me.'

She squatted down beside his chair.

'You're leaving the Votivkirche, dear Herr Kapellmeister?' she asked.

'I'm of an age now, my dear,' he told her.

He had heard the unhappiness in her voice. To her surprise, he reached out to touch her cheek; never before had he given her such a sign of affection. She took his hand to guide it.

'My world has almost vanished,' he said. 'Bruckner is retiring to Schönbrunn – he's very frail now, they say. And Brahms never comes in from Ischl. He's a sick man. He'll never admit it, of course. Doesn't care for mortality, poor fellow. It's the end of a line: the line of Haydn, Mozart, Beethoven, Schubert, and my old teacher, Sechter. Now it's all waltzes and waltz kings, eh? Did you know there's even a Viennese waltz in *Parsifal*? In the second scene of Act Two. Mahler conducts Johann Strauss's operettas at the State Opera in Hamburg instead of leaving them to the *opéra comique* houses. Frivolity is everywhere. This nation is going to perish from its own frivolity – you mark my words!'

He laughed, reproaching himself for having become so serious with her.

'Take care, my dear, that the Dual Monarchy's first great woman composer doesn't find herself becoming its first waltz queen instead! ... It's time for an old fuddy-duddy like me to go out to Grinzing, eh?'

She took his fingers from her cheek so that he would not feel the damp on it and gave his hand a squeeze before releasing it.

'They drink the new wine at Grinzing,' she said.

'That's true. I'm not opposed to everything new, you see. Haven't I provided you with a nice young teacher, a leader of the new music?'

'May I come out to Grinzing and visit you sometimes?' she asked.

'If my sister permits,' he replied. 'Yes, my dear. Indeed, I hope that you will. But probably you'll forget me very easily – even if you find it difficult to believe just at the moment. Though not, I hope, all that I've taught you.'

She drew herself to her feet.

'I never forget the people I love,' she said.

'Thank you, my dear child.' He spoke so quietly that she found it difficult to hear him. He had not raised his face to her so that she wondered if he knew that she had stood up.

It was only later that the full implications of Dr Labor's departure struck her. The fact that von Zemlinsky came to 6 Theresianumgasse to give her lessons meant that she had no excuse, other than her visits to Dr

Burckhard at the Burgtheater, for going out alone – and even Dr Burckhard had taken to calling for her at home to take her driving on the Ring. The subject was never discussed; no decisions were ever arrived at. The freedom she had enjoyed ever since Pappi had decided she should study under Josef Labor wasn't rescinded exactly, it just seemed to suffer a natural erosion.

Dr Burckhard was becoming more and more closely drawn into the domestic circle. Since Mutti and Herr Möll had made a public declaration of their intention to marry that autumn, Herr Möll held dinner parties for his friends and allies of the Academy – the Künstlerhaus – at the apartment in the Theresianumgasse, with Mutti as his hostess. Alma-Maria knew that Gustav Klimt was one of his allies in his opposition to the ruling faction to the Künstlerhaus; she had even heard that Herr Möll and his friends had elected Klimt to be the president of their group. But though she longed for it, and waited expectantly every time there was to be such a dinner party, Klimt never appeared. She could only suppose that now Mutti was reverting to being a respectable married lady once more, she couldn't permit him to enter her home in view of his notorious relationship with Emilie Flöge.

Others came who were not painters – Alfred Roller, the famous stage designer, architects like Otto Wagner and Josef Hoffmann, and Hermann Bahr, the distinguished journalist. There was also Dr Burckhard, who was invariably placed beside Alma-Maria. Very soon, Dr Burckhard was invited alone; Mutti made a great fuss of him, which he clearly enjoyed. There was serious talk of Mutti and Alma-Maria going to stay with him for a month in the summer at his country home above Pertisau in the Tirolean Alps. Mutti had even begun to follow Herr Möll's example in addressing him as Max; she even suggested mildly that Alma-Maria should follow her example.

Alma-Maria fantasized encounters with Herr Klimt in which she would reproach him for never having made the slightest attempt to get in touch with her again. But since she was rarely out on her own, there was little chance of the fantasy being realized.

One night as she was sitting at her dressing table mirror, about to brush her hair before going to bed, Grete appeared at the door in her nightdress, a familiar-looking book in her hand.

'*Man shall be trained for war, and woman for the recreation of the warrior,*' she read aloud.

Alma-Maria turned round on her stool.

'Where did you get that?' she demanded.

'Where you left it, on the piano,' Grete replied sweetly. '*All else is folly . . .*' she continued reading.

Alma-Maria stood up holding her hairbrush in her hand. *Thus Spake Zarathustra* had been lying neglected on the piano, on the small heap of music manuscript she had been using in setting it. Von Zemlinsky had forbidden her from engaging in the composition of any large-scale work until she had mastered sonata form and instrumentation.

'*Let the woman be a plaything, pure and delicate as a jewel*,' read Grete, assuming a lisp.

'You stole it!' Alma-Maria exclaimed.

'I did not. I borrowed it ... *Let the women's hope be, Would I might give birth to the Superman....*'

'You didn't ask me. You stole it!'

Alma-Maria rushed at her and tried to grab the book from her. Grete held it behind her back and retreated down the passage.

'*Man's happiness is "I will"*'!' she called from a safe distance. '*Woman's happiness is "He will"* ... Just think, Almschi....'

Alma-Maria caught up with her; she struggled with her to seize the book.

'... If you marry Dr Burckhard,' Grete gasped. She managed to turn her back against Alma-Maria and hold onto the book. '... When you've *let him take his recreation* – that's what it says here – ' She giggled, the giggling rising to a shriek – 'you might give birth to the Superman!'

Alma-Maria reached round to snatch the book. Grete swung round, striking Alma-Maria's breast with the edge of her shoulder. Infuriated by the sudden pain, Alma-Maria hit her on the thigh with her hairbrush as hard as she could. Grete screamed. Clutching onto the book so that the pages were crumpled in her grip, she stroked her thigh gingerly. She called, 'Beast! Beast!' several times. As Mutti came running up the stairs, she pulled up her nightdress to see where Alma-Maria had hit her.

'You've bruised me!' she shouted with an unmistakable note of satisfaction.

'What on earth's going on?' Mutti demanded.

'Alma-Maria hit me with her hairbrush,' announced Grete. 'Look! She's bruised me!'

In fact the red mark had not yet developed into a bruise. Grete realized it, and quickly dropped the edge of her nightdress.

'I was only trying to get my book back,' Alma-Maria explained with some show of calm. 'Gretl took it without asking me.'

'You didn't want it,' said Grete. 'You hit me for nothing!'

'Is it one of the books Max gave you?' asked Mutti, as if it would have made a serious difference.

'No it isn't!' said Grete before Alma-Maria could speak.

'Why don't you let her borrow it then?' Mutti asked. 'If you don't want it.'

Alma-Maria felt like saying, 'It was given to me by somebody I love much, much more than Max Burckhard' – but it all seemed far too complicated.

'Go back to your room, Gretchen,' Mutti said. She turned and followed Alma-Maria into the bedroom.

'You must learn to be a little more generous, Almschi,' she said. 'And not only with your sister. I sometimes think it's because of the way your Pappi encouraged you to devote all your time to thinking about music. It's not right for a woman. I mean you're not, thank God, in the position I was at your age. You don't have to cultivate a talent because you have to help your family earn a livelihood. You see, I can't believe that God ever intended women to be – I don't know! – explorers, artists, philosophers, all that sort of thing. He gave them the wrong sort of brains. . . .'

She smiled and patted Alma-Maria's hand.

'Sisters always quarrel,' she said. 'It can't be helped. But you know what would make you truly happy? Not composing a great big symphony or something. Just marrying a man who is considerate and gentle and kind to you, and making *him* happy. And then bearing his children, and watching them grow up to be as nice as your Pappi.' She sighed. 'Surely,' she added regretfully, 'no woman could think of anything more beautiful than to create a happy home?'

Before she left Alma-Maria, was was sitting once more at her dressing table, she stooped to kiss the crown of her head.

'Think about it, *liebchen*. I don't mean you should stop having your music lessons with that extraordinarily ugly little man. I only mean that you should have a proper sense of values about things.'

Dr Burckhard was wealthy and influential, thought Alma-Maria. He was also gentle, kind and considerate. Marrying him would provide a certain escape from the increasing restrictions of home. It would also allow her the opportunity to become, like the Frau Hofratin Zuckerkandl, the centre of her own literary, artistic and musical salon. In fact, there was every reason to suppose that if she married someone as eminent as the Director of the Burgtheater it wouldn't take long for her to become a Hofratin herself. On the other hand, the thought of close physical contact with Dr Burckhard – the thought, let alone the reality – nauseated her. It made her wonder how the women she had seen loitering in the Stadtpark and in the streets behind the Naschmarkt could become what they had become. There was hunger, of course; but surely even hunger might be preferable to having to submit to Dr Burckhard in the way a wife was expected to submit.

Fasching – the pre-Lenten carnival season – was a particular irritant. Even the temporary relief afforded by visits to the Burgtheater was denied her, since Dr Burckhard's duties required his attendance at the Imperial Chamberlain's department at the Hofburg throughout the period. Instead, there were private, afternoon *bals masqués* to be attended with Mutti and Grete, where everybody pretended they didn't recognize one another but where everybody's Mutti kept a watchfully protective eye on her own daughter, and an eye greedy for potential gossip on everybody else's. At the same time, the maids, Noni and Hannele, went scampering off in borrowed *crêpe de Chine* and rhinestones, with masks glittering with sequins and with nodding feather plumes, to the dance-halls and cabarets on the Prater.

It was a relief one morning when Herr Möll arrived to ask if he might take Alma-Maria to a special exhibition of a newly completed work at the Kunsthistorisches Museum. It meant her absence from an afternoon party at the home of one of Mutti's friends, but Mutti simpered prettily and said,

'You know very well, *liebe* Carl, you don't need my permission to take my daughters out of doors.'

'Is it one of your exhibitions, Uncle Carl?' asked Alma-Maria.

'I'm afraid not,' he replied. 'I wish I could say that it was.' Herr Möll cultivated a reputation for modesty as assiduously as he did for a business-like approach to fine art. 'It is the work of a painter whom, I fear, you admire much more than me.'

'Klimt?' Mutti asked. It was wonderful how all her archness could fall away in the utterance of a single syllable.

'Klimt it is,' Herr Möll smiled. 'But I give you my solemn assurance, Anny, that Gustav Klimt will not be there.'

Mutti sighed.

'I suppose,' she said, 'one must not judge an artist's work by his moral character.'

They drove the short distance in an open *fiacre*. It was the first warm afternoon of early spring, in which the freshly shooting grass gleamed and the heavy statuary along the Ring glistened like pillars of salt. They turned off the Burgring into the Maria Theresienplatz, where small clusters of pedestrians strolled blinking in the unfamiliar sunlight. As they drove round it, they were greeted frequently by raised hats or a discreet wave of small gloved hands; Alma-Maria was surprised to observe how well known Herr Möll appeared to be. They drove up the sweep of the carriage ramp, and got down at the great domed entrance hall. Placing her arm in his, he led her inside and down the length of the hushed vestibule to the side of the main staircase.

The stairs mounted on a façade of ever-rising half-columns. The panels between the columns had recently been painted with figures representing the historical development of the visual arts. Herr Möll led her to a panel set between two of the taller columns. On it was painted the life-size figure of a young girl. One of her pale, slender hands rested on the edge of a fountain basin; on the far side of the basin stood a giant amphora decorated in the style of fourth-century Boeotia. The girl represented the working girls of ancient Boeotia who helped in the manufacture of such pottery. She wore a loose flowered gown with wide, flowing sleeves which had been pulled up her slim arms to just above the elbows – like the sleeves of young Viennese laundrymaids. A girdle of some coarse, ragged material, stained and splashed with white, was bound about her hips and waist so that it both protected her gown and also showed off her figure and the fullness of her bosom. Her luxuriant honey-blonde hair was gathered in thick bunches on her shoulders. She was leaning forward as if she had just emerged from behind the left-hand column – indeed, part of the lower half of her torso was still concealed behind the column. One hand, fingers stretched upwards, was rising toward her chin in a gesture suggesting her uncertainty at what she might find in the world beyond her safe apprenticeship in the workshop. There was also, however, a dazzling clarity in the blue of her eyes, and a firmness about the chin under the small parted lips.

Alma-Maria felt excitement and amazement so that she wondered if she might faint. It was like looking into a mirror. She saw the inscription painted in *trompe-l'oeil* relief onto the pediment at the foot of the panel: 'The Girl From Tanagra'. She saw the signature in the bottom right-hand corner, the thick, bold, tailed-off brush strokes: Gustav Klimt. She heard Herr Möll say dimly, from afar off,

'You haven't been sitting for him behind your Mutti's back, have you, Almschi?'

She replied in a whisper through dry lips,

'There was only that one time. At Demel's.'

She gripped his arm. She was shocked – shocked by the way Klimt had understood her, her longings, her hesitation, her arrival into womanhood; shocked by the way he had revealed his understanding of her to anybody who cared to look at the panel.

'Your Pappi would have approved of it, I think,' Herr Möll said.

'Would he?' she whispered.

Would he? Would he have approved of her incontinent longing for the man who had understood her secrets so clearly and who had betrayed them to the world with such virtuosity? She had prayed to be allowed to become the Beatrice to some present-day Dante, hadn't she? And this was the mocking answer to her prayer. To be left with an aching desire for something more – much more? For some star-burst of creativity which would utterly consume her . . .?

2 THE INFANTA'S BIRTHDAY: 1896-1901

 MÖLL ASSISTED them into the carriage. Mutti was reluctant to climb up inside until she was certain all the baggage was safely stowed onto the train. Once in the compartment, she leaned painfully out of the window, attempting to peer through the steam which gushed up from the couplings.

'Everything is quite safe,' Möll assured her. He stood on tiptoe to put his lavender-gloved hand over hers. His small beard jutted upwards. Alma-Maria took the opportunity of inspecting the crowds on the platform to see if von Zemlinsky was among them. Rashly, she had told him when she and Mutti were due to depart from the Westbahnhof. She was relieved not to see him.

A horn sounded; carriage doors were being slammed up and down the train. Above the hiss of steam and shouting, Mutti called down, 'À bientôt, Carly'. Alma-Maria winced.

The carriage jolted; platform arches, the heads of porters and bystanders began to glide past. Mutti pulled up the window and settled her back against the embroidered upholstery of her seat. She sighed comfortably, made a lap, and straightened her skirt over it.

'You know, liebchen,' she said. 'I'm not at all sorry you should be away from Vienna. My only fear is that it won't prove long enough ... I can't deny,' she continued, 'that I've been quite concerned at the amount of time Herr von Zemlinsky spends with you.'

'You have nothing to worry about, Muttichen,' Alma-Maria replied.

'He behaves quite properly toward me – and I hope you don't think I'd let him do otherwise.'

'I'm sure you wouldn't, *liebchen*. The poor fellow is as ugly as a monkey. I just wonder whether you are being fair to him.'

'Whatever do you mean, Muttichen?'

'I'm sure you don't actually discourage him – I mean, from the way your lessons drag on . . . What I want to tell you is this – a girl like you has a responsibility toward a man like him, a man who . . . well, isn't used to having young women falling at his feet. You could very easily find yourself being cruel to him without meaning to.'

'Muttichen! We make music together. Nothing else.'

'I haven't accused you of anything, Almschi. I just don't think you've learnt everything there is to know about life – even if you are cleverer than me.'

Alma-Maria sat back and gazed out at the passing fields and white, domed churches. Supposing Alex von Zemlinsky was attracted to her because of her looks, she thought. Did that mean that she wasn't musician enough to justify the time he spent with her?

As they stepped down from the carriage at Jenbach, they were met by the cold smell of damp pines. Behind them, across the tracks, meadows stretched out under a drizzling sky to the Kitzbühler Alps, their snowy peaks hidden under cloud. Before them, gloomy rock and forest rose like an encroaching, giant wall about the small railway town.

Dr Burckhard came to greet them from the ratchet mountain train which stood tilted upwards, billowing woodsmoke, against the cliff side at the eastern end of the station. He wore cord breeches, heavy woollen stockings, and climbing boots under a more formal black coat; over his head, as he saluted them, he held a vividly green bowler hat. He looked every inch the prosperous Viennese tradesman fancy-dressed as a countryman.

'*Meinen Damen!*' he exclaimed with facetious formality. He bowed over each of their hands in turn.

'I'm afraid we aren't yet dressed for climbing,' Mutti laughed.

Both she and Alma-Maria were wearing fashionable summer-weight linen suits. They had draped their short raincoats over their shoulders.

'But you do have some luggage with you?' Dr Burckhard asked, glancing anxiously down at the handbags they were carrying.

'Oh yes!' exclaimed Mutti.

She pointed vaguely in the direction of the van from which more than a dozen matching valises and trunks were being lifted down.

'I'd better obtain some assistance – excuse me,' Burckhard said. He looked somewhat put out, Alma-Maria noticed, as he recruited a small band of porters to carry their luggage over to the waiting ratchet train. There, the bags occupied most of the seats in one of the two small wooden carriages behind the heavily steaming engine, forcing the other passengers to huddle disapprovingly on the remaining benches.

They began the slow, laboured ascent up between the pine trees into the cloud. Through the billowing, smut-filled smoke, Alma-Maria caught sight of sudden steep chasms in the sheer rock faces below, and torrents hanging against the broken stone. Once or twice they passed stands of hewn tree trunks stacked in glades of man-high fern. She felt a sense of awed desolation, and longed to be back home in Theresianumgasse.

They emerged from the cloud as they descended between meadows to the foot of the Achensee, chugged past the inn by the lake shore and the two farmhouses which constituted the village of Maurach, and came to a halt between the two boardwalks and fencing in an open field which formed the end of the line. Despite their raincoats and parasol-umbrellas, they had become soaked to the skin and chilled in the open carriages. Burckhard led them back down the line to the inn; he had already ordered a horse and trap to take them up to his house in the woods above Pertisau; now he needed to hire a cart to carry their luggage.

During the first few days of the holiday, far from being distanced from Mutti, Alma-Maria felt they had never been closer. From the upstairs bedroom which they shared, and its quaintly carved balcony under the eaves, they could see over the village rooftops and domes, across the wind-flurried surface of the Achensee to the cliffs of the Rofanspitze – the steep mountainside which plunged abruptly into the unfathomed depths of the lake. It would have been a spectacular view if it had not been shrouded in a curtain of mist and rain.

While they had been unpacking and changing, Alma-Maria had not dared to utter a word of complaint. Not until she was almost dressed, buttoning up her skirt at the back, did she catch Mutti's eye. Mutti gazed at her as if challenging her to speak her mind; then Alma-Maria saw her lip begin to twitch. They broke into smiles and then laughter simultaneously. They threw their arms round one another.

'Whatever are we going to do?' said Mutti, still laughing. '*Leibling! Leibling!* I *hate* the country!'

'So do I!' Alma-Maria said, giggling helplessly.

They had hardly got downstairs, when Burckhard suggested they should all put on their coats and go for a brisk walk before dinner. Mutti treated this suggestion as a joke – she might even have thought it was intended as a joke.

'We've only just got warm and dry,' Alma-Maria explained. She knew Burckhard was being serious.

'We'd catch our death!' Mutti exclaimed.

'When you are in the mountains,' said Burckhard, 'the weather doesn't matter. The weather is what you want it to be – it is a state of mind. The will is everything. It is in weather like this that man proves himself the master of Creation. As for Death – Death exists only in the mind of him who believes in its existence. For me, Death has no existence.'

'I'm sorry, Max dear,' Mutti told him with a great show of solemnity. 'I have buried a dear husband ...'

Alma-Maria found it difficult to conceal her astonishment at Mutti's funeral sincerity of tone.

'... *I* know about Death,' Mutti added for Alma-Maria's benefit.

'*Behold the lesson we have been taught*,' Burckhard quoted, ignoring her. '*That all things recur eternally and we ourselves with them.* Alma can explain that to you, can't you Alma?'

'*Thus Spake Zarathustra?*' asked Alma-Maria. But she didn't understand a word of it, and admitted as much when he had tramped off down the forest path in his gleaming oilskins.

She sat at the cottage piano while Mutti, who had offered to prepare the evening meal, retired to the kitchen. She started to play a nocturne by the Irish composer, John Field. It was a charmingly wistful little piece. Mutti came to the parlour door tying on a pinafore over her smart matinée-gown.

'That's nice,' she said. 'Much nicer than so much of the music you and your musical friends like, these days.'

Alma-Maria felt like improvising a few clashing dissonances but decided against it.

'Von Zemlinsky gave it to me,' she said deliberately.

'Do you mean, he composed it?' asked Mutti.

Alma-Maria pretended she hadn't heard. Let Mutti think so.

The rain dribbled in thick streaks down the window like glass bars. Supposing Alex was developing a strong ... tenderness ... toward her. While Mutti was probably right about taking care not to be cruel with the feelings of some men, the more dull-souled sort, it was different with men who were creative spirits. The condition of being in love was surely a spiritual necessity for the searcher, the poet? It was a motive force like the fire in the furnace of a steam-engine; and even more powerful than love requited was the pain of a love which could know no earthly fulfilment.

During the second week of their stay, the weather cleared and the sun shone. For the first time, Mutti and Alma-Maria could stand on their balcony and see the light, bright green of the still waters of the Achensee where it reflected the dense mass of forest above the cliffs opposite, and stare upwards to the broken white on the jagged peaks of the Seekarspitze and the Rofanspitze glittering against the dazzling blue of the sky.

Alma-Maria felt a sort of peace. Burckhard taught her to ride a bicycle. She loved the sensation of freedom – the untrammelled movement as she pedalled along the road round the lake, and the air on her face. Leaving Mutti at home, they rode to the northern end of the lake, to Achenkirch, and looked down over the frontier into Bavaria. They had lunch outside an inn, in the shade of the linden trees, and listened to a band of village musicians who had come from over the border.

He suggested over dinner that he should take her to see what he called his mountain eyrie, a hut on the summit of the Rofanspitze. It was agreed that Mutti would bring a pony and trap with a picnic supper to meet them when they descended to the mountain foot on the opposite shore of the lake, and they would drive home together.

Alma-Maria was unaccustomed to walking such a distance, let alone climbing. But the day was glorious; the resinous smell of the forest was all about them, and through the trees as she clambered up the path behind Burckhard, she caught ever-widening glimpses of frosted peaks against the brightness of the sky. Her legs were aching as they emerged from the trees onto the upper meadowland. She had to ask Burckhard to pause and let her rest. He had been striding on easily; he apologized. The spectacle as they turned to look back astonished her – the entire length of the Achensee was spread below them like a strip of gleaming silver, the outlying farms, the houses and shops clustered about the village churches, were tiny and as neatly placed as toys in a shop window. The air she breathed was fresh and thin; despite the discomfort in her stiffening calves and thighs, she felt euphoric – as if nothing could ever go wrong again.

She let him take her hand to help her up the meadow toward the stillness of the huge, overhanging crags. 'I can't take great strides like you,' she gasped, as if she needed to provide him with the excuse for this show of intimacy. A small herd of goats pattered away to one side of them, their bells tinkling across the empty air. She needed his support: her feet slipped on the shining grass where the snow had recently melted. She clutched the edge of her skirt about her knees to see where she was treading.

It was cold under the shadow of the rock face. Snow lay in a crisp, uneven-edged carpet, ending abruptly at the point where the sun reached it, but several inches thick. The air struck the back of her throat until she became accustomed to it. Burckhard took her arm.

'My anchorite's cell is this way,' he said.

Still holding her hand, he pulled her up a bank of loose scree until she realized that what she had taken to be a rock face in the summit of the mountain was, in fact, a gigantic outcrop, and that behind it, reaching to the foot of another cliff, was a stretch of snow-covered meadow. Far above the ragged cliff top, a cloud billowed white and solitary. He led her, her boots sinking into the snow and crunching the frozen grass below, under the cliff. In a bowl-shaped dip in the meadow where, out from under the shadow of the cliff the sun had melted the snow, stood a black, creosote-painted wooden hut, like a mountaineer's night shelter. He took her arm, holding her both more closely and more securely. She was weary enough to welcome the support, even to enjoy the warmth and protection of his male strength. On the path leading to the door –

a path consisting of scattered stones gathered together and trodden into the ground – he said to her,

'What I told you and your mother is true, you know. You are the first person I have ever brought to this place.'

She felt the first pang of anxiety she had experienced that morning. His short, nervous laugh grated on the cold, empty air.

'For me,' he said, 'it is like welcoming another spirit into my private soul.'

Had it been any other man, she would have wondered how many women he had said it to. Knowing Burckhard as she did, she was sure he had prepared it especially for her. It was not a reassuring thought.

He released her arm and opened the door. It was not locked, she noticed. She stepped cautiously under the lintel, and peered into the obscurity.

'Sometimes I remain here for as much as a week,' he said. 'What philosophy I have, I have found here. What religious teachings still clutter my intellect, I manage to discard here. It is here I am most myself.'

There was a blackened stove with a kettle, but there had been no fire lit in the stove for a long time. In the fresh mountain atmosphere, no smell lingered save that of the plank walls and the creosote. As her eyes became used to the gloom, she saw the rough, unpainted wooden cot with its pallet covered in rugs and sheepskin. There was a shelf with stained and peeling enamel cooking vessels, and tattered books. There was a chamber pot under the bed, and a pair of climbing boots scuffed and still soiled with dried mud. In the bright light through the door, a large, startled spider, a tough survivor of the mountain cold, scuttled across the plank floor into the pitch-painted darkness of a far corner. She was about to turn round into the daylight when she felt his arm about her shoulder.

'I am very happy you let me bring you here, *liebe Schatzi*.'

She persuaded herself that neither the rudely familiar endearment, nor her own slight tremor at it, had occurred.

'Aren't you ever afraid to be up here alone – I mean, for days by yourself?' she asked.

Both his arms were about her. He was looking down, smiling at her. She had thought that when the moment came, she would feel complete revulsion. She didn't. On the contrary, it was the attraction of his warmth, his strength, his maleness which was drawing her toward panic.

'I think,' he said, 'I could not have brought anybody else up here – because I was waiting to bring you. Do you understand?'

'You mustn't say things like that, Max,' she told him.

He stooped and kissed her on the mouth. She did not reciprocate, but she did not struggle. He murmured, '*Schatzi, liebe Schatzi!*' several times. She felt his hand pressing through her skirt, drawing her body to his. This was what it was like, she told herself; this is what happened between lovers. It would have been quite easy to have consented – surprisingly so, frighteningly so.

'Please Max! No! Oh please! I want us to be friends!' she cried out.

He let her go quite easily. She felt her skirt hem drop down about her ankles. She stepped back into the cabin. She wished she could have explained to him – but she couldn't, of course, not without hurting him more.

He was perfectly calm and collected.

'Of course, *liebling*. You are quite right. I hope I may be forgiven.'

'Oh Max! Don't be silly. Naturally, I forgive you.'

She wiped a tear off her cheek with the heel of her hand.

'I mean, we are friends, aren't we?' she went on. 'It was a mistake. Friends forgive mistakes.'

'You are very generous,' he told her.

'I am?' she asked. She laughed: at that moment it was the last thing she would have thought of herself.

'Perhaps we'd better go on,' he suggested. 'Unless you are too tired.'

She was tired. But she did not wish to remain in that place. As they trudged through the white glare to the summit, the air needle-sharp, their boots squeezing into the snow, she let him grasp her hand once more. A path like a narrow, steep-sided causeway led them up to the peak. There they stood on the edge of a precipice so high she had never imagined such a place – a sheer, overhanging drop of many thousands of metres. Far below her, birds were gliding with wings outstretched; the lake was now no more than a tiny thread, the woods, fields, and villages of the valley mere details on a small-scale relief map. At eye level from where she was standing, all about stretched an infinity of snow-covered pinnacles, crags, and smooth glacial slopes.

There was a cairn of loose stones on the narrow platform of rock which formed the highest point. Burckhard scrambled up it eagerly, as if he wished to climb as close to the sky as he could. When he reached the top, he turned to take hold of her, to pull her up beside him. When she hesitated, he asked her,

'Don't you trust me to keep you safe?'

Because of what had happened earlier, she felt bound to join him, though she could feel the stones slipping from under the soles of her boots as he helped her up. A sudden gust of wind billowed against her skirt, pushing the back of her legs like a giant hand. She grabbed and clutched at his arm. She prevented herself from looking into the void only inches from her toe-caps.

Burckhard spoke into her ear:

'Will you marry me, Alma?'

She couldn't understand why he said it: she wondered if he were joking. When he saw she wasn't going to answer, he said,

'Well, Alma? *Will* you marry me?'

He could let her go if he wished. The slightest push, and with a gust of wind she would slip from the cairn in a cascade of stones and fall, fall, fall down into the valley. People had said that if you had to fall far enough, you fainted before you struck the bottom (but how did they know?). She thought of Marie Vetsera and Crown Prince Rudolf at Mayerling. Her stomach clenched; her legs felt weak. She desperately wanted to crouch or sit down.

'Please, Max. I don't like it up here.'

She couldn't speak any more – not properly. It was like being in a nightmare. But he had heard her. He turned to her. In a voice he might have used with a child, he said,

'When you've given me an answer.'

Again the wind banged her skirt against the back of her knees, pressing it between her legs.

'Please, Max!'

She could feel the approach of that moment when it would be easier to let go than to endure the terror.

'Max!' It sounded more like a strangulated whisper than a scream.

'What are you afraid of?' he mocked. 'Even if you did fall, Death subsists with Time, and Time is the invention of the human imagination.'

He had gone mad, she decided. She stood on the brink of nothingness with a madman. A moment longer, and she would have been whimpering for mercy like a child.

'Come on then,' he said with a weary patience at her folly, and lowered her down from the cairn.

She walked alone along the rough, exposed path from the peak. When he joined her, she was standing with her back against a smooth wall of rock, sheltering both from the wind and her own fear. She was still trembling. As he came up to her, she was sure he would now recognize the state he had reduced her to. He stood in front of her. The expression on his face was that of a stern parent.

'You have been deceiving me,' he said. 'You've led me to think you felt a closer affection for me than you really did.'

'I thought of you as a friend,' she answered. Her voice sounded sulky – scarcely reflecting at all the sickening misery she was feeling. 'I thought you looked on me as – well – a sort of daughter, I suppose.'

She could just make out his shape towering over her, blurred through her tears.

'Oh yes! Yes!' he exclaimed. 'And you regarded me as a father, did you?'

Even if she had been capable of replying, she could not have said yes. There was nobody on earth could have taken Pappi's place.

He trudged away from her down the slope, through the snow. For a moment, she thought he was going to leave her there with the words spoken between them hanging in the cold emptiness. He turned back abruptly and climbed back several paces through his own footsteps.

'Perhaps in future you had better let men know it's a father you want!' he shouted, his voice echoing in the stillness. 'You could hang a placard round your neck, like a farm maid at a village hiring – *Experienced Daughter Requires Father!*'

She followed him down the mountainside, down from the snow line, down from the shining meadows into the darkness of the forest slope, down the winding path along the edge of a clashing torrent. She scarcely noticed the weariness of her legs; she knew they ached, but the pain had somehow separated from her, like the pain of somebody who had been drugged. She was on the verge of tears all the way, and there was a darkness about her brain which excluded the sunlight even before they had reached the trees. Burckhard had recovered his temper – perhaps it would have been better if he had not. He assisted her down the difficult slopes, and warned her of pitfalls in the woodland track. He asked her from time to time if she wished to rest. It was she who could not bring herself to speak.

They found Mutti waiting for them with the trap at the foot of the Rofanspitze, by the lake side. 'Such a lovely day!' she said. 'It has been a pleasure waiting here.'

Burckhard congratulated her on the stamina displayed by her daughter. The way Mutti glanced from one to another of them, Alma-Maria realized that she expected something further to be said. Then she knew that Mutti had known Burckhard was going to propose once he had got her alone up in the mountains.

During the picnic and the drive back, Burckhard talked and behaved as if nothing untoward had happened. With a great deal of effort, Alma-Maria tried to do the same. As soon as she and Mutti were upstairs alone together, Mutti asked her what had happened. Alma-Maria could see that she was close to anger already. She explained the day's events as truthfully as she could.

'You've been leading him a fine dance, of course,' said Mutti. 'I suppose I ought to blame myself for not keeping a closer eye on what you were up to.'

She spoke quietly to start with, but the anger was coming on in the same way it had done when she had been annoyed with Pappi.

'Did you actually suppose I wanted to come to this awful place?' she continued. 'Do you think I wanted to leave Vienna, and Carl? Just as we were starting to get things ready? Have you the slightest idea what a disappointment you are . . ?'

They had become strangers again, thought Alma-Maria.

'Your father's to blame, I need hardly say. He spoiled you beyond redemption. Most young women of your age would be over the moon at being proposed to by a Privy Councillor, not to mention the Director of the Burgtheater.'

'Mutti! He tried to ... to make love to me. He tried to make love to me and *then*, when I wouldn't let him, he asked me to marry him.'

'What did you expect?' snapped Mutti. 'You don't think he was going to propose to you *after* you'd let him have his way with you?'

It isn't true, thought Alma-Maria. It isn't happening.

'Gentlemen – true *Herren* – only ask girls to marry them whom they can respect,' Mutti said. 'It's surprising to me that Max does still respect you considering your behaviour. Apart from anything else, you're completely insensitive to the feelings of others, even though you regard yourself as a highly sensitive and artistic young woman. The only thing that pleases me is that Max Burckhard has probably had a very lucky escape.'

During the days which followed, Burckhard behaved as affably as before. They went on gentle excursions, all three together; he took care to see that he and Alma-Maria were alone together as little as possible. Mutti, for her part, remained as distant as she could from one who was sharing her room and bed. On their return to Vienna, having left Burckhard – he was due to return a day or two after them – they were met by Möll at the Westbahnhof. They were driving from the station when Möll, unable to contain himself, asked,

'Well? Have you any news for me?'

'None, dear Carl,' Mutti replied.

'My mother means that Dr Burckhard proposed ...'

'Alma-Maria!' Mutti warned her.

'... Proposed marriage to me,' Alma-Maria carried on stubbornly. 'And I refused.'

'I told you ...' Mutti began.

'You refused him?' Möll asked.

'Yes,' Alma-Maria said.

Möll took Mutti's hand. 'It's for the best, Anny,' he told her.

'For the best? Why?'

'Max Burckhard was dismissed as Director of the Burg three weeks ago. Dismissed, asked to resign – it comes to the same thing.'

There was a pause while Mutti digested this information.

'Well I never!' she said at last. Then she said to Alma-Maria, 'You never mentioned it ...'

'It will mean he'll probably lose his seat on the Privy Council,' Möll added.

Alma-Maria had been about to say that she had known nothing about it, but she thought better of it.

'What will become of him?' she asked.

'He won't starve,' Möll laughed. 'He has his law practice to go back to.'

'That's not the same thing at all,' said Mutti. 'The poor dear.'

'Apparently there has been disapproval in certain quarters of Max's choice of new plays for the Burg,' Möll told them over dinner that evening. 'Encouraging immorality, that sort of thing. And it has been remarked on that he has favoured a disproportionate number of pieces by Jewish writers. . . .'

He leaned across the table to address Mutti and Alma-Maria as if to keep what he was saying from the ears of the servants. Grete, who was sitting on the same side of the table as himself, he ignored.

'I'm afraid, he didn't accept his dismissal with a very good grace. The Freiherr von Wetschel went in person to his offices at the Burg to present him with the news from the Hofburg. As soon as von Wetschel's back was turned, our friend rushed across to the Josefstadt Theatre to have a word with Katherina von Schratt in her dressing room . . .'

'Carl, *mein liebe*!' said Mutti. 'Please let the girls leave the table first.'

Möll continued, driven on by his zest for a good tale, 'I've been told the poor fellow was in tears – that he actually fell on his knees on Frau von Schratt's dressing room floor and begged her to intercede for him with the Old Man next time he . . . paid her a call.'

'Carl!' Mutti exclaimed in a shocked voice.

'I do know about the Emperor and Frau von Schratt,' Grete said aggressively. 'Everybody does.'

'I suppose it'll remain a mystery whether she did intercede with him or not,' Möll went on. 'The story is, of course, that as she got him the Directorship of the Burg in the first place, she might also be under a cloud. At any rate, if she did speak to the Old Man, it doesn't seem to have made any difference.'

In the privacy of her own room, Alma-Maria wept again. She did not know what she could have done even if she had understood Burckhard's depairing hope, up there on the Rofanspitze; one can't marry a man just because he's kind and one feels sympathy for him. But she could have comforted him. She had noticed nothing of the appalling misery he must have felt. Mutti was right: she was dreadfully insensitive.

Mutti came in quietly. Alma-Maria managed to wipe her eyes before she could notice that she had been weeping.

'You should have told me about Max, you know,' Mutti remarked. 'I would not have been so hard on you. And also, *liebchen*, I could have warned you. Men are always ready to bid for sympathy – and there are times when a show of distress in a man can be a more seductive weapon than flattery. Your father was a virtuoso at it . . . So, I suppose we have to admit that all's well that ends well.'

She kissed her cheek.

'Good night, *liebchen*.'

Two mornings later, Alma-Maria slipped out of the apartment, and made her way to the Burgtheater. It was closed up for the summer; the massive foyer was gloomy with drawn-down blinds and canvas sheets. The passages leading from it echoed with the clatter of workmen's boots and pails and paint buckets, and the air was heavy with the smell of distemper.

Burckhard met her as she was coming up the stairs to the first-floor foyer.

'I wanted to say how sorry I am,' she told him. 'I hope you don't mind my coming here.'

'Of course I don't mind. I'm delighted as always. But why are you sorry?'

'Because of what has happened ... The way "they" have treated you,' she corrected herself. 'And sorry I won't be able to come and see you here next season.'

He smiled and relaxed visibly. She felt quite relieved.

'You are very kind, *liebchen*,' he said. 'But here in Vienna the way I've been treated is "par for the course" as they say. I too will miss our little meetings ... By-the-by, I have to apologize to you. I behaved very badly towards you.'

She looked away from him. She breathed deeply.

'You should have told me, you know,' she said.

'Would it have made any difference?' he asked.

'Not really. But it would have made a difference to the way I felt.'

He nodded. 'Yes, I know that. It is why I did not tell you. Shall we remain friends, do you think?'

'Please! I hope so,' she replied.

'That is good,' he said seriously. 'That makes me happy.'

'Max,' she asked, 'will you take me across to Demel's?'

'With the greatest pleasure in the world, *liebchen*. But what will your mother think?'

'I don't know,' replied Alma-Maria. 'And I don't really care.'

She put her arm into his, contented that she should have put all to rights.

'Supposing Major Picquart's evidence is the truth – I merely present it as a hypothesis, you understand – and this – er – Colonel Henry actually did forge the evidence against Dreyfus, is it not still possible that Dreyfus was guilty of being a spy?'

Several of the gentlemen around the dining table nodded their heads thoughtfully. One or two rolled the stems of their wine glasses between their fingers.

The ladies, including Mutti, who was sitting at the opposite end of the table to Möll, observed the conversation with the conventional expressions of admiration on their faces that their menfolk should have such a shrewd understanding of international affairs.

Since Mutti's marriage to Carl Möll, and the birth of little Marie (despite there aleady being an Alma-Maria in the family), the entire character of the apartment at 6 Theresianumgasse had changed. There was the establishment of Möll in the apartment, with a domestic routine fixed around his work; there was baby-worship, and the priority-bustling of nanny and nursemaid. Möll had, moreover become the principal mover and agent of those artists and architects who had broken away from the Kaiserlich-Königlich Academy of Arts to found the Vienna Sezession. As a result, Mutti had blossomed forth as hostess to an artists' salon and had arranged a full calendar of dinner parties, buffets, and late-night suppers. She was as pretty, and more vivacious, than Alma-Maria had ever seen her. Möll even talked of their having a new home, a thoroughly modern villa built by his friend and associate, Josef Hoffmann, up on the Hohe Warte, Vienna's most fashionable suburb.

At nineteen years old, Alma-Maria was expected to assist her mother in her newfound role. Despite that, she felt pushed to the margins of her own home. She felt suffocated by the velvet drapes and carpet-hung walls, the heavily framed photographs, and the china ornaments which Mutti, freed from Plankenburg and Pappi's tastes, regarded as suitable decorations, and angry that nothing of Pappi should have been allowed to remain.

Grete's behaviour in response to this new mode of existence took the form of noisy showing off, bouts of uncontrollable rudeness to visitors, stealing – on one occasion she had even taken a purse from one of the housemaids –, so that it had been impossible for her to be permitted to join the family when there were visitors present. She had withdrawn into a sullen solitude which, at least, was more restful than her previous behaviour. At tonight's dinner party, at which a half-dozen of Carl Möll's closest friends and colleagues with their wives had gathered to celebrate the first anniversary of the Sezession, her absence was unremarked.

Somebody said, 'I'm sure nobody at this table would deny that our Jews' contribution to South German letters and science is considerable. Yet the only reason for supposing Dreyfus to have been a spy is that he is a Jew – an alien.'

The portly gentleman who was sitting on Alma-Maria's right – whom she understood to be an influential art dealer – leaned forward. His starched shirt-front creaked as he did so.

'I believe we must make a distinction, my dear Winkel, between our respect for the contribution made to our culture by intelligent and intellectual Jews, and the extent to which one may rely on their loyalty to the fatherland. Only forty years ago, it would have been difficult to have found a round dozen educated Jews in Vienna. So where have they come from? They've come from Poland and Byelo-Russia and Transylvania. And why have they come? They've come because they know that it's a damn sight more comfortable to be subjects of the Old

96

Man than subjects of the Tsar, eh? But don't let's rely on them to be loyal to Austria – that's not something the Jew understands.'

'There are Jews in important offices in the Rathaus,' Alma-Maria suggested. 'Even though Mayor Lueger says he doesn't like Jews.'

The portly gentleman turned to her.

'Ah, my dear young lady! There you have stumbled on another reason why Jews come pouring into Vienna. As long as there's a Vienna, there will be Viennese inertia, and as long as there is Viennese inertia, Jews know they are free to prosper as far as their talents and their natural cunning will allow.'

There was laughter round the table.

'Almschi?' Mutti said anxiously. 'I'm sure our guests will want to hear you play, afterwards.' There was a general murmur of assent. 'If you are finished, perhaps we may excuse you and let you go to get your music ready?'

'Very well, Mama,' Alma-Maria said, a little cross because she knew she was being sent away for having joined in the conversation.

'You will, of course, play us one of your own compositions, won't you, Fräulein Alma-Maria?' Professor Winkel asked. He turned to the lady sitting to his left and remarked, 'It's said Fräulein Schindler is a very accomplished young composer.'

Alma-Maria went through to the drawing room. The first thing she noticed was that the statuette which usually stood on the piano when she wasn't playing was missing. It was a clay figure representing the birth of a tree nymph, the naked torso writhing from the trunk of an ancient tree like a butterfly emerging from its chrysalis, her long tresses entangled in the branches, her eyes and lips wide open in wonder at her new-found world after the dank confinement of the tree's roots. Pappi had made it for her as his last Christmas present. It was the only relic of him and his love for her that she had brought with her from Plankenburg. As she glanced about her, she recalled, in a vague way, Grete's voice calling down to her in the hall outside.

She returned to the hall.

'Almschi! Look!'

Tilting back her head, she looked up to the top landing. Grete was leaning over the turn of the rail above her. The statuette was held between her hands, over the rail.

'Gretl!' Alma-Maria called up.

Grete smiled sweetly down on her. She held the statuette further out over the stairwell.

'Please, Gretl!' Alma-Maria pleaded. 'Don't!'

'I'm sure Mutti and Uncle Carlchen don't want souvenirs of Pappi lying around the place,' Grete sang down in notes of pure reasonableness.

'Gretl!' Alma-Maria shouted.

Grete parted her hands as Alma-Maria dodged back against the wall.

The statuette did not drop so much as sail down. It exploded in fragments at Alma-Maria's feet.

Alma-Maria's scream brought Mutti, Möll and their guests tumbling out of the dining room to see what was going on.

'She made me do it,' Grete called down from the top of the stairs. 'I was only looking at it, and she shouted so loudly she gave me a fright ... And I dropped it.'

Alma-Maria stood looking down at the shattered fragments at her feet. She felt numbed.

'I'm very sorry, Almschili,' Grete continued in a simpering little voice. 'But you are partly to blame, aren't you, dear? If you hadn't startled me like that, it would never have happened.'

'Go to your room immediately!' Mutti snapped up at her. She turned to apologize to the guests.

Alma-Maria was still staring at the broken pieces, some of which were smashed almost to powder. It was all gone now – everything. If she didn't visit the park to gaze at his statue, she would even forget what he had looked like.

Mutti took her arm gently.

'Remember, *liebchen*, you are to play for our friends. There will be time for regrets later.'

'Of course, Muttichen,' she whispered.

The following afternoon, Mutti called her into the drawing room for a private chat.

'Uncle Carl has decided,' she told her. She had her handkerchief twisted round her fingers. Her pretty face was blotched and creased with crying.

'Gretchen is to go away to school. A friend of Uncle Carl's told us about it – quite a long time ago. A special school ... only I didn't want ...'

She broke into sobbing. Alma-Maria put her arms round her. 'Muttichen!' she whispered, but didn't know what else to say.

'It's so far away,' said Mutti, dabbing at her eyes. 'Near Zurich – I expect it's very beautiful there ... Oh Almschili! It's all my fault! I can't explain ...'

'Muttichen?'

'No, *liebling*. You couldn't possibly understand – not yet. But it's all my fault!'

She began to weep inconsolably.

Alma-Maria went to Alex von Zemlinsky's studio. She told him what had happened. His ugly, emaciated face seemed to radiate peace. He took her hand.

'It couldn't be much worse, could it?' he said. 'Your father's last gift to you destroyed; your sister being sent away under such circumstances. You must find it upsetting.'

She nodded, was silent for a moment, then said, 'Thank you, dear Alex.'

He lifted down a heavy, bound volume of music.

'I wanted to give you this anyway – not as something to console you for present sorrows, of course,' he told her.

It consisted of Haydn's piano sonatas. On the flyleaf, Alex had written in a bold hand: 'This, in gratitude for all the happy hours you have granted me, and with a solemn promise that I shall never let pass from my lips anything you should not wish to hear from me . . .'

'Dear, dear Alex,' she said.

She kissed him with deliberate lightness on his lips. He insisted on coming to the Karlsplatz with her and paying for a *fiacre* to take her and the heavy volume home. As she drove through the gardens of the Theresianum, she thought of him, and wondered why she couldn't return his love for her. It wasn't because he was ugly; she knew him too well even to take his ugliness into account. Perhaps it was because, in all his gentleness and kindness, there was no observable trace of Nietzsche's sublime Hero.

'Dearest Alma! They liked it – they really did!'

His long simian fingers clasped her arms. Eyes gleamed with tears in the disproportionately long, bony face. He was happy for her, and radiant in his pleasure.

'It was your playing, Alex,' she said. 'Yours and everybody else's. You made it sound so much better than it really is.'

She was not engaging in mock modesty. Despite the enthusiastic applause which had greeted her as she walked from her chair in the auditorium to let Alex kiss her hand and to take her bow, she was convinced that her Fantasy Variations for piano quintet had been dull – technically competent (otherwise Alex would not have allowed its public performance), but dull. She had tried to persuade herself that it had sounded that way to her because it had been preceded by Schubert's incomparable Piano Quintet in A major; but if a piece was worthy of public performance on a concert platform, it would always have to take its place with works by Haydn, Mozart, Beethoven, Schubert.

'My congratulations, Alma. It was warmly received. I'm all envy,' Schoenberg came forward to tell her.

Amidst the scraping of chairs, the audience had largely turned its back and was filtering out through the doors at the rear of the auditorium. Schoenberg had fought his way in the opposite direction. He was only a year or two older than she. However, his short-sightedness, plump features, receding hair and generally threadbare look, gave him in Alma-Maria's opinion the appearance of a rabbinical schoolmaster. And, unlike her, he was a veteran of the public concert hall, having often been booed by audiences and scalded by the critics. But Alma-Maria noted that he was complimenting her on the way the Fantasy Variations had been received, not on its musical qualities.

As the tide of audience receded, the ushers started to remove the rows of cane-bottomed chairs from the front. On the dais, the four string-players, drawn from Alex's pupils, had fastened up their instrument cases. They jumped down to the floor and ringed Alex and herself, reaching out to shake her hand and bow over it, and to offer their enthusiastic congratulations. She accepted them charmingly enough, expressing her gratitude to them. But nothing could remove the heavy sense of anticlimax, the bathos between what she had heard in her mind's ear as she had started to compose and what had actually been put down on the ruled manuscript. The musicians themselves – fellow students, her friends and comrades of heaven knows how many afternoons and evenings of music-making and heated debate – were no fit judges. They were her family who had played over her work even as she was writing it, had advised her, taught her, and above all, accepted her in the same way they accepted Alex's sister and Schoenberg's betrothed, the vivacious, button-nosed, Mathilde von Zemlinsky who now came up, kissed her, and slipped her arm into hers. Mathilde in taffeta evening dress, with high-collared sable cape over her shoulders, but with her chestnut hair tumbling untidily over her cheeks, looked like an impudent, observant maidservant from a Venetian comedy who had managed to appropriate her mistress's clothes.

'Carl Möll and your mother aren't here to witness your triumph?' she asked.

Alma-Maria shook her head.

'Good,' said Mathilde. 'You can come and celebrate with us!'

Alma-Maria was intercepted as she left the auditorium.

'So – you never did come and call on us, Fräulein Alma! Very remiss of you!'

They were at the back of the now almost deserted auditorium: two small, beautifully dressed and coiffeured middle-aged ladies with intelligent bird-like features. There were three gentlemen with them, one of whom was obviously a soldier for all he was in civilian evening dress. He wore a clipped moustache and tiny tuft of beard in the French Imperial style.

'We met at the Burg – oh, ever so long ago. Three, even four years,' one of the ladies said.

'Frau Hofratin Zuckerkandl?' Alma-Maria suggested cautiously.

Frau Zuckerkandl laughed. 'So you do remember!' She turned to her companions. 'Fräulein Schindler and I met when we were both guests of poor Max Burckhard at a *répétition générale* at the Burg. *Egmont*, wasn't it? With Kainz and Mildenburg. Fräulein Schindler was seeing her first play at the Burg. I shall never forget her look of wonder when Mildenburg appeared to Egmont as the Spirit of Liberty ...'

She smiled up at the military-looking gentleman. The latter picked up his cue:

'I believe that if the Spirit of Liberty had appeared to me in the form of this charming and talented young lady,' he said in a thick French accent, 'I too should have been reconciled to fate.'

He bowed over Alma-Maria's hand. The ladies applauded and said, '*Très galant!*'

'As you may have read in the newspapers,' Frau Zuckerkandl explained to Alma-Maria, 'Major Picquart here has only recently been released from prison. His crime is that he regarded loyalty to truth and justice as more important than loyalty to his military superiors. He has joined us for a well-deserved rest. He is not only a great lover of justice, but also of music. Not, however, of our German music, or so he claims. So we have brought him here tonight to show him the error of his ways.'

'I am utterly converted, Mademoiselle,' said Major Picquart. 'A sinner come to repentance.'

'Converted, I hope, by the music of Schubert,' said Alma-Maria.

'Partly, Mademoiselle. But not entirely. You are to be congratulated.'

'It is a great achievement, Fräulein Schindler,' said the second lady. 'You inherit your honoured Papa's artistic genius.'

Alma-Maria shook her head. 'No,' she said. 'That's not possible.'

It was the one compliment she could never have accepted.

'This is my sister, Madame Sophie Clemenceau,' Frau Zuckerkandl explained. 'And her husband, if I may present you to him, Monsieur Paul Clemenceau.'

She took Alma-Maria by the hand and drew her close enough to whisper loudly in her ear:

'He's brother to that dangerous radical atheist, Georges Clemenceau.'

Alma-Maria had to prevent herself from starting. There had been a rumour at the time of the suicide of Crown Prince Rudolf at Mayerling that it had been an assassination engineered by agents of Georges Clemenceau.

'My most sincere congratulations, Mademoiselle,' said Paul Clemenceau. He had a heavy peasant stoop, and spoke through thick, curling moustaches. 'You compose music with such assurance,' he added. 'Surprising in a woman, and so young and attractive a one. A beautiful experience.' He peered into her face with watery eyes.

'Thank you, Monsieur,' Alma-Maria replied.

'And this is my husband,' said Frau Zuckerkandl. Dr Zuckerkandl took off his pince-nez to bow over her hand. The most distinguished Professor of Anatomy in the Dual Monarchy, perhaps in Europe, and a Minister of State, he too congratulated her:

'My companions are right. A quite remarkable achievement. It would seem our Viennesse young women will soon become as musical as our men.'

She was grateful for the reassurance of the praise. She offered none-theless what she hoped was a suitably bashful smile:

'You are very kind, Herr Hofrat,' she replied.

'We mustn't keep you from your friends, my dear,' said Frau Zucker-kandl. She acknowledged Alex von Zemlinsky's bow with a slight wave of her hand. 'But perhaps you could dine with us tomorrow night?' she asked.

'It would be quite delightful,' Madame Clemenceau agreed. 'And I'm sure the gentlemen would be pleased.'

There were grunts and murmurs of approbation from the gentlemen.

'It's a great honour, *gnädige* Frau Hofratin. I shall ask my mother if I may accept.'

'We shall have to warn the *gnädige* Frau Möll that we shall not be allowing her daughter to return home to her bed tomorrow night,' said Dr Zuckerkandl.

'We have promised to take my husband and Major Picquart to Hei-ligenstadt, to see the sunrise over the Vienna Woods,' explained Madame Clemenceau.

'We'll send a servant round tomorrow morning with a letter for your mother,' said Frau Zuckerkandl. 'No! Better still – my husband will send a letter from his Hofburg office, won't you, Emil? By Imperial messenger.'

'Thank you *very* much, Frau Hofratin,' said Alma-Maria, allowing the excitement to creep into her voice. The gentlemen smiled in spontaneous indulgence.

As she rejoined her own group, Schoenberg said,

'I see you're about to be gathered up into Olympus. Only the greatest dine at Berta Zuckerkandl's table – don't they, Alex?'

Von Zemlinsky's features twisted into a smile of embarrassment. He had been a dinner guest at the Zuckerkandls' on several occasions, but he had always shunned the notion of becoming a celebrity.

'Mahler dines there,' added Schoenberg. 'They say Berta Zuckerkandl is the only hostess who can persuade him to dine out.'

Alex, Schoenberg, and the others closed about her with their protective affection. She was their mascot, their beloved younger sister. She won-dered what would happen should a Faust appear to seduce her from their midst. And if he did, could he give her a happiness greater than she felt at that moment?

The following morning, even as Möll was reading the largely favourable if not wildly enthusiastic reviews of the Fantasy Variations – it was enough they weren't larded with the vicious abuse which passed for music criticism much of the time – the messenger from the Hofburg duly arrived. He caused a great stir in the courtyard among the maids with his plumed shako, blue black-frogged pelisse, silver-stitched sabretache, and mirror-polished boots. Möll opened the crested envelope; Mutti was with the nursemaid in the nursery, playing with baby Marie.

'So, Almschi, it seems the Zuckerkandls wish to take you up,' Möll said. 'Distinguished admirers, eh?' His eye ran down the deckle-edged paper. 'Monsieur Paul and Madame Sophie Clemenceau ... Major Marie-Georges Picquart!' He sounded taken aback. 'You know who Major Picquart is, Almschi?' he asked.

Alma-Maria felt a sense of danger – of imminent disappointment.

'I know he was put in prison by the French military,' she said. 'He knew Captain Dreyfus was innocent, and he insisted on saying so. Wasn't that it?'

She looked down from the window into the courtyard. The messenger from the Hofburg was sitting on the edge of the well in a far corner in the company of four admiring young housemaids. He was smoking a black cigarette in an attitude of studied indolence.

Möll cleared his throat. 'He claimed, as Commandant of the Military Intelligence Bureau at Rouen, to have proof that the evidence against Alfred Dreyfus was a forgery. The Ministry of War in Paris maintains he was paid to perjure himself by a Jewish syndicate organized by the Rothschilds. It would seem unwise of him, to say the least, to take his leave in one of the most famous Jewish households in Vienna.'

One of the housemaids had approached the Imperial messenger more closely. The messenger reached out and took her by the hand; she was talking to him with an air of flirtatious arrogance, but she did not remove her hand. The other girls were eyeing one another and smiling.

'It's just that he happens to be a friend of the Clemenceaus,' Alma-Maria suggested. 'He came to Vienna with them.'

She wished she could have sounded more convincing.

'They say the Clemenceau newspaper – l'Aurore – which caused all the fuss in the first place ... they say that it's funded by Jewish capital,' Möll told her. His voice was heavy with reasonableness. 'Read this, Anny,' he said as Mutti came rustling in. 'It's addressed to you.'

'The Frau Hofrat Doktor Professor Zuckerkandl!' she exclaimed. 'Whatever ...? Oh, Almschi! You are being honoured, aren't you? Real press barons – well, baronesses, perhaps!'

'It is, perhaps, the wrong time for us to let our Almschi ..'

Möll broke off as Mutti tripped round the table to come and put her arm about his shoulder. It was, thought Alma-Maria, the sort of perfectly contrived movement she might have employed between the verses of a song in one of her *ingénue* roles at the Josefstadt Theatre.

'You're not jealous are you, *liebchen*? Because you've never been invited to the Zuckerkandls?'

She laughed prettily and drew back a lock of his hair from off his balding forehead with her forefinger.

'I don't want Alma-Maria to be drawn into politics,' he said.

'Almschi isn't interested in politics,' Mutti said. 'She knows no more about politics than I do. In any case, Mayor Lueger dines at the Zuckerkandl house, and we all know what he thinks of the Jews! Almschi just wants to have important people to make a fuss over her – and there's no harm in that, is there? The Zuckerkandls can open a great many doors. And, my darling Carly, they do say Professor Zuckerkandl has the ear of the Emperor, direct.'

'I begin to see how much I'm going to regret returning to Paris,' Major Picquart told her. 'Everything is so peaceful here ... and so beautiful,' he added, looking down at her.

They had left the rest of the party seated in the gardens of the Golden Kettle by the Abbey church. Frau Zuckerkandl had suggested Alma-Maria should take him up through the woods overlooking the Abbey to show him the spot where, by tradition, Beethoven had sat composing the Pastoral symphony.

'It's clear you have become great friends over dinner,' she had added.

Major Picquart had proved no exception to what Alma-Maria had previously observed to be true: that gentlemen loved her attentiveness, and responded to it greedily.

He had told her how the authorities at the Ministry of War in Paris had attempted to prevent him from testifying to Captain Dreyfus's innocence by unearthing *billets-doux* he had written many years before to Madame Ramazotti, the wife of the President of the Courts of Justice at Rennes, a lady ten years his senior. As a result of the ensuing scandal, Judge Ramazotti had discarded his wife, and Major Picquart had been imprisoned. Now he was released, Major Picquart had felt it necessary to take Madame Ramazotti under his protection. Alma-Maria had asked if he would be returning to her.

'Naturally,' he replied.

'And do you still love her?' she asked seriously.

Major Picquart smiled and stroked his tiny black beard with his forefinger.

'Did I ever?' he suggested. 'Who knows? I was no more than a boy then, you understand. And now? Well ...' He shrugged. 'Our names are entwined in history books which have yet to be written.'

She had been deeply moved by the mixture of chivalry and regret in his reply. The notion that the testimony of such a man could have been bought with Rothschild gold was quite ridiculous.

When they left the others, she had led him up past the Abbey, up the trodden path in the darkness of the wood, between massive boles of ancient trees, the exposed roots of great oaks, and out into the first sunlight of the morning. Before them lay, under scattered shreds of mist, the gently rolling landscape of meadows and gnarled trees which had inspired Beethoven's symphony and Schubert's 'Die Schöne Müllerin.'

'Are you afraid of what might become of you when you return?' she said.

Her eyes were smarting slightly from sleeplessness. There was a dreamlike quality over everything.

'Are you concerned for me, Mademoiselle Alma?' Major Picquart asked.

'Of course I am,' she replied. Then, rather for safety's sake, she added, 'I'm sure we all are.'

'You cannot imagine what consolation it is for a man to know that a lovely young woman is concerned for his well-being,' he told her.

The words were flirtatious, though spoken seriously. Alma-Maria saw that he was embarrassed.

They returned past the high Abbey wall. Beyond the orchard on the far side of the village street, they could see the Zuckerkandls and their party seated at tables under the trees. 'Our hostess,' said Major Picquart unnecessarily. He cleared his throat.

He set off ahead of her, across the road and into the orchard. She followed him.

'Have you, Fräulein Alma, ever heard the story of Nostradamus and the little peasant girl?'

She recognized the voice immediately, and thought she would faint. She turned. Klimt ducked his huge square frame under the hanging branch of a cherry tree, brushing off the dew-covered strands of webs which had been suspended glittering between the leaf-covered forks. Alma-Maria was not only unprepared for so sudden an encounter, she was equally unprepared for her own nervous response. She found herself staring at him; she was afraid her mouth had been open.

'What are you doing here in Heiligenstadt, Herr Klimt?' she asked.

'Looking for you,' he said.

He had a straw Panama hat on his head such as was customarily worn by wealthy people's gardeners. He was wearing a loose robe or habit. It trailed in the long damp grass.

'No!' he smiled. 'There's no need to feel disturbed. I was invited by Berta Zuckerkandl, but I was unable to join the party till this morning ... As I was saying, Nostradamus was walking near the woods one fine morning, when he saw this little peasant girl about to go into them. "*Bonjour, ma petite fille!*" he calls. An hour or so later, the little peasant emerges from the woods. Nostradamus is still there. "*Bonjour, ma petite femme!*" he calls.'

It took Alma-Maria a moment or two to understand the implications of the story.

'I realize your case isn't exactly the same,' he continued. 'But there must have been a thought – the passing shadow of a notion – of offering consolation to our French Regulus before he returns to captivity or worse.'

'Herr Klimt,' she protested.

But there was a thread of truth in what he said, like an almost imperceptible hair on a sleeve.

'You're a romantic, you see,' said Klimt. 'It's been a long time, but I remember that . . . Did you like my "Girl from Tanagra"? Möll told me he had taken you to see it.'

'I thought it very well done,' she replied.

'Only that?'

'I thought you took a very unfair advantage of me.'

'Because it wasn't kitsch?'

Precisely so, she thought. 'Because you didn't ask my permission – or even warn me,' she replied. 'And because I was young.'

'I knew your mother would object.'

'You could have caused me a great deal of trouble,' she said. 'And then, having made use of me, you just vanished.'

'I've continually asked after you. Has Möll never told you? I see him two or three times a week. Perhaps he's grown careful now he's a married man – and a father, I hear. I notice I'm not invited to the family home.'

He steered her in the direction of the group round the tables. She tried to speak sensibly, but emotionally she felt completely bewildered – overwhelmed by the strength, the potency of his masculinity.

'I shall tell you the truth, Fräulein Alma. I came here to ask you to sit for me again.'

'I don't believe you.'

The trouble was she hoped that it was true.

'You may ask Berta Zuckerkandl. I had no intention of coming here this morning – not until she told me that you would be here.'

'So it was a conspiracy?'

'If you like. She knows the subject I wish to paint. She agrees with me that you would be the perfect model.'

'What is the subject, Herr Klimt?'

'The personification of German Poetry.'

A confused babble of names sang in her weary brain: Schiller, Goethe, Heine, Rückert, even one of Pappi's dearest friends, Hans Bethge.

'What's the matter?' Klimt asked her gently.

'I had always imagined the Muse of Poetry to be tall and graceful,' she said. 'Not small.'

'Who better to represent German Poetry than the young woman the chattering world calls the most beautiful in Vienna.'

Frau Zuckerkandl came across the grass to meet them.

'So here you are at last!' But the tone of her voice was indulgent.

Alma-Maria avoided looking in Major Picquart's direction.

Although they travelled back into Vienna in the same carriage, she and Klimt could scarcely continue their conversation as they sat knee to knee with others. It wasn't until they were standing together in the carriage yard before the Zuckerkandls' baroque town house, that he was able to ask her,

'Will you come to my studio tomorrow?'

'Does my stepfather know anything about this?' she asked, staring up into his broad, red-bearded face. He shook his head.

'Unnecessary,' she heard him say above the creaking of wheels and harness, and the clopping of hooves on the cobbles. 'Best he shouldn't know, eh? I believe he would prefer us not to ask him. The work is for Olbrich's new Sezession Gallery – it's to be another mural, so it won't be kept secret from him for long. But if we don't ask his permission, he won't feel he needs to discuss it with your mother. Will you come to my studio?'

'I don't know,' she replied.

Frau Zuckerkandl joined them. 'Major Picquart will be leaving Vienna tomorrow with my sister and her husband,' she said.

'I must say goodbye to them,' Alma-Maria said.

Frau Zuckerkandl took her by the hand. 'I am grateful to you, my dear. Poor Major Picquart speaks of you as if you were an angel.'

'I've very much enjoyed his company,' Alma-Maria said.

'You must tell him so. And then Sandor will drive you home.'

Alma-Maria was glad to be taken away from Klimt without having had the opportunity to reply to his suggestion. She was glad, in her blurred state of weariness, to be absolved for the moment from the necessity of deceiving Mutti, even though she knew inevitably she would do so in the end.

'We couldn't possibly have the incarnation of Poetry resembling a *fin-de-siècle* virgin, now could we?' Klimt called to her.

She had retired behind the black, Japanese-decorated screen under protest. A bar of bright, afternoon sunlight struck at an angle past its inside edge, as if searching her out; she drew back from it as she pulled down the bodice of her white linen summer frock from off her arms and bust, then peeled it down off her hips.

'How do you think Poetry should look?' she called back.

There was a hoarseness in her voice, the result of nerves. Although she was nowhere near naked, she *felt* naked.

She had left the apartment saying that she was going for a walk in the Theresianum gardens. Nobody would deny her the right to a walk in the sun, and even as she walked out of the gate and crossed the street to the gardens, she was not sure that she had decided to go to the Josefstädterstrasse and Klimt's studio. She was still telling herself she could turn back as she boarded the tram on the Karlsplatz.

She had not stopped thinking about him for a moment since she had left him the previous day. He was the biggest, the most alive man she had met since Pappi died – whom he resembled, only he was more dangerous. She had been drawn on as if mesmerized, by an abrogation of will like the invalid who allows herself to die from a lack of inclination toward life.

She draped her frock on the back of the chair, placed her foot on the seat, and unfastened her stocking.

'The Spirit of Poetry could never be Vestal,' Klimt said from the other side of the screen. 'It does not shrink from the appetites and desires of the world. It is reconciled to them and interprets them. In the same way that you are reconciled to your femininity. That is why neither you nor Poetry could ever descend to kitsch.'

'I don't know what you mean,' she replied in a disapproving tone of voice.

In fact, she felt wonderfully flattered.

'Anybody with eyes to see can see you enjoy being a woman. You enjoy the power it confers upon you. Don't deny it!'

'I've never given it a thought,' she said.

Freed from the confines of her corset suspenders as she drew off her stocking, the hem of her slip fell round her knees. She could hear the scratch of paper being laid out on the table at the far side of the studio. It was reassuring.

'Will you let down that magnificent mane of yours?' he called.

She was wearing her hair swept up onto her head like some copiously brimmed satin hat. It had taken her half an hour to arrange.

'Is it absolutely necessary?' she asked.

'The moment a woman puts up her hair, she proclaims the epoch in which she lives. You are to be not only the muse of Heine and Goethe, but also of Walther von der Vogelweide and Hans Sachs.'

She took the loose Grecian robe hung over the screen and pulled it on over her head. Obediently, she unpinned her hair and shook it loose down her shoulders and back. Barefoot, she stepped out into the studio, praying that she was not committing some dreadful folly. Between the busy traffic of the Josefstädterstrasse and the wide studio window overlooking the garden and the trees beyond there was, mercifully, a high wall.

Klimt was at the table, his back turned to her. He had unrolled a wide strip of paper and was pinning it down across the surface. The studio was bare and functional, with none of the Biedermeier clutter and cosiness either of Pappi's or Möll's. It was quite unlike any studio she had visited, and she had seen many. The walls were bare save for a full-length mirror, the occasional stiff, gilded reproduction of a Byzantine mural or icon, and a long, high, black-framed Chinese painting of birds, trees, and waterfall – the style of which she recognized from Pappi's presentation copy of his friend Hans Bethge's verses, *The Chinese Flute*. The floor was bare save for the pile of canvases leaning facing the wall, the easel and work table, a single chair and couch, and the heavy field camera on its tripod, facing a sheet pinned to the wall, The place was a cross between an empty conservatory and a laboratory; a place devoid of function, awaiting some new event to give it character.

Without turning to look at her, Klimt beckoned her over.

'See? This is the plan – the stage on which we're going to set you.'

She padded over to join him, her slight white arm close to his thick, freckled one exposed below the rolled and tucked sleeve of his paint-stained monkish robe. She pushed her hair back over her shoulder so that it should not brush against him. He leant across her, pointing with his pencil to the extreme left of the paper.

'Here's where we start,' he told her. 'The entire design, when completed, is to occupy three walls of the Sezession's central chamber – twenty-seven metres or more in length. The centre of the chamber will consist of a large seated figure of Beethoven, carved by Max Klinger. My frieze around it – this – will represent Schiller's *Ode to Joy* ... the Ninth Symphony. What do you think, eh?'

Alma-Maria was not entirely sure he expected a reply. In any case, it was difficult to know what to say. The pencil marks on the bare paper showed no more than the figural components in his design; they had no further character. She was aware that the sleeve of his smock had slipped off his shoulder. He put his hand round to pull it up again, so close that he almost touched her.

'It's very grand,' she said. 'What do the figures represent?'

'The visitors will enter through a doorway arch here.'

He pointed past her. She stood motionless, afraid lest, if she backed from his outstretched arm, he would suspect she was flinching from his touch.

'The whole of this left-hand wall will be given over to a representation of Humankind's longing for happiness. These here are naked figures symbolizing the sufferings of weak humanity. They are imploring this figure here to undertake the struggle to achieve happiness on their behalf; he is a Knight, a Crusader, in full armour but without his helmet, who symbolizes Pity and Compassion, but also Ambition, Aspiration, the drive to win some control over Destiny ... Now here, on the wall facing the visitors as they come in – except that at first they won't be able to see it because of Klinger's massive statue ...'

He pointed to the centre of the sheet. Moving up the table, he reached out and, placing his fingers gently under her bared arm, he drew her beside him.

'We have the Hostile Powers. This is the giant Typhon, see? The bastard child of Earth and Hell. And here are his daughters – Sickness, Madness, Lust, Melancholia, Material Greed, Wrath, whatever – all of them seemingly unconquerable evils which the Knight must conquer.'

She knew she should draw away from him now, while it would not appear too telling a gesture. Before she could make up her mind to do so, however, he said,

'And here, *liebchen*, is you ...'

He took his fingers from her arm to point again.

'The Knight, over there, sees past the seated figure of Beethoven, to the wall opposite where, beyond the awful figures of the Hostile Powers, stands the Spirit of Poetry. She is inspiration, the unbidden Grace, a power greater than Pity or Ambition. It is she who gives him the strength to pass through the Kingdom of Typhon – the Valley of the Shadow – until he reaches here ...' He pointed over to the scribbled group at the right-hand end of the paper. He drew her closer so that she should see it. '... A choir of Angels is singing. Angels fly over his head guiding him onwards until he reaches this.'

Leaning across him she could just make out that the swirl of pencil lines represented two naked figures in a close embrace .

'The Kingdom of the Ideal Attained. The Knight ... naked because there is no longer any need for armour – embraces poetry in a kiss. Human Strength and Inspiration are fused into one – *Diesen Kuss der Ganzen Welt*, remember?'

The whole vast scheme was in his mind; what lay before her was no more than a series of largely indecipherable scribbles. Yet his explanation excited her in the same trembly, near-incontinent manner she had experienced when she had first seen 'The Girl from Tanagra'. He had an unerring knack of penetrating to her deepest fantasies. She said in a low, serious voice which she was sure would betray her feelings,

'Is the Knight to be a self-portrait?'

His laughter took her by surprise. He took his hand from her shoulder.

'Good God no!' he said. 'I can't think of anyone less suited to the role!'

His hearty self-deprecation, his physical withdrawal, made her feel foolish. She was tempted to insist that, in appearance at least, he was heroic.

'To work,' he said, still smiling.

He placed her between the sheet pinned to the wall and the wide black lens of the field camera.

'You will have to be very still and patient, Fräulein Alma,' he told her. 'And do precisely what I say.'

He stood back to examine her. If she were honest with herself, there was no need for her to exercise patience; it was sufficient that he was devoting his entire attention to her. He came up behind her and arranged the tresses of her hair about her cheeks and shoulders.

'A touch of wildness is necessary, I think,' he said. 'Of unpredictability.'

His fingers were on her face, tousling her hair.

'We must have you holding an open book. Verse – like the Evangelists are always painted holding the Gospel.'

He went over to the shelf above the table where stood a mere dozen books. He took down one.

'At heart,' he called over his shoulder, 'I'm a peasant – a simple Styrian peasant. If you ask your stepfather, I'm sure he'll tell you that I never open a book. But, in fact, I do read, every day, for half an hour before I begin work.'

'What do you read?' she asked.

'The Bible of course; *Faust*; Dante's *Vita Nuova*. And this above all.'

He brought it over to her. Opening it and removing the leather marker, he placed it in her hands.

'Hold it out, and up – as if it were a work of meditation. That's it. Stiff. Formalized.'

In the awkwardness of her attitude she could read only the running title on the top of the page: Canto XXX, *Earthly Paradise*.

'Hold it!' he called. 'For a minute only.'

He was fiddling with a plate in a wooden holder, loading it into the camera. She allowed herself to relax her pose just sufficient to read the verses under the title:

> In a white veil beneath an olive crown
> Appeared to me a lady cloaked in green,
> And living flame the colour of her gown.
>
> There came on me, needing no further sight,
> Just by the strange outflowing power of hers,
> An old, old love in all its mastering might.

She lowered the book slightly once more. She sensed that he was still fiddling with the camera. Without moving her head more than a fraction, she looked at him out of the corners of her eyes.

'Perfect!' he shouted. 'That's absolutely perfect! That sidelong look.'

His head had disappeared under the black velvet cloth. His voice was loud but dulled. She had frozen into immobility, anxious to please him. She heard the click of the shutter.

'Don't move!' he called. 'And keep that look!'

He stooped to take another plate from the box under the tripod. He was fiddling again with the back of the camera. He had meant her to read the passage, she was sure of it. He had marked it. And there was something else. The moment she had entered the building, she had looked for signs of Frau Flöge having been there – and there had been not a trace of her. Had the notorious friendship come to an end without café *Klatsch* having recorded the event?

She heard once again the heavy click of the shutter. He emerged from under the black velvet with his ginger hair ruffled about his bald crown.

'Is that all?' she asked. 'Have you got what you wanted?'

'I think so, thank you. It must be a difficult pose to hold for long.'

Her eyes felt strained. But she was let down. Was he inferring that if he had taken the photographs he needed he wouldn't want her to pose for the painting itself? As he took the book from her, she asked him,

'Are you always so quick at getting what you need, Herr Klimt?'

'At what I *think* I need, perhaps,' he replied.

He returned the book to its shelf. She retired behind the screen and began to change back into her white frock. Did he mean that sometimes he found himself mistaken? she wondered. About Frau Flöge, for instance?

'Would you be so kind as to come here again, Fräulein Alma?' he asked. 'Tuesday morning, perhaps? At eleven? Would that be possible?'

'I'll do my best,' she said.

The sense of relief was past all describing – but she must not betray her feelings. She tied the satin bow at her waist, at the back of her dress. She put up her hair in an approximation of the style in which she had arrived, and pinned on her straw sailor hat. She twitched the fullness of her fashionable leg-of-mutton sleeves into place, and stepped out from her temporary refuge. Her purse and parasol were lying on the end of the table, at the edge of the sheet of paper with his roughed-out design.

'Would you be very kind, Herr Klimt, and fasten up the collar of my dress at the back? I think I must have left it undone.'

It was both cheeky and very risky.

'I should be honoured, Fräulein Alma,' he said blandly.

He stood behind her. He had to lift the heavy brim of her hair from off the back of her neck to fasten the hooks and eyes of the lace choker.

'You have a very practised hand,' she said.

She had scarcely sufficient breath to utter the words, so conscious was she of his closeness to her.

'You have a very graceful neck, *liebchen*. You hold up your head like a swan. Did you know that?'

'It's only because I'm a little hard of hearing,' she whispered.

She felt the touch of his fingers on her neck, and the warmth of his breath. For a moment she was uncertain as to what was happening; then she knew that his lips were on her shoulder. She shivered and turned:

'Don't, Herr Klimt! You mustn't!'

His smile was gently indulgent.

'Have you never let a man kiss you before?'

'You know I couldn't come back here. Not if . . .'

She stopped. She had intended to warn him off. Too late, she saw that her tone of voice had betrayed a quite different interpretation.

'You are quite safe with me,' he said. 'I wouldn't do you harm for the world.'

As much as anything, it was his giant's gentleness which caused her to tremble inwardly.

'Let me tell you, Fräulein Alma: since you sat for me, that afternoon in Demel's, not a single day has passed when I haven't thought of you. Your peculiar magic has never ceased to work on me.'

He spoke so calmly.

'Please,' she appealed to him. 'It isn't fair, you know it isn't.'

She looked away from him.

'You know why I put that passage open into your hands just now, don't you?'

'I didn't read it,' she lied.

'I never fully understood what happened to Dante – I mean, when he met Beatrice that second time, on the Ponte Vecchio. His obsession with her seemed too fanciful, absurd. Until I met you, that afternoon by the tram stop on the Währingerstrasse. You are my Beatrice, Fraülein Alma, do you know that?'

'Oh stop called me *Fräulein* Alma, for heaven's sake! It makes me sound as if I was one of your Süssenmädeln.'

'Laundrymaids and milliners' apprentices have never interested me,' he assured her.

Not even Emilie Flöge's apprentices? she wondered.

'I said you could call me Alma, that afternoon. You've forgotten, haven't you?'

He shook his head slowly.

'No. But you've grown up.'

He reached out for her.

'You *are* my Beatrice, you know, Alma.'

'Oh please don't!' she whispered.

But she had neither will nor inclination to resist. Everything had drawn her to this moment, as she felt his lips on hers, parting them, and the strength of his arms all about her. As her breasts pressed on his chest, her mouth was welcoming his, while the voice in her head was telling her, 'This is what happens – there will never be a going back.' It was a voice which changed from eagerness to a chatter of fearful warning – like the monkey in Bethge's poem, the wild ghostly form cowering among the graves, which howls shrill warnings into the sweetest scents of life. She found herself welcoming the unfamiliar sense of arousal his enveloping presence was exciting in her as a fountaining spring which would silence the monkey's chatter.

But quite suddenly, he released her.

'You will come back?' he asked, as if he was afraid he had gone too far.

She was taken aback by his uncertainty. He too had heard the monkey. She was pleased in a way, although she was still secretly trembling. He stood behind her as she looked in his mirror, adjusting her hair and straightening her hat. She smiled shyly into the glass.

'I promise,' she said.

All the way home, up the Josefstädterstrasse, on the tram to the Karlsplatz, through the park and gardens of the Theresianum, she rehearsed what had occurred, and tried to dull the turmoil of her feelings. When all was said, she had only allowed him to kiss her – that was all. But it wasn't all, and she knew it very well. The truth was, she had recognized the symptoms of desire. Klimt had released her before she had opportunity to indicate her willingness to yield herself to him. Probably she ought to be grateful to him. In the meantime, she wished God would stop the agitation inside her.

Under the courtyard archway, by the janitor's window, she caught up with the nursemaid, Beate. Beate had been wheeling baby Marie in her bassinet out in the Theresianum Gardens.

'Thank God you're here, Fräulein Alma-Maria. I can't see Alfred anywhere. Will you give me a hand with baby up to the apartment?'

Thus her everyday world opened its forgiving arms to receive her back. Clutching her skirt with one hand while holding up the prow of the bassinet with the other, she knew she would be sufficiently disarrayed by the time she reached the top of the stairs to conceal any earlier dishevelment.

She bought a parcel of school exercise books in which to confide the day-to-day course of the most exciting experience she had ever known. She was aware of the folly of committing such experiences to paper, but she felt there was no way she could contain emotions over which she had so tenuous a control.

She spent many afternoons either posing for Klimt in his studio, or sitting under the trees of his walled garden. Mutti was so obsessed with playing with baby Marie when she wasn't busy being hostess to Möll's business and artistic friends that she was growing accustomed once again to letting Alma-Maria go her own way.

In the studio she posed in her loose Grecian robe, book open in her outstretched hands, her arms aching. As a reward for her patience, Klimt allowed her to sit on the settee beside him. He taught her how to draw, using the pencil economically. She listened, followed his directions, fearful lest he move away from her. Sometimes he put his arm about her as if he was going to embrace her again. He praised her slight efforts, and she even played with the idea of giving up music in order to dedicate herself to fine art.

That July, on the recommendation of Dr Bleuler at the Burgholzli Institute near Zurich, Grete came home for a short holiday. She was quite changed when she was in the apartment with the family: grown-up, genteel, watchful of her own behaviour. She had also grown prettier than Alma-Maria had remembered. Alma-Maria was deputed to look after her when she went out walking. She took her down the Praterstrasse, out to the palace gardens of Schönbrunn. Grete would slip her arm into hers, and chatter about her fellow pupils and their problems; she even chattered openly about her own problems. She said she was beginning to understand her own nervous excitement, her neurotic compulsion to seek attention, and that Dr Bleuler had told her that it wasn't all that uncommon in older children, particularly girls.

'Poor Almschi! I do see how awful I must have been! Can you forgive me, Almschili? I do need forgiveness you know. Dr Bleuler says it's an essential part of the treatment.' She laughed. 'Like not drinking strong coffee, and not having baths which are too hot.' Then she went serious again. 'I know I must have made you suffer. Dr Bleuler made me see how jealous I was, you see. About you and Pappi. I mean, I know Pappi was always the kindest Pappi in the world to both of us, and I hope I'm not ungrateful. But there was your music, wasn't there? And you loved his work. So you had to be his favourite – it was only natural. I never realized how jealous I was. Dr Bleuler has made me understand how things go on inside you, very deep down, like hate and jealousy, which your mind doesn't know about at all! Dr Bleuler says it's because you're always taught that they're sins, and that God won't love you if you're full of hate and jealousy. So you just daren't admit to yourself you've got them. And then they all come bubbling up – you know, like a volcano erupting. So, I'm a volcano!' She laughed again.

Two attractive young women in light summer dresses, walking arm-in-arm in the dappled yellow shade of the linden trees, were bound to attract attention to themselves. As they passed the open windows of a pavement café, a group of Light Cavalry officers, their arms resting on the vine-shaded sills, called out to them. Amid calls of encouragement, a hunchbacked fiddler came from inside, gap-toothed, with lank, greasy-black hair; he followed Grete and Alma-Maria down the pavement, playing, 'I Kiss Your Hand, Madame'.

'Do you know?' said Grete airily. 'Dr Bleuler even asked me if I'd ever thought of murdering you.'

'What did you tell him?' asked Alma-Maria.

'I said, of course I hadn't! . . . But it's funny. I think he'd have rather liked it if I'd said yes!'

She gave Alma-Maria an affectionate squeeze.

An open *fiacre* passed, travelling in the opposite direction. The horses were walking. The coachman's head lolled forward; he was asleep in the afternoon heat. The two gentlemen passengers raised their hats as they went by. With encouragement, they would have woken the coachman and stopped; it was the sort of thing to which Alma-Maria was accustomed. She noted, however, that Grete had turned her head slightly, smiled mischievously for a moment or two, and then had frowned, biting her lip. It was as if she enjoyed raising the gentlemen's expectations only to dash them.

'Dr Bleuler's a wonderful man,' said Grete. 'Eugen Bleuler. Of course,

I don't call him Eugen. But he addresses me as *du* – I think he rather likes me. He always makes a point of coming over and walking with me when he sees me in the garden at exercise time. Actually, he's just like you – in one way, that is. He doesn't mind me chattering.'

But Alma-Maria minded very much indeed. She couldn't help thinking that she could have been in the Josefstädterstrasse with Klimt, sitting in the peace of his studio garden. For all the sisterly affection Grete now offered – and claimed – it was a stranger who had come home from Zurich.

One wet afternoon when Mutti had taken Grete shopping Alma-Maria went back to Klimt's studio. She had Alfred call her a *fiacre*, then directed the coachman to drive her down the Naschmarkt to the Freihaus. It was not until they had reached the Karlsplatz that she asked him to continue round the Ring to the Josefstädterstrasse. No doubt, like all his kind, he was used to such deceptions. As she paid him off, however, he raised his bowler hat and begged the *gnädige* Fräulein to convey the compliments of Fritzl the Cabbie to the Herr Painter Gustav Klimt.

She went through the garden. Klimt saw her through the studio window, and opened the door to her. He was holding his palette resting on the stained sleeve of his smock.

'I had not expected to see you, *liebchen*,' he said. 'I thought you had deserted me.'

She peered into the studio, afraid of what she might find. Emilie Flöge, for instance.

'No! No!' he smiled, reading her thoughts. 'There's nobody else here.'

'I have to look after my sister,' she explained. 'I have to snatch what time I can.'

She thought suddenly she was going to cry. Klimt pointed to the easel in the centre of the room.

'Finishing touches,' he said. 'But the light is abominable. It's a commission. Doesn't do to keep rich and influential patrons waiting.'

'Aren't you rich and influential?' she asked. 'For a painter, I mean. The cabbie who brought me here asked me to present his compliments to the Herr Painter.'

'Now that *is* fame!' Klimt replied. 'But it could all vanish with the next change in fashion. An artists's fame is fool's gold – until he's dead, of course.'

He led her round to the front of the canvas. He put down his brushes and palette.

'It's intended as a *sopraporta* for von Dumba's music room. Sheer pretentiousness on his part, of course. So I thought I'd take patronage as my subject.'

He was standing close to her so that she was able to rest lightly against him, to share the experience of looking at it with him. The principal figure on the canvas was clearly that of Franz Schubert seated at the

116

piano. It was set in the drawing room of a wealthy family, at night. In the shadows behind the composer stood two young women, sisters; their *coiffeur* and their loose flowing tea gowns were, however, in contemporary style. A portly, middle-aged gentleman, evidently their father, looked on, smiling in both a benign and proprietorial manner. Schubert's features, familiar from a hundred paintings and busts, were bathed in light from the four candles in brackets on the music stand of the piano. In the fragmented outer aureole of the candlelight was another face, another figure in present, contemporary dress, with her thick mass of light brown hair piled about her head, her blue eyes jewel-bright in the candle flames smiling at Schubert in tender, understanding longing.

Just as when she had first set eyes on *The Girl from Tanagra*, so now she felt the same sensation of seeing herself as if reflected suddenly and unexpectedly in a shop window. Then, immediately after, although there was neither title nor words, she recognized the notes on the score lying open between the branched candle holders on the piano. How many others, she wondered, glancing at the painting, would recognize the solemn, grim opening passage of 'Death and the Maiden'?

'I think you have painted me into one of your nightmares,' she said.

'Why?' he asked. Then, when she didn't answer immediately, he said: 'Would you like to tell me what you see there?'

'*Vorüber! ach vorüber* . . . Pass by! Pass by, Go, you savage skeleton!' she quoted.

'Well?' asked Klimt.

'Schubert,' she said. 'At Zseliz? With the Esterhazys?'

'Go on.'

'My portrait represents Caroline Esterhazy? Schubert has fallen in love with her. Only he already has the' – she hesitated – 'the sickness which killed him?' She sighed heavily.

'You know about such things?' asked Klimt.

Who didn't in Vienna? – the family whose son had been quietly removed to spend his days in a private institution in the mountains, or the daughter who was never seen in society because you couldn't say what she'd get up to next. Alma-Maria did not reply.

'There's the second verse of the song,' he reminded her. '*Gib deine Hand* . . . Perhaps I was thinking of the "little Death".'

He looked down at her to see if she understood what he meant. She felt overburdened with knowledge – knowledge of things which she had never experienced, and which, at least in Mutti's opinion, no unmarried girl of her age should have known about. She was uncertain what Klimt's reaction would be to finding out the extent of her knowledge.

'Death is the ultimate completion, fulfilling in us everything we have lacked,' he told her. 'It is also the germinator, without which life could not continue. It's not a nightmare – it's a celebration. I painted this in the same spirit as I am painting our "Ode to Joy".'

'Our "Ode to Joy"!' She felt a thrill of delight at the notion of herself as collaborator.

He turned her to face him. He looked down into her eyes so that she couldn't avert her gaze.

'I've been haunted by your beauty,' he said. 'The look of someone who sees into the heart of things; who is too young to know what she sees, but who isn't afraid. I swear to you, dearest child, if I hadn't encountered you, I'd never even have thought of our Beethoven Frieze.'

'Then why aren't you painting yourself as the Knight?' she asked.

'Because I can't believe I could ever possibly deserve an inspiration like you,' he said.

'Please – you mustn't say things like that. I don't think I can bear it.' She struggled to smile.

'I was so frightened – terrified – you weren't going to come back here!' he told her.

'You couldn't have believed that.' She saw tears in *his* eyes. 'Oh you couldn't!' she whispered.

That night she sat cross-legged on her bed, writing the afternoon's events into her exercise book. She had stood the bolster on its end beside her so that, should Mutti or Grete come knocking at her door, she could quickly drop it over the book.

'. . . I found my ignorance had been quite appalling. But he drew me to the Ultimate with such gentle consideration. He knew where to find my every sensitive spot and played with it so cleverly. When he brought me to the Ultimate, it was like when I was on the very edge of the Rofanspitze with the wind about to blow over me – except it wasn't in the least like being with poor Max Burckhard, as Gustav's embrace was so strong and terrible.

'When *it* happened, we truly shared it – Wonderful!'

She underlined wonderful three times, driving the pencil so that it furrowed the page. In the dazed reverberations within her mind, there were fragments of physical reality: the dull throb and smart between her legs – the shock of glimpsing the bulk of his tumescence, for which no plaster cast of classical statuary had prepared her, which for a moment of panic she had thought she could never contain without terrible pain. There had been the smell of his body, a momentary fear of oppression and suffocation. When she had cried out, however, it had been from quite another sort of fear: the fear that he would not take her over the edge, that she would not quite experience the star-burst annihilation for which she was crying so greedily.

Afterwards, he had sat beside her on the settee. She had lain in his arms, feeling marvellously, drowsily lethargic.

'. . . There can be few young women,' she wrote, 'who are so fortunate and so happy' – again, she underlined *happy* three times – 'in their first experience of Love . . .' She underlined *love* so hard that her pencil went through the page.

He had shown her a sketch pad: page after page of studies of herself, draped as for the Beethoven Frieze; fully dressed, with hair up, hair down, sitting, standing, profile, full-face, or smiling sidelong over her shoulder. There was one full-length study which showed her walking away, her head turned from him, as if he had sketched her as she went away up the path to the garden door. Across the sketch, he had scrawled in bold script,

'*Gib deine Hand* . . . Give me your hand, you lovely and tender creature, I am a friend and do not come to punish.'

He said in his most kindly, gentle voice,

'You're never going to escape me, you see? There'll be paintings of mine when you have almost forgotten me – when I am gone, perhaps – and there you'll be.'

How do you think I'll ever forget you? she had wanted to ask him.

'You'll be there to haunt the minds of people who look at my work, just as you have haunted my mind since I first saw you, that morning in the Burg.'

Sitting on her bed, she smiled to herself, and concluded her entry in the exercise book by writing,

'*Bonjour, petite femme!!*'

Truly, nothing could ever be the same again. For better or worse, let the wheel turn:

> Welcome, world that is
> so full of joys!
> Thanks to you for the act of love.

It had been a kind of marriage, she told herself; it was going to procreate great works of art rather than children, just as the love between Beatrice Portinari and Dante had done. That was why Klimt had talked about 'our' Beethoven Frieze.

She slept that night with the exercise book under her pillow, returning it to its hiding place in the wardrobe, under the shoe drawer, in the morning before Noni brought in her hot water.

Two nights later, the night before her return to Zurich and the Burgholzli Institute, Grete came in, creeping round the door without knocking. Alma was still undressing, and had not yet taken out the exercise book. Grete sat down on the bed, sinking into the eiderdown cover. She curled her legs under her.

'It's been ever so nice,' she said.

The sad regret in her voice made Alma-Maria stop her unbuttoning and turn to her.

'I've been happy,' said Grete. 'Really happy.'

'I've been happy, being with you,' Alma-Maria told her.

It wasn't quite true, but it was near enough. She sat down beside her and took her hand. Grete went on,

'Some people are quite nice and kind – at the Institute, I mean. Dr Bleuler, of course. And one or two of the teachers. Mademoiselle Thomas is nice – she lets me call her Madeleine when we're on our own, and she even takes me down to the village to have a cup of coffee with her sometimes. But a lot of the girls are quite horrid. I suppose it's because they're a bit disturbed. They're coarse – really vulgar – when they think nobody's going to hear. There's one, Lili Muller – a Jewess, of course – who told me something really disgusting. She said that when a Jewess gets married, the morning after her father-in-law inspects the sheets. You know – to make sure that she was – well – *pure* when she got married. And, would you believe it? there are people who actually sell bottles of something, secretly, to Jewish girls who are going to get married, just in case, so that they can pour it onto their sheets!'

She was looking Alma-Maria straight in the face. Alma-Maria felt she could have been mistaken, hoped that she was mistaken. Yet she could have sworn that as Grete finished her recital, there had been a momentary, fleeting look in her face of intense, searching malice.

Alex von Zemlinsky and his coterie were in a state of excitement. The players of the Vienna Philharmonic had petitioned Mahler to be allowed to give the first Viennese performance of his symphony, 'The Titan'. It was to be performed that night, in the great Golden Hall of the Musikvereinsgebäude, under the direction of the composer.

Alma-Maria was having a lesson with Alex in the early afternoon.

'You're going to be able to come with us, aren't you, Almschi?' he asked.

There was a suggestion in his carefully controlled voice that he was going to be very disappointed if she said no. She had become dreadfully conscious of neglecting him in favour of Klimt. She had always imagined that when a 'good' woman surrendered herself to a man for the first time, she experienced a total, exclusive emotional commitment. It had not prevented her from becoming haunted by the thought of hurting Alex.

'Oh Alex, I'm afraid I can't come with you!'

At least she could tell the truth, this time. But she felt no easier as she saw his face fall.

'The Zuckerkandls have invited me to join their party. I'm dreadfully sorry.'

'You knew we'd all be going,' Alex said, reproaching her as a child might reproach a grown-up for breaking the promise of a treat.

Worse – it would almost certainly be more stimulating to listen to Mahler's music properly for the first time in the company of Alex and his friends.

'We'll talk about it very soon,' she promised. 'Oh Alex! I am sorry – truly I am.'

She turned to him and took both his long, bony hands. He stared down at them, at his grimy, inky fingers.

'You know my ballet?' he asked, changing the subject abruptly.

'*The Golden Heart?*'

He had written the music to a fairy story by Hugo von Hofmannsthal. They had played over movements from it together on the piano.

'I sent it to the Court Opera weeks ago,' he told her. 'They haven't even sent me an acknowledgement.'

'Alex, dear,' she asked. 'Did you submit it scored?'

'In short score.'

'You should have scored it! You know instrumentation is your strong point ... One of them,' she added.

He looked up, a sheepish expression on his face.

'It's going to be such a big score,' he said. 'There's so much I want to get done. There's my B-flat Symphony – your symphony if you'll allow it to be. And I've got another subject for an opera on the brain. I don't want to spend weeks fully scoring – you know, eighteen, twenty staves a page – a work I can't be sure will ever be performed.'

'I'll help you,' she told him, almost without thinking. When he looked doubtful, she said, 'I can produce a very legible manuscript – you know that.'

'I couldn't possibly ask it of you.'

'I should like it. Working with you. And I'm sure it would teach me a great deal about scoring.'

'You are an angel – my good angel!' he whispered.

He lifted her hands and kissed them, first one, then the other. She felt his tears on them, falling on either side of where his beak of a nose pressed on her knuckle.

She went to the Musikvereinsgebäude that night, with the Zuckerkandls and another middle-aged couple, Dr Thalberg, a colleague of Emil Zuckerkandl's at the University's Department of Anatomy, and his wife. Their manner was amiably conventional, their every remark predictable.

After they had arrived, when she had retired into one of the closets in the ladies' *garde-robe* behind the Grand Tier, through the door she heard Frau Thalberg say to Berta Zuckerkandl,

'My dear Berta! The Schindler girl – I had no idea she was such a lovely creature! Those amazing blue eyes! Where did you find her?'

She felt she was being talked about as if she were a doll whom Frau Zuckerkandl had taken up only so that she might adorn her social circle. She felt a strong inclination to run off, to go and seek out Alex and his party where they would be sitting under the dusty cornices of the amphitheatre slips high above the platform. Berta Zuckerkandl appeared to have sensed she had been put out. When they reached the *loges fauteuils* which the Zuckerkandls rented for the entire orchestral season, she placed her husband with the Thalbergs so that Alma-Maria and she could sit together.

'Alex von Zemlinsky looks on Mahler as his master,' she said. 'I'm sure he must be here. You are very fond of Alex von Zemlinsky, aren't you?'

'He is a wonderful teacher,' Alma-Maria replied guardedly.

'But as a person?'

'He's the kindest, gentlest man I think I've ever met – after my father, that is. He's so brilliant, and yet so humble. You can't help being fond of him.'

Her own outburst of frankness made her feel comfortable. In her euphoria, the thought, light as a thread, passed through her mind that her relationship with Klimt might prove to be no more than a distraction from her destiny – an *ignis fatuus* to lead her astray from the true path of music.

'I shall ask your mother if you may stay with us at our house at Steinbach on the Attersee. We are having a small party there, just for three weeks, next month. And if I ask the Freiherr von Zemlinsky as well, do you think your mother might be offended?'

'Oh no!' said Frau Zuckerkandl. 'Mutti knows that our friendship is a musical one.'

'Very well,' said Frau Zuckerkandl. 'That's what we shall do.' She patted Alma-Maria's hand.

The members of the orchestra were all in place; a ripple of applause greeted the leader as he walked out onto the platform, his violin extended in front of him. The tuning stopped; an expectant hush fell over orchestra and auditorium. For all the sneering and joking about the little Jew-dwarf who had got himself baptized on Cosima Wagner's orders, Gustav Mahler's reputation as martinet of the podium affected the entire Musikverein. Even the fashionable audience sat still as schoolchildren awaiting the arrival in the classroom of a particularly ferocious head-master.

He came limping on, up the platform steps. There was scattered applause from individual members of the audience, greatly daring. He glared down at them through the flashing, steel-rimmed pince-nez perched just above the hook of his unmistakably Levantine nose. Alma-Maria recalled when she had last seen him, walking with that same rapid, jerking limp from his cab to the entrance of the Burgtheater. She remembered how she thought he had caught her glance. Now, unlike his predecessor with the Vienna Philharmonic Orchestra, the portly, amiable Willi Jahn, who would have bowed obsequiously and kissed his hands to the audience like a true Viennese performer, he gave them a look suggesting it was an impertinence that they should be there at all.

She noticed also that though his evening dress was clean and pressed precisely, his tie was badly tied and hung loose from his collar (there was a café story of how it had come undone during a performance of the *Liebestod* from *Tristan* and he had taken it off and hung it on the podium rail behind him as if on a washing line), and that his receding mane of black hair stuck out in every direction.

He raised his baton. The orchestra, whose members, though they had freely elected him as their director, mimicked him and told scabrous stories behind his back about his relations with female opera singers, came rigidly to attention. The soft, sustained opening phrase of Wagner's Prelude to Act One of *Lohengrin*, floated into an absolute stillness. As the music continued, Alma-Maria realized that she had never been to a concert where the conductor exercised such a complete control over the playing of the orchestra, or held an audience so enthralled. She herself felt half afraid to draw breath.

When the symphony began, she appeciated from the very beginning that he had the same grasp of orchestral writing as he did of orchestral playing: the horn cadences rising steadily from the initial *sostenuto* on divided strings, the birdsong candences on the woodwind like the awakening of a summer's dawn. As the performance continued, however, she felt herself becoming more and more irritated – to the point of anger. She could perfectly understand why Alex and his pupils admired him so much: there were passages in which the sheer virtuosity of the scoring, when the instrumentation was so exactly right that excitement took her by the throat. But immediately afterwards, the sublime effect would be demolished by a section of clod-hopping vulgarity or sentimental kitsch. The first movement ended with a *tutti* worthy of Wagner. It was followed by a movement in which shimmering string writing was used to support a solo trumpet passage of such hideous banality that it was scarcely worthy even of the description *Schrammel-musik* – suburban coffee-house music. In the third movement, a perfectly scored *Ländler*, as gently yearning as any by Brahms, was framed in the heavy-footed parody of a bottom-kicking, thigh-slapping Tirolean peasant dance – material which had no place in a symphony.

The whole work bore out something Schoenberg had told her: how no Jew could ever make any important or great statement without immediately afterwards making a joke about it or trying to apologize for it. She was relieved, after all, not to have been sitting with Alex and the rest. She could not have borne their enthusiasm. The intensity of her own feelings took her by surprise.

The end of the performance was greeted, at least from a greater part of the audience, with rapturous applause. Mahler accepted the ovation with a series of jerky, uncomfortable little bows, as if he were a puppet controlled by a puppet-master who had not yet entirely mastered the strings. He walked off with the same rapid limp with which he had entered, ignoring both audience and orchestra.

When Alma-Maria was at the top of the staircase leading down to the main vestibule, her arm in Berta Zuckerkandl's, a gentleman behind her, speaking to his female companion, remarked, 'A Hebrew event, you will observe.' His companion, a youngish woman in white satin trimmed with white fur and tiny crystal drops, replied, 'I hadn't realized there were so many Jews in Vienna – of a certain class, of course. It makes one feel quite overwhelmed.'

Alma-Maria noticed that Berta Zuckerkandl's bird-like face offered no hint that she had overheard the remarks.

All through the night, Alma-Maria kept waking up. The funeral march from the symphony, with its sardonic, mocking repetition of 'Frère Jacques' alternating with the jigging, sobbing dance from a Jewish village band, kept playing insistently through her head however hard she tried to concentrate on other things.

She was posing for the Beethoven Frieze when she told Klimt that she was going to Steinbach to stay with the Zuckerkandls there. She didn't tell him that Alex von Zemlinsky was going as well. Even so, the vehemence of his response took her by surprise.

'Three weeks!' he exclaimed. He dropped the pen he was using, then kicked it across the floor. 'What do you suppose I'm going to do for three God-damned weeks?'

'I'm sure you can manage without me for three weeks,' she told him quietly.

She relaxed from the pose she was holding. As she lowered the book, her arms and calf muscles glowed with the sense of ease.

'You fill this place with life,' he said. 'It's dead without you.' Anger dwindled into a brooding sullenness. 'You know how much I need you,' he said, not looking at her. He slammed his drawing board down on the chair by the easel.

'Do I?' she asked. Then she added provocatively, 'You don't need me for your work. You even draw and paint me without me.'

There was the unseen, unmentioned third person of her love drama – Emilie Flöge – never quite to be put from her mind. Berta Zuckerkandl had pointed her out at the theatre one evening. She was the antithesis of Alma-Maria: a tall, slim beauty with cropped, frizzy hair, and only the slightest mammary swellings under her loose-flowing silk gown. The gown had a peacock feather design like great eyes with heavy lashes staring in all directions; Alma-Maria had wondered if it had been Klimt's work. She had glided down the aisle to her place, conspicuous in the front of the stalls, in a cloud of sycophantic acolytes. She had glanced about her, acknowledging the greetings of acquaintances with the slightest of smiles and inclination of the head. She had been all grace and elegance, and, above all, assurance.

Remembering the scene, Alma-Maria began to feel a certain trepidation about being away for three weeks – about the possibility of returning to find that Frau Flöge had reasserted herself in Klimt's life.

'I watch you as you move,' he said. She could see the effort it cost him to transmute his feelings into words. 'I observe the movement of your features. I try to photograph them, to fix them in my memory for ever. Sometimes the thought of them fading so that I cannot recall you terrifies me.'

She had given up hiding behind the screen to undress and then dress again. She was about to take off the Grecian smock she wore when posing for him. Her back turned to him, she had drawn it up under her arms so that she was naked from above the waist down. Glancing over her shoulder, she saw that he was watching her, and was pleased.

He sat down on the settee. She turned to face him. 'Come here!' he ordered, She pulled the smock off, over her head, dragging her hair up with it so that it fell back onto her shoulders and down her arms.

'Come here, Almschi,' he repeated. He reached out and took her wrist. She dropped the smock on the floor, and stood in front of him.

'There are only two sorts of people in the world,' he told her. He swept her hair where it had fallen forward, Eve-like, off her breasts and back over her shoulders. The edge of his hands touched her raised nipples so that she sighed. 'There are those who breathe life and those who breathe death. You breathe life.'

He drew her down, over him where he was reclining. She did not wait for him to pull off his paint-smeared smock fully, but reached under it and mounted astride him. She went down, pushing his erection into herself, holding it there on the edges of pain. Her knees were only just supporting her on the upholstered verge of the settee. She might easily slip off it to the floor in her effort to tug at him between her legs. Always at these moments, there was Bethge's ghostly monkey waiting to chitter with mocking laughter among the misty graves.

He reached for her breasts as she jerked and trembled over him, her hair spilling and trailing over his arms. He pressed her nipples between forefingers and thumbs. She pushed down further, trying to take more and more of him into the clenching cavity between her legs. She felt her hair about her face matting with sweat. Occasional jabs of pain shot through her breasts when he squeezed too tightly, but then pleasure danced through her so fiercely that she shouted out loudly enough for Emilie Flöge to hear it in the Casa Piccola under the shadow of the twin towers of the Mariahilf. The moment came when she knew she would climax. She let out a sustained yell of excitement which took all her breath from her.

She lay drowsily in his arms, on the settee, her legs sprawled shamelessly apart, his great paw resting lightly on the mat of hair under her belly. She said,

'You'll see. Three weeks will go very quickly. At least, I'll pray every night they go quickly.'

He bent his head. Smiling, he kissed her cheek. 'Child!' he said.

She was dressing, buttoning the cloth buttons of the camisole top of her slip. As before, she had her back to him, the short skirt of the slip bunched about her waist. She was about to pull it straight when he called to her, 'Don't! Stay exactly as you are!'

At first, she didn't understand. Then she heard the almost imperceptible hiss of pencil shading on sketch board.

'Move your bottom over slightly to the right,' he said.

'Gustl!' she protested.

'Only a study. Nobody will see it except ourselves.'

'Even so . . . Besides, I must go home.'

'A moment of truth,' he said, still stroking away with his pencil. 'One single moment of un-kitsch – the moment when a newly grown woman hallows a wanton's gesture with her innocence.'

'Oh Gustl!' she exclaimed softly.

She posed as he asked. The faint sound of his pencil was like a feather touch on her body; an act of love. Again, she felt the urge to tell him her own feelings: how much she was in love with his strong, intelligent face, with its occasional looks of pain recalled, and with his great, bearish shape. That she wanted to be his, body and soul.

But she didn't say it. Because, even as she stood there with an immodesty which, only a few weeks previously, she would not have thought herself capable of, there was something which told her that feelings could alter, hers as well as his.

In fact, she decided, she was not really innocent at all and wondered, indeed, whether she ever had been.

She returned to Klimt's studio the afternoon before she set off for Steinbach. She wanted to reassure herself as much as him. He started to make love to her. She had to tell him that although he was her great darling greedy bear, it was the wrong time for her. Because she hated having to hold anything back from him – particularly when she was having to leave him for an eternity of three weeks – she sounded apologetic. Taking his cue from her remorseful tone, he turned sulky, pretended to be preoccupied in stretching a canvas, and addressed her in monosyllables as if she was an unwelcome visitor. She found his attitude hurtful and infuriating. Later, when she had had time to think, she would find it laughable, and all too typical of the male sex. It was inconceivable that an Ivanhoe or an Egmont or even an egotist like Faust would have behaved so; but then, of course, Rowena and Klärchen and Gretchen, since they were the invention of men, probably didn't suffer anything as inconvenient as a period. At the time, she was simply angry. She picked up her hat and purse, told him he was childish and stupid, and she would certainly not write to him – not even send him a picture postcard of the Attersee. As she went to the door, he said over his shoulder.

'You must do exactly as you wish.'

It wasn't until she had stormed out into the garden and had reached the street door that he realized that she had walked out on him, and ran after her.

'Almschi!' he called. 'Almscherl!'

But she was being carried along on a wave of indignation. Once outside, however, she began to pray that he would go on following her. She walked rapidly for some metres up the street to put a distance between herself and him. Then she started glancing over her shoulder to see if he was coming, running after her. There was no sign of him. She paused at the end of the Josefstädterstrasse to no avail. As she turned the corner into the bustle of the Langegericht, she began to cry with disappointment; but she did not retrace her steps.

That night she was too busy selecting her clothes and supervising Noni's packing her cases to give Klimt much thought. It was not until she was alone in bed that she thought that she might write a letter to him after all, and what she should put into it. But what should she say? It was he who had been inconsiderate and insensitive. She began crying again.

There was no time for brooding the following morning. The Zuckerkandls sent round for her early. There was the journey to Linz in the luxury of the transcontinental express, then the trip to Gmund in the open carriage of the small wood-burning train, through the hayfields and Alpine meadows of the Carinthian countryside. Berta and Emil Zuckerkandl made a fuss of her, treating her as if she were a favourite daughter; and there was the thought of Alex von Zemlinsky, who had been conducting at a Mozart festival in Salzburg and who would already have arrived and be waiting for her in Steinbach.

The other guests who arrived at the Zuckerkandl house that evening were Jewish – friends of Dr Zuckerkandl's from the Institute of Comparative Anatomy in Vienna and the University Hospital, and journalist acquaintances of Berta Zuckerkandl's. As on a previous occasion, she felt, with Alex – and she wasn't altogether sure about Alex – a stranger, albeit a welcome one, in a slightly foreign world where people talked in private asides about relatives and friends who lived not only in the outlying provinces of the Empire, places she could not picture like Galicia or Ruthenia, but also in cities she could not have placed on a map, like Leeds and Manchester and Chicago. Yet those same people were greedy for long hikes up into the mountain forests – not at all to her taste – as if they could not breathe enough of the air or take in enough of the scenery of their Austrian homeland; and this in a self-conscious way which she found rather ludicrous. Despite all this, she knew she had nothing to complain of in the flattering attention and kindnesses paid to her.

It was towards the end of the first week. The whole party was sitting in Berta Zuckerkandl's Turkish drawing room, after dinner. From the open window, in the warm dusk, a meadow sloped directly down to a woodland fringe of dark beeches between whose thick trunks gleamed the surface of the lake; voices sounded from scattered boats, distinct across the water.

Frau Zuckerkandl had had the two baby grand pianos brought together. Her other guests lounged on the divan settees, and on the floor cushions around the arabesque, ivory-inlaid coffee tables. It was not Alma-Maria's favourite room: she disliked the oriental décor, the fringes of beads, the giant blue and white porcelain amphoras with their burden of tall, dry reeds and bullrushes, and the febrile star, crescent, and archway motifs on the cushions and upholstery. It oppressed her in the way it seemed deliberately intended to deny the simplicity of the land outside.

She and Alex sat at the keyboards, facing one another across the cases of the two pianos. They played duets: Brahms's 'Schumann Variations' and the waltzes opus 39, followed by Mozart's Duo Sonata in D. After the Mozart piece, there was enthusiastic applause.

One gentleman said, 'They play with such sympathy – not only for the music, but for each other's playing.'

Frau Dr Hofmayr said to her husband, a colleague of Emil Zuckerkandl's, 'Fräulein Schindler plays Brahms just like a man. I wonder she has the finger span!'

There were murmurs of agreement. Alma-Maria glanced across at Alex's face. He smiled back with such an affectionate warmth that his bony, crooked features were suffused with a sort of beauty.

Berta Zuckerkandl suggested they should all walk down through the gloaming to the lake shore. As they descended the meadow, the gentlemen's cigars glowing in the half dark, Alex dropped slightly behind. Alma-Maria, knowing that he was hoping she would do so, dropped back to join him.

Somebody ahead of them said, 'I've heard Brahms is a sick man.'

'Cancer,' Dr Zuckerkandl confirmed. 'Mahler has been trying to persuade him to go into the Loewe Institute. He's refusing to accept any treatment. Mind you, he's probably better off without it, if he's happy where he is.'

'Are you thinking of going to see him, Alex?' Berta Zuckerkandl called back.

'I . . . I don't know,' Alex replied.

Even while he was stammering, Berta Zuckerkandl added for the benefit of everybody else,

'Of course the Freiherr von Zemlinsky is Brahms's favourite pupil, aren't you, Alex? We can lend you a bicycle, you know. It's a lovely ride, up over the Weissenbach Pass and down into Ischl. You could be there and back in a day very easily.'

'Darling Alex,' whispered Alma-Maria. 'I think you've been given your marching orders.'

They reached the lake shore. The surface was utterly still; the last boat had been rowed back to its mooring. One of the younger men of the party played ducks and drakes: the stones left a brief wake of phosphorescent stars as they bounced and skidded across the surface. Alma-Maria put her arm into Alex's.

'Would you like me to come with you?' she asked.

He thought for a moment. Then he said doubtfully, 'Brahms can be an ogre sometimes.'

'Not a very dangerous one, from the sound of it,' she replied.

'He's quite the rudest man I know.'

'Are you trying to put me off, Alex?'

'Oh no! No! I couldn't imagine anything more wonderful than spending a day alone with you ... I was just trying to be fair, that's all. You can ride a bicycle, can't you?'

'Don't be silly! I wouldn't have suggested coming with you if I couldn't, would I?'

Berta Zuckerkandl appeared out of the darkness.

'I could recognize your voices,' she said. 'Sound carries so precisely here, doesn't it? I was going to ask Almschi if she would like to go with you. I expect you'd like a change from climbing up mountains, wouldn't you, *liebchen*?'

There was a sudden plop in the water close by. Alma-Maria thought for a moment that somebody had thrown a pebble, but the sound had been too soft. It must have been a fish jumping to catch an insect, she decided.

'We do have a lady's bicycle up at the house,' said Frau Zuckerkandl. 'And I'm sure we could find a divided skirt which would fit you. Of course, they do keep on saying what a threat to young women's morals the bicycle is, don't they?' She laughed. 'But I'm sure Alex can be trusted not to take advantage of you.'

The following morning, when the dog carts came round to the house to take the rest of the party on the first leg of their picnic journey to the summit of the Hollergebirge, Alex and Alma-Maria set off on their bicycles down into Steinbach, and then up the long, winding road to the Weissenbach Pass. She followed just behind him, struggling to keep up with him. The blue serge skirt she had borrowed – it belonged to one of the servants – was slightly too tight for her on the seat, adding to her discomfort as she pushed up the last two or three kilometres to the head of the pass. Her legs ached, the sun was hot, there was sweat dribbling under her arms and running from under the stiff brim of her straw boater freely into her eyes. As she battled to each the top, she began to wonder whether uphill walking wasn't altogether preferable.

They rested for a few minutes in the shadow of the small baroque chapel overlooking the spectacular Weissenbach Gorge. Alex spread his jacket for her to lie on. It smelt of tobacco, and she found it comforting. He sat a few paces from her, and smoked a cigarette.

'Happy?' she asked him.

'I shouldn't say it,' he replied. Then he burst out, 'How can I be anything else when I'm with you?'

'No. You shouldn't say it,' she told him. 'Not really.'

'But it doesn't make you angry?'

'Oh Alex! Why should it?'

There were several good reasons she could think of. But she remembered the way his face had been transformed the previous night as he smiled at her. Perhaps God had graced her sufficiently even to avert Brahms's notorious rudeness.

She watched Alex through drowsily half-closed eyes. He had rolled his shirt sleeves to just below his elbows. His fingers were long, prehensile; his arms, under their covering of downy black hairs, were sinewy and strong. She had noticed as she cycled behind him uphill, how compact and strong were his hips and thighs. There was a sort of beauty conferred by intelligence, she decided – Socrates, notorious for his ugliness, had just such a beauty. Even so, she could never imagine devoting herself to Alex, for all his genius, as she could imagine herself as handmaid and muse to Klimt.

As a consolation prize, because in a sort of way she had grown to love him, she reached out and took his hand.

'I too am glad to be here,' she told him.

They mounted their bicycles once more and coasted down the road into the open valley. Above the trees, enfolded in Alpine meadow, gleamed the roofs and spired domes of Bad Ischl. The Wolfgangsee stretched glittering into the lap of the mountains. At first, Alma-Maria found the descent frightening. The brakes scraped as she clutched them; stones shot from under the wheels; the breeze in her face made her eyes water and snapped at her unfamiliar skirts. As she gained confidence, however, she felt wonderfully free and irresponsible.

They dismounted at an inn a short distance from Ischl, and drank ice-cold wine and had a meal of bread, sausage and cheese, sitting in the orchard garden. Across the meadows, the white square tower of St Wolfgang's church quivered in the sunlight. The wine maintained Alma-Maria's sense of euphoria. When the moment came to complete the short distance to Brahms's house, she felt quite reluctant to move.

They left their bicycles at the inn and walked the half-kilometre along a meadow path. As they reached the end of the path, where stood a small, old-fashioned house, with whitewashed walls and carved, painted gables, she paused, hiding behind a heavily boled wych elm. She unpinned her straw boater and gave it to Alex to hold while she attempted to arrange her hair, thrusting her combs upwards through it to secure it.

'He'll not be concerned with your appearance,' Alex assured her.

'Never mind,' she replied. 'He is the last of the giants – Gluck, Haydn, Beethoven . . . Wagner. It's a bit like going to church – it isn't a question of whether anybody *notices* your appearance.'

'I wouldn't include Wagner's name in your litany of saints; not in his hearing; and don't mention Bruckner's name, whatever you do!'

'Bruckner!' she laughed, and it sounded forced. Already she was beginning to feel shy. She could see that Alex was nervous.

She pinned on her hat once more, carefully.

'Ready,' she announced.

A dumpy little grey-haired woman greeted them. Below her apron and rusty black dress, her black woollen stockings had fallen down her swollen legs.

'*Grüss Gott* – the *gnädige* Freiherr von Zemlinsky isn't it?'

She blinked inquiringly at Alma-Maria, and pulled a pair of wire-rimmed spectacles from her apron pocket to examine her more closely.

'*Grüss Gott*, Fräulein.'

'Fräulein Schindler is the daughter of the artist who painted the view of Ischl which the master has hanging in his studio,' Alex explained.

The housekeeper's face beamed. 'It is so like the real thing,' she exclaimed. 'You recognize it straight away. Your Papa is a very clever man, Fräulein.'

She led them round the side of the house.

'The Herr Doctor Composer is in the garden,' she explained. 'You must not mind him, you know. He has not been at all well – not well at all. People tell him he should seek help – clever people. But he pays no attention. He just gets cross. With me – with everybody. You mustn't mind him, Fräulein.'

He was standing under a tree, in the ragged, unkept grass, silhouetted against the shimmering haze of the mountan slopes which enclosed the valley. Because of the brightness, she could not see at first whether he was looking at them as they approached, or had his back to them. Even before she could make out his features and his full beard, she noticed how his suit hung baggily from his frame. Then as she saw his face, she realized that his skin hung sagging and empty under his eyes and about his jowls – the body of a fat man which sudden sickness has left half-vacant.

'*Grüss Gott*, youngster!' he called to Alex. '*Grüss Gott!*'

He folded him into an embrace. As he released him, Alex turned to Alma-Maria.

'Honoured Master, may I present my pupil – my gifted and well-born pupil – Alma Schindler. Fräulein Schindler is the daughter of the late Jakob-Emil Schindler, the painter.'

She held out her hand to him. Brahms did not see it, or ignored it. He gave her the most fleeting of glances with his weary, rheumy eyes, and turned back to Alex.

'Female pupil, eh? I had a female composition pupil once. Damned Englishwoman, believe it or not. She had some slight aptitude – but then she was three quarters a man!'

He laughed painfully, grotesquely, his discoloured fingers clutching at his waistcoat. Alex took his arm to help lower him onto the rustic seat under the tree.

'You know, youngster?' said Brahms. 'If I wanted to give myself nightmares, I'd imagine trying to copulate with Fräulein Smyth, eh?'

Beads of sweat stood out on the top of his bruised, bald pate. He patted the pockets of his creased, shapeless linen jacket.

'Cigar,' he said. 'Cigar.'

Alex produced a case from his pocket.

'Ah yes!' said Brahms taking one. He bit off the end and spat it into the long grass at his feet. Alex lit a match for him.

'Should you be smoking, Magister?' he asked.

Brahms coughed and cleared his throat. He peered up from the seat as if he had difficulty seeing Alex as he stood over him. His beard was discoloured with nicotine. His appearance was one of neglect. He pointed his cigar at Alex.

'Don't you go telling me I'm a sick man, youngster. They all keep telling me I should go to Vienna, to the doctors. Even Frau Klinger. A man can't be allowed to grow old decently these days. Mahler says I look ill – comes here to see me every month – tells me I should get myself examined at the Loewe Institute. Wants to put me in the hands of his Jewish medical friends, I dare say.'

He gave Alma-Maria a bleary glance.

'Composition pupil, eh?'

'Yes, Magister,' Alex replied. 'I believe Fräulein Schindler has a very real talent.'

Brahms coughed and cleared his throat.

'Take her to the Court Opera. Let her hear Mahler conducting Mozart; it'll teach her what *real* music should sound like. That should cure her.'

He addressed himself solely to Alex. It was as if he had decided quite pointedly to ignore her physical presence.

'Hasn't cured Mahler himself, mind you,' he continued. 'Fellow left me with one of those vast scores of his. Calls it a symphony – my God! Has a nice little scherzo, but a choral last movement the length of an oratorio.'

He cleared his throat again, then sucked on his cigar. Alex relit it for him.

'Garbage,' he went on. 'Shit. Except where he's borrowed from my *Requiem*. That's the Jew for you: devoid of any spark of originality. Did you ever hear any of Joachim's compositions? A joke – a joke in bad taste. Though they're damned fine executants, Jews. Do you know? Tchaikovsky wept when I took him to hear Mahler conduct his *Eugene Onegin* in Hamburg; said it was the most sympathetic interpretation of his music he had ever heard – other than his own. You have to give it to them; damned responsive to other people's feelings. That's why Jewish women make the best whores, eh?'

He laughed, wheezed bronchially, and spilled ash from his cigar down his waistcoat, He went on laughing. Alex was obviously worried. Brahms began to wheeze noisily as if fighting for breath. Alex stooped over him, his hand on the older man's shoulder. Brahms recovered. He brushed away Alex's hand in a gesture of irritation and tried to wipe the ash from off the front of his waistcoat, but only succeeded in establishing a grey smear.

'Mahler had to get himself christened before he could take over the Court Opera,' he declared. 'Frau Wagner made the Jew crouch under the yoke, eh?'

Didn't he realize, Alma-Maria wondered, that it was a topic which had been talked and sniggered over in Vienna to the point of exhaustion? She was seized with an anger which came so quickly she had no control over it. She saw that poor Alex was torn between the respect he felt he owed to his revered master and his boundless admiration of Mahler's genius.

'Perhaps, Herr Doctor,' she heard herself saying coldly, 'The Herr Director felt it was a price worth paying for a post in which he could exercise his God-given talent to the full.'

Brahms didn't look at her.

'Perhaps,' he grunted.

A heavy silence fell between them. Alex stood as if waiting for his old master to say something more. Brahms prodded the grass with his toe.

'He is a very kind man, Mahler,' he said in a gruff, low voice.

Alex glanced across at Alma-Maria. Brahms did not look up.

'The last time he was here,' Brahms went on, 'he took me up into the Ischl Woods. We went up beside the Traun to the waterfall. He supported me all the way, and he's only a little fellow. We smoked a cigar and talked about the new music. I told him what I thought of some of it. Do you know, he had the temerity to answer back? He pointed his stick at the water and said, "You see? That wave there passes on, but it is always followed by another." Do you know what I said to him, eh? I told him, "Let's hope they are all flowing into a lake and not a frog swamp!"' He laughed at the recollection. Then he said, 'It was a beautiful day, youngster. I wonder if I'll ever see the Traun again.'

'You must take care of your health, Magister,' Alex told him.

They left him sitting under the tree staring out towards the mountains. When they had reached the summit of the Weissenbach Pass – they had to walk their bicycles up the last kilometre and a half – they rested again. Again, Alex took his jacket from where he had tied it on the crossbar, and spread it on the ground for her to sit on. This time they sat in the sun, near the edge of the gorge.

'I expect it was a very painful experience for you,' he said.

'He ignored me,' she said. 'I might have been invisible.'

But that wasn't what she really wanted to say.

'How can such music spring from somebody so selfish – so loveless?' she demanded.

'If it's in the music it must be in the man,' Alex replied. 'He's always been boorish and insensitive at times – particularly, I'm afraid, to women. But he hasn't been unloved. Schumann loved him. You've heard how Mahler tries to look after him. Clara Schumann would have married him after Schumann's death, if he'd asked her. He did love her in his way. His illness only started after her death last April. He missed her funeral, you know. He thought it was to have been at Frankfurt. He didn't realize that she had asked to be buried beside Schumann at Bonn. He arrived at the graveside after all the other mourners were gone, and the grave-diggers were filling in the grave. The truth is, he can't forgive himself for not having said goodbye to her.'

They arrived back at the Zuckerkandl house to find it deserted: the rest of the party had dined and gone rowing on the lake. The two of them dined alone, then went to the Turkish drawing room. At first, they sat at the open window; they couldn't see the boats, but they could hear voices laughing from off the lake.

'I remember hearing Brahms's C-minor Symphony for the first time,' Alma-Maria told him. 'Pappi took me to hear von Bülow conduct it at the Sophiensalle. I was twelve, I think. I remember I felt quite ecstatic listening to the last movement – it seemed so majestic, so triumphant, so full of faith. And there's the man who composed that wonderful hymn – so lonely and afraid! It's frightening.'

'He's dying,' said Alex. 'He knows it. He's afraid of death.'

'He wouldn't be if he had somebody with him who really loved him. *Love casteth out fear.* I don't mean Mahler visiting him once a month, or anything like that. I mean somebody who'd be with him all the time, to comfort him in the dark and try to take the pain away.'

She saw that across the window seat Alex was smiling at her myopically. He had his glasses off and was polishing them with his handkerchief.

'I don't see what I've said to amuse you!' she said angrily.

He waved his hand in front of him in a vague gesture, his wrist sticking out from his frayed cuff.

'Not at all! Not at all!' he demurred. 'It's the way you speak the truth so directly. But Brahms would never let anybody get that close to him.'

'It *is* frightening!' She shivered.

Alex got up and went over to one of the pianos.

'It isn't a state you're ever likely to experience, Almschi,' he said.

He spread out a score in front of him, and sat down at the keyboard. He started playing.

'Because this is you,' he said.

She recognized the duet from Mozart's *The Magic Flute* – *Bei Mannern, welche Liebe fühlen*. She got up and stood behind Alex, her hands resting on his shoulders. She joined her own, slightly husky voice to his:

> Love's lofty aim shows there's nothing more fine,
> Nothing more noble than woman and man –
> Man and woman, woman and man –
> Seeking together the presence of God . . .

As the final note of the duet drifted away as if through the open window, she whispered,

'It's the desolation we saw this afternoon. It haunts me.' She blinked back tears.

'*Bei Mannern, welche Liebe fühlen,*' he said gently. He drew her down, and she allowed him to, so that she was sitting on his knees. ' "*Any man who can accept love, will not lack a kindly heart*".'

Once again he had removed his glasses.

'Oh Alex!' she said. She cupped her hands on his cheeks and kissed him.

'I can accept love,' he murmured, half in warning.

'I know,' she replied, and kissed him again.

There was the slight absurdity of his long beak of a nose pressing into the edge of her cheek beside her own small one. But she needed to feel herself in his embrace. When he eased her off his knees, and led her to the soft-cushioned divan, her desperate need to put the panic fear of loneliness from her prevented her from giving any rational consideration to what was occurring. As he drew her down, she continued to return his kissing with a passion equal to his. When he began drawing up her skirts, she knew very well she had encouraged him to do so.

'I'm taking advantage of you,' he said.

Poor, ugly Alex! It was quite ridiculous he should think himself capable of taking advantage of her.

'I want you to!' she whispered.

Would Alex find she wasn't a virgin, and be shocked? And what was she doing? What would everybody think of her if they found out? Words came unsummoned into her head. *Zarathustra*: '*We must become what we are – to deny one's instinct is corruption!*'

She heard herself laughing in shocked but amused surprise at her own wantonness. And Alex's ugliness? Her own aroused appetite set all considerations aside, washed around as it was by a great feeling of tender friendship for him.

Freed from the restrictions of her divided skirt, she clutched at Alex as if to drive him to take her as fiercely and as deeply as he could. But as he rode her to her climax, it was Klimt who possessed her mind.

That same night when she retired, she found a note from Alex slipped under her door:

> Nobody is like you! How can I thank you for what has passed between us this evening? But you must promise me, my love, that you will tell me when you want no more of me. I know it will happen in time – and when it does, I promise you there will be no reproaches, no attempts on my part to keep you closer to me than you wish. Believe me, I shall forever be only too grateful for what you have already permitted me....

Utterly wearied as she was by the activities of the day, she found it impossible to sleep. Pictures floated through her mind: the Weissenbach Gorge in the heat of the midday sun; Brahms crouched under the tree, his clothes hanging from his sagging frame as if he were vanishing from this world before her eyes yet pleading to be allowed to remain; the ugly furnishing of Berta Zuckerkandl's drawing room vulgarizing passion. She forced herself into full consciousness to draft a reply to Alex's note:

> ... It was the most beautiful thing, *mein liebe* Alex. But you have guessed, I know, that we must not let it happen again. I do love you. I shall always love you as my very dearest teacher and friend. I do not want to lose your dear companionship. What happened this evening was good – very good. And it was right and true for the moment it occurred. But the moment has passed, and it would be wrong to pretend that we could ever re-create it ...

Alma-Maria had not found Venice boring when she had been there with Pappi. But that was many years ago and in a different world. In those days they had left Mutti, Grete, and Fräulein Weyss in Danieli's Hotel, nursing headaches caused by the heat, and had gone off together to explore the labyrinths of alleys, narrow embankments and unweeded *campos* (squares), for quaint, evil-smelling courtyards and glorious, neglected churches.

Memories of heat and headaches had resulted in Mutti insisting this time that they stay at the Hotel des Bains on the Lido instead of in Venice itself. Only in the evening did they take the hotel steam-launch across the lagoon to the landing stage in St Mark's. Möll and Mutti would only explore where there was no fear of their losing their way – which was no exploring at all. They drank an aperitif with all the other German-speaking visitors at Quadri's in St Mark's Square: they felt more at home there than at Florian's opposite which, though it was more famous, was full of Italians and Americans. Then they would take a stroll, just like everybody else, among the Riva degli Schiavoni to the lion gates to the Arsenal and the Public Gardens, before returning to St Mark's and the hotel launch. Back in the hotel on the Lido, they would have a buffet supper before going to bed. So precise a daily routine made even sunset over San Giorgio Maggiore and the domes of the Salute seem wearisome.

Afternoons were the worst. Möll and Mutti retired for the siesta until four o'clock. Because of the siesta, Alma was forbidden to play the piano; there was nothing left to her but to sit in the lounge reading, surrounded by old people in varying states of somnolence. Or to walk under the dusty pine trees and palms of the garden, evading the stares of the young men in vulgarly striped blazers and straw-topped shoes, who lounged, sprawled, and swung on the seats, and blew their cigar smoke at her to attract her attention as she passed by. Once or twice, she found herself wanting to cry to relieve the tension of her boredom.

The reason given out for their retreat to Venice – though baby Marie had been left behind with her nursemaid – was the removal of the household from the Theresianumgasse apartment to their newly built home up on the fashionable Hohe Warte. The possibility gnawed in Alma-Maria's mind that there might be other reasons: that Möll might have guessed at her visits to Klimt's studio; that her careless abandonment with Klimt after her return from Steinbach the previous autumn might have left tokens in her underwear which the maids had spotted and talked about; that while Mutti and Möll had not voiced their suspicions, they had agreed to remove her from Vienna for the summer.

One evening, three weeks after their arrival at the Hotel des Bains, having crossed the lagoon to Venice as usual, they walked further than they were wont to do, penetrating the Merceria to the Santa Maria Formosa and its market stalls canopied like a medieval knights' encampment, and on to the massive gothic façade of the Zanipolo. Uncle Carl had announced that Venice filled him with a restless urge to paint – it was the sort of predictable remark he would make – and was searching for a subject. While he moved from position to position around the wide square, with Mutti on his arm listening to his commentary, Alma-Maria went to the steps leading down to the still water of the canal by the steeply arched little bridge. The decaying palaces of fourteenth-century merchant princes, the barber-shop mooring posts were mirror-reflected on the surface as in the dampened glass of a mildew-stained window.

There was a reek of carbolic spilling from the watergate of the Free Public Hospital concealed behind the lofty, ornate porch of the Old School of St Mark's. An object like a single grey inflated water-wing floated sedately in front of her. At first she thought it was a cat. Then she saw that it was the swollen body of a huge rat, its small stick-like legs thrust upwards, its tail stretched stiffly behind it. Even upside down, its pointed head and bright eyes had a look of malign intelligence as if, in the complexity of its scheming, it was unaware that its torso was likely at any moment to explode with gaseous decomposition.

She turned away. Uncle Carl had decided that the Zanipolo was an unsuitable subject for his genius. He and Mutti joined her on the canal-side. Uncle Carl noticed the swollen object on the water; he regarded it with a look of contemptuous distaste.

'One would not see such things if we Austrians still governed here,' he said.

They returned to St Mark's Square and Quadri's. Möll ordered iced Moselle and they sat close to the orchestra for Mutti's sake.

Their waiter came out of the restaurant. He twisted and writhed his way between the tables to where they were sitting. Mutti nodded happily to the music. Möll tried his Italian on the waiter as he placed the drinks and the small wicker basket of dry biscuits on the table. Alma-Maria turned away to peer once more into the crowds. The whaleboning of her chemise collar pressed into her neck like narrowly pointed fingertips. She was sure the edge of the collar was soiled with sweat.

A fissure opened in the dense mass of the seething currents of the crowds, leaving a cobbled entry into their midst. A figure, tall and heavily built, emerged from the side of the fissure. It was only for a moment, but the impression left was vivid and unmistakable – Klimt, red-haired, red-bearded, in a very untypical dazzling white suit, a vivid red necktie about his wilting, open shirt collar, his face purpled and moistened. Their eyes met; there was a look of expectation and excitement in his recognition of her, as if he had been searching her out. Then, across the mouth of the gap in the crowds processed a column of jabbering north European tourists – Scandinavians of some sort – following a lean schoolmasterish guide waving a blue umbrella in one hand and his inevitable Baedeker in the other. When they had passed, the fissure had closed up and the apparition of Klimt was gone.

They walked to the Molo, to take the hotel launch back to the Lido. Alma-Maria sat silent in the prow, under the awning. She tried to rehearse over and over again the moment when the fissure appeared in the swirling currents of tourists in the Square, and she saw Klimt standing there. She had to re-create the moment to convince herself that there had been no mistake – that she had not been hallucinating as a result of too much exposure to sun and heat. But each rehearsal proved more difficult, more exhausting than the last until she reached the edge of nausea. Back at the hotel, she pleaded the conventional headache and went straight up to bed.

After lunch the following day, she continued to plead a headache. In the solitude of her room and a silence broken only by the sound of children playing among the beach huts on the shore, she lowered the blinds, took off her shoes, and lay down on the settee under the window. Mutti came in on her way to her own room and her siesta. Alma-Maria suggested she might not attend their customary evening excursion across the lagoon. She was not normally prone to headaches. Mutti looked curiously at her.

'You're not due for at least a fortnight,' she pointed out, 'You haven't been drinking the water, have you?'

'No, Mutti.'

When Mutti was gone, she listened for her voice and that of Möll on the corridor outside. She heard their door close, and waited as the heavy afternoon silence returned. Then she rose, put on her shoes, and very quietly left the room and went downstairs.

Klimt was in Venice. Perhaps he was looking for her, not realizing that she was staying out on the Lido. She walked down the steps from the garden terrace, and crossed the sparse, sandy lawn to the gate which led onto the narrow road behind the hotel. Letting herself out, she made her way between the private villas with their gardens to the main public landing stage of the island across the square from the Church of Santa Maria Elizabetta. There, on the edge of the clusters of would-be passengers awaiting the docking of the *vaporetti* which chugged laboriously to and from Venice, she looked out across the glittering water, and wondered where, under the dazzling skyline of domes and pointed campaniles, in the jungle of alleys and embankments, Klimt might be looking for her – if he was looking for her.

A *vaporetto* came in, bumping the wooden pontoon, sending black, scummy water splashing against the embankment wall, and pouring smoke across the square so that people coughed as they jostled down the landing stage. A group of young men – scarcely more than gymnasium-school age, and as handsome and lethal as supernumeraries in a Shakespeare play or a Verdi opera – were sitting or swinging on the embankment rail. Alma-Maria noticed that they were examining her admiringly. Their eyes flashed into hers, and she knew she had made a mistake. They leaned out at her, calling to her, beckoning, blowing kisses, and laughing contemptuously. She moved round the kiosk at the top of the landing stage and she heard rather than saw the boys as they jumped down from the rail. At the ticket booth she took her place behind a fat woman whose dress scarcely contained her. A family carrying shopping baskets and battered magazines closed in behind her. The boys at the rail jumped up and down and called out to her as the family behind her pushed her down the landing stage onto the boat.

She hadn't set out with any intention of crossing to Venice. She had with her neither duster-coat nor parasol, and only the little purse she always carried on her wrist. The small straw boater she wore for strolling about the grounds of the hotel made her feel slightly naked. She looked down into her lap, and did not look up again until it was San Giorgio Maggiore rather than the Lido embankment, across the expanse of water.

She was so confused that she followed the crowd off the boat at the Zaccaria instead of St Mark's. She was drawn into the noisy, polyglot crowds seething backwards and forwards over the steep bridges of the quay. Since most around her who hemmed her in were taller than herself, she scarcely knew which way she was heading. It was not until she was on the summit of the Ponte della Paglia and caught the briefest glimpse of the Bridge of Sighs that she knew she was at the Doge's Palace.

She was stepping out of the shade of the covered façade of the Doge's Palace into the garish sunlight of the Piazzetta, when she saw him. He has seen her first: he had been sitting in the open-air café under the shadow of the Library of St Mark's, where he could command a view of the entire Piazzetta and the Molo. He had got up and was pushing his way between the people crowding round the tables; his height enabled her to spot him before he emerged from the throng. She tried to run at him, but a mob of English visitors clutching guide books and postcards came between them. He reached above them: she could see his outstretched arms, straw hat in one hand, red silk bandanna in the other, and the flash of his gold wristwatch. The tidal current of visitors caught her and swept her along. She cried out 'Klimt!' several times, with the desperation of somebody who was in danger of drowning. A moment later, she felt a grip on her arm; he had reached her, and was drawing her to the edge of the crowd.

She smiled up at him. 'Klimt!' she repeated.

He put his hat back on his head and wiped the palms of his hands with his red bandanna.

'I've been here since ten o'clock this morning,' he said reproachfully.

'How did you know I'd come at all?' she asked. 'And here.'

'I didn't know you'd come. I knew you'd try. As for here – everybody who is looking for anybody must start by passing through here.'

He pointed to the two tall columns – one supporting the Lion of St Mark, the other, the figure of the saint himslf – which form the entrance to St Mark's Square.

'How long would you have waited?' she asked.

'As long as it took you to come.'

'I didn't know I was going to come. I didn't have any intention of coming.'

'You couldn't help it.'

'You're very conceited,' she told him.

'Not at all. I couldn't help myself from coming to Venice after you.'

'Don't pretend you came here simply because I was here!'

'That is the absolute truth, Almschi ... Do you want me to swear it on the mortal remains of St Mark?'

He pointed to the Byzantine doors of the Basilica. As he did so, he put his arm close about her waist.

'Not here, Gustl! There's bound to be people from the hotel.'

He held her firmly to him. She could feel the strength of his thigh against her hip. Despite her fears, she longed to turn to him. His arm still about her, he guided her across the square, between the ranks of tables of Florian's and Quadri's toward the Correr Arch. They passed through the shaded coolness and, still in the shade, made their way along the shops on the galleried passageway below the San Moisé bridge. The black gondolas were moored on either bank of the canal, their gondoliers waiting expectantly on every water step. Klimt drew Alma-Maria into the deeper shadow of an empty *calle*, a narrow defile between the high, unbroken walls of two ancient buildings which led onto a cramped, deserted courtyard like the bottom of an empty well.

He stopped and put both arms about her.

'The only discreet place in all Venice,' he said.

'I think it's a place for murders, not love,' she told him.

But she reached up, putting her arms round his neck, pressing herself against him.

'I've taken a studio,' he said, still holding her to him.

'So you didn't come to Venice just because of me, you liar!'

'I didn't know how long I would be staying here. Would you want me to stop painting for love of you?'

'Of course not. I want you to paint because you love me!'

'Will you let me take you there?'

She ran her fingers through the thick red stubble of his beard.

'I love your beard,' she teased him. 'It makes you look like a Hephaestus – blacksmith of the gods.'

'Will you?' he insisted.

'Where?'

'Over on the Zattere. It looks out across to the most beautiful of all Venetian churches – the Redentore. I shall paint you with your hair flowing down your back, framed in an arabesque window, looking across the canal to the church – *Alma-Maria, Stella Maris*: tender Mary, Star of the Sea, watching over the shrine of the Redemption.'

Looking up into his face, she felt the tears of sheer joy welling up. She wanted to tell him she would go with him, stay with him, live with him for as long as he wanted her. Was Emilie Flöge gone for ever? she wondered.

'I have to go back,' she heard herself say. 'Back to the Lido. They think I'm just taking a short stroll in the hotel grounds ...'

She gave a little laugh.

'I shall come across to the Lido with you,' he told her.

'No – no you mustn't.'

'Then I shall come tomorrow. I shall go to Santa Maria Elizabetta, and pray there and light candles until you come to me.'

'You'll be seen. Somebody's sure to recognize you.'

'Almschi! I'm not as famous as that.'

'Möll might see you. Mutti knows what you look like. You shouldn't look so grand and so distinctive. It isn't fair!'

'Are you telling me I'm not to see you at all?'

'No, I don't mean that. I couldn't bear that.'

'What then?'

'I don't know what to suggest . . .'

'But you want to see me?'

'Don't be so ridiculous!'

Klimt stood silent for a moment, his arms round her shoulders. The shouts of the gondoliers, the creak and slap of the oars as they struck the water, sounded from the mouth of the *calle*. He drew her close to him once more. He spoke into her ear as if speaking so were a form of kiss.

'Tomorrow, ask if, when Möll and your mother are taking their siesta, you can take one of the hotel boats across to San Giorgio Maggiore to visit the church. Nobody would find the idea at all strange of a young lady going across to visit an island monastery. And I shall wait for you in the church.'

'I'll do my best – my very best.'

She turned her face to his, reaching for his mouth. She kissed him, seeking to let him know that she would be his whenever opportunity permitted.

They said goodbye at the Correr Arch. She returned across St Mark's Square and out to the Molo alone. She avoided the hotel launch which was moored at one of the piers, and joined the crowd jostling onto the *vaporetto*. She met Möll and Mutti as she was returning up the garden terrace past the windows of the hotel lounge.

Mutti said, 'Oh, there you are! We were just coming out to look for you. Uncle Carl is about to set off on his painting expedition. I thought I'd take a gentle stroll up the *lungomare*, perhaps as far as the old fortifications. Would you like to keep me company, *liebchen*?'

It was strange – as if she had been dreaming, and had woken to find nothing like the amount of time had passed that she had imagined.

She took the opportunity of strolling with Mutti along the shore among the reeds and the dunes to broach the idea of her visiting the monastery the following afternoon.

'I don't see why not, *liebchen*, if you take one of the boats from the hotel moorings. It must be rather dull for you, walking in the garden every afternoon.' She paused, staring out across the fluttering little waves to where a ship was sailing southwards from one of the Austrian ports, to its white superstructure, and the long trail of grey and white smoke from its tall funnel which hung motionless between silver sea and sky. 'You know,' she carried on, 'you could find out whether there are other people at the hotel who want to go to the island. It is very beautiful, after all. I've wondered myself what it must be like inside. Cool, I expect, with all that white marble. You might find yourself making up a party. That would be fun.'

'I expect it would.'

Alma-Maria decided not to pursue the matter any further, but to wait for the following afternoon and then go, now she could claim that Mutti had given her permission. She couldn't imagine anything worse than arriving on San Giorgio with an escort of chattering tourists.

The blow came at breakfast.

'*Liebchen* – Uncle Carl and I have decided: we shall come with you this afternoon instead of having our usual forty winks.'

Möll smiled and nodded his agreement, and dabbed brioche crumbs from his moustache and beard with his napkin.

There was no way Alma-Maria could prevent them from coming with her.

Her sense of disappointment was almost more than she could bear. She prayed that something, anything would happen to change their minds.

They crossed over to San Giorgio Maggiore in a *traghetto* from the hotel landing stage. The heat was intense, the water of the lagoon as still as the surface of a mirror. The small islands between the Lido and San Giorgio were a blazing, impossible green and white. Möll stared out across to the skyline of St Mark's and the Doge's Palace. The boat rocked slightly as the boatmen dipped their oars. Mutti sat beside Alma-Maria, their skirts spilling over one another's as they lay back on the cushions. More and more, as they glided past the high, rotting mooring posts on the unkempt lagoon shore of the island, with their half-sunk skeletal boats, Alma-Maria felt she would have preferred never to have met Klimt, than to have suffered the fear and suspense she was now experiencing. The shadow of the church's tall campanile struck across the water like a sudden chill. Somewhere behind the pale red brick of the high, severe monastery walls he was waiting for her, expecting her, unaware of danger and disappointment.

They landed on the step in front of the white marble façade of the church, and crossed the black and white lozenge tiles of the forecourt. Water lapped against the steps as the boatman pushed off the *traghetto*. They entered the cold white, classical interior. Möll genuflected and signed himself with the cross. Mutti sighed, and looked up into the great dome. Alma-Maria glanced all about her. There was no sign of Klimt. Without waiting for the others, she walked to the centre, where she could see into the side chapels. Mutti came over to join her, her high heels clicking on the stone floor.

'You mustn't be in such a hurry,' she said.

'I'm not, Muttichen. It's just that I wanted so very much to see the Tintoretto in the sanctuary.'

The sense of relief made her voice sound excited. He wasn't there. But she hardly dared to raise her eyes to Tintoretto's 'Last Supper' for fear that he might emerge from some side door, or out of a confessional, and suddenly confront them. What had happened? she wondered. Had God or her guardian angel intervened to protect her? That was what peasant girls and kitchen maids believed, she told herself – but she still accepted the possibility.

A monk appeared and spoke to Möll. He showed them the carved wooden choir stalls, describing them and explaining their motifs while Möll translated his commentary into German. He took them through the cloisters to the monastery refectory, to show them Tintoretto's 'Marriage of the Virgin'. He suggested, through Möll, that the signor and signora might like to rest from the heat of the day in the shade of Palladio's garden cloister, and led them outside through the church once more, through the great sacristy to a small sacristy with a cobbled floor and smelling of stale incense and mildew. The first thing which Alma-Maria noticed, after the ranks of slender columns supporting the cover of the walkways, was the brilliant green of the lawns and topiary beyond, and the splashing coolness of the fountain in the centre.

The monk suggested that Möll and Mutti sit on white garden seats in a laurel arbour in one corner. Möll asked if he might smoke a cigar. When the monk, smiling, agreed that he could, Möll offered him his case. The monk, after the sketchiest demurral, took one and put it carefully inside his scapular. Möll lit his cigar, letting smoke and scent trail out across the open lawn. Mutti sighed again, sat back, and closed her eyes. Alma-Maria sat with the monk on the stone balustrade between the columns.

'The garden. Very beautiful. Yes?'

He spoke in deadly slow, carefully enunciated German.

'*Bellissima, molta bellissima*,' she ventured.

'Good. Very good Fräulein.' He laughed. 'We have a bigger beautiful garden.'

He stopped. She wondered why he was waiting. The atmosphere of somnolence was infectious. Mutti's eyelids were drooping. After a minute or two, it seemed as though Möll would let his cigar go out. Perhaps the monk was waiting for a tip. Then he said to Alma-Maria, as Möll deliberately opened his eyes,

'You see the bigger garden, yes?'

He turned to Möll. Indicating Alma-Maria, he spoke in Italian. Möll nodded dismissively, and the monk said to her,

'Your father says you come with me . . . to see the big, beautiful garden . . . yes?'

Anything was better than sitting watching Mutti and Möll sleeping. She slid down off the balustrade, exposing her silk-glazed legs above her cream raffia-topped, button-strapped shoes. The monk deliberately averted his eyes. She followed him round the cloister until they reached the opposite corner to that where Mutti and Möll were resting. He opened a small door in the wall; above the lintel, set in a triangular marble pediment, two plump-cheeked *putti* clutched carved linen folds over their genitals.

Beyond lay another world. A garden of green lawns, privets and ornamental shrub hedges spread over more than half the island's surface, stretched to the shore where the Canale San Giorgio met the open Adriatic. Hosepipes, their rose mouths propped on forks, sprayed the grass carpets between the dusty paths; beads of moisture scintillated on individual blades, and there was a smell of greenery she had not encountered since they had arrived in Venice.

The monk led her to the end of the monastery wall. Beyond a glade of umbrella pines was a wooden landing stage to which was moored a *traghetto*. The two boatmen were standing, leaning on their long oars, at the end of the landing stage. A third man, taller and burlier than the boatmen, stood with them. Against the brilliance of the water he was in silhouette, but she could see the shape of his straw Panama and the flowing kerchief about his neck. As he came towards her, between the dark pines, she saw that it was Klimt. Amazed, she watched as he took a wad of creased and discoloured paper lire from the pocket of his linen jacket and placed it in the monk's outstretched hand. The monk beamed with childlike delight, thrust it under his scapular, and bowed and gestured that Alma-Maria should go to him. Klimt held out his hands to receive her.

Had the clocks all stopped in a time of enchantment? she wondered. Were Mutti and Möll encased in a single still moment?

'Now will you come to my studio?' Klimt asked. 'It's just over there.'

He pointed across the water, across the mouth of the Giudecca Canal to the opposite shore, where a line of restaurant pontoons were moored under the white façade of the Santo Spirito. She nodded. As if in a trance, she allowed him to help her to the *traghetto*, to climb aboard and settle into the cushions. He sat down opposite her. She glanced up at the monk.

'The good brother will be waiting here for you when you return,' Klimt assured her. 'He has been well paid for his patience.'

It was like the Venice of stories, thought Alma-Maria, Would the monk assassinate someone if one paid him enough?

The oarsmen stood, one on the prow, one on the stern of the boat.

They rowed with easy, relaxed movements, steering the boat down the Canale San Giorgio and out across the Giudecca Canal where tiny waves slapped the black varnished bulwarks and a breath of sea wind touched Alma-Maria's cheek. She took off her wide-brimmed summer hat and fanned her face with it. She said to Klimt,

'Möll and Mutti decided to come. It wasn't my idea. I was afraid something horrible would happen, like you not realizing they were there, and kissing me in front of them – something like that.'

'I was waiting for you, watching from the end of the island. When I saw them with you, I thought perhaps you had decided – well – to demonstrate something to me.'

'Gustav! How could you!'

He shrugged. 'My worst fears,' he explained. 'Anyway, I retreated into the church. I found our clerical friend sweeping the floor of the great sacristy. He's only a lay brother, a menial really. Very susceptible to bribery: "for the poor people of Mestre, Brother" – that sort of thing.' He laughed heartily. 'So we arranged matters: that Möll and your mother should be encouraged to take a rest from the heat, while he took you on a little excursion of your very own.'

She glanced back past the oarsman's legs, to the landing stage of San Giorgio.

'Supposing they come back there?' she said. 'They'd see us quite clearly.'

He leaned forward, took her parasol from her, and pushed his Panama down onto her head.

'There!' he said. 'You are in disguise.'

She was about to remove it when the bow oarsman looked back at her, and exclaimed, '*Ah, bella, signorina!*' He pressed fingertip and thumb together in a gesture of appreciation. She tilted the hat rakishly and sat back. Removing one lace mitten, she dangled her hand over the side of the boat, trailing her fingers in the water.

She was still wearing the hat when they landed on one of the pontoon restaurants which gave the Zattere its name. Carrying her parasol over his shoulder like a tourists' guide with his umbrella, Klimt steered her across the embankment to a side door of the restaurant building, past the kitchen, and up three flights of narrow stairs to the top. The studio stretched, under the roof, the full length of the house. It was comfortably furnished – even luxuriously compared to the bare shabbines of the entry and the stairs – and was cool despite the long skylight which had been set into the slope of the roof. Halfway down the room, where Klimt had set up his easel, there was a window in a pointed Moresco arch, with a cushioned seat. Alma-Maria went and looked out. Across the broad greenish surface of the canal, directly opposite, supported on either side by crumbling tenements with ragged washing hanging out over the unweeded embankment on flagpoles, stood the Redentore, with its great flight of steps leading up to the single-columned façade, and its massive dome and bell towers.

'It is beautiful,' she said.

'Nobody goes there,' Klimt said. 'It will die of neglect like everything else on the Giudecca.'

She moved back to the canvas on the easel. He had painted the arabesque frame of the window. In pencil, he had lightly sketched in the tympanum, dome, and belfries of the Redentore. Over it, occupying somewhat less than the right-hand half of the window space, he had sketched in very lightly the ghostly outline of a female figure.

'You weren't teasing me?' she asked, 'About painting me at the window?'

'*Alma-Maria, Stella Maris*? Do you think I would joke about such a thing?' His voice was soft, carressing. 'With your hair down,' he said.

His hands were gentle as they unpinned her hair, lowering carefully the heavy tresses and spreading them over her arms and shoulders. Again, the tears stole into her eyes. He knew so well how to play on her feelings, it wasn't fair. He turned her about.

'Let me look at you.'

He drew her tresses forward so that they covered the swell of her breasts and poured over her lap almost to her knees.

'The old masters would have killed for the chance to paint you as Eve. Do you know that?'

'Why? Because my hair is long enough to cover me?'

'That – and because you would look like a child in Eden.'

He picked up the Panama hat which he had taken from her when they had entered the building, and replaced it on the back of her head.

'A child in Eden, but still Mankind's mother . . . and seductress.'

He put his hands on her waist.

'Klimt!' she protested. 'You make me sound like Kundry, in *Parsifal*.'

'Do you always take your reference points from opera and drama?' he chided her.

'What else can you do when you're young and haven't lived very much?' she asked gravely.

'Almschi! You are wonderful!'

'What do you mean? You're laughing at me, aren't you?'

'Oh no! No!'

He embraced her, and kissed her with the passion of someone who could not contain his feelings.

'Klimt! It isn't fair.' She said it aloud this time.

'It wasn't fair the first moment I set eyes on you. My God, Almschi! You transfigure everywhere you go with your beauty.'

'Oh don't! Please!'

But when he released her, she was disappointed.

'Why did you make me look so ... sly, in the Beethoven thing?' she asked.

'Sly? I hope not. It wasn't what I intended.'

'What was it, then?'

'Knowing? But not in a knowledge of the common world. Of deep time, perhaps. *I* shall paint you as Eve, sitting framed in that window, who at one and the same time lures men by her beauty into a City of the Dead, yet stares out across the window at the Church of the Redemption.'

'You know what you are, Klimt? You're a symbolist, a decadent. You're a better painter than Levy and Khnopff, I admit – you're not a Jew. But you're infected with the same unhealthy notions.' She stared up into his face. 'A child-like seductress with mysterious, dark knowledge, who leads men to redemption through sin! Is that how you think of me?' she asked. 'I just want to be yours.'

It came out quite suddenly, unintentionally, from her lowered voice.

He took off his linen jacket and tossed it over the corner of the stretcher on the easel. He loosened the kerchief at his throat.

'You must see my sanctuary,' he told her.

Lightly resting his arm on her shoulder, he guided her to a small door at the far end of the studio.

'A garden!' she exclaimed, as he held it open for her. 'A real garden!'

There were beds of flowers against the walls and in the centre, surrounded by a gravel path. There were patches of shade shed by arrangements of potted trees. A grotesque lead face in the wall slopped water from a distended pendulous lower lip into a zinc trough – the very sound of it was cooling.

Klimt came up behind her. He lifted her up by the waist, drawing her bottom into his lap as her feet left the ground.

'Gustav!' she gasped.

For a moment, before he lowered her, she caught a glimpse of the mouth of the Grand Canal and the Piazzetta of St Mark's in a blaze of reflected light so that she was blinded. But even in the midst of the glory, she had been aware of the pressure of his body on hers through their light summer clothes.

'There is a bed,' he said into her ear. 'Over there.'

'Klimt! You put it there on purpose. You've no shame at all!'

It was a divan couch under an awning on a wooden frame set in the far corner of the wall. Plants and two small palms were set about it for shade.

'You take it for granted, I'll ...'

He took advantage of her momentary hesitation:

'I've been longing for you since you left Vienna,' he said. 'I've been unbearably restless. You alter all my perceptions – my whole being. I

148

don't believe there is anything in the whole of creation as beautiful as you.'

'Gustav! That is incredibly stupid!'

There were other women – Emilie Flöge, and many others besides, it wouldn't surprise her. But they were all on the far side of the Alps.

'You have no idea how much I've been wanting you,' he said.

'I've dreamed about you, thought about you, talked to you even though you weren't here, every single day. Many times a day.' She dropped her voice. 'And night.'

Lies. All lies. And yet, given the way she felt now, it ought to have been true. Wanting it to be true made it so.

He kissed her again, enclosing her small size in his great strength. He led her round the gravel path to the small arbour, and the divan couch. As he drew the kerchief from around his neck, and dropped it over the back of a lime white iron chair, she spread her hand across his shirt, slipping her fingers between the buttons. He stooped over her, and unfastened her blouse at the back as if she had been indeed a child. She felt her hair falling about her bared shoulders and arms. He unbuttoned the cloth buttons of her satin bodice. The satin clung to her breasts and under her armpits where she had been perspiring. She felt the warm, empty air on her hardened nipples. She prayed he wouldn't touch them. She dreaded the thought of asking him not to; at the same time, she could not have borne any further excitation.

He lifted her again as he laid her on the bed – effortlessly, so that she had the sensation of hanging on air. She drew her skirts from under her as she was lowered. She spread her legs so that he could come close to her. She watched as he uncovered his distended erection.

He stood between her legs, his hands under her buttocks raising her. As he pushed into her – there was always that first moment of alarm that she might not open far enough – she struggled to raise herself to embrace his thrusting hips, her wrists pressed on her knees. She was desperate to force all the sensations mounting inside her into one single cataclysmic release before he was finished. Sweat ran from under her arms. She could feel drops tickling under her breasts then dribbling off her ribs onto her flanks; beads of sweat spilled into her eyes like tears seeking their source.

Blinded and crying out, she climaxed while he was still jerking and pushing inside her. The sense of release ebbed and flowed, rose to overlapping waves of climax as she struggled for breath, then flooded away as if seeking escape in a wider sphere than she could provide. She let go, and sank back against the cushions. She felt him slipping out of her.

'Oh Klimt!'

She smiled. He leaned over her and kissed her cheek through her damp hair. Her eyes were very heavy.

She said, 'I suppose I ought to go back now, if we're not to be found out.'

His face was close to hers. She kissed him just above the downy softness of his beard, then let her head fall back again. There was no resisting the overpowering somnolence of the afternoon: the voices calling on the *riva* below, the lapping of waves from passing boats on the creaking pontoons, the smell of salt water and damp stone, the splash of the grotesque little fountain which sounded so close compared to other sounds that she fancied she could feel the cold water drops on her cheek . . .

She woke up slowly. She was lying with one leg extended, the other with her knee still drawn up. The warmth of the afternoon air bathed the naked lower half of her body and her exposed breasts. She looked past her raised knee to where Klimt was sitting on the white iron chair. He had reclaimed his straw hat; somewhat battered, it was placed forward on his head to shield his eyes. He was in his shirtsleeves, his kerchief loosely tied once more about his neck. He held a sketch pad and charcoal on his knee. He had just lit a cigar; fresh smoke curled in a ribbon, drifting almost imperceptibly in the still air.

'Gustav! You haven't been drawing me again?'

He looked guilty, like a schoolboy found out. She said, 'My God! How long have I been asleep?'

'A quarter of an hour. Twenty minutes. That's all.'

'I must go.'

She sat up, struggling against weariness. Even buttoning up her bodice was a physical exertion. She stood up, letting her skirts fall about her legs. The cream linen skirt of her summer suit was terribly creased and there was nothing she could do to smooth it.

As she tidied herself, Klimt folded back the cover of the sketch pad. He scribbled something at the bottom of the exposed page, then took the page from the pad, rolled it up, and gave it to her.

'It is for you – to keep or destroy, as you wish.'

She placed it carefully at the bottom of the small embroidered canvas bag she carried on her arm. He led her downstairs. The restaurant kitchen at the bottom was clean and quiet – there was only one cook and a waiter there – and there was only a scattering of customers at the tables on the pontoons. Klimt called out for a *traghetto*. As she followed him in the direct sunlight along the *riva*, her legs felt weak, and the bruised feeling inside her crotch was heavier than on previous occasions, the price she supposed she had to pay for the mutual greediness of their coupling. She only hoped that when she reached Mutti and Möll, her stiffness would not betray her.

On the gently swaying landing stage, she offered her cheek for Klimt to kiss. He held her hand.

'How shall I see you again?' he asked.

'I'll come to you, now I know where you are. In the afternoons when I'm given the chance.'

He lifted her fingers and kissed them.

'I shall wait for you. Every day.'

'I may find it difficult. Especially if I get into trouble over this afternoon.'

He lowered her down into the cushioned seat of the boat. The oarsmen pushed off from the wooden stage. He raised his hat and held it up for as long as she watched him over her shoulder. As she met the cooler air of mid-channel, she tried to put up her hair satisfactorily.

The monk was waiting at the garden landing stage behind the monastery buildings. He dismissed the boatmen, then led her back across the garden and through into the cloister where Mutti and Möll were still sitting, apparently at their ease. The thought occurred to her that they might have enjoyed her absence; it quite irritated her.

'You've been gone a long time,' said Mutti.

She eyed Alma-Maria's skirt.

'You've been exploring!'

'Yes, Muttichen. It is such a big garden.'

'You look quite exhausted. And you'll have to change when we get back to the hotel. You're such a child still – isn't she, Carly?'

Möll smiled at her in an avuncular manner.

'It is nothing to be ashamed of, Almschi,' he said.

'Was it *very* interesting?' asked Mutti.

'Oh yes, Muttichen.'

The monk decided it was time to come to her assistance. 'The *schöne* Fräulein was much interested, Signora.' He nodded ingratiatingly.

'Thank him, Carly!' Mutti prompted.

Möll took out his purse. He counted out several hundred lire notes with some concentration. He gave them to the monk.

'*Per i povere,*' he said.

The monk bobbed his head enthusiastically.

'*Grazie. Grazie, signor.*'

He thrust the money under his scapular. It was going to be a good day for the poor, thought Alma-Maria. She followed the monk and Mutti and Möll out through the sacristies, and under the white dome at the centre of the nave and transepts. The monk unbarred the west door of the church, and they stepped onto the black and white chequered terrace in front of the portico. Across the Bacino with its myriad small vessels darting and gliding like water insects amidst the glitter, lay the panorama of St Mark's and the Doge's Palace crowded with tiny, multi-coloured figures. In the merciless sunlight, it was like consciously sleepwalking through a Carpaccio painting with only the pulsating ache from lovemaking to remind her of concrete reality.

Alone in her room, with the sunlight seeping between the slats of the blinds, and comfortably naked except for her slip, she took Klimt's sketch from her bag and unrolled it. It was quite small, no larger than the page of an exercise book. Once again, it showed her in post-coital sleep. Because of the way she was lying, with one leg raised, her sexual parts and the dense thatch of blonde hair surrounding them were displayed without the least concealment, so that they seemed to her not only shocking, but strange. The ribbons which attached the tops of her stockings to her blue satin Swedish girdle were like those of a laundrymaid turned can-can dancer in a dockside tavern cabaret.

He had drawn her face in complete contrast to the lower part of her body. She was smiling in her sleep with the contentment and whole-hearted ease of spirit of a child, so that if she were shocked by the indecency of her posture she was astonished by the innocence which he had recognized in her. It wasn't at all fair, she told herself; he knew that, however much she might disapprove, she would recognize it to be a work of art. Across the bottom he had written, *Alma Redemptrix*, and had added his strange, thick-lettered signature.

She lay on her bed, on her side, propping her head on her palm, and staring at the drawing as if, by so doing, she could tame it. With a reassuring feeling of affection, she began to see that really what he had portrayed was his own feelings toward her: the Faustian unity of disparate attractions, the carnal satisfaction of animal desire and the promise of spiritual sinlessness and peace. *Eternal Womanhead*, again. That was what it was.

She drew herself round on her bed so that she could see herself in the pier glass on the wardrobe door. With some daring, she drew up the single satin garment she was wearing, and parted her legs. She gazed into the mirror to see what Klimt had seen. She pressed one finger through her body hair to touch and caress one single, sensitive spot in a furrow of dampness.

'Darling Klimt!' she murmured aloud.

She was awoken by a knocking on her door, and Mutti's voice inquiring as to whether she was dressed for dinner. Mercifully, she had locked the door – the drawing was there on the bed beside her. She called out for Mutti to wait while she put something on. Fighting a heavy drowsiness, she slipped off the bed and tiptoed to the wardrobe. She extracted her exercise book journal from under the paper lining the bottom of the wardrobe, slipped the drawing between the pages, and replaced it. She snatched up a clean petticoat and tied it on round the waist of her slip, then took down an evening dress and spread it across the bed. She went to the door and unlocked it.

'Oh Muttichen – I am glad you've come! I was lying dreaming; I had lost all notion of time. I don't know how I'd have got ready it you hadn't come in time to wake me up.'

*

Within the week, Möll returned to Vienna. He was compelled to go because of the impending exhibition at the new Sezession Gallery which the Old Man had consented to inaugurate with his Imperial Royal presence. There was also the near completion of the furnishing and decoration of the Villa Möll up on the Hohe Warte. Mutti and Alma remained at the Hotel des Bains. With Möll gone, Mutti was less inclined to cross over to Venice to sightsee; she passed her days reclining under the awning of a private beach hut, resting in her room or sitting in the lounge chatting to other guests – 'I've never met so many really *interesting* people.' In the mornings, Alma-Maria would accompany Mutti to the beach, remaining for an hour or so before returning to her room to practise on the piano. In the afternoons, she would walk in the gardens until she felt it was safe to slip away to the public landing stage; from there, she would take the *vaporetto* to the Molo, and hire a gondola to take her round to the Zattere.

Klimt painted her, made love to her and took her to explore the most obscure and sometimes the most unexpectedly beautiful places.

She could never have imagined – even when she had first let him have his will with her – that she could ever have been so wonderfully, so joyously, in love. There were moments when he would be explaining something to her and she would see him detached from her, and marvel at the beauty and intelligence in his face, his strength and astonishing good looks. She would feel weak with desire and long for him to take her back to his rooms.

As days and weeks passed she saw no reason to suppose that things wouldn't go on as they had been for ever and ever, or something like it. Then a letter arrived from Möll announcing that the Villa Möll was ready, the servants installed, and it only required the presence of its mistress. Mutti shook off her lethargy and announced that they would leave for Vienna as soon as they could pack. No sooner had she returned to her room for an afternoon nap, that same day, than Alma-Maria set off immediately for the Zattere, and Klimt's studio.

Klimt was sitting on the restaurant pontoon moored under the windows of his lodgings. He lounged under the striped awning, the crust of a pizza in front of him like a well-picked bone, and a litre wine flask three-quarters empty. He looked as careless and relaxed as she had ever seen him. She waved her glove to him. He drew himself from his chair and lumbered across the gently swaying planks to the embankment. He fanned himself with his straw hat; the wine had made him sweat more profusely than usual.

'I didn't expect you so soon,' he said.

'We're going home,' she told him.

He stood, mute. The news clearly took him by surprise; perhaps he had come to feel, as she had done, that they were caught up in some fragment of eternity.

'When?' he asked. 'Not tonight?'

She shook her head. But the relief vanished from his face when she told him, 'Tomorrow, in the morning sometime. I'll have to go back to the hotel straight away, just about. Mutti's taking her siesta, but she'll want to start on the packing and arrangements.'

He dragged his kerchief from his throat and mopped his face.

'Wait a second,' he said.

He dredged a fistful of lire notes and coins from his pocket and went back across the pontoon to pay the waiter. When he returned, he said,

'Time for a short stroll, surely?'

'A very short stroll,' she replied.

He looked at her curiously. 'You don't want to go back to Vienna so soon?' he asked.

So soon? she wondered. It had seemed like half a lifetime. She slipped her arm into his.

'You'll be going home soon, won't you? You said you'd come here because of me.'

He led her down a narrow alley under the shadow of the Santo Spirito Church. They crossed a small sunlit square where ragged but spotlessly clean children played like tousled cherubim on the church steps. He led her down a second, darker alley and through a low archway. To her surprise, she found they were standing in the pretty, cobbled Campiello di Ca' Barbaro, one of the places they had discovered during their explorations. She went across the little bridge over the narrow canal.

'Remember, you said you wanted to paint me standing here?' she asked.

'I still want to,' he told her. 'If you'll let me.'

'What do you mean?'

She felt just a little afraid.

'Stay here with me. Don't go back with your mother.'

'Gustl! You are joking, aren't you?'

'I'm perfectly serious.'

'I couldn't do that!'

'You love me, don't you?'

'Haven't I proved it?' she asked.

'Very well. Stay with me. I have money; there's no need for you even to go back to the Lido. We can go back to my rooms. I'll get a launch to take us straight across to the railway. We'll catch the first train out, to Pisa, Florence, Milan, anywhere. We'll be away before your mother finds you're gone and sends the *carabinieri* out looking for you. Then we'll come back here and set up home together . . . We'll find a maid for you,' he added.

'But Gustav – you can't just vanish from Vienna. I mean, there's the Sezession exhibition, your Beethoven Room, and . . .'

'Max Klinger's Beethoven Room, you mean ... Vienna will forgive me soon enough.'

Alma-Maria was about to say, 'It's all right for you – you're a man,' when he realized he'd said the wrong thing.

'We can make our own world,' he went on. 'We don't need Vienna. It's become a city of neurasthenic Jews. Everybody's in love with death. I know: I was dead from the time my brother Ernst died. I fell in love with his sister-in-law because she was his sister-in-law. You were what brought me back to life; you *are* life. I was stifled until I found myself breathing the same air as you. Almschili! You are all life, all beauty. I want to paint you rising from the ripples in a moonlit sea. I want to paint the world through the wonder in your eyes ...'

There was a moment, albeit a fleeting one, when she was swayed by the intensity of his declaration. But it came as a warning.

'My music,' she said. 'What about my music?'

She thought of playing the piano beside Alex von Zemlinsky – dear, ugly, adoring Alex; the sound of Mozart and Schubert, true Vienna, amidst the caged birdsong, the riotous window boxes, the cheerful, noisy squalor of the Freihaus; of dawn trips with his associates and pupils to Heiligenstadt to drink toasts outside the comfortable, picturesque little house on the Pfarrplatz, where Beethoven had composed.

'It's very silly,' she told him. 'You know that really, don't you?'

It was a cue to give him a chance to agree with her – to make it easier for both of them. But his face displayed a quite extraordinary disappointment.

'I thought we felt a deep commitment to one another,' he said; 'that what was between us was something more important than any other consideration. Almschi? If your talent for music is great enough, you don't need Vienna ...'

The little canal smelt of decay. There was a dampness about the acacia shade.

'It's no good, Gustav,' she said. 'I'm going back with Mutti.'

'With Mutti!' he mocked.

She picked up her parasol. Getting up from the wall, she opened it. She was vaguely aware of other tourists sitting, open Baedekers in hand, under the trees, watching curiously.

'Almschi! How many others have you led on like this?'

It was terrible, and so unexpected. He was talking in exactly the same way Burckhard had talked, up on the Rofanspitze. When he had asked her to marry him. She turned and walked away down the alley towards the Santo Spirito and the embankment: it was all she could do to prevent herself from running. She could hear his footsteps coming after her.

'Almschi! Don't you realize ...? Don't you see you made me believe ...'

In the mouth of the square behind the Santo Spirito, she stopped and turned round. Better to face him than listen to those awful footsteps echoing between the high walls.

'Almschi . . .' He spread out his hands, appealing to her.

'No doubt Frau Flöge is waiting for you in Vienna,' she said, struggling to conceal her shortness of breath.

She saw the look of pain on his face and wanted to cry out in hurt confusion. She turned away from him once more; this time she did run, clutching at her muslin skirt, her parasol stick bouncing clumsily on her shoulder.

She ran down the passage beside the high white wall of the church, and out onto the Zattere embankment. He came after her. By chance, a *vaporetto* was drawn up at the landing stage. She ran towards it. He managed to clutch at her arm.

'Almschi!'

'Don't touch me! I never want to see you again!'

He released her instantly. As she reached the landing stage, she saw people sitting on the pontoon. Their faces wore quietly condescending smiles, as if they were watching the playing out of a familiar Venetian *commedia*.

She boarded the *vaporetto*. He did not follow her. She walked along the rail into the brilliant sparkle of the sunlight bouncing off the wavelets of the Giudecca, placing the deckhouse between herself and him. As the boat drew out, heading for the Dogana point and the open waters of the lagoon, she took a seat in the bows, under the awning. Her mind was enclosed in a twilight muddle of thought and emotion. It hadn't been fair – not fair at all – that on an instant, with no preparation of any kind, he should have broached the idea of her giving up everything that was familiar in her life, for the exile and social isolation of a *demi-mondaine*. In any case, the love of a Gretchen or Klärchen was meant to support the hero, not to tempt him away from his destiny. She would not have been showing true love for Klimt if she had encouraged him to desert his colleagues of the Sezession. As the boat approached Santa Maria Elizabetta on the Lido, she was irresistibly reminded of the black cypresses and white mausoleum columns of Arnold Böcklin's painting 'The Isle of the Dead'.

She reached the Hotel des Bains, and went upstairs to find the door of her room open and the blinds inside drawn down. Her open cabin trunk had been placed in the window alcove. The wardrobe door was open. Skirts and chemisettes, evening gowns, slips and petticoats lay spread out on her bed. There were footsteps along the corridor. A chambermaid looked in at the door, then hurried on before Alma-Maria could speak to her. She saw that her shoes had been wrapped carefully in tissue paper and had been placed in a neat row beside the cabin trunk. She glanced into the wardrobe. The paper which lined the bottom had been pulled slightly askew, perhaps by the maid in gathering up her shoes.

'Don't try to lie to me about where you've been, Alma-Maria.'

Mutti stood in the doorway, her blue patterned tea gown like a tent round her small plump body. Her face was obscured in shadow, but in her hands was a wad of waxen-covered school exercise books.

'How could you?' She waited, but there was nothing for Alma-Maria to say. 'To write it all down ... every detail ...'

Alma-Maria still said nothing. She had neither words nor energy to match the situation. She wished she could escape this whole dreadful day by fainting away. She felt a weary drowsiness behind her eyes; the gloom of the closed blinds enveloped her; but her legs continued to support her.

'Serafina found them. A hotel maid!' Mutti said.

Why should that be especially terrible? Alma-Maria wondered. No doubt hotel maids knew a lot about people's errant behaviour – a lot more than ordinary family servants.

'She found them in the wardrobe – hidden under the liner. She wanted to know whether they were yours, or whether they'd been left behind by somebody else. Please God, oh please God she didn't look inside!'

'I don't suppose she can read German,' said Alma-Maria.

Her voice sounded dry and harsh, quite unlike the way she felt. She couldn't swallow.

'She doesn't have to read German to understand this! ... Does she? *Does she?*'

Mutti thrust out at her Klimt's line drawing. Even in the shade, through the darkness of her mind, Alma-Maria could see the exposed genitals, each tousled hair, each crease between her thighs. She felt sick, but with a dry, torturing nausea which told her the vomit would never come. How much could consciousness bear? Beyond the blinds, below the *lungomare*, children were playing, their voices ringing on the heavy afternoon air so that even their quarrelling sounded carefree.

'How could you bring yourself ...?' Mutti broke off. 'I can't understand ... Such ... such filth!'

Alma-Maria wanted to say something about love and art and the difference between kitsch and truth, but there was no way the words would come.

'To pose for this ... To let yourself be ...' Mutti broke off again. 'Be loved – I suppose that's how you think of it – by any man who'd want to draw this kind of thing! And then for you actually to keep it!'

She pushed it towards Alma-Maria's face, as if expecting her to take it, to do something with it.

'What would your precious Pappi have said?' Mutti demanded grimly. 'Do you think he can see you now? Oh, I pray not! Do you honestly think your Pappi would ever have drawn anything like this – eh? Well, do you?'

Many artists had – Alma-Maria knew that now. Rembrandt, for instance.

'No,' she whispered. She sat down on the edge of her bed. 'Please, Mutti. It's over now.'

'It's over? So everything is all right? I don't know what you mean, it's over. How many of these delightful little works of art are going to be passed round Vienna, do you think? Pictures of my daughter . . .'

'None. He gave it to me – it wasn't meant for anybody else to see.'

The violence of Mutti's blow across her face sent pain, like conducted lightning, shooting from her cheek and behind her eyes, through her neck and into her shoulders. The shock forced her other cheek to rest on her shoulder.

'Mutti!' she gasped.

She heard Mutti catch her breath.

'Did Carl know you were going to Klimt's studio? Tell me that. Did Carl know you were sitting for him behind my back? Did he?'

'Of course he didn't!' Alma-Maria sobbed.

'Does he know you've become Klimt's latest mistress?'

She clutched at Alma-Maria's hair. Almost immediately, the stinging pain became a leaden agony pressing down through her skull into her jaw. Her head was being shaken to and fro as if Mutti wanted to tear it from her shoulders.

'Stop!' she screamed. 'You're not so virtuous yourself, are you, Mutti?'

'What do you mean? What do you mean?'

'You did it behind Pappi's back! Who got you with Grete?'

Mutti suddenly released her hair. Alma-Maria gasped again and tried to brush the blur of tears away from her eyes with her wrist.

'Was it Möll? Is that why you don't trust him, Mutti?'

Mutti, too, was trying to catch her breath. Her plump cheeks, which had always made her look absurdly young and pretty, were now an apoplectic purple as if rouged like a female clown. She clutched at the brass bedpost; Alma-Maria's tears were flowing freely. She struggled to speak through them:

'Oh I knew all about it! Children notice things like that – like Möll coming out of your bedroom in the afternoon.'

The room had suddenly become silent. Tears flowed and flowed; where did they all spring from? Children were still calling out and laughing as they played in the sunlight outside.

She turned her head away, hiding her face behind her hand.

'Once, when you were having one of those terrible rows with Pappi, I went and hid in the old summerhouse,' she said. 'I think I wanted to die . . . Then Möll came looking for me. Dear old Uncle Carl! Do you know what he said to me? . . . He said married couples always have their ups and downs – it's just nature's way. He said that quarrels clear the air. He was so kind and understanding, was dear Uncle Carl.'

She lowered her hand and looked at Mutti, who had sat down on the stool by the dressing table. She was slumped over, her elbow among the hairbrushes and bottles, her head resting in her hand.

'Carl Möll is not Gretl's father,' she said.

'Who is? Not Pappi, at any rate. Has nobody ever told you – "Judge not, lest ye be judged"?'

She laughed. Mutti said nothing; she was staring in front of her. In an onrush of feeling, Alma-Maria rose from the bed and went and knelt down, resting her hands in Mutti's lap. She saw the tears running down Mutti's face.

'Who? Tell me, Muttichen,' she said, in a quite different tone of voice.

'I have been judged – dreadfully judged. I suppose I'm afraid of you being judged in the same way.'

'Tell me. Please,' Alma-Maria begged.

Mutti took her hands in her own, and stared into her face through her own tears.

'Hans Makart,' she whispered. 'Hans Makart was Grete's father.'

Alma-Maria sat back on her heels, astonished. She still kept her hands in Mutti's.

Hans Makart – the great Hans Makart – flamboyant stage manager of Imperial-Royal pageants, the darling of the Hofburg, of the prosperous arrivistes who haunted the smoking-rooms of the Hotel Bristol and of the waltz kings who haunted the Café Zauner alike; Pappi's idol and friend, the amiable woodcarver giant who had carved an oaken crib for baby Alma-Maria with his own massive hands. Hans Makart, Austria's most acclaimed painter, who spent the final year of his life strapped into a canvas jacket in the Alsenburg Hospital for the Insane until syphilitic degeneration rendered him harmless at last both to himself and to others.

Of course – Pappi had first been introduced to Mutti when she was a young actress modelling in Makart's atelier. Had she already become Makart's mistress? Was the relationship in which Grete had been conceived a relapse into an old affair?

'Grete?' she said in a low voice.

'What?' asked Mutti.

'Is she ever going to get better?'

'We have to pray . . .'

'Pray?'

Mutti squeezed Alma-Maria's hands.

'Isn't despair the greatest of sins? Isn't that what you Roman Catholics are taught? . . . Almschi? Oh, please God you'll never be punished the way I've been punished. You see, men like Klimt don't confine their seductions to decent, respectable women.'

She clenched and unclenched her fingers over Alma-Maria's knuckles.

Emotional exhaustion, the release of long-ignored and suppressed guilt, Mutti's tears as much as her own, brought Alma-Maria to the point of surrender.

'Muttichen! Muttichen! I shall never see him again, I promise. Never!' She tried to bury her face between her arms on Mutti's lap.

'But Almschi, how could you . . . write it all down like that? And those terrible drawings . . .!'

'I don't know . . .' What didn't she know? 'I don't know what's happened to me! . . . Oh Muttichen! Muttichen! I hate it – I hate all of it! Can you ever forgive me?'

She thought of the creeping madness which sometimes took years to take possession of its helpless prisoner, and of the desperate solitude of insanity. She thought of the nightmare suffering Schubert had distilled into 'Death and the Maiden', the Unfinished and the great C-major symphonies. She thought of Hugo Wolf in Pappi's studio in Plankenburg so many years ago, screeching out his delusions and thumping at the piano. She thought of the malevolence leering behind the smile of false innocence in Grete's face.

Mutti stooped over and gathered her into her arms. She felt Mutti's breasts, soft against her cheek. Her tears soaked into the silk of the loose tea gown; they seemed to activate Mutti's mimosa perfume. Mutti's hand stroked through her dishevelled hair.

'Liebling . . . liebling, of course I forgive you,' Mutti's voice caressed her. 'We shall keep our secrets. Nobody need know. We'll make amends and be strong from now on, won't we?'

It was easy enough for Mutti to say. Mutti did not feel the emptiness at the very heart of Alma-Maria's existence.

The Villa Möll stood at the very edge of the Hohe Warte. It represented the first bastion of what Josef Hoffmann and others of Carl Möll's friends intended to be a colony of financially and socially successful artists, musicians, and writers. It was the antithesis of the over-furnished apartment on the Theresianumgasse. Two floors built over a basement, with a spacious servants's attic in the roof, looked out over the undulating leaf-green sea of the Vienna Woods to the rooftops and church domes of Heiligenstadt. The windows were high and wide, the rooms bright and uncluttered with shiny parquet floors and tall, angular furniture in the newly fashionable Glaswegian style. When they had first returned from Venice, Mutti had wandered with Alma-Maria from room to room exclaiming, like the Holsteiner Protestant *Hausfrau* she really was, 'It'll be so easy to keep clean!' There was not a hint that Pappi had ever existed, not a memento of Alma-Maria's childhood at Plankenburg. Everywhere was a monument to the apotheosis of Möll.

The villa next door was completed within weeks of the Villa Möll. Its master, Hugo Henneberg, a wealthy printer and a collector of Japanese prints and oriental *objets d'art*, took up residence a fortnight after Alma-Maria and Mutti had arrived, together with baby Marie, and the day and night nurses who had been looking after her in Mutti's absence. No sooner had he settled in, than Henneberg asked Möll to view his new house. He was getting down from his new Adler motor car at his front gate when Alma-Maria was with Möll in the garden. Möll and Herr Henneberg chatted at the gate as the handyman-chauffeur parked the motor car in the shed beside the house. Herr Henneberg remarked to Möll that he had several pieces of furniture, notably a wall cupboard, designed and built by Mackintosh in his Glasgow workshop, and suggested that he might care to go in and inspect them. When Möll readily accepted, Herr Henneberg suggested that Fräulein Schindler might also be interested. As he said it, he looked directly into her eyes and smiled the familiar kindly, admiring, older man's smile. He took Möll's arm to steer him up the steps to the street door, then she followed after like a dutiful daughter.

She recognized the style of the painting with a shock of jealousy all the more painful because it sprang at her as if out of ambush. It was a full-length portrait of Herr Henneberg's wife, Marie, and it hung facing the door, over the turn of the hallway stairs. There was the unmistakable suggestion of erotic self-awareness in the subject's pretty, slightly florid features, and the shining parted lips; in the dishevelment of her coal-black hair and the satiated manner in which, clad in a loose, lace-fringed *peignoir*, she was reclining among satin cushions. Alma-Maria did not need to read the signature impastoed onto the bottom right-hand corner to suspect who had provoked that look of languorous fulfilment.

Herr Henneberg turned from speaking to Möll.

'You are admiring the portrait of my wife, Fräulein Schindler? Or may I, since we are to be neighbours, address you as Fräulein Alma-Maria? ... Do you like Klimt?' He paused, gave a little laugh, and added, 'His work, I mean?'

For a moment she was afraid that he, and probably half Vienna, had discovered about herself and Klimt.

'I admire his technique,' she replied carefully.

She was glad Mutti was not with them.

'He can be a little – er – too frank at times for a young lady's taste, eh? Not at all like your Papa's style.'

He smirked down into her face. He knew nothing, she realized; he was merely patronizing her.

After the inspection of the reception rooms, the furniture and pictures, they went out onto the terrace, into the sunlight. As with their own terrace, young shoots of clematis and wisteria were being trained so that they would later conceal the garish newness of the brick. Across the parapet was the same vista – a heaving sea of oaks and ancient chestnuts stretching north to the Danube and west to Heiligenstadt and beyond.

While Herr Henneberg and Möll sat at the rustic table and smoked their cigars and talked, she stood staring out over the tree tops.

'He's causing us a great deal of anxiety, I'm afraid,' she heard Möll say clearly.

'What's he up to this time?' asked Herr Henneberg. 'I hear he's been abroad these past few months.'

'Exactly. He's supposed to be completing this frieze to surround Klinger's Beethoven piece. And now he's back, he's got himself arrested.'

'A serious offence? Would it be possible to have a quiet word in an ear in the Hofburg?'

'It's a police court matter,' said Möll. 'Drunk and causing a public disturbance. Not so bad as long as Frau Flöge doesn't prefer charges. It seems he paid a visit to the Casa Piccola yesterday afternoon, after he'd lunched a little too well. I don't know what sort of a quarrel he'd been having with Frau Flöge – she'd caught him chasing one of her little seamstresses, I dare say. Anyway, he was up in the workrooms at the top when he opened the windows and started throwing down the stock – gowns, muslin wrappers, hats, anything he could lay his hands on – to the crowds in the Mariahilferstrasse and, of course, the Café Centrum is just opposite, so you can imagine the scramble. And he was shouting his head off, and singing. Finally, he vomited – they say, into a passing perambulator ...'

He glanced in Alma-Maria's direction, and lowered his voice so that only scraps of the ensuing conversation were audible to her: Herr Henneberg saying, 'Of course, there was that temporary *crise de nerfs* when his brother died,' and Möll saying, 'Some passers-by were honest enough to bring gowns and suchlike back into the shop.'

That night, she could not sleep. She was haunted by the idea that she might have been responsible for Klimt's lapse into insanity. But there was an even worse fear which crept up on her like a ghost out of the gnarled, damp roots of the forest trees outside. It was a fear that his behaviour might have quite a different cause: the infection which had crawled into Hans Makart's brain to rot it until he had to be carried to the madhouse – that same infection which had been passed in Mutti from him into Grete – might also be in Klimt. The terror of the thought forced her to crouch up against the pillows, her tongue pressed against the back of her teeth to prevent herself from crying out. Mutti had said they should pray for Grete. Perhaps they should pray for Klimt; more so, even for herself. How many mothers in Vienna were praying that night as their sons or daughters drifted into delusion, mania, and from thence into a merciful vegetable torpor? It was God's punishment for sin; token and punishment in one.

Night turned to earliest dawn. Grey mist hung in heavy, miasmatic cloud on the forest trees below. The more dreadful imaginings dried up into a dull ache of leaden emptiness. She fell asleep for several hours.

When she was woken by Noni bringing in her hot water, the dull empty ache was still there. She began to feel that the relative cheerfulness she had enjoyed between her return from Venice and that moment had been a delusion in itself, a remission to mock the progress of some dreadful spiritual degeneration.

Driven by the need to exorcize the demons of fear and regret which possessed her, she crept from the Villa Möll before either Möll himself or Mutti were up, and made her way down the Wollergasse and past the park benches where once had been the ramparts and palisades of the bastion which gave the Hohe Warte its name. Her eyes stung with weariness. Her own dry thoughts were more real than the skirts of the woods through which she was passing.

At the bottom, she took the second car of a train of tramcars. It was crowded with shabbily suited, hungry-faced clerks, and female typists and telephonists in serge and gaberdine, all travelling in to jobs at the Rathaus or government offices. The pungent smell of cheap scented soap mingled with that of the previous day's tobacco. Normally it would have gripped her with nausea; now she felt at one with the sad, sallow faces, and the shoddy, servile tidiness of her fellow passengers. She got down at the Schottentor opposite the dear, familiar precinct of the Votivkirche. For one moment, as she was cuaght in the warmth of the early sunlight, she thought that perhaps, if she went into the church, she would find Dr Labor sitting up in the organ loft waiting for her. The illusion was dispelled as soon as it was formed, leaving her in her solitary confinement of misery.

She walked rapidly, with an empty purposefulness, behind the University, round into the Josefstädterstrasse. Coming in the opposite direction, up from the tenements of Hernals, and pushing her from the pavement, were weather-stained and leathery-faced workmen and gnarled-fisted scrubbing women in ragged, soiled aprons. They smelt sour from the unequal battle with hunger and poverty. Only a couple of milkmaids – little more than children – with their dog cart and battered churns and ladles, and a postman in his ill-fitting uniform and greasy shako, were walking in the same direction as herself.

She reached the familiar garden door. She had no idea what had brought her here; as she raised the latch, and opened it slowly, cautiously, she felt no desire to find Klimt inside. She felt no desire for him. There was nothing left in her imagination of the *Übermensch*, the moral giant, the greatest artist of the age, to whom she had given herself with such abandonment. Inside her the hero had died with God. But possessiveness and fear were left and, like the person alone in the house at night who senses the presence of a ghost, she felt, in her desolation of spirit, the need to confront the cause of her misery rather than to have it lurking in the dark corners and under the staircases in her mind.

She stared across the derelict, weed-entangled garden to the dust-smeared windows of the studio. The high enclosing wall isolated her from the clatter of boots hurring up the cobbles of the street outside. There was a heady scent of late honeysuckle; but, instead of coming as a grace, it only added to the confusion behind her stinging eyelids, sour-tasting mouth, inside her throbbing head.

She wandered back through the confused alleys and courtyards of the old city. She was aware that, by this time, her absence from home – if that was what the Villa Möll was – would have been discovered, and that Mutti would be anxious. The knowledge seemed remote, disconnected from her. She was aware in some dull fashion of passing the Volkstheater, and of giant, angry trams clanging and spitting past her, only inches from her, as she crossed the Mariahilferstrasse. She took no notice of the noise and bustle of the Naschtmarkt, and the ribald, mocking, obscene comments shouted at her by the market women whose stalls she so completely ignored. Rather than by any volition of her own, she found herself entering under the street archway of the Freihaus. As she mounted the outside stairs of the inner courtyard, she met a tatterdemalion girl of eleven or twelve years, carrying a stinking pail and trailing a damp mop behind her as if it were a hobby-horse or toy cart. Without waiting to be spoken to, the child announced,

'Herr von Zemlinksy isn't here. He's gone out – with his best hat on.'

With a self-satisfied smirk, she continued on her way, splashing Alma-Maria's skirt hem with the dirty mop as it banged down the stairs behind her.

Alma-Maria continued on her way till she reached Alex's studio. A woman who was watering a window box filled with petunias, on the far side of the yard, bawled out for the entire population of the area to hear.

'The honourable and well-born Freiherr has gone out, Fräulein!'

The voice rasped with authority, commanding her not to enter.

'I shall wait for him,' Alma-Maria called back.

Her voice sounded ineffective, it was so hoarse.

She went in. The room was in its customary state of squalid untidiness, but she found that the very confusion eased her pain a little. On the piano, on top of a substantial pile of printed scores, was a battered, enamelled coffee pot. She felt it, and it was still lukewarm. She sat down at the piano. Open on the stand was a sonata by a composer – Vilhelm Stenhammar – of whom she had never heard. She began to sight-read it, the notes she played intruding into the silence, the suspended motion of a well-inhabited room. She wished Alex would return.

There was another large pile of music manuscript on a stool by the piano bench. Recognizing Alex's hand, she picked it up, placed it in her lap, and read the title page: THE DWARF: *a tragic fairy tale for music, in one act – after the story by Oscar Wilde.* She turned the pages with some curiosity. The music was densely notated in four-stave short score – *spartivi* – as if the composer had the entire orchestration in his head and couldn't commit it to paper fast enough. She could not read it clearly, particularly as Alex had composed with such obvious urgency and had dashed the myriads of notes onto the staves, together with scribbled directions for full orchestral scoring between them.

With growing fascination, she decided to follow the libretto. It told the story of an Infanta – the King of Spain's eldest daughter –, a spoilt child of thirteen or fourteen: how, at her birthday feast, she was presented by a group of young noblemen with the gift of a hideous dwarf boy, a charcoal-burner's son whom they had found in the depths of the forest and had carried off to be her court jester. The Infanta realized that the dwarf had never been away from home before – had never been out of the forest – and knew nothing of the outside world. To tease him, she told him that if he sang nicely to her, he could choose any of the girls in the room to be his bride. He sang, and having sung, chose her. The Infanta then realized that he had never seen his own reflection, and had no idea of how hideous he was. It amused her to encourage him, to make him believe she had fallen in love with him. One of her maids warned him that he was being led on and took him to a mirror. On seeing his own reflection, he screamed out in horror and pain. When the Infanta hurried back to continue the game, she found him in a state of collapse. Bored with him, as she would have been with a broken doll, the Infanta wanted nothing more to do with him. He died; and when the maid explained it was from a broken heart, the Infanta replied that she preferred that they should give her, in future, presents which didn't have a heart.

As Alma-Maria read, turning the pages in her lap, the room seemed to grow dark; misery closed in around her once more. She had no doubt about what had inspired both the opera and the fever of inspiration in which it had been written. She stacked the pages neatly and replaced them on the stool where she had found them; he must never know that she had seen it. But the enormity of the injustice appalled her. She had never played with Alex's feelings – she had never shown the least repugnance at his dwarfish ugliness. Rather the opposite: she had always regarded him as her very dear friend; it was not her fault if his feelings for her occupied a different dimension from those she felt for him. Now that Klimt was gone from her life, Alex and what he represented was all that was left to her. What had she ever done to make him think of her as spoilt and callous?

She fled from the studio, from the Freihaus with its sour cabbage smells, its Galician Jews screaming at each other from basement to basement, its burgeoning window boxes and chattering caged birds. She stumbled out once more into the bustling crowds, round the stalls and the piles of straw and smashed wooden boxes of the Naschmarkt. She walked on and on, down narrow, dirty cobbled streets she had never walked before, under threatening, crooked, overhanging gables with their weather-worn, carved bird-prisons, under the shadow of grotesque, sugar-stick spires, and statuettes of the Blessed Virgin leering over plant pots from the corners of houses. She had no idea where she was going, only that she was being drawn on by some volition not her own. She passed rows of mean shops, with cracked and broken windows, selling unwholesome food and second-hand garments so soiled that the maids at home wouldn't have torn them up for cleaning rags. There were noisy taverns already filled with vicious, quarrelling voices; she passed under the arches of tall, decaying tenements, from the doorways and staircases of which spilled fat, blotch-faced women with matted hair under their headscarves, and ragged, futile aprons, and children with matchstick limbs glimpsed through their rags, and faces with sores, listless with hunger. Some, women and children both, tried to clutch at her and beg from her as she went by, in accents which betrayed origins far removed from the Archduchy of Austria.

A long sidestreet reeking sourly of anthracite dust, between blackened, gritty warehouses, led her out onto the broad quayside of the Donau Kanal. She looked about her in a dull bewilderment as to what she was doing there, at the squat, tarpaulin-covered barges moored against the steps, at the cranes thrusting into the merciless brightness of the sky, and the uncompromising fronts of the warehouses with huge broken doors like smashed teeth in black, foetid mouths. On either side of her, railway lines stretched away down the quay, raised bands of silver-topped rust lifted from the withered knot grass and weeds which had sprung up from under the surface of coke embers.

She walked a little way along the deserted quay. Was it Sunday? she wondered. Or a public holiday? In front of her rose a great bridge with iron panels in the form of shields above its piers, and huge lanterns on fantastically wrought iron columns rising at intervals along its iron parapet. It stood like a fortress gateway, a series of portcullis arches across the canal. A long flight of brick steps between dank walls led up to the pavement and roadway above. They were too steep, the treads too high and slippery; she did not have the energy or will to mount them. Instead, she was drawn to the edge of the quay, out of the sunlight, under the shadow of the bridge.

There was a sudden coolness, which was comforting. The surface of the canal below the curved edge of the coping stone at her feet was as still as oil. From the reefs of broken timbers and rotting hay amidst the scum and froth came a cold estuary smell she remembered from summer days on the island of Sylt. It was wonderfully dark and peaceful. Unexpectedly, she began to sob. There was nothing to hold on to; she just stood there staring down into the water, her hands clenched against her lips, until her tears prevented her from seeing anything. Her sobbing was so violent that her breasts ached. She kept moaning, 'Pappi! Oh, Pappi! Pappi! Take me home!' – while, in her mind, Plankenburg in the olden days when they had first gone to live there grew more and more real about her, drawing her back into its woodlands and quiet vineyards, to the piano in Pappi's studio looking out on the overgrown, fairy-tale rose garden.

'Alma? Alma Schindler?'

The woman's voice came from the iron parapet of the bridge above.

'Alma? Whatever are you doing down there?'

She brushed the tears from her eyes with the edge of her glove and stared up. Berta Zuckerkandl, her inquiring face, under her extravagantly wide-brimmed hat with its piled black veil round the rim and its peacock feathers, looked even more bird-like than usual.

'Are you going to come up to the street? Or are we going to shout to one another?'

Frau Zuckerkandl was laughing. She hadn't noticed her tears, thank God, thought Alma-Maria. She turned to the steps. As she climbed them, Frau Zuckerkandl called down to her.

'My sister saw you as we drove across the bridge. She thought you were one of those poor housemaids – you know, betrayed and discarded *Süssenmädeln* – about to throw herself into the canal. It's a favourite place for broken-hearted women, this. She was determined it was our duty to prevent you from doing anything – well – too drastic.'

'I went to call on Alex von Zemlinsky,' said Alma-Maria. The climb was steep, and she was short of breath. 'He was out. So I decided to go for a walk – to explore, really.'

'Not the most salubrious spot for exploration,' suggested Frau Zuckerkandl.

She glanced curiously into Alma-Maria's face as she reached the pavement.

'I meant to take a short cut to the Prater,' replied Alma-Maria. 'I got lost, I'm afraid.'

It might explain the ravaged state of her face. Frau Zuckerkandl took her arm.

'We shall take you back to the Opernring, at least,' she insisted. 'In our brand new acquisition.'

She pointed to the large Daimler-Benz parked against the pavement halfway across the bridge. Alma-Maria recognized Sophie Clemenceau, Frau Zuckerkandl's sister, sitting in the cushions of the high basketwork seat behind the driver.

'Only one breakdown between Leopoldberg and here, wasn't there, Hans?'

'Exactly, *gnädige* Frau Hofratin.'

The chauffeur clicked his heels. In his grey, brass-buttoned duster-coat and peaked cap, he looked like a Prussian infantry officer.

'Hans comes from Magdeburg,' Frau Zuckerkandl confided. 'You can't get decent mechanics here in Austria – Austrians don't have the application ... You know Madame Clemenceau, my sister?'

The chauffeur held open the rear door. Supporting her elbow lightly, he assisted Alma-Maria up the step.

'Of course we know one another,' Madame Clemenceau said graciously, taking her by the hand and helping her into the seat beside her. 'Such a surprise, meeting you here of all places! Berta didn't even know you were back from Italy.'

'It was rather naughty of you, you know,' said Frau Zuckerkandl, squeezing into the cushions on her other side. 'You should have let us know – particularly since we are all on the telephone ... Our little Alma was exploring, Sophie. She was trying to take a short cut to the Prater and got lost. Wasn't it fortunate – and quite extraordinary – that we should appear just in time to save her?'

It was painfully true. Alma-Maria wished that she too had a veil behind which to hide her face.

The chauffeur bent down in front of the two big, polished headlamps of the car. He cranked the wheel. After a series of grinding noises and reports, the motor started and he mounted into the driving seat in front of them.

'Put this about your face,' said Frau Clemenceau.

She had taken a light angora wool scarf from a box at the side of the car. She hooked it over Alma-Maria's head and wrapped it about her chin.

'There's always dust,' she explained above the rattle of the motor. 'We have a duty to look after the most beautiful girl in Vienna.'

It couldn't have been by chance, thought Alma-Maria. Destiny, not chance. Nor, necessarily, the good fairy. It was comforting to have Frau Zuckerkandl to look after her, to feel her hand touching her own. But Frau Zuckerkandl had been responsible for bringing Klimt into her life. She sighed involuntarily, and hoped her sigh had not been heard over the sound of the motor.

They were climbing now, rattling explosively, up towards the Ring and the old city. People on the pavement stared curiously as they drove by. Sophie Clemenceau called in her ear:

'Berta was wondering only yesterday if you were back. She and Emil are having a small dinner party on Saturday, you see. Rather too many gentlemen ...'

'Burckhard is coming,' said Frau Zuckerkandl, glancing shrewdly at her, 'and Alfred Roller, and Richard Heuberger, whom I'm sure you've met – amongst others. What made us pray you were back in Vienna was that we simply don't have enough ladies who are young and beautiful, and who can keep pace with the gentlemen's conversation. Which means we need you, my darling.'

'It's a rather special occasion because it's so difficult to persuade him to attend private dinner parties ...' said Sophie Clemenceau.

The name was lost in the grind of the motor.

'Or his sister doesn't usually grant him ticket of leave. She's a terrible little woman – a real Jewish mother, by all accounts.'

Berta Zuckerkandl looked directly into Alma–Maria's face. Alma-Maria hadn't intended asking whom they were talking about. She didn't really care. But it felt as though Frau Zuckerkandl were compelling her.

'I'm afraid I didn't hear the name. Who is the special guest?'

'Gustav Mahler, my dear,' Berta Zuckerkandl replied.

3 FIGURES ON A
BEETHOVEN FRIEZE:
1901-1902

'OH ALEX!'

There was nothing to be done except to throw herself with as much confidence as she could summon on the *tendresse* he had always shown for her. He was standing in the doorway of the music room with the maid, Hannele, behind him staring questioningly at her. The wet was dripping from the sleeves of his overcoat and from the limp cap he was holding between his fingers. His glasses were still smeared with the rain – he was blinking behind them – and there was no telling how much he knew about what had been going on since she had last seen him so many strange and terrible adventures ago, or whether he had learned about her visit to his studio the other day.

'Why didn't you give your coat to Hannele?' she asked.

He looked like a bewildered owl through the blur of his spectacles.

'I didn't know whether you'd wish me to stay,' he said.

He fumbled with his coat buttons. Hannele reached out to take the coat from his shoulders. He was carrying a battered music case under his arm; it slipped and fell to the floor. He stooped to pick it up just as the maid took hold of his coat, so that he was caught half-crouching like a suspected felon in the clutches of a policeman. Alma-Maria went to his rescue.

'Oh Alex! You really are silly, you know – a darling, but silly. Why should I have telephoned you if I didn't want to see you?'

'You'll soak your dress,' he warned her, as she helped Hannele to remove his coat.

She was wearing a loose silk tea gown. It showed off her figure flatteringly, if her figure needed any flattering.

'Do you think I care?' she asked. 'I'm so pleased to see you!'

'Truly, Almschi?'

'Oh very, very truly, Alex.'

She waited for Hannele to take away his coat and hat.

'I thought perhaps you just wanted to start your lessons again,' he said.

'That – of course,' she replied.

Hannele closed the door after her.

'So much wasted time!' she added. 'Alex! It's been like a dream. I need to know I'm waking up.'

'Then it wasn't a good dream?'

'I must have thought it was going to be, mustn't I?'

The thought of a life of routine, including seeing him for lessons at regular times, making music with him and Schoenberg and Mathilde and others of his circle, whispered a return to an old contentment.

'It was a mess! It was hateful!' She reached out, inviting him. 'I don't know how I could have been so utterly stupid.'

He took her into his arms. She drew back her head and looked into his gaunt swart face. It was wonderful how love could transform something so incredibly ugly into a kind of beauty. It had to be true that love was the centre of all true being.

She removed his spectacles, placing them on the small table behind her, and stared into the deep black of his eyes. The network of lines about them suggested he had not slept since she had last been with him.

'Do you remember,' she asked, 'me telling you that I thought I'd only be truly awakened by a Great Love?'

He nodded.

'I know now that it isn't true – that it's nonsense,' she went on, still holding him with her eyes. 'The things which really matter are things like our friendship – and music. Do you know? I don't think I can separate our friendship from music.'

She could see that he couldn't find the words to reply to her, that his eyes were swimming with emotion. She moved her lips to his, giving him permission to kiss her as passionately as he wished. As he did so, she pressed herself against him, reassuring herself that he loved her as much as ever.

When he released her, she had to gasp a little. She laughed.

'It's wonderful, Alexchen! Knowing that one is forgiven.'

'Forgiven?' he asked. 'For what? It's a glory just to know that you're back and that you want to see me again.'

She took him by the hand.

'*Just* to see you again?' she asked. 'Don't you think I value a loving friendship more highly than that?'

'Love can be very exclusive,' he said.

He picked up his spectacles and wiped them on his sleeve before putting them on.

'Not for me, Alex,' she told him seriously. 'Never again. Never – when one realizes what one almost lost by being so blind and stupid.'

She sat down on the piano bench. He smiled and bent over his music case.

'You can't imagine how I've been longing to make music with you again,' she said. 'But I never imagined it would be like this. It makes me feel ashamed.'

She felt his hand on her shoulder. He leaned over and spread some music in front of her. She rested her head for a moment against him.

'I'm so glad,' she said softly. 'Home again.'

As he sat on the bench beside her, she remembered to ask,

'Have you heard anything from the Opera about our ballet? Has Mahler accepted it?'

He shook his head.

'But that's wicked!' she exclaimed.

'I've telephoned the Director's office – oh! – I don't know how many times. Always the same: whoever it is deeply regrets, but the Herr Court Opera Director is in rehearsal, or is in conference with His Highness the K-K Chamberlain.'

'Poor Alex! That is really disgusting!'

He had taken out the Mozart Duo Concerto in E flat. They played it through together.

'I feel like I felt at Steinbach, Alex,' she said. She sounded uncertain, like a child confessing to something. 'That evening, after we had bicycled back from Ischl. I've never felt so alive ...' She turned her face from him. 'I think,' she added hesitantly, 'it must be because I'm sharing music with somebody who is very dear ... I'll tell you something, Alexchen. I'm going to the Zuckerkandls' tomorrow night. Do you know who's going to be there? Mahler! I shall ask him what he's doing about our *Golden Heart*.'

'No. Almschi, I don't think ...'

But she wasn't going to listen to his doubts.

'I shall absolutely insist. He's had your score long enough, hasn't he? And I'm not going to have anyone treat my Alex like that! I don't care how great a personage he's supposed to be – I shall take him by storm!'

'I believe you will,' he said.

His look of adoration was the most perfect of rewards, she decided.

She had known the party was to be a small one. Nevertheless, as she entered the hall, the sound of lively conversation from upstairs added to her sense of trepidation. She had felt sleepy all day – a sure sign of nervousness – and as weak as if she were convalescing from some serious illness. She had made great efforts with her appearance, but no amount of attention to her looks could arm her against her sense of insecurity.

Frau Zuckerkandl's maid, Antoinette, took her furs from her shoulders; she was a strange, dark pretty little creature who always watched her mistress with attentive adoration and seemed to have no existence save that of satellite.

The double doors of the salon upstairs were open, bathing the landing with light. Looking up between the wrought-iron banisters, she could see the distinguished figure of Emil Zuckerkandl talking with Max Burckhard. They were framed in the doorway. Standing in the light behind them, and several centimetres taller than either of them, was Klimt, perfectly dressed in evening suit and white tie, his hair and beard groomed and trimmed. They turned to acknowledge Berta Zuckerkandl as she came out of the salon dressed all in red, then returned to their conversation as she swept down the stairs.

'Alma!' she said, holding out her arms in greeting.

She spoke quietly enough for those upstairs not to hear. Alma-Maria felt the touch of her fingers on her bare arms above the edge of her long satin gloves, and the dry peck of her kiss.

'I feel faint,' Alma-Maria told her.

Antoinette hesitated, hugging Alma-Maria's furs to her so that they concealed her small black apron.

'I think I'd better leave,' Alma-Maria whispered.

Quickly, she thought. Before anybody else realized she had arrived.

Berta shook her head at Antoinette. With a tiny inclination of the head, the maid carried the furs away.

'Come into the library, *liebchen*,' said Berta. 'There is nobody there.'

She took Alma-Maria's arm, and led her across the hall in the opposite direction to that taken by Antoinette. She opened the library door and let her in. It was quite dark. She switched on a single light: it was uncosy, utilitarian, like the work light over an unused stage.

'Well!' she said.

Alma-Maria sat down on the edge of a deep-winged leather armchair. The room was cold but still smelt of Dr Zuckerkandl's cigars.

'Klimt is here,' she said.

'Of course,' said Frau Zuckerkandl. 'I invited him. My husband stood surety for his release ... But you've heard about all that, I dare say.'

'You didn't tell me he'd be here,' said Alma-Maria.

Berta rested against the edge of the table, the palms of her hands on the surface on either side. She surveyed Alma-Maria for a moment.

'I invited him after I invited you.' She paused. 'My dear, I thought it best for both of you.'

She waited as if for an answer.

'You belong to the same world,' she continued. 'You can't avoid each other for long, you know. Like planets, you move on fixed courses – the Beethoven Exhibition, for instance. Sooner or later the world is going to know that you sat for him.'

How much else did Frau Zuckerkandl know? Alma-Maria dared not try to find out.

'I shall ask him to come and speak to you here,' said Berta. 'He can bring you upstairs.'

'I'd rather go home. Truly, I would.'

'That would be exceedingly foolish,' said Berta Zuckerkandl firmly.

She went to the library door. 'Antoinette?' she called. The maid joined her at the half-open door. Alma-Maria could not hear the conversation but when the maid had disappeared Frau Zuckerkandl said, 'Antoinette has gone to fetch him.'

They waited. Alma-Maria wondered if she could maintain any sort of grasp over her feelings. The door opened a little further and he came in softly.

'I must return to my guests,' said Berta Zuckerkandl.

Klimt stood aside for her. When she was gone, he said, 'I was told I must escort you upstairs.'

There was no sign about him in the cold, bare light of the single lamp either of dissoluteness or his imprisonment.

'They didn't tell me you'd be here,' she said.

'And you wouldn't have come if you'd known?' he asked in a serious tone of voice.

'I don't think so,' she replied so quietly that she could not hear her own voice.

'Haven't you forgiven me?'

She could not reply.

He stood patiently, then he said, 'If you wish, I'll leave you. Emil Zuckerkandl will bring you up, I'm sure.'

'No Gustl. That won't do. Frau Zuckerkandl . . .'

'Would be cross? I'm sure she would. With me.'

Alma-Maria looked up at him.

'I was afraid that what happened to you,' she began; 'those awful things people have been talking about . . . I was afraid it was all because of me!'

'Almschi!' he smiled down at her. 'What a conceited child you are!'

Her eyes misted with tears.

'I'm the cause of my own trouble, Almschi.'

'We're friends?' she asked anxiously. 'I looked for you. In the Josef-städterstrasse. It was very deserted.'

'You went there?'

'Yes.'

'I haven't had the heart to go back there. Not yet ... Perhaps now I will.'

He had always known where she could be touched. Somewhere something was telling her there was a spark of devilry still there. But for her, the fire was gone out; she did not think it would ever burn again in quite the same way. There had been too much turmoil and too much fear.

'Will you look after me this evening, Gustl? That's all I ask.'

'I couldn't have hoped for any greater pleasure.'

She went up the staircase on his arm. She hoped that all the emotional disturbance had not affected her appearance. There was a pier glass between the potted palms at the turn of the stairs. She saw herself: her hair was still perfectly arranged; she could see no disfiguring redness about her eyes; her silk gown remained uncreased. As she passed into the salon, however, she felt the little confidence she had managed to build up slipping away again. She saw Emil Zuckerkandl talking to the reassuring figure of Max Burckhard, who was a little more portly than in the days she had visited him at the Burg. She saw Sophie Clemenceau shimmering in oyster and pearl. Between Burckhard and Dr Zuckerkandl on the one hand and Madame Clemenceau on the other, stood a slight figure no more than two or three inches taller than herself whose black evening suit hung from his meagre frame. He had a long, lean, aquiline face, with a lofty, shining forehead under a tangled mane of black hair which looked as if it had been combed by his running his fingers through it. His whole head looked as though it were disproportionately large for so slight a body; his mouth was thin – rather cruel-looking, she decided – and his brown eyes were hypnotic in the intensity of their gaze which, at that moment, was directed onto her. The intensity and brightness was exaggerated by the thick lenses of his steel-rimmed spectacles, so that she recalled their effect on her when, long ago, she had previously encountered that stare directly on the carriage ramp of the Burgtheater the morning she went to see *Egmont* rehearsed.

She had forgotten all about his being at the Zuckerkandls' in her confusion on discovering that Klimt was there.

'Alma!' Berta Zuckerkandl came rustling over to her as if she had never greeted her in the hall downstairs. 'You must meet our guest of honour – the Herr Director of the Court Opera.'

Berta pushed her forward gently. Mahler advanced, limping slightly, to meet her. He had a tense, forced smile as he took her hand and bowed over it.

'I kiss your hand, Fräulein Alma.'

'I'm honoured to make your acquaintance, Herr Director,' she replied. Her voice rasped hoarsely.

Through her gloves his fingers felt as dry as sticks. She saw Burckhard smiling in her direction, easily, affectionately. She wanted to go to him as if stepping onto a safe shore.

'Our charming and well-born hostess says that you are a most accomplished musician, Fräulein Alma,' Mahler told her. He still held her hand, as if he had forgotten to let go. 'A composer too – a woman composer. I should be interested to hear something of your work.'

She recognized the slightly sneering tone of 'woman composer'. Dislike of his attitude worked on her like a whiff of sal volatile.

'I don't think I'd like to submit any of my compositions to your judgement, Herr Director. I've heard you are a very severe critic.'

She looked down at her hand. He let it go.

'I hope we all strive for a certain standard of musical excellence,' he replied stiffly.

Alma-Maria turned to Burckhard, offering her hand. He bowed over it.

'Before you arrived, I was asking Max here,' Klimt told her, 'whether he found his return to the practice of law and his elevation to the Kaiserlich-Königlich High Court of Justice an anticlimax after dealing with all those theatrical temperaments at the Burg.'

'Anticlimax?' Burckhard said. 'Perhaps. At least I sleep more easily at night. You can't live your life in a state of perpetual excitement, eh?'

'Do you agree with Max?' she asked Klimt.

Klimt smiled down at her – messages passed between them.

'I'm entirely of his opinion,' he said. 'Life in perpetual excitement induces its own form of neurasthenia.'

'Which I know you believe to be one of the plagues of Viennese society,' she replied, remembering a conversation on his roof garden in Venice. Her self-confidence was returning.

'One of them,' Klimt agreed.

The word 'neurasthenia' had drawn Dr Zuckerkandl's attention to them. He spoke to Burckhard about one of Freud's recent publications – *The Psychopathology of Everyday Life*. Berta and Sophie Clemenceau continued to occupy Mahler's attention.

She went into dinner on Klimt's arm. She wondered what Mutti would say if she knew – but Mutti and Möll had always seemed remote from the Zuckerkandl establishment. She sat between Burckhard and Klimt at table; they encouraged her to feel as if she were between two affectionate elder brothers intent on protecting her from the attentions of other guests on her side of the table. Opposite her Mahler was sitting between Berta and Sophie Clemenceau. Emil Zuckerkandl sat at the end.

Berta attempted to draw Mahler's attention to Alma and her partners.

'There are three of you here with something in common: the Beethoven Memorial exhibition at the Sezession in May. There will be Klimt's "Ode to Joy" frieze. Alma will be there in spirit, at any rate.

And the Herr Director is to conduct a special performance of the Ninth Symphony there on the opening night.'

'I'm sure the Herr Director will be there in spirit, not only on the opening night,' said Klimt.

'Of course. Of course,' Mahler replied impatiently, and continued his conversation with Sophie Clemenceau.

Klimt sighed pointedly. He turned and whispered to Alma-Maria, 'Have you noticed, dear Almschi, that there are some people who can hold conversations with only one person at a time?'

She laughed light-headedly, like a noisy schoolgirl. Mahler broke off what he was saying to Madame Clemenceau. He glared across the table at them.

'May I not be allowed to share the joke with you?' he asked.

Alma-Maria told herself that he looked like an irate country schoolmaster, but she felt overawed none the less.

'A joke between old friends, Herr Director,' she explained.

'Shared past experiences,' Klimt added.

She felt a terrible urge to start giggling again. Mahler was staring fixedly at her. Candle flames from the table centrepiece shone in his spectacle frames so that his eyes were hidden from her. At last he said, 'I must apologize, Fräulein. Most sincerely. I am intruding on a private conversation.'

She was glad when he turned away once more. It had been unnecessarily serious, she felt.

A maid came in and said something in Berta's ear. Berta rose and left the dining room.

'Walter! How delightful!' Her voice came from the landing outside. 'So you were able to get away in time.'

She led in a slim young man, holding him by the hand.

'You see, Sophie? Emil? I told you Walter wouldn't be able to resist Frau Weidel's Beef Esterhazy. Walter, have you met Herr Director Gustav Mahler?'

'I haven't had that honour,' the young man replied.

Berta led him round the table to Mahler. His eyes caught those of Alma-Maria. He had a lean, sensitively intelligent face, with a delicate, feminine mouth. He had a down on his upper lip, and his cheeks were as smooth as if he had never had to shave. He was beautiful rather than handsome, Alma-Maria decided; and quite conceited, the way he stared at her a moment or so longer than was necessary.

'This is Walter Gropius, Herr Director,' said Berta. 'Herr Gropius is an architect.'

'Not yet, Frau Hofratin,' Gropius corrected her. 'In two years' time if I am fortunate enough to qualify.' He turned to Mahler. 'I've just come from the Konzertverein. One of your most fervent disciples was conducting there, so I was informed.'

'And who was it?' Mahler asked.

He looked disconcerted.

'Von Zemlinsky, Herr Director.'

'Fräulein Schindler is one of Alex von Zemlinsky's pupils, aren't you, Alma?' said Berta.

Mahler stared across at her.

'Von Zemlinsky's, eh? A fine professor, von Zemlinsky. You are a fortunate young lady.'

'Fräulein Schindler isn't the daughter of Jakob-Emil Schindler?' asked Gropius.

'Of course,' replied Berta.

'My congratulations, Fräulein,' said Gropius. 'Your father was a great painter.'

He was bowing over Alma-Maria's hand when Mahler said,

'Von Zemlinsky is a good conductor. He has a particular feeling for Mozart.'

Gropius took his place at the end of the table opposite to Dr Zuckerkandl.

'I'm afraid I didn't go to listen to von Zemlinsky's conducting,' he said. As the maid served him, he glanced across at Alma-Maria. 'I'm sure he is an excellent conductor. But with Kubelik playing Mozart's G-minor Violin Concerto, how could anyone notice anything else?'

'Do you know?' Alma-Maria asked rather loudly. 'I find I'm not the slightest bit interested in virtuosi and their performances.'

She was afraid it had sounded rather like a challenge. Everybody fell silent. Berta asked,

'Why not, Almschi?'

'Because it's just the same as when you go to the opera, and instead of the audience between the acts talking about the music or the drama, they're all discussing whether Fremstad has a better *portamento* than Sembrich and things of that sort. You wonder whether they appreciate the actual music at all. The only thing about a soloist worth discussing is whether his playing is worthy of Mozart's or Schubert's music.'

Mahler clapped his hands.

'Very well said, Fräulein Alma!' he called. 'Wagner would have agreed with every syllable, and so should every serious-minded opera director. Virtuosi use music as a pedestal on which to stand so that people can marvel at them. True musicians are the servants of their art, not its conquerors.'

'I think you must be a neo-Platonist, Fräulein Schindler,' Gropius remarked.

'Really, Herr Gropius?'

She turned her head toward him. She hadn't the faintest idea what he meant.

'You believe that the particular may only be judged in terms of its involvement in the general – in the total harmony which surrounds it.'

'Yes. I do.'

'It is a good architectural criterion. But do you also believe with the Ancients that physical beauty is indicative of the presence of spiritual beauty?'

'Forgive me, Herr Gropius,' said Mahler; 'but I don't believe Plato ever suggested that his teacher, Socrates, was a good-looking fellow. Yet if one is to argue that physical beauty is the outward manifestation of spiritual worth, then the corollary must hold true – that a virtuous spirit bestows physical beauty on the body which contains it.'

Gropius certainly should be the possessor of a virtuous soul, thought Alma-Maria. He was strikingly beautiful – the more so when his lip was curled in sullenness.

'I suppose so,' he said.

'And yet, I can't believe that Fräulein Alma here would try to persuade us that Alexander von Zemlinsky is a handsome man!'

He laughed, his shoulders shaking.

'I believe Alex has great beauty for those who have eyes to see,' Alma-Maria replied.

She did not quite dare to believe it. The middle-aged Gustav Mahler and the eighteen- or nineteen-year-old Walter Gropius were both showing off to impress her.

'Zemlinsky!' Gropius forced a laugh, making it sound strident. 'Zemlinsky's the ugliest man in Vienna! Everybody says so.'

'It is intelligence which informs a face with real beauty,' she said. 'Which is why I regard Alex von Zemlinsky as a beautiful man.'

Mahler had taken off his spectacles to wipe them on his napkin. He blinked myopically.

'Come now, young lady, I think you're taking the argument a little too far. Loyalty to your professor is very commendable, but the fact remains, von Zemlinsky is nobody's idea of a handsome man any more than I am. In any case, is he so very intelligent? I suppose one must admit he is musical – but that isn't always the same as intelligent.'

'You're never going to find out whether he's intelligent or musical,' Alma-Maria said, 'if you hang onto the scores he submits to you for over a year without looking at them.'

'What do you mean, Fräulein Alma?'

He put on his spectacles again, and in so doing, reassumed his air of authority.

'His ballet score – *The Golden Heart*.'

She hadn't meant to bring the matter up so abruptly. But now she had begun, there was no going back.

'You've had it in your office for over a year now, and I don't suppose you've so much as opened it.'

'Let me tell you, young lady, I directed all rehearsals and performances of your professor's *Es mar Einmal* at the Court Opera. I think I may claim to as exact a knowledge of his ability as a composer as you.'

'That has nothing to do with what I'm telling you!' she retorted. 'You've no right to keep a score that's been submitted to you for so long. Dr Burckhard never held on to play scripts that long when he was Director at the Burg – did you, Max?'

Max Burckhard smiled and lifted his hand to indicate that he wouldn't involve himself in the argument.

'Especially,' Alma-Maria continued, 'when it's composed by a true musician like Alex von Zemlinsky – who, by the way, regards himself as your pupil ... You could at least have written him a letter of acknowledgement.'

Mahler pushed his chair back from the table. He lifted the ankle of one leg onto the knee of the other, and began to massage it.

'The book is sheer nonsense,' he growled, in his deep bass, so that Alma-Maria had to strain to catch what he was saying. 'None of my staff can make head or tail of it – choreographers, musicians, dramaturges, nobody ...'

He lifted his head to face her across the table.

'I must tell you also, since you are a most persistent young woman, that I cannot understand how anyone who takes a serious interest in music, let alone someone who is studying music with the intention of becoming a composer, could possibly defend such sentimental milk-and-water trash!'

'It is not trash!' Alma-Maria shouted back. She almost slammed the table.

Even so, there was a secret little voice in her fiery brain which told her that the charge of sentimentality was justified. She became aware of the silence about the table.

'I helped Alex to score it,' she said more quietly. Then, defiantly again: 'And even if it isn't brilliant, that's no excuse for being hurtful about it!'

'Ah!' Mahler exclaimed. He pointed a long finger into the air. 'That explains it ...' He smiled his thin-lipped smile. 'So you helped him to score it. That explains why the orchestration is its strongest point.'

There was a ripple of friendly laughter. One or two applauded, and Sophie Clemenceau called across to her,

'There, Almschi, see? The Herr Director has paid you a fine compliment!'

Alma-Maria did not reply. She was seething with anger – anger at the patronizing way Mahler had dismissed her complaint, anger at the way he had tried to mollify her with flattery. It would take some minutes for the fury to simmer down.

Afterwards, when they had all returned to the salon – Berta Zuckerkandl did not hold with leaving the gentlemen to smoke their cigars –

Mahler came limping, hopping almost, over to her with his hand extended.

'Come now, Fräulein Alma. Let's make peace, eh? I can't promise to put on von Zemlinsky's ballet at the Court Opera, of course. But as my tribute to your loyalty to your professor, I do promise to send for him tomorrow – no later – to discuss the score with him. Will you accept my terms for an armistice?' She took his hand and looked into his face. Holding onto her hand, he said, 'Perhaps you would care to come to the Court Opera to see me, and to explain the symbolism in von Hofmannsthal's story – it is von Hofmannsthal, isn't it?'

'I'll tell you what, Herr Director,' she challenged him. 'I'll come to your office and explain *The Golden Heart* to you, if you can explain to me, here and now, the book of Bayer's *Die Braut von Corea*. After all, you conduct it every ballet season at the Court Opera.'

He laughed quite spontaneously.

'I admit defeat,' he conceded. 'You'll have to ask some of the thousands who pack the auditorium whenever we play it.'

There was a look of rueful distaste on his face. He gave her fingers a gentle squeeze and released her hand.

'Would you do me a very great favour?' he asked, lowering his voice.

'What's that, Herr Director?'

'Would you consider showing me some of your compositions? I would be greatly interested to see them. Some of your more recent work – work that you yourself are proud of.'

Nervousness returned to replace her anger. The opportunity was there to advance into unknown and unknowable territory; she was uncertain as to whether she wanted to commit herself.

'I don't know if . . .' she began.

She was going to say that she didn't know if she had composed anything she was particularly proud of, just now. But that would have sounded like false modesty. She shrugged slightly, and shook her head.

'Whenever you wish,' urged Mahler. 'I am always at the Opera. I shall leave instructions that you are not to be turned away.'

'Perhaps,' she replied. 'If I can think of something good enough.'

She felt Berta's hand on her sleeve.

'Forgive me, Herr Director,' Berta said, 'But poor Gropius, over there. He's only got my husband to talk to, and I know he wants to make Alma's acquaintance.' As they crossed to the other side of the room, Berta said, 'You stood up to him. That was very brave; he can be more destructive than he realizes. It doesn't help him to be well liked. Have you made it up?'

'He wants me to go to the Court Opera to show him my music.'

'Well, well! Things do move fast!'

They came up to Gropius.

'Here we are, Walter. Now you can stop pretending to be interested in what Emil is saying to you.'

She led her husband away.

'You are not Austrian, Herr Gropius?' Alma-Maria asked him.

'Nor am I a Jew, Fräulein Alma.' He had lowered his voice momentarily. 'I'm from Westphalia. May I ask if you've inherited your father's talent as a painter?'

'My father's talent, perhaps. But not for painting – for music, as you may have gathered. Are you just visiting Vienna, Herr Gropius, or are you living here?'

'Studying. England and Vienna are the world's centres for architecture at the moment. Vienna – Hoffmann, Olbrich . . . it's really quite exciting . . . Would it please you, Fräulein Alma, if I said I was living here in Vienna?'

She wondered if he had meant by the words 'Nor am I a Jew', that she had spent too much time talking to Mahler.

'I was merely making conversation, Herr Gropius.'

Mahler left early. 'He's really not a very sociable being,' Berta explained. 'Sophie telephoned him and invited him: she has a way with him – the Clemenceaus look after him when he's conducting in Paris, and he's grown very fond of my sister. Besides, Justine – that's his sister – always fusses if he's late, or so I've heard.'

Gropius was to escort Alma-Maria home in the Zuckerkandls' car – 'He can help Hans push you, if it breaks down halfway up the Hohe Warte,' said Berta. He had gone to look for Hans. One of the maids was helping Alma-Maria into her furs.

'Mahler has asked Sophie and me to persuade you to come with us to the Opera tomorrow. We're attending the *répétition générale* of his new production of *The Tales of Hoffmann*. It's usually left to the light opera companies, of course, but Mahler has managed to persuade the Chamberlain and his committee to let him give it the full grand operatic treatment.'

Alma-Maria paused only for a moment.

'I should like to, very much,' she heard herself reply.

She noticed she had not even managed to keep the excitement out of her voice.

'It has been a strange evening for you, hasn't it, darling Almschi?' Berta said, as they were going downstairs to the hall. 'You've been sitting at table with your past on one side, and something very close to your present on the other. And opposite – who can tell? – perhaps your future.'

'He made me feel so shy and awkward. I hope my behaviour wasn't too noticeably embarrassing. It's always the same when I'm feeling shy:

either I refuse to talk at all, or I give the impression I'm terribly forward,' said Alma-Maria.

They were sitting on the back seat of the car at the entrance to the Court Opera. Hans was waiting at the step to help them down, but Alma-Maria was reluctant to move. She felt secure, wedged between the two older women. Besides, she was so much at ease with them, was able to say exactly how she felt in a way she hadn't been with anyone since Pappi's death.

'He was captivated by you. Anyone could see that,' Sophie Clemenceau told her.

'You're not shy at the thought of seeing him now, are you?' asked Berta Zuckerkandl.

'I'm afraid I am – because I feel I behaved badly.'

'You couldn't behave as badly as he does,' Berta said. 'He's so used to acting the tyrant, he forgets how to behave in ordinary company. He needs the friendship of somebody like yourself.' She slipped her hand round Alma-Maria's arm. 'Somebody young and beautiful – who isn't a soprano looking for a way to success ... We'd better go in, or he'll have to start the rehearsal wondering what's become of you.'

They got down and went up the steps into the foyer. Mahler was standing at the top of the grand staircase, in the Schwind Foyer, on one leg like a gaunt, black-crested heron. When he saw them, he came running down to meet them with no regard for the dignity of his position. He addressed Alma-Maria with complete disregard for the others.

'So you've really come, eh? I was afraid you wouldn't. Here, let me take your coat.' He grabbed at the fur lapel as if afraid some attendant might intercept and prevent him. As he held it while she slid her arm from the sleeves, he said, 'I'm so very pleased, you know. *The Tales of Hoffmann* is a work of which I'm particularly fond. I think it's because, all his life, Offenbach wanted to escape from operetta and compose a real opera. And then, in his old age, when he was at death's door, he succeeded – and produced his masterpiece. I sometimes wonder if I shall be so fortunate.' He threw her coat over his arm.

'We shall put it in my office,' he told her.

'I think the Frau Hofratin and Frau Clemenceau might like to leave their coats,' she suggested.

'Of course! Very remiss of me!'

But he didn't really sound apologetic. He helped Sophie Clemenceau off with her coat and Alma-Maria assisted Berta to remove hers. Carrying Berta's coat, she followed Mahler across the foyer to the door of his office. Just inside, he turned and took it from her. With all three furs threatening to fall from his arms, he asked, her in an urgent tone of voice,

'Fräulein Alma, tell me. Did you sleep well last night?'

'Very well indeed, thank you, Herr Director. Why do you ask?'

'I didn't sleep a wink all night. Do you understand me?'

'Really, Herr Director!' she exclaimed softly.

He put the coats over the back of his black leather sofa, and gestured they should return to the foyer. As he led them through into the great horseshoe of the auditorium, he took care to address himself to the two older women.

She had not been entirely truthful. On the one hand, she had not passed an uncomfortable night. On the other, she had not slept well in the accepted sense. She had woken frequently, and always there had been uppermost in her mind, as if it had been there even while she slept, the rivalry for her attention between the young architectural student, Herr Gropius, and Mahler. The previous evening, when the Zuckerkandls' car had brought her home to the Hohe Warte, and had drawn up outside no. 8 Steinfeldgasse, the Villa Möll, Gropius had sighed as if he wished the drive had been much longer. Even before, she had been conscious of his eyes on her, watchful as a cat's. His hand grasped at hers before she could get out.

'Fräulein Alma, may I see you again?'

Was he attempting to steal a march on Mahler? she asked herself. Who could tell what the future held? She had bestowed on him a smile so dazzling he must surely have seen it, even in the dark.

'Of course you may, Herr Gropius,' she had replied.

Mahler took his leave of the three of them when they were settled into their comfortable gilt-backed *fauteuils* in the centre front of the orchestra stalls. A liveried attendant was hovering in the side aisle, waiting to escort him down into the orchestra pit where the musicians were already tuning up. Mahler leaned over the backs of the chairs in front of them to bow over Sophie and Berta's hands. When he turned to Alma-Maria, he said to her in a loud whisper, as though nobody else was present.

'You will come again, won't you, Fräulein Alma? When we have a little more leisure? And you will bring me the best of your work, eh? I'm impatient to see it.'

'If you want me to, Herr Director.'

'You promise?'

'Yes. I promise.'

'Word of honour?'

'Herr Director! ... Oh, all right! Word of honour!'

Satisfied, Mahler loped off down to the orchestra pit, and disappeared behind the red plush hanging on the rail. Berta leaned across her sister's lap to talk to Alma-Maria.

'Whatever have you done to the tyrant of the Court Opera?' she asked. 'You've got him behaving like a schoolboy!'

Alma-Maria was troubled. Tomorrow she had a lesson with Alex. Would he be hurt if he were to find that Mahler was offering his friendship to her? There was that terrible little opera, *The Dwarf*, to tell her how hurt he had been already, even if she had tried to persuade him there could be nothing deeper between them than what already existed.

The orchestra had fallen silent. She heard the click of Mahler's baton on the desk. The opening chords of the prelude crashed out, followed by the off-stage chorus of the Spirits of Wine. She had never previously seen *The Tales of Hoffmann*. She found it strange, ominous. It was very Jewish, of course – the grotesque mingling of charming little operetta melodies with the grim story which was being unfolded of Hoffmann's three tragic love affairs. Was this the shadow-side to Goethe's Gretchen, where Eternal Womanhead led the poet not to Salvation but to drunken despair? The darkness of the piece was made all the gloomier for the quality of the stage production, and the superb performance of the musicians under Mahler's direction.

The third episode began seductively enough: gondolas swayed behind a façade of slender arabesque arches, discharging their carnival-masked passengers, while soprano and mezzo-soprano voices sang the Barcarolle off-stage. Gutheil-Schöder made her entrance as Giulietta down a sweep of stairs, reaching to welcome Hoffmann while dismissing the protests of her current lover.

Her outstretched arms were naked to the shoulders, her silk and jewelled bodice slit under her armpits so that it was possible to glimpse the swell if not the peaks of her bare breasts underneath. Her billowing satin Turkish trouser legs were slit from ankle to hip so that, as she crossed the stage to Hoffmann – '*Nous avons un poète étranger parmi nous*' – they fell open to reveal the entire length of her naked leg.

She had scarcely sung the words when, above the sound of the orchestra, there was the fierce click of Mahler's baton on the edge of the podium desk, and a rattle as it snapped and fell to the floor. The music collapsed into a discordant halt.

'Frau Schöder? Forgive me!'

Mahler's voice had an unpleasant edge to it.

'Who is responsible for the costume you are wearing?'

Gutheil-Schöder stepped forward to the footlights. It was extraordinary how the bedizened hardness of the role cracked and melted from her like a wax mask before the fire as she stooped toward the conductor's podium. Alma-Maria couldn't catch what she said.

'My dear woman . . .!' Mahler's voice was all too audible. 'Your dress was not like that on the design sheets . . . Frau Weissler?'

A plump, middle-aged woman in widow's black, with a chatelaine and scissors suspended from her girdle, hustled out from the wings. With her was a young girl in a maid's white pinafore. The entire house was absolutely silent. Gutheil-Schöder held the slits in her Turkish trousers closed between her fingers.

'Frau Weissler? Will you please see that Frau Schöder's costume is stitched up correctly. Now, if you please; as quickly as possible.'

At first, when Gutheil-Schöder had been escorted off the stage by the wardrobe mistress and her assistant, Alma-Maria felt nothing but sympathy for her. She was angry at Mahler's cruelty in making an example of her in front of the entire cast, orchestra, and the audience scattered about the stalls. After Gutheil-Schöder had returned, and the act had been recommenced, she began to modify her opinion. By the time Giulietta's contemptuous rejection of Hoffmann had been reached – '*Je te l'abandonne!*' – the singer had fully assumed the Messalina-like quality of the role, that of the vampiric apparition who renders her victim supine by the erotic impact of her personality before destroying him. The scandal which her costume in its more revealing form would have caused would have distracted from, not enhanced, the integrity of the characterization, and would have drawn the audience's attention away from the music. Mahler had been right, not only to insist on the costume being modified but in being angry about it.

Afterwards, when she was being driven back up to the Hohe Warte, Berta asked her,

'Well Almschi? What do you think of our little Jew-dwarf now?'

She was taken by surprise by the epithet coming from Berta's lips, so that she replied without hesitation,

'I admire him enormously.'

'You were not put off by his harshness? That Puritan response to poor Schöder's dress?'

'I believe he was being loyal to the composer.'

'Many people will say that his behaviour was cruel. Gutheil-Schöder is still very young, and quite devoted in her admiration for him.'

'Then many people will be wrong,' Alma-Maria said. 'It is the duty of somebody in Herr Mahler's position to be single-minded in his service to music.'

Berta embraced her impulsively.

'I was right,' she said. 'Gustav does need a friend like you.'

On thinking about it in the quiet of the music room, later, Alma-Maria was surprised by the uncompromising attitude she had adopted in her defence of Mahler, and not at all sure she had been correct. She felt quite confused by her own feelings about him.

The following morning, Noni came to her room with a letter. She had only just got up, and was at the wash stand with her nightdress pulled down about her waist.

'It has to be important, Fräulein Almschi,' Noni told her. 'It came by pneumatic.'

Alma-Maria hastily dried her hands. There was nothing on the envelope to suggest its origin. She tore it open. Inside was a single sheet of paper: four verses with no address and no signature. The handwriting was spidery but clearly legible. She sat on the edge of her bed and, with ever increasing excitement, she read to the third and fourth:

> It happened overnight
> – I spent it wide awake –
> That when there's a knock, immediately
> My eyes fly to the door!
>
> I hear 'Word of Honour'
> Ringing in my ears constantly
> Like the battering of cannon-fire:
> I glance at the door and keep watch!

She read and reread. Walter Gropius, the beautiful young architect, had sent her flowers the previous morning. She would be bitterly disappointed to find that the poem too had come from him – there was no satisfaction in being the object of so young a man's infatuation. It was the phrase 'Word of Honour' that made her sure of its authorship.

Through the mist in her brain, she saw Noni still standing at the door.

'There's no reply, thank you Noni.'

She reached for her chemisette and buttoned it over her breasts as if afraid of what Mahler might think if he could see her sitting there stripped to the waist.

> I hear 'Word of Honour'
> Ringing in my ears constantly . . .

There couldn't be any mistake.

After breakfast she showed Mutti the poem.

'Well, *liebchen*! Somebody's very smitten with you, I must say! Can you guess who it is?'

'Yes, Muttichen. I'm quite certain who it is.'

'Are you going to tell me?'

There must be no repetition of the dreadful business over Klimt.

'Gustav Mahler. I met him at the Zuckerkandls' the other night. I told you, Muttichen.'

Mutti laughed.

'*Liebchen*! Even before I was twenty, like you, I had become accustomed to receiving dozens of poems through the post. If I'd allowed myself to dream they came from the Director of the Court Opera, or the Principal Conductor of the Vienna Philharmonic, I don't know what would have become of me! A man in Mahler's position isn't going to send anonymous rhymes to unknown young girls – not even one as pretty as my Almschi . . . Gustav Mahler!' She laughed. 'You'll be telling me it comes from the Old Man himself next!'

Alma-Maria left Mutti to go and get ready to set off into the city for her music lesson with Alex. She had reached the end of the Steinfeldgasse and had turned off onto the gravel path through the park below the road, which would take her to Döbling and the tram stop for the Ring, when she saw a *fiacre* come toiling up the road in the opposite direction. Through the glass of the closed window, she saw, under a Russian-style fur cap, the unmistakable features of Max Burckhard. She wondered what business he had up on the Hohe Warte, and whether he had been coming to speak to her. He hadn't noticed her, and she was anxious not to be late for her lesson and so hurried on.

'Do you know who called here, this morning?' Mutti said, when she returned home that afternoon.

By that time, Max Burckhard was far from Alma-Maria's thoughts.

'Max – Max Burckhard,' Mutti continued. 'It seems, when he left the Zuckerkandls' the other night, he found Herr Mahler waiting for him round the corner, in a *fiacre*. Max says Mahler wanted to ask all sorts of questions about you. He says Mahler told him that he didn't like you at first – he thought you were too pretty and fashionably dressed to be serious about anything, but that you soon changed his mind for him. Then, Max says, he started asking the most personal questions about you. Max told him off: he told Mahler that those you admitted to your friendship knew what sort of a person you were, and that other people had no right to try to find out ... So what do you think of that? I suppose I have to admit I could have been wrong about that poem.'

What should she think? Alma-Maria wondered. That she felt tremendously flattered? That she couldn't exclude a man who was twice her age, far from good-looking, who suffered from a slight deformity, shortsightedness and was a Jew, from her mind?

'I don't know, Muttichen. I honestly don't know.'

'*Liebling*,' Mutti said, 'you'll take care, this time, won't you?'

'Yes, Mutti.'

'I'm afraid of my daughter being too lovely – too lovely for her own happiness, I mean.'

The plump prettiness of Mutti's face, Alma-Maria noted, no longer disguised the crow's-feet etched about her eyes.

Gropius called two days later. He brought with him three tickets for the orchestra stalls for the première of *The Tales of Hoffmann*, in the hope that Frau Möll and Fräulein Schindler would accompany him. Alma-Maria had rather hoped that Mahler would have sent complimentaries – perhaps even for the Director's box. She wondered if the work involved in introducing a new opera into the Court Opera's repertory had put her from his mind. Disappointed though she might be, she was not averse to being seen in the midst of the glitter of satins and diamonds and ivory white and silver *Chevau-légers* uniforms. It was even possible that Mahler might catch a glimpse of her to rekindle his interest in her, though that was in the realm of daydreams.

It was always a little humbling on such occasions to discover how well Mutti was remembered from a career which had ended over twenty years earlier, how lines of middle-aged and elderly gentlemen formed between the rows of gilt-backed *fauteuils* to bow over her hand and to compliment her on her looks. She was as much aware of the opera glasses and *pince-nez* which were turned in her own direction; she chatted to Gropius with a deliberately charming affability, taking what she assured herself was an innocent delight in the admiration she provoked.

Above their heads, the electric lights in the huge chandelier dimmed. The footlights mounted like fountains rising on the vastness of the red and gold proscenium curtains. There was a scatter of applause as Mahler mounted the podium. There was something absurd about his short, slight figure, with only his unruly mane of black hair and the edge of his shoulders visible above the rail of the orchestra pit. When he turned to acknowledge the applause, he looked like a precociously serious schoolboy peering over a garden fence, with his chin resting on the rail. Then, quite suddenly, she found that his spectacles were on her where she was sitting in the fifth row. The awkward severity vanished from his face and a spontaneous, broad grin, even more boyish, took its place. The radiance of his pleasure in seeing her there suggested that, for a moment at least, he had forgotten the existence of the rest of the audience. However, he bowed to left and right, and turned back to face the orchestra. She glanced at Gropius to see whether he had noticed what had happened. He was peering down at the programme open on his knees. She looked about her. Apart from a couple of Mutti's erstwhile admirers who were finding their chairs, the audience's attention was on the curtain, while over the entire house there was the stillness on which Mahler insisted before even the first chords of an overture were played.

Mahler did not look at her again, either during the intermission or after the fall of the curtain when taking his bow on stage. At the end of the performance, she left the auditorium with Mutti on one side, nodding her head to acquaintances, and with her arm in Gropius's. No liveried footman, no member of the staff of the Opera, intercepted them with an invitation to call on the Director in his office.

Mutti only went to the Court Opera to hear works by Gluck, Mozart, or Grétry. *Fidelio*, Wagner, even Gounod, were all too heavy for her – 'Too many notes being played at the same time; I'm sure one's ear wasn't designed to listen to so many different noises all at once!' But, sitting in the dark interior of the *fiacre* taking them home, she sang snatches of the waltz song from the first act of *The Tales of Hoffmann*, and the love duet from Act Two. She seemed happier and more carefree than at any time since their return from the real Venice. The following morning, another basket of flowers arrived, sent by Gropius – 'Such a handsome boy!' Mutti exclaimed. But handsome and eligible though he was, he was still a boy; compared to a man such as Mahler, he could occupy a place only on the periphery of Alma-Maria's mind.

The next visit she paid to the Court Opera, two weeks later, was also with Mutti – to hear Gluck's *Orfeo ed Euridice*. To her disappointment, she found that it was to be conducted by one of Mahler's assistants, Bruno Walter, even though it had been Mahler himself who had introduced the work to the Court Opera in the edition by Berlioz for contralto lead. As they were making their way to their places, however, she recognized him up in the Director's box. Just as she was about to sit, she saw that he had noticed her. Without the least concern for what coffee-house *Klatsch* would make of it, he rose and bowed to her, smiling broadly, so that she wondered whether he had been looking out for her at every performance. She found it difficult to pay attention to the music, and kept glancing up at the face, pale in the light from the proscenium, craning forward over the parapet of the box. She thought she had never seen such intelligence, such sensitivity of feature. Several times he turned his head to look down at her; quickly, she attempted to assume an interest in the performance.

When the curtain fell on Orpheus journeying through the infernal regions, Mutti decided they should take a stroll in the foyer, hoping, Alma-Maria had no doubt, to find herself holding court over old admirers. Mahler was waiting to intercept them at the exit. He advanced toward Alma-Maria and reached out to take her hands, ignoring everybody passing by on either side who expected at least a nod of recognition from the Court Opera Director.

'I did not expect the great joy of seeing you here again so soon, Fräulein Schindler!'

'May I have the privilege, Herr Director,' she said quickly, 'of presenting you to my mother?'

He bowed over Mutti's hand, kissing the knuckle of her forefinger.

'I have not previously had the honour, Frau Möll. I know you by reputation, of course. I have been told often what a sweet soprano voice and delightful stage manner Fräulein Anna Bergen had.'

'Oh Herr Director, you are so kind!' Mutti simpered.

'Perhaps you and Fräulein Schindler would care to take tea with me in my office? I'm sure you would find it more comfortable than the promenade or crush bar.'

Alma-Maria wondered whether Mutti would be disappointed at not mingling with her old admirers, but she was delighted; she slipped her hand under Mahler's arm and Alma-Maria followed them dutifully up the stairs to the Schwind Foyer.

'Did you never consider coming here, Frau Möll, and auditioning for us?' Mahler asked.

Alma-Maria could hardly believe her ears. Nothing she had heard or observed about Mahler had suggested he was capable of such outrageous flirtatiousness.

'I'm sure you could have played a most attractive Susanna in *Figaro*, or Mistress Ford in *The Merry Wives of Windsor*. Indeed, I wish we could have seen you in such roles.'

'You are so very kind, Herr Director, but I really did have such a little voice ...' She paused. She wasn't going to deny his compliments completely. 'Quite satisfactory for the Josefstadt, or even for the Volksoper, but it would have been lost in a great place like this. I believe I can say in all honesty that I do know my limitations.'

The years fell from her under the spell of Mahler's attentiveness. Gravely, he replied to her,

'Alas, Frau Möll, I wish all singers shared your self-understanding. It would make the life of us poor opera directors so much easier!' As they stepped out of the foyer into the quiet of his book-lined office, he said, 'I hope you don't consider my accosting you during the intermission an impertinence ...'

'Not at all, Herr Director!' Mutti replied. 'I'm sure both Alma-Maria and I feel greatly privileged!'

It was the first time Alma-Maria had been past the doorway. She was struck by the precise tidiness of the room, the orderliness of the music scores, the books, the pencils and pens all in their proper holders, the cut hot-house flowers in their vases, and not a sign of dust anywhere, not even on the leaves of the potted plants. It was so unlike poor Max Burckhard's office at the Burgtheater.

'It is the only chance I have of the pleasure of speaking with you,' Mahler continued. 'I shall have to leave during the third act. I'm catching the night train to Munich.'

'Will you be going for long, Herr Director?' asked Mutti.

'A few days only. I'm conducting at the Residenz.'

'Your own work, Herr Director?' Alma-Maria asked.

'The German première of my Fourth Symphony, I'm delighted to say.'

'You compose, Herr Director?' Mutti asked, her face bright with interest.

'When my Imperial and Royal duties allow, Frau Möll. Which is all too rarely, I'm afraid.'

It was ridiculous, thought Alma-Maria; like watching two actors on a stage. He made himself sound like some Sunday composer who writes music in his free time as a hobby.

'I expect that is why you have such a sympathetic understanding of the music you conduct here,' said Mutti. 'Trying to write music yourself must give you great insight into the work of other composers.'

Alma-Maria felt quite put out by the way Mahler was indulging Mutti, and the way Mutti believed she was being indulgent with Mahler.

They were sitting together on the heavy black leather sofa. Deliberately she sat at the great Broadwood grand piano – a magnificent instrument, she realized, even without touching the keys.

'You must come and call on Alma-Maria and me up on the Hohe Warte,' said Mutti, 'the moment you return from Bavaria.'

'Nothing would give me greater pleasure, dear lady,' Mahler replied.

'The Villa Möll – that's number eight, Steinfeldgasse. Now, you won't forget, will you, Herr Director?'

'I certainly shan't forget, I assure you. But I must put the address in my diary.' He got up and went over to his desk. 'Would the afternoon of Wednesday the twenty-seventh be agreeable to you?'

'Alex von Zemlinsky has arranged for me to have a lesson in counterpoint with Dr Gound on the afternoon of the twenty-seventh,' announced Alma-Maria.

She was sitting with her back to them. She did not turn round.

'I'm sure the Freiherr von Zemlinsky will be happy to make your apologies to Dr Gound when he learns who it is who is calling on us,' Mutti told her.

Alma-Maria was far from sure Alex would be pleased to find out who was calling on her. When she realized that Mahler had no intention of suggesting an alternative date, she said,

'Very well. I shall be seeing Alex tomorrow. I suppose I'd better ask him to change my lesson with Dr Gound.'

Her voice was sulky, but Mahler and Mutti appeared to be enjoying one another's company too much to notice it. She felt excluded as they continued chatting to one another over the teacups. There was a heavy, freshly bound manuscript score on the piano lid. She took it down. As she suspected, it was a photographed fair copy of the Fourth Symphony, set there, she presumed, for Mahler to take away with him. She turned the pages until she reached the final movement. She saw that it took the form of a song for solo soprano and orchestra, *Wir geneissen die himmlischen Freuden*:

> We enjoy heaven's delights,
> So can dispense with earthly things.
> No worldly turmoil
> Is to be heard in heaven . . .

She picked out the melody of the orchestral accompaniment to the main section of the vocal part, with one hand, until she reached a lovely, slow chorale theme in E minor –

Saint Peter in Heaven sees all . . .

Here, she managed with both hands an approximation of the brass and woodwind, while rendering the vocal line in a husky *Sprechstimme*.

Mahler stopped talking. Mutti followed suit. When Alma-Maria stopped playing, he applauded.

'Bravo, Fräulein Alma! Excellent! The praise I've heard for your sight-reading appears entirely justified. I'm almost sorry the excellent Hermann Behn has already arranged the keyboard transcription of my Fourth.'

He got up again from the sofa and came over to the piano with his curious limping gait. From a side table he picked up an even larger bound volume of photographed manuscript.

'Perhaps you would care to take this with you and look through it while I am in Munich? Or, since it is rather heavy, I shall have a messenger bring them to you at eight Steinfeldgasse tomorrow morning. These are folk *Lieder* – settings of words by Achim von Arnim and Bettina Brentano, charming, simple rhymes from the beginning of the last century. They have not yet been published in their present form, for voice and orchestra.'

This last comment was directed at Mutti, who beamed at him from over the back of the sofa. Alma-Maria was well aware that the Arnim-Brentano *Des Knaben Wunderhorn* poems, though they might have the superficial appearance of naivety, were far from simple and not always charming – not, at least, as Mutti would regard charming.

'I'm sure Almschi feels very privileged,' said Mutti. 'Don't you, Almschi?'

'Yes, Mutti,' Alma-Maria replied dutifully.

She could afford to be dutiful now that she had drawn Mahler to her side.

They were returning out into the foyer on their way back to the auditorium, when she said to Mahler,

'Herr Director? Do you suppose you could ever consider me for the post of your assistant conductor?'

Mahler laughed at her impertinence.

'I don't know that Dr Walter is ready to give up his position. He is still a young man. But I will tell you this – if your technical mastery of the stick is equal to your sympathy for music at the keyboard, I would have no hesitation in letting you conduct for me.'

Aware of her own boldness, she moved closer up to him and said,

'Is that judgement a truly objective one, Herr Director?'

'Whose judgement is ever truly objective?' Mahler asked in reply.

His deep brown eyes, magnified through his spectacles, gazed into hers.

'I shall ask *you* a question, my dear. Would you want my judgement to be entirely objective?'

She could scarcely breathe.

Heavy though the volume was, she took the *Wunderhorn* songs to her lesson with Alex. It was, she decided, one step towards letting him know what was happening. He looked them through at first with apparent interest. Then played through three of them, with her half-singing the vocal parts. Alex said nothing until they had finished. His look of suppressed anger frightened her.

'What do we have?' he asked. 'First, a piece of *Schrammelmusik*, nothing more. Then a little melodrama masquerading as tragedy. Then an oafish, clod-hopping attempt at humour. What is a complex, subtle musician like Mahler doing, producing rubbish like this? Never able to stay with one mood for longer than a moment!' he continued. 'Typical of the man who's afraid of his own emotions.'

All the songs were similar to the one which concluded the Fourth Symphony, she had decided. She said nothing, shocked as she was by Alex's condemnation of the work of his adored master and idol.

'Even Mahler can't prevent the Jew from emerging,' said Alex. 'The self-indulgent display of ersatz emotion; the lack of any fixed principles ... So unworthy!'

The vehemence with which he spoke made her wonder whether he was about to burst into tears. She felt dreadfully guilty. She tried to tell herself that it was quite uncalled-for, that there was no reason why he should suppose that there was anything between herself and Mahler, and even if there was, there was no justification for his becoming so emotional about it. At the same time, though she had never committed herself to anything more than a fond friendship with him, or so she told herself, she could not bear to see him fighting back his distress.

It was difficult to know how to comfort him, since nothing had been said other than his comments on the songs. So she just looked at him and said, 'Alex,' softly, and stroked his cheek, hoping that he understood that she had realized his attack on Mahler's music was no more than a statement of his distress.

That same night, Möll could hardly wait for the maids to withdraw from the dining room before announcing,

'Alma-Maria, I think I'm bound to tell you what I told your dear Mutti this evening.'

He was puffing himself up like some huge pink-faced toad.

'It was quite wrong of either of you to have accepted Herr Mahler's invitation to his office last night. I'm sure that we do not lead such sheltered lives that you are unaware of his reputation as a roué – a rake – nor of the succession of young female opera singers with which his name has been connected.'

She sat staring at the crumbs on her plate. She noticed that Mutti had nothing to say.

'Any friendship between you, Alma-Maria, and Herr Mahler is out of the question,' Möll continued. 'It would be quite grotesque! He is over forty – twice your age. He lives recklessly, beyond his means. He has allowed his health to deteriorate as a result of his intemperate living.

He is not liked either at the Court Opera or the Musikverein. They say all the players in the Philharmonic detest him for his bullying, sarcastic manner. I don't suppose he will be allowed to remain in his present, lordly position for very long. And then where will he be? I understand his so-called composing isn't worth the paper it's written on.'

As they filed out of the dining room, he grasped her arm to hold her back, so hard that she was sure he had bruised her.

'You haven't answered me, Alma-Maria!'

'I wasn't aware you had asked me anything,' she replied angrily.

'I'd be obliged to you if you at least said you would think about what I told you.'

'I'll think about it, Uncle Carl.'

'Do you imaging your Pappi would have liked the idea of the name of his beloved daughter becoming connected, in popular gossip, with that of a Jew – and not even an Austrian Jew, one of our own?'

'There is no reason whatever why my name should be linked with Herr Mahler's,' she said. 'My God! I've only spoken to him on three occasions!'

'It is best it should remain that way,' said Möll.

But her name was already linked to that of Mahler. The following afternoon as she sat in the drawing room, watching the first snowflakes of winter hovering and falling against the darkening sky outside, one of the maids announced the arrival of Dr Burckhard. Mutti was paying a social call down in the city. Alma-Maria greeted him alone; she allowed him to kiss her.

'I'm afraid this is presuming on our old friendship, Almschi,' he said. He hesitated. Then he said, 'If Mahler were to ask you to marry him, what would your answer be?'

It was the impertinence of the question which forced it out of her – the aggressive tone of his voice.

'I would accept.'

Immediately she had said it, she wanted to take it back.

'Max! This is perfectly ridiculous! Why does everybody seem to suppose there's a friendship between Mahler and myself? We've met three times – each time in company. The first time you were present yourself.'

'It's common knowledge, Almschi – and not just coffee-house *Klatsch* either – that Mahler is head over heels in love with you.'

'It isn't common knowledge to me! Do stop talking nonsense, Max.'

'I just want to warn you. As somebody who still loves you. It would be an unspeakable disgrace for a creature as lovely as you are – the well-born daughter of a distinguished Viennese family – to throw herself away on a degenerate, rachitic Moravian Jew, one who doesn't even have good looks to recommend him.'

Alma-Maria went very cold.

'I'm surprised by you, Max. And disappointed. The man you've just described is a great artist – has any one tried to deny that? He is the Director of the Imperial and Royal Court Opera. He is the principal conductor of the Vienna Philharmonic Orchestra and president of the Musikverein. In fact, your degenerate and whatever-it-was Jew is just about the most distinguished musician in the entire world. And if I choose to be his friend, let me remind you, Max Burckhard, that I'm a grown woman now, not a child. I make my own judgements about people, thank you very much. Because I am still fond of you, I'd be happy if you wouldn't try to say anything more to me at the moment. In fact, I think you'd better go.'

As soon as he had gone, she went across to the music room. She would have liked to cry. Instead she found herself trembling. She sat at the piano, but did not play. Outside, the snow was falling thickly, silently, dark flakes becoming white as they pressed against the windowpane before sliding down to the sill.

She couldn't make out what was going on inside her. She hadn't been able to put Mahler out of her mind since she had first met him. But was it because of the glamour and authority attached to anyone who held his place in the world of music? She didn't feel desire for him the way she had felt desire for Klimt, and even for Alex, particularly after that night at Steinbach. And yet she could imagine lovemaking with him, and the joy of serving such a man by giving him all the pleasure and satisfaction she could – there was a sort of arousal in that.

Once more, she opened the volume of *Des Knaben Wunderhorn* and leafed through the ten songs. There was one song she recognized as being more daring for the singer than any of the others, because she would have to sing the opening phrase slowly, unaccompanied: *Urlicht* – Primal Light.

> ... then as I stepped onto a broad pathway,
> There came an angel who wanted to turn me away ...

As in the Fourth Symphony, a brass and woodwind chorale underscored the vocal line with a strong, devout melody – a declaration of sturdy religious faith.

> Ah, no! I would not be turned away!
> I am from God and would return to God.
> The dear God will send me a lamp
> To lighten me to eternal, blessed light!

The dear God will send me a lamp ... What had he been thinking of when he wrote that wonderfully tender line? Surely the lamp God sends can only be Love? What other light is there to lighten the soul to heaven? He was the first man she had ever encountered – after Pappi, of course – who could give meaning to her life, for he surpassed all the men she had

196

ever met in talent, in genius, perhaps even in intelligence. Was it presumptuous to suppose – perhaps *hope* would be a better word – that God might have caused their paths to cross so that she might be the lamp.

'I trust you gentlemen are devising some scheme to mark the sixtieth anniversary of the Imperial-Royal succession, eh?'

Mutti glanced anxiously down at General the Imperial Count von Steindorf's plate, as if his question had been an implied criticism of the hospitality he had been receiving.

She called the maid over. 'Hannele, would you help His Highness the Herr General to another portion of cherry sorbet?'

'No, no, dear lady!' Count von Steindorf demurred with a wave of his hand. 'You tempt me to the sin of greed … *inter alia*,' he added, casting a sidelong, roguish smile in her direction.

His monocle fell from his eye and swung like a pendulum over his empty plate.

'The sixtieth anniversary?' asked Gropius, who had been placed next to Alma-Maria. 'That's seven years away.'

'Six – almost six, that is,' Möll corrected him hastily. 'Young men always imagine five or six years to be an eternity.'

The other guests – Max Burckhard with some half-dozen artistic colleagues of Möll's from the Sezession – nodded their agreement.

The aim of the dinner party, Alma-Maria knew, was to seek Count von Steindorf's good will in securing the Old Man's presence at the opening of the Beethoven Festival next May. Gropius had been asked to keep her company.

'I put it to you, gentlemen,' said Count von Steindorf, 'an Austrian celebration would be a fine thing. Nothing to do with your damned Croats, Serbs, Czechs, Eyeties, or Galicians, eh? A celebration of the fine old Archduchy! And not a hint of your damned Prussians!'

Alma-Maria glanced across to Mutti, who was staring down at the tablecloth.

'I hope his Highness the Herr General doesn't hold it against me that I'm half North German,' she said.

'Hey? Hey?' Count von Steindorf looked from her to Mutti. He laughed, and wagged his finger at Mutti. 'It must be you, dear lady! For certainly our beloved and honoured Emil Schindler was Austrian to his fingertips.'

'I am from Holstein, Your Highness,' Mutti admitted.

'But your beauty and your talent confers full Viennese citizenship on you, my dear,' he replied archly.

'The idea of an *Austrian* festival has a great deal to commend it,' said Max Burckhard, ingratiating himself with Count von Steindorf by his apparently judicious tone of voice. He leaned forward over the table.

'The truth is, since the Compromise of 1868, Hungary has remained a Magyar nation – but what has happened to Austria . . .?'

'Quite so!' Count von Steindorf grunted his approval.

'We are swamped by the influx of Moravians and Slavs from the east, and Jews from every quarter of the globe. Do you know? The entire governing body of the National Credit Bank – not just Herr Director Fischer, but the entire board – is made up of Prussian Jews?'

'Jews are a particular case,' said Gropius. 'Having no state of their own, they have no culture of their own . . .'

'They assume the mantle of philosophy,' Burckhard interrupted enthusiastically, even rudely, thought Alma-Maria. 'Because they are nationless, they have no armies to make them political tyrants. So they wield words: they invent philosophical systems to enslave their fellow men. Think of Spinoza – or Karl Marx.'

'Or Dr Sigmund Freud?'

'Sig*i*smund Freud!' somebody laughed.

'Has anyone noticed how Dr Sig*i*smund Freud's patients always seem to be women – hysterical women?' asked a plump, crop-headed gentleman, an art critic for a Christian-Socialist journal. 'The sort of people who are susceptible to Jewish – er – charm.'

'That character in the novel – what is it? – by an Englishman with a French name . . .' somebody said.

'Svengali?' Möll suggested.

'Svengali, quite. Was he meant to be Jewish?'

'Oh, certainly,' replied Möll. 'The description of him tells all.'

'A few weeks ago,' Gropius began in a quiet voice which compelled the others round the table to pay attention despite his youth, 'I enjoyed the inestimable privilege of escorting Frau Möll and Fräulein Alma-Maria to the Opera. We heard Offenbach's *The Tales of Hoffmann*. The music, I have to admit, is quite charming – melodies which linger in one's ear. But the charm of the music sugars the blackest, most cynical view of womanhood it is possible to conceive. Our own poet, E. T. A. Hoffmann – . . .' He smiled. 'I speak as a fellow North German, my dear and honoured Frau Möll – is depicted as a hopeless drunk. But that is quite consistent with the work as a whole, for there isn't an aspect of it which isn't a denial of every Christian German value.'

Somebody said, 'Hear, hear!'

Count von Steindorf grunted heavily:

'That's what happens when those fools in the Chamberlain's office appoint a Jew to direct the Kaiserlich-Königlich Court Opera,' he said.

Alma-Maria rose from the table and made for the door. Mutti called, 'Almschi!' after her, but she went on until she had reached the foot of the stairs outside.

Mutti came after her.

'Almschi! whatever's the matter? Leaving like that without so much as excusing yourself! And with His Highness present!'

'You heard them!' Alma-Maria told her.

'Heard what?'

'All that talk about Jews!'

'Our guests have been saying nothing more than I've heard you say yourself,' Mutti told her. 'In fact, Herr Gropius was saying exactly what I've heard you say about Jewish music.'

Alma-Maria turned on the first step to face her.

'Don't you realize, Muttichen? They're talking about Mahler! Uncle Carl, Max, Herr Gropius – they're all determined to poison our minds against him.'

'Oh what nonsense, Almschi! You're being far too sensitive about this new friendship of yours. I'm sure they mean nothing of the kind.'

'Yes they do! Max is still jealous … And Gropius is trying to pay court to me.'

'You should count yourself lucky! A good-looking, intelligent young man like him …'

'Muttichen! I'm not a child any more to want to be flattered by the attentions of any good-looking young man!'

'You are growing into a very conceited, vain, young woman.'

'Why? Because I think Mahler's a greater man than any of them – even if he's a Jew?'

Mutti gave up.

'I warn you, Almschi: you're too headstrong for your own good. I'd better tell our guests that you've gone up to choose some music to play after dinner.'

'No, Mutti. I've a better idea. Tell them I was taken suddenly – with a woman's sickness. Then they can all feel thoroughly self-satisfied.'

She was seated at the piano working out figured basses in preparation for her next lesson with Alex's friend and colleague, Roger Gound. Although it was scarcely mid-afternoon she had had to call Hannele to light the lamps. The weather, she suspected, had entered into a conspiracy with Möll, Burckhard, and everybody else to punish her for her bad behaviour: to keep her confined to the house. Downstairs, the snow had drifted up against the windows like buttresses.

She was interrupted just as she had managed to achieve some concentration on what she was doing, when Hannele rushed in.

'Fräulein Almschi! You'll never believe it! Gustav Mahler is downstairs – Gustav Mahler, in person, asking for your Mutti!'

It was wonderful. You could be sure the girl hadn't heard a note of classical music in her life except what she heard played here, on the piano. And yet the name of the Court Opera Director was as familiar to her as that of the Crown Prince – probably more so in view of Franz Ferdinand's grey opacity.

'And is Mutti at home?' asked Alma-Maria.

'No. There's only you, Fräulein Almschi. Shall I tell him there's nobody at home?'

'I'll go down to him.'

Hannele followed her out of the room.

'Fancy Gustav Mahler coming here in person,' she exclaimed. 'And your Mutti not here!'

'Hush!' Alma-Maria told her.

She arranged carefully her light silk shawl over her sleeves. She went to the stairs and started down at a deliberate pace, with Hannele restraining herself behind her. Mahler was standing in the vestibule, his heavy, caped tweed coat over his arm, his wide-brimmed velvet hat in his hand.

'Herr Director! Has nobody taken your things?' asked Alma-Maria.

'The young lady there told me your honoured mother and your stepfather were out, so I didn't let her take them. I didn't know whether I should stay.'

Alma-Maria noticed how he shifted his weight from one foot to another.

'Of course you must stay!' she said. She offered him her hand to bow over. 'You've arrived in the nick of time. Dr Gound has set me some truly dreadful – diabolic – exercises in counterpoint. He's set me a ground bass on which I've got to compose a nine-part chaconne. God must have sent you here to assist me.'

'Supposing I help you, Fräulein Alma, and the excellent Dr Gound tells you it is very poor – not academic. What then?'

'Oh, I promise I won't tell on you, Herr Director!' she laughed.

Hannele was watching and listening in amazement.

'Take the Herr Director's coat, Hannele,' Alma-Maria told her.

She took Mahler's arm and led him to the stairs.

'I'm forgiven for intruding on you like this?' he asked. 'I'm two days earlier than we arranged, I know. But on the train back from Munich, all I could think of was that I was drawing ever nearer to you.'

'Please, Herr Mahler!' she whispered. She glanced at Hannele who was carrying away his coat and hat. She was on the stairs, two steps above him, and thus a fraction taller than he. When Hannele had disappeared, she turned to him. 'I know what you mean, my dear,' she said.

He lifted his wonderfully intelligent, leonine face to stare at her. She leant down slightly, and brushed the lightest of kisses onto his dry cheek.

She amazed, even shocked herself. She wondered if she had actually done what she had done. She retained enough composure to say, 'Let me take you to my music room,' and to turn and lead him on as if nothing had happened for all the vertiginous feeling inside her head.

'And this is your room?' he asked, following her in.

He stared about him as if, by doing so, he was exploring her interior life.

'It isn't really – but I'm the only one in the house who uses it,' she told him.

He went over to the piano. He opened the bound volume of *Des Knaben Wunderhorn* where she had placed a leather marker.

'You've been playing my *Urlicht*?' he asked.

'It is beautiful,' she said, happy to be able to say so in complete sincerity.

'I use it to preface the final movement of my Second, you know,' he said.

Without sitting down, he played the accompaniment, the serene, solemn melody. She sat down beside him on the bench and as he lowered his hands from the keyboard, she felt the light touch of his knuckle against her leg, and the abruptness with which he moved it away.

'How does a Jew come to write such Christian music?' she asked.

'I am a Christian,' he said. 'I thought the whole world knew that,' he added wryly.

She knew that he was referring to the condition of his appointment to the Court Opera.

'I don't mean theologically speaking,' she said. 'I mean the quality of the music.'

'When I was a boy, I sang in a church choir – St Jacob's parish church in Iglau. We had an excellent choirmaster – we studied Beethoven's "Christ on the Mount of Olives", Haydn's "Seven Last Words from the Cross", and Rossini's "Stabat Mater". Not a bad grounding for a provincial, small-town boy, eh? And when I was twelve, I was allowed to accompany rehearsals on the piano of Mozart's Requiem in D minor – now that was an education!'

'But weren't you brought up a Jew?' she asked.

He looked at her as if his naturally serious face might break into a laugh. She wondered if she was being more than ordinarily naive.

'Certainly I was. My father was most observant. But I'm afraid he had to accept from very early on that, musically at least, I was a Christian. When I was little – so I've been told – every time our cantor opened his mouth in the synagogue, I'd start screaming for him to stop making such a dreadful noise.'

'Didn't your father mind you singing in a church choir?'

'Not in the least. There were several Jewish boys in the St Jacob's choir. It was one of the few ways open to us of studying how to make music – and, I suppose, it was a way of being acknowledged by the German-Christian community. For a Jew living beyond the borders of the Archduchy that is important.'

He got up from the bench and began to walk about the room, studying the books which she kept on the shelves because she had no bookcase in her bedroom.'

'Nietzsche!' he exclaimed. 'So much Nietzsche!'

She noticed how he shifted from one foot to the other – a certain sign of agitation.

'Dangerous!' he said. 'Not for young women to read!'

'Really?' she asked.

'It would be better if you burned them,' he said.

'My old, dear teacher, Dr Labor, told me that you had composed a perfect setting for Nietzsche's words.'

'Ah yes. "What Deep Midnight Says". I did not know Josef Labor approved of it ... It is a beautiful poem – and it suited my mood at the time.'

'What mood – may I ask?'

'Of course you may. There had been an unhappiness in my life, a great misfortune – I won't trouble you with the detail. Like Nietzsche, I had come to dislike the way philosophers claimed to seek out the truths of existence. It seemed to me then that the only result of pondering over such matters was to discover one's own hopeless inadequacy – that earthly existence is essentially tragic. Then I read *Die fröhliche Wissenschaft*. I can't express the relief I felt to find that somebody else had experienced the same feelings as myself; that it is in attempting to penetrate the mysteries of existence, one denies all joy in living; that the art of living is to seize on one thought, one experience at a time, and to rejoice in it. It became the philosophical basis of my Third Symphony.'

He smiled, but not at her – at some unspoken memory. He limped back to the piano bench and sat beside her once more.

'*Was mir die Liebe erzahlt*,' he said, as he began to play once more, a long, gentle melody. 'What Love tells me ... One experience at a time: what Christ meant by "take no thought for the morrow".'

He played on. The melody seemed to continue so that first statement and development merged into a single ocean-like calm of sound. She sat afraid to move, to break the melodic stillness. When at last he ceased playing, he told her, 'It's no longer Nietzsche, of course. I should have called it "What God tells me".' He glanced at her. 'Nietzsche would not approve of that, I think.'

'What could you write to follow such a movement?' she asked.

'Are you so impressed by it?' He sounded as if he was amused by her seriousness.

'It is a slow movement, isn't it?' she asked.

'It's an adagio. But it is also the finale of the symphony.'

'The last movement?'

'Why ever not?' He laughed. Then he became serious, schoolmasterly: 'In an adagio movement, everything becomes still, one approaches Truth. Haven't you heard Bruckner's Eighth Symphony?'

She shook her head.

'To write an adagio finale like that is to achieve real greatness! In a perfect universe, all symphonies will end with an adagio.'

Why then, she wondered, hadn't Mozart, Beethoven, Schubert, or even Brahms, ended symphonies with an adagio? There was arrogance here, she suspected. This suspicion was reinforced when Mahler, remembering what he had been saying originally, told her, 'No young woman should have Nietzsche on her bookshelf. Women are not philosophical beings. Intuition and logic don't mix. Women are by nature intuitive.'

He turned about on the bench and pointed to the shelves.

'Burn them!' he commanded.

'You remember what Heine said about burning books, Herr Director?' she said. ' "Start by burning books and you end by burning people." I shall read Nietzsche more fully, even if I don't have a man's logical mind; and when I've read them, I shall make up my mind whether to get rid of them or not.'

'She has always been such a wilful child, Herr Director!'

Mutti came bustling in. She hadn't even removed her scarf or coat.

'I hadn't the faintest idea you'd be here this afternoon. In fact, I swear I thought you were still in Munich. Please forgive us.'

'Nothing to forgive, *gnädige* Frau Möll.' Mahler rose to his feet. 'Any fault is entirely mine.' He bowed awkwardly. 'I returned from Munich last night. I found myself drawn here.'

Alma-Maria noticed with amazement that his left foot was twitching violently.

'You mustn't flatter our Almschi, Herr Director,' Mutti said. 'She is quite badly behaved enough already. Fancy coming all the way up to the Hohe Warte, and on such an afternoon as this! There's no help for it – you shall have to stay for dinner. We're having *Paprikahändl*.'

'You are too kind, dear Frau Möll. To tell you the truth, I've never cared much for *Paprikahändl* ...' He corrected himself abruptly. 'But I'm sure that yours will be a revelation.'

Mutti laughed the coy laugh which always embarrassed and infuriated Alma-Maria.

'Then you'll stay, Herr Director.'

'I shall have to telephone my sister, Justine, to tell her I won't be home for dinner,' said Mahler.

'Oh dear!' Mutti exclaimed. 'And our telephone is out of order. Snow on the lines, you know.'

'There's a telephone at the inn down in Döbling,' Alma-Maria suggested.

Suddenly it occurred to her that Mutti had been allowing Mahler an opportunity to take his leave.

'Very well,' Mahler replied. 'I shall have to walk down to Döbling.' He glanced at Alma-Maria. She did not hesitate. 'I shall keep you company, Herr Director. I know the quickest way to the inn ... Not that I go there, you understand.'

'I should think not!' said Mutti, amidst laughter.

Their feet crunched into the impacted snow between the park benches as they made their way down the hill. The street lamps cast multicoloured shadows across the snow; above them bare branches formed weird skeletal arches against a sky dimly lit by the lights of the city which spread all about the foot of the Hohe Warte. The air was bitter: even through her furs, Alma-Maria felt the cold.

Mahler's bootlaces kept coming unfastened. He had to stop to tie them several times, apologizing as he did so. Each time, he would choose the least practical foot-rest – the arm of a park bench, always a little too high, or the pedestal of a balustrade which was both too low and too narrow for practical use. Finally, when she had become thoroughly impatient and chilled by their stopping in mid-path, she sat down on the nearest bench and made him place his foot in her lap, between her knees while she secured his laces in a double bow.

'There!' she said.

He was holding his head turned from her so that she shouldn't see how embarrassed he was. He mumbled his thanks, and they completed their journey to the inn uninterrupted, but in silence.

The innkeeper's wife recognized the Herr Director – 'from the news-papers, Your Excellency'. She stood a little apart as Mahler, now tho-roughly embarrassed, fumbled through his pockets trying to find a sheet of paper which would remind him of his own telephone number. In the end, he had to ring the Court Opera to ask his secretary for his own home number.

When he had talked to his sister, he replaced the receiver on its cradle, took out a handkerchief and wiped the palms of his hands.

'Oh dear!' he said. He dabbed at his face, then removed his spectacles and wiped the lenses. 'Do you know?' he went on. 'In the nine years my sister Justine has kept house for me, I have never done such a thing.'

'What, Herr Mahler?' asked Alma-Maria. 'Never told your sister you weren't coming home for dinner?'

'Not by telephone.'

He fumbled in his purse and gave some coins to the innkeeper's wife. Alma-Maria could see by the way the woman smiled flirtatiously and curtsied that he had given her too much.

'I'm afraid she won't understand,' he said.

'You didn't offer her any explanation so that she could understand,' she told him.

He shrugged. 'It wouldn't have made any difference,' he replied.

She took his arm as they stepped out into the lamplit snow once more.

'You need looking after,' she said. 'Not even knowing your own telephone number!'

'You mean, I need telling off. That's what you really mean!'

'Just a little bit, perhaps. I don't suppose a man in your position gets told off very often – except by the critics, of course.'

'Oh yes! By the critics, of course!' He laughed.

They climbed back up the hill, clutching firmly onto one another's arm to prevent them from slipping on the frozen surface of the snow. Above them, the lights of the villas at the top of the hill twinkled through the branches. They were two-thirds of the way up, when he said,

'Beethoven was right. Beethoven loved – but he would not marry. He knew that it wouldn't be easy for a woman to marry a man like him. He knew that he had to be entirely free of that sort of responsibility.'

Alma-Maria had always understood that the reason why Beethoven never married was because of an unfortunate tendency to fall in love with women far above his station.

'I too cannot allow myself to be bound by material responsibilities,' he went on.

Was he really telling her that he would not be able to marry her?

'Do you often compare yourself to Beethoven, Herr Mahler?' she asked.

'No. No, of course not,' he said hastily. 'Only in the one respect, that is. Beethoven never had the responsibility for the Opera placed upon him. You know, my dear ...' He stopped in his tracks and turned to her. 'I could lose my place at the Opera and with the Philharmonic at any moment. They are virtually my entire livelihood.'

She looked up at him with great seriousness, accepting the challenge she believed was there.

'Have you never considered, Herr Mahler ... I hope you won't think me very impertinent ... Have you never thought of the possibility of someone binding themselves to material responsibilities on your behalf? Wouldn't that be a way of keeping yourself free?'

He reached for her and drew her into his arms. As he kissed her, she parted her lips against his. His spectacles fell forward onto her face.

'Do you always kiss so dogmatically, Herr Mahler?' she asked him softly, as he replaced his glasses on his nose.

He put his arms round her again.

'Almschi. That's what they call you, isn't it? Almschi! Almschi! Almschi!'

Back inside the Villa Möll, they went straight upstairs to the music room without disturbing anyone. Mahler did not even remove his scarf and coat until Alma-Maria had closed the door.

'What will your mother say?' He looked at her quite anxiously. She warmed her hands at the stove, smiling back at him over her shoulder. He was wiping his glasses again and blinking myopically. 'May I address you as Almschi?' he asked.

She nodded, then said "Yes" in case he still couldn't see.

'I will take you into my confidence, my dear Almschi, and you must treat me with kindness. You have made me feel as if I have returned to my adolescence. I daydream about you when I should be working. I wake up at night picturing you. Every day, I want to send you verses. When I'm on the podium, I imagine that you are in the audience – I imagine I'm conducting for you, only for you.'

She reached out her arms to him, to reassure him. She was not entirely sure she enjoyed physically the act of being kissed by him: there was a sour smell about him, the sort of neglectful smell she could associate with bachelordom. But his need for her – the need of the forty-year-old Director of the Imperial-Royal Court Opera, the Principal Conductor of the Vienna Philharmonic, for her love – cried out to her. She was adult enough, surely, to know that she could not expect love with him to be of the same quality as love with Klimt, or even with Alex.

'Promise you'll think about it very carefully, Almschi. That must be your first act of kindness. If you think you would find disappointment in me, you must say so immediately. Today or tomorrow I could get over it, even if I'd find it hard to take. In four months' time, let us say ... I couldn't bear to think of it.'

Very shortly, they would have to go downstairs, to a dinner of Mutti's *Paprikahändl*. Already they were addressing one another as *du*; it was as good as a public proclamation of their engagement. She scarcely understood her own feelings. Did she feel for him as a woman for a man should? Or was it just for the man-boy who couldn't tie his bootlaces properly, who didn't know his own telephone number, who was made nervous by the possessiveness of his own sister? Supposing he wasn't the Director of the Court Opera, the world-famous conductor, the acclaimed composer?

But then, he wouldn't be the same person at all, would he? One could spend a lifetime agonizing over such things.

' "Wilt thou, my heart" ... Those lines you sang to me before we went out,' she said. 'They reminded me so much – so very much – of *The Magic Flute*.

> There's nothing more noble than woman and man –
> Seeking together the presence of God ...'

'You understood that!' he exclaimed, beaming with pleasure.

He stared down into her face. Then he went all solemn; he was blinking as if he might be about to weep. She too felt as if she might melt in his embrace.

'I believe our souls have touched,' he told her.

She nodded.

He turned his eyes from her as if afraid to let her see his emotion.

'I never believed anything like this could happen to me,' he said.

She pressed herself against him.

'My Mahler!' she whispered.

The following morning – it was Sunday, and she was hardly out of bed – a messenger arrived from the Court Opera bearing a large, heart-shaped box containing almond *Kugler*. A handwritten note had been slipped under the ribbon:

> You gave me such joy yesterday. You listened to my foolishness and answered me with wisdom. How short the afternoon seemed, the evening, a mere coda, so I felt a great sadness as I drove back to the Auenbruggegasse. Tomorrow I have to go to Berlin – to the Palace Hotel. I shall be there for the next ten days; I am conducting three concerts, including a performance of my own Fourth Symphony. But tonight at the Opera, I shall give *The Magic Flute* for you – entirely for you. You shall be my inspiration through every bar. Every moment of Pamina and Tamino's pilgrimage will express the truth of my love for you. Mozart understood that truth supremely – how only through the trials of love one learns to know one's own soul. Do you think that you too might learn, through a love for me? Is that possible? To me, you seem to grow in wisdom and understanding every time we meet!
>
> Adieu for now, my teacher, my comrade, my dear and only Alma . . .

She went down to breakfast and sat at the table. Holding the letter between her fingers, she said, 'Muttichen, I want to go to the Opera this evening.'

'Not tonight, *liebchen*. That's quite impossible. Herr Gropius is coming to dinner.'

'I want to go to the Opera just the same.'

'The only reason Herr Gropius is coming is to see you.'

'That's not my fault, Muttichen. I've no particular wish to see him.'

'Alma-Maria my dear, I think you are in danger of making a great mistake – of giving Herr Mahler the idea that you can't keep away from him. Herr Gropius is a handsome young man with a most promising future – that's what Uncle Carl says, at any rate. He would make a much more suitable companion for a girl like you than a middle-aged . . . well – cripple.'

'I thought you were going to say "Jew", Mutti.'

'That too. It's quite one thing to admit Jews into one's house or acquaintance – in Vienna, one can hardly live in the world of the arts without doing so. But to admit one into one's family, that's something entirely different. They really are not the same as us, you know. At least, that's what Uncle Carl thinks, and he should know better than you about such things. In any case, who is there to go with you. Somebody has to entertain poor Herr Gropius.'

'I shall go and ask Frau Zuckerkandl to take me,' Alma-Maria announced.

Mutti sighed heavily.

'My dear, what a delightful surprise! And such a splendid excuse to hear *The Magic Flute* once more. Particularly since Emil is in The Hague attending some boring medical congress or other. I positively refused to accompany him this time – The Hague is such a tedious place any-way . . .!'

They dressed for the evening in Berta Zuckerkandl's bedroom, with her little maid, Antoinette, in attendance.

'You are so beautiful, my darling, especially by candlelight – the way it glows through your hair. I do understand your poor mother's anxiety, certainly if she's afraid you might marry a Jew.'

Alma-Maria was shocked; it was as if Frau Zuckerkandl intended to use the opportunity of intimacy between them to take Mutti's side.

'I didn't expect you to say anything like that,' she said. She sounded almost sulky.

'Why not?' Berta asked. 'I ought to understand these things – better than most, I should think . . . 'Toinette, you may leave us. I shall help Fräulein Schindler to finish dressing.'

The maid looked at her mistress, her small, sallow face and dark eyes expressionless. She curtsied slightly, and left.

'She too is Jewish,' said Berta Zuckerkandl. 'From Rumania – the poorest of the poor. Her father disowned her for loving a Rumanian boy: not that it made a great deal of difference to her materially. I doubt if the family could have provided her with an adequate dowry.'

'I've noticed the way she looks at you,' Alma-Maria remarked.

'Oh yes. Dog-like gratitude. I took her in. I named her; her real name is Anya. A new name seemed appropriate when she was starting on a new life. There can't be anything more wretched than a *shtetl* Jew or Jewess who has been cast out by their family. They have no community, nothing they can relate to, scarcely a notion left of who they are.'

'She is so obviously fond of you.'

'Quite so. I am her entire world.'

'There's nothing like that about Mahler,' said Alma-Maria.

'No. He is not a child of the *shtetl*. His problem is quite different.'

'His problem?'

'It happens often that one boy from a large family – you know, of the small tradesman class – will be selected and set apart from his brothers and sisters to be educated to take his place in the professional class. The rest of the family sacrifice themselves – or are sacrificed – to give him his chance in life. So you can see what happens, can't you?

All their hopes, dreams, and aspirations are centred on that one poor boy.'

'And that was what happened to Mahler?' asked Alma-Maria.

Berta Zuckerkandl nodded. 'It's just as much of an exile as being disowned by your family, in a way. Just think: what has Mahler got in common with a family of the smallest of small shopkeepers in a place like Iglau? I imagine great success like Mahler's only makes matters worse. You can see for yourself what an uncomfortable creature he is socially. Even in the company of musicians, he's nervous and suspicious. He sometimes seems as if he sets out to create an atmosphere of hostility around him.' She took Alma-Maria by the hand. 'I think what I'm trying to tell you, darling, is that if you take up with Gustav Mahler, there's no question of any half-measure of love. You'll have to create a world about him just as surely as I've become my little 'Toinette's world.'

'But Mahler's a great man!' Alma-Maria exclaimed.

'Certainly Mahler is unique. He may not be the world's greatest composer − only time will tell. He is probably the world's greatest conductor, certainly of opera. But if you marry him, it won't be the world's greatest conductor of opera, or of anything else, you'll be marrying, but a very lonely, insecure man.'

Alma-Maria took her hand from Berta's. She sat down on the stool at the foot of the big double bed.

'I don't know,' she said. 'I'm not sure I'm in love with him in the way I've been in love before. I'm not even sure I believe in him as a composer. I don't know what's going on inside my head . . . In any case, how can you separate a man like Mahler from the musician? He's made of music.'

The lonely, tormented hero pursuing his Destiny, she thought, who has renounced his familiar world in the quest for the realization of his vision.

'I'll tell you one thing which worries me,' she went on. 'It's whether he will encourage *me* in *my* work. Will he love my music for itself like Alex von Zemlinsky does?'

Berta shook her head, smiling.

'You have to make your choice, I think,' she said.

'Oh, I've made my choice,' Alma-Maria replied.

But, in fact, there had been no choice to make, any more than there had been for Gretchen in the summerhouse; any more than there was for a would-be postulant nun called to the seclusion of the cloister.

Destiny: it was her sense that Destiny was leading her, that she was in the hands of a Higher Power, which filled her with a wonderful calmness as she went with Berta to the Court Opera. There were glances as they passed through the foyer, a glinting of jewelled buttons and earrings as heads were turned in their direction; she glimpsed rather than heard the whispering of the curious and was left quite impervious to it. When Mahler mounted the podium, the applause was warmer and more welcoming than usual. He glanced across the front stalls, and then directly into the Zuckerkandl's *loge*. Despite the distance, Alma-Maria was quite certain she had seen a look of wonderful tenderness in his face as he saw that she was present. It was as if a thread was suddenly spun between them invisible to all but themselves. Knowing the number of pairs of opera glasses which would be on her at that moment, she did not dare to signal to him.

She sat motionless through the performance. She felt that, for the first time, she understood that it was indeed a heaven-sent work, and that Mahler's incisive interpretation revealed in all its grandeur and beauty its celebration of the redemptive power of human love. With the final defeat of the Queen of the Night and the elevation of Pamina and Tamino to the realms of Light, she knew what it was to be ravished by loveliness.

She did not try to speak with Mahler before leaving the Opera; she hardly wanted to speak with anybody. But after they had got into their carriage, she saw, across the concourse, the figure of Mahler in the lamplight, his wide-brimmed velvet hat crammed down on his head, his tweed cape, caught by the wind, flapping about his arms, hurrying across to a waiting motor car. He was clutching a bulging, battered music portfolio. With him was a dumpy little woman in a hat with a dead bird, its wings spread on the veiled brim on either side of her head. She was scuttling along behind him. Alma-Maria had no doubt that it was his sister, Justine. She did not look in the least like the terrible dragon she had imagined; if anything she looked nervous, in need of protection rather than over-protective. On the other hand, her presence made Mahler himself look *petit-bourgeois* – a village schoolmaster, perhaps. Alma-Maria just caught a glimpse of porters placing suitcases into the motor car before losing sight of it as their own carriage swung out onto the Ring. She would accompany him, her looks would complement his golden intelligence into a single presence. With her love, he would gain the physical stature he presently lacked.

'Have you considered the possibility that Mahler is seeking a replacement housekeeper?' Berta asked.

Alma-Maria felt rather than saw the smile on the small, bird-like face buried in the shadow of Berta's huge fur collar.

'A *replacement* housekeeper?' Alma-Maria asked.

'Justine Mahler is to marry Alfred Rosé in March. Hadn't you heard?' Alfred Rosé was the leader of the Vienna Philharmonic.

Alma-Maria shook her head. She wondered if she should feel angry: as if Mahler has been trawling for somebody to take his sister's place. Instead she experienced a wonderful sense of relief – even of elation.

She was restless that night. She sat up in bed, clutching his framed photograph to her. Once she opened her nightgown to place his face against her naked breasts, but the glass was cold and she felt ridiculous, so she put it back on the bedside table, buttoned up her front once more and stared at the photograph instead. The more she stared, the more wonderfully strong and intelligent it looked. There was no hint of the cringing anxiety to please, the vulpine acquisitiveness, the smug self-conceit which marred the features of so many Jews. But then, as some-body had once remarked to her, however the Jews preferred not to admit it, even to themselves, there had been so much interbreeding with gentiles down the ages that in many such distinctive racial characteristics had become concealed if not actually bred out.

She whispered aloud, 'I love you! I *know* I love you!'

The clock over the parish church down in Döbling struck three as she turned out her light and settled down to sleep.

'Herr Gropius was disappointed – grievously disappointed – to find you weren't here.'

'Grievously disappointed, Mutti?' Alma-Maria mistrusted Mutti's occasional moments of theatricality. 'What did he say?'

'He didn't *say* anything. He's far too good mannered. It was written all over his face . . . You don't have to look at me like that, Alma-Maria.'

'Like what?'

'Like you think I'm making a fuss about nothing. You may live to regret it, my girl. There's one string to your bow you've snapped, I'm sure of that!' She paused. When Alma-Maria didn't say anything, she continued of her own accord, 'I do know what I'm talking about. There have been times in my younger days when I turned away an admirer. And you have a bad habit of encouraging gentlemen to suppose you like them a great deal more than you really do. If you are blessed with looks, there are certain responsibilities to be accepted with them.'

'What on earth makes you think I ever considered Herr Gropius a "string to my bow", as you put it?'

'You've allowed him to escort you – to the Opera, for instance.'

'Only in your company, Müttichen.'

But she had snapped one string to her bow; the thought of having to explain to Alex how far things had gone, when she remembered his look of unhappiness the last time they had been alone together, was something she wished she could set aside.

Mutti held out to her a letter which she had opened.

'This one is addressed to me,' she told Alma-Maria. 'But you may read it. There is one for you by your cup.'

There was an envelope half concealed under her coffee cup. She took Mutti's letter and looked at it. It was a brief note in which Mahler expressed his regret to the dear and well-born Frau Möll at having to tear himself away for two weeks from Vienna, and 'from a family with whom I've already come to feel so close and so at home'.

'Do you see what I mean, *liebchen*? Herr Mahler wouldn't write like that unless you'd offered him a great deal of encouragement.'

'But, Muttichen, it was you who insisted he stayed for dinner,' Alma-Maria pointed out as she handed back the letter.

'Only because you'd made it impossible for me to do otherwise.'

There was no point in arguing, Alma-Maria decided. Mutti had seemed more than welcoming at the time. No doubt Möll had been having a few words with her.

She finished her coffee and brioche, and picked up her own envelope, slipping it into her wrap pocket unopened. She went upstairs and sat at the piano. She even played through the opening movement of Haydn's C-minor Piano Sonata before removing the letter from her pocket. When finally she could defer the pleasure no longer, she read, in Mahler's neat, precise handwriting,

Please don't go to any trouble writing to me – just put down the first things that come into your head. Everything you tell me about yourself is adorable and precious to me, even the most insignificant things. Always imagine, if ever you write to me, that I'm sitting beside you and that you're chatting about anything, everything, under the sun. You see? I want to know all about your life *in detail*. Except – just one thing, my Alma: please do write legibly!

I've told Justi everything – there was no avoiding it. The other day, we were out strolling on the Ring together when we met your stepfather. Justi remarked afterwards, 'What a charming fellow he is, that Herr Möll!' and I said without thinking, I'm afraid, 'Yes, indeed, but wait until you meet her mother!' That let the cat out of the bag, of course. And then when I stayed away for dinner, and told her I had been up at the Villa Möll, she realized the truth. Now that she understands everything, you'll find she'll be a good friend to us.

It's too cruel I have to be away just at this time. I'm so unhappy about it, and yet it's almost as if the voice of God is calling out, 'Be brave, be forebearing, be patient above all!' There's so much noise, so much busyness going on around me here, I can't write about really important things. But there's one voice louder than any other, and I know now that it will never be stilled in my heart. It's a voice which only utters one sentence – I love you, my Almschi . . .!

She folded the letter carefully, replaced it in its envelope and put it back in her pocket. She would continue practising at the piano for an hour, maybe two, before she allowed herself to read it again.

That afternoon, she walked in the park watching the winter sunlight across the snow, and the purple shadows lengthening. She wished Pappi could have met Mahler: surely they would have adored one another. She had never felt so happy in her life; she only wished she could have told

Pappi how happy she felt. Perhaps she could. Perhaps the simple peasant religion was true and all the saints, great and humble – and surely Pappi was a saint if there were such things – could hear what those who loved them offered them in prayer. She just wished it didn't seem silly, praying to Pappi. Perhaps there was a season in people's lives for silliness.

She had to summon all the moral courage at her command to go to Alex in his studio. She knew that she had to go to him: that to expect him to come to her would be to suggest she needed the security of her own home. She stood in his doorway, hesitating like a guilty child. The raucous voices of children at play echoed round the open galleries.

'You got my letter?' she asked.

'Yes . . . Come in, Almschi. You're blocking out the light.'

That was his first gift to her, the use of her familiar name.

'I haven't stopped loving you, you know,' she told him.

He reached out to take her music case.

'I didn't imagine you had come to hate me . . . so quickly,' he said.

He put her case on the piano and sat down, motioning her to sit down beside him.

'Mahler has won me,' she said.

'There can only be one person like that in anybody's life,' he replied. 'At any one time. Otherwise things tend to become very untidy.'

'Alex!' she protested.

She began to cry. She hadn't intended to – it seemed too much like a defensive weapon. She struggled to find her handkerchief in her purse. He handed her his own. It was clean. She dabbed her eyes.

'I knew it would happen, in my heart,' he said. 'I knew that Alma would be satisfied with nothing less than the greatest musician of our age. A hundred years ago, and I would have had to have given you up to Beethoven. Worse things could have happened: eighteen hundred years ago, I might have had to have surrendered you to Nero.'

'Oh Alex! Don't be ridiculous.'

'Some people would say Mahler is half Beethoven, half Caesar – over the realms of music at least.'

'It's funny, Mahler himself says if I'd met Beethoven or Wagner, I'd have worshipped at their feet . . . But I much prefer your music to his.'

'Do you really, Almschi?'

There was a hint of irony in his voice.

'I wouldn't say it if it wasn't true,' she told him.

'Then your instincts are more highly tuned than your ear.'

'At least I don't hero-worship him like you and Schoenberg and everybody else seems to do! Not for his music, at any rate.'

'Alma-Maria Schindler, if you were living at the time of Jesus Christ, you would have wanted to be the Magdalen. I'm quite certain.' He gently reclaimed his handkerchief. 'You might not have regarded the parables

213

highly as literature. You'd have told everybody there were better stories, in your opinion, in the Book of Daniel. But I bet you'd have knelt and dried his feet with that magnificent hair of yours, just the same.'

'You think I'm by nature a handmaid?' she asked.

'To those whom you regard worthy of your service. It is, after all,' he continued, 'an easy way of recognizing one's position on life's map. I expect the Magdalen felt safer at Jesus's feet than on the noisy, busy streets of Nazareth or wherever she lived.'

It was then she noticed the thread of his bitterness, well concealed though it had been. She began to cry again, and reached for his hand.

'Please, oh please, stay my friend, Alex!' she said.

Palace Hotel
Berlin
17 December 1901

My dearest Almschi! (that is how you spell it, isn't it?)

I'm writing to you, my beloved Alma, with rather a heavy heart. I'm afraid of hurting you and yet I can't think of what else I can do. I have to tell you the feelings aroused in me by your letter which I received this morning, because I'm sure they are absolutely basic to our relationship.

Admittedly I'm reading between the lines (I have to tell you it is only with the greatest difficulty that I manage to read the actual lines – and do you have to use purple ink on azure paper?). There does seem to me to be a glaring contradiction between this letter and so many of your assertions to me, 'I want to become the sort of person you *wish* and *need*!' etc.

You tell me about your chat with Burckhard. I wonder how he knows that your personality and mine could never be happy together. Does he have a personality himself which enables him to recognize one in somebody else? You don't develop a personality simply by *wanting* to have one. A personality – yours, my darling Almschi, theirs, anybody else's – grows by what the spirit feeds on, and everything you absorb is a form of nourishment to the spirit: it can *form* it, but it can also *deform* it. You – adorable, infinitely adorable, and enchanting young girl that you are – are as yet unformed, unspoken, spiritually undeveloped. Your entire youth, and therefore your entire life, has been constantly impeded in its true growth, escorted, directed (even when you thought you were most independent) by those highly confused companions of yours who spend their entire lives groping about in the dark and following false trails. I'm referring more to Burckhard and others than to Zemlinsky who is, I know, a good, humble fellow, for all he's confused and insecure. People like Burckhard – camp-followers of the Arts, we may call them – constantly seek you out because you are beautiful and enormously attractive to men. On account of your extraordinary physical charm, they seek to keep you in their company by permitting you to argue with them, and because of your inexperience, you are a most comfortable because unthreatening antagonist. Just suppose, for a moment, you were a very plain girl. How much interest do you think they would take in you then?

In their eagerness to flatter you, to keep you by them, they have deliberately fed your single abiding obsession. And what is that obsession which has fixed itself so firmly in that head I love so indescribably dearly – that obsession without which you are convinced you would no longer be yourself?

This obsession – *forgive me, but this has to be discussed*! – is with what you describe as 'your' and 'my own' music. So I have in a sense to set *my* compositions against yours and to defend them against you who scarcely know them and certainly don't understand them. Would it not be possible from now on for *you* to regard *my* music as *yours*?

Let me put it this way: how do you picture the married life of a husband and wife who are both composers? Have you the remotest idea how ridiculous and, in time, how degrading for both of us such a ludicrously competitive relationship would inevitably become? What would happen if, just at the time you decided the Muse was upon you – you were called upon to do some housework or provide me with something I needed, since you yourself tell me you wish to relieve me of my troubles and to serve me?

This point *must* be settled between us before we can ever contemplate a union for life. You tell me you are prepared to curb all your desires and passions, as if there were only the one sort of desires and passions – those of the more gross sort. In the same breath, you tell me your conscience is bothering you because you are not working on your lessons for v. Zemlinsky.

Now, I really do have to go out and work in a moment. There are three hundred orchestral players and singers gathering out there to wait for me. It is my profession, as surely as if I were a physician, a lawyer, or even a bricklayer or Donau bargee. And if you marry me, Alma, you too will have a profession – *to make your husband happy*! Please don't misunderstand me; don't imagine for one moment that I hold a 'Doll's House' view of our future relationship. I'm never going to regard you as my plaything-squirrel who is also, coincidentally as it were, my housekeeper. Would you really suspect that of me? *I realize very well that you must be happy if you are going to make me happy*! But if we are to be husband and wife, then the worker's role falls to me – in this case, one of composer as much as opera director. Your role is that of the loving companion and partner in my work.

The question you must ask yourself clearly and honestly is, will you be satisfied with such a role?

What a terrible moment I'm causing you! I do know that, Alma. But you must appreciate that I myself am suffering while I await your reply – though I know that must be poor consolation for you. God bless you, my dearest, my love, whatever you decide to tell me. I won't write tomorrow but will wait for your reply when I return to Vienna. I'll send one of the servants to fetch it when I get back, so please do have it ready.

A thousand loving kisses, my Almschi. Be truthful to yourself when you write.

Your Gustav

She let Mutti read it, while she herself sat on the sofa, her tear-smeared face turned to the wall. She stared at the carpet hanging, seeing every close-worked warp and weft of the loom. Her anger and misery had been uncontainable: she had had to share it with somebody – and there was only Mutti.

She had never been swollen-headed about her music. She had always known in her heart that her compositions were accomplished without having that originality, that spiritual purity, which might lead to greatness. But that he should tell her to choose between her music and him – it was the last thing she could ever have expected, and from him of all people! Give up her music? Music was the only thing she had lived for up to now; it was her entire life. Poor darling Alex would have understood that. Perhaps she should go to Alex, throw herself at his feet, and tell him she had made the most ghastly mistake and that she wanted to be his for ever.

'But I love him!' she cried out.

She hadn't meant to, not to say it aloud, at any rate. It had been her reply to questions sounding in her head.

Mutti sat on the sofa at her side, and rested her hand on her shoulder.

'Mahler?' she asked.

'Who else?' Alma-Maria replied, sounding more bad-tempered than distressed.

But tears poured down her face, dribbling onto her breasts. She sobbed so violently her ribs began to ache. Through the turmoil she noticed that her bosom really did heave, which was interesting.

'I feel he's tearing out my heart,' she wailed into Mutti's consoling, mimosa-scented arm.

'It's a very self-centred letter,' Mutti remarked.

'He could have put it to me more gently – what he wants of a wife.'

'It shows exactly how he regards you, *liebchen*. I know you've never accepted Uncle Carl in your Pappi's place – but I can tell you this: he'd never have dreamed of treating me the way Herr Mahler is treating you.

Carl has always been the most considerate of men.'

That part of Alma-Maria's brain which was regarding and noting what was happening told her that it was an impertinence on Mutti's part to compare Möll's commercial attitude to art with Mahler's driving genius.

'*Liebchen*,' said Mutti softly, stroking Alma-Maria's head. 'It isn't too late, you know – to have second thoughts, I mean. Why! Herr Mahler even suggests the possibility of your refusing his ... his *terms*. And you have only known each other for a few weeks.' She went on soothing Alma-Maria's brow. When Alma-Maria said nothing in reply, she pressed on. 'Perhaps you ought to break with him while he's away. It would make it so much easier – for both of you. And it would be better now than later ... I'll tell you what – will you allow me to talk about the letter with Uncle Carl?'

Alma-Maria nodded helplessly.

Möll spoke to her as they were leaving the dining room after dinner. It was Saturday night. There had been a cold buffet; the maids always left a cold buffet on Saturday night, before they went out for the evening.

'Almschi? Your dear Mutti showed me Mahler's letter. Shall we have a little chat about it?'

He had put on weight and gravitas simultaneously; both had come with his assumption of leadership over the Sezession.

He led her through into his study and motioned her to sit down. He stood behind his desk. Mahler's letter lay on the blotter.

'Very Hebraic,' he observed. 'I imagine it is the result of our Jewish friends' unfortunate history as much as the old notion of their being the Chosen Race which makes them so insensitive to the well-being of any but themselves. I'm sure, my dear, you have been attracted by the sheer brilliance of the man, particularly since it shines over a sphere which you regard as peculiarly your own. He is a brilliant musician, there's no denying it – by far the best Court Opera director there has been in my time ... or anybody else's, I suspect. But when it's a matter of personal relationships, he can be as grasping as any of his tribe. So from now on you are to regard *his* music as yours, and have none of your own, eh?

'But ethnicity apart, I think you might also consider this: even if he were a purebred Austrian Christian, his demands on you might prove more than you would wish to accept. By all accounts, his health is not of the best. He is also deeply in debt – he couldn't possibly afford, even with the income your father settled on you, the sort of household which could make the burden of looking after an invalid an easy one. It may be true he wouldn't regard you as a plaything who is also his housekeeper. But he might have to regard you as a housekeeper – and a frugal one, at that – who is also his nurse.

'You see? You do have to regard your future most carefully. You have to be quite sure what you might be letting yourself in for. And if I might go back to the question of race: any physician who isn't a Jew himself – and there are one or two left! – will tell you that Jews make the worst patients. They tend to make a great deal of fuss if they imagine they aren't being paid enough attention – hysterical at times. And they invariably imagine the worst about their own condition ...

'Almschi, will you give me your word that you'll think seriously about what I've been saying? So that I can tell your Muttichen ...'

She whispered, 'Yes,' and took back Mahler's letter from him.

'There's a good girl,' he told her. 'Do you know? I believe we are becoming friends at last.'

She took the letter up to her bedroom. She felt sleepy – the effect of expending so much emotion, she decided. She could not find the energy even to undress properly, but got under the quilt still wearing her underwear and stockings. She slept heavily with her bedside lamp still on. But it was not yet morning when she woke up with the light in her eyes. She reached for the letter. In the night stillness, she forced herself to reread it. Strangely, she heard a new tone in it – one of a great longing, a longing for her, which filled her with its own yearning warmth. As she lay back experiencing it, she felt a pleasant excitement which demanded a response from her. How would it be, she wondered, if she were indeed to commit herself wholly to him – to give up everything for him, even her music, an ultimate self-denial? Her longing for him was greater than she could have described; surely she could live for him? In fact, there was nothing else in the world she wanted except to be his, and to bear his child.

Mutti, and all that Möll had said, had made it quite clear. She felt no resentment toward them; they had cleared her mind. Her own music was never going to match that of the least among the great composers, but her knowledge and understanding of music had equipped her marvellously to be the helpmeet to a true composer (so much more so than Mozart's Constanza).

As for her friendships with other men ... Burckhard? Burckhard had flattered her, just as Mahler had described in his letter; her frivolity, her flirtatiousness, had stemmed from that episode in her life; she hadn't been like that before she met him. Klimt? It was when she had been physically close to Mahler that she had fully appreciated the *vulgarity* of the sort of passions Klimt had aroused in her. She was appalled by the thought of how close to disaster that adventure had brought her. In fact, that sense of how close she had been to becoming irrevocably soiled was the true reason why she could not bring herself to speak of it – to anyone, let alone Mahler. And Alex? What of poor, dear Alex? He was the worst of all precisely because he was so dear to her. It was he who had sustained her pride in her work, who had insisted she form an estimation of herself which was dangerously false.

She need only to talk with Mahler to know how vain, frivolous, and vulgar she had become. Unlike the others, he had the power to uplift her; he offered her a beautiful, a sublime vision of the world. He had showed her the way; she must live her life entirely for him, allow herself to be subsumed into him. She was filled with a sense of elation. She wrote in her diary:

> Everything about him is dear and familiar to me, even though we have known each other so short a time; his breath is so pure, I want nothing, nothing, nothing more than to submit to him absolutely ...

The morning of his return to Vienna – she knew he would have taken the night train from Berlin – she set out for 10 Auenbruggergasse in the crisp December sunlight. If Mahler had not yet come from the station, then surely Justine would allow her to wait in their apartment.

She was making her way down the main street of Döbling to the tram stop, when she was accosted by a uniformed messenger. He saluted her.

'The excellent and well-born Fräulein Schindler?' he asked. 'I have a letter for you, from the Herr Court Opera Director Gustav Mahler.'

He held out a light brown manila envelope.

'You recognized me!' Alma-Maria said.

'Of course. The excellent and well-born Fräulein Schindler is well known ... for her beauty.'

Behind his thick black moustache, the man's face leered in what was supposed to be a smile. She took the letter from him.

'I am supposed to receive a letter for the Court Opera Director in return,' the man said.

'I am on my way to Herr Mahler's apartment now,' she told him.

'The Herr Director was good enough to pay for an *Einspänner*.' The messenger pointed to the tavern, where a cab was standing at the kerbside. 'If the excellent Fräulein Schindler will do me the honour of riding with me.'

As they drove down toward the Währingerstrasse, Alma-Maria was unpleasantly aware of the messenger's leg, squeezed against her own, as they sat together on the narrow leather seat. She took her hand out of her muff, breathed on her fingers, then tore open the envelope and took out the letter. She read it despite the lurching and swaying of the light carriage, and the possibility that her companion could read it across her arm.

> My last letter to you has weighed so heavily on my soul these past three days, as I thought of the impression it must make on you. I hope for both our sakes that you read only my love and devotion into it, and appreciated their strength and depth. You have understood, haven't you my darling, how adamantly and implacably truthful I can be when I'm in love? I felt that everything had to be clear between us before we embraced once more – I know that I will never again

have the serenity or self-control to tell you and ask you about ... well, all these things. I have never awaited the reply to a letter of mine with such trepidation, such fear ...!

She got down from the *Einspänner* under the archway on the Auenbruggergasse and ran up the stairs. Before she had even reached the front door, it was opened for her, with Justine holding it, almost concealed behind it. As she ran in, Mahler emerged from the lounge, in his shirtsleeves, his waistcoat unbuttoned, his jacket dangling from his hand, as if she had caught him in the last stages of his dressing; his collar hung open, she noticed, and his necktie was hanging around his neck.

She called a greeting to Justine. There were two maids watching from the end of the passage. She didn't care. She ran straight into Mahler's arms.

'Gustav! Dear Gustl, welcome back!' she cried.

The torn envelope of his letter was sticking out of the muff she was holding in one hand. She heard Justine, behind her, shooing the maids back to their quarters.

Mahler drew her into the lounge. She put her arms round his waist, pressing herself against his shirt front.

'I'll be anything you want, Gustav!' she said. 'I love you so much!'

'I expected my man to bring me back an answer to my letter,' he said.

'He has,' she replied. 'Me.'

He held her tightly.

'I daren't believe this is you,' he said. 'I've thought of little else – except dreaming of a moment like this, and fearing it would never happen.'

'As far as I'm concerned,' she told him, 'you only need to want something to happen, and it will.'

He sat down on the sofa. She started to sit beside him, but changed her mind. Instead, she sat on his lap. They kissed.

'I shall try to be exactly as you wish me to be,' she said. 'I shall try never to be wilful again.'

'Do you believe two people can merge into one another so that they really become one person?' he asked. 'At least as far as the outside world is concerned?'

'Oh yes!' she replied. 'And we're going to prove it.'

She put her arm round his neck and kissed his mouth with her lips open. Her abject surrender of all her hopes and ambitions to his, her commitment to his will, excited her. She let him feel her breasts pressing against his chest. When he tried to put his hand there, she drew back a little and helped him to unbutton her jacket. When he cupped his fingers over her blouse, she whispered, 'Oh, Gustl! They're yours! Yours!'

She took off his spectacles, and kissed each of his eyes. 'Almschi! Oh Almschi!' he groaned as if in pain. He took his hand from her breast. 'I have to go across to the Opera,' he said. 'I have a band rehearsal.'

She pressed herself against him again.

'Can't Dr Walter take it?' she asked.

'It's the new production of *Tannhäuser* – for St Stephen's Night. The first full band rehearsal. Can you imagine the talk if I didn't show up? Particularly since my secretary arranged my schedule weeks ago so that I should be back from Berlin for it.'

This, she decided, was her first test. She got off his knees. Very seriously, she said, 'Of course you must go, darling Gustav.'

She leaned over and kissed his cheek. He started to tie his tie.

'You don't know how I wish I could go, knowing that you would be here when I got back – here as my wife.'

'It will happen,' she replied.

She stroked her fingers round the hollow of his cheek and along his jaw.

'You'll have to shave twice a day,' she said. 'That's my condition for marrying you: that you shave twice a day.'

'Even when I'm not conducting in the evening?'

'Particularly when you're not conducting in the evening.'

He took her hand from his face. Opening it, he kissed her palm.

'I feel so close to you now that I can't imagine how we could be any closer,' he said. Then he added, 'You've forgiven me for writing to you like I did?'

'There was nothing to forgive. You brought me to my senses.'

As she looked into his face, she saw the hollowness of his features, the bright, haggard intensity. She remembered what Möll and others had told her about his health. It frightened her a little.

'I want to give everything of myself, everything, to you, my husband,' she told him. 'I want you to receive me as yours, to instruct me in what you want me to be.'

The wetness in his eyes filled her with happiness. She put her arms round him again so that the warmth spilled from one to another.

When he was ready, she followed him out to the stairs. One of the maids handed him his hat, gloves, stick, and music portfolio. She made a mental note that when they were married, she would do that herself. She watched him go down to the motor car with its radiator hood and its huge headlamps gleaming copper against the snowlight beyond the arch. He climbed into the back seat; he turned and waved a gauntleted hand to where Alma-Maria was standing with Justine.

'That's his one real show of pride,' said Justine, 'driving in that hired motor – always that one – to the Opera, and to the Musikvereingebäude of course. It makes him feel very up to date, I suppose.'

Justine took Alma-Maria back inside. As they sat together in the lounge drinking coffee, Justine looked at her with big, anxious eyes.

'Is it going to happen?' she asked. 'I mean, he's asked me already, when he's only been back an hour or two – he's asked, "Surely it's a crime for me, Autumn, to chain Spring to me like this? There'll only be Winter to look forward to; she'll miss out on Summer altogether" ... He is so uncertain of himself, particularly where you're concerned, Fräulein Alma. It's so surprising in somebody whom everybody seems to think of as a real tyrant.'

'Dear Fräulein Justi,' Alma-Maria assured her, 'you will leave this apartment to join your husband, and I shall move in to join mine. And we shall be sisters, won't we?'

'Do you really believe that?'

'Believe it?' Alma-Maria asked. 'I'll make it a promise!'

Alma-Maria and Mahler became formally engaged just before Christmas. On Christmas Eve, as they decorated the tree standing framed in the drawing room window, she vouchsafed to Mutti,

'I'm never again going to look at another man. I know in my heart I'm giving myself, all that I am, to my husband. I know how foolish I've been in the past, but I'm quite sure of myself now.'

'I hope you are – with all my heart,' Mutti said.

Möll was standing at the open stove, watching them.

'So you've made up your mind, Almschi,' he said. 'It's your life, of course!'

Little Marie came running in, pursued by her nursemaid, Beate. Möll caught her and lifted her up.

'Hey, little one! You're not supposed to come in here till your Muttichen and Almschi have finished decorating and lit the candles.'

So that was the end of the conversation. Not that it would have signified very much: Möll wasn't going to say or do anything to cross Mahler – not, at least, until after the Sezession's Beethoven Festival next May, for which Mahler was arranging and organizing the music.

Mahler came to the Villa Möll to eat with them at their Christmas feast. He brought a large, expensive Dutch-girl doll whose clothes came off, for Marie. He talked to Marie very seriously about things which mattered to her – a facet of his character Alma-Maria had never previously suspected – and won over Mutti absolutely ('little children can always tell, you know').

'I hope poor Fräulein Mahler hasn't been left all on her own for Christmas Day?' Mutti asked.

'I think Justine was very happy for me to leave her,' Mahler replied, and smiled at Alma-Maria who was seated beside him.

Mutti glanced from one to the other, then she too smiled broadly.

'Is that why you wish to marry my daughter, Herr Gustav?' she said archly. 'You think you might need a new housekeeper soon to look after you?'

'All things are possible,' Mahler said.

He did not seem in the least displeased. How unnecessarily, thought Alma-Maria, brother and sister had worried about one another's attitude.

After the meal, she sat with Mahler at the piano in the music room. They played over the first movement of his Fourth Symphony in Behn's reduction for four hands.

'Well? What do you think?' he asked her when they had finished.

'Honestly?' she said.

'Naturally. What use would it be if you, of all people, weren't honest?'

She was affected somewhat by the warmth from the stove and the wine she had drunk at the meal.

'I think Haydn does this sort of thing much better,' she replied.

Mahler looked at her, taken by surprise. He burst out laughing.

'I wish you had said Mozart,' he told her.

'If I'd meant Mozart I would have said Mozart,' she said stiffly. 'There is a joyous quality in Haydn's music which isn't in Mozart's.'

'Then you haven't heard enough Mozart. But I'm glad you recognize the element of joy in my poor effort, even if I don't reach Haydn's sublime heights ... Will you indulge me by playing over the *adagio* section with me? It's not at all the sort of thing Haydn would have done – it's not really in the *Humoreske* vein of the symphony's title.'

He turned the pages until he came to the opening of the third movement.

'*Ruhevoll*,' Alma-Maria read aloud. Spiritual calm.

'Calm, but also a yearning for tranquillity of soul,' Mahler explained.

They played it through to the end of the *allegretto* variation. He touched her fingers to stop her.

'Well?' he asked her.

She would have to sound very perspicacious, she decided.

'I much prefer this. You are speaking with your own voice.'

'You wouldn't compare it to Haydn?'

She shook her head. She wondered if he were laughing at her.

'Did you know you stole a note from me – a sixteenth?'

He turned back a couple of pages and pointed. He played the run, counting as he did so.

'You see?'

She was about to tell him that he wrote too many notes. Then she remembered it was what the Emperor Leopold II had said to Mozart after the first performance of *Die Entführung aus dem Serail*, and thought the better of it.

'I'll make you a present of it,' he told her. 'Of an entire quaver, if you'll accept the gift.'

He took a pencil from his breast pocket and ringed the note. Above it, he wrote neatly, 'For my beloved Alma, to do with as she pleases.'

Alma-Maria put her arm in his.

'I'm very greedy, you know. One quaver only excites my appetite.'

'I would have given you the entire symphony, but it was completed at the engraver's by April last, over six months before we met.'

'For whom did you write it?' she asked.

She was fearful of what the answer might be to what was, she knew, a Bluebeard's Castle question. Calm, yearning, regret, and toward the end, in the fourth variation, something approaching a dead march – until it was broken off abruptly to be replaced by a gentle, happy *pesante* dance which, in its turn, led back to the calm of the movement's opening: she wondered if – and dreaded the possibility – it might have been inspired by his feelings for Anna von Mildenburg. She was aware, as everybody in Vienna was aware, that von Mildenburg had become the dear friend of Hermann Behn. But Behn was nothing more than Mahler's shadow.

'I find it difficult to speak about it,' Mahler admitted, and Alma's heart sank. He stared at the score in front of him. 'But if I don't entrust my deepest feelings to you, where will we be? ... When I was writing the two last movements, I kept seeing my mother's face. She was weeping, but she smiled at me through her tears exactly as she did in life. I kept seeing it as clearly as in a moving picture.'

Alma-Maria's sense of relief came as a surge of happiness.

'My mother died eleven years ago. I was at Budapest then. The telegram arrived telling me she was on the point of death just as I was about to mount the podium to conduct a first performance of *Lohengrin*. The leader had actually taken his seat. There was no way I could refuse to go out in front of the orchestra. The following morning, I tried to find someone to replace me for the evening performance. But there was nobody in Budapest who knew *Lohengrin*. I couldn't expect an entire opera company to lose several days' salary on my account.'

'But you still reproach yourself?' asked Alma-Maria.

It was as if her sense of relief lent her understanding.

'I didn't even arrive for her funeral.' Then he said, 'She never had the life she deserved. My father never showed her the least affection – he fathered children on her when he was drunk, but servant girls were more to his taste. Our servant girls – the cheapest – the sweepings of Iglau. Nine of my brothers and sisters died young. My mother's life was punctuated with following small coffins to the graveside.'

He fell silent for a time. Alma-Maria waited. Finally, he gently played over the chorale *motif* of the final movement.

'My mother,' he said, 'believed that she could cure all human suffering by love. Her own bereavements only made her the more loving to us who were left ... I suppose, in the *adagio* section, I tried to lead my vision of her to the gates of heaven. It's a Jewish mother's notion of heaven, of course: the children come running to greet her, to lead her to ultimate happiness. And the ultimate happiness is somewhere where saints and archangels prepare the meat –

Wine costs not one farthing
In Heaven's cellars,
And angels bake the bread.'

Alma-Maria said nothing at first. Then she told him, 'I'm sorry about what I said, comparing it with Haydn.'

He shrugged his shoulders. 'There's no need to apologize for criticizing honestly.'

She wondered whether there was a slight hint of sarcasm in his voice. She dared not look at him.

There was no awkwardness when they returned downstairs, to the tree.

'I have just presented Almschi with her engagement present,' Mahler announced to Möll, Mutti and little Marie. 'An entire quaver from my Fourth Symphony.

He held open the score.

'Perhaps,' said Möll, beaming as amiably as any paterfamilias, 'I should draw a circle round one of the houses in my painting, "A View of Grinzing in Late Autumn", and make you both a present of it!'

Everybody laughed. Mahler put his arm round Alma-Maria's waist.

'Seriously, Mama ...' He pronounced *Mama* in the English fashion. 'After spending time playing the piano with your daughter, I long for the pleasure of asking you for her hand a second time.'

Mutti laughed again. She embraced and kissed them both. Möll kissed Alma-Maria, and put his arms round Mahler and embraced him. It was as if nobody had expressed the least doubt of Mahler's suitability as a husband.

Nobody ever found out who broke the news to the press, but on 27 December, every morning newspaper carried a report of the engagement of the Director of the Imperial-Royal Court Opera and Principal Conductor of the Vienna Philharmonic Orchestra to the Noble and Well-Born Fräulein Alma-Maria Schindler, the daughter of the late and much lamented Jakob-Emil Schindler – Austria's most distinguished landscape painter – and of Frau Anna Schindler, remembered by all music-lovers as the lovely and greatly admired actress and singer Anna Bergen whose retirement on marriage from the stage and concert platform twenty-two years previously had been such a blow to the Vienna musical theatre. Article after article proclaimed Alma-Maria's youthful beauty and her wonderful musical talents. Much was made of her handful of publicly performed compositions, as if they had been rapturously acclaimed through the German-speaking world.

28 December saw the commencement of a flood of congratulatory letters, telegrams, bouquets. The signatures on many of the communications arriving at the Villa Möll during the days which followed

indicated to Alma-Maria what sort of a world she was about to move into. Not only were they sent by distinguished members of the Viennese musical establishment whom she had met, or of whom she knew, but also from famous instrumentalists all over Europe, and opera singers who had sung under Mahler's direction in Cassel, Laibach, Budapest, Hamburg, London, and Vienna. There were deckle-edged notes from composers who, although they were very much alive, were already half-legend: Rimsky-Korsakov, Saint-Saëns, Puccini, Charpentier and, of course, Richard Strauss.

Mahler telephoned. He was far from happy about the furore. Not only was it an intrusion into their private lives, it was also the most hectic period of the Opera and Concert season. He sent a motor car to fetch her to Auenbruggergasse on the afternoon of the twenty-eighth. The pair of them, with Justine and her fiancé, Alfred Rosé, drank a glass of sweet wine in mutual congratulation and friendship. Mahler and Alma-Maria left Rosé and Justine alone together in the lounge, and went through into the music room.

They sat down at the piano.

'Now we can pretend that nobody knows.' He put his arm round her waist. They kissed. 'There are only you and me – in the limitless space of eternity.'

He leant forward and opened the manuscript book on the music stand.

'Your scores are always so neat and precise,' she said. 'Are you always so tidy?'

'You can read it?' he asked.

'It's quite simple. Is it yours?'

'It's yours. My belated Christmas present to you.'

The piece was marked *adagietto*. Although laid out for two hands, it was already in *spartivi* – its instrumentation, for divided strings and harp indicated.

'I mean to enshrine it in my Fifth Symphony – the other four movements I wrote in my *Hauschen* by the lake at Maiernigg last summer. I don't normally compose here at all – just scribble down ideas, if they ever come to me with all the commotion of the Opera. But the inspiration of your presence: that excluded all other considerations. I couldn't help myself.'

She was already exploring the opening phrase, stretching her hands across the keyboard and gently stroking the notes. She lowered her hands.

'You must play it to me, Gustl,' she said.

Had he known what the effect on her would be at what he had told her? she wondered.

'I don't want to play it for myself,' she added. 'Not the first time. Play it to me.'

She rested her head on his shoulder for a moment. Then she got up and went and sat on the *chaise-longue* in front of his work desk. He began to play – a long, easily identifiable melody of elegiac beauty and quiet. It was difficult to recognize anything of her own spirit in such tranquil, almost sad music – except, of course, her looks, the looks which were (unspoken secret) so foreign to what went on inside her head, but whose impact, she could scarcely help knowing, had such an effect on the men she met.

As he played on, she experienced a sense of quiet anger, though she could not have said whether it was directed at him or at herself. There was so much of his music which she had heard which struck her as post-Wagnerian bombast. Yet there were always these movements of an indescribable loveliness and originality which poor Alex von Zemlinsky could never have begun to aspire to.

He lowered his hands from the keyboard, allowing the final notes to vanish into the limitless space of which he had spoken. He turned about on the stool.

'Third or fourth movement – I haven't made up my mind. The complete work begins with a funeral march and ends with an *allegro giocoso*. With this *adagietto*, the secret of that transformation is revealed – the saving power of human love. Our love; the love you inspire in me.'

He removed his spectacles, took a large red handkerchief from his shirt cuff, and wiped them.

'It is very beautiful,' she said. 'I can't believe you've ever written anything so beautiful.'

'That's because the person who inspired it is so beautiful; more beautiful than anything I could have imagined.'

She rose from the *chaise-longue* and went over to him. Her vision was as blurred as his must have been as she sat against him to embrace and kiss him.

But deeper inside her mind, she was wondering why the movement should have been so sad – why, however calmly, it should have made her think of loss, of bereavement.

The following evening, 29 December, she attended a revival of *The Tales of Hoffmann*. For the first time at the Court Opera, she sat in the Director's Box. The moment she entered unaccompanied and took her seat, she heard the rustling and whispering all round the great gilded horseshoe of the auditorium. The briefest glance across the huge pit told her that she was the cynosure of every lorgnette, opera glass, or naked eye, and that her satin dress, her dressed hair and tiara, her diamanté bracelets, her complexion, every nuance of her facial expression, were being minutely examined. She was tempted to turn and flee precipitously, but she dared not move while the lights were up. She froze into immobility, staring fixedly at the Imperial monogram embroidered on the curtains.

When Mahler mounted the podium and turned to take his first bow, there was a storm, a tidal wave of applause. The audience in the stalls rose to their feet. Mahler bowed his usual stiff little bow. But then, instead of shrugging his impatience at not being permitted to start the performance as he did usually, he clutched at the brass rail and bowed a second and third time. Alma-Maria noticed that his gaunt face was suffused with happiness. He turned his head and looked at her briefly, smiling up at her amidst renewed applause. She managed to smile back at him. Then he turned and rapped the edge of his desk with his baton – several times before the tumult subsided – and the house lights dimmed.

'Please accept my best compliments, Fräulein Schindler.'

Alma-Maria only just heard the low soprano voice from behind her above the singing of the Spirits of Wine from the semi-darkened set of Auerbach's wine cellar on the stage. 'You see, my dear? The whole of Vienna rejoices for you – and so do I.'

Alma-Maria turned. She had not missed the hint of malice in the voice. She recognized the statuesque figure, back-lit by the dim red glow from the antechamber of the box – the thick, curly shoulder-length hair, the strong jaw, the more than generous bosom of Vienna's most famous female singer.

'Anna von Mildenburg,' she introduced herself. 'Gustav and I have been musical associates and, I hope, friends, for a number of years ... May I join you?'

Alma-Maria had risen. She took advantage of the darkness to move to the rear of the box.

'Please sit down, Fräulein,' she said.

She drew the curtain, excluding them from the auditorium.

'I've always been so glad Gustav chose Schöder to sing in *Hoffmann*,' von Mildenburg said in a low, rich voice. 'It needs a younger voice, particularly for Antonia. But it really is rather a trashy work, don't you think?'

Alma-Maria would almost certainly have found herself agreeing had it been anybody else. Instead she felt outraged that von Mildenburg should have entered the box as of right, unannounced, after the curtain had gone up, and have filled the entire space with her overpowering presence; and then have criticized Mahler's choice of production.

'I find it quite a fine work,' she replied.

She felt nervous. Von Mildenburg's eyes were watching her like those of a cat in the semi-dark, hard, bright, unblinking yet with all expression filtered out. Was it true, she wondered, that von Mildenburg had been Mahler's mistress when he had launched her on her international career from Hamburg, and that he had brought her with him to Vienna on that account? It was astonishing that, all those years ago, at the *répétition générale* in the Burgtheater, she should have thought von Mildenburg the ideal Goethean heroine.

'It's true I don't think *Hoffmann* is an opera of the first rank,' she went on. 'But it's both melodious and effectively dramatic.'

She hoped she sounded suitably judicious.

'Then we must agree to differ, my dear.'

Alma-Maria felt the touch of von Mildenburg's glove on her own.

'So you've succeeded where all others have failed,' said von Mildenburg. 'You have persuaded Gustav to abjure the monastic life. I'm very happy for you both.'

Did she really mean it? Monastic? Or was she being ironic – or even kind?

'His friends had really come to believe that he had decided to doom himself to perpetual bachelordom. I wonder if we are about to witness the appearance of a new Gustav Mahler – a sunny, lyrical composer, perhaps of a Mozartian opera!' She laughed an abrupt little laugh. Then she said, 'As you say you enjoy *Hoffmann*, I won't keep you any longer. I'm sure we're going to meet again very soon. I know men often tend to discard their old friends when they get married, but Gustav is a little older than most, isn't he? Perhaps a little more set in his friendships? ... Anyway, my profoundest congratulations, my dear, and *auf Wiedersehen*.'

She got up, drawing the chain of her gilt purse up her sleeve. She embraced Alma-Maria, planting an *eau-de-nil* scented kiss on her cheek.

'You know, I'm sure, I shall be singing for Gustav – *Das Klagende Lied* and the final movement of his Fourth Symphony – at the Musikvereingebäude on the twelfth of January? I shall be dedicating my performance to the pair of you. You'll remember that, won't you, my dear?'

As von Mildenburg stepped down from the box onto the concourse behind it, Alma-Maria returned to her seat, and tried to put the intruder's suffocatingly patronizing behaviour from her mind. It wasn't easy.

At the end of the performance, Mahler himself took ten curtains, bowing awkwardly as if he hadn't spent the past twenty years acknowledging often very appreciative applause. Flowers were thrown – some, both bouquets and single blooms, into the Director's Box. Alma-Maria didn't know whether she was supposed to acknowledge them or not. She pretended she hadn't noticed their arrival. She felt a strong sense of panic.

After he had changed, Mahler with Alfred Rosé took her to Hartmann's Restaurant for dinner. Möll, Justine and Mutti were waiting for them. There was no chance of privacy; as they dined, gentlemen kept coming to the table to congratulate the Herr Director of the Court Opera and to kiss Fräulien Schindler's hand. Any reservations Mutti might have had regarding the forthcoming nuptials were fast melting in the warmth of celebrity; she smiled radiantly on the occasion. Despite interruptions, it was decided that the wedding of Alma-Maria to Mahler, and Justine to Alfred Rosé, should take place on the same day, 9 March, so that Alma-Maria should move into 10 Auenbruggergasse the day

Justine left. Toasts were drunk to seal the arrangement, but Alma-Maria could not help noticing that Mahler scarcely pretended to share in the conviviality.

When dinner was over, Mahler and Alma-Maria walked alone, arm in arm, along the Ring. On either side, the colonnaded public buildings with their statues and pinnacles reared snow-covered into the frosty sky, One one or two carriages drove by them along the wide, deserted boulevard. Alma-Maria told him about von Mildenburg's visit to his box.

'We'll have to make some arrangement for you to meet my friends and colleagues,' he said. 'We can't have them sending spies to inspect you.'

'Is that what she was?' asked Alma-Maria.

'Perhaps. I don't know.'

She noticed his look of unhappiness – his face looked more sallow than usual in the yellow lamplight under his fur hat. She wondered if he was embarrassed, or even guilty.

'You look so pleased when you were accepting your ovation tonight,' she told him. 'Now you look quite miserable. Tell me about it . . . Trust me.'

'When I went back to my dressing room,' he replied, 'she was waiting for me. She said she wanted to return . . . certain letters to me. Then she fainted. Or, rather, she pretended to faint. I'm afraid Anna doesn't draw any great distinction between substance and histrionics.'

'What did you do?' Alma-Maria asked, managing to keep the anxiety out of her voice.

'I splashed cold water onto her face. I forced a thimbleful of slivovitz between her teeth, and showed her to the stage door. The cold air revived her, if she actually needed reviving . . . I can't pretend it wasn't upsetting, I'm afraid.'

'Of course it was upsetting,' Alma-Maria said. 'Particularly since you have been friends for a long time. She congratulated me on succeeding where she had failed.'

'She imagines you . . . to be my mistress. She thinks all women are as she is, except that most are hypocrites.'

Alma-Maria tightened her arm round his.

'Did you love her?' she asked.

'Not in that way. No – whatever the world may say. She has been a good friend in some respects, though. She is a great artist, and a fine interpreter of works of mine. I wouldn't wish to seem ungrateful.'

He stopped walking abruptly, so that she tugged at his arm. They stood at the very edge of a street lamp's glow.

'Almschi,' he said.

'What is it?'

She felt anxiety opening up inside her.

'I must tell you, Almschi ... I have to. I have never loved anybody that way.'

'You mean – slept with anyone?'

She searched his face. He was standing on one leg, then on the other, as he always did when he was disturbed or worried. He wouldn't look directly at her.

'I had to tell you, Almschi.'

'That isn't something to be ashamed of, Gustl.' She laughed. 'It's supposed to be virtuous!'

'It isn't with me. Not now ... Do you understand what I'm telling you?'

'Yes, Gustl.' She took a deep breath of cold air. 'You're afraid that now ... you might not be able ...?'

He nodded.

'My father never had any difficulty!' he said. 'I came on my father once, in the stable behind our factory-distillery.' He shrugged as if he had already made an admission but wished to disregard its significance. 'I used to climb up into the hayloft when I was little, to dream, and to read sometimes ... above the dray horses' stalls. It was warm and safe there. I could see strips of sky between the slates. I was lying there just dreaming, I think. I heard movement below me. I thought it was a horse moving at first, only then I heard whispering. I remember looking between the floorboards and seeing the stall below dark but empty – at least, I thought it was empty ...' He took his cigar-case from his pocket.

'You'll permit me?' he asked. He pinched off the end of a cigar and lit it. She noticed in the flicker of the match flame that his hands were shaking. She waited without moving.

'Yes,' he said. He paused, smoking. Then he continued. 'After a little time I heard groaning – a woman groaning. I was frightened. I was ten years old – just the right age to have to accept responsibility while being terrified of its obligations. Then the crying started. Crying and even screaming.' He grimaced. Like somebody listening to a tale of terror, Alma-Maria was afraid of what she was about to hear yet was enthralled by the story.

'I knew it was my duty to find out what was wrong, and help if I could. But you know what it's like with children: there was always the likelihood of being no use at all – just horrified at what I might find.

'I plucked up all my courage, and dropped down from the loft onto the ground. There was a lantern hanging over the door out to the yard – a paraffin lamp. It was turned down very low. It was too dark to see what was in the stall the crying had come from, so I took down the lantern and turned up the flame. I can recall the smell of the paraffin and the oily gritty touch of the wheel as I tell you about it. There was a woman. She was sitting up in the hay. I remember how thick her legs were, and her torn black stockings, and the white all round her – her underwear, I suppose ... And a leather apron dangling from round her neck – she was one of my father's distillery maids, I imagine. I couldn't see her face at all. But she started shouting at me, filthy, obscene words, in a harsh baritone – I'd never heard a woman's voice sound like that before, corroded, I suppose you could call it. I remember among the obscenities, the ordure she was shouting, that she accused me of spying, and how unjust I thought it was when I'd only come to try to help her. Then I saw my father: he rose like a giant out of the hay. He ordered me to come to him, several times. He had his thick black belt in his hands.

'I turned and ran. They both called after me – not too loudly, but it was terrible ...'

He put the heels of his palms to his ears as if, even now, he had to try to shut out the sound.

'Gustl!' Alma-Maria said softly, but he did not hear, lost as he was in the recurring nightmare.

At last, he said, 'I realize now that, brute though he was, he might well have not meant to hurt me. He might simply have been holding the belt before putting it on. More likely, he intended to swear me to silence about what I'd seen – he might have tried bribery rather than blows for all I know. But I was terrified by everything – the whole wretched scene. The world was gone dark.

'I ran away, out of the yard and up the street. I'd no idea where I was going. I didn't run very far. There was a street organ under the second lamp up from our house. There was a group of ragged children gathered round it – not Jewish children, of course, you wouldn't catch Jewish children out after dark, not even habitual outcasts like me. The organ was playing "O du lieber Augustin" and the children were jogging up and down, sort of dancing to the rhythm ...'

He sang the opening line of the nursery song twice over, softly to himself ... 'You see how one is in the grip of one's own past?'

Alma-Maria waited some minutes before asking the question:

'Did your father use his belt on you?'

'No. Not on that particular occasion. I suppose he was afraid I might have blurted out the cause. So I lay in bed at nights waiting for him to find another pretext for thrashing me ... My father never had difficulties in finding reasons for whipping us. Drink was the real cause on most occasions. On one occasion he beat and kicked my mother so badly he lamed her for life ... Justi was the one he picked on most – even after she had become a woman. Once, when she was nine years old, my brother Ernst found her lying in her bed. She'd stuck candle stubs all round the frame and had lit them. Ernst asked her what she was doing. She told him the candles helped her to pretend she was dead ...'

His voice cracked. He dropped his cigar and buried his face in his hands. Alma-Maria was taken by surprise: he had been talking in a quiet, even voice, almost a monotone. She placed her hands on his shoulders.

'I've never spoken about these things before,' he explained.

'Isn't it just as well you should?' she asked.

'You are so beautiful,' he told her. 'So magnificently beautiful! Why should you want to commit yourself to somebody like me?'

'Gustl!' She couldn't help laughing. 'Don't be absurd! ... Dear Gustl, in the few weeks we have known each other, I've learnt more about myself than in all the rest of my life – that's why. Because there is so much truth about you, my dear, I couldn't bear to be anywhere else or with anybody else.'

'Oh, my dear! ... My dear, I shall thank God for you always.'

> '... If woman's love, also from on high
> Can help you through your sorrow,
> Hallowed legions of the sky ...'

She broke off. Then she said, almost by way of an apology, 'My father thought *Faust* was the most beautiful book – the most precious book – in the world.'

'Your father was a most discriminating man,' Mahler said.

'So I shall be your Gretchen, you see?'

She pressed herself against him the way she remembered Gretchen pressing against Faust in von Kreling's illustration of the summerhouse scene. She offered her mouth to be kissed.

'We'll cause a scandal through the whole of Vienna,' he told her.

But he kissed her as she had wished. She unbuttoned her coat and opened his to enclose herself against him. There was a jingling of harness. Carriage lights wobbled between the trees.

Oh shit! she thought.

There were ribald shouts from the open windows of the carriage; young cavalrymen driving back to the Hofburg. She noticed how Mahler turned his face from the light.

'You see?' She smiled at him, after the carriage was gone. 'I can be wicked enough for both of us. Are you sure you still want to marry me?'

She was entirely confident.

'There is nothing wicked about you, my Almschi,' he said. 'Nothing which you do not consecrate.'

His eyes shone brightly as he looked at her.

'I wish that were true,' she replied. 'For your sake my darling.'

As she was going to bed that night, or morning, for it was four o'clock by the time they got down from Mahler's motor car outside the Villa Möll, she told herself that it had been the most wonderful day ever. The discovery that he had not slept with Anna von Mildenburg, or any of the other women with whom his name had been linked, was its crowning jewel. Any misgivings which still lurked in her mind were well out-weighed by her sense of quiet joy.

233

A week later, Mahler and Justine held a dinner party at 10 Auenbruggergasse with the purpose of introducing Alma-Maria to his oldest friends.

She spent the entire day calculating, worrying over, her appearance, so that had she been making an appearance in the foyers and landings of the Burg or the Court Opera all eyes would have turned in her direction. As it was, Justi came out to the stairs to greet her, and exclaimed, 'Oh Alma! You're so beautiful!' in a tone of voice which suggested not that she was a pleasure to behold, but rather that she should have made an effort to place her good looks under restraint.

Then, just as Mahler was slipping her cape from her bared shoulders, she beheld through the salon door the statuesque figure of von Mildenburg – Mildenburg in an evening gown cut so low that even from that distance, Alma-Maria could see the pink edge of her nipples peeping, where the tiny lace scallop of her basque strained to bursting point against her over-generous bosom.

Knowing that she was wrong to do so, but unable to help herself, she whispered to Mahler, 'You never told me you were inviting Mildenburg!'

'I could scarcely not do so,' he replied quite severely. 'She is a very old acquaintance. Besides which, she is – enjoying? – a relationship with an even older friend, Professor Siegfried Lipiner.'

'I thought it was Hermann Behn,' Alma-Maria said.

Mahler smiled. 'That was last year's fashion . . . Actually Behn is here. So we're all friends together. And we have dear Bruno – Bruno Walter, and one or two others whom I'm sure you've met.'

He escorted her into the salon, with Justine fussing behind them. The men rose to their feet. She recognized Dr Walter and Hermann Behn. There were several she knew quite well – Arnold Rosé, for example, and, because he had been a dinner guest on several occasions up at the Villa Möll, the painter Kolo Moser. In fact, she could have felt herself among friends had the mood of the occasion been right. But Mahler stood at her shoulder blinking proudly at her as if showing off some rare *objet d'art* he had recently acquired, while Justine was too awkward and shy to create any sort of atmosphere save one of anxiety.

There were four persons who were complete strangers to her: the poet-philosopher, Siegfried Lipiner; his ex-wife, Nanna Spiegler with her husband, the scientist Albert Spiegler; and Guido Adler, the distinguished musicologist and physician.

Mildenburg set the tone. In her creamiest voice, she said, 'Fräulein Alma! It should be forbidden absolutely! Your looks and appearance put the rest of us poor women into the shade!'

Lipiner, tall, stooped, white-haired and grey-bearded, kissed her hand and said, '*Mädchen*, may I tell you what a long awaited delight it is to make your acquaintance?'

If there had been any one thing to set her teeth on edge, it was to be addressed as '*Mädchen*' – as if she were some pretty waitress in a tavern garden. It set the tone of ersatz formality which pervaded the entire occasion. Lipiner and his gentlemen friends and admirers – notably Dr Adler – dominated the dinner table, throwing compliments about the food to Justine as they might have thrown scraps of meat to a grateful lapdog. Alma-Maria was painfully conscious of being inspected by a jury comprised of men who regarded themselves as existing on a loftier intellectual plane than any woman could hope to aspire to, least of all an attractive young woman.

The conversation, presumably in honour of Mahler and herself, turned to the subject of human and divine love. Dr Spiegler suggested that the present company could be compared to that which had gathered round Socrates – at this he nodded ingratiatingly in Lipiner's direction – in Plato's *Symposium*. Alma-Maria remained silent for a full fifteen minutes while this subject was pursued, until Professor Lipiner inclined his head in her direction, and said, 'I'm afraid all this theorizing is a little above the head of our *kleine Mädchen*. Socratic discourse is a masculine pursuit and rational philosophy a male element. We are forgetting that we have ladies in our midst, and one who is exceptionally young, charming and beautiful ...'

Bruno Walter caught Alma-Maria's eye. He too had remained silent through the discussion, perhaps because, despite his distinction as Mahler's deputy conductor at the Court Opera, he also was young. Hastily, he intervened.

'I believe Fräulein Schindler to be an exceptionally well-read and well-informed lady. I am sure she is familiar with the arguments of the *Symposium*.'

'Indeed? Now that is an interesting thought,' said Lipiner.

He smiled at the company round the table. Alma-Maria lost her temper.

'I have read Plato's *Symposium*,' she said. 'I was tickled pink by it. All those effeminates sitting round a powdered old sodomite, justifying their homo-erotic antics in high-flown verbiage.'

She saw Kolo Moser's mouth twitching with suppressed amusement. Beside her, Mahler cried out, 'Bravo! Well said!' and clapped his hands. Professor Lipiner and most of the rest looked scandalized. Anna von Mildenburg decided to come to the rescue: 'I think what Fräulein Alma is really telling us is that Professor Lipiner is being most unjust to our sex. Isn't that so, Alma? ... You see, what Professor Lipiner appears to have neglected is that it was a woman – an attractive woman, the Lady Diotima – who provided Socrates with the true definition of love.'

It was the turn of the others to applaud. Alma-Maria realized that von Mildenburg had given the company permission to ignore the statement she herself had made. She lapsed again into sullen silence.

The conversation turned to fine art. Lipiner remarked that he regarded an allegorical study by Guido Reni as his favourite painting. He turned once again to Alma-Maria.

'I'm sure your eminent and respected father, our great Jakob-Emil Schindler, spoke to you about Reni's work?'

'I've seen the painting you described,' she retorted. 'The colouring is certainly good. But it would be a great deal better if it was possible to see what it was supposed to represent.'

Lipiner didn't even pretend to respond politely. He sighed impatiently, drummed his fingers on the table, and said, 'Well!'

Mildenburg again intervened.

'I'm afraid, my dears, we're not making a very good job of finding out where Fräulein Alma's tastes lie. Perhaps she will let us know what she thinks of Gustav's music?'

Alma-Maria took up the challenge in defiance of the laughter round the table.

'I know very little of it,' she said calmly. The laughter ceased. 'And what I know, I'm afraid I don't care for much.'

The silence which greeted this was one of shock. She understood immediately that this time she had gone too far. She put her arm into Mahler's.

'It is Gustl I want to marry,' she said. 'Not his music.'

Mahler said, 'She is a fierce critic – just what every creative artist needs in his home.' He smiled at her. He smiled proudly, not covering for her rudeness but in genuine tenderness so that she wanted to cry.

When they were gone, and Justi was supervising the servants, he closed the music room door and pressed his back against it. She was about to tell him how sorry she was at her own behaviour when he burst out, 'Oh dear God! What a mistake! Such dear friends, yet put them together round a table and they all behave like children showing off to one another. How you must hate them!'

She was astounded.

'Only one or two of them,' she told him. Suddenly, hers was the voice of moderation. 'I think Professor Lipiner is the most sterile intellect I've come across,' she added.

Mahler shook his head.

'I don't understand what he was up to this evening. Almschi! When I first arrived in Vienna, I was scarcely literate except in music. That man taught me all I know of poetry and literature and thought. He's opened my eyes to so many things.'

'Perhaps it's women, then,' she suggested. 'Perhaps it's that he's contemptuous of women ... *Mädchen! Kleine Mädchen!* As if I were some half-idiot skivvy waiting to be seduced by the grand gentleman!'

'I'm sure that was never in his mind.'

'Oh no? Then why does he take it for granted I wouldn't be able to understand Plato? Why should I have to like Guido Reni's work because he does – or even because my father told me about it? Haven't I got an intelligence of my own? ... I'll tell you something: Pappi – "our great Jakob-Emil Schindler" regarded Reni's work as puerile compared to Caravaggio's.'

She realized she had raised her voice. She saw the pained discomfort on Mahler's face.

'Oh Gustl!' she said. 'I never mean to make you unhappy.' She put her arm round his neck. Raising herself on her toes, she kissed him on the forehead just above the bridge of his spectacles. 'I'm sure Professor Lipiner has never talked to you like that,' she told him. 'Because you're a man, you see. A very, very talented man with a great big intellectual forehead which I adore ...'

He was supporting her in his arms so that her toes scarcely touched the floor.

'And because you're a man – because you've proved yourself in the world's eyes – he's never going to talk to you like that. He wouldn't dare!'

'He was trying to be kind ...' Mahler began to explain. But already she was distracting him.

'You're the kindest man in the world, my own darling Gustl,' she said. 'But *you* don't patronize me.'

She pressed her cheek against him, secure in the belief she had said the right things.

Four afternoons later, he called on her at the Villa Möll. Mutti was downstairs: Alma-Maria was sure she would not disturb them. Before the maid came to tell her of his arrival, she had already made sure there were copies of Mozart – beloved Mozart – scattered about the piano, and that the volumes of Haydn Sonatas given her by Alex and signed by him were nowhere in evidence. Mahler brought a score with him, a symphony he would be introducing to the Vienna audiences later in the season. He told her he had prepared the third movement for four hands so that they could play it together. The name on the score was not that of a composer whose music she knew: Vilhelm Stenhammar, Symphony in F.

'A young Swedish composer,' he explained, as they settled down beside one another at the piano.

He made no reference to the events of their last meeting.

'It is very charming. Very accomplished. And to tell the truth, not very demanding, so our Viennese audiences will love it. But I wanted you to see this movement, to find out if you share my admiration of it.'

When they had tried out the lyrical opening melody, she laughed and said, 'It sings. It really sings.'

'It is always enchanting to discover that one is absolved from expressing something in music because another composer – usually Mozart – had already expressed it perfectly.'

'And what does this express?' she asked, though she knew, or hoped she knew, the answer.

'I'm working ... I'm entirely preoccupied ... then suddenly there's your face – your smile, those wonderfully blue eyes, those perfect little teeth, the light in your magnificent hair – quite unsummoned, but there, absolutely clear before me. And there is the most perfect lightening of my spirits ...' He played over the melody once more. 'This expresses it absolutely.'

She looked at him. 'Gustl.'

'What?'

'Nothing – just, Gustl!'

She began to unbutton his shirt front. He looked down over his large floppy bow tie.

'What are you doing?'

'I want to feel your heart,' she explained.

She slipped her hand under his shirt, into his singlet and the warmth beneath.

'It beats strongly. I'm good for you,' she told him.

'It beats for you, Almschi.'

'Oh, I hope so!'

They embraced, and began fondling.

'Music benches weren't made for passion!' she laughed.

They slid down onto the thickly piled rug on the floor.

'Almschili!' he groaned.

He raised himself up. For a moment, she was afraid she had made the most dreadful mistake. But he reached out to a chair, pulled the cushion from it, and placed it under the small of her back. He put his spectacles on the piano bench.

'You'll sit on them later,' she said. 'Just you wait!'

He unbuttoned her shirt and bodice, exposing her breasts.

'Kiss them, Gustl! You kiss them beautifully, my darling!'

She lifted the lower half of her body, dragging up her skirts. She wished it had been his own music she had found so melting. Poor Gustav!

'Oh yes!'

His member was hard. Thank God she didn't wear drawers: unbuttoning could have proved disastrous.

He was over her. She determined not to avoid his breath.

'Don't stop ... feeling my breasts, my darling.'

He had entered her – right inside her.

It wasn't good, but she had never expected it would be – not like with Klimt, or Alex, if it came to that. But that had been animal passion – informed by friendship, of course. This was the Sacred Mystery, holy, set apart. She tried to suppress her shaking as she lay in his arms, to exorcize it by repeating, 'Joy beyond joy! Joy beyond joy!'

She felt she was Sieglinde awakening to the glory of the forest glade. He should have fathered his child upon her at that sanctified moment. That was the supreme hope: the sovereign remedy against all uncertainty.

The last two weeks of January and the first two of February, two months before *Fasching*, were the busiest in the Director of the Court Opera's calendar. Alma-Maria saw little more of Mahler than the moments they could grab together between rehearsals, and before and after the performances she attended. On one such occasion, she was wandering restlessly about the music room of 10 Auenbruggergasse, waiting for Mahler to finish dressing for the evening; he was to conduct one of his particularly favourite works, Schubert's Great C-major Symphony, at the Musikvereinsgebäude. Like a priest vesting for a particularly devotional Mass, he, who hardly knew what he was wearing most of the time, took special pains over his appearance when directing a work he regarded as an object of veneration.

The room was overheated; she let her fur-caped silk cloak slither off her shoulders across the back of the *chaise-longue*. Then she saw the letter on the Persian table. It lay there as if it had been intended she should notice it: certainly, it had not been received only recently; it had been folded and refolded. She recognized the woman's handwriting in the green ink on the creased paper. Listening for a moment to ensure that neither Mahler nor Justine were approaching, she picked it up. Immediately she noted that the writer addressed Mahler as Gustav and used the familiar, affectionate *du*:

... I see no reason why Siegfried, or myself if it comes to that, should make any allowance for what you choose to describe as the youth and inexperience of your bride-to-be, and what your friends must regard as her intolerable rudeness toward them and, by implication, the lack of consideration for your own feelings. In fact, I can hardly understand how you could have permitted yourself to let her behave toward us in the way she did. Is it possible, because you've become so besotted with her looks that you feel you don't have to regard us as people any more, but rather as objects you can drop when you feel like it (and, I suppose, pick up again if need arise)? I'll tell you one thing: I, personally, want nothing more to do with your beloved Alma Schindler. Perhaps you think she alone will satisfy your needs – in which case, you won't mind living with her in *Splendid Isolation* ... undisturbed by all of us troublesome useless people.

As for Fräulein Schindler. Can you really not see how superficial and heartless she is? How deeply does somebody love you, who can make so little effort to be pleasant to your friends; who is so loath to associate with people who have achieved enough, surely, to expect some little respect from one who is still a very young woman; who finds it so disagreeable to be 'judged', as she terms it, by her future husband's long-standing acquaintances? And whose response to the best-intentioned efforts to make conversation with her and to put her at her ease is to be impudent, opinionated, and hypocritical ...?

The signature at the bottom was a simple 'Anna'.

However much she told herself that the letter was the work of a defeated rival, Alma-Maria was shaken by the vehemence with which von Mildenburg had expressed her evident pain. She snatched up her cloak and trailed it across the room to the bookshelves on the far side, as if to put as great a distance as she could between herself and the letter lying on the table. Had Gustav left it there? Had he intended it as a reproach? Or was it something he had been reading and re-reading – something, like the disparity in their ages, to be used as an impediment to his marrying her?

He came through from his bedroom. His smile was as alive as always when he first saw her. He was going to embrace her when he saw the expression on her face. He didn't even glance at the letter.

'Whatever is the matter?' he asked.

She shook her head. 'It's nothing,' she said. But when he persisted, staring, inspecting her face, she blurted out,

'Gustl ... I think, perhaps ... I think I might be pregnant.'

So she might. She was three or four days late. On the other hand, she had never worked like clockwork – had always been slightly envious of women who were regular.

His face was utterly transfigured. She noted that its radiance made him look quite beautiful.

'Almschili! Oh my golden, glorious Almschili!'

She had to laugh in relief, in his arms. Mildenburg was gone, utterly vanished.

'I can't be absolutely sure, my darling Gustl. Not for another two or three weeks. Perhaps I shouldn't have told you – not yet.'

'Why ever not?'

'Well, it isn't as if it's going to show and we'd have to have our wedding earlier, or anything like that ... And I'd hate to disappoint you ...'

'Oh my Almschi!' He dragged off his spectacles to let his tears flow unobstructed.

She laid her head against his shoulder. So that was all right – thank God!

She was not so foolish as to suppose that married life could possibly be as she had imagined it. Still less did she suppose that she and Mahler would dwell in a perpetual mutually fulfilling golden haze; what she had known vicariously of marriage armed her against some of the pitfalls. Even so, she was scarcely proof against such a complete disillusionment as occurred.

The date and venue of the ceremony had been announced in the morning and evening newspapers, both in advertisement and in the social columns. No time for the wedding had been announced, but it was generally assumed that it would take place, like most society weddings, at the great Karlskirche, in the evening. Mahler, because of his dislike of unnecessary publicity, decided that it should take place in the morning as early as possible, even before the first scattering of tourists arrived, Baedekers in hand, to explore the treasures of the side chapels and to read the life of St Charles Borromeo in the reliefs of the triumphal arches.

Rain poured down. Alma-Maria was brought by carriage by Mutti and Möll, who was to give her away. She would have liked to have enlisted Mutti's support for having the ceremony at a more sociable hour, but Mutti's only response was, 'I'm sure dear Gustav knows best, *liebchen*,' while Möll was anxious to put in at least half a day's work at the 'Golden Cabbage' – the name the ordinary Viennese had given to the golden-domed Sezession Gallery. Mahler arrived with Arnold Rosé and Justine on foot. He was wearing galoshes: they splashed as he walked, and left patches of damp up the aisle all the way from the porch steps to the sanctuary gate. Neither Rosé nor Justine knew how to behave in church, so it was just as well it wasn't a full society affair. When the sanctuary bell rang, and the priest and his acolytes made their entrance, Mahler knelt at the prie-dieu beside Alma-Maria, missed the kneeler and fell sprawling across the floor.

Only the six of them attended the wedding breakfast in the private hotel room overlooking the Kärntner Ring. The same group drove to the station where Alma-Maria and Mahler were to catch the Vienna-Prague-Warsaw-Petersburg express to carry them off to their honeymoon in the Russian capital. Although glad to settle into the wood-panelled, deep-cushioned comfort of the Pullman car, Alma-Maria couldn't help feeling that the whole thing had been as furtive as an elopement, and she envied Justine and Rosé who were going off immediately to their own wedding which would be attended by the entire Jewish complement of the Opera and Philharmonic players – a considerable proportion – and many other musicians besides.

Nor was the three-week stay in St Petersburg a honeymoon in any sense but the name. Mahler was conducting two major concerts in the Assembly Hall of the Nobility – including Beethoven's *Eroica* and Schubert's great C-major Symphony, and the orchestral excerpts from Wagner's *Ring*, all of which, given his demanding musicianship, required intensive rehearsals with the aid of an interpreter. He had also been invited to conduct several performances at the Maryinsky Theatre of

The Queen of Spades, Tchaikovsky having placed on record his own opinion that Mahler was his finest interpreter.

At first, Mahler's preoccupation with work did not worry her overmuch. His first cousin on his mother's side, Gustav Frank, had risen to a senior rank – that of Departmental Head, equivalent to a general in the Tsar's army – in the Imperial Chancery. He was a charming and amusing fellow without the least trace of his Jewish origins, and only too willing to escort his Austrian cousin's astonishingly attractive wife to see the sights of St Petersburg. His position in the Government gave him entry into the Winter Palace, into all but the Imperial Family's private quarters; he showed her the Hermitage, the Peter and Paul Fortress, and took her for troika-rides on the ice of the frozen Neva, and skating on the canals and under the bridges of the islands on the Little Nevka.

In his safekeeping, she allowed herself to enjoy the flirtatious advances of guards officers and high ministry officials. At night, in the Assembly Hall of the Nobility, or at the Imperial Opera, she found herself revelling in the attention assiduously paid to her as the beautiful and fashionable wife of Europe's most famous conductor. To top it all, there was the ecstatic, adulatory applause with which each of Mahler's appearances was received.

There was one performance – the second orchestral concert – when his conducting of two of her own favourites, the Rhine Journey and Funeral March from *Götterdämmerung*, filled her with an intense excitement, as though for the first time she was appreciating his real greatness as a conductor; when the applause from the glittering audience, as wild and uninhibited as if it had been made up of Viennese students rather than beribboned and jewelled society, brought home to her the extent of his international acclaim. In the midst of the noise, as she sat smiling, almost in tears, next to the Imperial Box, she wondered why on earth he should want to expend so much of his precious time and energy on compositions which, however accomplished, could never hope to match the music she had just heard him interpret and his talent as a conductor must surely be unique. Her hands, inside her ivory satin gloves, stung with her own clapping, as if she, by applauding hard enough, could persuade him of the truth of her thinking.

Halfway through their stay, Mahler caught a chill. He cancelled neither performances nor engagements. The remainder of the time, however, he kept to their hotel bed, covered his head in Turkish towels and inhaled balsam and eucalyptus infusions till the sweat dripped onto the sheets. In a muffled voice, he compared the medicinal preparations from the apothecary on the Nevsky with those he used in Vienna, and argued persuasively that Russian aspirin was adulterated. He discussed medicines with the same gravity and display of learning as he did philosophy, a discovery Alma-Maria shared with Gustav Frank when he was taking her in a hired sleigh along the dazzling snow-covered shore to visit the Imperial Summer Palace at Peterhof. Frank laughed.

'You mean you've come as far as marrying my cousin Mahler without finding out his favourite hobby?'

'Hobby?' she asked.

'Medicines – whether apothecary-dispensed or patent: he loves them all. He has only to learn about a new nostrum and he'll discover he has just the right symptom to try it out on!'

'I have found it out,' she said. 'Now. Here in Petersburg.'

Frank patted her knee through layers of fur rug.

'You poor darling!' he laughed jovially.

The first night of the new production of *The Queen of Spades*, after taking twelve curtain calls, Mahler almost fainted and had to be helped into a chair in the wings. There was no mistaking his utter exhaustion. The following morning, one of the physicians to the Imperial Family, a distinguished-looking nobleman, Baron Kozlovsky, was sent to see him. In the drawing room, when he had left Mahler's bedside, he told Alma-Maria in heavily accented German, 'In terms of sinew, your husband is strong, I dare say.'

Alma-Maria nodded.

'The wiry sort usually are. But constitutionally – that's another story. Poor – hungry – as a child, perhaps?'

'Yes. I think so.'

'That would explain it. The effects of ill-nourishment in earliest childhood, as with mental ill-treatment – fear, you know – can never be entirely conquered. You must make sure he does not overtax himself.'

She took advantage of Baron Kozlovsky's presence to consult him herself. She forced herself to admit to him that she and Mahler had anticipated their wedding.

'Then the answer is plain, my dear young lady,' he smiled. 'Nature has taken its proper course, and you have cause for rejoicing. My congratulations to you both.'

She saw him out of the hotel suite. Before summoning the lift, he turned to her.

'You'll forgive me, dear lady. It is my duty to remind you. You are a most attractive, healthy young woman. Your husband is much older than you. You should not encourage him to overtax his strength. I'm sure I do not have to explain to you ...'

He pulled the bell lever. As if in response, there sounded a loud sneeze in the suite followed by a noisy wheezing of breath. As the lift clattered up to the landing gate, Baron Kozlovsky bowed over her hand and touched her fingers with his moustache and beard.

He had told her she had cause for rejoicing, she thought to herself as she returned into the suite and the lift clattered down to the reception hall below. She wasn't sure. The possibility that she was pregnant had served well enough to subdue what she had supposed had been Mahler's misgivings regarding an alliance between spring and autumn; but at that time, she had had none of her own.

They had avoided the boredom of Lent. The Easter season was come, with the frenetic resumption of concerts, opera, and ballet – all that the Viennese public regarded (together with *Skandal*) to be the essentials of civilized living.

Mahler said the Easter bells, as they rang out over the glow of a midnight sky under which everybody was still awake, reminded him of *Faust*. He was already in bed, the book he had been reading resting face downwards on his raised knee. Alma-Maria was sitting at the dressing table brushing out her hair; she was perfectly aware that the light on the dressing table shone through the satin of her nightgown.

'"You heavenly music",' he quoted, '"strong as you are kind. Why do you search me out in the dust?"'

'Then I must be your Gretchen,' she teased him.

He adjusted his spectacles to examine her.

'Helen, I think. You're too beautiful for Gretchen. "What then remains but to transfer to you/Myself and all I wrongly thought was mine?"'

'But in Arcadia Helen vanished from Faust's arms, leaving only her dress and her veil.'

'Perhaps I'm afraid that's what is going to happen in my case.'

'If that's what you think ...' She put down her hairbrush and got up off the stool ... 'I won't even leave you my dress and my veil.'

She drew her nightgown over her head and dropped it by the dressing table. Naked, she lay down beside him on the bed. He gathered her into his arms; she removed his spectacles and laid them on the bedside table under the lamp.

The bells fell silent. He mounted her, covering her. She wrapped her legs round his slim athlete's body. He brought her to the point of crying out before slipping from her. It was tantalizing – but it was getting better ...

After Easter, the season was resumed for six or seven frenetic weeks before the Opera and the Musikvereinsgebäude closed for the summer. Mahler took up what Justine had warned Alma-Maria was his invariable routine. The maid brought in his morning chocolate at six-thirty exactly. At seven exactly he rose, shaved and dressed, breakfasted in his study while scanning the morning papers, spent an hour glancing through the scores he would be working on during the day at the Opera or with the Philharmonic, and then, at nine precisely, he left the apartment to walk to the Court Opera.

Shortly before one o'clock, his devoted secretary, Lenerl Sgalitzer, would telephone from the main office at the Court Opera to announce that the Herr Director was on his way home. Cook would have the soup placed on the dining room table at the exact moment he came in through the front door. Lunch would be followed by a rapid walk round the entire Ringstrasse, during which Alma-Maria, who had never cared much for walking anyway, was hard put to keep up with him. After his walk, he took tea and cakes, and returned to his room to study scores and manuscripts submitted to him. At five-thirty, he went either to the Court Opera or the Musikverein. If he was conducting, he would not come home until late, and usually Alma-Maria would go to hear all or part of the performance. If one of his assistants was directing the performance, he would stay for the first act before returning home for dinner; if a distinguished guest, then he would remain to escort his colleague to Hartmann's or another fashionable restaurant for dinner afterwards, at which Alma-Maria was usually present.

On the evenings when he returned home for dinner – which occurred all too rarely – they would talk over the meal (Mahler was always too preoccupied over lunch to make conversation, and the pace he set on their walks on the Ringstrasse was too sharp), then, as the maids cleared the table, they would go to his room and play the piano together, their favourite composers – for her, Wagner; for him, J. S. Bach; for both of them, Mozart and Haydn. On one such evening, he ate in silence, refusing to be inveigled into conversation. When it came to dessert – *Marillenknödel*, apricot dumplings, a speciality of their cook – he pushed the dish aside, untouched.

'Gustl, what is it?' she asked.

He sighed. At length, he replied, 'I shouldn't burden you with office problems.' He changed his mind, unable to contain his feelings. 'It's this damned Pfitzner business.'

'You mean, *Die Rose vom Liebesgarten?*'

He nodded. They had played parts of Hans Pfitzner's opera – submitted to the Intendant of the Court Opera – over together. She had liked the Prelude: there had also been a raindrop *motif* in the second act, and the fourth act Funeral March, which she had found very impressive.

'I knew it would happen,' said Mahler.

They had argued over it. Mahler had regarded most of the second and the whole of the third acts as being turgidly post-Wagnerian. To that, he had added his objections to the libretto – that it was a mass of stodgy, incomprehensible symbolism.

'You've never approved of symbolism,' she had told him. 'You much prefer literalism – it comes out in your own music.'

She had restrained herself from pointing out that it was probably one of the peculiarly Jewish traits in his personality. Whatever the reason, the Court Opera had rejected *Die Rose vom Liebesgarten* on his recommendation.

'It seems that there's a cabal formed round Pfitzner,' he said.

He nodded to the maid to take the dish of *Marillenknödel* from in front of him.

'I strongly suspect *Die Rose* itself was put up as a stalking-horse.'

'Gustl! Even you can't think it was as bad a piece as that,' she protested.

'Prince Montenuovo's office has been bombarded with letters from his supporters – quite influential, some of them. Abusive in some cases. And I have to waste my time replying to them, justifying my decision. It's painful: I know perfectly well Pfitzner has talent, even if he's not a Strauss. I'm not saying *Die Rose* is without merit . . . Read this!'

He pushed across the newspaper which he had brought in. It was a copy of the popular mass-circulation *Reichspost*. It had been folded to expose the centre page. The first leading article began:

Readers with a retentive memory will recall that, with our customary concern for objectivity, we declared our intention of postponing comment on the appointment of an unadulterated Jew to the most elevated and responsible position Vienna – universally accepted to be the world's musical capital – affords. Not even the prospect of the Jewification of the Opera could spur us to its defence until 'Herr Mahler commences his Jew-boy antics on the podium'.

The moment has come. Indeed, there are many who will regard our patience as culpable. In his rejection of what the finest, most truly German critics regard as an authentic German work of art, by a composer whose purity of blood is as evident as his attachment to the German soil – we are, of course, referring to *Die Rose vom Liebesgarten*, and its composer, Herr Pfitzner – our worst fears are realized. The Jew-Tsar of the Court Opera has only to detect the true soul of the German race reflected in the work of any of our younger composers (the Hebrew is too cunning to attempt to suppress the works of Mozart or Wagner, but will Hebraicize them if he can) to slam the doors of Opera and concert hall against him. . . .

And there was more – much more – in which it was suggested that Mahler's parentage had resulted in his moral and physical degeneration, the inherited effects of alcoholism and venereal disease, and also that he had married "Vienna's loveliest girl-child" to mask his true, homosexual, nature.

She stared at it as if, by keeping her eyes on it, she could somehow destroy it so that it might never have been. She heard herself whisper, 'Oh Gustl!' There was no way she could tell if the nausea which had taken hold of her was caused by the obscenity of the attack on him, or by her first realization of the sort of abuse to which she had laid herself open by marrying him.

'Oh Gustl!' she repeated.

By swallowing hard several times, she prevented herself from being physically sick.

'Always a Jew enters this world with one short arm ...' He smiled and hunched up his shoulder to demonstrate what he meant. 'It's difficult to cope with the deformity which doesn't exist except in other people's imaginations,' he added. 'But so many other people!'

She made herself get up and go to him, to squat beside him and hold his hand.

'Do you mean you knew that there'd be this sort of response if you rejected *Die Rose?*' she asked. 'That it would have been easier to have accepted it?'

'Quite. And then there follows the terrible curse of self-pity.'

He put his fingertips to his spectacles to push them up to the bridge of his nose. She saw that it was a gesture of self-deprecation.

'I know you, Gustl.' She forced herself to smile up at him. 'You wouldn't compromise like that. Ever.'

'No?' he asked. 'Not even the Jew who accepted baptism?'

'Him least of all. What? After all those saints – Peter and Luke and Mark and the rest – in the Fourth Symphony? And the Three Angels and Jesus in the Third?'

'Did you know that Walter changed his name on my advice? From Bruno Walter Schlesinger? I told him I did not think Vienna would accept two Jews directing the Opera.'

'I also know that you turned down a commission to compose a Mass because you said you couldn't in all honesty compose a *credo*. Everything else, but not a *credo*.'

'Who told you that?'

'Schoenberg. It's true, isn't it?'

'Yes. It's true.'

'Schoenberg would have composed a *credo*.'

'Schoenberg wasn't brought up in the Jewish faith,' he said.

She sat back on her heels. They were at ease now, talking like this, and trusting one another. It was a time to take risks.

'Gustl? You know what you said about being born with a short arm? ... Do you think it's possible you might be over-anxious about keeping your integrity? I mean, is it possible you could be unfair to Herr Pfitzner because you know he's favoured by ...' She pointed at the copy of the *Reichspost* ... 'this sort of lout?'

To her relief, he was not angry with her. Quite the opposite. His face was transformed with tenderness.

'You are so wise, my Almschi,' he said. 'So beautiful and so wise. Already I can't imagine how I could live without you.'

She sat up. Gratefully, she allowed herself to be enfolded in his arms.

The event which most preoccupied Alma-Maria – even more, much more, than what people insisted on calling her 'interesting condition' – was to take place in early May, just before she and Mahler were due to retire to his summer retreat at Maiernigg, on the very shore of the Wörthersee. This was the Beethoven Festival at the Sezession Gallery. It was the point at which so many fragments of her life would come together to form a synthesis of her past experience. At the centre would be the unveiling of the Beethoven Memorial sculpted by Pappi's old friend and drinking companion, Max Klinger. There would be Gustav Klimt's long-awaited Beethoven Frieze (the thought of it filled her with suppressed excitement and some misgiving), which fellow artists were already insisting should be preserved for posterity. The exhibition would be of the work of artists she had met up at the Villa Möll, or long ago in Pappi's studio at Plankenburg, all presided over by Carl Möll. In the hall where Kimt's masterpiece would be on display, Mahler would conduct soloists and chorus from the Opera and musicians from the Philharmonic in his own arrangement for voices, wind, brass, and percussion of the finale of Beethoven's Ninth.

Before that, however, she attended another gala occasion. The Opera season was to end with the première of Richard Strauss's second opera, *Feuersnot*. Though Strauss himself would conduct the initial performances, it was an extraordinary compliment both to Mahler and the Vienna Court Opera. Except among those whom Hugo Wolf and others had called the Brahmins – those who, like Hanslick and Neuberger writing in the *Neue Frei Presse*, affected a slavish adherence to Brahms's pedantic classicism – Strauss was held in adulation throughout the German-speaking musical world. He was, moreover, Director of the Berlin Court Opera, where he could perfectly well have mounted the work.

Alma-Maria alone knew that had *Feuersnot* been the work of any composer other than Richard Strauss, an old and valued as well as very distinguished friend, Mahler would have rejected it. They both enjoyed the music as they played it over, exploring the score together in their evening sessions at the piano. It was filled with wicked *pastiches* of Wagner and Brahms, but there were also passages of marvellous originality and breathtaking transitions, and two glorious waltz duets which transcended in melodic inventiveness the Viennese waltz duets which Mahler was compelled to conduct as part of the Vienna Opera's standard repertoire.

Alma-Maria arrived at the Opera on the arm of the distinguished concert pianist, Josef Schalk. Usually, she went to the Director's box discreetly, by a side entrance. This time, in a new silk gown designed by Kolo Moser to conceal the first signs of her condition, she let Schalk lead her through the fashionable crowds in the foyer and up the stairs. The faces turned in her direction, the whispers by the informed to the uninformed that she was the wife of Herr Director Mahler, and the glances of undisguised admiration from young light cavalry officers concealing their extreme youth behind ferocious moustaches, and aged bewhiskered senators, the breasts of whose evening suits glittered with Imperial-Royal orders, still had power to gratify her, even though she told herself that by this time she should be indifferent to such attentions.

Mahler and Franz Schalk, Josef's younger brother, were already in the box when she and Josef arrived to take their places. So was Richard Strauss's wife, Pauline. Mahler introduced Alma-Maria to her.

'You do indeed have a very attractive wife, Herr Mahler,' Frau Strauss told him, as if Alma-Maria were less a person than an artefact.

She herself had turned forty. Once she had been petite and pretty. Now she was plump, but this had the effect of preserving her complexion and her prettiness. She wore scented face powder, and an enormous lace collar on the neck and shoulders of her taffeta dress which looked incongruously childish on a woman of her age. She gave her hand to Alma-Maria, and, to Alma-Maria's surprise, said,

'Honestly, Frau Mahler, I wonder how you can be bothered to come with all these musically illiterate numbskulls . . .' She waved airily at the crowds filtering into the *loges* around them . . . 'to listen to the nonsense we're going to hear tonight.'

Alma-Maria laughed, imagining that Pauline Strauss was joking. She found herself being rebuked.

'My dear young woman, there's nothing the least amusing in what I've just said – any more than there is in my husband's latest offering.'

Mahler helped her to the seat beside his own. He bowed to one or two people sitting nearby. Alma-Maria smiled and inclined her head. She tried to catch his eye but he avoided her glance, she knew quite deliberately.

Applause cascaded downwards from the four circles of the auditorium, gathering in tumult, then spreading more discreetly among the fashion-ably and militarily dressed in the stall *fauteuils*. The house lights dimmed; Alma-Maria noticed Pauline Strauss resting the several chins of her pretty face on the velvet parapet of the box, and staring down at her handsome genius of a husband, a sturdily erect six-foot-three whose bearing and close cropped blond curls made him look like a Bavarian cavalry colonel. He bowed several times over the podium rail, and spread his hands, inviting and relishing the applause which had greeted him in a way Mahler would never have done. Alma-Maria was sure she heard Frau Strauss call down, 'Show-off!' quite loudly.

They were ten minutes into the work when Alma-Maria realized that the succession of noises she had heard were disapproving grunts emanating from Frau Strauss. A moment or two later, Frau Strauss looked around the others in the box and asked,

'Is there anybody here who can honestly say he likes this horse manure?'

There was a rustle of protest from the *loges* on either side. Again, Alma-Maria glanced at Mahler. The stage lights glinted on the gold rims of his spectacles; he kept his eyes fixed on the stage.

Lack of response inspired Frau Strauss to greater effort.

'Anybody who claims to like this garbage must either be hopelessly ignorant or a musical cretin!' There were hisses for her to keep quiet from all sides. 'We all know there isn't an original note in it!' she announced.

From the way she sat forward, it seemed she was calling down to her husband.

Amidst scattered calls of protest, and to the studiedly masked relief of those around her, she sat back in her chair. For fifteen minutes or so, they were permitted to listen to the performance in peace. Then suddenly and all too clearly:

'Wagner, you know. He's stolen everything from Wagner. If not from Gluck. Or Mozart, of course . . .' She leaned forward. 'But mostly Wagner!' she called. Heedless of the rising if muffled noise of protest all around, she turned to Alma-Maria and Mahler. 'And Berlioz. We mustn't forget Berlioz. He keeps Berlioz's *Treatise on Instrumentation* on his desk, you know. All that praise he gets for his tricks with orchestration! Stolen from Berlioz – every last bit of it!'

Mahler too kept Berlioz's *Treatise* to hand in his room. It occurred to Alma-Maria to say so, but she didn't dare. In any case, Frau Strauss hadn't finished.

'The poor fool thinks if he steals a *motif* from Wagner and scores it like Berlioz . . .' She leaned forward again. 'People will think it's original!' She turned to Alma-Maria, and added conversationally, 'And most people do, the fools!'

Alma-Maria dared not catch her eye. She was afraid Frau Strauss was hopelessly drunk. The latter lapsed into silence for a time. Then she leaned over to Alma-Maria, and whispered hoarsely.

'*Lohengrin* – that's what he used for the hero's triumph in *Ein Heldenleben* – his triumph!' There was not a trace of drink on her breath. 'Think of it. The introduction to Act Three of *Lohengrin* – a theme played by every village band from Moscow to Lisbon! He really is such a *vulgar* creature!'

Feuersnot, being in a single act, was mercifully short and without an intermission. Strauss himself received no fewer than fifteen rapturous curtain calls, during which Pauline Strauss groaned and swore. Mahler had booked a private dining room at Hoffmann's for Alma-Maria and himself, the Strausses, and the two Schalk brothers after the performance. The audience was filing out when Strauss, his face shining with his exertions on the podium – he had given a performance on the podium quite unlike Mahler's restrained style, quite as rich, in fact, as anything up on the stage – arrived at the box. He ran his fingers through his receding curls, wiping the sweat from off his forehead with his wrist. He was beaming with pleasure at the audience's enthusiastic approval of the work.

'A great success,' Mahler told him, embracing him. 'My heartfelt congratulations!'

There was something ridiculous about Mahler with his small stature embracing the giant Strauss. Alma-Maria noticed also that Mahler had not congratulated him on the quality of the work. Not that Strauss would notice – he had come to expect universal approval and there was only the question of the amount of it to be considered.

'Thank you! Thank you, my dear friend!' he replied to Mahler. 'Well, Pauksl?' he turned to his wife. 'Aren't *you* going to congratulate me? This is Vienna, after all – not Berlin or Munich. And they loved me! Didn't they all love me? – you have to admit it!'

Without waiting for her answer – she sat staring fixedly out across the rapidly emptying auditorium – he turned again to Mahler.

'The festival of the *Algemeine Deutsches Musikverein*,' he said. 'Ninth of June, at Krefeld. The first full performance in Germany of your Third, eh?'

'That is so,' Mahler smiled.

Strauss turned to Alma-Maria.

'You see before you, my dear, beautiful young lady . . .'

Alma-Maria heard Pauline Strauss snort.

'. . . one of the very first Mahlerians, converted to the new religion on hearing your husband's Second Symphony in Berlin, in '97 was it?'

'December '95,' Mahler corrected him.

'Of course. And your husband paid me the greatest of compliments – grater than all this . . .' He waved his hand across the sea of empty chairs below them. 'He told me that there was nobody in the world he would rather have in his audience than myself.'

Pauline's snort at this was so loud that everybody started except Strauss himself, who did not appear to have heard it.

'I shall be there at Krefeld, my dear fellow,' he assured Mahler. 'I shall be conducting in Düsseldorf the previous week. We shall stay over . . . shan't we, Pauksl? Even if it is going to be one of your symphonic Behemoths, eh? . . . Did you hear that, Pauksi? I told Mahler his Third is bound to be another of his symphonic Behemoths!'

Pauline twisted round to face him.

'You know what you are, Richard? You're a thief! I wonder you have the impertinence to come in here among musicians whose shoes you're unworthy to clean, let alone to tie, to boast about your success! Don't you think they recognize Wagner, Gluck, and Spohr when they hear them . . .?'

'Spohr, my dearest?' asked Strauss, evidently taken by surprise only at the charge of having stolen from that particular source.

'And Liszt, and Berlioz!'

'Pauksi! . . . Dearest . . .!' Strauss pleaded.

'How dare you address me! I wonder you have the gall to come in here after a display like tonight's!' She rose to her feet, gathering her coat about her. Timidly, Strauss made as if to place it over her shoulders. She stepped away from him as if avoiding stepping in dog dirt. 'I'm not coming to have dinner with you, I can promise you that! The very sight of you makes me sick!'

She had begun to shout. The Opera staff who were clearing up between the rows of *fauteuils*, and extinguishing lights, looked up at their Director's box. Mahler took Pauline by the arm. She did not shake him off.

'It would be better, perhaps, if we continued discussing our evening's arrangements in my office,' he suggested gently.

Pauline smiled sweetly at him, and allowed him to lead her out of the box onto the concourse. Strauss and Franz Schalk – who had been responsible for preparing *Feuersnot* at its early rehearsals – followed.

Josef Schalk took Alma-Maria by the arm.

'You mustn't worry, Alma my dear – I may call you Alma, may I?'

'Please,' she replied.

Suddenly she felt like a little girl again, secure in the protection of a distinguished but kindly grown-up.

'They behave like this all the time,' he said in her ear. 'I expect it's a sort of game with them.'

'It's a game that makes everybody else feel embarrassed, then,' she objected.

Schalk smiled down at her. 'That's true of most love games, isn't it?'

She still felt it was all very odd and ugly.

They caught up with Mahler and Franz Schalk outside the door of Mahler's private office. The two men had lit cigars – 'To calm the nerves,' Mahler explained. The sound of shouting could be heard even through the thickness of the baize-covered double doors.

'You make me sick – I mean, vomit! You can go to your precious dinner, and welcome! Though what you think you have to celebrate about, I can't imagine!'

'But, dearest . . . our friends . . .'

'What they do is up to them! They probably have stronger stomachs than me – they don't have to share a bed with a thief and a liar and a cheat! . . .'

'Pauksi! . . . Please, Pauksi . . .!'

Strauss sounded as if he was in tears. Alma-Maria was horrified. She wanted to shout at them to stop. The men around her – even Mahler – were quietly smiling. Their look of complacent superiority filled her with disgust.

Mahler stepped forward and knocked at the door.

'A moment!' Strauss's voice called.

The door opened almost immediately. Pauline emerged, her satin and fur coat wrapped tight about her.

'I'm going straight back to the hotel!' she shouted over her shoulder. 'Alone! And don't imagine you're going to share my bed tonight!' She turned to confront her husband as he came out after her, clutching his hat and gloves, his coat over his arm. 'In fact, you'll be doing me a great favour if you stay out all night!'

'Oh Pauksl!' Strauss begged in deep distress. 'Can't I see you back to the hotel ... Please?'

She stared coldly up at him.

'Please Pauksl,' he whispered.

'I don't suppose I can prevent you,' she replied. 'But only if you walk ten paces behind me. I insist on that!'

Strauss pulled on his coat. 'I'll join you all at Hoffmann's,' he told Mahler, and he ran off down the promenade after his wife.

'*La commedia è finita*,' Mahler observed. 'For the time being.' He took Alma-Maria's arm. 'Shall we go, gentlemen?' he asked.

The entrée was served by the time Strauss rejoined them. He took a seat beside Alma-Maria. He appeared to be in reasonably good spirits so that she supposed there to have been some sort of reconciliation between himself and Pauline. After several mouthfuls of food and a glass of wine, he reached across the table and picked up the menu. Still chewing, he took a pencil from the pocket of his white dress waistcoat and, to her surprise, began to scribble figures on the back of the menu. He looked across to Mahler.

'Rehearsal fees, my dear chap. Three hundred and fifty kreutzers a morning? Is that what was agreed?'

Mahler was taken aback.

'It would result in a total of twelve hundred kreutzers approximately,' Strauss went on, impervious to any hint.

'It's a matter for His Highness Prince Montenuovo's office,' Mahler said. He leaned across the table. 'Telephone me tomorrow after midday. I'll make sure everything is ... cut and dried.'

At last Strauss recognized his embarrassment.

'Oh, my dear fellow!' he laughed. A look of cheerful wickedness came over his face. His blond moustache bristled as he pursed his lips. 'In Reichmarks,' he said, rather more loudly than was necessary. 'I wonder what it all comes to in Reichmarks, eh? Plus the return fares from Berlin and our bills at the Central – I won't set my losses at *Skat* on my account ...'

He thrust his pencil behind his ear like a cashier in a dress shop and resumed eating. He turned to Alma-Maria and said to her with his mouth still full,

'You mustn't judge my Pauline too harshly, dear Frau Mahler. I know she's a bit rough on me at times – but it's what I need. Now your husband: he's quite the opposite. What he needs is encouragement. I've always encouraged him, and so must you. As for me, well, I need somebody to scold me, you see. It revives me no end ...' He leaned towards her, almost brushing her ear with his moustache. 'And afterwards,' he whispered, 'we make love ... magnificently!' Without pausing so much as to take breath, he swung round to Mahler. 'Puccini, Herr Director ... I believe you are giving a first German performance of a Puccini opera. Next season.'

'November,' Mahler replied. '*La Bohème.*'

'And how much does Signor Puccini expect to receive from the Imperial-Royal Court Opera?' asked Strauss.

Mahler removed his spectacles. Removing his handkerchief from the breast pocket of his evening dress, he wiped them. Blinking myopically, he asked Strauss,

'How much would the Royal Court Opera in Berlin expect to pay Puccini for the right to a first performance?'

Strauss laughed aloud. 'A lot less than the Vienna Opera, I can tell you!' he replied.

He took the pencil from behind his ear, picked up the menu and started calculating figures once more. He raised the menu to hide his face, then inclined his head to Alma-Maria.

'The trouble is, Frau Alma,' he said in a low voice, 'I'm an exact antithesis to your husband. There's not a trace of spirituality in the entire Strauss family – least of all in myself. Now Mahler's music is all meditation, prayer, profound thought. As for me – I just tell stories in music.'

She looked him straight in the eyes.

'Like *Till Eulenspiegel*?' she asked.

He laughed delightedly.

'Quite, my dear! Absolutely! You are sharp ... Mahler, you lucky devil! You've got a wife here who's as sharp as she's beautiful!'

Alma-Maria concealed her bewilderment at not seeing in him the least trace of the poor henpecked creature who had been reduced almost to tears by his wife's cruelty. She explained it to Mahler, as she prepared for bed.

'There's more than a touch of masochism there, I imagine,' Mahler replied.

'Masochism?' she asked.

'You better ask Berta Zuckerkandl to get Freud to explain, or one of her husband's friends who are of Freud's turn of mind,' he replied. He was sitting up in bed watching her. She was at the dressing table again, brushing out her hair. 'Personally, I've no patience with it,' he said.

'Strauss – or Dr Freud and his followers?'

'Both. Certainly not with Strauss's attitude towards his wife ... I suppose he thinks he's had success so easily all his life he feels he ought to be punished.'

'Perhaps it's because he knows he doesn't deserve the admiration he receives.'

'Doesn't deserve it?' asked Mahler.

'Well, he's such a materialist, isn't he? You can't be a materialist like that, and a great artist.'

'Richard Strauss is a very great artist.'

Alma-Maria turned to face him.

'I don't know how you can say that, Gustl. His dreadful materialism aside, he's so literal. He said himself all he does is to tell stories in music.'

'Only?' asked Mahler. He smiled in a thin-lipped, superior smile: the smile of someone who is indulgent towards another from a position of vastly greater knowledge.

Weariness – it was early morning – made her irritable. He sat up in bed with the front of his nightshirt unbuttoned, his wiry hair standing up all on end, and his spectacles gleaming at her in the lamplight. He was going to lecture her.

'We've passed the stage, I hope, where a composer of Beethoven's calibre had to apologize to the Viennese public for including literal effects in the "Pastoral" Symphony. Strauss has a grasp of orchestration superior to any composer since Berlioz – greater than Wagner even, greater by far than Brahms. I'd go so far as to say that there is not and there never has been a composer with such a command of tonal colour. He has revolutionized use of the orchestral palette. We are all his pupils.'

'You only say that because he's a friend of yours ...'

It was so ridiculous! His success as a conductor, as a director of opera if not as a composer, had been as meteoric as that of Strauss. Yet he grasped at friendship as if he were about to drown in an ocean of bullying and contempt – as if he were some poverty-stricken Jewish boy who was fearful of being stoned if he set foot outside the ghetto.

'You always idolize your friends,' she added lamely.

He had idolized her in the same way, she realized. The suspicion had occurred to her – it had been put to her – that he had acquired her as an ornament with which to impress the world. But it was not that way at all. He had acquired her in order to impress – to reassure – himself. That was why she was not allowed to compose any longer: he could not permit her any creativity of her own; even the child she was carrying would be *his* child, would bear *his* name. It would have been endurable, she told herself, if she were to be sacrificed to his sense of his own genius (though, in all probability, the sacrifice would never have been demanded), but to have allowed herself to become the victim of his belief in his essential inferiority – *der Ewige Jude*.

'You said yourself something about how he would never achieve the heights if he went on sticking out his tongue at audiences,' she said, not to win a debating point, but to mask the sense of purposeless bleakness in the life before her.

'A moment of exasperation,' he replied. 'At least we agree on the stupidity of the libretto.' He peeled off his spectacles. 'It's very late,' he remarked. 'And I must be in the office as usual in the morning.'

He lay down pulling the bedclothes over him as if all problems had been resolved.

She slept soundly because she was very tired. When she rose, the sense of bleakness was almost gone. Her condition, far from causing her nausea in the morning as everybody had led her to expect, filled her with a lethargic well-being. She went out into the hallway to call to cook to send her breakfast into the dining room. She was standing in her wrapper, her fingers buried in her hair, massaging her scalp – or her brain – into activity, when Mahler came out of his room, his thick, battered portfolio under his arm. It was a sunny morning and he wasn't going to need his coat, but she took his hat and stick – which he invariably carried uselessly under his arm – from the tallboy.

'You know, Almschli: thinking about what you were saying last night about Strauss's materialism . . .'

It was too early, she felt. Her brain wasn't going to work properly.

'Not know, Gustl. I'm still asleep. I may not look like it, but I am.'

She held out his hat and stick, praying he'd just kiss her on the cheek and leave. He took the hat and stick from her.

'He is my friend, whatever you may say,' he insisted on continuing. 'I think it's important you should understand.'

'Gustl – I was very tired when we were going to bed . . .'

'No. Listen to me. About this materialism you were accusing him of. He's quite right, you know, when he says – as he has said – that one doesn't have to be a shopkeeper to want a decent remuneration after sitting up night after night over some vast orchestral score. The sheer effort of scoring – I mean, the labour with the pen, let alone the brain – deserves a decent return on one's work. Strauss only says out loud what so-called idealistic composers think about privately.'

'Even you, Gustl?'

'Of course, *liebchen*.' Being him, he had not noticed her sarcasm.

He kissed her cheek and departed, leaving her angry enough to have entered into competition with Pauline Strauss. He wasn't even sufficiently aware of the reality of her existence to notice when she was too tired to be lectured at.

And since returning from St Petersburg, she had discovered a new activity for the morning, other than practising on the piano and planning the replacement of the musty old furniture: bookkeeping. It was the height of absurdity: the thought of the Bavarian card-playing, *bon viveur* Richard Strauss, meticulously working out the monies owed to him to the last schilling and pfennig on the backs of menus, while Mahler, the

Moravian Jew, kept his books in a state resembling long disused birds' nests, for which there was no excuse considering the extraordinary neatness and clarity of his manuscript scores. Nor did he have the least notion or apparent concern regarding his financial standing. She had discovered that, despite his considerable salaries from the Court Opera and the Musikverein, and his income from royalties which were reasonably substantial, they were deeply in debt – a fact of which he had been blissfully unaware, thanks to Justine having, for many years, kept all tradesmen's bills out of his sight. With the help of her own income, Alma-Maria was now struggling to take matters in hand. There was no reason why they should not become reasonably well off, given a little care and attention. Had she not accepted responsibility for keeping the accounts, it would only have been a matter of time before they had run into bankruptcy. Mahler, far from expressing appreciation at her endeavours, seemed incapable of taking the least interest in them.

When he returned for lunch on the dot of one, as usual he monologued on those aspects of his administrative work which were plaguing him at the moment, or lapsed into self-absorbed silence. He did not even ask how she was feeling. She supposed, when lunch was concluded, that he would walk her round the Ringstrasse as usual. She doubted that, when the time arrived, he would notice that she could scarcely keep up with the brisk pace he set. Today, however, as he folded up her napkin, he suggested they should retire to his room.

'You've been playing *Die Walküre*. I noticed you'd left it up on the piano. I should like to hear you play over *"Wie dir die Stirn"*,' he told her in a strangely forced voice which made her suspicious.

'I'm not in the mood for it. Really, Gustl.'

'I should find it most relaxing,' he insisted.

'I don't feel like playing. I mean it.'

The note of exasperation in her voice communicated itself to him at last.

'Do you feel tired, little wife?' he asked, all solicitous of a sudden. 'It's your condition, of course. I'm sorry! I'm very inconsiderate.'

She wanted to say that it had nothing to do either with tiredness or her condition, but she left it a fraction too late. He had taken her hand and was leading her to his room.

'You must sit down,' he was telling her, 'and I shall play for you. If you want to doze off, please do so. We shall forget about our walk – there's a sharp breeze this afternoon.'

He led her straight to the piano, removed the copy of *Die Walküre* from the stand and gave it to her. Immediately she noticed the sheet of manuscript paper between the pages which had not been there before. It had been placed between the opening pages of the ecstatic love duet of Siegmund and Sieglinde. She removed it. Across the top of the page was written, 'For My Dearest Almschi'. It was a song set out in Mahler's fastidiously neat hand. The accompaniment was in two staves as for piano, but already indications of instrumentation had been pencilled in. Excitement as much as curiosity compelled her to read it:

> If you love for beauty's sake,
> Do not love me:
> Love the sun,
> It wears hair of gold.

There was a fleeting moment when the old, bleak depression which had been possessing her since last night might have persuaded her to screw it into a ball and throw it at him – or even to tear it into scraps. But the simple melody in all its tenderness seemed to sing itself into her head even as she gazed at the notes – a true German *Lied* in the tradition of Schubert and Schumann.

Mahler sat down and began to play it, singing the words in his conductor's growling but musical *Sprechstimme:*

> If you love me for youth's sake,
> Do not love me:
> Love the spring
> Which is young every year.

She sat beside him. As he played on, she surrendered herself to it. It compelled her to let go her hurt and frustration. But resentment remained like an opiate-subdued pain lurking in a bedroom corner waiting to rejoin the sufferer when the drug had worn off.

Between their first playing it over and the maid's bringing in afternoon tea, they played it and sang it – one, other, or both together – twenty times. And made love:

> If you love for love's sake,
> Yes, then love me!
> Love me always,
> As I love you, for ever.

The Emperor paid an informal visit to the Beethoven exhibition at the Sezession Gallery, one afternoon, three days before it was due to open to the public. Mahler was rehearsing his orchestra and singers in one of the main galleries where Klimt's great frieze was being presented. Alma-Maria was with her stepfather in the central gallery where stood Max Klinger's white marble Beethoven Memorial.

Before the Old Man's arrival, everybody moved about talking in whispers, stilling the atmosphere like a maid scattering droplets of water from a pail to lay dust. Only Mahler was unaffected by the mood of expectancy, hunched over the music desk, riding the musicians along Beethoven's score with monomaniac intensity, signalling emphases in phrasing here, booming out his bass voice there to draw out some detail in orchestration, while the orchestral players who mocked him and mimicked him and complained endlessly about him behind his back followed every detail of his interpretation with fearful concentration.

From her place beside the Beethoven statue, Alma-Maria was able to watch the Old Man's arrival at the top of the Gallery steps. Möll had gone out to greet him: now he stood in the centre of the group of brilliantly uniformed equerries, a subfusc figure in the midst of the silver braid and epaulettes, golden sword knots and tall shako plumes. Beside him stood the bowed representative of a millennium of Hapsburg rule, slightly smaller than Möll and a little shrunken so that his plain pale blue military jacket and blue-black uniform trousers hung creased and baggy on him. Only his unplumed shako sat on him stiff and erect as he advanced up the hall, using his silver-scabbarded sword as a walking stick.

He paused momentarily at the entrance to the gallery where Mahler was rehearsing. He nodded his head in time to the march variation of the 'Ode to Joy' as if, notoriously unmusical though he was, he recognized that at least, then continued on his way. Alma-Maria knew that she would be presented. It was only now she began to feel butterflies fluttering in her stomach. He was the Old Man, she had been telling herself – King-Emperor perhaps, not at all well read, unsuccessful on the field of battle as in marriage, whose wife and son had died violently amidst rumours of scandal, his sight and hearing not what they had been. She had not taken into account the aura with which he had been endowed by more than fifty years of reigning over the greatest empire in Europe. Though he was more frail by far than those around him, and more dull in appearance, he carried with him authority. Had he been alone instead of surrounded by a glittering and attentive entourage, she decided, he would still have made her feel nervous.

She was dully aware of Carl Möll presenting various acquaintances of hers to the Emperor. Somewhere on the margin of her consciousness she remarked that, though it was mid-afternoon, Klinger was still slightly sober; that Klimt, whom she had not noticed before in the throng and whom she saw in a sort of mist, was dressed in a well-tailored suit and wore a fob and watch chain on his stomach, and that Emilie Flöge did not appear to be with him. Then Möll turned to her, reaching out his hand to indicate her to the Emperor.

The Emperor's rheumy eyes gazed on her as if out of the concealment of a medieval knight's jousting helmet. His bushy white moustache with his full side whiskers, which all but met on his chin, hid the lower part of his face. The visor of his military shako all but covered his eyes so that he was staring at her by tilting his head slightly back. She saw that his nose was a network of tiny veins, and that there was a purple underlay to the dead-ash pallor of his cheeks. He approached her, tapping his way with the steel tip of his sword scabbard. She curtsied – a full, Imperial curtsy, despite the detectable swell of her stomach – and thank the dear God she remembered how.

'My stepdaughter, Imperial Majesty,' murmured Möll. 'Frau Court Opera Director Gustav Mahler.'

'Beautiful!,' wheezed the Emperor. 'Beautiful woman!'

'Thank you, Your Imperial Majesty,' Alma-Maria managed to reply. Her voice sounded thick, as if she were imitating him.

The Emperor beckoned her with an upward movement of his gloved hand to rise. She managed to do so without touching the ground with her hand. He stared at her. She did not know whether protocol demanded that she should gaze back at him attentively, or that she should avert her eyes.

'Frau Mahler, you must tell your husband he should write me an Imperial march. Our composers no longer write Imperial marches. It is a bad thing ... Say what you like, it means there is no pride in Empire any more ...' He cleared his throat, holding his clenched knuckle to his mouth. 'They tell me your husband is a genius at composing, Frau Mahler. Don't know anything about music myself. Don't know anything about genius. I only know about hard work, eh? A hard-working composer should find the time to write an Imperial march, what d'ye say? You tell your husband ... Because if there's no pride in Empire left, it will all fall apart – apart. Yes! And what will become of your husband and his sort then, eh? The first to be devoured ... Tell him to write an Imperial march!'

Alma-Maria bowed her head. She heard the click of the Old Man's scabbard tip as Carl Möll led him away from where she was standing.

'Do you feel all right, Frau Alma?'

Somebody stood at her side, his hand cupping her elbow. It was Alfred Roller, whose paintings hung about the Beethoven Memorial. He was a friend and colleague of Möll's whom she had grown to like. Earlier that month, she had invited him to dine with Mahler and herself. The conversation over dinner had resulted in Mahler commissioning him to design the new production of *Tristan und Isolde* at the Court Opera next season.

'Yes. Quite all right. But I should like to sit down.'

She felt safe and comfortable in Roller's company. He was a big, robust man with a kindly face set in a fierce black beard – a man from the same mould as her Pappi.

The Old Man and his cortège were passing out into the daylight at the end of the vestibule.

'Something of an ordeal, eh?' Roller remarked.

He continued supporting her by the arm until the Old Man was gone, then he took her across to the Café Museum. He knew, of course, that she was pregnant – the whole of Vienna knew that she was carrying *Der*

Mahler's child. But while demonstrating his concern for her, he was sensitive enough not to mention it.

'Will you be joining Gustav now?' he asked, over chocolate and whipped cream.

She shook her head.

'He'll be going back to the Opera,' she said. 'I may go there tonight.'

She was careful. Roller admired her. But over the past few weeks he had come to idolize Mahler. There were many artists and writers like him, who were so astonished to meet a distinguished musician who was also literate and informed in the other branches of arts and science that they came to think of him as a centre, as a peripatetic Parnassus where the Muses met. They were less ready to appreciate – or at least to express their appreciation – that such meetings took place over *her* dinner table in the Auenbruggergasse, forming a salon which depended on herself entirely, as hostess.

'I shall return to the Sezession in a moment,' she continued. 'I haven't looked at the pictures yet – not properly.'

'I could drive you home?' Roller suggested.

There was a *fiacre* rank along the pavement opposite, the cabbies in a waking sleep, nursing their whips, the horses chomping into burlap nosebags.

'No, Alfred. You're very kind. I'll be perfectly all right, I promise you. One has these little turns.' She reached for his hand and, smiling, gave it a squeeze. 'One learns to put up with them.' She realized she sounded quite matronly. 'Besides which,' she added, 'they attract the attention of nice men like you.'

She stood searching round the walls of the gallery for her own figure. She was alone under the brutal, colourless glare of work lights. Orchestra and choir were gone: upright chairs were scattered about; many of the music stands had tumbled to the floor.

She saw it. She had not seen it at first because it was above her, on the wall panel immediately beside her. It had all been so long ago – a lifetime's experience ago. Yet there it was, in the familiar Grecian costume, the tangled mane of her hair caught in a Grecian filet, a figure a metre and a half high, and placed high enough to be clearly visible above the heads of choir and orchestra ...

She was no longer holding a copy of *The Divine Comedy*, she noticed – perhaps it was considered unsuited to the Muse of German Poetry – but a gigantic gilded lyre, one of whose horns rested on her shoulder. Her head was tilted forward so that her ear touched the curlicued vent of the lyre's sound box, a reference to her slight hearing impediment, perhaps. Above her, a choir of angelic figures, golden, jewel-encrusted, floated horizontally on a sea of calm. Her fingers touched the thread-like strings of the lyre: was she transmitting the angelic melody? The eyes glanced mischievously out across the gallery to the opposite wall, while a smile played about her lips conveying some secret, even disreputable, message.

She turned to inspect the object of the Muse-figure's glance. It too stood a metre and a half – perhaps two metres – high, the Hero-Knight encased in dull, brick-coloured armour. He was grim-faced, purposeful, his hands resting on a great two-handled war sword, dulled like his armour with use. He was framed by two supporting figures, one erect and smiling in steely pride holding a wreath above his head, the other, her hands together in the formal indication of prayer, her head stooped to whisper tenderly into his ear. Pappi and Möll between them had taught Alma-Maria enough of the iconography of painting to recognize the Spirit of Ambition on the one hand and of Pity on the other. And the Knight himself: the face staring over the bowl-shaped collar of his cruel plate armour, gaunt, aquiline, Semitic, was as unmistakable as her own.

It should have been ludicrous ... should have been. But there was nothing ludicrous about Klimt's vision. There was artistic licence certainly: the figure was made to seem tall. There was nothing false, however, about the impression of sinewy physical strength, the athletically sprung tension which Klimt had conveyed as lurking beneath the steel shell; though only Alma-Maria and a handful of very intimate friends knew of its reality. Nor was anything false about the puritan zealot's fixed stare on the haggard face. Klimt had caught the authority there which caused people – even those who mocked and imitated him as he limped up the Opernring shortly after nine each morning, and back shortly before one in the afternoon – to stand still to watch him go by, and to crowd the café windows.

She forced herself to follow the Knight's journey. Behind him stood or knelt the emaciated figures of Suffering Humanity, imploring him to go forward. Five more huge panels spread round the three walls continued the progress. She pushed her way through the chairs and fallen music stands to inspect the centre panels.

Here were the Hostile Powers painted in gilt on a base of casein in which were set in febrile richness patterns and decorations in semi-precious stones. Here was the Giant Typhon, vast, squat and hairy, grinning through broken teeth. His right shoulder supported the Gorgons, Sickness, Mania and Death. On his left shoulder sat Desire, naked, leering sidelong, open-lipped, with lard-white buttocks oozing over Typhon's fur in perverse invitation.

Standing apart, staring in lubricious approval at Desire, was Impurity. Here was the most obscene object Alma-Maria had ever seen in a painting. Its face with its rolling suet chins peered from the half-concealment of a gaudy, jewel-encrusted headpiece. Her Indonesian sarong, a mass of painted eyes which stared outwards at the viewer as if to hypnotize and paralyse, was tucked into a heavy gold and jewelled belt. The belt itself was clasped under the creased overhang of her vastly pregnant belly on whose grease-gleaming surface lay her two fat, pendulous breasts with their red, cow-like teats. Did Klimt himself know, Alma-Maria wondered, what monstrous foetuses crouched in the wet darkness of that stretched and swollen belly, waiting to be debouched, stinking, into the world?

The Gorgons too were naked except that they were draped in their hair. Asps writhed as thin as earthworms from the tresses, while the women themselves stared balefully from blue eyes, each from a different angle and in a different direction, so that, between them, they took in the entire gallery. Each had between her legs a growth of hair precisely similar in colour, shape and density. They were, in fact, identical sisters – all of them: Sickness, Mania, Death, Desire . . . and, Alma-Maria realized, the Muse of German Poetry. They were all *her* identical sisters. Even the gross figure of Impurity, swollen as a drowned corpse in its dropsical fecundity, shared some of the others' features – features which, in one or two instances, only a lover would recognize.

She groped behind her to find one of the musicians' chairs and lowered herself onto it. Pappi – dear, dear Pappi – would have read the fresco immediately. She recalled how he had explained to her Mantegna's paintings of the Nativity, the Deposition, and Botticelli's Adoration of the Magi – the winding roads with identical figures at each turn and twist, revealing in their tribulations the full development of the scriptural story.

She twisted herself round to look at the conclusion of the progress – the Kingdom of the Ideal revealed in the panel beyond the figure of the Muse. There, close by the entrance, were the final figures, those symbolizing Pure Joy, Pure Happiness, Pure Love. And with them, to illustrate the apotheosis of Beethoven's great choral episode, surrounded by a choir of heavenly angels and framed under an arch of fire-trailing comets, the now naked figure of the Knight, his taut, sinewy frame being embraced by, and closely embracing, the nude figure of the Muse in a lover's kiss.

It was as if Klimt had entered Mahler's skull: had perceived the experiences, the puritan terrors and revulsions *and desires* which racked his sexuality. It was if he had some private intimation of what had drawn Mahler to her; had known also what she had hoped for, what Mahler had longed for – *Diesen Kuss der Ganzen Welt* ('With this Kiss, greet the World'), Schiller and Beethoven's paean to the liberation of the human spirit – and had taken it, in their case at least, as having been accomplished.

'The janitor told me you were here.'

He had thrown his coat over the shoulders of his smart, unaccustomed suit. It lent him a proper, Bohemian air.

'Do you approve, Frau Court Opera Director? Does it receive your *imprimatur?*'

'Don't call me that, Gustav.'

She was struggling to contain herself. He took his hands out of his trouser pockets, and let his coat fall over one of the chairs. He stared with his good-humoured, peasant face around him.

'I'm thinking of changing the title,' he said, to *Mein Reich ist nicht von dieser Welt*, "My Kingdom is not of this World". What do you think? Do you think Mahler would be willing to alter one line of Schiller's *Ode?*'

Just as if she were drunk, she heard herself say, word for word, inside her head, I'm still in love with him.

It was so unfair – so dreadfully unfair.

'Why don't you ask him yourself?' Her voice was cold.

'Because he would certainly say no – to me,' said Klimt. 'Mahler regards me as semi-literate. In which, of course, he's perfectly correct.'

'Have you asked him whether he approves? He's spent the day rehearsing in here.'

'He hasn't spoken to you? I was going to ask you.'

'I didn't have a chance to speak to him. He had to go straight back to the Opera.'

'He glanced at it before he started,' said Klimt. 'He laughed. I don't think he saw it really. I think he was too full of his music.'

'Why didn't you paint yourself as the Knight?' she asked. 'I know you told me from the start you weren't going to, but it would have been more honest.'

'Why, Frau Alma?'

'And don't call me that, either!'

He caught the urgency in her voice.

'Very well. Almschi?'

She nodded. There were tears, but mercifully they did not fall.

'Two reasons. First of all, I'm not Mahler. You have to realize who your husband is, Almschi. The Court Opera is to Vienna what the Temple was to the Jews. And the High Priest is Gustav Mahler. They may not like him, they may even want to take him out and stone him from time to time, but he's the one who enters the holy of holies at the appointed times and comes out to reveal the great truth to the people.' He paused, as if uncertain if he should continue. After a moment's silence, he made up his mind. 'Secondly, I've never thought of you like that ...' He pointed to the figures of the Gorgons... 'Or that! ... Or that! ... Or that!' He ended at the figure of Impurity. 'Mind you ...' He turned back to the figures representing the Despairing World ... 'I've thought of myself as this.' He pointed to the painfully etiolated, huddled figures of Melancholia and Self-Hatred. 'Even if I have painted them as women. Nor ...' He swung about to take in the farther side of

264

the gallery ... 'have I ever expected to achieve such a degree of blessedness.' He pointed to the naked figures of the Kiss. 'Not even, my dear Almschi,' he said softly, 'when we were together.'

She stood up and turned as if to leave. With these vivid carbuncle-encrusted walls surrounding her, with self-images smiling, leering, mocking down at her, she felt as if she had been imprisoned in somebody else's brain. She would have liked to burst into tears – great choking sobs of self-pity for the poor entrapped delusion she had become.

'Almschi!' Klimt called, seeing her to be upset. 'This is supposed to represent an ideal experience. I planned it before ever I knew you properly – or Mahler at all. You know that perfectly well.' He hesitated. As she made her way to the door of the gallery, pushing chairs aside as she did so, he came after her. 'I *cast* you for the part.'

'Oh quite! Like Burckhard cast me for a part. Like everybody casts me for a part.'

'I cast you for the part because you have the sort of beauty which inspires men to venture for something beyond themselves.'

She stopped and turned to face him.

'Yes?'

'I cast your husband as the Knight because he *is* a crusader. The only truly dedicated crusader I've met.'

'And you painted my husband armoured from head to foot, and me stripped naked.'

'It is your husband who's finally stripped naked.'

'And the look you've given me – even what no doubt you regard as an idealized me!' She pointed in the direction of the Muse. 'That coquette's look! You know better than anybody I've never been a coquette.'

'A glance of enticement? The Lorelei smile? ... But not an enticement to destruction, Alma, my dear. It's an enticement to the utter fulfilment of Love – the fulfilment which leads to untrammelled creativity. "Love which casteth out fear", remember.'

'It's pornography.'

She knew that would hurt him.

'*Et tu*, Alma?'

She should have left before they had come to this; she did not want to hurt Klimt, even when he had imprisoned her in the midst of his nightmare apparitions.

'Alma, you know that erotic love can be a lure to salvation. *Faust?*'

She nodded.

'Gretchen in the summerhouse,' she said.

'There, then. You understand this.' He waved around him.

But it hadn't been that way at all – no ecstasy, no angelic choirs. There had been no arrival in the Kingdom of the Ideal for either of them. Just herself without either her freedom or her own music, living as the figment of men's fantasies as if she had been condemned to a life sentence in this garish, enamelled cistern.

Klimt looked down into her face.

'You are astonishingly beautiful, you know,' he told her. 'You always were. But there's a radiance about you now.'

Oh, the longing – the awful longing! But it was all far too late now. She patted his sleeve then, quite gently, removed her hand from his arm.

'That's what they always say,' she said, 'about women in my condition ... I must go home now, to make sure they have Mahler's dinner ready. He'll be famished after all this.'

She laughed, and pulled her handbag up her glove and over her sleeve. 'He always has a very good appetite, even if he doesn't know or care what he's eating most of the time. Goodnight, Gustl.'

4 IN THIS WEATHER...
IN THIS TURMOIL: 1907

MAHLER HAD taken the children out for a row on the lake. Normally after lunch, when they were at Maiernigg for the summer, he would insist Alma-Maria leave three-year-old Guckerl and five-year-old Putzi with Miss Turner, the girls' young but pernickety English nanny, and accompany him on his unvarying four-mile walk up and round the mountainside. Alfred Roller described him as a 'narrow-gauge walker' because he kept his legs brushing close together to occupy the least possible space, would lean forward with his chin thrust out like a ship's prow as if to break the surface of an airy ocean. He also stamped the ground noisily, altering his pace according to the music sounding in his head. He rarely talked, often sang or even shouted themes as they came to him, and sometimes stopped abruptly to note down a passage which had come to him in his pocket manuscript book. On these latter occasions, Alma-Maria was expected to keep her distance so as not to disturb his concentration. After his second experience, as a house-guest at Maiernigg, of walking with him in the mountains, Roller declined to do so again. No such option was open to Alma-Maria even though, being small and encumbered with skirts, she found it a strain to keep up with his brisk uphill pace. There was a deeply inculcated sense of her duty as wife and companion which her resentment would not negate.

On an afternoon as close and as heavy as this one, his unexpected decision to take the children for a row was more than ordinarily welcome. Not that it was unusual for him to take the children out in the boat –

he did so frequently after his walk, in the cool of the evening, his considerable power and skill as a swimmer ensuring their safety. Indeed, Putzi and Guckerl were encouraged to take liberties with him which were not permitted to any other member of the household, including their mother. If they escaped from Alma-Maria or Miss Turner and found their way to their father where he was working, far from being rebuked, they would emerge from the music room, or the 'little composing house' up in the woods, with their mouths and fingers sticky with chocolate, jam or cake. Alma-Maria's pointing out that this positively encouraged them to disturb him took no effect whatever. In the evenings, he would play with them, dance with them or read to them with a fierce commitment which sometimes frightened her a little: it was as if he were afraid he might not see them for very long, and he had to give them all the love which he had not received from a father in his own impoverished childhood.

Since yesterday afternoon, Putzi, the elder of the two, had been complaining of being uncomfortable because of the heat. At lunch she said her head was aching, and she had eaten only very little because, she said, her neck was sore. The previous evening, Alma-Maria had noticed that her glands were slightly swollen, but in the morning the swelling appeared to have subsided. Over lunch, Mahler had suggested a row in the boat – a voyage of exploration for a place where Putzi would feel cooler, in the middle of the lake perhaps. Guckerl laughed and banged her spoon, shouting, 'In the water, Pappi! In the water!'

'It might be a little too cold,' Miss Turner suggested.

She shivered violently to make her point. She spoke a pedantic, schoolroom German which made Mahler imitate her behind her back (he was a little afraid of her), and which she always thought the Viennese might not understand clearly.

'It won't be cold,' Alma-Maria reassured her. 'There's not a breath of wind.'

'Then we'll row very fast,' said Mahler, 'and make a wind, shan't we!'

Guckerl laughed so hard at her father's imitation of rowing very fast that she dropped her spoon on the floor. Putzi looked very solemn and pretty: with her mass of blonde hair and her big blue wondering eyes, already she was taking after her mother and maternal grandmother rather than the Jewish side of her family.

'It'll be nice,' she said gravely, in a strange, masculine voice.

After they had left the table, Alma-Maria had told Mahler,

'I know what you're like when you play up to the children, Gustl.' He had already taken off his alpaca summer jacket, was unbuttoning his waistcoat and unfastening his shirtsleeves. 'You're going to play at being a paddle-steamer or something equally stupid. Don't go over-exerting yourself in this heat.'

He looked slightly sheepish.

'Please, Gustl,' she urged.

There had been a rehearsal of a new production of *Das Rheingold* at the Court Opera the previous winter, at which she had been present. At the point in Scene Two, when, in accordance with Wagner's stage directions, the giants Fasolt and Fafner were supposed physically to lift up Freia, Goddess of Youth and Beauty, and carry her away, the two basses refused to do so. The young soprano playing Freia was, for once, ideally cast. She was taller than average, but slim. Mahler, who regarded Wagner's directions as a sanctified rubric, insisted. The two basses, playing their boorish roles for real, argued that in almost every opera house it had become the tradition to ignore this particular instruction. Mahler had exploded.

'Tradition is slovenliness!' he roared like thunder.

He had stormed up the gangway from his desk in the auditorium onto the stage – for one terrified moment, Alma-Maria had been afraid he was furious enough to have attacked them. Instead, in spite of her being taller than him, he had lifted the soprano in his arms and had carried her up the ramp between the lathe and canvas cliffs. A few moments later, he had reappeared, his arm about her shoulder and had returned her to the sulky-looking giants.

He had returned to his table in the auditorium, and the rehearsal continued according to Wagner's expressed wishes. Alma-Maria noticed, however, how heavily he slumped into his chair, and how the remainder of the rehearsal passed with virtually no comment. Afterwards, ashen-faced and tight-lipped, he returned with her to his office, accompanied by his devoted production assistant, Alois Przistaupensky. There, he lay on the settee, breathing short, staccato breaths as if afraid to breathe deeply.

'The damned pain!' he groaned once.

'Where, darling?' she had asked. 'Where do you feel it?'

'Across my chest. Up my arm. In my jaw, like toothache.'

'Telephone the Loew Institute,' she told Przistaupensky. 'Ask for Professor Kovacs.'

Mahler clutched at her arm. 'It'll pass,' he said. 'There's no need for more fuss.'

'Gustl!' she had rebuked him.

'It's happened before. It'll pass as if nothing has happened.'

Alma-Maria looked to Przistaupensky who was standing behind the settee. Przistaupensky was going to admit nothing at first, but he wore a guilty expression behind the waxed tips of his moustache. Out-stared, he admitted,

'It was during the rehearsals for *Lohengrin*, last March.'

'Alois!' exclaimed Mahler, confirming by his albeit weak display of indignation that secrets had been kept from her.

There was a scratch at the door. Lenerl Sgalitzer bustled in without awaiting a reply. She had her shorthand pad and pencil clutched against her wrist, ready to take Mahler's post rehearsal notes. Pretty and neat as always, nevertheless she looked suspiciously flustered at the sight of Alma-Maria; a lock of the blonde hair, which she kept secured in the severe bun befitting a married woman who was continuing to pursue a career, had escaped and was straggling down her face. She pushed it back, away from her nose.

'Not now, Lenerl!' Mahler groaned. He lay back against the cushion Alma-Maria had placed at his back. 'This afternoon – after your lunch.'

Frau Sgalitzer looked down at him.

'You've had another of your attacks, Herr Director,' she said accusingly.

'What happened at the *Lohengrin* rehearsal?' Alma-Maria demanded. She was determined not to be excluded by Gustav's Opera House *familia*.

'It was Act Three, the first scene,' Frau Sgalitzer replied briskly.

Mahler groaned again, this time at the extent of the betrayal.

'The slaying of Duke Frederick in the bridal chamber,' Frau Sgalitzer continued. She looked to Alois Przistaupensky to fill in the details.

Mahler was past limiting the damage already done.

'Your honoured husband didn't think the action quite forceful enough,' Przistaupensky explained. 'He felt the scene required – well – more violence. Panic – hysteria among the bridesmaids.'

Alma-Maria could picture what had happened, given Gustav's passion for *Realismus* in music drama. He had acted all the parts himself, screaming bridesmaids, Frederick's vengeful blood lust, Lohengrin's death-dealing blow, Frederick's monstrous last agony.

'He demonstrated till he was satisfied everybody was doing exactly what he wanted?' she asked.

Przistaupensky and Lenerl Sgalitzer nodded their agreement.

'He exhausted himself,' said Frau Sgalitzer.

'Lenerl!' protested Mahler.

'Well it's true, Herr Director!' said Frau Sgalitzer. 'You were holding your hand on your heart and gasping for breath. Poor Herr Alois here had to help you back to your seat.'

'It's true,' Przistaupensky confirmed.

'This is all the most utter nonsense!' Mahler protested. 'It was nothing more than a passing discomfort. Indigestion. You see? . . . The pain is passing now.'

He sat up and put his feet to the ground. Alma-Maria had to admit to herself that the colour was returning to his cheeks. She asked Przistaupensky and Frau Sgalitzer to leave them. When they were gone, she had said,

'You swore your staff to secrecy, didn't you?'

'I didn't want you worried by trivialities,' he had replied, his boldness returning. 'They're just passing turns. You know very well how fit I am most of the time.'

'Gustl, I'm supposed to be the person who looks after you, not your salaried assistants!'

'You do, Almscherl. Beautifully ... Look, Almschili: the attacks have never been bad enough for me to stop a rehearsal. Nobody would have known anything had happened in that *Lohengrin* scene if that fool Przistaupensky hadn't seen me put my hand inside my shirt.'

'You've been overworking. You're always overworking. You ought to let Kovacs have a look at you.'

She should have sounded sympathetic. Instead she had sounded sullen. When Mahler had replied, it had been to pacify her.

'Very well, *liebchen*. At the end of the season.'

But when the season had ended, they had come as they always came, to Maiernigg, to the two-storey retreat he had built seven years earlier in the wood on the shore of the Wörthersee.

She had reminded him of his promise that first evening. She had been sitting on the upholstered lounger on the first-floor bedroom balcony, smoking a cigarette – an occasional after-dinner luxury. The mirror surface of the Wörthersee had stretched unbroken to the mountainside opposite; the sunlight had still been glittering on the snow-caps of the peaks high above them. He had been leaning, half-sitting, on the Tirolean-style carved balustrade (a decorative kitsch she secretly detested), his jacket slung over one shoulder, smoking his evening cigar. His attitude suggested a man *acting* as if he were at leisure.

'You have no need to concern yourself about my health a moment longer, *liebchen*,' he had told her with a vast assumption of airiness. 'I have resigned the direction of the Imperial-Royal Court Opera – as from the end of December.'

It took several moments for the implications of his statement to sink in. When they did, her response was one of shock.

'Gustav! What on earth shall we do?'

She saw suddenly how appallingly wasted was all that her careful book-keeping had achieved – the cook and four maids, Miss Turner, Anton, his manservant-chauffeur, and the luxurious Mercedes-Benz of which both he and Anton were so immensely proud, the small army of occasional music-copyists, shorthand typists, and piano tuners (there were two concert grands in the Auenbruggergasse apartment, two in the Maiernigg house, and the cottage piano in the 'little composing house'). There was also the upkeep of two homes, and the dream of a third one – a Haus Mahler to be built by Josef Hoffmann up on the Hohe Warte, close to the Villa Möll. Very little of this could be supported by his royalties, and even his appearances as a guest-conductor – though he would no doubt be much in demand – would scarcely maintain such a standard of living.

But there was a deeper cause of unease in the fact that she was aware that much had happened of which she had been deliberately left ignorant. So that she was not mollified when he told her,

'I am to be treated much more generously than poor old Burckhard ever was. I'm to receive an annual pension of 14,000 kronen instead of the customary 10,000. I'm to receive 20,000 in compensation for my loss of office, despite the fact that I have chosen to resign. And you, my darling, are entitled to a Privy Councillor's widow's pension – even though I'm not a Privy Councillor, and I never did write an Imperial march. We shall not be badly off, I think ... In any case, Conried is after me.'

Heinrich Conried, Director General of the Metropolitan Opera, New York, was feared as a notoriously successful headhunter by every opera house management from Covent Garden to La Scala. Tetrazzini, Melba, Caruso, and Scotti had all been filched from under the noses of European managers. Mahler himself has lost Fremstad and Sembrich from the Vienna Court Opera.

'He wrote to me from Berlin. He wanted to own me body and soul, mind you, for 180,000 kronen a year. I told him I wouldn't even consider the offer under 73,000 a quarter.'

'How long has all this been going on?' asked Alma-Maria.

'He telegraphed me when I was conducting my Third in Frankfurt – mid-January, wasn't it? – accepting my conditions. I suppose he'd heard rumours about my approaching demise – or débâcle – at the Court Opera.'

'So you did know you might be forced to resign?'

'Of course. I've always known.'

'But you didn't think to tell me?'

'I warned you from the very beginning. Don't you remember? I told you I could only regard my tenure at the Opera as running from day to day.'

'That was six years ago, Gustav!'

He shrugged. 'So what has changed?'

The answer was that, to set against the interminable hurling of abuse by the Nationalist and Christian Socialist press which owed allegiance to the anti-semitic Mayor of Vienna, Karl Lueger – *schöne Karl* to the adoring multitudes who attended his Sunday carriage drive round the Ring – there were the packed houses and the international acclaim which had been accorded to Mahler's cycle of the five major Mozart operas which he had produced both for Vienna and Salzburg. The London *Times* had written of his production and conducting of *The Marriage of Figaro*, that it was 'the ideal *Figaro* in its enchanting grace ... Nobody who was present at Salzburg's opera house last night will ever forget the experience – unique, perhaps, since the composer's own production in Prague.' *The Magic Flute*, with Roller's magical settings, Selma Kurtz's astonishing coloratura as Queen of the Night, and Gutheil-Schöder's enchanting *ingénue* Pamina, had been the sensation of the Vienna season. In the coffee houses and wine cellars, tickets had changed hands at astronomical prices.

With the cycle complete, and the acclamation at his achievement still ringing in his ears, Mahler took three weeks leave to conduct in Rome. The Nationalist press had leapt at him as if out of ambush. The *Deutsche Zeitung* wrote,

> Herr Mahler is doing a tour of Italy gathering laurels – and, more importantly for one of his tribe, even more money. We shall, one of these days, as a responsibility toward our music-loving readership, calculate how many months' paid leave he has extorted from his employers to pursue his personal money-making schemes . . .

The *Reichspost* reported,

> Once again we are provided with a striking illustration of the current mismanagement of the Vienna Court Opera. Jew-Director Mahler, having secured an enormous salary which can only be described as exorbitant, is now abroad, peddling his inferior symphonic products around Italy as his father peddled rot-gut brandy round the villages of Moravia . . .

And there had been much more of the same kind, together with the usual cartoons depicting him as a hook-nosed, slobbering deformed dwarf eyeing lubriciously from his podium the young female singers under his baton.

Few people could have stood the stream of vilification which had been directed at him from all but the Jewish-owned press, and the constant plotting and manoeuvring against him that went on in the management committees of the Imperial theatres. She had known about it because everybody had known about it: that he could never have maintained his position but for his extraordinary success at the box office and his international acclaim as a conductor.

And yet he had refused to talk to her about it. He would expect her to lavish loving sympathy on him if he had a common cold or an attack of indigestion, but she was allowed no part whatever in the real struggles of his life. Once, unable to contain herself, she had burst out – at a dinner which they had been giving for some of his collaborators at the Opera, Kolo Moser, Roller, Bruno Walter and his wife, and Hugo von Hofmannsthal –

'Can't they *see* and *hear* what Gustav has achieved at the Opera?'

Mahler had reached over and put his hand on hers to quieten her.

'One has to remember what Mozart wrote to his father. In fact, every Director of the Court Opera should have it engraved in front of his eyes. "The Viennese public are utterly incapable even of beginning to understand what seriousness means." '

There was no discussion. The Viennese public was the product of
Fate. To have discussed such a phenomenon with her would have been
to admit that there was some possibility of modifying the Viennese
public – or Fate. It was, she had decided, a peculiarly Jewish trait that
towards Fate one either adopted a quietist, fatalistic attitude, or one
defied it. One never entertained the possibility that one could modify it.
So Mahler's attitude toward the strident and often cruelly libellous
attacks made on him by the press was to ignore them as if they had not
occurred. Never for a moment had he allowed her to see that they might
have hurt him.

Sitting in the stillness of the bedroom balcony overlooking the lake,
with the last sunlight catching the pinnacles of snow on the mountain
summits up on the far side, she had asked,

'Did they make you resign?'

He appeared not to have heard at first. In a gesture which never failed
to irritate her, he examined the damp end of his cigar and picked from
it a shred of tobacco which he then had to brush off the tip of his thumb.

'I had a number of conversations with Prince Montenuovo,' he replied
at last. 'He appeared to think that in view of the state of public opinion,
I should curtail my private – independent – musical life.'

'So you actually did resign?'

'Yes . . . I realized how tired I felt.'

This was an admission and a half.

Of course, as well as his Levantine inability to perceive the possibility
of modifying the operations of a malign Fate, there had been his refusal
to compromise to the least degree. So, when the Crown Prince, the
Archduke Franz-Ferdinand, had sent to him the young soprano Mitzi
Gunther, with a letter suggesting without subtlety that she be accepted
by the Court Opera for the following season, he had glanced at the letter,
had torn it up immediately, and had told the simpering girl, 'Now sing
for me.' When she had done so, he had sent her away and telephoned
Prince Montenuovo.

'Fräulein Gunther's voice is trash. I can do nothing with her.'

'It is his Imperial Highness's express wish she should appear on the
stage of the Court Opera.'

'She may certainly appear, so long as she doesn't open her mouth.'

'It is a long-standing promise on the part of His Imperial Highness
that she should sing with the Court Opera. Her salary will be paid from
the Imperial Privy Purse . . . Gustav, you must understand that it *is* the
Imperial-Royal Court Opera, and that you are a servant belonging to
the Imperial Household, as I am.'

'Very well. I consent. The programme will contain a note to the effect
that Fräulein Gunther appears "Upon the Highest Command".'

274

'You know very well that is quite impossible. It would give rise to the greatest scandal.'

'Then I'm supposed to bear the onus of apparently remaining unaware of Mitzi Gunther's lack of even a modicum of talent?'

'There is surely a small part . . .'

'Not while I'm Director of the Court Opera, Excellency.'

'Then, my dear Mahler, you'll have to send me a report on Fräulein Gunther's ability as an operatic singer which I can pass on. Quite frankly, I dare not pass on your refusal by word of mouth. You might not feel the need for friends in the highest places. I do.'

At first, when she had heard about it, Alma-Maria had been proud of him. Then it had occurred to her that by giving Mitzi Gunther a role so small the critics would scarcely have noticed it, he could have won the support of the Crown Prince at a most trying time. After all, the Archduke Franz-Ferdinand hadn't been particularly interested in Fräulein Gunther's career – he was merely offering a sop to a discarded mistress. Mahler, she had decided, had been displaying the wilful incorruptibility of the psychologically insecure.

Equally stubborn had been his advocacy on behalf of Strauss's *Salome*. That evening in Krefeld when, for the first time, he had conducted a complete version of his Third Symphony in Germany – and she had been pregnant with little Putzi – Strauss had kept the promise to be there he had made on the first night of *Feuersnot* with addition. He had bounded onto the stage at the end of the final *adagio*, and had walked up and down in front of the orchestra, clapping and whipping up the applause of the audience. He had then publicly embraced Mahler like a gigantic but amiable mastiff embracing a whippet.

There was no mistaking the affection which existed between them. Over dinner at the hotel, they argued exclusively with one another as if their wives weren't present – over Socratic-Platonic religious belief, the Athenian institution of slavery, and Mommsen's *History of Ancient Greece* – while Pauline Strauss moaned to Alma-Maria about clothes ("Where *can* one buy chic blouses or a decent jabot in a place like Düsseldorf?' and 'Really, my dear Frau Alma, *are* there any *really* smart dress shops in Vienna?'). Mahler had remarked to Strauss that he had received overtures from the New York Philharmonic Society regarding the possibility of his conducting the New York Philharmonic–Symphony Orchestra for a summer season, while the Court Opera was closed, but that he had not been convinced he would be allowed sufficient rehearsal time to suit his own standards of performance.

'My dear old fellow!' Strauss had exclaimed. 'Why don't you do what Toscanini does? Stand in front of them. Wag your stick like any damned actor. Then pick up your pailful of cash and catch the next boat back to Cherbourg and civilization!'

Alma-Maria had found both Strausses detestable, without a grain of moral integrity between them. She couldn't understand Mahler's reaction. He had laughed heartily at Strauss's suggestion. The same night, when she had asked him if he was seriously considering the invitation from New York, he replied,

'By the time one completed the season, one would have gone a fair way to losing one's soul. I'm sure my little Almscherl wouldn't approve of that!' as if his refusal was entirely for her sake.

When Strauss had sent Mahler his outline for a proposed opera based on Oscar Wilde's play, *Salome*, with a view to its being commissioned by the Vienna Court Opera, Mahler's response had been anything but enthusiastic. He took a violent dislike to the subject, which offended against his ingrained puritanism. He had been sitting at her escritoire one evening, writing back to Strauss, when she put her arms round his neck and said to him,

'Don't you think it'll only encourage him, Gustl, darling? Trying to persuade somebody like Strauss not to compose the opera he's set his heart on is surely a bit like telling a man he shouldn't try making love to a woman he's become obsessed with. Anyway, isn't a true artist like an alchemist? Can't he transmute base metal into gold?'

Mahler had drawn her arms tight about him until her cheek was pressed against his own.

'I didn't know my Almschili was such a romantic!' he told her.

Twelve months passed. Strauss turned up in Vienna and insisted on taking them both out to lunch at a restaurant on the Grabern. With him he had a pile of manuscript. They were leaving the restaurant to walk back to the Opera when Strauss noticed the piano showroom with its enormous plate-glass window opposite the Leopold Fountain. He dragged at Mahler's arm.

'Come on. I'm going to play you my *Salome*.'

Mahler pulled his watch from his fob pocket.

'So that's the reason for this pleasant little occasion,' he remarked in a tone which would have withered anybody less self-confident and ebullient than Strauss.

'One act – that's all,' said Strauss. 'I'm sure the Serene Highnesses and Excellencies of the Hofburg can dispense with your services for a mere ninety minutes.'

He started to drag Mahler physically across the square. Alma-Maria trotted after in her fashionably tight skirt. All round the fountains, passers-by, recognizing the three of them, stopped to gawp.

The showroom manager was only too delighted to allow such very distinguished figures in the musical world the use of any of his stock.

'An English Broadwood,' Strauss insisted.

'Of course, gentlemen. The only instrument for orchestral reductions – the sonority . . .'

The manager led them to a Broadwood concert grand which stood actually inside the big plate-glass window.

'The best light, gentlemen,' he explained.

Strauss sat down and started to arrange his heap of manuscript.

'Shall I turn for you, Dr Strauss?' Alma-Maria offered.

'Please, Frau Alma! How very kind!'

The crowd was already forming outside the window as she took her seat on the stool offered by the manager. The manager stood back. She noticed he really was rubbing his hands together in an uncontrollable gesture of satisfaction. Mahler, on the other hand, was hopping from one foot to the other.

He continued to show his impatience as Strauss played, sang, chanted, grimaced his way through the opening scene. Halfway through the first encounter between Salome and the Baptist – *Deinen Mund begehre ich* ('It's your mouth I most desire') – Alma-Maria noticed that he was absolutely still. He remained motionless for most of the remainder of the recital, as if hypnotized by the erotic charge in Strauss's extraordinary score, moving only once to signal to the manager to bring him a chair.

When they reached Salome's 'Dance of the Seven Veils', Strauss stopped playing abruptly. Stepping instantly out of the voluptuous sensuality of the scene he was communicating, he remarked cheerfully.

'Haven't written it yet. Bit of a musical prop, eh? Shove it in when we've seen if we can find a singer who can dance a bit.'

'Isn't that a bit risky?' asked Mahler. 'Leaving it, and writing it later when your mood may be quite different?'

'No, no! Scenery, my dear fellow. Paste and canvas. I can botch it up any time.'

Strauss returned to his recital. He seemed wholly unaware of the ugliness and horror of the final scene – of the physically sickening sudden transition to a grunted B-flat on double basses which illustrated the decapitation of the Baptist, and Salome's final transports of lust as she sang to the severed head, 'I want to kiss your mouth, Jokanaan!' Or rather he was quite aware, but in a different mode to his audience: he was laughing and beaming mischievously as he lowered his hands finally from the keyboard.

Neither man looked for Alma-Maria's opinion of the work.

'It could very well be the finest thing you've written,' Mahler told Strauss.

Strauss was enchanted.

'My dear Mahler! Do you really think so? That's praise indeed!'

'The quintet – the Five Jews – that might be a little difficult to stage . . .'

They began to discuss a hypothetical production. The crowd at the window melted away. Alma-Maria wandered from piano to piano, ignored by both of them. It was not until late that evening, when he had returned from the Opera, that Mahler had put his arm round her waist and had kissed her.

'Darling Almschi, you were right all those months ago! The alchemist Ricardus has indeed transmuted base metal into gold! You are an extremely perceptive and intelligent little wife, and I shall never doubt your judgement again.'

But that had been a sop to her after all the hours she had been ignored.

Mahler had obtained a copy of the libretto from Strauss. He presented it to the General Management of the Court Theatres with the strongest recommendation that it should be given its première by the Vienna Court Opera. Astonishingly, in view of the leisurely proceedings of the Hofburg staff, he had a reply from Privy Councillor Dr Emil Jettel von Ettenach within forty-eight hours.

> My dear Mahler – Even you must surely have realized that the figure of the Baptist appearing in an erotic drama would prove anathema to Christian susceptibilities. We are not, of course, in a position to examine the validity of your opinion that it is a work of exceptional musical power; but if it were, it would hardly mitigate the revulsion which must be felt by decent people at the nature of the story. One might also be tempted to remind you that the representation of events which belong in the realms of sexual psychopathia has no place on our Court stages . . .

She had begged him to leave it at that. *Salome* could scarcely have been turned down more emphatically by his employers.

'Honestly Gustl! You said yourself that the subject was a repulsive one.'

'That was before I heard the score.'

'I bet he only composed it to see how much he could get away with. I bet you anything you like he was laughing up his sleeve with every note he wrote, thinking how it would scandalize people! You know Strauss as well as I do.'

'And Bach, when he wrote the B-minor Mass, thought he was writing a demonstration piece, a bit of advertising with which to win commissions from Catholic courts. And Mozart thought he was writing a pantomime for the riffraff of the Naschmarkt when he wrote *The Magic Flute*. And perhaps even the Blessed Virgin only wanted a very ordinary son. Nobody ever *intends* the descent of the Divine Spirit.'

'The Divine Spirit? Richard Strauss!' she retorted.

Mahler had given her a very cold look indeed. The sort which could frighten even her – temporarily. He had written to Strauss:

> On Tuesday next, my dear Strauss, I am going in person to the Hofburg to take the bull by the horns. And I shall not let go, I assure you. You may regard your *Salome*, at least as far as Vienna is concerned, as my personal commitment . . .

His discussions with the members of the General Management Committees and their rejection of his applications were selectively leaked to the Nationalist and Christian Socialist newspapers.

> It cannot rightly be said that Dr Strauss's new opera is the work of a Jew. But it is significant perhaps that its most enthusiastic advocate is the Jew-Director of our own Imperial and Royal Opera, and that it is he who seeks to subvert the standards of wholesomeness and decency set by his Christian predecessors by the production of an open and palpable blasphemy ...

Salome received its first German performance at Dresden. Mahler – they had retired to Maiernigg for the summer – was engrossed in working on his Sixth Symphony, and in completing a new cycle of settings of poems by Rückert. He had been in his usual withdrawn state of abstraction when he was deeply involved in composition. He had refused to talk to anybody, dressed like a tramp, and had forbidden her to play the piano in case it distracted him up in his 'little composing house'. Only the children had been exempt from the Trappist regime.

Then the embossed, gilt-edged pasteboard had arrived. It was an invitation from the Mayor of Graz:

> Sir – I take the liberty of extending to the Celebrated and Distinguished Director of the Imperial and Royal Court Opera and to his Admired, Highly Esteemed, and Well-born Wife, the most respectful invitation to attend the first performance in the Dual Monarchy of an opera – *Salome* – by Dr Richard Strauss, as my guests in my box.

The Graz City Opera, being neither Imperial nor Royal, was exempt from the censors of the Vienna Hofburg. The Trappist silence was shattered.

'Gustl, you can't possibly go! Everybody will know about it! They'll think you're slapping the faces of your own Management Committee!'

'There's the question of friendship, Almschi. Loyalty to a friend.'

'Gustl!' She was almost screaming at his obduracy. 'When has Richard Strauss ever done the least thing for you? Oh yes! He stood up and applauded when an audience was already applauding you. But supposing you produced something which was unpopular – something audiences didn't understand? You wouldn't see Richard Strauss for dust. You conduct his work. When has he ever conducted yours? Frau Pauline wouldn't let him – it might lose money! And they're rich! They've both always been very well off. Putzi, Guckerl, and I, we depend on you utterly – well, almost utterly.'

'My position imposes on me a duty to advocate and uphold music I consider to be of exceptional merit. Strauss's score is just such music.'

Aspects of Jewishness – the defiance displayed by the prophet, the need to bear witness in the face of heaven knows what contumely – was as strong as the belief in the immutability of Fate. Karl Kraus, Sigmund Freud, Artur Schnitzler, even Berta Zuckerkandl – all were capable of defying public opinion, of obstinately persisting in a course of action which defied popularity, to invite being branded as outsiders.

She had gone with him to Graz. And if she had had to be conspicuous, then she had been conspicuous in style, in a vivid blue *crêpe de Chine* gown designed by Kolo Moser, with jewellery worthy of Salome herself, designed for the Wiener Werkstätte by Carl Otto Czeschka. There had been the most gratifying whispering and rustling of excitement when she had entered the box in the opera house escorted by the Mayor.

The response to Mahler's appearance in Graz that night had been so violent that an old friend of Pappi's and Möll's, the critic Hermann Bahr, who had never quite forgiven Mahler for Anna von Mildenburg's having fallen in love with him when Bahr himself had wanted to marry her, wrote a letter of sympathy to Alma-Maria:

> So once again your poor Mahler is to be hounded, hounded, hounded! Why do these people hate him so? From the way they write, one would think it was solely because he is a Jew. But they hate Klimt equally. So perhaps it is because he is true to himself and what he believes – because our fickle Viennese public know that integrity is freedom, and they resent the freedom which is his but which they will never have the courage to enjoy ...

Mahler had been protected over the *Salome* episode by the K-K Court Chamberlain, Prince Montenuovo. But more recently, only a few weeks before they had come to Maiernigg this summer, there had been the Schoenberg *Skandal*. Because Schoenberg was her friend and frequent dinner guest, Mahler had insisted in giving his Chamber Symphony his seal of approval by attending its first performance at the Bosendorfersaal.

Almost from the very first notes, the audience had fidgeted restlessly in protest at the strange dissonances in the music and the lack of identifiable melody. Mahler himself was as bewildered as Alma-Maria by the strange musical paths Schoenberg had elected to follow. But when, halfway through the performance, a group of men at the back began to grind their chairlegs on the floor and to excite laughter by walking in and out of the auditorium slamming the doors, he sprang up and, with the powerful bass voice and intimidating authority which had enforced discipline on singers, stage staff, and orchestra at the Opera, he demanded the work be heard in silence. The tumult died, the mischief-makers either returned to their seats or left the hall. Only their ringleader remained standing. He was a very erect, bull-necked man with cropped hair and imperial whiskers and a satin order across his evening dress. Alma-Maria recognized him immediately to be the Archduke Franz-Ferdinand's personal favourite, General Franz Conrad von Hötzendorf. Mahler was in bad enough odour with the Crown Prince over his refusal to employ Mitzi Gunther at the Court Opera, without courting further unpopularity in that quarter – but of course matters had already gone too far. In a voice to rival Mahler's own, General Conrad von Hötzendorf's rang out above the orchestra's attempt to continue Schoenberg's symphony:

'No decent Austrian would wish to hear any more of this Jew filth.'

Whereupon the General turned and strode out of the auditorium.

It was most unlikely that he had come to hear Schoenberg's music, thought Alma-Maria, as the performance continued to a sullen silence from a thinned-out audience – or had even heard of Schoenberg except as a protégé of Mahler. She had no doubt his master the Archduke had sent him, and that the intended victim of his interruption had been Mahler rather than Schoenberg.

Her worst suspicions were confirmed when, as they came out of the Bosendorfersaal, they found General Conrad von Hötzendorf waiting on the steps in the damp glare of the carriage lamps. His gleaming top hat was at an angle and he was holding his stick as if it were a sabre at his side. Around him was a small group of the aides who had been with him inside the auditorium. Below the steps, Möll, who was invited to dine at 10 Auenbruggergasse, was waiting with Anton and the motor. Mahler, with Alma-Maria on his arm, chose to ignore the General and his young cronies, and started to step down toward the motor.

'Pity they didn't give the young Jew-boy the thrashin' he deserved!' General Conrad von Hötzendorf called out. 'Pollutin' the ears of decent citizens with his damned caterwaulin'! Damned impertinence, I say!'

'No, Gustl!' she said.

But Mahler had already turned.

'It is astonishing, Herr General,' he said quite gently, 'to find a nobleman of your distinction bawling out insults in a public place like any street urchin.'

General Conrad von Hötzendorf's eyes glared in the lamplight. His breath steamed in the March night air. He thrust out his stick at the top button of Mahler's coat.

'By God, Herr Director! I know you, sir! You may think yourself safe, sir, because no true *Herr* can challenge one of your sort to an affair of honour. But I can thrash you, sir! By God, I can thrash you!'

He raised the stick above his head. Mahler pushed Alma-Maria aside; she stumbled, but was caught by a gentleman coming out from the vestibule of the Bosendorfersaal. At the same time, Möll rushed up the steps and grabbed at the General's arm.

'I beg you, sir!' he said, as the General struggled to free his arm. 'Not in a public place, sir! Think of the disgrace ...'

General Conrad von Hötzendorf's belligerence subsided. He allowed himself to be steered down the steps by his aides to a carriage waiting below. As he mounted the carriage step, he turned and shouted,

'You needn't have got so excited, my dear Herr Director! We boo and catcall at Mahler's music as well!'

For all the excitement, on the short drive back to the apartment, Mahler seemed wholly preoccupied with Schoenberg's music.

'I have to confess I haven't the foggiest notion of what he's up to,' he said. 'But he's young, so I expect he's right. When one is growing old, you know, one's ear loses its sensitivity.'

Alma-Maria and Möll had been left alone for a minute or two in the drawing room.

'Your Mutti, you know, *liebchen*,' said Möll, 'believes Gustav to be something of a saint. It's quite a rare thing for a mother to feel about a son-in-law, I dare say. In spite of all I said to you when he first began to show an interest in you, I'm beginning to see him in the same light.'

He wiped his hands with his handkerchief.

Within a week of the Schoenberg concert, Mahler had been summoned to the Hofburg, to Prince Montenuovo's office, to justify his application for leave in order to conduct in Rome.

Saint, visionary, beloved teacher – and monk. It wasn't just to those people who saw him in those roles – which seemed to be everybody except his declared opponents – she had to conceal the extent of her resentment, but to herself. And their attitude helped to separate her, not only mentally and spiritually from him, but even physically. Two days after the Schoenberg concert, Guido Adler, professor of History of Music at the University and one of the guests at that ghastly dinner party intended by Mahler to introduce her to his friends, had arrived at the apartment when Mahler was at the Opera. He had sounded as if he were about to burst into tears:

'Oh my dear Frau Alma! I have been so distressed these past two days, I can't tell you! I felt I had to talk to you about Gustav, to place my trust in you as between two people who truly love him. Frau Alma, it has to be said! He made the most painful exhibition of himself the other night. It may very well cost him his job, you know ... Frau Alma, it's hard for me to say it, but I do believe you could have stopped him ...'

'I?' Her voice rasped, jagged as a badly sharpened knife. Professor Adler didn't appear to notice.

'Friendship, and concern for a younger man, is one thing. But for a man in his position, and one of *us* – you understand my meaning, dear lady – to risk destroying a career of world distinction for the sake of the frightful cacophony we had to endure at the Bosendorfersaal the other night ... It's insane! I tell you, I went straight home and I shed tears. You can ask my wife: I shed tears, and it is no figure of speech, I do assure you. I thought of Gustav, and I thought of the way music is going and I wept dreadfully. Poor, poor music! And you know, Frau Alma? It has to be said: Gustav will have to bear as much responsibility for what happens as anybody.'

He reached for her hand, but she avoided his grasp.

'Thank you for coming, Professor Adler,' she told him. 'I'll pass on what you said to my husband.'

'No! No, Frau Alma! You have to *persuade* him, before it's too late.'

There had been a time, a once-upon-a-time, when she had dreamed of being helpmeet, Muse, persuader. But even if she had felt inclined to do the lachrymose Professor Adler's bidding, it was a time long since departed. Even when they were supposedly on holiday, the leaden, pre-marital routine Mahler had set himself travelled with them, with the books and the mountain of manuscript scores.

Since he had no time to compose while he was administering the Court Opera as well as producing and conducting, every minute of the summer on the Wörthersee had to be utilized properly. At five-thirty in the morning, long before she was up, he went out for a swim in the icy lake. He then walked the half-kilometre up through the pine woods to his 'little composing house', to remain there for the next seven hours in complete isolation. He would return to the house for lunch, for a quick game with the children, then there would be his dreadful four-mile walk, which for her was almost a run. There would be tea and cakes, and then he would take the children away, to bathe, to go out in the boat, to read stories; she had become painfully aware that she was growing jealous of the children as she heard from a summer distance his laughter joining with their high-pitched giggling and screaming. Only after dinner were they together, by themselves, and even then, more often than not, what communion there was between them was through the mediation of music, their playing together of Bach, Mozart, and – as a concession to her – piano reductions of Wagner. And, of course, work-in-progress, which, in its more early stages was not open to discussion.

Guests came and went. Alfred Roller was a frequent visitor, as were Alex von Zemlinsky and Schoenberg. There were singers with a particular rapport with Mahler, Marie Gutheil-Schöder with her husband, Selma Kurtz whose unpinned hair was almost as long as Alma-Maria's own, and the vastly popular Czech tenor, Leo Slezak, whose loyalty to and love for Mahler kept him at the Court Opera despite inducements to go elsewhere. There were artists – Kolo Moser, who was designing the Imperial postage stamps as well as Alma-Maria's clothes, and Klimt. None of them – not even those dearest to his heart, like the soprano Lilli Lehmann whom alone among his female friends he addressed as *leibchen*, or the most beloved of his assistants, Bruno Walter – was allowed to disturb his routine. All of them had come to identify themselves by their relationship to him.

This included those she herself had loved. So Alex's torments of jealousy at having lost her had been overcome by his near-slavish adoration of Mahler, while she had dwindled into Frau Alma Mahler. Even more exasperating was the case of Klimt whom she, through her stepfather, had introduced to Mahler. Painfully she came to realize that they had had similar formative experiences – both had reached positions of eminence in their art from which they could scarcely have risen further; both had suffered bereavement at the loss of brothers whom they had dearly loved; both were targets of the most vicious and persistent abuse of which the Viennese newspapers were capable, even if Klimt could not be accused of Mahler's ultimate sin of being a Jew. So they seemed to grow closer together in a friendship which excluded her even more effectively than did Alex's worship of Mahler.

Apart from such interruptions, Maiernigg for her meant the water-lapped stillness of the lake shore, broken by the distant chatter of servants and children, and the peremptory commands of Miss Turner. Not that she couldn't keep herself busy. With Alex von Zemlinsky she had learnt how to prepare and copy full orchestral scores, and even to assist in scoring as the pupil of a great and much sought after portrait painter might assist in painting the background to the subject. From the moment, even before their wedding, Mahler had realized how neat and precise a copyist she was, and how competent an arranger, he had been only too glad to make use of her skills, particularly as her own musical training gave her a clear understanding of what she was about. In her doing so, she had discovered that under Mahler's show of self-will and arrogance, his insensitivity toward others' feelings – and her own drives and desires – there was a great humility. She could suggest modifications in scoring and even in melodic development which he would invariably consider and occasionally accept. When he allowed her to discuss his work, he never manifested the quick impatience he displayed on the podium; once, with the draft of his Sixth Symphony, he re-ordered the inside movements on her recommendation, and in the case of his First Symphony, 'The Titan', dropped one movement altogether. His readiness to entertain her suggestions and even to act on them, filled her with an awesome sense of responsibility.

For all that, however, she had grown aware that the interior of his mind was a Bluebeard's chamber, locked against her, into which she obtained occasional keyhole glimpses which disconcerted her or, occasionally, even horrified her.

There had been the mid-morning, the previous summer when, to her astonishment, he had suddenly appeared in the house, ragged and dishevelled as he usually was when he had been working in his hut since dawn (he who had his shoes, shirts, and city suits made for him in London). He had insisted she come with him to his 'composing house'; had clutched her wrist in his long, prehensile fingers, and had dragged her there, ignoring the twigs and briars which plucked at her dress. In the hut, he made her sit beside him at the keyboard. On the music rest a manuscript score was propped up, the score of some immense choral work covered in erasures, corrections, and details of scoring pencilled in tiny but pedantically formed letters. She saw the words of the chorus stretched out below the staves.

'Two movements,' Mahler exclaimed. 'Parts, some people will call them – there are bound to be idiots in Vienna who'll insist it's an oratorio, not a symphony. The first is a setting of the *Veni Creator Spiritus* – the old medieval invocation of the Holy Ghost...'

He splayed his fingers to the limit, and crashed out the opening chords: 'Organ!' he shouted in her ear; 'full diapason! ... Then – *Veni! ... Veni Creator Spiritus!* ... The prayer for divine grace – *imple superna gratia* ... For spiritual strength ... Then, most important of all, the prayer for love – *Accende lumen sensibus,*

> Illuminate our senses,
> Pour love into our hearts ...'

He lifted the top sheets from the music rest and placed them on the piano lid, and played over the passage he had just quoted. He turned to his work table.

'The second movement,' he said, picking up a pile of completed manuscript, 'constitutes the answer to the prayer of the first. It's a setting of the final scene of *Faust* ...'

He set the music up in front of him and sorted through the pages.

'The Mage's soul is imbued by the Holy Ghost with a longing for Paradise which leaves him restless, dissatisfied with the created world. He is guided and urged on by the Spirits of Wisdom, of Vision, of the Muses and the Graces. But in the final instance – in the moment of pre-Judgement – he is drawn upwards by that which is most sacred of all: his own, personal, experience of Love.

> Gaze upwards in the tenderness of your penitence!
> Gaze on her who has saved you –
> Thus you cast off all earthly garments
> And are washed in Salvation ...'

He played the opening of the Angelic chorus. From the piano and the sheet manuscript in front of her, she could appreciate the affirmation in the music, the mighty swell of '*Blicket auf* ... Gaze upwards!' It was followed by an extraordinary modulation into a warm, peaceful, yet strong *cantabile*. When he had finished playing it, he turned to her.

'And that,' he told her, 'is you, my darling Almscherl. Your love casting out my fear.'

He played it again, murmuring Goethe's words as he did so. It seemed to her that it was the loveliest thing in terms of sheer melody he had ever written.

'That is for me?' she asked like a child astonished by an unexpected present.

'Not *for* you,' he told her. 'It *is* you.'

So there it was. He could ignore her emotional needs, deny her passion for months at a time. He would even shrink from her if she so much as touched him in bed. Then out of the blue he would produce some extraordinary, some breathtaking expression of his love for her; something which, while it gratified her beyond words, still left her rankling with a sense of injustice.

She got up from the piano. Across the table, the window was open: the room was filled with the deciduous smell of pine needles and of dried creosote. Between the chintz curtains and the dark trees, she could see far below a strip of lake water. Miss Turner would be taking the children for their morning exercise along the shore.

An abstraction came to her mind. If he saw her as Gretchen to his Faust, drawing his soul toward Heaven, who was the instrument of her salvation? Or were all women supposed to reflect the Holy Mother's immaculacy? A monstrous selfishness was lurking somewhere, she felt. But she was pleased and flattered by his tribute to her, so that she tried to suppress her more negative feelings. Sunlight fell across the manuscript of the first movement, which he had placed on the piano lid.

'Would you like me to start laying out the full score?' she asked.

She picked it up to look through it.

'Would you like to do it?' he asked.

She nodded, quite truthfully. She tried to tell herself there were more acts of love than one.

'It's going to be massive, isn't it?' she said, laughing.

They infected one another with pleasure.

'As massive as one of Strauss's operatic scores.' He smiled at her. 'I think you'll find I've indicated the scoring of the first part fairly completely. I've still got most of the instrumentation for the second part to do. But there's enough there to keep you going for a bit.'

Another pile of manuscript lay on the table, under a title page as clear and legible as all his completed scores. It was headed 'For Alto Voice and Chamber Orchestra, after Poems by Friedrich Rückert: *Kindertotenlieder*'.

' "Songs for Dead Children" . . . What is this?' she asked, leaning over again. Clutching the symphonic movement she was holding to her breast, she turned the pages of the new work. Mahler maintained his silence – as if *he* were guilty of something for a change. She read,

> In this weather . . . In this turmoil,
> I would never have sent the children out.
> I was not allowed to say anything against it –
> I knew there was a risk they might die tomorrow,

But there's nothing to be done about that now.

'Gustav!' she exclaimed. 'How can you write such things?'

He put down the pen he was holding.

'What do you mean?' he asked.

'How can you tempt providence like that – you who love the children so much?'

He was quite calm – maddeningly so.

'Perhaps it's because I love them so much.'

'Rückert wasn't playing when he wrote those poems, you know!' she said. 'He was mourning the death of his own little son.'

'Perhaps I was using Rückert to exorcise my own deepest fears,' he suggested.

Between the trees, the sun was shining so brightly on the lake surface she could not bear to look at it.

'I don't know half of what goes on in your head!' she said.

There was so much more she could have told him that morning – how he had stopped her from working at her music while he, instead of giving her something in return, was pouring all that was most important, all that mattered most about him, into his. She went to the door of the hut; before she opened it to go out, she said,

'You keep me away from you most of the time. And then you write dreadful things like that!'

She had intended having the last word, but before she could step down onto the woodland path, he said,

'These are not the things I'm working on now, Almschili – not principally. It's the turn of the final scene from *Faust* now, and do you think I would ever have discovered the truth in that without you to show me?'

The cheat! she thought; the rotten, wicked cheat! He couldn't help but win over her.

'Oh Gustl!' she cried helplessly, and ran to him, dropping his precious score as she did so, to enfold him, and be enfolded, all frustration, anger, remorse lost in a sudden surge of joy that her deepest aspirations and his creativity should have merged so miraculously.

That summer and the early autumn which followed had been a fever of composition on his part. For everybody else, life had had to go on tiptoe. Even the children had not been allowed to laugh or cry except for the hour or two each day he played with them – an indulgence he could not deny himself even under the extremest demands of inspiration. Alma-Maria herself dared not play the piano because he swore he could hear it up in his composing house. Servants, nursemaid, children, all were slaves to his current work. Even the postman was asked not to sing or whistle as he came down the woodland path.

Under this tension, all her old resentments started to return. There were mutinous murmurings of complaint from the female servants, though the loyalty of Anton, Mahler's manservant, was undinted. This made Alma-Maria's task the more difficult, since she found herself in complete sympathy with them. Then one September afternoon, he had come down to the house for lunch half an hour earlier than usual, his face radiating joy. He had been setting the most exalted section of the poem, the vision of the *Mater Gloriosa*. He insisted on playing over his sketch to her –

> Yonder go women's shapes
> Over me drifting:
> And wreathed in her seven
> Bright stars, they attend her,
> The High Queen of Heaven ...

As he played on, so her own excitement mounted. There was no letting up in his inspiration. He had set stanza after stanza in a tidal flow of unforced melody, bearing Faust's soul upward:

> Encircled by the noble choir of spirits
> The newly arrived is scarcely conscious
> Of himself,
> Hardly conscious of the new life ...

And then, Gretchen's soul's cry to the Blessed Virgin,

> O let me be his tutor, for
> The new dawning dazzles him still ...

'It is *your* music, my Almschili! Every note of it is yours!' he told her.

Throughout the past winter, she had prepared the full score for publication. From the immense opening chorus with its huge sustained pedal chords to Gretchen's reunion with Faust in Paradise, she had become increasingly certain that she was working on Gustav's supreme masterpiece. Occasionally, as she realized how he had clothed Goethe's words in the glory of music, she had not been able to stop herself from weeping.

Just before they had left Vienna for Maiernigg, this year, Mahler had written to Willem Mengelberg in Amsterdam:

We have just now completed my Eighth. It will be something the world has never heard the like of before. All nature is endowed with a voice in it. It is the greatest thing I have done so far. Imagine the universe beginning to ring and resound. It is no longer the sound of human voices. It is the voice of planets and suns revolving in their orbits. All my other symphonies have been but preludes to this one.

Below his signature, to his delight, Alma-Maria had written as a postscript: 'Every word true. A-M. Mahler-Schindler.'

Perhaps it was in part his belief that, at last, he had touched his genius's fulfilment that made him accept the idea of resigning from the Court Opera so readily. That, as well as his declared weariness.

Concerned about his state of health, she went up to the bedroom, out onto the balcony. Sitting there in the padded lounger, gently swaying, she could hear the sound of voices across the water and the gentle splash of oars. He was almost certainly overdoing it. He was always overdoing it, and the painful attacks he had suffered at rehearsals this past season would make no difference whatever. He shared the view held by Miss Turner that the infallible cure for physical weakness was ever more strenuous exercise; he was, of course, no more Viennese than Miss Turner. There was a diamond glitter across the water. On the mountain peaks under the gathering shreds of cirrus, there was a corresponding glitter in the rarified atmosphere: it was a portent of storms in the days to come. Even a natural city-dweller like herself could spot that.

She heard the splash of the oars coming closer, and the creak of the rowlocks. But now there was no shouting or laughter. This worried her. She got up off the lounger and went to the wooden balustrade. Leaning out over its carved edge, she could see the rowing boat approaching in the intervals between the trees on the shore, slicing the surface of the lake. Mahler was rowing at speed like a machine. The girls were sitting quite motionless in the stern cushions.

Even before Mahler brought the boat round to row into the little bay beside the house, she knew that there was something very wrong. She ran inside and down the stairs faster than she had done since she had been a child.

'Ilse!' she called. 'Maddalena! ... Miss Turner? Would you come to the shore, please!'

She ran out of the house without waiting to see if the maids and the nanny were following her, and down between the trees to the water's edge. The boat was coming straight in, with Mahler stooped over the oars rowing strongly to beach it immediately. In the stern, Putzi was sitting still and dull-eyed as a waxwork, with Guckerl crouched and unhappy beside her. The bows crashed up over the pebbles. For a second, Putzi looked as if she might fall forward into the boat like an off-balance puppet.

'Gustav, what is it? What's the matter?'

Little Guckerl was sitting gripping the side of the boat, face ashen with terror. Alma-Maria splashed into the water. Mahler was swaying on his feet as he stood up and bent down to pick Putzi up. As he lifted her, Alma-Maria saw and smelt the state of her drawers and petticoat. He clutched the child to him with none of his usual fastidious revulsion at the condition she was in. Alma-Maria saw the gaunt anxiety in his face.

'Oh, my dear!' she cried.

The freezing water soaked through her skirt around her knees.

'Take Guckerl,' Mahler told her.

She took his arm, steadying him as he stepped from the boat into the water still clutching Putzi to him. Putzi's head lolled on his shoulder as if she couldn't support its weight.

'My neck hurts, Muttichen,' she croaked, so that Alma-Maria could barely catch the words. 'My throat hurts bad.'

Mahler waded ashore. Miss Turner had come down to the bay followed by the two maids, but he shook his head at them. Alma-Maria picked up Guckerl and carried her onto dry ground.

'Will you take Guckerl, Miss Turner?'

She put down Guckerl and, clutching her cold, dripping skirts, ran after Mahler, into the house. He had stopped in the narrow hallway.

'Smell her breath,' he said.

The ordure smell from her garments was bad enough, but as Putzi struggled to raise her head to speak to Alma-Maria, the stench of foetid decomposition was asphyxiating.

'My neck hurts,' she croaked again.

Alma-Maria tried to sound calm.

'I'll telephone for Dr Blumenthal to come out here immediately,' she said. 'Gustl, take her up to our room. That'll be best . . . to keep her out of Guckerl's way.'

Mahler nodded.

'Get one of the servants to go and fetch the electric torch from up in the hut. And tell Anton to get the motor out – we'll send him over to Klagenfurt to fetch Blumenthal.'

He went on upstairs. She went into the music room and put a telephone call through to Klagenfurt. The freshly polished empty room was so peaceful, but above the trees outside the cirrus had closed up over the mountain peaks and the western sun was casting a lurid red over the gathering clouds. Please God there wouldn't be a storm so violent it would prevent Dr Blumenthal from reaching them – there was only the village apothecary in Maiernigg.

The telephone was answered by Frau Blumenthal. The doctor was out on his afternoon round, but by the time Herr Mahler's manservant had arrived with the motor, he would have returned and had his afternoon tea. Alma-Maria hung up the telephone and went upstairs to reassure Mahler that Dr Blumenthal would be on his way shortly. Miss Turner was undressing Putzi.

'I've sent Ilse for warm water,' she told Alma-Maria.

Mahler was standing at the foot of the bed.

'Go and see to Guckerl's tea, please, Miss Turner,' said Alma-Maria. 'I'll manage here.'

The servant arrived with the torch. When she had finished cleaning and changing Putzi into a clean nightgown, and had put her into the big double bed, Mahler sat down beside the child, put his hand on her forehead and made her open her mouth. Putzi was flushed with fever, and when she coughed or groaned she made a rasping noise like the scraping of dead leaves. The smell of her breath hung over the entire bed. He shone the torch down her throat. Alma-Maria heard the sharp intake of breath like a sob. For a moment she did not realize that the sound had come from him.

'What is it?' she asked. She must not allow herself to show poor little Putzi she was anxious.

Mahler switched off the torch and got up from the bed. He took her by the arm. There was such a look on his face she was afraid he would collapse. Putzi's voice came from the huge lace-flounced pillows,

'Muttichen! Don't leave me!'

'No, *liebchen*. I won't.'

'Muttichen! My neck hurts inside. It hurts so much!'

'I'm just going to talk to your Pappi for a moment. I won't be long, I promise.'

The room was growing dark. The clouds closing in round the mountain summits had brought a false dusk. Mahler drew her to the door.

'Don't let the maids in here,' he said. 'Miss Turner, yes. She's been exposed to the infection. But there's no need to put the servants at risk.'

'At risk?'

'It's diphtheria.'

'How do you know? ... You're not a doctor!'

Intolerable anxiety brought anger in its wake – anger at Mahler, who couldn't see a new patent medicine without detecting symptoms in himself which required its immediate application, making so dogmatic a diagnosis.

'The marks of diphtheria are quite clear on her rear palate and throat.'

'What do you know about it? You don't know anything!'

'My brother Ernst died of it – in my arms.'

'You were fourteen!'

She tried to calculate how many years ago that would have been. Her brain refused to function properly. She heard the terrible cackle of Putzi's breathing behind her. Mahler clutched at the doorjamb.

'It could be just a chill.' Anger turned to pleading. If she pleaded hard enough, she could make it true. 'A chill which has inflamed her throat and got onto her stomach. A summer fever – it isn't uncommon.'

Mahler sighed. For the moment there was no strength left in him to argue something in which she had not the least wish to believe.

'Please God you're right, Almschi! Oh please God!'

But she knew very well she wasn't.

'Go to Guckerl, Gustl. She'll need somebody to reassure her and love her.'

She went back to Putzi.

It was dark by the time Dr Blumenthal arrived, and thunderstorm rain was falling across the lake like a bead curtain. He took off his cap and shook it, and peeled the rain-smeared goggles off his forehead. One of the maids helped him off with his tarpaulin coat. The other maids were carrying lamps upstairs, bowls of livid yellow casting angular shadows on wallpaper and ceilings. Upstairs, there was a ring of such bowls about the bed; Putzi was clenching her eyes against the glare from them as she croaked for breath.

Dr Blumenthal asked Alma-Maria and Miss Turner to remain with him while he examined the patient. He urged Mahler to wait outside.

'Sickrooms are the reverse of usual procedure, my dear Herr Director,' he said with the bonhomie which never seemed to desert a member of his profession even under the most critical circumstances. 'It is the ladies who must work, the gentlemen who can only watch and pray. Isn't that so, ladies?'

'Precisely so, Herr Doctor,' replied Miss Turner.

Alma-Maria could never quite grasp the truth that the authoritative Miss Turner was four years younger than herself, scarcely more than a girl. Recognizing her efficient self-control, Dr Blumenthal presented Miss Turner with the enamel kidney bowl from his bag containing spatula, cotton wool, and torch speculum. Alma-Maria stood looking on helplessly as Miss Turner drew the lamps closer round the bed and, as Dr Blumenthal knelt on the bedside to examine Putzi's throat with spatula and torch, held one up to give him a more general light, apparently ignoring Putzi's choking distress as she herself could never have done.

Wind and rain beat against the windows and pattered on the balcony floor outside. Putzi gagged and choked as Dr Blumenthal, murmuring all the time, 'There! Only a moment, my darling!' pressed the spatula closer to the back of the throat. The child's terror affected Alma-Maria. She had to clutch the rail at the bottom of the bed to prevent herself from trying to drag Dr Blumenthal away from her.

Suddenly, Putzi let out a sharp little bark. She jerked up into a sitting position and began to retch. Dr Blumenthal got up and stepped back as Miss Turner held the kidney bowl and a cloth under Putzi's chin. Putzi choked, gasped, wheezed, and caught her breath as if she were being strangled. In the glare of the oil lamps, Alma-Maria saw the cloth which Miss Turner was holding turn to blood. The stench of foetid putrescence filled the room. There was blood and matter on Putzi's chin; her face gleamed with sweat. Dr Blumenthal stooped over her. As her head sank back on the pillow, he mopped her brow with a fresh lint pad.

'There,' he said. 'There, little one, you'll feel easier now ... There's no more to be done for the present,' he told Alma-Maria. To Miss

Turner, he said, 'See that the cloths and waste matter are burned immediately . . . We must let our young patient rest. Tomorrow morning, we'll see if she can take a little liquid.'

Mahler was waiting out on the landing; they talked on the stairs, in as low voices as the beat of the rain and Alma-Maria's hearing defect permitted.

'Diphtheria,' said Dr Blumenthal. 'Not a doubt of it, I'm afraid. Your little girl will breathe more easily tonight – the false membrane which forms on the back of the throat was already in a state of decomposition. It has detached itself.'

'So she is getting better?' Alma-Maria asked.

She noticed the way Dr Blumenthal glanced at Mahler. Didn't he realize who was likely to prove the stronger of the two of them?

Mahler removed his spectacles to wipe them – a nervous, betraying gesture.

'Another false membrane will grow,' said Dr Blumenthal. 'The disease is still at its early stage.'

'Early stage!' Alma-Maria exclaimed. She stopped herself.

'As long as the tissue remains infected,' Dr Blumenthal explained, 'the so-called "false membrane" – scab would be more accurate – grows to protect it from worse damage. That is nature's way.'

He made it sound positively benevolent.

'But it makes it difficult for her to breathe!' Alma-Maria protested.

For a moment, Dr Blumenthal did not reply. It was when he addressed her as 'Dear lady', and took her hand, that she realized how bad poor Putzi's condition was.

'It grows and detaches itself,' he went on, 'until the infection passes.'

She did not take her hand away. Speaking a little louder so that her voice would not shake, she asked,

'Tell me honestly. What is the worst that can happen?'

Again Dr Blumenthal glanced at Mahler, but Mahler refused to meet his eyes.

'Tell me, Dr Blumenthal,' she urged.

'There is a tendency – just a tendency – it's far from invariable – for the false membrane to grow larger than its host tissue, the mucus membrane.'

'It stops the breathing? It chokes . . .?'

'It means one has to have recourse to surgery – a simple tracheotomy. It's a common enough kitchen table operation these days – a bypass of the obstructing matter, that's all.'

'How long will it take before we find out?'

'Whether surgery will be required? Three or four days. No longer than that.'

Dr Blumenthal stayed that night in one of the two small spare bedrooms. She insisted that Mahler sleep in the other, refusing his offer to take turns with her sitting up with Putzi. With part of her mind she told herself she did not trust his emotional stability as far as children and their suffering was concerned. But there was another part of her which positively wanted to prove that he was weaker than herself in this respect.

Putzi slept that night – feverishly, it was true, but sufficiently to allow herself several hours of anxiety-ridden, dream-filled sleep in the armchair by the bed. Once, in the middle of the night, Putzi woke up. Through a heavy, uncomfortable drowsiness, Alma-Maria heard her ask in a strange, husky voice as if she were possessed,

'Muttichen, am I going to die?'

'No. No of course not, *liebchen*.'

Putzi breathed steadily as a sleeper breathes. But it was becoming noisier again. Suddenly, out of the lamp-lit silence:

'Muttichen, what's it like – dying?'

What was the answer? – 'I don't know. It's never happened to me'? Or – 'You'll be with Jesus and Mary, and Grandpappi, and be happy for ever and ever'? ... It would have been nice to have told Putzi that, if only she could have said it convincingly instead of seeing nothing but a wall of blackness before her.

'What's it like?'

'You're not going to die, *liebchen*.'

'I don't want to!' The voice croaked up into an approximation of a wail.

'I promise you shan't. I promise! I promise! I promise!'

But as Putzi dozed off once more, and she settled back for a return to sleep, unbidden, she heard in her brain, Schubert's grim setting of Claudius's poem, the melody and words repeating themselves in her head,

> Pass by! O pass by!
> Go, you savage skeleton!
> I am still young ...

The following morning – a heavy, damp, thunderous morning, with sunlight penetrating the thickness of the dark cloud over the lake sufficiently to tinge it with a livid, unnatural hue – she telephoned the Villa Möll and Mutti. Mutti came by the first train to Klagenfurt, and was brought by Anton to Maiernigg in the motor. Scarcely had she arrived when she insisted that she take her place with Miss Turner and Alma-Maria at the bedside. She also displayed the utmost solicitude toward Mahler, whom she had come to adore, insisting he go to his hut and work rather than distress himself to no good purpose.

Mahler meekly did as he was told. The second morning after Mutti's arrival, leaving her by the bed where Putzi was struggling for breath,

Alma-Maria went up through the woods. The clouds had rolled down among the tops of the pines to form a roof which leaked incessantly. The clinging moisture formed on her cheeks, in her hair, and soaked through the light summer coat she had thrown over her shoulders. After a night without sleep, she had intended to go straight into the little composing house, flop down on the floor at Mahler's knees and rest her burning eyes in his lap. She saw him through one of the windows, between the small chintz curtains. He was sitting erect at his work table. Beside him, the lid of his piano was closed. On the table in front of him there were no books or scores. There was only the ruled staves of the manuscript sheets she had prepared for him some days ago, and they were empty. He sat as motionless as a statue, staring at the bare half-dressed plank wall in front of him. As she looked, she was certain that he had found, in that oriental stillness for which he had on several occasions expressed admiration, a way of bidding farewell to Putzi in his heart.

And she hated him for it. She hated him for his fatalism. She hated him for having detached himself like one of Putzi's suppurating scabs from her own utterly fatigued misery. She hated him for his desertion of an anxiety which had entrapped her and wouldn't stop gnawing into her entrails.

She turned away and ran down between the tall, dripping trees to the edge of the lake. Clutching a bough which reached out over the pebbled shore to the water, with the rain soaking through to her skin, she gave herself up to a violent fit of sobbing. She sobbed to try to comfort her aching self-pity; she sobbed because she couldn't take Putzi's hand and journey with her to comfort her on whatever journey into pain-streaked darkness awaited her; she sobbed because there was no big, bearlike Pappi to come and take her own hand. She sobbed because all the piles of music in the world – Mozart, Haydn, Beethoven, Schubert, Wagner, or Mahler – could never alleviate the agony or match the spiritual enormity of one little child's suffering.

She lost count of the days and nights as Putzi's struggle to breathe grew more terrible, more wasting. They were few, but they seemed endless. The febrile yellow of lamplight was exchanged for the heavy grey which passed for daylight, and back again. And the creaking and rasping from the small, increasingly haggard frame continued. From time to time Mahler came down from the hut. He stood at the bedroom door, wishing to be close to his little daughter, but unable to face the horror of the physical reality; he who had composed symphonic movements, elegies, on the deaths of children. It was Mutti who drew him away, urged him to lie down, or to return to the hut in the woods.

There was an afternoon in the grey, humid twilight, when Alma-Maria and Mutti were sitting together in the sickroom. Putzi had sunk into another world – one where the only consciousness lay in the need to draw breath past the leathery membrane which burned her small throat. Mahler came to the door. He stood there like a somnambulist, a ghost. Alma-Maria wanted to scream at him to go away. No doubt in future years, as with the deaths of several of his brothers and sisters, it would all be distilled into some great symphonic *Trauermarsch*, and God's obscure but cruel will would be justified to sleek, pompous concert subscribers the world over. It was the Jewish way, of course. It was what the Old Testament was all about: the helpless acceptance of a callous, barbaric Deity's will elevated into a demonstration of virtue. And what a wonderful comfort such quietism must be!

Mutti – plump, pretty, indulgent Mutti – went to him and took his arm. Gently, she led him away. When she returned and sat down beside Alma-Maria, she said,

'Poor Gustav! He never had your happy childhood, you see. He feels it dreadfully when something happens to stop Putzi and Guckerl having the happiness he never had. It's unbearable for him.'

Alma-Maria's sense of necessarily suppressed outrage at her mother's complacent sympathy was aborted by Putzi raising her head from the pillow. She was fighting for breath, her veins pounding round her temples, her face empurpled. She managed to creak, 'Muttichen!' in a hideous distortion of a voice. Alma-Maria tore open the little nightgown. She pressed against the cavity of the chest as if she could force the child to breathe.

'Telephone Dr Blumenthal,' she called to Mutti. 'And tell Anton to be ready to drive to Klagenfurt immediately.'

'I'd better tell Gustav,' Mutti said.

'No!' shouted Alma-Maria. 'Gustav is useless! Useless! Go and telephone! Straight away!'

'But Almschi!'

'Go!' she screamed.

Her own tears fell hot on her bared arms as she attempted to massage Putzi. At that moment she understood how close she was herself to hysteria. She heard Putzi's croaking sob. She reached over for the damp cloth in the bowl by the bedside and started mopping the child's forehead.

'Do what I say, Mutti,' she said with an assumption of calmness. 'We must have Dr Blumenthal here before Putzi has another attack.'

Mutti left the room looking quite disapproving at the disrespect with which she had spoken of her husband – Mutti, who had been anything but respectful with Pappi when he had been alive. Putzi and she were afloat – barely afloat – on a sea of folly.

Dr Blumenthal arrived in the early evening. Mahler emerged from his room to greet him. He behaved with automatic courtesy. Alma-Maria waited as they came up the stairs. All afternoon, thunder had rumbled about the clouds between the mountain tops, and jagged threads of lightning lit the rippled surface of the lake.

'You've kept our young patient in the same room, eh?' asked Dr Blumenthal. 'That's good. An even temperature is best, even in this weather.'

He took his bag from Mahler, and went inside.

'Well, little lady. How are we this evening?'

Putzi lay staring up at him, eyes bulging from their sockets with the effort of breathing. They took up positions as if they had been pre-arranged in a theatrical production: Dr Blumenthal sitting on the edge of the bed, Miss Turner holding the lamp for him, Alma-Maria at the foot. The tableau was held only for a moment. Almost immediately – even before Putzi had started to gag – Dr Blumenthal withdrew his speculum from her mouth and switched off the torch. He got up and took Alma-Maria by the arm to the window leading out onto the balcony. There was a crash of thunder; lightning threw curtain-shadows across the room.

'We must resort to surgery, I'm afraid,' he said. 'It's not a moment too soon. In the ordinary way I would have waited for the assistance of a colleague, but we must operate tonight – there's no help for it.'

Mahler was waiting in the passage with Mutti. Alma-Maria went to him.

'He says he must operate,' she told him.

'We must open a passage in the upper trachea to enable her to go on breathing. It is a perfectly simple operation. It has saved countless lives. But before I ask your permission, I'm afraid I must warn you . . . In the case of a young child, the windpipe is deeply placed among – well – other important structures. Some of these are blood vessels which are vastly over-full and swollen because of the effort she is having to make in order to breathe.'

'So she may die as a result of the operation?'

Mahler sounded deadly calm.

'There is the danger of severe haemorrhageing. Yes. But there is one thing I can promise you absolutely. If we don't operate, she will die tonight.'

'Then we have no choice,' Mahler said.

'None at all, Herr Director – if you want your daughter to live.'

One of the maids was sent to the village to fetch the apothecary to assist Dr Blumenthal. Alma-Maria and Miss Turner prepared the scrubbed kitchen table which was brought up by Anton and a woodman from the village to the bedroom. They spread over it a blanket folded in a sheet. Every available lamp in the house was brought in.

Alma-Maria picked up the trembling, panting little body, and laid it on the table. With Dr Blumenthal and the apothecary in their shirtsleeves standing out of the child's sight behind her, she applied the chloroform pad. Putzi offered no resistance: it was as if she welcomed unconsciousness. As soon as she was limp, Dr Blumenthal asked her to leave. Only the apothecary, who would continue administering the chloroform, and Miss Turner, who was holding a lamp in either hand, were allowed to remain.

She went down the passage. She passed the open door of Mahler's room; he was sitting on an upright chair set by the wardrobe and was staring across the room. She thought of going to him, but a cruel pity prevented her. Let him remain in his trance; it was preferable to the agony of waiting. She went on down the stairs. Without pausing to put a coat over her shoulders, she went out into the storm. Walking along the shore, she wept, sobbing aloud and wailing like an animal in pain, the drenching wind snatching the consolation of the noise from her. The tree tops swirled and snapped above her; the rain stung her shoulders and beat at the back of her legs. She crouched on the turf on the wet mould and crawled beast-like to the foot of a tree, pressing her cheek against the ragged bark as though it might offer her comfort. If there was a Christ, she thought, surely He would come to her now to still the storm without and within. But the darkness howled, lashed, and was empty, and took nothing of her pain from her.

It was five o'clock and a grey half-light of a morning still heavy with cloud when she stumbled back bedraggled into the house. Miss Turner was in the hall putting on her waterproof coat to come to look for her.

'They're finished, Frau Mahler,' she said.

She looked very weary and unwontedly young.

Alma-Maria pulled herself up the stairs. Anton was standing with Maddalena at the top.

'Where's your master?' she asked.

They stared at her as if trying to comprehend the state she was in.

'He's asleep,' Anton told her.

He took down a shawl which was hanging on a wall bracket and placed it over her shoulders.

'He cried himself to sleep,' said the maid.

'That's good. Let him sleep,' said Alma-Maria.

She went through to the bedroom. There was the same gasping rattle from the bed. In the glare of two lamps, she saw that the sheet on the empty kitchen table had turned a scarlet satin where the flow of blood was still fresh. Dr Blumenthal, who was fastening his cuffs, came forward to intercept her.

'I'm sorry, Frau Mahler,' he said in a low voice, 'your little girl's condition is still critical.'

He tried to draw her from the room, but she refused to go.

'Is my Putzi dying?' she asked.

'We can always hope,' he replied. 'We have succeeded in opening up a vent in the trachea, but she has lost a great deal of blood.'

The apothecary, still in his shirtsleeves, was wrapping up the blood-drenched sheet in the blanket, as if its disappearance would comfort her.

Anton had come in behind her.

'Shall I wake the master?' he asked.

'No. No.' She heard herself laugh. 'Why should anybody in this world have to suffer more than he has to? Let him sleep on. Tell Maddalena to fetch Frau Möll. Ask Frau Möll if she'll be so good as to sit with Putzi while I change.'

In clean, dry clothes she returned to the sick bed. Mutti stayed with her. Dr Blumenthal returned to Klagenfurt, to his other patients, promising to come back at nightfall. The apothecary remained. Later in the morning, Mahler came and stood just outside the door. From the bed, Putzi whined, occasionally emitted a strange whistling noise, but for the most part continued the rasping, grating noise of the past days.

At four o'clock in the afternoon, the dreadful sound of forced breathing stopped. Mutti had left the room briefly. Alma-Maria had dozed off into a shallow sleep; the silence woke her instantly. Putzi was sitting up. She was staring at her, her eyes bulging. Blood was pouring from her mouth and throat, crimsoning nightgown and sheets. But she wasn't choking. She wasn't breathing at all. Alma-Maria jumped up. As she did so, Putzi fell back into the pool of blood on the pillow. Alma-Maria's screaming brought the apothecary running in, followed by Mutti. Putzi was lying wide-eyed, still staring up at Alma-Maria. The apothecary made the sign of the Cross. Alma-Maria leant over: with two outstretched fingers, she managed to close Putzi's eyelids into a semblance of peace. Kneeling down at the bedside, she too made the sign of the cross – not through any belief in its efficacy, but because it seemed appropriate. Then she got up and went to the door. Mahler was standing ashen-faced, himself drained of life. She took him by his ice-cold hand.

'It's all over now, Gustl,' she told him calmly.

She led him downstairs as if he too were a child.

All that night, the three of them – Mutti, Gustav and herself – sat together in the drawing room. Sometimes they held hands. They did not speak. Each in their desolation had nothing to offer the others.

On the second day after Putzi's death, in the afternoon, Mahler said to Alma-Maria in a tone of authority she had not heard him use since they had come to Maiernigg that summer,

'The clouds have lifted. It isn't good to stay indoors all the time ... Muttichen, will you see that Almschi takes a walk along the shore? The sunlight will do her good.'

The same night Putzi died, they had sent little Guckerl with Miss Turner back to Vienna, away from the house of mourning, to spend the rest of her quarantine period up on the Hohe Warte with Möll and her young aunt, the ten-year-old Marie Möll who, since she had been in contact with Putzi before her coming to Maiernigg, was also in quarantine.

Mahler's own recovery had been grim-faced but almost immediate. It was as if his helpless, hopeless quietism during his elder daughter's life-and-death struggle had furnished him for bereavement. Now he was taking responsibility for all the affairs consequent on a death in the family; he made arrangements, and wrote the necessary letters, with a strange, awesome calm.

Once, however, Alma had gone quietly up to the second floor where Putzi's worn out little body lay to find him standing in the twilight, his hand clutching the doorjamb, and his face pressed against his wrist, weeping so that his shoulders heaved. She had turned softly, and gone back downstairs. Once again she had caught him out withdrawing himself from her, hoarding his sorrow from her.

The habit of obedience remained – Mutti would have been shocked had it been otherwise. They put on their coats and went out into the fresh sunlight. The air was warm, but there was a brisk wind on the lake, whipping the surface into wavelets. They walked a little way along the pebbles, the wind catching at the chiffon scarves with which they had secured their summer hats – there had not been time to procure mourning – and flapping them into their faces.

They walked arm in arm, but had little enough to say to one another. Then Mutti said quietly and quite calmly,

'Almschi, *liebling*. I think I'm going to faint.'

Clutching at her mother's arm, Alma-Maria took off her own long duster-coat and laid it on the bank above the shore.

'Sit down, Muttichen,' she said.

She saw Mutti's legs give way, the edges of her summer gown spilling round her. She grabbed her as Mutti's face fell forward. She was a dead weight; Alma-Maria was forced to let her slump down on the outspread coat. She stared in dull shock as pale yellow urine spread out across the lap of Mutti's muslin skirt. She took off her jacket and bundled it under Mutti's head for a pillow. The wind felt sharp through her blouse as she ran back to the house for help.

As she approached it, running up through the trees, she saw on the driveway the white hearse and the two horses with their white nodding plumes. She saw the coachman standing holding his whip between the hearse and the front door – saw his black cape edged with gold and his braided cocked hat. She saw Mahler, his face set grim, standing on the porch with Anton beside him, watching as two men in black suits and crêpe-bound hats brought the small, unvarnished coffin out of the house and carried it to the hearse.

So that was why Mutti and she had been sent out for a walk. At that exact moment, she felt no resentment. It was true that she could not have borne it if she had been present when the small lid had been screwed down ... Oh please! Please God! ... Make it true – Gustav's vision of a child's heaven! That heaven he had envisaged for his mother – the gentle Jewish girl bound to poverty and ill-treatment, whose forgiving nature had taught him love. Please God, let his mother be there to welcome little Putzi – to a place where

> Everything lives in peace and calm, and
> we lead the life of Angels ...

There was a strange darkness, though it was only mid-afternoon. Then came the buzzing through the brain. Mutti was still lying by the water's edge. She must tell somebody about Mutti. But it was too late. The ground swerved up to meet her ...

'Sleep,' said Dr Blumenthal. 'Sleep and the grace of tears. That's the best medicine for you, ladies. Time and prayer, eh? You've exhausted yourselves, and no wonder. It's all quite natural, under the circumstances.'

Alma-Maria was sitting beside Mutti. There was the smell of Mutti's mimosa scent. It has always been like that: however much she had hated Mutti for her shallowness, her stupidity, her vanity, her behaviour towards Pappi, at times like this she longed to be physically close to her.

Neither had been unconscious for long. It had only been a minute or two (though it had seemed like days) between the time she had collapsed and the time she had warned Mahler of Mutti's collapse. Mutti had come to before the servants had reached her, though she had still been lying on Alma-Maria's coat. She had walked back to the house, supported by Anton.

Mahler was aware of the closeness which was between them. As if, even at that moment, he needed to overcome his exclusion, he said,

'Come along, Doctor. Perhaps you'd better examine me as well.'

Weak and unwell as she felt, Alma-Maria was shocked by what she took to be the pettiness of his suggestion.

'You'd better remove your jacket and lie back on that sofa, my dear Herr Director,' said Dr Blumenthal, taking the suggestion perfectly seriously.

He opened Mahler's waistcoat and shirt. He tapped at Mahler's chest. He applied his wooden stethoscope four or five times. Alma-Maria assumed that this thoroughness was a way of demonstrating his disapproval of Mahler's levity. Then she noticed the increasingly severe expression on his face. He knelt down on the floor to listen through the stethoscope more intently. Finally, he rose stiffly to his feet. He dropped the stethoscope into his bag.'

'Well!' he said.

Mahler swung his feet to the floor and sat up. He began buttoning his shirt.

'You know, my dear fellow,' said Dr Blumenthal, 'you have absolutely no cause to be proud of a heart like that. No cause at all.'

'What do you mean?' asked Mahler.

'You must have been aware of certain symptoms. You couldn't be in your condition without your body sending you some pretty strong warnings. Pain in the chest? The jaw? The arm?'

Mahler nodded.

'You chose to ignore them?'

'I thought it was indigestion. Toothache.'

'Take my advice, my friend. I'm just a plain country practitioner. Take the first train from Klagenfurt tomorrow. You're acquainted with Professor Kovacs, aren't you? Very well, I'll telephone the Loew Institute from here and warn him of your arrival. In the meantime – no physical exertion whatever. I'm absolutely serious.'

He turned to Alma-Maria. 'I'm sorry this should come at this time, Frau Mahler, but your husband has – in my humble opinion – behaved very foolishly. We cannot be absolutely certain, of course, until he has been thoroughly examined by more eminent medical men than myself – Professor Kovacs and Dr Chvostec, for instance. In my view, however, he has been suffering from a vascular dysfunction of the heart for several years – not weeks or months. He is lucky to be alive ... And, needless to say, the tragic events of the past few days cannot have improved his condition.'

As soon as Dr Blumenthal had taken his leave, Alma-Maria went back to where Mahler was sitting on the sofa. She sat on the floor beside him, where Dr Blumenthal had knelt when he was examining him. Mahler looked ashen and shaken, the old man he had so often, and prematurely, claimed to be. She herself still felt weak, overwhelmed by the cruelty with which Providence, or something, was treating her.

'Gustl, why didn't you tell me it was as bad as this?'

He turned his face away.

'Gustl!' It was a rebuke.

He took her hand.

'I didn't want to worry you unnecessarily.'

'Unnecessarily!'

'I thought it was heartburn. Tiredness. That's all.'

He had been afraid she might insist on him going to Professor Kovacs and being told to curtail his work. His work was always more important than anything else.

As if to confirm her bitterest thoughts, he sighed heavily and lay back against the cushions.

'*Nunc dimittis,*' he said.

'What do you mean?'

He did not appear to hear the note of accusation in her voice.

'My Eighth,' he said. 'Our *Faust* symphony. It's finished. Revised and completed. I have looked at it and seen that it was good.'

He sighed again.

She could not believe it. There was no music – not all the music which had ever been written – which came anywhere near the reality of individual human experience: the brutal, driving fulfilment of a lover; the heaving, elemental discomfort and release of giving birth; the agonizing nightmare of death. And only that afternoon, Putzi's little body had been buried in the village graveyard.

'Gustl! It's only music! Music, do you hear me? Dots on paper! Rows and rows of lines and dots! Nothing else! It's just dreaming!'

She knew she was being unfair. Mahler did not allow himself to be unduly disturbed.

'Dear Almschili,' he said, his voice trembling with what sounded very like pity for her. 'That is what our dear God has put you and me into this world for. I certainly can't imagine he put anybody as ill-made as myself here for any other purpose.'

She sat back on her heels, away from him. She buried her face in her hands and howled – howled into the black vaults of her own terrible isolation.

5 DRUMBEATS AT A FIREMAN'S FUNERAL: 1907-1908

 SHE WAS STANDING at the rail of the sundeck watching the huge bows of the SS *Augusta-Viktoria* as they lifted on the Atlantic swell then plunged and smashed into foam the crestless waves. It was the second day out; gulls still glided and swooped and screeched overhead before falling back behind the towering smokestacks to search for refuse in the wake. Beyond the flagstaff on the bow, beyond the heaving of the waves, ocean and sky met in grey nothingness.

Mahler was spending the day lying on his bunk wondering if he was going to be seasick.

She had lunched alone in the saloon since – alone, if she discounted the attentions of the amiable young deck officer who had been assigned (presumably by the Purser) to be her escort at table. He had shown not the slightest inclination to return to his duties, and had been happy to supply her with a second glass of Benedictine to go with her coffee. She had felt a slight sense of liberation at Mahler's absence, in being able to have her wine glass refilled without being conscious of his puritanical watchfulness. Afterwards, she was disinclined to return to their state room, comfortable though it might be, and had sent Kathi, her personal maid, to fetch her waterproof coat.

A gentleman, his neck and ears buried in a collar of Russian fur accompanied by a boy of fifteen or sixteen, emerged from the hatchway door under the bridge. They stood on the far side of the deck-walk overlooking the ship's bow. There was nobody else braving the wet, heaving deck and the cold drizzle in the wind. She listened to the melancholy screeching of the gulls overhead, and wondered how they knew when to turn back, how they found their way to shore through the universal grey of sea and sky.

Curiosity made her turn her head – to see if she recognized the gentleman and the boy from the first-class dining saloon. The gentleman recognized her; clearly, he had been waiting for her to turn her head. He moved his stick to his left hand, raising his hat to her with his right and bowing slightly. She inclined her head and smiled before turning away. She waited a decent interval, then walked away round the deck out of his sight.

She stood at the rail, staring down into the ragged lace of foam far below, spreading away from the ship's side to be dissipated in the confusion of the sea. For the quarter-mile length of the deck there was nothing but empty boards, empty seats. The thin rain, the desolation, reminded her, as the gentleman raising his hat had reminded her, of an afteroon in the Stadtpark twelve years before – was it *only* twelve years? – when she had been sitting in the drizzle with empty benches on either side of her, gazing at Pappi's statue. Her sadness then had been sadness in an age of innocence: when, all around her, the possibility of happiness had remained inviolate.

Poor Max Burckhard! *Tout passe, tout casse, tout lasse* . . .

When the news of Mahler's resignation had broken, and his appointment as principal conductor at the Metropolitan Opera, New York, Burckhard had taken a risk worthy of Mahler himself by writing an uncompromising article in the *Neue Frei Presse* on Mahler's forthcoming departure from Vienna:

> Austria has, after all, been finished as a great power for quite a while. Once upon a time, we could pride ourselves on being a true nation-state. Now, we are merely one half of something – the Dual Monarchy, Austria-Hungary – something in fact which has no real name of its own.
>
> But we do *have* something – something in which we Austrians really and truly *are* something. We have the Vienna Opera: the Vienna Opera which Director Gustav Mahler has turned into one of the cultural glories of our entire continent. Director Mahler has only to step onto the podium and raise his baton to command the attention and unbounded admiration of the musical world, whose productions are held to be outstanding, altogether incomparable as artistic achievements the world over.
>
> And we will simply let this man go. Indeed, how many of us are actually crowing over his imminent departure, as if we had accomplished an act of true patriotism . . .?

In fact, the situation was not quite as Burckhard believed. The general management of the Imperial-Royal theatres had found it virtually impossible to replace Mahler. Some conductors declined to accept the post as a matter of principle – believing, like Burckhard, that Mahler's resignation had been forced on him because of the vilification and abuse poured out by a nationalistic and anti-Semitic press. Others, like Felix von Weingartner, the General Management Committee's first choice, simply had no wish to have their talent publicly measured against that of Mahler. As a result, Prince Montenuovo and his superior, Prince Leichtenstein, had both appealed to Mahler to withdraw his resignation. A month or two earlier, he might well have done so, but Professor Kovacs and Dr Chvostec were of the opinion that his heart was in worse condition than even Dr Blumenthal had diagnosed. From his retreat at Toblach in the South Tirol, where he had gone alone to come to terms with Putzi's death, he had declined. His appointment to the Metropolitan Opera House meant that he had only to produce and conduct – not administer – and that he had the summer and autumn in which to return to Europe to compose and arrange performances of his own work. His pension, royalties and American salary would ensure that Alma-Maria and Gucki were amply provided for.

Above the lifeboat davits and the drifting black smoke from the great funnels, the seagulls were falling back to hover and glide, screeching over the ship's wake. In the grey dankness, they knew their point of no return.

She was still on deck. Stepping back under the cover of a door leading to a companionway down to the lower deck, she took her cigarettes from her purse and lit one. Then she went back to the rail. Should anyone approach her along the deserted deck, she would have plenty of time to drop it over the side undetected. Now that she and Mahler were alone together, sailing to a new, strange city together, she felt the old entrapment enclosing her.

Their separation in the aftermath of Putzi's death had been a convalescence for both of them, though it had not seemed so at first. They had agreed they would never want to return to Maiernigg so, while Mahler went to recuperate in the South Tirol, she had left Gucki in the care of Miss Turner and Mutti, and had taken a suite in the Hotel Carinthia in Klagenfurt from which she could supervise the clearing out and make arrangements for the sale of their house on the Wörthersee.

During the first two evenings there, she had wondered if she could bear it. It had not taken long for the other guests at the hotel to learn who she was. All the good manners in the world could not have suppressed the surreptitious glances thrown in her direction and the sense rather than audibility of curious murmuring. A number of gentlemen sent their wives or female companions to her table in the dining room to offer their condolences at her recent so terrible loss. The staff, too, had taken their cue from the other guests; if the hotel had been a sanatorium she could scarcely have been treated with a more hushed consideration.

There was no avoiding driving out to Maiernigg. She could not leave the packing of manuscript scores, pictures and books, many of which were by friends or colleagues of Mahler's, to unsupervised workmen. Stripped, however, of familiar hangings and furnishings, the entire character of the house was changed. As a result, the pain was not nearly as acute as she had anticipated. She could not bring herself to go up to the bedroom on the second floor – she had to entrust that to Kathi, her maid. Otherwise, she walked through the half-emptied rooms, and stepped down from the veranda onto the shore, testing and awaiting the coming of uncontrollable sorrow.

When it came, its form took her by surprise. She had left the house and Kathi, and had walked alone up to the tiny village church. There, in the graveyard, among the wrought-iron crosses, the marble Calvarys under the scented lime trees, and the small, sad, sepia photographs in their oval frames, she had wanted to wail out her loss over Putzi's grave. The hot tears, which spilled down her cheeks under her black veil, were those of a fierce indignation that Mahler should have prevented her from kissing her little child goodbye as she lay sleeping in her coffin that afternoon. It was anger rather than grief which she found uncontrollable. She beat her fists on the edges of the granite cross till she grazed the surface of her knuckles through her gloves.

Surely it was a severe Providence which ensured that, when she returned from her final visit to Maiernigg that afternoon, there was a letter waiting for her, postmarked Alt-Schluderbach, Toblach in Tirol. She cut open the envelope reluctantly.

My Almscherl! – I'm feeling most anxious. I know your silence means that you are weary, not in good spirits. Are you well? Tell me. And now all this packing is bound to be the last straw. Almschi, just let it happen. What does it matter if some of the crockery gets smashed, or even if a picture ends up with a hole in it? It is you who matters. You must let Kathi look after you.

I feel in the best of health. If Blumenthal *et al.* had not found anything, I'd have continued in the same old way. Certainly I would not have been going to bed at nine o'clock and rising at eleven – Anton is being very strict with me, you see! I have to confess that I am composing – Bethge's poems which you gave me seem to reflect my own feelings so precisely. I've no doubt you knew that they would, and it was why you gave them to me – you have the perception and sympathy which is vouchsafed only to angelic beings. I look down the lake to Schluderbach and I fancy that I am Bethge's 'Lonely Man in Autumn' (or is it Tchang Tai's?)

> A blue autumn mist hovers over the lake,
> All the grass blades are rimed in frost ...

and then, you recall, those wonderful lines –

> My heart is weary. My little lamp
> Went out with a hiss, reminding me of sleep.
> I am coming to you, my beloved, my resting place,
> To you who gives me peace ...

It makes me think that, as I walk back from the shore in the evening light, I'm going to see you and Guckerl running down the meadow to meet me. And then I feel lonely.

But the poems have set a stream of musical ideas going in my head so I can honestly say that, if only you were with me, I believe I might be truly happy. I think of you and Guckerl continually, my dearest. I kiss you tenderly. Mind you behave yourself, as I promise I'm behaving myself. *And don't lift a hand over the packing.*

All my thoughts, my angel,

Your Gustav.

Oh! I must tell you. Mengelberg wrote to me asking if he and the Amsterdam Concertgebouw might be permitted to give the first performance of our 'Faust' Symphony. I refused, naturally, though I was immensely touched. First – it is *your* symphony, nobody else could have taught me the reality of Goethe's closing lines. Second – it is a setting of what is, perhaps, *the* German poem. Therefore it should be revealed in Vienna or possibly Munich. G.

She had never felt so remote from him. While he might be concerned for her welfare, he did not begin to approach her innermost feelings. On the other hand, there was, in his lack of understanding, the innocence of a child, the innocence which his admirers took for sainthood.

During the weeks subsequent to their return to Vienna, and Mahler's concert tour of northern Europe, and prior to their departure, it had seemed as though, now that they were finally to lose him, the Viennese could not find ways sufficient to express their love and respect for him. There was the gala performance of his Second Symphony (the 'Resurrection') given for the Vienna Musikverein by the Philharmonic, and the ecstatically received final production of Beethoven's *Fidelio* at the Opera. On the platform of the Westbahnhof, to send them on his way had been asssembled two hundred of Veinna's leading composers, musical scholars, and performers, including a majority of the Opera orchestra players and the Philharmonic. Mahler was embarrassed and awkward – his limp was accentuated and, as he stood hat in hand to receive the commendations of three of the younger generation of composers, Schoenberg, Alban Berg, and Anton Webern, he stood first on one leg and then the other, so that she had been afraid, given his tiredness after his farewell concerts, that he might topple over.

Their compartment had been filled with flowers. As the train pulled out of the station, she had leant forward and taken his hands. Guckerl was being left behind with Mutti and Miss Turner. Their personal servants, Anton and Kathi, who were accompanying them to New York, were behind, in the second class. They were alone for the first time for months.

'Are you sad to be leaving?' Mahler asked.

She shook her head. 'Are you?'

'No. No regrets at all – except that we can't take Guckerl this time. It's a good way to put off the old.'

He peeled off his spectacles to wipe his eyes. Was it possible, she wondered, by wishing something to happen and by acting it out, to make it truly occur? She put her arms about him and kissed him – not passionately, not to frighten him, but as tenderly as she could manage.

They had stayed a week in Paris before travelling on to Cherbourg. Rodin had expressed a wish to sculpt a bust of Mahler. Through the Clemenceaus and the Zuckerkandls, arrangements had been made for the General Management of the Court Opera to commission it. By breaking the journey, Mahler provided Rodin with the opportunity to make preliminary studies. Alma-Maria attended the first two sittings, and was fascinated to watch how Rodin began with a pellet of clay and proceeded to build up the shape of the head, instead of following the practice of Pappi and his friends, of taking a large lump of clay and reducing it. After two sittings, however, she found Mahler's restless twitching on the dias – of which Rodin probably remained scarcely aware but which she was afraid would become more and more obvious – and the presence in the studio of a succession of silent young girls in cheap finery, their lips waxen scarlet, their cheeks rouged, more and more embarrassing. So she remained in the hotel suite for the second two sittings.

On the evening after his final sitting, Mahler returned to their suite with a look of utter delight on his face.

'Do you know what Rodin has just told me?' he said. 'He says my skull is exactly the same shape as Mozart's!'

The drizzle had turned to rain. There was a canopy over the deck, but the rain swept in over the rail. It caught her face through the thin net of her veil and trickled down under the collar of her raincoat. Reluctantly she was forced to go below; the movement of the ship, the rolling of the decks, was unnerving when the pannelling of the landings and the staircases, and the furnishings and fittings were all designed to suggest the interior of some princely hunting lodge.

In the stateroom, she found Mahler stretched rigid on the bed. He wasn't seasick. He hadn't been seasick, even when they had sailed out of Cherbourg across a choppy sea on the tender to board the SS *Augusta-Viktoria* where she lay at anchor, offshore. They had dined very pleasantly last night, with Mahler the guest of honour at the Captain's table, and had then gone up on deck so that he should enjoy his after-dinner cigar while looking across to the lights along the coast of the Cherbourg peninsula. Then he noticed that the ship was under way and that there was a slight swell. Instantly, he had begun to examine himself for symptoms of seasickness. He had gone down to their stateroom convinced that if he lay down motionless, seasickness would be averted. He resembled nothing so much as one of the carved effigies of a cardinal-archbishop on his tomb in St Stephen's.

She stood at the foot of the bed.

'You don't feel unwell?' she asked.

'Not at all,' he replied. Without a trace of humour, he added, 'Lying still is obviously the answer.'

'I don't feel ill either,' she told him.

A sudden lurch of the deck made her grasp at the brass bedrail. As a result, the point of her remark was lost on him.

'Will you read to me?' he asked.

'If you wish.'

She enjoyed both reading and being read to. It was something – reading and discussing what they read – which bound them, however insecurely, together.

They were reading Novalis. She had been reading the *Journals* while staying at Klagenfurt. The reason she had selected them was because they were the only books among those which Burckhard had sent her so long ago which she had not either read or dipped into. It was as if God had deliberately held her back from them until they were necessary to her. Novalis's account of the loss of his child-sweetheart, Sophie von Kühn, the pain of his bereavement and his reconciliation to what had to be endured as he prayed by her grave had been a wonderful comfort to her, and as soon as she had finished them, she had sent them to Mahler at Toblach, enthusiastically recommending them. It was one of the stupid inconsistencies of life that, however distant she might feel from him in all sorts of ways, there was one thing of which she could be certain: that his appreciation of something which had deeply affected her, whether it be music, painting or literature, would find a response in him.

She released the bedrail and went to the table where the book was lying. Another heave of the deck under her feet, and she had to grip at the tiny rail round three sides of the table. Beside the book, on the blotter, was a completed wireless-telegraph form – the new Marconi Wireless had been installed on the SS *Augusta-Viktoria* for the benefit of first-class passengers. She glanced at it. It was addressed to Frau Hofratin Berta Zuckerkandl, in Vienna:

> ... I have no regrets. After all, I take with me the only true home I have ever known – my blessed Alma. And it is only now, when I am released from the crushing burden of administrative work, that I know what will be my dearest task. Alma has sacrificed six years of her youth to me. No one can ever know with what absolute selflessness she has subordinated her life to me and my work. With her, I go on my way with a light heart ...

He had made himself the centre of her life whether she wanted him to be so or not. He had entrusted himself, his weaknesses and his genius, to her. Never would she be able to tell him of her longings, her emptiness of soul.

She drew up a chair beside the bed. She began to read.

> Now I know when the last morning will come, when daylight ceases to dispel Night and Love – when sleep becomes a single inexhaustible and eternal dream. For everything that is visible clings to the invisible – the audible to the inaudible – the tangible to the intangible. Already I feel a celestial tiredness within ...

They heard the noise of excitement in the passage outside the stateroom – voices of children begging their parents or governesses to come and see, and running footsteps and adult voices calling – although it was only just after seven in the morning, and the light through the portholes no more than a dull grey. They got up and dressed themselves, not waiting for Anton and Kathi to come up from the second class. A cold, offshore wind caught Mahler by the throat as he stepped from the hatchway out onto the deck, causing him to cough violently and to reach back for the hatchway rail. Alma-Maria noticed afresh in the morning light, under the black stubble his shaving never quite succeeded in eradicating, how gaunt was his face.

'Would you like to go back, Gustl?' she asked him.

He shook his head quite violently. 'This must not be missed,' he said between coughs. 'What would we say to Strauss if we missed it?'

They went forward to join the crowds who had already gathered along the rail overlooking the bows. Below were the crowds who had poured up from steerage, a jam-packed mass of peasantry from Poland, Byelo-Russia and the Baltic in peaked caps and head shawls, men, women and children, Gentile and Jew, all wrapped about the shoulders and chests in the ubiquitous woollen comforters of the poor. There was no excitement down there. Only apprehension as, already, men from the Purser's office began to herd them into position for their disembarkation onto the tenders which would take them to Ellis Island. If Gustav and she were fleeing persecution, thought Alma-Maria, and had to subject themselves to the United State immigration inspectors, there was no doubt whatever that, given Gustav's state of health, they would be returned to their native land.

The spectacle beyond the bows of the SS *Augusta-Viktoria* was as spectacular as they had been led to believe. They were in the Narrows between Staten Island and Brooklyn with their eighteenth-century bastions and ravelins covering the entrance. Beyond lay the Upper New York Bay, a ruffled, white-crested inland sea over which gulls circled and screamed. Across two miles of water stood Liberty Island and the Statue of Liberty in sharpest focus, its crown and torch gleaming gold in the bright slant of the December morning sunlight. Beyond that lay the grim black outline of Ellis Island, and the mouths of the East and North Rivers. Between the river mouths like a grotesque exaggeration of the Dogana of Venice seen from the Lagoon, lay Manhattan Island with its skyscraper skyline, its tall rectilinear pinnacles caught in an empty dazzlement of sun while their bases lay submerged in the inhospitable menace of dark, cold shadow.

For a quarter of an hour they stood watching as the Statue of Liberty drew nearer. Mahler suggested they should go down for breakfast. The familiar, German comfort of the saloon excluded the strangeness outside, while, through the portholes, there were glimpses only of the sea. At tables around them, however, the sound of American voices were more assertive, as if, now their owners were surrounded by an American shore, the ship itself was no longer a foreign place, despite its sailing under the Hohenzollern eagle.

The ship had come to anchor. There was the sound of sirens outside and a general busyness as sailors ran past the saloon windows. Someone remarked in German, further down the table, that the tenders were alongside to take off the immigrants from steerage. A number of passengers got up and left their breakfasts unfinished to watch or gloat over the scene from the sun deck. Mahler dunked his brioche into his coffee bowl.

'"There is nothing so reassuring for the man beloved of fortune than to behold the misfortune of others,'" he remarked. 'Aristotle, *The Poetics*.' There was a note of misliking if not of contempt in his voice. Alma-Maria looked at him. He dabbed at his mouth with his napkin. Then he added, 'Some of those people – the way they were dressed, you know? – could have been my father, my relatives, in the most exact sense.'

'But not your mother?'

'No. Certainly not my mother.'

He winced, she noted.

They returned to their stateroom for the last time. As they descended the mock baronial staircase, there was a gentle shudder and the prolonged bellow of the ship's siren. They were under way once more. Cabin staff were wheeling great linen baskets filled with discarded sheets, pillow cases and quilt covers up the passages. Cabin maids and stewards shouted to each other, teasing, laughing, or, in the case of their superiors, urging them to greater speed, with no regard for the comfort of passengers. In the stateroom itself, Alma-Maria found the heavier bags already gone, the bed stripped, and the towels removed. Even the cut flowers had been taken from the vases. It had been their comfortable home for five days and nights, made familiar by the toilet articles, the books, the garments which had been spread about. Now, all tokens, all rights of tenure were gone. It had become a hygienic void, and they were, however temporarily, in a state of homelessness. After a few minutes, Anton and Kathi joined them to take their hand luggage. Kathi was crying. At first, Alma-Maria pretended not to notice. A semi-darkness like a false twilight covered the portholes, plunging the cabin into gloom. Outside, she could see cranes reaching upwards and massive, steam-driven gantries, and behind them, interrupted by the swooping of gulls, corrugated iron roofs and cliff walls of buildings with tiny smoke-stained windows. There was no trace of tree, or green, or beauty of any sort. Her sense of depression was not improved by the fact that her period – ever the most movable and uncomfortable of feasts – had just started. A sense of homesickness and loss came over her such as she had not experienced since she was removed from her home – Pappi's home – of Plankenburg. Impulsively, she put her arms about Kathi. Gratefully the girl sobbed against her shoulder, unaware that her mistress was seeking vicariously to comfort herself.

A pageboy was sent to request Herr Mahler and the noble and well-born Frau Mahler's presence on B-deck as there were gentlemen boarding the ship to greet them. Alma-Maria dried the maid's eyes and left her in Anton's charge. At the top of the stairs, she took Mahler's arm. They stepped out on deck. It was crowded with first-class passengers waiting to disembark. On the quay below, there were dense crowds packed behind crush barriers, all staring upwards, searching along the ship's rails. As those below recognized friends or relatives, they tried to shout up above the noise of the docks, or waved handkerchiefs at the full extent of their arms. Women had handkerchiefs pressed to their eyes, men held little children above their heads to see and be seen.

'This way, sir! This way, madam!' The pageboy led them through the crowd on deck, which parted to let them pass.

A number of gentlemen passengers raised their hats and bowed as they went by. She heard the name 'Mahler!' murmured through the throng as if their fellow passengers had just discovered his degree of eminence. Despite physical discomfort and the sense of sadness which had afflicted her, she felt her self-confidence returning. She smiled and nodded to several of the ladies she recognized from the dining saloon and strolls on deck.

Two elegantly dressed middle-aged men were waiting with one of the ship's officers at the head of the steep, covered gangway. As Mahler and Alma-Maria approached through the crush, one of them stepped forward. He was a stout, shortish man with pince-nez dangling on the end of a blue velvet ribbon. He raised his hat from off a polished bald head.

'The so-distinguished and honoured Herr Director Gustav Mahler?' He held out his hand. 'Andreas Dippel,' he explained. 'I have the honour to be manager of the Metropolitan Opera.' He bowed over Alma-Maria's hand. 'Beautiful – quite beautiful!' he exclaimed. 'The Herr Director is the most fortunate in such a beautiful wife.'

His German-Swiss accent with its American twang reminded her of provincial hotel managers and restaurant head waiters.

'Welcome to the United States of America,' he added.

The second and taller of the two came forward.

'Henry Theophilus Finck, at your service, Herr Director ... *gnädige* Frau Director ...'

For all his American accent, he spoke the purest Viennese. 'I have to confess to being a critic, I'm afraid: music editor, *Evening News*, and self-elected delegate of the New York musical press ... I had the very great pleasure of hearing your *Magic Flute* at the Court Opera, a year last spring.'

His eyes met Alma-Maria's. She gave him a slight yet, she hoped, winning smile.

'Are you Viennesse, Herr Finck?' she asked.

Dr Finck was obviously pleased and flattered by her calculated mistake.

'No, Frau Director. I'm third generation American. It must be my accent, eh? I obtained my doctorate at the University of Vienna.'

'Then you are acquainted with Professor Adler?'

'Guido Adler? Why yes. He's a good friend of mine.'

Two ship's officers saluted as they reached the head of the gangway. She felt Dr Finck's arm supporting hers as she stepped up onto the gangplank.

'Guido Adler is a very dear friend of my husband – and myself, of course,' she said.

They descended to the pier of the Hamburg-Amerika Line in a lonely little cortège – Andreas Dippel with Mahler, Dr Finck escorting Alma-Maria, and the two servants behind them. Above them and in the crowds against the crush barriers on the pier there was an awareness that these were people of significance: faces were turned in their direction, and discussion began as to who they might be.

Dippel turned to speak to her.

'The Opera has taken a suite on the eleventh floor of the Hotel Majestic. I hope you will find it comfortable, Frau Director. The principal rooms overlook Central Park – not the Wienerwald, I'm afraid, but the best prospect New York affords.'

She was about to reply to the effect that she was sure it would be very pleasant when Mahler said dryly,

'Our home in Vienna doesn't overlook the Wienerwald.'

The bald little man's anxiety to please had irritated him. Alma-Maria said,

'As long as we have two pianos ...'

'In the drawing room as you requested, Frau Director. Broadwood grands.'

'You play, of course, Frau Director?' asked Dr Finck.

'My wife is an accomplished pianist,' Mahler called back over his shoulder.

'We play four hands,' said Alma-Maria. 'It is our favourite leisure occupation.'

They were reaching the bottom of the gangway. The front of the waiting crowd was very near. Although the majority were preoccupied with the friends and relatives who were still packed against the ship's rail waiting to disembark, there were plenty of people watching them as they stepped, for the first time in five days and nights, onto *terra firma*. Alma-Maria raised her veil slightly with her gloved fingertips. She held her skirt off the ground very precisely.

'This way, if you please, Herr Director, Frau Director,' said Dippel.

She noticed out of the corners of her eyes the number of well-dressed men at the barriers who looked in her direction. Despite everything that had happened to her, her looks were a passport she still held in her possession. For the moment, at least, homesickness was removed to a safe distance, though, as she entered the pierhead buildings of the Hamburg-Amerika Line she was conscious that the leaden sense of exile had been driven only as far as the margins, and was waiting there like the watchful eyes of wild beasts lurking in the darkness about the circumference of a cave-mouth fire.

'Petersen, *Herald*. Mr Mahler, was the decision that the first opera you would conduct at the Met should be *Tristan and Isolde* your own or Mr Conried's?'

The gentlemen of the New York musical press had gathered in the lobby of the Metropolitan Opera House. They had formed a semicircle between Mahler and Alma-Maria and the way out. There were twenty or thirty of them. They ranged in appearance from Henry Theophilus Finck who, with one or two others, could have been, from their distinguished and scholarly appearance, members of the Viennese musical press, to the unshaven and shabbily dressed reporters who had come in hope of a story.

'It was a matter for mutual agreement,' Mahler replied in English.

Alma-Maria, who was standing with her hand tucked into Mahler's arm, looked to Andreas Dippel to translate. As she inclined her head to listen, she favoured the pressmen with her profile. Camera flashes snapped and flared in her face leaving a pungent smell of sulphur and saltpetre.

'Krehbiel, *Daily Tribune*. Somebody must have been the first to suggest *Tristan*. Was it you, Mr Mahler?'

Even when she couldn't understand what was being said, Alma-Maria could detect the hostility in the voice. It took her by surprise. It was only their second day in New York, and Mahler's first public appearance.

'I believe I suggested that I might regard Mr Conried's flattering invitation in a more favourable light if I were to be allowed to direct *Tristan*.'

He was smiling. Some of the pressmen also smiled, reducing the tension in the air.

'Finck, *Evening News*. Herr Mahler, your own production at the Vienna Court Opera of *Tristan* was famous throughout Europe, and, I believe, won the enthusiastic endorsement of Frau Cosima Wagner, the composer's widow ...'

He paused, both to allow his colleagues to take in Mahler's very considerable credentials, and for Mahler himself to confirm them.

'That is true,' Mahler replied. 'Frau Wagner was good enough to express her gratitude to me for the production by Dr Alfred Roller and myself.'

'How do you feel about directing performances staged by somebody else?' Finck asked.

'It is honour enough to be in charge of interpeting Wagner's sublime score with the orchestral players of a first-class opera house – not to mention singers of the quality of Fremstad and Knote.'

Clearly his mention of 'first-class opera house' had the desired effect. There was a general rustle of satisfaction.

'Krehbiel, *Tribune*. Mr Mahler, it is well known to all of us here that Signor Toscanini expressed a wish to conduct *Tristan* at the Met either this season or the next. Am I not right in suggesting that Toscanini has made *Tristan* his own particular masterpiece?'

'Not in Greater Germany, Mr Krehbiel. There it is regarded as Richard Wagner's particular masterpiece.'

There was open laughter at this riposte.

'In any case,' Mahler continued. 'If you're suggesting that I should have declined the opportunity to conduct *Tristan* simply because Maestro Toscanini wishes to conduct it here, I can only reply that Dr Mottl conducted it here before either of us.'

'Huneker, *Times*. Mr Mahler, do you intend conducting any of your own music during your time with the Met?'

'Certainly. If anybody will be kind enough to give me an orchestra.' He paused, then added, smiling again, 'Try stopping a composer performing his own music when he has been given an opportunity to do so.'

Again there was the approval of laughter. Another question was called out. Alma-Maria realized it was intended for her. Dippel said,

'The gentleman from the *Daily News* wishes to know what you think of New York so far?'

'Oh my God!' She laughed, falling into the more relaxed mood which prevailed. 'We've only been here a day.' Then she said, 'I'll tell you one thing, though. Reports of the New York skyline are not exaggerated.'

Another question – Dippel translating:

'What do you think of New York women, Mrs Mahler? Are they as fashionable as Viennese women?'

The answer came straight into her head.

'No ladies are ever as well dressed as Viennese ladies ...' She paused for effect, then, with a girlish giggle, slightly embarrassed, 'You must forgive me, gentlemen. I'm so prejudiced!'

More laughter. They liked her.

'Who designs your dresses, Mrs Mahler?'

'Two famous designers in Vienna – of course. Bertold Loeffler and Koloman Moser.'

'Are they very expensive?'

Alma-Maria paused before replying. She said,

'I think you will have to ask my husband.'

She glanced at him and saw his smile, thin as a thread. He would never admit – not even to himself, in fact least of all to himself – but he was jealous of the attention being paid to her.

'I shall tell you, gentlemen, what I think of the way New York ladies dress when I have come here to hear my husband conduct. I shall observe the Diamond Horseshoe most carefully.'

The Diamond Horseshoe was the horseshoe-shaped crescent of boxes on the grand tier, each of which cost its lessee $60,000. She was pleased with her little display of knowledge acquired.

'Is that a promise?' somebody called out.

'Of course,' she replied.

For a moment, she was happy.

The gentlemen of the press dispersed giving every sign of having been pleased with the occasion. Dippel took Mahler and Alma-Maria to lunch at Heinrich Conried's flat in an apartment block adjoining the Metropolitan Opera House, on 39th Street. Entering Conried's abode was like entering somebody else's fantasy. The Director and virtual proprietor of the Metropolitan Opera received them in his salon, a circular room with small stained-glass windows whose amber, magenta, blue and red panels were artificially lit from the outside. The walls were draped in sombre, deeply flounced satins and velours on which rested paintings in lavishly encrusted and ornamented gold frames, the subjects of which could hardly be made out. The guests, of whom there were a dozen including Alma-Maria and Mahler, sat on tapestried upright armchairs which were set in a circle about the satin walls. In the centre was a gondola-shaped seat, suspended by plaited golden ropes from a velvet-covered baldaquin with a tasselled fringe, in which lounged their host smoking a cigar.

'You must forgive me, friends,' he said in faultless Austrian-German. 'I am not as well as I would wish to be.'

It was true he had the hollow look of a cancerous tabes. As he swayed, half reclining in his strange black seat, the smoke from his cigar hung still in the perfumed air.

'I hope Dippel has seen to it, Herr Mahler, that you and the lovely Mrs Mahler are as comfortable here in New York as we can make you?'

Mahler assured him that such was the case. Coppelius, thought Alma-Maria: Dr Coppelius's salon in the first act of *The Tales of Hoffmann*. That's what the room reminded her of, with the suspended lounging seat for the automaton-doll, Olympia, set in a room curtained off from the real world.

'Do you know, Gibson?' said Conried. 'They tell me Hammerstein and his so-called Manhattan Opera have cost us $1,200,000 in five years. Well, this season we shall have Fremstad, and van Rooy – Cosima Wagner entrusted Wotan to him at Bayreuth, you know! And Chaliapin for Leporello. And Caruso, and our own sweet Geraldine Farrar – I've captured her from Berlin! And here we have the greatest conductor in the world – Herr Gustav Mahler. Do you think Hammerstein can match that, eh?'

He had to break off in a paroxysm of coughing. He concluded by spitting into a spitoon of burnished copper which stood on the floor by his lounger. Alma-Maria caught Mahler's eye. He was on the very edge of bursting into laughter. She looked away. She didn't feel much like laughing, herself. The gripping period pains which she had scarcely noticed in her excitement at visiting the Metropolitan Opera House and meeting the press, were now seizing her. She wished she could go to the washroom.

The man whom Conried had addressed as Gibson was discussing the sets for *Tristan and Isolde* and for *The Ring* which Mahler was to conduct later in the season. He was a dark, swarthy, beetle-browed man, portly with good living, who spoke in a German so atrocious she could not catch what he was saying. However, she turned her head to give the impression of taking an intelligent interest. In so doing she caught the attention of his young wife – younger than he by at least twenty years – a pretty girl with a small, sweet face, retroussé nose, small pursed lips, and mass of corn-yellow hair swept upwards and pinned in layers in a similar style to her own. She was wearing an extremely close-fitting, fashionable dress which fell in a swirl about her feet, hugged her hips, showing off her hour-glass figure, and was heavily looped and flounced below the square décolletage to emphasize her already full bust. As she caught Alma-Maria's gaze, she gave a little, amused shrug of her shoulders, and parted her lips in an apologetic smile.

When the guests were permitted to leave the audience chamber to go to take lunch in the dining room – in the absence of their host – the young woman came over to Alma-Maria. In rather better German than her husband's, she said,

'I'm going to freshen myself up before we go in to lunch. Would you like to keep me company?'

Alma-Maria was only too glad to comply.

'I'm Mrs Charles Dana Gibson, by the way.'

She said it as if expecting Alma-Maria to recognize the name.

'And you are Frau Gustav Mahler. You're quite as beautiful as they said you'd be. More so, in fact. And I didn't expect the great conductor's wife to be so young!'

'Oh, you are kind, Mrs Gibson!'

'No I'm not. I'm honest. Really and truly, I am. I've offended so many old hags because I couldn't flatter them – you know, the words won't come out!'

Alma-Maria did know. She couldn't return Mrs Gibson's compliment because, although she appeared young in almost every respect, the powder and blush she wore could not conceal the deep crows' feet about her eyes and the slightly weathered look of her cheeks, now she was standing in a clear light.

'You speak excellent German, Mrs Gibson.'

'You mean unlike my poor husband? My mother is Swiss. In fact, Mr Gibson met me in Switzerland, even though we both come from Roxbury, Massachusetts.' She continued talking even when Alma-Maria went into the cubicle, standing at the door and calling through it in her raised, childlike voice: 'I was lucky really. Charles Dana – Mr Gibson, I mean – had just signed a contract with *Collier's Weekly*, so he needed a fresh model.'

At that point, Alma-Maria realized who she was. Mrs Charles Dana Gibson – *the* Gibson Girl, of course. Even in Vienna there had been calendars, posters and magazine pictures displaying that sweet little oval face, the mass of hair as luxuriant as her own, the perfect hour-glass figure. She supposed being married to the artist made it seem all right to have portraits of herself in her petticoats and stockings, or bathing drawers, in journals all over the world.

As they sat side by side in front of the huge ormolu-framed mirrors, tidying their hair, Mrs Gibson said,

'You're the only woman I've met with hair as nice as mine.'

Indulging her childishness, Alma-Maria replied,

'I have been envying you your gown ever since I first saw you.'

Mrs Gibson was delighted.

'Have you? Truthfully, now?'

'Of course, truthfully.'

'It's a *Merveille*. I bought it in Paris. The first to make the Atlantic crossing. I'm so glad you like it.'

'It is beautiful.'

'It should be,' said Mrs Gibson. 'It cost almost nine thousand dollars ... We'd better be joining the gentlemen. They'll be dying of hunger, poor things. And Mr Gibson will be mad at me – except he won't because I'll tell him I had to show you where the rest room is.'

After lunch, Mahler and Alma-Maria took their leave at the same time as the Gibsons.

Flakes of snow drifted between the tall buildings, from a cold leaden sky. A large coupé drew up against the pavement. The grey-uniformed chauffeur dismounted to hold open the rear passenger door. Alma-Maria noticed the panelling inside, and the crystal epergnes containing cut orchids fixed between the windows on either side.

'May we carry you anywhere?' asked Mr Gibson. 'To your hotel?'

'I'm returning to my place of work,' Mahler replied. 'My first real ordeal since our arrival – meeting my fellow musicians. My wife, on the other hand ...'

'Yes, dear Frau Mahler,' said Mrs Gibson. 'Can we take you?'

Alma-Maria allowed herself to be driven back to the Hotel Majestic. She had been inclined to walk: she knew it to be no more than a mile away, across Bryant Square and up Fifth Avenue, but nagging period pains defeated her. She just wanted to take an aspirin and lie down.

As the chauffeur opened the door for her to get down, and the uniformed and braided commissionaire came down the hotel steps to hold his large umbrella over her head, Mrs Gibson asked,

'May I telephone you in your suite sometime during the next week or two, Frau Mahler?'

'Elvira! You must give the Mahlers time to make themselves at home,' Mr Gibson reproached her in his uneven German. 'My wife is always in a hurry,' he explained to Alma-Maria.

But it was clear he doted on her whom he still regarded as his child-wife.

'Having friends is part of feeling at home, silly!' Mrs Gibson retorted.

Lying on the bed under the satin coverlet, liberated from corset and suspenders, with the aspirin ease taking its effect, Alma-Maria decided that things could be a great deal worse. There had been German speakers every step since they had left the ship. Mahler was being treated with all the respect owed to him, and flattering attention was being paid to herself. And although at home in Vienna she would not have approved of advances as direct as those of Mrs Charles Dana Gibson, she was amused that her first offer of female friendship on arrival in New York should come from the original Gibson Girl. It was certainly something with which to amuse Berta Zuckerkandl, when she first wrote to her.

That night, Mahler returned to the hotel in the best of spirits.

'Conried came over in person to introduce me to the orchestra. Do you know? They played a *Tusch* in my honour! The *Heldenmotiv* from *Siegfried*.'

He sang out the exultant horn theme.

'Then Spiering – he's the leader – insisted I should rehearse them in the *Tristan* prelude. We began. There was a chorus practice going on in a room behind the stage. I stopped the orchestra immediately and told Conried, 'These gentlemen and I cannot possibly rehearse when there are other rehearsals going on in the building. We can none of us hear each other properly.' I think Conried was a little taken aback. The orchestra was pleased. We sat absolutely still till there was silence. Spiering told me afterwards that Mottl and other conductors had grumbled about the noise, but nobody ever did anything about it before. I actually believe the orchestra likes me.'

Never before had he displayed the least interest in whether his orchestral players – or any others of his colleagues and collaborators – liked him or not. But she was pleased to see his spirits so raised.

'Do you think Conried likes you?' she asked, smiling.

She got up off the bed. The pains had returned, but were milder than they had been.

'Conried is a sick man – there's no doubt of that.'

'Do you think that's what Herr Gibson meant about you being the next Director of the Met?' she asked.

Mahler laughed.

'So you managed to understand so much English, *liebchen*! That was nonsense. He didn't know what he was saying – he probably meant Musical Director. At least, I hope it was nonsense!'

Alma-Maria went through to the closet. She left the door ajar while she washed and changed. He called after her,

'*Tristan, The Ring, Don Giovanni, Figaro*. It would be a bit of a tall order for somebody directing the whole Met. But for anybody concerned only with music – heaven! And with singers like Fremstad, Scotti, Chaliapin, Caruso ...' I shall take you down to dinner this evening – for the best dinner the Majestic provides. I walked home up Fifth Avenue. It's so easy to find one's way in New York. I bought these for you on my way.'

He came in, holding out a brown paper packet lined with tissue. She took it from him and drew out the gossamer thin stockings with their filigree lace windows.

'Gustl! How much did these cost you?'

They flowed through her fingers like fine grains of sand. It was quite ridiculous. In six years of marriage he would have died of embarrassment before he could have bought such things for her. Attracted though he had been by Lehar's score for *The Merry Widow*, he had regarded it as hurtful to his dignity as Director of the Court Opera to be observed handling a copy in a shop. He had sent her to buy it for him (and then had the gall to quote from the waltz in the triumphantly joyous finale of his Seventh Symphony). Still less could he have allowed himself to have been seen handling items of women's apparel.

'Since it seems everybody talks about the price of everything in this city – two hundred dollars.'

'Oh Gustl!' Then, seeing the shadow of disappointment on his face, 'You are absurd! And I do love you!'

Did she? It seemed the right thing to say.

She sat on the quilted stool by the washstand and rolled them on up her legs. Her bodice was still unbuttoned from making her toilet; her breasts were exposed. She saw the way he was looking at her. It had been a long time – months, a year even – since he had looked at her in that way. She rose with her stockings still rolled about her knees, and went and kissed him. That was a mistake, to let him embrace her so closely. It excited him.

'Oh Gustl! We can't, you know. It's the wrong time.'

How typical it was that he shouldn't know when she was suffering her period. She could have gratified him, of course, to build on the changes he had manifested in his behaviour in order to recreate what she had given up as lost. She could have handled him, or even taken him between her lips; such practices had long since ceased to be entirely strange to her. But the inclination to do such things with him had long since passed. She eased him away gently, and buttoned up her bodice.

The following morning, in the *New York Times*, there was the report of an interview with his Isolde – Olive Fremstad – as well as a most favourable account of his meeting with the press at the Metropolitan Opera House. He translated it for her over the breakfast table.

'Dear Fremstad!' he said with the gentle affection he normally reserved for Lilli Lehmann alone among his singers. Alma-Maria wondered. Was it the unquestioning respect with which he was being greeted in New York? Singers and, indeed, some of his players had worked under his baton in the Old World. They knew of his martinet reputation, and still the Opera orchestra had greeted him with their highest accolade, a *Tusch*, a fanfare in his honour. And in return he had softened almost beyond recognition. Perhaps the son of the poor Bohemian-Jewish brandy peddler, the grandson of the beggar woman who trudged from Jewish settlement to Jewish settlement in all weathers selling petticoat strings for a few copper hellers each, no longer felt he had to fight to hold his place in the world. For ten years he had held the highest position the world of music had to offer. Perhaps now he felt he could let those who worked under him see the sweetness of disposition which previously had been revealed as a secret to those who loved him.

A few days later, she was attending a rehearsal at which this view was reinforced. He was holding a preliminary practice with the ladies of the Opera chorus who were to sing the parts of Valkyries in *The Ring* later that season. At the end of the principal Valkyrie chorus from *Die Walküre* itself, he laid down his baton and announced.

'Ladies, I must pay you the compliment that never before – never – have I heard voices of such quality assembled for the Valkyries' chorus. Not even in Vienna. Not even at Bayreuth.'

There was a gasp of delighted astonishment. Over forty women fell in love with him instantly. He held up his hand to indicate he had not finished. It was the old Mahler, thought Alma-Maria; some terrible sarcasm was going to engulf his poor victims.

'And now, ladies, having discovered from me that you are uniquely gifted with such voices, I must ask you to use them so that an audience will be able to hear them!' And then he laughed aloud, as if his severity was all a joke – and they laughed with him, still loving him. 'Shall we take it from *Halt ein o Vater*, if you please?'

This time the quality of sound was transformed.

'Thank you, ladies,' he told them.

He was still smiling – and so were they. People at the Vienna Court Opera would never have believed it, Alma-Maria told herself.

If he had succeeded in shaking off one form of insecurity, he suffered another. If he did not need to go to the Opera house, he remained in bed in the morning. He worked in bed, at his settings of Bethge's poems from the Chinese, *The Jade Flute*, or over his sketches for another enormous instrumental symphony. The settings of the poems, *The Jade Flute*, constituted, Alma-Maria realized, a symphony for voices and orchestra. But he wasn't going to admit to it. Beethoven had composed only nine symphonies; Schubert's great C-major Symphony was his ninth and last; Dvorak had died while planning a ninth symphony; Bruckner's last completed symphony was his Ninth. By maintaining that the new work was a song cycle despite its symphonic structure, he had sought to deceive Providence. The trouble was that his locomotive creativity was beyond his control. Behind the supposed song cycle, another symphony was on its way. One of them was going to have to be accepted as Mahler's Ninth.

In the afternoon, if he wasn't rehearsing, they would cross the avenue and walk in Central Park. Untaxing though this was, he asked her from time to time to feel his pulse; occasionally, feeling or imagining he felt the onset of palpitations, he would insist she fetch one of the horse-drawn cabs to take him back to the hotel.

For the most part, except for the evenings, she was left to her own devices. There was none of the reassuring familiarity of home. If he was composing or studying scores, she dared not play the piano in the drawing room. The hotel was luxurious, even if the food was not as austerely plain as Mahler preferred; there was no housework to be supervised. It was hard enough to find employment for Kathi to prevent the girl from lapsing into one of her bouts of homesickness.

When Mahler was out, the suite became an empty, silent place – which the metallic clatter of the elevator out on the landing, the noise of traffic coming up from Central Park South outside, seemed to make only the more oppressively silent. When the hotel chambermaids and housemaids came in at their appointed times, she couldn't understand what they said.

Mahler returned each night buoyantly cheerful. His mood was one she had never seen in him before – hectic with the exultation she had heard was experienced by people doomed to die of consumption. His attitude to his work, to composition in particular, had included rigid obedience to a timetable, a regimen as precise as that of a dedicated bureaucrat. Now he went to it greedily, jealous of his time. They still played over his work-in-progress at night, if he had time and energy left over from the day. Once, when he was already in bed and she, having brushed out her hair as always, was about to join him, he lay staring up at the ceiling as if into a starry sky and announced.

'There will never be a *Tristan* to equal this one – not this side of heaven.'

She had no wish to curb his enthusiasm, but secretely she wondered if he could be deluding himself. She had seen for herself backstage that the scenery was old and worn and fustian, and the staging thirty years behind the work he and Roller had devised for the Vienna Court Opera. Moreover, it was Fremstad's début in the part of Isolde, one of the most musically and dramatically demanding soprano roles in opera.

That night, when the lights were out, he took her with a potency which astonished her – and not pleasantly. The act was performed quickly and without tenderness, as if he had needed to use her for the sole purpose of relieving his surplus nervous and physical excitement; as if it had been waste matter, she decided bitterly after he had turned his back on her, for which her body was a suitable receptacle.

The only break in the monotony of her days were the evenings when they were invited to dinner by one of the millionaire benefactors of the Metropolitan Opera. Mahler had never liked such social occasions at best; here, for all his fame and reputation, he was 'on approval', under the examination of his paymasters; except that he sat above rather than below the salt, he might have been Mozart at the table of Archbishop

Colloredo or the Emperor Josef II. There was the immensely fat, middle-aged widow who insisted on showing them her collection of paintings, all housed in a windowless brownstone cistern into which nobody was allowed save herself and very particular guests. There was an immensely wealthy doctor who had discovered – and patented, to his own considerable advantage – spinal anaesthesia. With him they had dined off side plates on which were tiny helpings, washed down with a half-bottle of champagne which was shared by seven guests. Another patron of the Opera had taken them round his private museum containing tiles, shards and clay figurines which, he claimed, were Sumerian and dated from 3000 BC. Even Mahler spotted that the exhibits were spurious. With the faintest hint of obsequiousness, he pretended to be taken in.

Alma-Maria suffered another disadvantage, that of language. Her hosts and hostesses as a rule spoke German – a German larded occasionally with Yiddish vocables at which Mahler winced, though so slightly that only she could have noticed. But the same was not true of their guests. Her natural looks even more than her fashionable dress always ensured the men's attention if not that of other guests of her own sex. Her impatience with heavily avuncular flirtatiousness was increased by her inability to hear and understand the compliments being paid to her. Surrounded by vulgarity and ostentatious display, she was revolted at the thought that Mahler had been bought into the service of the Golden Calf. Even the solitude of the mornings when Mahler was composing were preferable, even if she did have to keep silent as the grave.

Nor did she sleep well; it was at night, lying awake listening to Mahler's heavy breathing evolve into snoring, that loneliness came to devour her like the Promethean eagle. Repetitively, interminably, she would rehearse in imagination Putzi's last illness – the sounds, the lurid lamplight in which the doctor and the apothecary worked, and pain made cloying with weariness. She would think of Gucki, left behind with Mutti and Miss Turner so that her childish prattling in the narrow confines of an hotel suite would not impose strain on Mahler. She rehearsed the cold, grey rainswept day on the island of Sylt – the day Pappi died, and she not with him.

On the night of 23 December, the hot-eyed, memory-laden vigil became more than she could bear. The wind was beating snow against the cornices outside, carrying with it the jingle of harness and muffled creak of wheels from the avenue eleven floors below. Mahler was breathing the even, calm-sounding breaths of deep, restful sleep. There was also the sound of voices, at first wispy, hard to catch or recognize as voices, but then, after a few minutes, either through concentration or a change in the direction of the wind, clearer albeit far away:

> *Ein Kind geborn zu Bethlehem, Alleluja!*
> *Des freuet sich Jerusalem, Alleluja!*

It was a carol Muttichen used to sing long ago, in Plankenburg, where she had lovingly tried to recreate the North German Christmasses of her own childhood. Tonight, up on the Hohe Warte, there might be snow, and Muttichen, with little Guckerl, and Marie, and Miss Turner, all joining in.

> *Die König aus Saba kamen da, Alleluja!*
> *Gold, Weihrauch, Myrrhen brachtens dar, Alleluja!*

The voices rang quite distinctly. She clenched the lace flounce of her pillow, her knuckle pressing her teeth between her parted lips. But nothing would stop the hot tears from running down her cheek into the linen cover. And Mahler wouldn't be able to comfort her even if he were awake; he knew nothing of the Christian child's paradise.

She wiped the tears from her eyes with her fingertips, sat up and got out of bed very quietly and carefully. She did not bother with her wrapper which lay over the back of the dressing table chair, but went out to the vestibule of the suite and put on her sealskin coat. She let herself out onto the landing, opposite the elevator shaft. The lights had been dimmed. Through the windows behind the elevator she could see the constellations of pinprick lights from the skyscrapers of downtown Manhattan. There was no fear of people coming up the elevator and seeing her – there was only the roof above. From up the open shaft came the voices and the sound of a piano: they were coming from the suite on the tenth floor, immediately below.

> *Hie leit es in dem Krippelein, Alleluja!*
> *Ohne Ende ist die Herrschaft sein, Alleluja!*

She went barefooted down the carpeted stairs, and stopped, resting her shoulder against the wall, at the first turn. The singing ended. There was applause, laughter, and a burst of conversation. Even to that she listened greedily, self-pityingly, waiting for more tears to come.

Suddenly, and before she could turn away, the suite door was opened, spreading light across the landing to the elevator gate. The voices were much louder. A lady came out, in furs, followed by a gentleman holding his top hat, stick, and white gloves. After him came a young man similarly encumbered and a young woman, a pretty, fresh-faced girl who still wore her thick yellow hair loose, shoulder-length spreading from under the tilt of her white fur hat, over the white fur collar of her coat. All were clutching gaily wrapped parcels.

They called final farewells and Christmas greetings to their hosts. The young man went to the elevator shaft to ring the bell. He turned and saw Alma-Maria standing above, at the turn of the stairs, her nightdress conspicuous below the knee-length hem of her coat, and her bare toes.

'Why, hallo!' he called.

The absurd notion occurred to her that she could pretend to be sleepwalking.

'Miles!' his mother rebuked the boy.

She blinked up to where Alma-Maria was standing staring down.

'Mrs Mahler, is it?' she asked. 'Is everything all right, dear?'

Her husband joined her.

'Can we help you in any way?' he asked.

Alma-Maria did not understand them, but she understood the concern in their voices.

'Forgive me ...' she began. 'I couldn't sleep. I heard the singing.'

The lady glanced at her husband.

'Of course, my dear! You don't speak English,' she said in German. 'I do hope the noise of the party hasn't disturbed you and Herr Gustav Mahler. Mr and Mrs Gellhorn would be so distressed!'

'No, no!' Alma-Maria assured her. 'My husband is fast asleep. I couldn't sleep for thinking ...' She hesitated. 'For thinking of my little girl – she's at home in Vienna with her grandmother. I miss her, you know? And then I heard you all singing *Ein Kind geborn*.' She smiled. 'I felt quite homesick.'

'Of course, dear,' said the lady.

'And you were singing it so beautifully. I just wanted to hear you. I didn't think I'd be ... well ... caught like this. I'd better go back upstairs before anybody else catches me spying. I'm embarrassed enough as it is!'

The girl with the long yellow hair came to the foot of the flight of stairs.

'Are you really Mrs Gustav Mahler?' she asked in Viennese-accented German.

'Yes.' Alma-Maria nodded.

'I remember everybody talking about you in Vienna, saying how beautiful you were. Only I thought you'd be much older.'

She had the soft peach-bloom complexion of a child, and forget-me-not eyes. She could not have been more than sixteen or seventeen years old. There was a steady, innocent frankess about her gaze. Alma-Maria prayed that she could not see the track-marks of her tears on her face.

'Mitzi! Don't be impertinent!' the young man called to her.

He was standing at the elevator shaft, his hand on the bell. He wasn't her brother; his eyes were dark, his complexion swarthy.

'You don't mind, do you, Frau Mahler?' asked the girl.

'Not in the least,' Alma-Maria assured her.

'The whole of New York is talking about the first performance of *Tristan and Isolde* a week on Wednesday,' said the girl. 'You can't get tickets – they're gold dust! And now I shall be able to tell everybody at college I've met the wife of the great Gustav Mahler!'

'I'm sure Frau Mahler wants to go back up to her suite,' said the lady.

'Goodnight,' Alma-Maria said. 'Thank you for being so under-standing.'

As she let herself back into the suite, she heard the rattle of the elevator from the floors below. It would have been an exaggeration to say that she felt happy as she took off her coat and replaced it in the vestibule wardrobe, but there had been an angelic quality about the girl they had called Mitzi – an unafraid quality about her good looks, which had touched her like the receiving of a blessing. She wondered if the boy was her courtier.

At a quarter past eleven, the following morning, Christmas Eve, when Mahler was preparing to leave for the Opera, the telephone rang. Alma-Maria answered it; it was to tell her that a Mrs Baumfeld with friend was at the porter's desk, wishing to know if Mrs Mahler was willing to receive her. Mrs Baumfeld wished it to be known that they had met on the tenth-floor landing the previous night. Without elaboration, Alma-Maria explained that it was a lady she had met in the hotel the previous day who wished to come up.

'Give me time to make my escape,' Mahler told her.

He stretched out his arms to let Anton help him on with his coat while she stood with her hand cupped over the horn of the telephone. He kissed her goodbye, took his music portfolio from Anton, and left.

Alma-Maria waited at the door of the suite. She went out to greet Mrs Baumfeld as she stepped from the elevator. The yellow-haired girl was with her.

'Dear Frau Mahler, you don't think I'm being impertinent do you? Returning so quickly, I mean.'

'No, of course not. Please come in. The chambermaids are gone now. So has my husband, I'm afraid.'

'To the Met?'

'Yes. Rehearsals.'

'Hello, Frau Mahler.'

The girl gave her the loveliest of smiles. Alma-Maria closed the door after them. Mrs Baumfeld held out her hand.

'My dear, I'm Elizabeth Baumfeld. My husband is chairman of the Hamburg-Amerika line. He is also an impresario in a small way. And this forward young lady whom you encountered last night is Mitzi Uchatius. Mitzi is the daughter of an old friend of my husband who lives up in New Hampshire. She's staying with us while she is studying here in New York City.'

Alma-Maria led them through to the drawing room.

'Where are you studying, Mitzi?' she asked.

'The Association of Decorative Arts College ... Only, I'm studying fine arts,' she added with a certain pride. 'Oh my? Did you stitch that?'

A silk chemise was draped over Alma-Maria's work basket. Around the hem and the upper edge of the bodice front she had embroidered a narrow frieze of tiny flowers.

'Yes. I did.'

She was not going to say that, as far as needlework was concerned, it was her solitary accomplishment, only to be used as a last bastion against boredom.

'They're exquisite. Look, Aunt Elizabeth!' Mitzi exclaimed. 'I wish I could do work like that! See?' She lifted her skirt to show her petticoat hem. 'Horrible little snags everywhere!' She dropped her skirt again.

'Will you let me send my maid to fetch coffee?' asked Alma-Maria.

'Oh no,' Mrs Baumfeld replied. 'We're only making the briefest of calls. We – that is Mr Baumfeld and I ... Let me put it this way. Mr Baumfeld has arranged a tour of the Eastern cities by the Dresden *Residenz Theater* Company. We have invited the players to dine with us tonight – a real German Christmas dinner, you know, with a tree, and singing, and children – everything. And we wondered whether you and Herr Mahler would care to join us.'

'Please, *gnädige* Frau Mahler,' said Mitzi. 'It would be wonderful to be able to boast that the great Herr Gustav Mahler had been to dinner with us.'

She looked appealingly into Alma-Maria's eyes.

'You know,' said Mrs Baumfeld. 'You two could be sisters. Same colour of the eyes – though perhaps Frau Mahler's hair is just a shade darker.'

'Perhaps Frau Mahler already has a younger sister,' said Mitzi.

Without giving the least consideration to her reply, Alma-Maria lied, 'No. No I haven't any sisters, so there is a vacancy for the job.'

They laughed.

'Except, that isn't quite true. I do have a half-sister, only she's twenty years younger than me. My mother married again after my father's death.'

'Oh well,' said Mitzi, 'she doesn't count.'

'Mitzi!' protested Mrs Baumfeld.

'You and Herr Mahler will come tonight, won't you?' Mitzi asked.

'Perhaps Frau Mahler is already engaged for this evening,' suggested Mrs Baumfeld.

Alma-Maria shook her head.

'I'll speak to my husband,' she said. 'I promise I'll do my best to persuade him. It's so very kind of you.'

'And perhaps, Frau Mahler, one day you'll teach me to stitch flowers on my petticoats as cleverly as you do,' said Mitzi.

'They're quite easy to do,' Alma-Maria told her. 'Believe me, if I can do them, they must be very easy.'

'You mustn't be too modest,' said Mrs Baumfeld. 'Mitzi is a student of art, you know.'

'Then she's flattering me, aren't you, Fräulein Mitzi?' said Alma-Maria.

The noise was deafening. The children were clamouring to go to the tree in the drawing room. The actors and actresses from the Dresden Theatre were playing up to them as if improvising a first act for E. T. A. Hoffmann's *Nutcracker and The King of Mice*. Alma-Maria glanced up the table at Mahler. There was a look of pain on his face so acute she wanted to laugh. Mrs Baumfeld had already suggested that he should play the piano for them after dinner, and when he demurred had insisted.

'But, dear Herr Director, everybody in this house has to play for their supper. Even little Lili. Don't you, Lili?'

Lili was about seven.

'Yes, Mama.'

'You see, Herr Director?'

'Perhaps I might be allowed to play as representative of the family Mahler?' Alma-Maria had suggested, knowing Gustav to be perfectly capable of getting up and walking out if pressed too hard.

'My wife,' he said, 'is a most accomplished pianist – certainly as accomplished as myself.'

'I just don't know how musicians manage to read all those thousands of little dots . . .'

Renata Paulmann, the theatre company's somewhat elderly *ingénue*, was speaking. Her gaunt angularity did nothing to conceal her years; nor did her dress, the way she wore her hair, nor the emphatic blush she had applied to her cheeks. Her voice sounded husky from drinking schnapps and smoking cigarettes, but it carried across the hubbub to the ends of the room.

'. . . And so many of them doing different things at the same time . . . You know they called him *Der Mahler* in Vienna? We played a five-week season at the Burg almost two years ago, and that's what everybody called him – *fiacre* drivers, trolley-car conductors, waiters, everybody. *Der Mahler*! . . . You don't mind me telling everybody how famous and important you were in Vienna, do you Herr Director?'

Alma-Maria could see the tightness of his mouth drawing his cheeks even more hollow than usual – or was it the candlelight? And dear God! She wanted to laugh so much, so near to letting go. Somehow he was managing to remain polite, sitting beside Mrs Baumfeld. There was a distinguished-looking, formidable, white-haired dowager sitting opposite him, her head held stiffly erect by the whalebone points of her lace collar. It was just as well she was engaging him in conversation, Alma-Maria decided.

She herself was sitting beside Mitzi Uchatius. Mitzi had confessed that she had asked to be placed next to her.

'I hope you don't mind. I wanted to ask you all sorts of things ... Like, have you ever met Gustav Klimt?'

'Oh yes. He is a friend – a very dear friend.'

'When we were in Vienna – we were in Vienna for two years while Papa represented the phonogram company there – I wanted to go and see Klimt's paintings at the University. But Mama and Papa said no.' She glanced across the table, then asked, 'Are they truly as scandalous as people say?'

'I hope not. I've sat for him on a number of occasions.'

'Was it for your portrait?' Mitzi asked.

'Oh no! I sat for him when he wanted some sort of Muse figure. Dante's Beatrice: the Muse of German poetry, the inspiration for one of Schubert's songs.'

'I can see that,' Mitzi told her.

'Can you, *liebchen*? You're very flattering, you know.'

'I expect you're Herr Mahler's inspiration too. He writes music, doesn't he?'

Alma-Maria didn't really want to be distracted from thinking about Klimt. What if, that afternoon in Venice, she had agreed to run away with him to Florence or Rome? The affair might not have lasted – but the excitement, the fulfilment might have justified everything.

'I'm sorry to have to say it, but I cannot share this seemingly universal approval of *Tristan and Isolde*.'

The stiff-necked dowager sitting opposite Mahler was speaking, her voice ringing down the table like that of a Prussian drill-sergeant.

'However accomplished the music – beautiful, if you wish – it is an immoral work. There is not the least hint of remorse shown by Isolde in the final scene. On the contrary – she is glorying in her adultery. It is an intemperate work: a self-indulgence on the part of its author; even, I would suggest, a self-justification.'

'You are referring, I take it, to Wagner's relationship with Cosima von Bülow?' Mahler asked.

There was a note in his voice which alarmed Alma-Maria. She wished she were beside him to try to restrain him.

'Indeed I am, Herr Director. And to the duty Wagner owed to Frau Cosima's father – a fellow musician and composer who had done everything to further Wagner's career.'

Alma-Maria remembered Pappi's personal reminiscences of Cosima Wagner's father. From what she recalled, she didn't suppose Liszt would have cared a bent heller what his daughter got up to. She could see the dowager's face: the way she was biting her lower lip. The woman knew she had said something stupid, Alma-Maria realized, if only that it was scarcely well-bred to denigrate the work which her dinner companion was about to conduct at the Metropolitan Opera House for the first time. She hoped that Mahler, too, would detect the look of regret.

'That is all *Tristan and Isolde* means to you, Madam?' he demanded. 'A score which many critics – including myself – regard as the greatest operatic score since Beethoven wrote *Fidelio*?'

His challenge caused the woman to assert herself once more.

'Do you suppose, Herr Director, that an artist's work does not reflect his moral condition?'

'I presume you have read Aristotle, Madam? – and that you recall that section of *The Politics* where he discusses whether the virtue of a good flute player is the same as that of a good man?'

'Aristotle was a pagan,' replied the dowager. 'I trust we can be said to have learnt something from our belief in Divine Providence.'

'Charity, for example?' suggested Mahler.

Alma-Maria felt a sickening tension in her stomach.

'I've always found *Tristan and Isolde* most disturbing,' intervened the skinny *ingénue* from the theatre company. 'I can never sleep after hearing *Tristan*.' She stared about her, looking for sympathetic understanding. 'The *Liebestod* simply sings through my poor brain all night . . .'

Nobody responded to her attempt to defuse the situation.

'Mind you, I haven't heard it all that often. Working in the theatre myself, you know . . .' her voice tailed off.

'There is a story, *gnädige* Frau,' Mahler continued, 'of the man in the art museum who is examining a painting by Rembrandt – "David watching Bathsheba at her Toilet" or "Susanna and the Elders", it doesn't matter which. His attitude is similar to yours: he uses expressions such as "reprehensible", "immodest", "immoral". He's on the point of leaving when the attendant says to him, "My dear sir, there are some works of art which one may not judge. It is you who are judged by them."' The swell of his rich bass filled the room. 'I suggest, *gnädige* Frau, that in attempting to set a value on Wagner's masterpiece based on your own Biedermeier standards, you tell us nothing about the work and everything about yourself.'

There was a heavy silence over the table. The servants waiting at the sideboards did not know where to look. The children wriggled uneasily on their chairs, but dared not make a noise. The Christmas bonhomie had been dispelled. There were one or two desultory attempts to renew conversation, but the elderly dowager remained stiffly silent throughout the rest of the meal. Alma-Maria felt a gritty buzzing in her head, a gathering darkness against the edges of her vision. She would have liked to have said that she was ill, to have asked Mahler to take her home, but dreaded confirming the oddness in her behaviour she had revealed the previous night to her hosts.

The ladies rose from the table to take coffee in the drawing room while the gentlemen smoked their cigars. The children were sent to play upstairs until it was time to gather round the tree. Crossing the hall, a woman Alma-Maria did not know said to her,

'Is your husband in the habit of creating scenes in other people's homes, Mrs Mahler?'

Alma-Maria ignored her because, in the wretchedness of her condition, she had no idea of what of say. Somebody took her arm and gently steered her into the dazzling lights of the drawing room. There was a rustling of silks, a chattering, a click of coffee cups and spoons all about her, hemming her in. She couldn't make out what was being said. She looked expecting to find that it had been Mitzi Uchatius who had guided her. Beside her, smiling at her was the actress, Renata Paulmann.

'I did *so* admire your husband's outburst, Frau Director,' she said in her raddled, husky voice. 'It's the artistic impulse, isn't it?'

The slightly bloodshot eyes framed in the powder which was intended to conceal the bruises from fatigue under the lower lids and the network of tiny creases, stared in appeal. It was *she*, Alma-Maria realized, who was seeking approval.

'I'm an instinctive creature myself,' Fräulein Paulmann added. 'An artist has to be in touch with her innermost being. I'm sure the Herr Director would not be the great conductor he is if he were not in touch with his innermost being.'

A maid emerged from the glare of the lights to offer them coffee. Behind her was another guest from the Dresden Theatre, a more motherly figure than Fräulein Paulmann.

'It is so irritating,' said this second actress, 'when one has devoted months of one's life, years perhaps, to the interpretation of a work, to have it put down . .' She lowered her voice . . . 'by some ignoramus.'

'My husband and I,' Alma-Maria heard herself say, quite calmly, 'are both great admirers of Wagner's work. My husband was introduced to Wagner in person, when he was a student in Vienna. By Anton Bruckner. It was a great moment in his life, I think. I'm quite envious of him.'

'But you're far too young ever to have met Wagner!' Fräulein Paulmann exclaimed.

'You're very kind, Fräulein Paulmann.'

She was about to explain that she had been four when Wagner died, when Fräulein Paulmann gripped her arm and said,

'Please call me Putzi. Everybody calls me Putzi!'

The eyes in the painted face were staring at her, begging for friendship. Alma-Maria felt the shattering of the fragile self-control she had been exercising all evening.

'No!' she heard herself say. 'No!'

For a moment, there was a chance of taking a grip of herself, or so she thought. But she wanted to let go, as somebody seized by vertigo wants to let go, to fall to a greater, more enveloping security. She was clenching her hands so that the nails dug into her palms. Her voice was rising to a scream: 'No! No! Go away! Leave me alone!'

There was a disturbed murmur of voices about her. She saw Mitzi

Uchatius's lovely child's face framed by the heads and shoulders of the women in front of her. It was filled with a wonderful concern. She heard her own voice sobbing and crying out. Other people's voices were sounding questions like waves beating against her. She heard Mahler's strong voice, his arm about her. She tried to tell him not to carry her like she had seen him carry singers in rehearsal, back to Vienna. He was explaining,

'Our daughter – we called her Putzi. She was taken from us, five months ago. My wife has not yet recovered from the blow.'

She realized she was supposed to have fainted. She let herself sink into oblivion through a lapping tide of sympathetic voices.

There were two doctors at her bedside the following morning. One of them spoke German; both exuded the mystique of all medical men.

'Nothing to give rise to any long-lasting anxiety ... Bereavement, arrival in a strange country ... Perhaps a little more wine than usual to drink – the festive season, you know.'

It was true she had taken several tots of Benedictine to give her confidence before setting out the previous night, but she had not felt in the least tipsy. Mahler was standing at the foot of the bed. The doctors led him away to the window. They stood there, talking. Kathi had been standing at the closet door. They called her over. Surely they didn't suspect her of being a secret drinker? They weren't sounding out Kathi about it? She strained to hear what they were saying, but could make out only an incomprehensible murmuring. She felt sick with anxiety.

The German-speaking doctor returned to the bedside.

'Nervous debilitation, dear lady. Nothing more serious. We prescribe a tonic – strychnine, iron, and quinine. Sounds much worse than it is. A stimulant to get the bodily machine functioning properly, eh? A little gentle exercise each day. That should put you on your feet in time for your husband's début at the Metropolitan.'

Which, of course, was all that mattered.

Mahler remained with her all day. It being Christmas Day, there was no call for him to rehearse. He was attentive and considerate to her. Anton was sent out for the medicine. She took three teaspoonfuls, three times during the day. Kathi brought her a glass of Benedictine each time, to take away the awful taste. Mahler had no objection. Far from stimulating her, the combination of tonic and liqueur made her drowsy. She sat at the drawing room window watching the people strolling and skating in the park, in the dying light of the afternoon, and nodded off from time to time. Mahler wrote letters: to Roller, to Gerhard Hauptmann, to Mengelberg in Amsterdam, to Bruno Walter and his young wife. Through a half-sleep she heard the gentle scratching of his pen; Jew though he was, and without orthodox beliefs of any kind, he would have regarded it as sacrilege to have worked on Christmas Day.

334

She would have been happy to have dozed and rested, half-watching the lamps as they flickered on across the snow-darkened city landscape – could have wished it to go on for ever, with Mahler quietly near her, waiting on her. Only somewhere, at a distance, vaguely, she was ashamed – not so much at having created a scene as having ruined the chance of a friendship. When she murmured occasionally, 'I'm so ashamed! I'm *so* ashamed!' it was to provoke Mahler into putting his arm about her, to comfort her through the moments of painful regret.

In the days which followed, Mahler spent more and more time at the Opera. Once again she was alone in the suite. She dozed, took her medicine and Benedictine, and dozed again. Accompanied by Kathi, she sallied out briefly into a world as lonely as the suite, only to return to doze again. It was not an unhappy existence, but there was always the knowledge that unhappiness was there, waiting for her.

On the fifth day after Christmas, two days before the opening of *Tristan and Isolde*, Mitzi Uchatius came alone to the Hotel Majestic. Kathi let her in. Mahler was, as usual, at rehearsal.

Alma-Maria could not restrain her pleasure.

'Mitzi! What a wonderful surprise!'

'I hope you don't think me terribly rude, *gnädige* Frau Mahler. Mrs Baumfeld said it wouldn't be proper, but I did so want to find out how you were.'

She was wearing her yellow hair down, tied back in a huge blue bow like a schoolgirl. Her clear young face glowed with health.

Alma-Maria took her hands and kissed her cheek.

'I can't think of anything more lovely,' she said. 'And please, please call me Alma.'

Thank God she had made her toilet and was properly dressed. Up until today, she had spent every morning with her hair loose, and wearing her wrapper.

'I didn't tell Mrs Baumfeld I was coming here. I said I was going to call in at the college. You won't let on, will you, Frau Alma?'

'No, of course not, *liebchen*.'

'And are you better? We were so dreadfully sorry to hear about your loss . . . And that awful Fräulein Paulmann!'

'I'm afraid it must have been very upsetting for her,' Alma-Maria said.

She had become secure in happiness, however temporary it might prove.

'Oh, her!' laughed Mitzi. 'She recovered *very* quickly. You turned a spotlight onto her, you see.'

'I was just being over-emotional, I'm afraid. Nervous debilitation, the doctors say. I really feel very much better this morning. Much better for seeing you. You look like spring – beautiful!'

'I'm never going to be as beautiful as you, Frau Alma. I remember hearing about you when we were in Vienna – Frau Gustav Mahler, the most beautiful woman in Vienna!'

'How disappointed you must be!' – protecting herself, not fishing for compliments – 'seeing me as I really am.'

'You are just as they said you were,' Mitzi told her seriously.

'You are very, very kind,' Alma-Maria replied, equally seriously.

When she told Mitzi that she was supposed to take a walk each day, Mitzi, as she had hoped, suggested she come with her instead of Kathi.

'I'm sure Kathi will be delighted,' Alma-Maria said. 'I'm afraid she's been very bored these past days, looking after me. She'd much rather be at her English class. I'm sure she has made friends there – the sort she doesn't talk about to me.'

She wondered if Mitzi too had admirers – like the young man she had seen on the landing, that first evening.

They walked arm in arm on paths dusted with snow, through a maze of snow-burdened trees and bushes. The air was cold, grasping at the throat. Children were tobogganing down a tree-lined avenue; their voices hung frozen in the air.

'There's the Metropolitan Museum of Art.' Mitzi pointed across the margin of the park. 'I don't think they have any of Klimt's paintings there. Not yet. It would be marvellous if I had a painting hung there one day.'

'So you are going to be painter?' asked Alma-Maria.

'Oh yes! A portrait painter – but a creative one, like Rembrandt. Not just somebody who paints senators and Supreme Court judges.'

The vapour from their mouths drifted on the air.

'My father managed to paint our equivalent of senators and Supreme Court judges and be creative,' Alma-Maria told her.

'Do you paint, Frau Alma?'

'My father used to give me lessons. And Klimt tried to teach me to draw . . .'

'Klimt taught you?' Mitzi exclaimed.

'Not very seriously. I always wanted to be a composer. The world's first great woman composer.'

They were climbing a flight of ornamental steps. For the first time that morning, Alma-Maria felt weary and was glad of the support of Mitzi's arm.

'Shall I take you back to the hotel?' Mitzi asked.

'Not yet.'

She didn't want the companionship to end so soon.

They reached the top. A stone balustrade curved in a semicircle, forming the back of a stone bench.

'Tramps sleep here in the warm weather,' Mitzi explained.

It was deserted now. Voices floated from far away among the trees. Above the very centre of the balustrade stood a stone classical figure –

a goddess or nymph half draped. From one of her pointed nipples hung a thin, vitreous icicle.

'So you write music, as well as your husband?' Mitzi asked.

'I'm not supposed to.' She mustn't allow any hint of bitterness into her voice. 'I had to stop composing when I got married. One composer is enough in any family.'

She felt an involuntary empathy with the statue. Her own nipples had stiffened uncomfortably against the silk of her bodice.

'I expect that is what your husband told you,' said Mitzi, in a matter-of-fact voice which was almost a rebuke.

'He made it a condition of our marrying,' Alma-Maria told her before she could prevent herself.

'Did you keep the music you had composed?' Mitzi asked.

'Yes. I take it with me everywhere – the still-born children of my imagination.' She laughed self-deprecatingly. Mitzi hugged her arm to show sympathy. Too late, Alma-Maria added, 'I don't suppose I was ever going to be a very great composer. Probably I'd never be as great a composer as you'll be a painter.'

They walked, arm in arm still, down from the terrace, across a narrow stone bridge to skirt the zoo with its smell of dank, soiled straw, and the cawing, screeching, honking of its inmates hanging on the wintry air. Returning towards the avenue, Central Park South, they passed the lake with its crowds of skaters gliding and swirling, scarves swinging, and blades hissing and crunching on the ice.

Alma-Maria said,

'You are very patient to spend time with me like this.'

'It's nice being with somebody who is artistic like me. Mr and Mrs Baumfeld are very sweet to me. But they're like all their friends. They talk about nothing except money and how much somebody is spending on something – and who is going to marry whom, of course. All terribly dull, really.' They walked on. 'It must be terrible not being able to do what you want,' said Mitzi. 'I mean, like painting or composing music.'

Alma-Maria was conscious of having been disloyal to Mahler, and that with one who was little more than a child. But the feeling stood off from her, at a distance, without pain.

'But I suppose you do compose in a way – I mean, as Herr Mahler's inspiration. Does your music sound like Herr Mahler's at all?'

'Oh no. Not at all,' Alma-Maria replied. 'My husband is a Jew, you know. Christian – but once a Jew, always a Jew.'

'Mr and Mrs Baumfeld are the same. They don't actually go to church, though.'

'You're not Jewish?'

'No. Not German, either. My parents are Lithuanian so we're Roman Catholic.'

'Like myself,' said Alma-Maria. 'I knew you were baptized as a child.

There's a special brightness about those who were baptized as children. That's why I say my music and my husband's could never be alike. Music by Jews nearly always begins with a dissonance. Think of the opening of Mendelssohn's "Midsummer Night's Dream" Wedding March – or the barcarolle from *The Tales of Hoffmann*. And then think of music by Catholics like Haydn, Mozart and Schubert, how often Christian music begins with a chord in C major, like *Die Meistersinger* for instance.'

She was aware of Mitzi gazing at her – those childlike, wide blue eyes gazing at her. She wondered if she had been talking stupidly, hadn't really explained what she meant. She carried this fear with her as they crossed the avenue and returned to the hotel.

'I must go back to the Baumfelds,' said Mitzi when she had seen Alma-Maria to the door of her suite. 'Or they'll be wondering what I've been up to.'

Alma-Maria felt a desperate need to bind the girl to her. Fighting her feeling of nervous apprehension, she said,

'Mitzi? *Liebchen*? On Wednesday night, would you like to come to the Opera with me? To hear *Tristan* from the Director's box?'

There was only the hesitation of a moment before the girl's eyes shone with excitement.

'The opening night?' she asked.

'As my guest, of course.'

'Oh, Frau Alma!'

'I shall telephone Mrs Baumfeld and seek her permission. Do you think she will have forgiven me? ... I won't mention this morning, of course.'

'Oh, Frau Alma! Please do try! I'm sure she doesn't think there is anything to forgive. But I've no idea what I can wear! Not for a seat in the Diamond Horseshoe ...!'

And she put her arms round Alma-Maria and warmly kissed her.

The thought of Mitzi Uchatius's companionship at the opening night of *Tristan* gave Alma-Maria the courage to telephone Mrs Baumfeld, ostensibly to apologize for her breakdown at the Christmas Eve party. Mrs Baumfeld was all understanding and concern – everything must have been such a strain on her, her terrible bereavement, particularly when caused by an illness like diphtheria, a new world, new people, and the natural anxieties surrounding her husband's début at the Met. And their young friend, Mitzi, had been *so* worried about Frau Mahler. This gave Alma-Maria the opportunity to say how grateful she had been for Mitzi's company at table, and what a charmingly considerate girl she was.

'Oh yes!' Mrs Baumfeld agreed. 'And *such* a nice family, the Uchatiuses – they've done so well. And when they came from Russia, they

338

hadn't a cent to bless themselves with, poor dears! But that was before Mitzi was born, of course.'

When Alma-Maria offered her invitation to Mitzi to be her guest in the Director's box, Mrs Baumfeld responded with a delighted acceptance. There was no need, she assured dear Frau Mahler, even to confirm it with Mitzi herself – the child would be *so* excited. She and Mr Baumfeld would be there, of course, in the stalls; Mr Baumfeld did not aspire to one of the thirty-seven boxes on the Grand Tier, but he would bring Mitzi up to the Director's box.

Alma-Maria had brought to New York two evening gowns by Loeffler, neither of which she had worn. She chose the one which suited her blonde hair and pale complexion best: a rich, blue close-fitting satin with the loose-skirted overskirt, medieval in style, which fell back away from the underskirt in a train. Over this she put on, for the first time, the sealskin coat with matching hat and muff which was Mahler's inordinately expensive Christmas present.

There was a telephone message from the porter's desk downstairs to announce the arrival of the cab they had ordered. Mahler was cross; he had expected the Metropolitan Opera to provide him with a car. He was also unwontedly nervous. He had eaten nothing since breakfast, and, though she had persuaded him to lie down for the afternoon, he had been unable to sleep. He let Anton sling his coat and scarf over his arm. he examined Alma-Maria, adjusting his spectacles in order to do so.

'Nobody will have eyes for the stage,' he said, making it sound like a rebuke. 'Not that it'll be any great loss – a little hard on poor Fremstad, of course.'

Alma-Maria took his arm to steer him to the elevator.

'Fortunately,' she teased him, 'they'll have ears for the music.'

'A debatable point from what I've heard,' Mahler replied. 'There is a scientific law ...'

'The Mahler law – one of several?' she suggested.

'Quite. That the more an audience pays at the opera, the less disposed they are to listen. Box-holders at the Metropolitan Opera House pay more than anywhere else in the world – and still they can't afford to send a car for the conductor!'

'Come on, Gustl! Even Strauss says the Vienna Court Opera is the lion house. After ten years in Vienna, you've nothing to fear.'

As the cage door of the elevator rattled open, he eased her forward. She was stepping into it, when she felt herself being pulled back by the train of her gown. She turned to see why he was tugging at her, and collided into him. She felt the ripping of her skirt against her hip. As he followed her into the elevator, he had trodden on her short train: it was torn clean away from one side of her gown, leaving a gaping rent in the seam of the underskirt.

For one moment, she tried to persuade herself that she could go on, that she could hold the train in place to conceal the tear, but it was ridiculous of course. She tried to silence Mahler's attempts to apologize.

'Kathi will just have to do what she can. You must go on. I'll follow as soon as she's finished.'

She returned to the suite. Mahler followed.

'I have no intention of going without you, Almschi!'

'You have to go, Gustl! Don't be silly!'

'I couldn't raise a stick tonight without you being there.'

'I'm not a lucky charm, Gustl.' To soften the bitterness, she added, 'I haven't much claim to being a guardian angel, either.'

'You're everything, Almschi. You know that.'

Since when? she wondered.

'Kathi!' she called. When the maid came out of her room, she held up the ragged hems to show her.

'Oh my God!' Kathi exclaimed. She examined the damage. 'It's all on the seams, fortunately. We'll soon have it done.'

She went to fetch needle and thread. Alma-Maria slipped her coat from her shoulders.

'They'll be waiting for you,' she said.

'Let them wait. They should have sent a car. In any case, from what I've heard, music is the last thing an audience at the Met wants to hear.'

In Vienna, he would never have stayed, least of all on a first night. She stood motionless in the centre of the drawing room as Kathi crouched at her skirts stitching rapidly and efficiently.

'You are a good, clever girl, Katchen,' she said softly.

She stared at the blackness of the windows between the half-drawn curtains. Mahler had taken his long, ivory-inlaid baton case from his coat pocket and was tapping it monotonously into the palm of his hand while shifting from one foot to the other.

The telephone rang, splitting the silence like a saw blade. Kathi looked up enquiringly.

'Let it ring,' said Mahler. 'It'll be Schertel at the Met. If we don't answer, he'll assume we're on our way.'

Schertel was stage manager.

'We're almost done, Frau Alma,' Kathi said consolingly. She stooped her head so that it rested against Alma-Maria's flank like the touch of a lover, and broke the thread with her teeth. She let fall the overskirt into place. 'There,' she said, looking up. 'Nobody will notice anything. And we can mend it properly tomorrow.'

The metallic grinding of the telephone ceased.

A quarter of an hour later, they dismounted from their cab at the stage door. Both Theodore Spierl and Anton Schertel were waiting by the doorkeeper's office. At the angle of the stairs beyond, a couple of musicians in evening dress were on watch.

'My profoundest apologies, gentlemen,' Mahler announced, his voice slightly raised. 'I had difficulty procuring a cab.'

'Even the Grand Tier is beginning to fill up,' Schertel remarked as he led the way up the stairs to the conductor's dressing room.

'They are still taking their places?' asked Mahler. 'That's good. We wouldn't wish to start before the audience is ready.'

He glanced back at Spierl. Alma-Maria noticed that the leader of the orchestra was smiling. Before them, members of the orchestra who had been on watch were scuttling back to the green room. Several Arthurian warriors and sailors appeared in the passage, then vanished rapidly. A brief melody was heard on flute, and a staccato cadenza on an E-flat trumpet.

Mahler entered his brightly lit, comfortably furnished room.

'Good evening, Frank,' he said in English to the servant who was awaiting him.

He turned his back on him to let him remove the coat from his shoulders, taking his baton case from his pocket as he did so. To Schertel, he said,

'Allow me two or three minutes to pay my respects to Madame Fremstad and Monsieur Knote, then we may invite the gentlemen of the orchestra to take their places.'

There was not a trace of nervousness about him now. Even the pallor of his gaunt cheeks had changed to a healthy glow. He was the Court Opera Director once more. She went over to him.

'I think it's time for me to go.' She kissed him on the cheek. 'Good fortune, and God bless you, Gustl,' she whispered.

He took her hand and squeezed it gently. As he left, accompanied by a liveried attendant, he was taking one of his batons from its case.

On the promenade behind the Grand Tier there were still groups of gentlemen in starched, diamond-studded shirt fronts, some with thick cigars stretching their fingers apart, and ladies in glittering tiaras, with fluffy swans-down stoles over their silver-encrusted satin and crêpe de Chine gowns, and clutching sequin and pearl-covered purses. One stately old gentleman whose shirt front curved out over the narrow lapels of his immaculately white waistcoat like the chest of a pouter-pigeon stepped out of one of the boxes to announce loudly to all within earshot,

'Damn' thing ain't started yet!'

Somebody said 'Hush!' Eyes turned to look at Alma-Maria. She wondered whether already she had become known. She kept her eyes in front of her, and tried to smile slightly with closed lips. The attendant opened the door of a box for her. She stepped up inside. There was a maid, a young negress smaller even than she, in white lace apron and streamers and smelling of good quality powder-of-violets who took her fur and folded it carefully. She drew back the curtain which separated the anteroom from the front of the box for Alma-Maria to pass through. Before her was the vast, gilded horseshoe, tier upon tier, enclosing the steeply raked stalls. The stalls was an ocean of heads; the tiers were in a state of traffic, most of the seats unoccupied, with groups visiting groups in boxes not their own, and everybody standing up and filling the whole enormous edifice with their chatter. Andreas Dippel and Heinrich Conried were in the Director's box, in rear seats, and had risen to greet her. She noticed that the black and white of evening dress only accentuated the consumptiveness of Conried's looks. A third gentleman towered over her, a white-haired giant with Bismarckian whiskers, gold-chained cufflinks in his polished cuffs and rubies like droplets of blood in his shirt front.

He took her hand, introducing himself:

'Otto Kahn, Frau Director. I kiss your hand.'

Otto Kahn, first among the group of millionaires on whose great wealth the Metropolitan was founded.

'I'm honoured, Herr Kahn.' She offered him her most brilliant smile, and detected the quiver of his lips in response.

'May I present my wife, Helene?'

There was a very grand, matronly lady sitting at the front of the box wearing a yellow, silk-covered toque on her head, with two red ostrich plumes pinned to it as if it were a turban by an opal the size of a small duck egg.

'Helene, my dear, this is Herr Director Mahler's wife.'

Mrs Kahn offered a mittened hand encrusted with the heaviest rings Alma-Maria had ever seen.

'How-de-do, Frau Mahler. You must be very proud of your husband tonight.'

She spoke very carefully as if she might crumble into powder if she spoke too sharply. It was one of those dreadful moments when Alma-Maria could not say the right thing.

'I hope I shall be, Frau Kahn.'

'I think Mrs Kahn thinks it's your duty to be proud of Herr Mahler,' said Mitzi Uchatius.

She rose from her seat in the front corner of the box. She looked very young indeed, all in white, with her hair up, revealing the smallness of her face and the thinness of her bared shoulders above the deep broderie anglaise flounces of her old-fashioned gown. 'Her First Ball', thought Alma-Maria: Pappi could have portrayed her in a genre painting.

'I'm sure it's a wife's duty to be proud of her husband,' said Mrs Kahn.

Alma-Maria embraced Mitzi. She felt Mitzi's genuine kiss on her cheek. It made her happy.

'You see?' boomed Otto Kahn, who appeared not to have noticed his wife's irritation. 'We have taken good care of your young guest, eh Frau Mahler?'

'Everybody's been very kind to me,' Mitzi confirmed.

Alma-Maria was aware that all round the horseshoes of tiers, opera glasses and lorgnettes were turned on her. She must talk and be natural, and behave as if she were not the cynosure of everybody's gaze.

'I'm so ashamed at keeping everyone waiting,' she said, as Dippel held the back of the chair between Mrs Kahn's and Mitzi's. She turned to Mrs Kahn. In order to win her approval, she admitted with what she hoped was winning honesty, 'I tore my gown when we were about to leave the hotel. It was so clumsy of me. And my husband was determined not to start without me. Fortunately my maid is a very good seamstress.'

'It is a very beautiful gown, Frau Mahler,' said Mrs Kahn. 'It suits you very well. From Vienna?'

'A very dear friend in Vienna designed it for me.'

'I think the whole audience is admiring it,' whispered Mitzi. 'Everybody is looking at you.'

Alma-Maria was about to say that perhaps it was she they were looking at, when Conried leaned forward, cleared his throat and said,

'I'm sure the young woman whom everybody called the loveliest girl in Vienna is used to being looked at.'

Otto Kahn also leaned forward to pass a programme to her.

'Well, Frau Mahler, what do you think of our little opera house, eh?'

'It is very grand, Herr Kahn. Very impressive.'

'Public subscription built it and sustains it,' Kahn went on. 'None of your kings, kaisers, or tsars. A people's opera house, eh?'

The orchestra was in place, and was tuning up. Spierl had taken his seat at the leader's desk amid a sparse applause from the stalls and gallery. The people to whom Kahn had referred were still engaged in shuttling from box to box, chattering, clattering and flashing jewellery like stars in a restless firmament.

As the lights began to dim, Alma-Maria glanced down into the orchestra pit. The podium was quite unlike that at Vienna or Munich or St Petersburg, or anywhere else she had seen Mahler conduct. It was raised like a round church pulpit with a short flight of iron stairs leading up to it, as if the conductor was to be regarded as being as much a performer as any of the singers. Mahler was entering between the desks of the first violins. The string players fluttered their bows on their instruments *con arco* to greet him. As he mounted the short, narrow stairs, a more robust applause spread through the house. Alma-Maria felt rather than saw Mitzi's smiling at her, and knew the girl was proud to be there, sitting beside her.

The lights were down, but the conversations along the Grand Tier, the rustling of silks and the muffled scraping of chairs continued. There was a crystalline burst of female laughter from three or four boxes round the sweeping curve of the horseshoe. Mahler laid his stick down on his desk. He appeared to be examining the score in front of him. The orchestra sat motionless, the violins and violas with their instruments resting on their knees.

'I'm afraid your husband doesn't appreciate that this isn't Vienna,' whispered Mrs Kahn.

Alma-Maria dared not add to the disturbance by replying that it had been Mahler who had taught the Vienna audience to be silent as soon as the leader of the orchestra took his place. He was about to attempt the same lesson with the Met, not taking into account, perhaps, that the noise-makers, not an Imperial Chamberlain, were his paymasters.

He picked up his stick. She saw it like a thread in the glow from the desk lamp. He drew himself erect. She heard above the restless noise around her the martinet click-click of the stick tapping the edge of the music stand. The violins and violas put their instruments under their chins. There was no lessening in the chatter from the tiers.

'Doesn't he realize they won't settle down until he begins?'

Conried was speaking to Andreas Dippel.

'Schertel warned him,' Dippel replied.

There was more laughter and louder chatter from the boxes nearby. She strained forward, her breasts pressed against the velvet ledge of the parapet. She felt panic, but also an involuntary swell of pride. She wanted to join her will to his, to strengthen him, to unite with him whether he needed her strength or not. He had lowered his stick once more. He was standing in a familiar stance, one elbow resting in the palm of his hand, and his chin cupped in his other hand. The mass of hair behind his great forehead was standing up in silhouette against the lights on the curtains like an angry coxcomb. There was no lessening in the noise being made by the lessees of the $60,000 *loges*.

After what seemed like minutes, but which was probably no more than thirty seconds, he turned to face the audience. Please God he wouldn't try to lecture them, she prayed. He gripped the brass rail with one hand, the stick dangling between the fingers of the other. He looked up and surveyed the Grand Tier from one end to the other. From behind the partition separating the Director's box from its neighbour, a man's voice said loudly.

'Good Lord! The fella's got the cheek of Old Nick!'

Mitzi whispered a translation into Alma-Maria's ear. Their fingers tightened round one another's.

Mahler released his grip on the brass rail. For a moment, he held his stick horizontally between the fingers of both hands. Quite deliberately and theatrically, he struck the rail with it three times. He waited, still staring up at the tiers. The Grand Tier whispered into silence. Alma-Maria heard the gentlemen behind her sigh in unison. Mahler turned to the orchestra once more. He raised his baton. The silence over the huge auditorium was palpable as if contemplating, but only contemplating, rebellion. Out of the silence, drawn and woven of its elements, came the

344

first, still notes of the *Vorspiel*, the three-times repeated love-spell. The music soared from the stillness; the silence of the auditorium remained unbroken. Nobody dared break the spell now it was uttered.

The *Vorspiel* died into the stillness from which it had been drawn. Now it was the sea, and the sailor's homesick cry. The scenery was tired, the staging old-fashioned compared to Mahler's collaborative productions with Alfred Roller at the Court Opera, but the audience remained spellbound. Beside Alma-Maria, Mitzi was motionless, eyes round and gleaming in the reflected light from the stage, her hand in Alma-Maria's. And Alma-Maria herself knew that musically, there had never been such a *Tristan*, had never been music so magically erotic. There was the astonishing purity of Fremstad's voice, but that alone did not explain the attentiveness of the fat, boiled shirt fronts with the bejewelled and powder-dusted women. Mahler was excelling himself, with the orchestra playing as if it were an extension of his will. At the same time, he was not only performing the music, but interpreting it, advocating it, revealing its treasures as if they had previously been hidden. She had heard *Tristan* more times than she could remember, had played it over on the piano alone and with him, but never before had she listened to detail of harmony and instrumentation as she heard it tonight.

When music and voices soared in the nocturnal garden scene, she glanced again at Mitzi and saw in the shimmer of the light that she was weeping – because it brought back some memory of adolescent love? wondered Alma-Maria, or because it revealed to her for the first time, the power and ecstasy of carnal passion?

Mitzi did not take her hand from hers until the curtain fell for the first intermission, and then it was to applaud, hands held level with the face. She stopped and wiped her eyes with the little lace handkerchief she had taken from the puff of her short sleeves. In fact, the applause was not wildly enthusiastic. Otto Kahn leaned forward between them.

'Your husband, my dear Frau Mahler, has convinced us all that we're in church.'

She would have to remember that; it would please Gustav no end.

Mrs Kahn said to her,

'Wonderful, my dear Frau Mahler! I've never heard such a performance . . . Not even at the Berlin Opera. Your husband is a magician!'

Only one or two people dared to rise from their places before Fremstad took her final bow. Most remained sitting even after the heavy, tasselled curtain had finally fallen into place. Alma-Maria heard Mitzi's sudden intake of breath.

'Did you enjoy it?' she asked unnecessarily.

Mitzi smiled apologetically and lowered her eyes,.

'I don't know what to say. I can't find words,' she whispered.

Conried moved in his chair.

345

'I think we can say New York has not heard Wagner performed like that. Not even under Seidl, or Mottl.'

He was pleased with himself for having acquired Mahler. Self-satisfaction started him coughing into his handkerchief. He looked into it as he removed it from his lips. Alma-Maria caught Otto Kahn's eye for a split second. Kahn had hoped she hadn't noticed Conried's behaviour. Why she did not know, but it made her uneasy.

'Should we go down and pay our respects to the *maestro*, would you say, Frau Director?' he asked. The audience along the tiers was beginning to move, to talk once again. Voices carried notes of wonderment. 'Shall you be going to the green room?' he asked.

'Not during the intermission, Herr Kahn. I know my husband prefers not to be disturbed until a work is over.'

'It's a trip to the powder room for me,' Mrs Kahn announced.

Alma-Maria looked to Mitzi, who nodded.

'We will keep you company, Frau Kahn,' she said.

'And you gentlemen,' said Mrs Kahn, rising, 'may take your cigars in the foyer. Follow me, ladies!'

Everybody on the concourse knew Mrs Kahn and acknowledged her as she swept by. Everybody eyed Alma-Maria, sweeping glances up and down her gown, and murmuring to one another when she had passed by. Mitzi said, clinging to her arm,

'I feel I'm going to be terribly famous just being with you.'

'I don't know why anyone should take notice of me,' Alma-Maria replied.

She didn't know why she said it. She had never been given to arch demonstrations of diffidence back in Vienna. Mrs Kahn turned round.

'It could be, my dear, that you have been seen sitting in Mr Conried's box, so that people realize that you are Herr Mahler's wife. Or it might be that your photograph was in the *Globe* the other day.'

'My photograph?'

She had a clear idea that Mrs Kahn had taken a dislike to her.

'You haven't seen it?'

Evidently Mrs Kahn didn't really believe her.

'It's one of the series,' said Mitzi. 'The Most Beautiful Women of the Twentieth Century', they call it. You were number seven of the series.

'Nobody asked if they could use my photograph!' Alma-Maria exclaimed.

'Nobody asked?' Mrs Kahn laughed at her. 'Oh my dear, you've a lot to learn about our New York press!'

'Aren't you pleased, Frau Alma?' Mitzi asked. 'I'd be terribly flattered. At least I think I would.'

They entered the powder room. It was like a wide, tented pavilion: the ceiling was of yellowing satin draped in wide flounces from the centre to the circumference. The walls were of red flock between the heavy gilt

346

of the mirrors. Young negro maids ran errands, dodging through the dense throng of ornately dressed women, or knelt or crouched adjusting gowns on their wearers. Voices were raised in accents far more strident and sharp-edged than they would have been at the Court Opera. Although Alma-Maria couldn't understand what was being said, she heard names being bandied – Fremstad, Sembrich, Mildenburg, Lehmann – and places – Dresden, Covent Garden, Buenos Aires, Vienna – and knew that those around her were playing the game played by fashionable opera-goers everywhere, that of comparing singers and houses in order to demonstrate how widely they had travelled.

As on the concourse outside, heads were turned to inspect her as she passed. Mrs Kahn was gone, sucked into a vortex of familiars. Mitzi led her towards the closet cubicles curtained off at the far end. Before they reached them, they were greeted by an enormously fat negress with a chatelaine containing pins and small change at her waist. Alma-Maria opened her purse to tip her, but had no idea how much she should give. Mitzi noted her hesitation. She took two small coins from her own purse and handed them to the woman.

'Mrs Baumfeld never gives more than a couple of nickels,' she said. 'She says its vulgar to give more.'

She gave Alma-Maria's arm a squeeze; she was happy to have been of service.

'Frau Mahler!'

More heads turned. Despite the extraordinary Turkish costume – fringed turban, high-buttoned brocaded coat, and sheer silk bloomers through which her legs were visible like shadows – Mrs Charles Dana Gibson's girlish prettiness, her small retroussé nose, her cupid-bow lips, were instantly recognizable. She had come from one of the closets.

'Darling Frau Mahler! Honestly! we mustn't keep meeting in ladies' rest rooms, must we? Something will have to be arranged.' She grabbed Alma-Maria's hands. 'I must tell you, darling. Your husband! He is – wonderful! There's no other word. Everybody is saying what a genius he is. I know I'm going to weep all through the *Liebestod*! And so will everybody else: poor Fremstad won't be heard for all the sniffles round the Diamond Horseshoe – and she is in such marvellous voice, isn't she? I expect that's your husband's work. They say he is *so* patient with singers – not at all what people expected . . .'

She broke off, noticing that Alma-Maria was looking at her costume. She giggled.

'It's all Charles Dana's fault. He absolutely insists on my dressing up as a heroine from an opera whenever we come to the Met. And tonight, because it *is* so very special, we decided I should dress as the only heroine in opera with my name – Elvira. And I'm not Donna Elvira from *Don Giovanni*, because she's not really the heroine. So I bet you'll never guess which opera I'm from!'

'Rossini,' said Alma-Maria straightaway. '*L'Italiana in Algeri?*'
Elvira Gibson pouted.

'Of course you'd know, wouldn't you, darling? I bet your husband's been conducting it all his life! But nobody else could guess.'

'May I introduce a young friend of mine, Mrs Gibson,' Alma-Maria said, 'who is studying painting here in New York: Miss Marie Uchatius . . . Mitzi, this is Mrs Charles Dana Gibson.'

Mitzi gazed wide-eyed at Elvira Gibson.

'*The* Charles Dana Gibson?' she asked. Elvira Gibson laughed delightedly. She clapped her hands.

'Adorable! Quite adorable! . . . You know, you really mustn't let Miss . . .?'

'Uchatius,' said Mitzi.

'My darling! I'm so sorry! Of course!' Elvira Gibson turned to Alma-Maria again: 'You mustn't let her near Charles Dana. He'll want to sketch her the moment he sets eyes on her' – she glanced at Mitzi – 'in bathing drawers, I shouldn't wonder. Or in knickers and holding a tennis racquet. Something *louche!*' She looked over Alma-Maria's shoulder. 'Mrs Kahn! Hi! . . . I was just telling Frau Mahler what a wonderful conductor her husband is. Charles Dana says he has simply got to be the next Director of the Met . . .'

Mrs Kahn interrupted her without the least pretence of good manners.

'I'm sure Frau Mahler has a very clear notion of how good a conductor her husband is.'

Alma-Maria excused herself and Mitzi.

'We must go through before it's time to take our seats.'

'Darling! I'm holding you up, aren't I? But we *must* get together – with or without our husbands – mustn't we?'

'I would like that,' Alma-Maria replied truthfully enough.

Elvira's chatter was infinitely preferable to the silence of an empty hotel suite.

Silence fell over the darkened auditorium the moment Mahler resumed his place on the podium. Nor was it the obedient hush he had imposed on the audience of the Vienna Opera; far more it was expectation, appetite for what was to come. Alma-Maria watched and waited. Certainly, no one was disposed to fidget, let alone move from their seats, as Fremstad's Isolde, kneeling beside Tristan's body, began in a voice of innocent purity, her final aria. Her voice and the expectation of the audience seemed to become one as the piece flowed on to its climax of reconciliation where passion is satiated, fulfilled, and love and death become one and the same. For the very first time, Alma-Maria felt that she understood the music. It caused her to wonder how Mahler, so puritanical, so inhibited in many ways, could command orchestra and singer in so public and powerful a demonstration of erotic charge and release. She wondered how many of the starched and jewelled audience around her understood the meaning of what they heard – how many of the plump, silken, powdered dowagers had experienced what Fremstad's Isolde was representing there in front of them:

> In the billowing sea,
> in the ocean of sound,
> in the world-soul's
> depths profound –
> to drown now,
> to go down now –
> swoon in night –
> ultimate delight!

What, for that matter, did Mahler himself know of it?

And yet, he did understand. He had once told her about the Oriental belief – she couldn't remember now whether it was Indian or Chinese – that the person who dies in the rapture of love is not destroyed but is one with nature and is subsumed into Eternity.

Fremstad's last note, and the sound of the orchestra, faded into the stillness in which they had found their origin. And in that stillness, Alma-Maria ached with love and longing and pride for her Gustl. It held for a long, long moment. Then there was an explosion of applause. The singers came from between the curtains. Footmen brought on the bouquets. The audience called for Fremstad again and again. Finally, she led on Mahler. As he bowed jerkily, like a marionette, the audience roared and rose to its feet. The roaring and shouting of 'Bravo!' went on and on. Mahler raised his head and looked along the Grand Tier until he reached her. She saw his thin lips stretch in a smile. She smiled back. In the midst of the tumult, she wanted nothing more than to belong to him.

Otto Kahn had arranged the traditional party at Sherry's to await the arrival of the first editions of the morning papers. For Mahler, such overnight functions after the fall of the curtain had always been a wearisome duty except when he was in the company of very dear friends. Mr Baumfeld came to the box to collect Mitzi and take her home.

The auditorium was almost empty when Mahler and Spierl came up to the box. Alma-Maria could see that Mahler was weary. It worried her. On the other hand, she could also sense that behind his restrained, tight-lipped manner, there was an excitement, a boyish pleasure in his success building up. Anxious for his health she might be, but she hadn't the heart or inclination on her own behalf to suggest they return to the Majestic. As they followed Kahn and Conried down the staircase to the main foyer, she put her arm into his, reaching for his hand. Others had been profuse in their congratulations. Now, she said in his ear.

'Darling Gustl! You were right: there will never be a *Tristan* to match this unless you direct it, my darling.'

His face turned to hers, smiling with a sort of wonderment, as if he had never realized how much she loved him.

Fremstad, huddled in a prima donna's Russian furs to outshine even Alma-Maria's expensive sealskin, was waiting with her Tristan, Knote, in her hired limousine parked on West and 44th Street, some thirty or forty paces from the entrance to Sherry's: just sufficient distance to allow her to make a progress up the pavement under the eyes of late-night revellers. Kahn had his chauffeur draw up immediately behind. He arranged that Fremstad should make her entrance on Mahler's arm, and that Knote should escort in Alma-Maria. Mahler gave Alma-Maria a quick glance of rueful amusement, as if to say that the theatricals were still not at an end. Knote was too raw-boned, sturdy, and broad for a nineteenth-century notion of an Arthurian knight, but he was good-looking as well as strong, and he smiled appreciatively, exuding success, as he offered her his arm.

As they entered the dining room – so much more like that of the Prussian junker's country-house banqueting chamber than the Viennese idea of a restaurant – every other guest rose and applauded. They remained standing and continued to applaud as the group passed through to the table prepared for them. Fremstad projected the sweetest air of astonishment and emotion. Knote smiled and waved as if he were simply a popular undergraduate among his college friends. Mahler, as he heard his name called out again and again, looked stunned with amazement. As they reached the table, he said to Conried,

'Does this always happen?'

'Only after a success, Herr Director.'

'Have they all been at the Met?'

Kahn laughed.

'No, sir. One or two perhaps. Most here are stage people; they've been working.'

'Then how do they know it is a success?' Mahler asked,

'It's in the air, Herr Director. Call it instinct if you like.'

In Vienna, in such a place, a considerable number of the clientele would have been dreaming up cutting phrases with which to belittle his achievement.

'You Americans are such a generous people,' he said.

Alma-Maria saw that he was on the verge of tears.

Some tables had already received their newspapers when the bellhop arrived stooping under the weight of newsprint he was carrying to Mr Kahn's party. There had been reassuring smiles, and even scattered hand-clapping like a flurry of snowflakes, as other groups read the music columns. The table was littered with a debris of coffee cups and smoked cigar stubs. Kahn and Conried swept the litter aside without bothering to summon a waiter. Beside her, Knote translated into German:

The *World* – This was the debut of Fremstad as Isolde, and the first appearance before an American audience anywhere of the celebrated Viennese conductor, Gustav Mahler. Both have achieved the most eminent of successes. Mahler captured and held prisoner his audience from the moment he raised his baton. From the first notes onwards there was no doubting his supreme authority as an interpreter of the music of Wagner. I predict for him the greatest popularity and influence with the American musical public. Here is a supreme talent . . .

The *Sun* – The audience could not have been larger, more wrapt in its attention, more enthusiastic in its applause had it been a Caruso benefit night. When Madame Fremstad brought Mr Mahler forward, everybody rose to his feet and cheered as if he were not to be allowed to leave. Nor was this enthusiasm undeserved . . .

New York Daily Tribune – Mr Mahler did the greatest honour to himself, to Wagner's music, to the New York public. Wagner's score is familiar – perhaps a little too familiar to opera-goers – but Mr Mahler gave it a strikingly vital reading so that one wondered if, despite its familiarity, one had truly heard the music before . . .

New York Times – Mr Mahler's conducting resulted in a reading of the score far excelling anything New York has hitherto known, and I include the readings of Anton Seidl and Felix Mottl. He is a conductor of commanding authority and profound insight. It is doubtful whether the audience at the Metropolitan Opera has ever heard music conducted with such finesse, subtlety, and with such poetic understanding combined with dramatic power . . .

Olive Fremstad was sitting half facing Alma-Maria round the corner of the table.

'Do you know what Dr Mottl said to me just before he left for Europe, Frau Alma? He asked me to go with him to the Karlsruhe Opera. When I told him I'd prefer to remain here, he said, "You're not going to make any headway in your career by staying her, in the States – and certainly not by singing under the Jew Mahler."'

Alma-Maria glanced quickly across the table to make sure Mahler had not heard.

'Not here, surely?' she said. 'Everybody I meet – of importance, I mean – is Jewish.'

Fremstad shook her head.

'There's no escape, you know,' she said.

'Mottl was Gustav's rival for the Directorship of the Vienna Court Opera,' Alma-Maria told her.

Ten long years ago, that had been. Was professional envy a substance which never dissolved, never decayed with time? And why had Fremstad said it? Was it because Mahler's name had been mentioned in the notices more frequently than her own?

But Fremdstad was smiling.

'Now if it were Herr Gustav who wanted me to sing for him over in Europe – that would be altogether different!'

The longer the night had worn on, the less inclined they were towards bed. The second dawn of the New Year was turning the city lights pallid, and she and Mahler were walking in Central Park, the occasional drifting snowflake touching their cheeks.

'You've never been greeted with such complete approval, have you, Gustl?' she said.

'They are a very generous people,' Mahler repeated.

'Would you consider accepting the Directorship of the Metropolitan Opera, if it were offered you?'

Her eyes were burning were fatigue, but she was afraid of letting the time go.

'I need to promote my own work,' he replied. 'As well as the time to compose.'

She clung close to him.

'They love you, Gustl. You could make them do anything you wish.'

'Do you love me, Almschi?'

He sounded as if he were not at all certain.

'Oh yes, Gustl! Of course I do!'

And that cold, pale morning, walking on the impacted city snow, she meant it wholeheartedly.

In their suite, they gave instructions to Anton and Kathi that they were not to be disturbed. As Mahler was undressing hanging up his tails for himself – his 'working-clothes' – Alma-Maria emerged naked from her closet; naked except for the stockings, the absurdly expensive gossamer silk stockings he had bought her a day or two after their arrival in New York. He saw her in the pier glass in his own closet.

She pulled the pins from her hair, letting the tresses tumble haphazard about her; so had she seduced him in their early days. For a brief moment, she was fearful lest he spurn her. He sat down on the bed. He was less than half dressed. He smiled stupidly, too tired to know whether he should keep on his spectacles to admire her, or take them off to love her.

She knelt on the floor at his knees. He plunged his fingers into her hair, letting it pour around them.

'Gustl! I was so proud of you, last night. So proud! I want to show you how proud I was!'

She parted his knees, prising them open gently, and stooped her head

352

into his lap. She quivered her lips, the tip of her tongue like a mouse nibbling, then, as he hardened, took him into her mouth. She heard him catch his breath then gasp. He was stooped over her, running his hands through the hair flowing down her back, and reaching for her flanks. She drew back from him to gulp for breath, holding him with both hands, caressing him with the tips of her fingers. As she was bending forward again, he said,

'O she sucks forth my soul!'

She looked up at him through a veil of her own hair.

'What's that, Gustl?'

'Helen of Troy. Another Helen – not Goethe's.'

She took him into her mouth again, lapping him with her tongue as she did so. His hands cupped her breasts; his fingers drew at her nipples. She thought, Please God, keep him excited, Oh please, please God! through her own mounting excitement.

The moment arrived. She released him, and scrambled onto the bed beside him, careless of everything except her crying need for him to couple with her.

'Take me, Gustl! Take me! Take me! Take me!'

She drew up her knees, her closed eyelids stinging with fatigue. She felt his still strong, athlete's torso pressing between her thighs. He was hard, he had stayed hard, thank God, as with one hand she teased him into her.

Take me! Drive into me, Gustl (and Alex, and Hansl, and Faust, and Egmont, and Tristan, and Siegfried, and Crown Prince Rudolf, and all the heroes of the world),

> to drown now,
> to go down now –
> swoon in night –
> ultimate delight ...

to be annihilated into a star-filled universe!

But that was too much to hope for. He reached climax, subsided, and fell back beside her, leaving her washed up on a bleach-dry shingle of nauseous dissatisfaction.

The cold draught about her nakedness forced her into bed.

All the same – it *was* a brief spell of happiness such as she would not have expected when they had first arrived in New York. In fact, she saw no more of Mahler than she had ever done. His schedule was a heavy one. As well as conducting *Tristan* twice a week, he was preparing *Don Giovanni*, the *Ring* cycle, and *Fidelio* for later in what was, by Viennese standards, a long season. In the mornings he worked for as long as he could on the new song-cycle or on the sketches for his projected Ninth Symphony. But she felt his presence closer than she had done since their first days together and, even in comparison with those, his attentiveness to her looks and appearance, his demonstrations of affection, revealed how much less fearful he was of letting his feelings betray him. He went on shopping expeditions with her down Fifth Avenue – something he could never have brought himself to do in Vienna – and he enjoyed, even revelled in, the hectic bustle of the pavements and in the conspicuous display of affluence around him. To her astonishment, he even encouraged her to buy frilly blouses and jabots and silken underwear, as if he had begun for the first time to celebrate her femininity. Occasionally he would bring himself to ask her if she would attend a rehearsal so that they might discuss it in detail afterwards.

She felt valued by him as she had never done before.

They were both surprised by the response to his appearances on the podium at the Met. That, too, was quite unlike Vienna. Flowers were sent, great baskets full, and bouquets which filled the drawing room, and cards and letters. This provided Alma-Maria with an excuse to telephone Mrs Baumfeld to ask if Mitzi Uchatius might come to the hotel to help her reply to the messages of appreciation and congratulation – to act as her English-speaking secretary. Mahler's success appeared to have quite wiped away all memory of his truculent behaviour as well as her own outburst. Mrs Baumfeld was delighted Alma-Maria should feel Mitzi could be of service to her.

'Mind you, should you find she doesn't match up to what you require, please don't hesitate to say so. I don't think the dear child has ever acted as a lady's secretary before – except for me in an informal capacity – but it'll be good experience for her, I'm sure.'

So Mitzi became her regular companion, not only in writing letters in English for her, but in acting as her guide on visits to places of interest, notably to the Metropolitan Museum of Art – which included a charming, leisurely stroll across Central Park – and to the galleries and studios of the Association for Decorative Arts. The work on display at the latter she found old-fashioned, even dowdy, compared to that being produced by friends such as Josef Hoffmann, Kolo Moser, and Carl Otto Czeschka in the Wiener Werkstätte.

In an empty classroom-studio, Mitzi took her own work down from a cupboard to show her. There were protraits, four of them: capable, conventional pencil studies which were then painted in watercolour. They were pleasing but typical examples of a drawing room hobby, a well-educated young lady's 'accomplishment'.

Mitzi looked anxiously at her.

'You are quite talented,' Alma-Maria told her. 'What do your teachers say about you?'

'They're pleased with me, I think.'

She was still watching Alma-Maria's face.

'So they should be. There's character there. You do say something about the person instead of just creating a likeness.'

'Do you really think so, Frau Alma?'

'Naturally, *liebchen*, or I wouldn't say it.'

She turned the broad sheets of cartridge paper over again: mother, father, elder sister – and the Baumfeld's son, the boy she had seen by the elevator gate on the landing that night before Christmas Eve. She held it up.

'I only did it to please Mrs Baumfeld,' Mitzi explained.

'Don't you like him? He's a good-looking young man.'

'I think he likes me more than I like him. It's not that I don't like him – not at all. It's just that I don't like him in quite the same way as he seems to like me. Do you know what I mean?'

Alma-Maria smiled.

'I know exactly what you mean.'

'I expect you do. It must happen *so* often to somebody as beautiful as you.'

'Quite often,' Alma-Maria replied. 'But don't you worry, *liebchen*. It'll happen often enough to you as well – with your looks.'

With her gloved hand, she caressed Mitzi's cheek where it was peach-bloomed from the warmth of the room after the snow outside. For a moment – two or three seconds, no more – Mitzi lifted her hand to hold Alma-Maria's fingers pressed against the softness at the corner of her lips.

'I don't want it to happen,' she said wistfully.

'Don't you like being pretty?' asked Alma-Maria.

'I suppose I would hate not to be pretty. But that isn't quite the same, is it?'

They were walking back across the park when Mitzi, who had been very quiet for ten minutes, said,

'Frau Alma?'

'What is it, *liebchen*?'

'Would you let me try to paint you?'

'You mean, I should sit for you?'

'I wouldn't take up too much of your time. At least, I'd try not to.'

'Of course I will. But why do you want to paint me?'

Shamelessly, Alma-Maria expected the girl to tell her that it was because she was one of the 'Most Beautiful Women of the Twentieth Century'. Instead, Mitzi blurted out,

'Because I think you're one of the most interesting people I've ever met!'

'Because my husband is who he is?' Alma-Maria asked gently.

'Oh no! Not at all!' Mitzi sounded quite shocked. 'It's because you're quite different from that. All the women I meet talk about nothing except what their husbands do – or what their husbands like them to do. Or what they're going to wear for this or that, and what their husbands have bought them to wear.'

'My husband bought me this,' Alma-Maria told her.

She stroked her fur coat.

'Oh dear!' Mitzi exclaimed. 'I suppose I shouldn't say what I was going to say.'

'What were you going to say?'

'I was going to say you weren't at all like that.'

'What am I like, then?'

'I'm afraid of being rude, Frau Alma.'

'Don't be afraid.'

She put her arm round Mitzi's waist and gave her a hug.

'It's as if you lived your life for yourself alone,' Mitzi told her. 'I don't mean that you're selfish or anything like that. I mean that you have your own way of looking at things; that you think your own thoughts, not somebody else's.'

'Do you think I dress for myself?'

'I don't know that ... Oh dear! ...'

'That was unfair,' Alma-Maria said hastily. 'I imagine most of us dress to be admired, don't we? But I do wear what I choose to wear.'

'I'd like to paint you sitting at a window,' said Mitzi. 'You'd be looking out. The light would be on your face. But we wouldn't see what it was you were looking at; it would be your dreams, your visions outside ... Really what I mean is that I think that you're not like all those other women – you don't live through other people, you inspire them ...' She hesitated only for a moment ... 'the same way you inspire me,' she finished.

'Mitzi! That is a lovely thing to say, do you know that?'

'I honestly think you are the most wonderful person I've ever met!'

Alma-Maria threw her arms around her, burying her face in the pile of her coat.

'After my appearance on the landing that night?' she laughed. 'And my behaviour at the Baumfelds' It's you who's wonderful, *liebchen*, believe me! And I can't wait to sit for you!'

It was in the morning, when she took the breakfast coffee and brioches from Anton and carried them in to where he was still in bed, that she told Mahler of Mitzi's request. She did not describe the conversation surrounding it in any way, but he looked up from the papers he was holding, adjusted his spectacles on the bony hook of his nose, and said in a dry voice,

'You should be careful, Almschili. The girl is in love with you.'

'Gustl! Don't be silly!'

She was sure that women couldn't fall in love with women – unless, that is, they were wretched schoolgirls mewed up somewhere like the Maria Theresia Institute where they never saw a man month in, month out, or were prostitutes with so low an opinion of men that they had to look for love elsewhere.

'You only have to see the way she looks at you,' Mahler told her, returning his attention to the manuscript in front of him.

It was, she decided, a touch of the old Mahler, the Mahler who could blight something beautiful through sheer thoughtless self-absorption.

Her resentment did not last long. That evening, he was at home. They went out to dinner together, by themselves, at an Austrian-Jewish restaurant on Amsterdam Avenue and West 125th Street. Afterwards, they drove back round Central Park in an open horse-drawn cab, huddled in travelling rugs. The lamplight glistened on the snow-covered branches like candlelight on the sugar-icing of a birthday cake, while the lights from the skyscrapers hung like regimented constellations in the glowing black of the sky. When they got in, she went to her closet and drank two glasses of Benedictine to drive out the night chill – Mahler did not approve of their drinking more than two glasses of wine over dinner – then they sat down, each at their own piano. He had arranged two of the completed pieces from the song-cycle for four hands. Neither piece, she found, had the sadness, the regret, of other sections of the work she had heard. On the contrary, they seemed to reflect Mahler's new-found gaiety and optimism. They sang together – Mahler in his deep growl of a bass, she in her husky mezzo, the relic of the voice she had ruined by chanting out Wagnerian roles long ago, in the days when she had been studying with dear old Dr Labor.

She sat at the drawing room window, the winter sunlight glowing through the glass onto her cheek and through her loosely stacked hair. She had asked Mitzi whether she should sit with her hair up or down. Mitzi had not hesitated:

'Up. Because that's how I always see you.'

Alma-Maria had compromised, arranging it as if she had been caught with it down and had had to arrange it in haste. Not that there had been any haste about it; she had taken as much care over it as if she had been about to sit for Roller or Moser or any other real artist.

Mitzi had brought her easel and stool, those which she would have used for sketching outdoors. She had buttoned on a paint-stained blue pinafore smock over her sailor top and dark blue promenade skirt. She had tied her own hair back in a thick plait like a horse's tail. She presented a very businesslike appearance. Alma-Maria watched her from the corners of her eyes. The sweet oval face and pursed little mouth showed the same seriousness as Mitzi moved her pencil about the stretched cartridge paper, preparing the preliminary outline. She was being an artist more intensely than any artist ever was, certainly not Klimt, not even Mahler – and was, therefore, adorably vulnerable and very innocent.

'Why are you smiling?' Mitzi asked.

'I'm sorry. I didn't know I was. It was just something passing through my mind. It was a song Gustav and I were playing over together last night.'

'One of your songs?' asked Mitzi.

For one perilous moment, Alma-Maria was tempted to answer, yes.

'No. It's part of something Gustav is working on at the moment.'

'Oh.' Mitzi sounded disappointed.

She busied herself with her pencil, her head stooped forward, concealed behind the easel.

For exercise, to ease the cramp of sitting for so long, they went out that afternoon into the park to skate on the lake which was overlooked, over the trees and snow-covered mounds, by the hotel. They made good partners, circling about the ice, linked hand in hand, avoiding the admiring glances from members of the opposite sex as they passed them, and enjoyably using the skill they discovered in one another to dodge the would-be Lotharios who sought to come abreast of them. They clung to each other a hair's breadth from a kiss, as they glided back to the ladies' enclosure, pleasantly exhausted, to remove their skates.

Mitzi's eyes glistened. Their breath clouded the air as they bent forward to unclamp their skates from their boots.

'I enjoy it so much, being with you, Frau Alma,' Mitzi said, her head still down. 'I've been thinking about it a lot. Part of it is because you're not always looking to find fault with things – and people. You're not always talking about what somebody is doing wrong, or what wrong clothes they wear, or how awful servants are these days. All the women I know carry on like that, except you. God! I hope I'm like you when I'm your age!'

She sat up.

'I hope you are like you are now, when you're my age,' Alma-Maria told her.

There couldn't be more than ten years between them, she thought.

'You do like me, don't you?' asked Mitzi.

'Of course I do.'

'I mean, you're not just being patient with me or anything?'

'*Liebchen*, don't be silly . . .!'

She reached round Mitzi's shoulder. As Mitzi turned her face to her, she kissed her lightly on the lips – just the sort of thing Gustav had been warning her against, she thought with amusement. 'And Mitzi, *leibling*, stop calling me *Frau* Alma.'

'What should I call you?' Mitzi asked.

She was clearly moved.

'Call me Alma – or Almschi – like a darling friend ought.'

'May I really?'

Mitzi looked like someone who had been offered the most wonderful gift. Alma-Maria was tempted to embrace her and kiss her again. But she thought the better of it. Instead, she took her hand.

'Come on. I must go back to the hotel.'

As they walked the short distance to the gate opposite the hotel, Mitzi asked,

'Alma?'

'Yes?' Then Alma-Maria laughed. 'You see? It's not so difficult, is it?'

'May I come again? I mean, to do your portrait.'

'Of course you may, *liebchen*. I shall look forward to it.'

She found Mahler dressing in his 'working clothes' when she returned to the suite. She told Anton to leave them, and helped him herself with his studs, collar, and white tie. The cold air had refreshed her. When he was standing in front of the full-length mirror, checking his appearance, she noticed his glance had turned from examining his shirt front, his tie, the state of his hair (an unnecessary precaution, since, in an unconscious gesture, he always put his hand up and mussed it the moment he mounted the podium), to gazing at her reflection. She smiled into the glass:

'What is it, Gustl?'

'If I were to be offered the musical directorship of the New York Philharmonic Symphony,' he said hesitantly. 'What would your advice to me be?'

'Gustl!'

It was not the sort of thing on which he usually sought her counsel.

'Tell me.'

'I think, all things considered,' she answered, 'that we would have to ask Mutti and Gucki to join us here for the season. Perhaps even Miss Turner. Just to make sure, dearest Gustl, you behave yourself with all those dreadful old pearl-dripping matrons!'

He caught the note of tenderness in her voice.

'You do love me, don't you, Almschili.'

'Yes Gustl. I love you. I'm glad to be married to you.' She put her arms round his neck. 'Go, darling Gustl,' she whispered and then kissed him

He held her quite passionately.

'And come back to me quickly!' she told him.

She went down to the lobby with him, to see him to his waiting motor. It was while they were descending in the elevator that he said seriously,

'My decision would depend very much on the pension rights, and how far they would extend to you. One has to think of these things.'

The next evening, Mahler returned from rehearsing at the Met looking as happy as he had ever done since their arrival in New York. He had persuaded Conried and Schertel to acquire the Alfred Roller designs from Vienna for the new *Ring* cycle. Even better, they had decided to leave the entire production of *Fidelio* – the final opera of the season – to him alone. It was, moreover, to have Sembrich, one of his favourite singers, in the lead. There could be no doubt that it was a move toward creating him supreme tyrant over the Metropolitan Opera as he had been over the Vienna Court Opera.

They both felt so triumphant at his news that, after they had come up from dinner, they sat down and played and chanted their way through the ecstatic, triumphant love duet from the first act of *Die Walküre*. The thought crossed her mind that Siegmund and Sieglinde's coupling in that opera was peculiarly ill-fated; it amused her for the moment.

His mood of elation continued. Though he rarely drank himself, he did not object to her taking the tray with the Benedictine bottle and a small glass to her piano. He even smoked his evening cigar sitting at the keyboard – something which normally was unthinkable. He played over a phrase from the final act of *Don Giovanni*, which he had been rehearsing that afternoon:

'"*L'ultima prova dell' amor mio* . . . Let me give you one last proof of my love." I suggested to Gadski that when the Statue takes the Don's hand to draw him down to hell, she should rush forward to the edge of the pit to try to pull him back. I suggested that all three women are secretly sorry to see the Don go . . . that he's given them a glimpse of something they weren't supposed to know about – something immensely exciting, bewildering. And now, without him to chase after, all that's left is dull and empty. I suggested they should sing the final sextet with the three men looking smug, as always, but with the women trying to conceal their misery under a pretence of rejoicing.'

'What did they say to your suggestion?' asked Alma-Maria.

'Gadski and Scotti were scandalized, I think. Sembrich thought I was joking, and was kind enough to laugh.'

'You were joking, weren't you, Gustl?'

She was not entirely sure. She had never heard of Gustl joking in rehearsal, except in Vienna, in sarcasm at some example of slovenly adherence to tradition.

'I wasn't precisely serious,' he agreed. 'As Sembrich said to me, "we'll never be allowed to play it like that in Philadelphia" . . . It's an American proverb apparently. But my interpretation, Almschi? Truthfully now? Isn't it the right one?'

He looked at her across the polished cases of the two pianos, his eyes, magnified through his spectacles, appearing peculiarly inquisitorial. And she knew what he was thinking: that if she had never actually met Mozart's Don, she had certainly known the excitement, the bewilderment, the exhilaration the heroines of *Don Giovanni* had experienced in his arms.

'Yes, I think it probably is. It sounds like a woman's interpretation ...'

But then Mozart nearly always showed his stories from a woman's perspective. Without thinking, she strummed a fragment from the Countess's aria – *Dove sono* – in Act Three of *Figaro*. She saw Mahler's smile. His face looked so gaunt and grey, the lines etched so deep on either side of his stretched lips, and so full of affection for her that her heart went out to him.

'So it must be the right one, mustn't it?' she concluded.

Mahler laughed outright. He got up from his piano, and came round to her. It was late. She was still taking the tonic prescribed for her at Christmas, so assumed that he was about to help her to her feet, and so to bed. To her surprise, he put one arm under her arms, and the other under her knees, and lifted her up.

'Gustl!' she cried out. 'You musn't!'

But she was already held in the air. She put her arm round his neck. As he carried her across the room, she asked,

'What would Professor Kovacs say? Or Dr Chvostec?'

He had not carried her in his arms like that for ages.

'They're not here,' he replied.

His voice was strained.

'Put me down, please Gustl.'

He reached for the door handle, carried her into the bedroom, and laid her across the bed.

'Gustl!' she exclaimed. 'Oh Gustl! We shouldn't ... Darling, we shouldn't!'

Probably, after the effort of carrying her, he should be offering her his pulse to count. Instead, they weren't even bothering to undress properly. She dragged her skirt up about her waist and drew up her knees.

'Gustl! Gustl! Gustl! ...'

As always, he climaxed far too quickly. It was just as well, she tried to tell herself; she couldn't have stood being excited more than she was, and then be left unsatisfied. He collapsed beside her. He was breathing noisily – fighting to take sufficient breath into his lungs. Heedless for once of her own discomfort, she scrambled up.

'Gustl?'

He stared up at her. There were beads of sweat on the bony surface of his face. Even in the orange light cast by the bedside lamps, she could see the bluish tinge of his lips. He smiled at her.

'Where do you keep the digitalis?' she asked.

He shook his head.

'No need, Almschili.'

'Gustl, you are an idiot.'

His gasping for breath was lessening as she leant over him.

'Do you think you have to prove something to me?' she asked.

'I'm possessive,' he replied, 'I want to hold you to me.'

'Oh Gustl!' she said. The tears coursed down her face. 'I'm bound to you,' she said. 'For ever. Frau Gustav Mahler. *In sempiternum, amen!*'

'I'm sorry,' he told her, 'to be in this condition for you.'

She thought of pointing out to him by way of reassurance the fact that she had not had a period since the time of their first arriving. That was now two clear months ago. She dried her eyes and reached out a hand to pull him upright. For the moment, however, she decided she had best not excite him any further. Tomorrow would be soon enough.

Lying beside him that night, she dreamed. She dreamed that she was woken up by a figure which looked like Mutti except that it was far too tall, and wasn't really a woman. It was standing beside the bed, but close to the foot. There wasn't a great deal of light except for a dull, greyish light which emanated from the figure, but it was sufficient for her to realize that she was back in Maiernigg – in the bed in which little Putzi had died. She wanted to cry out in fear, but could make no noise. She turned to wake Gustav, but he wasn't there. The figure, she realized, was speaking to her, although it wasn't uttering any words. What it was telling her was wonderfully moving: it was telling her that the dear God had decided to return her Putzi to her, and that already Putzi was back inside her body.

She didn't tell Mahler, the following day. *Don Giovanni* was due to open in Philadelphia in less than a week. She insisted he stay in bed till the very last moment before he had to go to rehearsal. She told him he wasn't to give her the sort of fright he had given her the previous night. After he had gone, however, she did confide in Mitzi Uchatius – even telling her about her dream. Mitzi kissed her and returned to her easel, looking very solemn as she pretended to concentrate on sorting out her brushes before setting to work.

The girl's response troubled Alma-Maria. She rose from her accustomed seat at the window and went and stood behind Mitzi. She put her arms round Mitzi's shoulders.

'You won't tell anybody, will you, darling?' she asked. 'I haven't even told Gustav yet. But I couldn't keep it from you, dearest friend.'

'Of course I won't tell anyone,' Mitzi replied.

Alma-Maria couldn't see her face, but she sounded almost sullen, as if she took offence at the unintended suggestion she might break a confidence.

Alma-Maria sat down at the window once more. She had been nursing the hope that she and Mitzi might go skating again; she felt better physically than she had done for weeks. But Mitzi proved so taciturn that she hadn't the heart to suggest it to her. Mahler's remark about the girl being in love with her nagged at her. At the end of the session, when

Mitzi had taken off her pinafore smock and had wrapped it round the nearly completed portrait on its easel, Alma-Maria decided to be open with her.

'Mitzi, *liebchen*, you wouldn't be sorry if I was going to have a baby, would you?'

'Of course not,' Mitzi said. 'Why ever should I be? I'm very happy for you.'

There was a slightly raised timbre in the way she spoke. Alma-Maria let her go, with a feeling of sadness.

She was back again, two mornings later. She was cheerful and friendly as ever, as if anxious that her manner on her previous visit should be forgotten. She wanted, she said, to finish with the sittings before Alma-Maria went off with Mahler to Philadelphia. Alma-Maria was sure, however, that there was an alteration in Mitzi's feelings toward her, difficult though it was to define: as if Mitzi might have been sensing that the tiny life growing inside her would displace her in her affections.

There was no scope for Alma-Maria to broach or even to reconnoitre this apprehension. Firstly, Mahler was still in the suite, in bed next door – propped up on pillows, a bed-table littered with music manuscript pulled to his chest – with Anton going in and out with coffee, his newly pressed evening clothes, his freshly polished boots, and finally his hot water. Then there was a telephone call from the lobby to say that Mrs George R. Sheldon's chauffeur was at the desk asking if it was convenient for Mrs Mahler that his mistress should pay an unexpected call.

Alma-Maria apologized to Mitzi, and went out to the lift to meet her unknown visitor.

'I'm sorry, my dear. I'm sure this is an intrusion,' Mrs George R. Sheldon told her in a hardly accented German. 'Perhaps I should introduce myself by saying that I am chairman of the Ladies' Guarantee Committee of the New York Philharmonic Society.'

Alma-Maria showed her into the drawing room. She explained that Mahler was still in his room, and that he was working on a score.

'Then we shall have to keep our voices down, won't we?' Mrs George R. Sheldon replied.

She unwound her astrakhan stole from off her ample bosom. Alma-Maria indicated to Kathi to take it. She presented Mitzi. Mitzi was smiling awkwardly, and looking embarrassed. Mrs George R. Sheldon drew her pince-nez from under her silk jacket and clamped them on her nose.

'No need to introduce us, dear,' she said. 'Marie and I are acquaintances of long standing, aren't we dear?'

She stared at Mitzi's paint-stained smock. Mitzi bobbed a slight curtsy and said something in acknowledgement in a voice too quiet from Alma-Maria to catch.

'So you've become friends, I see,' Mrs George R. Sheldon continued.

She went round and looked at Mitzi's work as Mitzi stood silent, her hands clasped in front of her.

'I've disturbed a sitting! I'm so sorry! You've been letting Marie paint your portrait. That is very forbearing of you, dear Mrs Mahler ... I hope you're grateful, Marie?'

There was a hint of disapproval – of which of them, or of both, Alma-Maria was uncertain. Mitzi murmured a shy reply. Mrs George R. Sheldon adjusted her pince-nez to examine the painting.

'A charming likeness,' she said blandly.

She looked for somewhere to sit. Alma-Maria felt herself as much a child as Mitzi as she helped her visitor to a chair. She called to Kathi to make them some mocha coffee with whipped cream, then felt ashamed at having raised her voice.

'Aha!' said Mrs George R. Sheldon. 'You've brought something of old Vienna over here with you!'

Over the coffee, she said 'The reason I came here, dear Mrs Mahler, was to thank you – both on my own behalf and on that of the other ladies of the Guarantee Committee of the Philharmonic Society: to thank you for placing no obstacle to your husband accepting the post of Director of the Philharmonic Symphony. We do know how you must miss your beautiful Vienna – and your family, of course. You have a daughter back in Vienna, don't you? You must bring her over, next season.'

Mitzi was sitting across the room, watching and waiting like an obedient child, her hands folded in her lap. As she was saying goodbye to Alma-Maria, Mrs George R. Sheldon turned to her.

'You are not to take up too much of Mrs Mahler's time, my dear. I'm sure she has much more important things to do than to sit for you.'

Mitzi had risen to her feet. Her lips moved slightly. She bobbed another curtsy.

Alma-Maria went out with her visitor to the elevator.

'My dear, don't let that chit take advantage of you,' said Mrs George R. Sheldon. 'I was most surprised to find her here, I can tell you. Really, you know, she should never have been more than a servant – her father is as poor as a church mouse. But she's a pretty little thing, and knows how to use her winning ways. And Dorothea Baumfeld is such an indulgent woman – too much so for her own good in the opinion of some of us. The Baumfelds have virtually adopted her.'

The elevator car drew up to the landing. The gate clattered open.

'Please don't mistake me, dear Mrs Mahler. I am not saying you should watch your silver in case she takes it – certainly not! What I am saying is that you should guard against finding yourself giving it to her.'

Alma-Maria returned to the drawing room. Mitzi was standing by the easel. She was playing with one of her paintbrushes.

'I bet she told you I shouldn't be here, painting you,' she announced.

364

'She doesn't like me. None of them likes me. They're all snobs!'

Alma-Maria was surprised by how clearly aware Mitzi was of Mrs George R. Sheldon's opinion of her.

'*Liebchen*! It doesn't matter what they think.'

There was the opportunity here, she decided, to regain the girl's confidence. Mitzi stared down into her lap. Alma-Maria thought she heard her say,

'You'll think just the same, soon enough.'

There was Gustav as well. She ought to go into him. She had no idea the Philharmonic Society had already made an approach to him. There was also her anxiety lest, if only by some nudge or hint, the suggestion should have entered his head that she had been approached behind his back. Then she realized that, since she had come back into the drawing room, she had been hearing the steady, insistent thud of a drum beat. She stood listening. Mitzi heard it too, and was distracted from her own misery. Alma-Maria stood beside her and looked down to the avenue far below. The snow had melted, leaving only a few ridges of slush on the roadway. The day was heavy and grey, with a thin drizzle. A few scattered groups of people had gathered on the sidewalks, waiting, their heads turned in the direction of Broadway and Columbus Circle.

Alma-Maria opened the window. Further along, Anton and Kathi had opened the window of their small parlour room and were leaning over the sill. In the damp air, the thud of the drum was accompanied by the sound of a military band: even before she recognized the melody, Alma-Maria detected the solemn grief of the sound. Gradually the notes became clearer, forming the unmistakable melody of Handel's 'Dead March' in *Saul* and, with it, the accompanying tread of boots and creaking of metalled wheels of a ceremonial funeral cortège.

Leaning out herself, she saw between the damp trees the procession turn into the avenue: mounted policemen at its head; the band in navy blue uniforms marching six abreast; the columns of uniformed, bareheaded men, in silver-buttoned coats with wide leather belts from which hung fire-axes like sidearms. One of the columns was dragging the hearse – a four-wheeled fire tender on which lay the coffin draped in the Stars and Stripes.

The slow tramp, the creaking, the ceremonial mourning call of Handel's music and the steady, increasingly noisy drumbeats, drew closer, with the dance-like clatter of the hoof beats of the mounted policemen, until it began to pass immediately below. Alma-Maria could now see the family mourners behind the coffin: the men in stiff white collars and unfamiliar suits, one or two with small boys beside them walking with stiff and severe expressions in imitation of their elders, and twitching their heads round quickly now and then to take in their surroundings; and the women and girls supporting one another in grief, the skirts of their Sunday dresses under their coat hems splashed sodden black and clay grey from the mud of the road and the wheels.

Mahler had come into the drawing room unnoticed. He was in shirt and trousers, without collar and tie. His jacket was slung over his shoulders. He had gone to the other window. Now he opened it. The cortège was immediately underneath. Two beats on the bass drum, beaten frenziedly, filled the eardrums like cannon shots, dulling all other sound. The cortège ground to a halt, filling the avenue in front of the hotel. Looking out to the right, Alma-Maria saw that it was waiting for the police to stop the traffic on Fifth Avenue before it moved on to bear the coffin to St Patrick's Cathedral, a quarter of a mile further down. The coffin was immediately below the window, a gilded helmet placed on the Stars and Stripes. A man with braid on his uniform – the fire captain perhaps – walked round the hearse to speak to the women. Everything waited in silence except for the occasional crunch of boots on the miry road and the neighing of a horse. Bystanders and even the carriage and automobile trade about the entrance to the hotel were at a standstill.

Alma-Maria looked across at Gustav. He was standing with his hands gripping the sill, one leg lifted slightly from the ground. His face was grey and sunken and there was a grit of stubble about his jaw. He was weeping. She went to stand beside him, putting her arm in his.

'Gustl, what's the matter?'

He tried to smile at her, but he looked ghastly.

'The stupid idea came to me,' he told her, 'that they'd arrived too early. Then I thought, perhaps they've come to tell me it's time for me to write a Requiem.'

She knew what he was referring to. Mozart was never far from his imaginings.

The double drum beat sounded again, shocking with its savage vehemence. The feet began to tramp again, and out of their sound and the steady pounding of the drum rose once more the fatalistic solemnity of Handel's *Dead March*.

'You're right, Gustl. It is stupid.'

Out of the corner of her eye, she saw that Mitzi was once again wrapping the painting up in her pinafore, preparatory to going.

'Gustl! It *is* stupid!' she pleaded in a sort of desperation.

The new production of *Don Giovanni* which opened in Philadelphia, then moved back to the Metropolitan Opera House, was received by the New York critics with something close to ecstasy. With the news, shortly after, of Heinrich Conried's impending resignation from the Directorship of the Metropolitan Opera Company came Mahler's own resignation. But this latter was no more than a necessary preliminary to his accepting the appointment as Director himself, with full artistic control over every aspect of the Met's productions. At the same time, he signed a contract as Principal Conductor for the next season of the New York Philharmonic Symphony Orchestra. There was talk, moreover, of arrangements being made, under the aegis of Mrs George R. Sheldon, for a season of concerts to form a showcase for the performance of his own compositions.

Alma-Maria wrote to Alex von Zemlinksy.

Dearest Alex – Everything is going so well here. There is nothing Gustav touches but it seems to turn to gold – at least in the eyes of the critics. His *Don Giovanni* is being received with as much adulation, if not more, as his *Figaro* in Salzburg, last year (even if Chaliapin suddenly, on the spur of the moment, decided to sing his recitatives in Russian to see if Scotti could pick up his cues!). But I am afraid. I've drawn up a timetable to which we keep as rigidly as Gustav's schedules allow – you know, resting, walking, writing and composing, bedtimes, all that sort of thing. He swears that never, since his first appointment anywhere as kapellmeister has he exerted himself so little, so surrounded is he by respect for his musicianship and by kindness. It is true we have here orchestras who are eager to play for him and to carry out his instructions to the most exact nuance. But for my part, I can't shake off the feeling that we are living from day to day. Dear Alex, I wish you were here to reassure me ...

A fortnight later, they were in Boston for a single performance there of *Tristan*. During the third act, during Tristan's rapturous recalling of Isolde's beauty, she noticed, looking down at him from her box, that with his left hand he was unbuttoning the top pearl button of his white evening waistcoat. Fear, like a fist, clenched at her stomach. She felt a buzzing in her head as she watched him slip his fingers against his shirt. As the act proceeded agonizingly slowly to its close, she watched how he gripped the edge of his desk, leaning slightly forward, then moved his hand back to his chest again. She waited for him to collapse across his open score. The buzzing in her head grew louder, drowning out all other music. She felt herself falling from her chair into blackness ...

She came to with her nostrils filled with the sulphurous smell of smelling salts, and a roaring in her head worse than the noise which had accompanied her fainting. It took her several moments to realize that it was, in fact, enthusiastic applause coming from the auditorium.

'He isn't ill?' she asked.

Anton Schertel, the principal stage manager, was leaning over her, the phial of smelling salts in his hand. A theatre maid had unbuttoned her collar under her jabot, and had opened her gown sufficiently to loosen her corset.

'Who?' asked Schertel. 'You are taken ill, Frau Mahler.'

'My husband.'

'Herr Mahler is out there receiving his ovation.'

She was lying on the couch in the rear of the box. The maid, a plump girl with a mass of red hair and a face covered in freckles, was standing at the foot of the settee.

'The doctor will be coming, ma'am,' she said.

Alma-Maria struggled up into a sitting position.

'I don't need a doctor!' she exclaimed.

Gustav would be looking for her. He always looked in her direction when he came out to receive his call if he knew she was in the theatre. He would be worried lest something had happened to her. It was important he mustn't be worried unnecessarily: that was the first thing Dr Blumenthal and all the others had said.

Against Schertel's protests, and with the maid supporting her arm while trying to persuade her to stay where she was until the doctor came, she stood up. The box swayed about her like a ship's cabin in a storm. The noise of the auditorium came streaming into her skull, into that small space which could not support so great a clamour. She was falling again, the cane-backed chairs spilling around her. . . .

There had been nothing really wrong with her, the house doctor said. A momentary, womanly weakness – that was all. She was fortunate she hadn't hurt herself when she fell. Back to New York, plenty of rest and a little regular exercise: that was what was needed, that and an abstinence from what was, in her case, completely unnecessary tight-lacing (but it *was* becoming necessary, she was sure of it, even if she hadn't told anybody except Mitzi), and repeat prescription of the horrible-tasting strychnine, iron, and quinine tonic.

The freckle-faced box maid accompanied her, with Mahler, back from the Boston Theatre to their hotel. Mahler came to her when Kathi had put her to bed. There was a dinner party for the cast and the senior members of the production team being given by the managing directors of the new Boston Opera House which was under construction on Huntingdon Street. He should have been there, but already he had unfastened his tie and collar. He, the reason for what had happened to her, she decided, was using his concern for her to excuse his absence from the party.

'How do you feel?' she asked from the softness of her pillows.

She did not mean to sound as aggressive as she did.

'How should I feel, Almschi? I was very worried about you.'

'During Act Three – you were taken ill. I saw it.'

'I felt a slight discomfort, yes . . . it was nothing,' he added.

'Where? Tell me, Gustl! Where did you feel it?'

It was so inconsiderate of him – so typically inconsiderate – that she, in her condition, should have to prise information out of him. He blinked down at her. He was embarrassed.

'A slight aching in my chest and right arm. It has passed. It's you we should be discussing.'

She shook her head. But she was too weary to explain that but for him she would not have fainted.

'You're taking on more and more work,' she told him. 'You should talk to a doctor – Dr Corning, for instance.' He sat down on the bed beside her. 'You're so stupid, Gustl! You stay in bed in the mornings. You want me to feel your pulse when we go for walks. Then you pick me up and carry me, just to show me what a big, strong fellow you really are! And then you talk about writing your own Requiem.'

She wanted to continue driving home the point of what she was telling him, but she hadn't enough strength.

'Gustl, what do you think would be left to me without you?'

She had sacrificed her music for him. She had left little Guckerl back in Vienna to be here with him. She had endured the aching tedium of the hotel suite because of him.

'Dearest Almschili! Do you really mean that?' asked Mahler.

He was deeply moved – happy, even. Dear God! she thought; he'd taken it as a declaration of love, which wasn't at all what she had meant. She wanted to cry – she was so often near to tears these days – but she was too weary even for that.

It was the beginning of March. From the drawing room window, looking out over the park, Alma-Maria could see specks of yellow bobbing between the trees where the wind was buffeting the daffodil buds. The painting sessions were over, but Mitzi called twice during the first week after Alma-Maria had returned from Boston. Alma-Maria didn't discourage her; she had no one else with whom she could fill an empty day. So they walked out together across the park, against the wind which blustered out of canyon-like streets, where gulls circled screaming dismally over mud-patched expanses of deserted grass.

Mahler had been invited by Walter Damrosch to conduct his Carnegie Hall Orchestra in three concerts commissioned for the New York Symphony Society. Nothing could have been more convenient: Carnegie Hall was virtually next door to the hotel. The first programme included Smetana's Overture and *Furiante* from *The Bartered Bride* – a particular favourite of Mahler's – and Schumann's B-flat Symhony in Mahler's own re-orchestration. Fashionably dressed men and women fought each other for seats, while the *Times* reported:

Mr Mahler conducts with perfect simplicity of gesture, yet exerts an influence over his players which can only be described as hypnotic. His readings are those of a master musician.

Once again, the following morning, elevator-loads of flowers were borne up to the eleventh floor until the Mahler's suite resembled a conservatory. A particularly large basket was a mass of fern leaves and blooms. On its handle was a label: 'In admiration from Mrs George R. Sheldon and the

Ladies' Guarantee Committee of the Philharmonic Society.'

The scent of flowers was everywhere, palpable as a counterpane.

That same night, in the darkness, Alma-Maria woke up to it as if it were drugging her. She was being tugged and pulled through a surf of half-sleep, sometimes too hard, so that the tugging ended in sharp pain. As she came to wakefulness, she realized that the pulling and tugging, as well as the shooting pains, were inside her body. She rolled onto her back, the heavy discomfort forcing her to lift her knees. She began babbling prayers through her head that it might not be what she suspected it was. Needle points shot down towards her thighs. She cried out softly as a contraction cramped her, urging her to roll over and jackknife. A knife-pain stabbed the base of her stomach. Then came the wetness between the fullness of her legs, leaking down the creases of her buttocks, sopping into the sheet underneath her.

She heard herself cry out.

'Gustl! Gustl! Oh dear God!'

Again there was the dreadful, unendurable cramping: the searing pain which shot through her insides.

'Gustl!' she screamed.

It had come like an ambush. One moment she had been fast asleep, the next she was embraced in this waking agony.

'Aah! Please God! Please, dear, sweet God! Take it away! Let me die! Oh God! Gustl!'

There was blood, stickily, cloying blood and mess around her, its smell mingling with the heavy smell of flowers. There was the gripping, stinging, nauseating pain, too low down in her body for her to contain it.

The electric light came on adding its glare to the sensory chaos in which she was trapped. Gustav had sat bolt upright.

'Almschi? Whatever is the matter?'

He was only half awake. He put his hand on her shoulder. (Didn't he understand that the last thing she wanted was to be touched?) He raised the quilt and saw the state she was in. Involuntarily, he exclaimed,

'Oh my God!'

She was afraid he was going to vomit. In fact, she was sure of it. Mercifully, the pain was receding, the cramping less violent. With as much self-control as she could muster, she said,

'Fetch Kathi here.'

'A doctor. I must telephone for a doctor!'

He was on his knees, retreating backwards across the bed. He slipped off the edge onto his feet, his nightshirt rucked up about his thighs.

'No Gustl. Kathi, please. Kathi will know what's to be done.'

Poor Gustl, she thought. He was shocked and disgusted to his puritan Jewish soul. All his upbringing was no doubt telling her she was unclean.

Unclean! O unclean! . . . Don't let him be sick, sweet Lord! Not, at least, until he's woken Kathi.

She sensed rather than saw his retreat to the bedroom door. Now, she was alone, and glad of it. Just to lie there; not to move until the aching, the throbbing with the stinging at its centre was drawn away to become part of the boundless ocean which was sounding gently in her ears . . . One thing she must, must do. She moved her hand down her body:

'I baptize thee, *in nomine Patris, Filii, et Spiritu Sancto*. Amen.'

Above her knees, she sketched the sign of the Cross with her forefinger. Then she was permitted to lie still.

Kathi arrived, pinafore over her nightdress and her jacket over her shoulders. She helped Alma-Maria to move over to Mahler's side of the bed, and cleaned her. If she was shocked and disgusted, she showed it only by a tightening of the lips; there was nothing neurasthenic about Kathi's strong Aryan peasant soul. She stripped the cover from the feather quilt, then she helped Alma-Maria to the bedroom sofa, adjusted the cushions, and wrapped the quilt about her. Alma-Maria shuddered. She took the girl's hand in her own.

'Dear Katchen. You're very kind to me. God bless you.'

Kathi smiled away from her, and shrugged slightly. She parcelled up the bottom sheet, interposing herself between Alma-Maria and the bloody effluvia which had drenched it. Only when she had carried it away did she ring for the hotel maid on duty to help her to remake the bed.

Mahler was sitting on the opposite side of the room where he thought he would be out of the way. When Kathi had gone to ring for the hotel maid, he came over to her.

'Are you sure you don't need a doctor?' he asked.

If he felt that she did, why didn't he take the initiative himself? she wondered.

'Tomorrow will do . . . Why don't you go and lie down on the drawing room settee? You need to rest.'

She wished he would go away and leave her alone.

'But . . . You've bled so much,' he said.

He shifted his weight from one leg to the other. She looked up at him.

'I didn't tell you. I wanted to be certain. I missed two of my monthlies.'

He hadn't noticed for himself, of course, but he understood the implication. He buried his face in his hands, pushing his spectacles up onto his forehead as he did so.

'It isn't terribly unusual in the first two or three months,' she told him.

She closed her eyes. She couldn't bear the thought of him becoming emotional.

'Go and rest, Gustl.'

He'd get over it quickly enough. He could always add a sixth song to his 'Songs for Dead Children'.

Pain and physical discomfort passed with the passing of the night. What replaced it was something worse. The physical sense of void – her womb, her crotch, her breasts sending messages to tell her that motherhood had been torn angrily from her – became a spiritual void. Purpose had been grasped away from her. She was nothing. An aimless nothing, capable of nothing: Frau Director Mahler, that was all. Now and again, for a fragment of a second, she forgot she was no longer pregnant. Such moments were intended to mock her, just as the dream of the Mutti-like figure beside her bed at Maiernigg, had been sent by a cruel providence to torment her with a false happiness.

A German-speaking doctor came to look at her, examining with electric torch and spatula the most ragged and useless part of her useless body. He was all bluff and hearty reassurance who understood all about the physical machine.

'No lasting damage ... Bleeding may last a few days longer than your normal monthly sickness, but it's nothing to worry about. A little discomfort, eh? That'll pass after two or three days. In a month or two everything will be back to normal – absolutely normal. Within four months, God willing, you could be in an interesting condition again, so *nil desperandum*, eh, Frau Director. And we'll have you out and about in time for Herr Director Mahler's second subscription concert, I can promise you that.' Then, with an arch little smile half-buried in the plump creases of his face: 'But no romancing till after your next monthly sickness, do you hear?'

She stared up at him – could not bring herself to speak to him. He was very understanding.

'Always a nasty shock,' he told her, patting her on the shoulder. (Why did everybody think that touching her would reassure her? Was it to tell her – or, more likely, themselves – that they didn't find her disgusting?) 'Time's the great healer, eh, Frau Director? Remember, at bottom you're a perfectly healthy woman. There's no reason to suppose it'll ever happen again – none in the world.'

She sat by the window staring after him as Kathi showed him out of the suite. Mahler hovered over her. He was already in his tweed coat, his battered, bulging portfolio under his arm. He was blinking, and standing on one leg. She was sure he looked far more ill than she did, but it didn't excite any response in her. She felt contemptuous that he couldn't find the words to say to her.

'You had better go to your rehearsal,' she said. 'You can't keep a whole cast and orchestra waiting. And there's nothing you can do here.'

He stooped and kissed her cheek – dry cheek and even drier lips. In half an hour or less, he would be surrounded by musicians and a handful of the greatest singers in the world, all of whom regarded him as little short of the Incarnate Deity, all of whom were anxious to demonstrate how much they longed to please him. She in the meantime was left on her bleak mountaintop, with no ring of fire to warm and protect her, and no gift of sleep to comfort and lull her out of desolation.

She sat all day. Kathi tried to look after her, coaxing her to eat and drink a little. But she preferred to be left alone. Sometimes she thought it might have been nice to have had Mutti with her – Mutti in lamplight, bending over her, in nightdress and shawl and with the long-remembered scent of mimosa between her breasts. A little funeral, a Requiem Mass said in a small village church, would have been appropriate. But nobody was ever going to admit – openly, at least – that there had ever been a child. Still less had they known that it was Putzi who had tried to return after so long and lonely a journey to her Muttichen.

She was there, in the same place, when Mitzi came, the following noon. Mitzi had not known she was ill – not until Kathi told her as she entered the suite. She offered to leave immediately, but Alma-Maria let her stay: she scarcely cared whether Mitzi came or went.

She had brought the completed portrait with her, stretched on a board and parcelled in oilskin. She untied the parcel, unwrapped it and held it up at easel height for Alma-Maria to view. Alma-Maria stared dully at it. She had to focus her mind as well as her eyes. She wondered why Mitzi was showing it to her: it was so very ordinary – accomplished, by schoolgirl standards, and, like all work by genteel and inexperienced schoolgirls, insipid.

'It's very nice,' she said.

'Do you really think so?' Mitzi asked eagerly. Then she grasped the situation somewhat. 'I'm sorry, Alma. I shouldn't be bothering you with it. Not today. I'll bring it back some other time.'

She crouched down and started to wrap it up again.

'Is it part of the same trouble you had in Boston?' she asked.

'I suppose so,' Alma-Maria replied. 'I suppose you could say that.'

A lock of Mitzi's corn-yellow hair fell loose from the tortoiseshell band which contained it.

'Oh dear!' She gave a little, self-conscious laugh. Propping the painting against her hip, she drew open the band and thrust her hair under it.

'I lost my baby,' Alma-Maria said.

Mitzi lowered her hand from the back of her head.

'Oh gosh!' she exclaimed, then, remembering herself, she said, 'Alma! I'm so sorry!'

She pushed the half-wrapped painting aside so that it leant against the arm of a chair, and stood up as if there was some sort of action she could take.

'The doctor says there's nothing dreadfully wrong,' Alma-Maria told her. 'I mean, it isn't as if I can't have another baby ... I expect you're quite happy about it, aren't you?'

She said it in a tone of quiet reasonableness, so that the look of incomprehension on Mitzi's face surprised her. She explained quite calmly,

'I know you thought my having a baby was going to get in the way of our friendship. You felt jealous, I expect.'

Mitzi's face assumed an expression of horrified astonishment quite out of proportion with Alma-Maria's mild remark.

'In fact, I know you did. I could see it quite clearly when I told you about it. So, you've got nothing to worry about now.'

But Mitzi looked as if she had been slapped across the face. She blinked several times, and her mouth twitched. Quickly, she pulled herself together.

'I think I'd better go and leave you alone,' she said.

So she should, thought Alma-Maria, if she wasn't grown up enough to keep her more childish feelings under control.

Mitzi picked up the half-wrapped painting. Then she put it down again.

'I did it for you,' she said.

She bobbed the appropriate curtsy of a well brought up girl to a married lady, and said in a voice which Alma-Maria could only just catch,

'*Auf wiedersehen*, Frau Mahler.'

As she left, seeing herself out, she was just about to burst into tears. Alma-Maria was sure of it, though she couldn't for the life of her understand what had provoked the girl to such a state.

Silence rushed in to fill the empty spaces of the room. With it came the distant sound of the elevator descending, carrying Mitzi Uchatius away – it was odd, because Alma-Maria had never been aware of hearing the elevator before from so great a distance. For a long time she sat staring out at the grey afternoon. Kathi came in – she wanted to see if she could go to one of her regular classes, of course, and to whoever it was she was meeting at them. Alma-Maria would have let her go if she could have found the energy to speak to her. But she felt extraordinarily weary, as if Mitzi's coming, and the child's stupid behaviour, had drained her. People were not very good about facing the truth about themselves, even when there wasn't much truth to face ... And that was quite a clever remark, really – clever enough to bear repeating to herself. After Kathi had left her, she found she was repeating it again and again, running it through her head because there was something else waiting to take possession there.

The scream came bursting through, filling her head and spilling out all over the room.

'Putzi! Oh Putzi! Oh Putzi!'

374

Scream and scream and scream. There was Kathi come back into the room, trying to restrain her, trying to hold her hands. She wrenched them away, clawing and clutching as she did so. She saw through a blur of flailing hands and hair and damp, Anton's shocked and bewildered face looking over Kathi's shoulders. She went on screaming, piling scream on top of scream, afraid that the noise would stop and the hideous, leaden silence would return to suffocate her altogether.

6 "YEAR AFTER YEAR I HAD LONGED FOR LOVE": 1909

'BATH-TIME, LADIES ! This way, please. All of you, now!'

Beyond the windows, which rose from the floor to the high ceiling, the mountainside soared upwards into ragged grey skirts of cloud. The same enclosed view obtained on the opposite side of the building – the side overlooked from Alma-Maria's bedroom window. The mountains enclosed the sanatorium buildings like the outer perimeter wall of a prison.

She stubbed out her cigarette into the saucer on which stood her half-drunk glass of buttermilk – she was supposed to drink buttermilk with every meal, and once between meals. The seven or eight other women who had been with her in the long, sparsely furnished recreation room were shuffling towards the door. All were dressed like herself, in loose white cotton night shifts and woollen shawls even though it was eleven o'clock in the morning. The duty nurse, a tall, sturdy Pomeranian girl whose pretty face was offset by a pair of steely grenadier sergeant's pale blue eyes, approached Alma-Maria at a brisk strut. The apron which cuirassed her figure was so heavily starched that it glittered like icing sugar and crackled as she moved; a garment so dazzlingly clean mocked its purpose.

'You know, Frau Director Mahler, that smoking is not good for you. It is not good for your nerves. It is not ladylike; it sets a bad example for a young impressionable female like myself.'

She said it without a trace of a smile. Cigarette smoking was not actually forbidden to the guests at the Tobelbad Sanatorium. By the same token, guests were not actually forbidden to dress in their ordinary day wear. It was simply that the ladies' clothes were kept not in their rooms but in a long attic garderobe – rows of individual wardrobe presses – at the end of the ladies' bedroom wing and up a narrow flight of stairs, so that one had to ask permission to fetch them from a nursing sister. Only at dinner and afterwards was the wearing of one's own clothes actively encouraged; they were removed by chambermaids when one had undressed for bed and were taken back to the garderobe or to the laundry.

'You must hurry along and catch up with your friends, Frau Director Mahler. We mustn't be late for our baths or we will put out our entire schedule, won't we?'

'I suppose we will, Sister Inge.'

If Sister Inge detected the note of anger in Alma-Maria's voice, she did not show it. The entire staff of the sanatorium were North Germans: nurses, doctors, chambermaids, even the gardeners for all Alma-Maria knew. Only the 'guests' were Austrian.

Alma-Maria followed the others out of the door and down the long gallery. The slippers were loose on her feet; she had to clench her toes to hold them on, and they slapped the floor as she walked. Sister Inge was immediately behind her; she could hear the rattle of keys on the chatelaine which Sister Inge kept hidden under her stiff apron. She felt Sister Inge's hand under her elbow, pretending to offer her support but in fact hurrying her along the bare, carbolic-smelling passage. She straightened her arm at her side, shaking off the girl's grip.

As Principal Conductor and Director of the New York Philharmonic, it had seemed Mahler could do no wrong, during his second season in New York. If possible, his *Figaro*, with Sembrich making her farewell appearance as the Countess, and his production of *Fidelio* with Alfred Roller's settings had been greeted with even greater adulation than his *Tristan* and his *Don Giovanni*. The ladies of the Philharmonic Guarantee Committee had raised by subscription $200,000 to enable him to conduct a series of concerts of his own works. Alma-Maria had been assiduous in her charm towards them and their millionaire husbands. Invitations poured in, and they could have dined out every night that Mahler was not actually on the podium. They were the weekend guests on Long Island, or Oyster Bay, of the Theodore Roosevelts, the Vanderbilts, the Havemeyers; Alma-Maria behaved faultlessly, so that the society columns of the newspapers glowed with references to 'Maestro Gustav Mahler and his dazzlingly lovely young Viennese wife'.

From the time of their marriage, she had taken charge of and ordered Mahler's business affairs successfully. The fact that she saw this new social whirl into which they were drawn as part of the business side of their lives enabled her to contain her emotional state. And yet always

she was conscious of the spiritual chaos which threatened to engulf her –
of a return of the hysteria which had seized her in the days after her
miscarriage. It was ironic, she decided, that they were better off now, in
semi-exile, than they had been during Mahler's musical primacy in
Vienna. She took advantage of the fact to secure investments and annuit-
ies for them in New York in case she should suffer a worse breakdown,
and thus be unable to supervise their financial affairs.

They had returned to Europe once more via Cherbourg and Paris,
where Mahler was to conduct a performance of his Second Symphony,
'The Resurrection', at the Trocadero. She had made all the arrangements
and bookings for the journey. From the beginning of their voyage, they
enjoyed perfect weather. Mahler was in the best of spirits, still in a
euphoric state following the extraordinary success of his second season
in New York. If the thought of seasickness occurred to him, he did not
mention it. He was filled with ideas for yet another symphony, his
Tenth – one that would have pleased old Brahms, he declared, by its
perfect academic symmetry, *Adagio, Scherzo, Allegretto, Scherzo,
Adagio*. It had always been a matter for regret with him that Brahms
had not approved of his compositions.

Alma-Maria, standing at the stern rail watching the American coastline
recede into an opaque yet shining haze, wondered if now, a year later,
it were possible she had finally left behind the wretchedness and violence
which had so nearly overwhelmed her behind in their eleventh-floor
suite in the Hotel Majestic.

On a sunny afternoon, as they were approaching the Breton coast,
they had sat on deck watching the seagulls come swooping down to the
ship's wake. He said to her,

'I have tricked the good Lord, do you see, Almschili? By not establishing *Das Lied von der Erde* as my Ninth Symphony, I have drafted a
Ninth Symphony and am spared to compose my Tenth.' He sounded
boyishly pleased with himself. *Das Lied von den Erde* was the title which
he had finally decided on for the song cycle based on Bethge's *Jade
Flute*.

'There's a Jewish word for it – *chutzpah*,' he added. 'There's no exact
translation in any language I know of. I suppose you could explain it as
meaning something like outrageous cheek.'

She saw the shadow come over his face.

'If my father had heard such a word on my lips, he would have flogged
me,' he said. 'There was no worse offence at home than betraying oneself
by using a *shtetl* word.'

On the quay at Cherbourg, the following morning, with a raw off-sea
breeze blowing through the open customs shed which the early sunlight
had had no time to warm, she left Mahler sitting on one of their boxes.
She went to fetch one of the inspectors so that she could arrange for
their baggage to be loaded onto the waiting Paris *rapide* as soon as

possible. The grizzled chief inspector gave her an admiring look, and was as affably cooperative as he could have been. With two porters in tow, he went with her over to Mahler and the heap of boxes.

'Don't vex yourself, Mademoiselle, I beg you,' he told her. 'We'll find a comfortable seat for your father in one of the Pullman cars, and you can settle the documentation with me then and there.'

At that moment, she saw Mahler as the chief customs inspector had seen him – a crouched grey figure two decades older than his forty-eight years, huddled inside an expensive Scotch tweed overcoat several sizes too large for him, his cheeks mottled, sunken and unshaven. It brought immediately to her mind an incident which had occurred only three weeks previously.

Dr Joseph Fraenkel, who had been looking after Mahler in New York and who had become something of a friend, had invited her to take a ride in his buggy among the giant trees of Inwood Park at the northernmost end of Manhattan Island. It had been pleasant, with the sunlight striking glittering shafts through the overhanging branches and dappling the carpet of last year's leaves, so the fact that Dr Fraenkel had driven her there to talk about Mahler's condition came to her as a disappointment.

'I don't have to tell you, do I, Frau Alma, that your husband's heart is in far from excellent condition?'

'No, Dr Fraenkel. You don't.'

'Dr Corning and I have discussed his case on several occasions. We are agreed that there is no exact prognosis to be made. A patient who takes proper care of himself – treats his condition with respect, shall we say? – may be expected to have ...' The hesitation was only momentary before he went on, 'quite a few years of productive life before him.'

'Forgive me, Dr Fraenkel, I don't think you're telling me anything I don't already know.'

But she felt a sickening sense of apprehension.

'I'm sure of it, dear lady. But bear with me. We do have a problem here. Not only, in your husband's case, do we have a patient who took great delight in athletic pursuits before the onset of his condition, but one who is, at this very moment, at the height of his creative and intellectual powers.'

Between the massive tree trunks, she could see the expanse of the Hudson River sparkling in the sunlight, and the budding leaves like a green haze over the farther shore.

'You see – if we were to take the case of the great Wolfgang Amadeus ...'

Ah, yes! she thought: Mozart, always the comparison with Mozart. Now she could be quite sure this conversation was the result of a previous one between Dr Fraenkel and Mahler.

'Supposing Wolfgang Amadeus had not felt impelled to set down all that music – what was it? *The Magic Flute? La Clemenza di Tito?* The three great final symphonies? The two last piano concerti? The Clarinet Quintet? The Requiem – all in the last eighteen months of his life. It is possible he might have lived several years longer.'

He might have died just the same, thought Alma-Maria, and the world be poorer for some or all of those works. She did not say so.

'I'm sure your husband has so much still to give us,' Dr Fraenkel continued. 'And what we have to do, my dear, is to take very good care of him.'

And what about herself? thought Alma-Maria.

'Of course,' she said aloud.

'Forgive me asking, my dear, but do you happen to have read Octave Mirbeau's novel, *Journal d'une Femme de Chambre?*'

What on earth ... ? Alma-Maria asked herself. She had read it. But it was the sort of book a woman would admit to having read only to certain people. She had been enormously struck by the eponymous heroine's admission to having, like herself, severely uncomfortable periods – the first and only time she had ever come across the mention of such a subject in print.

'I do know,' Dr Fraenkel told her, 'that you are an unusually well read young woman. Mahler has told me of your enthusiasm for Dostoyevsky, for instance.'

'But why do you ask about Mirbeau?' said Alma-Maria cautiously.

Dr Fraenkel took it as it was intended – as an admission.

'Do you remember the episode dealing with Monsieur Georges?'

Monsieur Georges had been the sick young poet whose mother had retained the services of Célestine, the novel's heroine, so that she might bring some light and joy into his life. Célestine had been too successful in her task: such was the pleasure he took in her that he died from his exertions. There was little need for the warning. Mahler had not so much as touched her since that terrible night – the effect, she had assumed, of his all-too-obviously appalled disgust at what he had seen.

The conversation with Dr Fraenkel, she had decided, had been the result of Mahler's prevailing upon him to talk to her, to give him a justification for withholding himself from her which she could not deny.

She had had to lock the anger it had caused her in her heart. And then, on the cold quayside at Cherbourg, the sight of him sitting stooped there on the boxes had come as a bitter reproach. She had given him her arm to help him across to the Pullman cars drawn up on the quay. The trouble was that remorse at her sense of anger no more obliterated it than it would have eased her period pains.

'You may take clean towels from the table, ladies ... Remember to hang your gowns on the peg with *your* name on the label. We don't want to find ourselves wearing another lady's gown, now, do we?'

The ragged file of white-robed women shuffled across the hall. Each took two towels from the bare utility table – a small one for a turban around their hair, and one with which to dry themselves. Some started tying up their hair as they went along, as if such a display of eagerness might impress the attendants. A cellar stairway led down to the changing room and the baths. Hot damp steam rose to meet them as they descended, and a choking smell of sulphur. Alma-Maria felt perspiration pricking through her pores. Like one or two of the others, she reached out to press her hand on the wet, white tiles of the wall to prevent herself from slipping.

The changing room was no more than a passage from the bottom of the stairs to the sunken baths. Here the steam was fog-like, shrouding the moving figures and providing more privacy than the few inches of wooden partition separating each peg in the pretence of forming cubicles. There was the sound of coughing as sulphur clutched at the lungs. The attendants stood on either side of the entrance to the baths like gaolers. The 'guests' stripped off their robes; one could tell the new arrivals by the way they wrapped their towels about them under their armpits as they filed through, only to have them snatched away by the attendants.

Each bath was a white tiled pit filled with sulphurous, mud-coloured water in which four women could squat neck-deep on a tiled shelf beneath the surface.

'Come on now, ladies. Take your places. Hot water relaxes muscular tension, opens the pores of the skin and eliminates secretions, and causes the natural bodily fluids to circulate freely!'

This recital was part of an unvarying daily litany. One woman after another stepped down into her allotted place in one of the baths.

'Over here on the right, if you please, Frau Hofratin von Eggelsdorf ... No, Frau Cavalry-Brigadier Straub, not there – over here if you would be so kind ...'

Hair straggled grey and damp from under towels, breasts drooped from the roughened skin of ageing chests, fat buttocks hung like soft pale sacks over quivering, creased thighs. On the far side of the bath into which she herself was about to descend, Alma-Maria saw, through the mist unexpectedly, a young woman as short as herself with firm, full breasts, slim waist, and well-shaped hips and thighs with a dense thatch which spread in a triangle from her crotch almost to her flanks below her hips. The face under the towel about her head was so clear-complexioned and unlined, the small chin and mouth so firm and determined, the blue eyes so clear, that it was difficult to understand how she came to be in a sanatorium at all. It wasn't until Alma-Maria took a first step into the bath, and the young woman opposite did the same, that she realized that she was looking into a mirror – a mirror so accustomed to the hot damp vapour that it no longer steamed over.

The hot water lapped upwards until it was over her shoulders and she felt her buttocks safely resting on the slippery tiled seat. It was only just bearable: the heat caused her to gasp at first and inhale the sulphur-tasting air so that she thought she would choke or suffocate. He nipples particularly stung as if pins were being inserted and, even as she became accustomed to the temperature of the water, she was still afraid she might faint. Even that, however, passed at last, and she could close her eyes and retreat into the privacy of her own thoughts – to encounter the notion that she was here not because of any condition within herself, but because it was convenient for others ...

Sophie and Paul Clemenceau, and Gabriel Pierné, the conductor-composer who had arranged the Mahler concert at the Trocadero, had been on the platform at the Gare Montparnasse to welcome them to Paris. Sophie, in consultation with Berta Zuckerkandl, had arranged for Mahler's final sittings for Rodin, for the completion of the bust which was to be placed in the foyer of the Court Opera in Vienna. Sophie and Paul had also brought with them – for Alma-Maria a particular antidote for her sense of depression – a personal invitation to herself and Gustav to lunch the following day with General Marie-Georges Picquart, no longer the victim of the anti-Dreyfusards, but Minister of War in Georges Clemenceau's administration.

The night of the performance of Mahler's Second Symphony, she had been invited to dine with Gabriel Pierné and his wife before going on to the Trocadero to attend the concert. Mahler himself was not present – he was resting as he always had to before conducting, these days, under the watchful eye of Anton. Apart from herself, the guest of honour that night was the composer and musician whose primacy in French musical circles was as unquestioned as Mahler's had been in Vienna – Claude Debussy. With him was his wealthy wife, Emma, and another distinguished composer, Paul Dukas.

At the table, Debussy sat on Alma-Maria's left. She found herself strongly attracted to his dark, somewhat florid, animal good looks. He talked to her of his time in Russia as a pupil of Rimsky-Korsakov's – whom he described as 'a musical illiterate' – and as music tutor to Tchaikovsky's patroness, Madame von Meck:

'A stupid woman ... stupid past belief. If she had been content to have regarded herself as a Russian musical Mycaenas one might have found it in one's heart to have forgiven her! But she regarded herself as a Muse. Can one imagine anything so stupid? Incapable of putting four bars of melody together, she believed she could inspire music in her protégés. Mercifully, she regarded me as a mere servant. No wonder poor Tchaikovsky turned out his Fourth and the 'Pathétique' under her influence – every note the work of a haunted depressive! ... Do you regard yourself as Mahler's Muse, my dear lady?' he asked Alma-Maria. Without waiting for an answer, he continued, 'No. Of course you don't ... Emma, my dear? Do you regard yourself as my Muse?'

Madame Debussy, plump and motherly-looking, simpered.

'The whole world knows,' said Debussy, 'I married her only for her money.' He bent his head to Alma-Maria's ear. 'You have only to look at her, eh? In the same way as one has only to look at you, my dear, to know that, however wealthy you might have been, Mahler was not such a Jew that he married you only for your money.'

She felt angry, it was true, and astonished by the crudeness of his attitude toward her. But at the same time, had he got up and left her alone, she would have felt quite extraordinary disappointment. She looked into his face; his small black beard and moustache gave him the cruel, satanic look of a Borgia prince.

'I heard your husband direct a performance of *Fidelio* once,' he told her unexpectedly. 'In London – Covent Garden. It was sublime. I would go so far as to say, it could never be bettered.'

'I shall tell Gustav so,' Alma-Maria replied.

'You had better tell him that it is a compliment from someone notorious for his lack of ear for German music,' said Madame Pierné from the end of the table.

Debussy raised his hand in a gesture of protest.

'Only German music *after* Beethoven, if you please, Madame.'

'Do you not like the music of Schubert?' Alma-Maria asked him.

Debussy cast a rapid glance about the table to ensure everyone was taking notice.

'Schubert's *lieder* ...' he began. 'I'll tell you exactly what Schubert's *lieder* reminds one of – the smell of underwear in an elderly spinster's bottom drawer.'

This provoked a general merriment, though the reason was lost on Alma-Maria. If anyone was spinsterish, she decided, it was Debussy – in the way he was picking fragments from the plate in front of him, eating them, and pushing most of his food aside.

At the concert, Alma-Maria sat with General Picquart and the Clemenceaus in the Presidential box. Debussy, Pierné, and Dukas sat in the third row of the stalls. They remained there until the end of the second movement. They then walked out, the length of the auditorium, Debussy talking loudly over his shoulder to the others behind him.

'Very rude!' General Picquart said to Alma-Maria. 'But all too typical, I'm afraid.'

The Colonne Orchestra played faultlessly; the chorus was perfectly trained; the applause at the end was as enthusiastic as Mahler or Alma-Maria could have wished. Gabriel Fauré was present with Ravel; both went back to congratulate Mahler afterwards, with André Caplet who had recently become permanent conductor of the Colonne Orchestra. But the behaviour of Debussy and of Pierné, who had been responsible for arranging the performance in the first place, had cast a shadow over the evening.

The next morning, Paul Dukas came round to the hotel to apologize. Mahler was out, at Rodin's studio, so Alma-Maria received him. She was stiff with resentment. She met him in the vestibule, and did not even suggest that they be seated.

'Dear Madame, you must try to understand,' he attempted to explain, his high-pitched voice expressing more anxiety than conviction. 'French composers have been so anxious to throw off a German influence which, many of us feel, stifles the authentic French voice. Wagner, you understand. Everywhere, Wagner. And this struggle has resulted in a certain fanaticism. Your husband's music, you see, is German music. You cannot deny it, Madame.'

'That does not excuse rudeness, Monsieur Dukas: hurtful rudeness.'

Dukas stretched out his hands and shrugged.

'Madame, there is also Debussy. Debussy is *un type* – there is no escaping the fact. He knows only one morality, one code of behaviour. Music. About music, he is desperately serious. He has never written a dishonest note of music – believe me, Madame. In everything else he is ... without morality. He said your husband's music reminded him too much of Schubert ... Much too much of Schubert.'

It was as if he had sent a message to indicate another secret had been broken open. So Mahler's music also smelt of elderly spinsters' clean underwear!

'And you? What made you walk out like that, Monsieur Dukas?'

'Ah, Madame! That is something different again.'

He took a deep breath, then sighed. Lowering his voice, he said.

'I am like your husband, Madame – a Jew. There are many who regarded what Debussy and I think of as the German influence over French music as a peculiarly Jewish influence. Meyerbeer, and Offenbach, of course. Both very Teutonic in their musical thought. And Mahler being what *he* is – please forgive me, Madame, I mean no offence! And I being what *I* am. And the political climate being what *it* is, here in France ... I dared not stay in my place when all the world had seen Debussy and Pierné leave. They would have said immediately that it was just another example of Jews sticking together.'

Her own uneasy desire made her irritable as well as angry.

'I thought Paris was done with all that nonsense,' she said.

'Ah, Madame!' Dukas trilled mournfully. 'Let's not delude ourselves. Neither Paris nor anywhere else, alas!'

She had returned to her suite after he had gone, to sit down quietly, to smoke a cigarette and drink a glass of Benedictine. She had been trembling slightly. Never before – absolutely never – had she experienced in herself so disturbing a separation of physical longing from love as Debussy had aroused in her. She had always supposed it to be characteristic of many, perhaps most, men; but in women, a peculiarity confined to whores ...

'That's enough now, ladies! We mustn't let our skin get wrinkled, must we, Frau Sussmayr?'

Alma-Maria joined the other gleaming, dripping torsos and sodden, dangling head towels slopping through the sulphurous fog back to the narrow partitions and pegs. She began to hurry, trying to pass the stooped, emaciated figure with the withered dugs, on the tiled walkway in front of her. It had come to her suddenly that Sister Ingeborg or Sister Petra were perfectly capable of filching her cigarette case and matchbox and locking them up in the Superintendent's office. The woman in front of her was not prepared to let her pass, so she had to wait her turn to reach her peg. Without so much as wrapping her towel about her, she plunged her fist into the pocket of her shroud and felt the reassuring touch of metal.

The case was of chased silver – a present from Ferruccio Busoni who had played Beethoven's 'Emperor' Concerto at the third of Mahler's Carnegie Hall concerts. There were four cigarettes remaining inside it. Heaven alone knew how she was to get any more – or her other particular desire, a bottle of Benedictine. She wasn't able even to bribe a chambermaid; her purse was locked up with her outdoor clothes and her valuables. She had not yet reached the pitiable state where she would have been prepared to offer a domestic Mahler's ring, or the gold sleepers from her earlobes, in return for cigarettes.

She pulled the shroud down over her head and tied the waist string in a bow at the back. She thrust her feet into her slippers and drew her sanatorium shawl about her. Two nurses in stiff white caps with precisely gophered edges, and gleaming white aprons, stood at the foot of the basement stairs. In their hands, they held stiff-covered exercise books and pencils.

'Did you pass a stool this morning, Frau Director Mahler?'

'Yes, Sister Ingeborg.'

'That's good. Was it hard or soft?'

'Soft, Sister Ingeborg.'

'Well done, Frau Director Mahler.' To the other nurse: 'The Frau Director may have *Wurst* with her lettuce and buttermilk for lunch this afternoon.'

The second nurse made an entry in her exercise book. Alma-Maria shuffled on, following the figures in front of her up the stairs into the cool of the fresh air.

When they had returned to Vienna, they stayed with Mutti and Möll up on the Hohe Warte. Mahler rested most of the time, convalescing from the journey before undertaking a concert tour – conducting the first performance of his Seventh, with the Czech Philharmonic in Prague, the Sixth, with the Württemberg Royal Orchestra in Wiesbaden, and another performance of the Seventh, this time in Amsterdam with the

Concertgebouw Orchestra. He was then to go to Munich to commence preparations for the first performance, later in the year, of what he had come to regard as his crowning achievement, his Eighth Symphony – the setting of the medieval poem, *Veni Creator Spiritus*, with the final scene of Goethe's *Faust*.

He spent his mornings in bed and most of the rest of the day in Alma-Maria's old music room, preparing his scores, revising, planning the new Tenth Symphony. Once more, Alma-Maria had to attempt to renew a close relationship with little Gucki, to separate the child somewhat from Miss Turner toward whom she found she was harbouring distinct feelings of jealousy. She took Gucki with her own half-sister, the ten-year-old Marie, for walks into Döbling, or down into Heiligenstadt. Once, as a special excursion, she took both the children down into Vienna, to the Prater. Marie, five years older than Gucki, took charge of both of them – 'And I am your sister, aren't I, Alma-Maria?' Gucki remained silent, withdrawn, prepared to buy peace by never crossing Marie. When Alma-Maria tried to buy ice cream from one stall in the Prater Gardens, deliberately offering one to Gucki first, Gucki refused.

'Miss Turner wouldn't like me to,' she explained.

'Why ever not?' asked Alma-Maria.

'Miss Turner says the ice creams they sell off stalls aren't good for you,' Gucki replied. 'Miss Turner says they aren't ...' She hesitated. 'Hygienic,' she concluded.

'That's stupid, isn't it, Alma-Maria?' said Marie. Then she added with a scornful laugh: 'It's as if Guckerl thinks she's Miss Turner's daughter – not yours at all!'

Alma-Maria went with Mahler to the Nordbahnhof, to see him off on the first leg of his tour. She told herself that she knew the importance of his presenting himself before an international public, that she did not resent being left at home to look after their affairs. But she went back to the Hohe Warte feeling wretchedly alone. She telephoned the Zuckerkandls, only to discover that Berta had gone with Emil to a medical conference in Edinburgh, and that they intended breaking their return journey for two weeks in London, and a further week with Sophie and Paul Clemenceau in Paris.

Möll was fully occupied in organizing a special exhibition at the Sezession galleries to commemorate the Jubilee of the Old Man's accession to the throne of the Hapsburgs – an exhibition to be, once again, opened by the Old Man himself. Over dinner, the night after Mahler's departure, Alma-Maria suggested that the term Sezession was no longer appropriate to an institution which so clearly enjoyed Kaiserlich-Königlich favour.

Möll laughed, but qualified his amusement by wagging his finger in the arch fashion which had irritated her for as long as she could remember.

'K-K favour, perhaps, my dear Almschi! But K-K comprehension of what we are about, no!' He sat back in his seat with an expression of complacent self-satisfaction. 'You see, my dear, it is the mark of Imperial decline – not merely here in the Dual Monarchy, but throughout the nations down human history – that an *Imperium* embraces the very elements which undermine its foundations.'

Alma-Maria had provoked this response, but did not have the mental energy to give Möll the argument he was after. In the silence which followed his statement, Mutti intervened to say,

'Carl was remarking just the other day ... do you remember, *liebling*, when Count Czernin was here to dinner? ... how extraordinary it is the way Christian rulers – our own Old Man or the King of England, for instance – allow Jews to occupy some of the most responsible positions in the state: chairs in the important universities, directorships of national banks, and ... well, England has even had a Jew as Prime Minister, hasn't it?"

'A baptized Jew, *liebe* Annerl,' Möll explained. 'Some of the greatest names in our German culture are those of baptized Jews: Heine, Mendelssohn, for instance, and gentlemen who have sat at this very table, I'm proud to say – the Freiherr von Hofmannsthal, and Dr Schnitzler, and of course, our own dear, glorious Gustav ...'

Alma-Maria watched Mutti's face soften with deep affection.

'Of course! Of course! I always find it so difficult to think of our dear Gustav as a Jew. He is so impractical in business matters – and I'm sure he'd give his last schilling to a beggar.'

The following afternoon, Alma-Maria went with Möll to the Sezession building. Leaving him in his studio-office, she wandered through the empty galleries. The cistern, as she had come to think of it, where Klimt had depicted her as inspiring Mahler as medieval knight to pass through peculiarly Klimtian nightmares in order to obtain with her an erotic ecstasy which would transform humankind, *vide* Schiller, was unlit and deserted. She did not bother to turn up the lights; over the passing of the years, the message of the painting had become a sterile mockery.

She walked on, circuiting the central salon under the dome, and making her way where sunlight poured through windows set in white walls. On the walls were landscapes of lake water and wooded, rush-banked shores, of vineyards and lakeside villages, all in the impressionist style but whose authorship was immediately recognizable without looking at the thickly applied signature at the bottom right-hand corners.

'Almschi! I had no idea you were back in Vienna!'

She told herself that she had known he would be there, as big and bearlike as ever, in a cream-coloured summerweight suit with the waistcoat undone to ease the swell of his increasing girth.

'Hello, Gustl.'

She sounded extraordinarily shy, she decided.

'Almschi! . . . Well!'

He rose from the seat from which he had been contemplating his own work. He held out his arms to her.

'You are glad to see me, aren't you, Gustl?'

'Of course! Of course! What do you think?'

Last time they had met alone, here in the Sezession building, she had kept him at a distance, albeit gently. Now she surrendered gladly to his big embrace.

'Mahler isn't with you?' he asked in her ear.

She felt a mounting excitement.

'No. He's in Prague.'

'My Almscherl! I was afraid we'd lost you for ever to the land of bronco busters and six-shooters.'

'I haven't seen one bronco buster – or a six-shooter!' she laughed. 'Just lots of fat millionairesses, all of whom fall in love with Mahler's genius and want to buy him whole orchestras.'

'Do you think they'd fall in love with me, and buy me whole art galleries for my own use?'

'I'm sure of it,' she told him.

She thought of Mitzi Uchatius and how she had longed to see his paintings. But Mitzi's memory filled her with the unhappiness which surfaced all too easily these days, so she did not mention her.

'I'm so glad I've found you here,' she told him. 'I was hoping I would. Actually, to tell you the truth, I even thought of going to the Josefstädterstrasse to hunt you down, I've been so longing to talk to you again.'

He only half released her, keeping one arm about her waist and resting on the swell of her hip, to hold her close beside him.

'It's good to see you, Almscherl. And you look so ridiculously young. Whatever the vicissitudes of your life, you've certainly the secret of eternal youth.'

She did not know how much he knew of what had befallen her over the past two years, but his tone of voice managed to sound both admiring of her and concerned for her.

'I think I wouldn't mind ageing a little,' she replied. 'Then people might take me seriously as a person.'

'Do you think I don't take your seriously?' asked Klimt.

She sighed.

'I was very young then, you know,' she said.

'And I took advantage of your youth?' he asked.

'I don't know. Did you? I didn't feel taken advantage of . . . At any rate, I've no regrets.'

She left his side and went over to examine one or two of the paintings.

'A new departure for you, Gustl,' she said. '*En plein air*.'

'But not in your Pappi's style?'

'No. Certainly not. Nor Monet's.' She glanced back at him, over her shoulder. 'Van Gogh?' she asked.

'Ah!' he smiled. 'And going back a little further, Waldmüller.'

'Then they aren't so far from my father's style,' she told him approvingly. 'He was a great admirer of Waldmüller.'

She should have been warned by the very radiance of the canvasses, the warmth and colour in the natural sunlight – that and the fact that they were all of the same region, the dappled ripples of the Attersee, with places which were familiar to her – Nussdorf and Steinbach, with the slopes of the Schiffberg in the background.

But the warmth of the gallery and her present sense of joy mingled with excitement were leading her on. There was, moreover, the feeling that she did not want to return outside onto the Karlsplatz and the lonely traffic turmoil of the Kärntnerstrasse.

'I think now, Gustl . . .'

Turn back! Turn back before it's too late!

'I think . . . I made a mistake.'

'A mistake, Almschi?' Klimt asked.

She nodded, and looked at him.

'A dreadful mistake, Gustl.'

'When?'

She was warned by the careful upturn of his voice – the expression of indulgent amusement.

'In Venice,' she said. 'That afternoon.'

She felt quite faint.

'It was I who made the mistake, Almschi,' he told her. 'You had nothing to reproach yourself with.'

'I made a mistake,' she repeated. 'When you asked me to go away with you.'

She sat down in one of the seats. She struggled to pull out her handkerchief from the bag on her wrist.

He did not come to her. He said gently,

'It was a long time ago.' He hesitated, then said, 'I must tell you that I believe I have found happiness since then. That is, Emilie and I have found happiness. I hope you have, too.'

'But you're not married – you and Emilie Flöge?'

'No, we're not.'

She stared up at him in one last desperate, futile hope.

'I should have gone with you, that day,' she said. 'To Florence, or Rome.'

He smiled down at her calmly.

'No, Almschi. You certainly should not. It would have been disastrous. Particularly for you – the woman is always the one who is hurt most, particularly if she's as young as you were. And I – I'll freely admit it – would probably never have found the happiness I know now.'

'I'm glad you've found happiness,' she said.

She squeezed her handkerchief into a ball in the palm of her hand. Involuntarily she breathed in deeply. She tried to release the breath without sighing audibly.

'I'm making a fool of myself, aren't I?' she said.

'No, Almscherl,' he replied. 'You are paying me a very great compliment.'

She pushed her handkerchief into her sleeve.

'Yes, Gustl. I'm paying you a compliment.'

Dear God! Dear God! Dear God! At least He got her back to the Hohe Warte and her own room before she succumbed to tears of frustration and appalled embarrassment.

At the end of the first leg of Mahler's concert tour, she joined him for a week's holiday in Salzburg. They took the garden suite at the Hotel Nelbock so that he could rest and recuperate. Alma-Maria had learnt that Burckhard was living not far away, in a villa at St Gilgen.

She decided to visit him one afternoon, while Mahler rested. Anton drove her over to St Gilgen and then returned with the motor to Salzburg. At first, she had difficulty finding where Burckhard was staying. It was only after she had enquired at the lakeside inns and in several shops that, at last, a saddler suggested that she might be looking for the gentleman from Vienna who had taken the old forester's hut up in the woods. She followed the saddler's directions – up the path from the road, under trees, between boulders, winding upwards until the Wolfgangsee was a broad silver ribbon between the woodland slopes on which she was standing, and the more precipitous mountain slopes of the Schafberg stood opposite.

What she found at the end of the path shocked her. Burckhard came out of the hut to greet whoever was climbing up from the town.

'Alma! What brings you here?'

'We are staying in Salzburg. I was told you had a villa in St Gilgen.'

The hut was as shabby, the interior as dark as the cabin up on the Rofanspitze she remembered from long ago. His hair was greasy and unkempt; he had allowed his beard to grow; his eyes had become puffy and bloodshot. He wore a pair of *Lederhosen* which were stained and cracked, a ragged jacket, and a pair of muddied mountain boots. His shirt had a crumpled look, with black smears about the cuffs and collar suggesting that he never removed it.

'My villa,' he said, bowing and waving towards the hut. 'Forgive me, but you would not wish to go inside, I assure you.'

'May I sit out here, in the sunlight?' she asked.

'Of course. It is nobody's property. Dear God! You must have heard I was in a bad way for Mahler to let you come and see me!'

She sat down on a flat surface of rock at the path's edge.

'Not at all,' she told him.

She unpinned her hat and laid it carefully beside her to show him she had no intention of being sent away.

'Gustav was perfectly agreeable to my coming. He would have come himself, I dare say, except he has to rest these days. And I had not heard you were in a bad way. Have you recovered from ... from the last time we saw you?'

'Did you come up here to listen to me pitying myself?'

'Oh Max! Sit down here with me, and don't be so self-defensive! Have you got something to pity yourself for? Or are you just being melancholic?'

'I'm going blind, Alma.'

'Oh Max!'

She said it reproachfully, thinking for a moment that he had meant it figuratively.

'At first I found I couldn't open my eyes in the morning for two or three minutes. I panicked, I can tell you! Only I found I always could open them finally, so I became used to it. Then, slowly, it became five minutes, ten minutes. Now it's twenty, twenty-five minutes.'

'I'm sorry, Max.'

'I expect you think it's God's way of being merciful. I'm sure that's how Mahler would look on it. He'd say God is very kindly letting me get used to blindness by degrees.'

'Have you consulted anybody about it?' she asked.

'Why should I? I expect I'm a sick man anyway.'

'Emil Zuckerkandl would help you. He knows everybody in the medical world.'

'I don't want to consult anybody. May I remind you that *you* came up here of your own accord.'

'That was uncalled for, Max, my dear.'

'Yes. Yes, I'm sorry.'

He sat down on the stone seat beside her. He smelt sour as the very poor smelt sour. She forced herself not to move away from him. She even reached for his hand.

'Alma, do you believe in an afterlife?'

She and Mahler had been reading Plato's *Timaeus* together.

'I think I accept what Socrates said,' she told him. 'I don't know if it *is* true. But since wise men hope that it is so, it is best to direct one's life as if it were so.'

She had tried to avoid challenging him – and tried to give him a little hope. He rejected it.

'Wise and foolish men alike are fearful of personal annihilation. But that is what we all face. Do you know why animals creep into the undergrowth to die? It's so that they don't infect others of their species with their own fear.'

'Who has told you that you are going to die, Max?'

'Why should I live when I can't be sure of my own sanity from one day to the next, and I'm going blind?'

Mahler came himself to fetch her. She heard him calling her from below, and saw him coming up the path between the trees, leaning on his stick. Alarmed to see him over-exerting himself, she called on him to stop where he was, and went down to meet him. She told him the state Burckhard was in.

'We must take him back to Vienna with us,' Mahler told her promptly. 'There's no question about it.'

His decisiveness took her quite by surprise.

'Where is he?' he said. He would have walked on up, but she stopped him.

Usually, after he had taken much less exercise, he would ask her to feel his pulse or put her hand into his shirt to feel his heartbeat. There was sweat all over his face.

'You'd better sit down here and rest,' she said. 'I'll go back up and see if I can persuade him.'

The thought came to her as she climbed to the hut once more that the reason for Mahler having come in person, and having climbed the path, was that he was jealous. On the other hand, his concern for Burckhard was genuine enough.

She put her hand in Burckhard's, and told him that he was to come to the Hotel Nelbock with them, and that they would take him back to Vienna and look after him. Unworthily, she wondered how the porters at the hotel would react to the spectacle of him in his present condition.

'Come, Max,' she urged him.

Rather to her surprise, he stared at her as if trying to focus his eyes on her, then nodded.

'I suppose it would be best,' he said.

'Of course it would, dear Max.'

He allowed them to drive to the outskirts of Salzburg, under the shadow of the Kapuzinerberg. But then he suddenly reached over and tapped Anton on the shoulder and, before the others had realized what he was up to, told him to stop. Despite Alma-Maria's and Mahler's protests, he got down onto the road and set off without a word in the direction from which they had come. Mahler stood up and shouted to him in a clear, ringing voice,

'Burckhard! Burckhard!'

But Burckhard did not so much as turn his head. They watched until, having followed the curve of the road, he disappeared behind the hill.

Yet again, she had wept helplessly, on and on into the night.

After Mahler had set out on the second leg of his tour, Alma-Maria with Mutti, Gucki, and Miss Turner, went by train to Lienz and the South

Tirol, to look for a suitable summer residence to replace the house at Maiernigg. They travelled on to Toblach by local train and stayed there at the inn while they trudged through the highland snow which was still lying, though it was well into May, until they found a suitable house. At last they found one – a rambling farmhouse, built as an inn in the fifteenth century in the depths of the country, in a favourite spot of Mahler's midway between Toblach and the village of Altschluderbach, among the mountains. Alma-Maria arranged that they should live in the eleven upstairs rooms, while the proprietors, a sturdy, sober, prosperous peasant couple, the Trenkers, with a twelve-year-old adopted daughter, Marianne, should live on the ground floor. There was also a summer-house, slightly larger than the little composing house at Maiernigg, among some lakeside trees, two meadows' distance from the house, which looked across the water to the high peaks above the foot of the lake.

She had been driven from this new summer home to the sanatorium at Tobelbad, not far from Graz, by Mahler himself, with Mutti sitting with Gucki in the back seat of the motor-car. All the journey, Mutti and Mahler had kept up a stupid charade about how she needed above all quiet and rest. When they arrived at the Tobelberg – the castle which housed the sanatorium – they left the car by the gatehouse and walked up the short path to the steps which led to the arched main entrance. They stared up at the summits which seemed to ring the close, forest-clad valley: not the razor-sharp, glittering peaks of the Tirol they had left the previous day, but vast grey granite caps with slimy, craggy walls shrouded in a perpetual drizzle.

Mutti said to Gucki,

'It's lovely and quiet here. Your Muttichen will be able to have a nice rest, won't she?'

Gucki, anxious to please, tugged at Alma-Maria's coat and said,

'Muttichen, you will be able to have a nice rest here, won't you?'

Alma-Maria, close to tears – it had become almost a permanent condition – and anxious above all not to hurt the child any more than she had been hurt already, had said,

'Yes, my darling. I think I probably will.'

Rest! As if there had been anything else but rest at Toblach! There hadn't even been a piano to play on until three of them were delivered – two for the house, one for the summerhouse – forty-eight hours before Mahler arrived from Munich. The silence of the countryside had been so palpable it had clung to her ears like mud.

She had walked about the woodland and meadows, often striding out fiercely as she had so often resented doing when Mahler had dragged her along on his furious four-mile daily routine – but now seeking to shake off the nervous restlessness which possessed her so much of the time. Then came an afternoon when she was returning across the lower meadow, skirting the woodland, when she saw a young forester sawing logs in the shade of the trees. He was a strapping young fellow with close-cropped yellow curls above a broad, sweat-beaded face, and broad shoulders. His arms and thighs were thick yet sinewy. Sweat gleamed in the hair of his chest as he worked. Then she noticed that a button had come off the front panel of his *Lederhosen* so that it was hanging open. With a disturbing feeling of excitement, she realized she could see the shape, the protuberance straining into the cotton inside. His eyes met hers. He smiled. But she had raised her own eyes in time, no question of that. He paused, laying his saw on the log he was cutting up, called, '*Grüss Gott, meine Dame!*' and wiped his forehead with his rolled sleeve.

She smiled back and hurried on up the meadow. There had been nothing to be embarrassed about, nothing for shame. Except for the hunger which the spectacle had aroused in her; the disturbance which made her recreate in her mind's eye again and again what she had seen, so that she found herself burned up with regret that the boy should not have come to her, and pulled her to the ground dragging up her skirts as he did so. She could not stop herself from imagining the smell of his sweat, the power of his loins, the bulk she had seen shrouded now thrusting and stroking against her as it penetrated her more and more fully. The longing was so great, she needed to cry out, wanted to part her legs as if by doing so she could assist her imagination to create reality. But beyond the hunger there was nothing: no possibility or hope of satisfaction. Back in the house, she clambered upstairs, ignored Mutti and Gucki's cries of welcome on her return, locked herself in her room and threw herself across the bed face downwards, burying her fingers into the pillows, clawing at them, and crying and whimpering in her nauseous longing for this dreadful appetite to be taken from her.

Her period started shortly afterwards – the worst she had known. It was as if some small, ferocious beast had entered her and was gnawing with sharp little teeth and tearing at her. Aspirin only obscured the griping pains, so that they lurched at her as if out of a cloud, burying little fangs into her. She lay in bed. For almost two days she yelped with each onset of pain, clawing at her own hands. Somewhere, in the centre of the tearing, she knew she was being punished for the raw desire she had felt, that this pain was the corollary of lustfulness.

So she stayed in bed even when the pain had receded. There in the security of her upstairs room, she was safe from both desire and the punishment for desire. She had made no decision. She had not determined that she would spend the remainder of her life in bed. In fact, each day she was tolerably certain that she would be up and about the following day. She told Gucki so every time she came to her room to see her – until Gucki said scornfully,

'You always say that, Muttichen!'

It was just that when it had come to the point of making a decision whether she should get up or stay where she was, she had decided to stay where she was for just one day longer. So she had still been in bed when Mahler arrived from Munich. He had insisted that a doctor be called. Between them – Mahler, the doctor, Mutti – they had decided that she needed rest in a sanatorium.

'Frau Director Mahler? If you wouldn't mind stepping this way for a moment.'

It was Dr Gessner, Superintendent Dr Foerster's assistant. He was a young man – younger than she – and his air of Prussian hauteur and his steel-rimmed pince-nez suited neither his slender build nor his girlish complexion.

'... if you wouldn't mind conferring on me the inestimable favour of a word with me.'

He held open the door of his office. She shuffled through it obediently.

'Please be seated, Frau Director.'

She sat on the simple wooden chair in front of his desk, and held her hands clasped in her lap. There was a small dispensary curtained off to one side of the desk. The curtains were parted enough for her to see the big glass bottles with their different coloured liquids and tablets, the sets of drawers, the scales for measuring dosages, and the gas jet with its blue flame for melting sealing wax. It only needed a skull with night lights burning in the eye sockets, or a stuffed alligator hanging from the ceiling, and it might have been the cellar of one of the great alchemists of the fifteenth century – Agrippa, Albertus Magnus, or Johannes Faustus himself.

Dr Gessner sat down in the swivel chair on the opposite side of the desk.

'I hope you are comfortable here, in the Tobelberg Institute, Frau Director,' he said.

He pressed the tips of his fingers together.

'Quite comfortable, Herr Deputy Superintendent, thank you.'

'That is good.'

'I would feel even more comfortable if I were allowed to keep my clothes in my own room,' she said.

'Ah yes,' he replied. 'That is quite natural, of course. Probably you feel you are something of a prisoner without them, eh?'

He smiled at his own perspicacity.

'Something like it,' she told him.

'But you know that you are not a prisoner, Frau Director?'

'Do I?'

'And that you would be allowed your clothes as soon as you chose to ask for them?'

'Would I?'

'Of course.'

'Then why may I not keep them in my room?'

395

She was a prisoner, she was sure of it: she was being kept away from Mahler because her behaviour caused him distress and prevented him from concentrating on his work. Mutti was an accessory to her confinement here – Mutti who had loved Mahler as if he were a son almost as soon as she had really got to know him, who loved Mahler with a far deeper affection and concern than she had ever loved any of her own children.

'We do not encourage you wearing ordinary daytime dress, Frau Director, because we wish you to spend as much time physically at ease as is possible. Ladies' attire – particularly that of ladies of a certain class of society – is somewhat restrictive, you must admit. Ease of body, ease of mind – our motto, if you like ... Now, by keeping your clothes away from you, we create a buffer between a guest of ours and what might be a rash decision brought by homesickness, a longing to see her family and loved ones, or a moment's despair. The need to ask one of our nursing sisters to have the clothes brought to a guest provides a breathing space – a chance for recollected thought, do you see? It is rather like that space in time in the world of international diplomacy which occurs between the issue by a government of orders for mobilization and the actual commencement of hostilities.'

He beamed self-satisfaction at the aptness of the simile. For the first time, Alma-Maria noticed the glazed skin over the duelling scar across his forehead and cheek.

'Now, Frau Director,' he continued. 'Let us turn to the matter which I wish to discuss with you.'

He turned over a sheet of paper lying on the desk in front of him.

'According to a report here from Sister Christiane, you positively declined to take your afternoon exercise in the grounds yesterday, the day before ... Yes! And the day before that!'

'It was raining, Herr Deputy Superintendent. And I was permitted to wear only a wrapper over my gown.'

'I wouldn't have said it was raining exactly, Frau Director. Not yesterday. There was a mist hanging over the woods, certainly. But it wasn't raining.

'There was a thin rain,' Alma-Maria told him stubbornly. 'The most penetrating sort of rain. And one is not permitted – all right then: not encouraged – to wear one's outdoor clothes.'

'You were provided with galoshes. And Sister Christiane writes here that she offered you a perfectly adequate waterproof cape, which you refused.'

'It had been worn by other people,' she said.

'Frau Director, you must understand that Herr Superintendent Dr Foerster insists that the afternoon walk in the grounds is an intrinsic part of the treatment we offer our guests.'

He waited for her to reply. There was stillness – the sort of stillness one heard in the mist-soaked woods where there was no creaking of starched aprons, no muffled jangle of gaolers' keys. It was a stillness like that in the Stadtpark where once, so long ago, she had sat clutching her music case under Pappi's statue to talk to him.

'If Dr Foerster thinks it best . . .' she began humbly.

Dr Gessner beamed at her.

'That's better!' he exclaimed.

She knew exactly how he would look after he had become portly and middle-aged.

He opened a desk drawer above his knee.

'For being a good girl, eh? . . . we shall give you a reward!'

He handed a letter across the desk. She saw the postmark, Toblach-in-Altschluderbach, and the neat, orderly handwriting.

'So you will take a walk after your lunch, this afternoon?'

'Yes, Herr Deputy Superintendent.'

She stood up, clutching Mahler's letter. There was always the hope that he was writing to tell her he was coming to take her away from this place.

'Frau Director?'

Dr Gessner had also risen to his feet.

'Yes?'

Suddenly she was filled with anxiety.

'Sister Ingeborg has told Sister Christiane that you do not join in conversation with your fellow guests.'

'I prefer to be quiet, Herr Deputy Superintendent. I have my books.'

'Reading is good. But so is a little social intercourse. It is a question of maintaining a balance, isn't it, Frau Director? . . . You know that we have dancing every evening, in our conservatory – to the piano, or our phonogram? The gentlemen from the other wing come and join the ladies, and there are one or two gentlemen come up from Tobelbad village to take part in our merrymaking. I am sure that you, Frau Director, are an excellent dancer. What do you say?'

Alma-Maria said nothing.

'Well then,' he went on. 'Think about it, eh? There's no need to jump to a decision – a little progress at a time is best.' He went to the door and opened it for her, clicking his heels and bowing his head stiffly. 'Thank you for a most agreeable little chat, dear Frau Director,' he said.

She wandered out onto the gallery. There was no one there. She sat in a window alcove where she could look out across the drizzle-soaked garden. There she would read Mahler's letter until the bell went, summoning her to lunch in the dining room.

She tore open the envelope. She had intended doing it neatly, along the top. Instead, she ripped it raggedly across the address. She drew out the paper inside, creasing it as she did so.

397

My Almscherl – Your moods are very understandable to me. I myself have been through such states many, many times. This may surprise you, but it may at the same time be a consolation to you, and make it easier for you to come to terms with yourself. In between the brief moments of life of men and women of fine sensibility and intellect when they find artistic or spiritual fulfilment, there are the long barren stretches of existence which wring the soul with unanswerable longings. It is this ceaseless struggle and its torments that give the life of us privileged few its special character. I truly believe, my dear Almschi, that this is the meaning of all that has happened to you, of all that Providence has laid on you. It is a necessity of the growth of the soul and the forging of the personality. And you have so much of life still before you ...

She crumpled the sheets of paper in her fist. She could scarcely believe what she had read. *I myself have been through such states many, many times!* What exactly did he suppose had been happening to her? Locked, as he was, in the happy, secure sanctuary of his own creativity, he had exchanged all true sympathy with her in her condition for dry-as-dust formulae dredged out of his reading of Hellenic philosophy. She longed to shriek at him, to demonstrate the intensity of her anger at his obtuseness toward her. But she knew that by committing her feelings to a letter, she would only confirm the view he already held about her.

She screwed the paper into a hard little ball, and pushed it deep into the pocket of her shift.

She found the small wooden gate through the wall, behind the gardeners' shed disguised as a miniature Greek temple, at the farthest, uppermost part of the grounds. She had gone there to avoid the company of her fellow 'guests', and the surveillance of the attendants who walked like turnkeys between the moss-stained baroque statuary which lined the terraces above the rose walks. There was a danger – she knew it – of becoming more and more withdrawn: letters from Mahler begged her to 'make yourself well, my Almschili, that is everything, remembering that it is what a man makes of himself, by his untiring effort to live and to be, that is the permanent part of him'; they showed, if nothing else, that Dr Foerster's and Dr Gessner's reports on her progress were less than favourable. But there was peace where the forest slopes and the walls of the Institute met; where tree branches overhung like hands from outside reaching to take hers.

She withdrew behind the gardeners' shed to answer the call of nature – a simple operation when one was clad only in a shift and second-hand outdoor coat, and infinitely preferable to begging Sister Christiane's permission to return indoors for the purpose. And there was the door, without bolt and padlock, like the secret door in every children's story.

So she passed through it, closing it behind her most carefully and quietly. A short climb up a steep grassy bank heaped with pine needles which clung to her linen shift led to a narrow pathway beaten up the slope under the trees. It could have been made by man, but was more likely a deer run. She followed it away and above the Tobelberg Institute stubbornly. Though she knew there was no escape – where could she go without clothes or money? – the sense of freedom came over her so that she wanted to sing aloud like some heart-free country laundrymaid.

She had climbed for a half-mile or more, the skirt of her night-shift becomingly increasingly stained and dirty round the hem, when she came across the fountain. At least, they would have called it a fountain in the French fairy tales Pappi had so loved to tell her long ago. In the sunlight, under a gap in the trees, was a deep rock pool, mirror-still except at the end under the shadow of the mountainside where a mass of bubbles siphoned to the surface and splashed and sparkled, sending ripples into the stillness. Far above, on the rock face above the tree line, above the broken scree, and framed against the dazzling blue of the sky, the source of the fountain was visible – a stream of water falling down the cliff, to the naked eye, still and white as a thread before disappearing under the scree and the trees.

She took off the shabby summer coat given to her by Sister Ingeborg, spread it on the flat stone surface beside the pool and sat down in the sun. It was a place for strange and wonderful happenings: the sort of place where Madame le Prince de Beaumont might have imagined her dying Beast to have come for his last drink of water and where he saw Beauty's reflection staring up at him, her eyes filled with saving love. Even so, the voice took her sharply by surprise when it called, 'So there you are!' and she turned her head to the sunlight across the surface of the pool, and there, on the opposite side, was the most beautiful man she had ever seen.

She scrambled up into a half kneeling, crouching position. Thoughts tumbled and somersaulted through her brain: he had been sent to take her back to the sanatorium, or at least sent to spy on her; he had been sent by Mahler; that she was imagining him.

'You don't recognize me, Alma? Or must I call you *Frau* Alma now?'

He took off the feathered Alpine hat he had been wearing tilted on the back of his head. There had been so many people in her life, artists, musicians, opera-house staff, orchestra players; so many different circles of friends and acquaintances. But this one claimed the right to call her by her first name: and surely she wouldn't have forgotten those strong blond features, and the mesmeric blue eyes. He was, moreover, about her own age.

She stood up. Supposing he hadn't known she was a patient at Tobelberg? Hadn't expected to find her like this – undressed, bareheaded, with her hair down, like a mad woman in an opera, *Lucia di*

Lammermoor for instance? His tirolean jacket had been draped over his shoulders. He swung it, using his finger as a hook, and slung it over his arm. His sleeves were rolled to the elbow: he had strong arms, and the sunlight burned on the hairs which stood on them. A sword arm, a shield arm, she thought: the arms of one of those Burgundian Rhinelander heroes who had defied and beaten back the hordes of Attila the Hun in the golden age of Teutonic legend.

'It *was* a long time ago,' he called sympathetically. 'We met over dinner at the home of the *Hofrat* and Hofratin Dr Emil Zuckerkandl ... It was the night you rebuked Mahler for not reading a score by your friend Alexander von Zemlinsky.'

She remembered, first one thing, and then a whole succession of events.

'Walter Gropius!' she said.

What excuse could there possibly be for not remembering a man who had courted you? He had, of course, changed from a boy to a man in the intervening years.

'May I come over and join you?' he called.

'Of course.'

He jumped from rock to rock round the fountain pool. The sunlight on the water dazzled her.

'It's so bright!' she said, trying to excuse herself.

And he would be telling himself: look what she's brought herself to! She felt slightly faint, but she knew the only thing she could do was to face it straight on. She pressed her fingers against the bodice of her shift.

'They won't let us dress properly, in the Institute. Not until the evening.' She offered a little, self-deprecating laugh. 'I suppose they're afraid we might run away.'

He reached for her hand, held it for a moment as if to let her wonder what he was about to do, smiled at her, then bowed over her fingertips in the approved Viennese style.

'It is very good to see you, Alma,' he told her.

He released her fingers with just a hint of reluctance. He had been an arrogant, good-looking boy when she had last seen him, who hadn't quite known how to dress the desire he had felt for her in civilized raiment. And she had not been looking for a boy; in fact, she recalled, she had found his manner irritating.

'I know you'll believe I'm merely flattering you when I tell you that you are even more beautiful than you were when we last met.'

'That is ridiculous,' she replied.

The hem of her shift was grey and damp; there were even pine needles clinging in the hair which fell about her arms.

'You have a beauty of spirit now, which you only learn from being alive. It is now informing the physical beauty which was there before. I tell you, Alma, I came looking for you eagerly. But I had no idea you were going to look the way you do.'

'I'm sure you didn't!' she laughed.

But he refused to laugh back. He held her eyes with his.

'I'll dare to say this: that the beauty you now possess could only have come through suffering.'

She nodded because the suffering at least was true, and because she did not know what to say else.

'How did you find me out?' she asked.

'I've been attending a series of meetings in Graz – work, you know. Somebody in the hotel I'm staying at mentioned that you were up here, near Tobelbad. Then it seemed as if everybody in Graz had heard that you were at the Tobelberg Institute. At first, I didn't mean to come to try to visit you. I wasn't at all sure you'd want to see me – I don't suppose you found me a very nice young man. Looking back, I don't think I *was* a very nice young man. But the more I thought about you, the more I realized I hadn't any choice.'

'Walter!'

'I've thought about you often, you know, Alma – wondering whether you'd found what you wanted. Whether you were happy.'

She had to sit down again on the stone platform. He squatted down near her, but not so close as to make her feel trespassed upon.

'How did you find me *here?*' she asked.

'Oh! By accident. I went up to the Institute and asked if I might see you. A pleasant young medical man who comes from the same part of Westphalia as I do said that you were taking exercise in the grounds. I couldn't find you, so I let myself out of a back gate and decided to walk back to Tobelbad through the woods.'

'You didn't tell anybody that you hadn't found me?'

'No.'

'That's just as well. They'd make sure I wasn't allowed to come here again if they ever found out. You wouldn't tell them, would you, Walter?'

'Certainly not. . . . So you come here to play truant?' he asked.

'This is the first time. Honestly.'

'Tell me. Would you run away if they let you have your clothes?'

'If you had to sit up to your neck in boiling sulphur baths every morning, and drink buttermilk four times a day, you'd run away,' she replied.

He laughed.

'I certainly would,' he said.

'Are you a great and successful architect now?' she asked. 'Have you got what *you* wanted?'

His shirt and striped jacket, his cream trousers and two-tone shoes were all well and expensively made, she noted. But then he had always been wealthy – so much wealthier than Mahler when she had first known him. That was why Mutti had favoured him until she had succumbed to Mahler's particular brand of little-boy charm.

'What cathedrals and opera houses have you built?'

He shook his head. 'I'm afraid factories and engineering shops are my *métier*,' he said. 'The project we were discussing in Graz was a hydroelectrical plant to serve Styria and the Dalmatian coastal regions. Electrical dynamo plants will be the cathedrals of the twentieth century as railway stations were the cathedrals of the nineteenth . . .'

She was partly listening to him, but only partly. The sunlight was dancing round his head. She thought of him as Wagner's Siegfried, but then she changed her mind. Siegfried was a beautiful hero warrior, but he was also a blunderer, who was easily deceived and misled. Walter Gropius's face was sensitive and keenly intelligent. Siegfried would have laughed only in the midst of carnage, in the high singing of his Teuton blood. The new Gropius could laugh at himself and at her without any unkindness.

'That afternoon when I told you . . . told you that I was going to marry Mahler . . .' She had interrupted him. Now she had to think what she was about to say. 'I didn't think you'd ever want to see me again.'

'I've never stopped wanting to see you. I've never stopped wanting to know what had become of you. I knew you were in Vienna, of course. I knew when you became a mother. And when you went to New York. Berta Zuckerkandl writes to me. I know you lost your elder daughter. I was deeply sorry to hear of it . . . What I wanted to know was how you really were. If you were happy.'

'I'm happy for seeing you, Walter.'

'Truly?'

'Of course. I'm only sorry to let you find me in such a mess.'

And it was true that she felt happy. Or at least she had experienced a quickening of joy, like the first movement of a child in her womb.

'What sort of a mess?' he asked. 'Do you mean the state of your appearance . . . or something else.'

'My appearance,' she said. 'But something else as well.'

He stared at her. 'I would be happy and privileged if you thought you could talk to me,' he told her, 'about the things which mattered.'

'You're very kind, Walter. But not this afternoon . . . The sky is far too bright,' she said with false gaiety. 'Until today – well, yesterday, to be truthful – it's been cloudy all the time. Nothing but mist and drizzling rain for three weeks.'

'How is your little daughter?'

Alma-Maria wondered if the false note she had introduced had driven him back to the formality of polite inquiries.

'Gucki? Oh, she's very happy. We had to leave her, of course, when we went to New York. A hotel suite is no place for a child, so she stayed with my mother and her nanny. I'm afraid she's much more attached to them than to me.'

'Don't you mind that?' he asked.

'Sometimes. But it's turned out for the best, hasn't it? I mean, with my being here.'

He said nothing for a moment. She was afraid she had, yet again, blundered into disaster.

'Alma, may I come and see you again? Tomorrow, for instance?'

She could scarcely hide her relief.

'Don't you have to go home?'

'My work in Graz is finished for the moment,' he said. 'I have a few days to do as I please.'

'Oh Walter! I would like that so very much!'

She would have liked to have told him how beautiful he was. Men were always allowed, even encouraged, to tell women they were beautiful.

'Walter, would you do me a great favour?'

'What is that?'

'Bring me cigarettes – and a bottle of Benedictine if you can find one.'

He laughed outright. 'Your medical advisers don't approve of ladies smoking and drinking, I dare say,' he said.

'They don't approve of anything except buttermilk, lettuce, and sulphur baths.'

'I will bring them. In the meantime ...'

He held out his cigarette case.

'Take them all,' he told her. 'No. Take all but one, then I have one to smoke on my way back to the village.'

As she filled her hand with his Turkish cigarettes, she said,

'I'll have to be ever so careful with them. I haven't brought my case with me. It's days since I smoked a cigarette.'

For a moment, she thought he might lend her his own case. He didn't, and she had to drop the cigarettes into the pocket of her shift.

'I suppose electrical power stations really are rather like the old cathedrals,' she said. She was so afraid she had just sounded like a greedy child asking for sweets; now she wanted to restore herself in his good opinion. 'I mean, both are built so that people can draw on resources outside their own natural strength.'

'I couldn't have put it better myself,' he said.

She wondered if he were mocking her.

'I'd better go back,' she said. 'I don't want them to become suspicious about where I've been. Will you walk back with me some of the way?'

'Certainly. And where shall we meet tomorrow?'

'Up here, if it's as fine as it is today ... I really do want to hear about your work, Walter.'

She saw again the faint amusement on his face. Before she could attempt to demonstrate her intelligent interest in industrial architecture, he said,

'May I ask why you are a patient here?' He offered her his arm for her to rise to her feet. 'You are in very good looks – and in reasonably good spirits, I'd say.'

She sighed.

'You don't have to tell me,' he said.

'That's all right. It's no secret. There was Putzi's death and I had a miscarriage, and two seasons in New York away from Gucki. And on top of that, as you probably know, Mahler isn't supposed to be in the best of health.'

Why had she done it? Why had she let fall that one drop of bitterness? She would never have done it under consideration: uttered that single word, 'supposed'.

'I imagine your own misfortunes, and the need to respect your husband's creative genius, have put you under a great deal of stress.'

'Yes. Something like that. To be honest, I have been rather distraught from time to time.'

'Very understandably, under the circumstances. And I imagine your husband is too busy to be able to look after you, the way you need to be looked after.'

'Thank you, Walter – for being understanding. And for wanting to see me again. But I'd better go back alone, now. We'll see each other tomorrow.'

That night, to the surprise of the nurses and of Dr Gessner, she dressed for dinner, and afterwards went to the conservatory. Dr Gessner in particular congratulated her on showing signs of recovery. She even danced to the strangulated sound of the phonogram music cylinders. She allowed herself to be chosen as partner by a courtly, somewhat elderly Quartermaster-Major of Uhlans who waltzed with drill-book perfection. Between dances, she sat out with him among the ferns and listened to his account of the injustices of Providence: how, while serving with Imperial Headquarters Staff in Bosnia, his young soldier servant had been assassinated, shot down in a dusty, dirty village street in Novi-Pazar by a revolver-wielding, Serbian so-called student. Alma-Maria listened patiently to the Major's description of 'what a dear boy' the soldier servant had been. The tears he allowed to accumulate behind his monocle testified to the breakdown which had resulted in his being hastily consigned to the obscurity of a mountain valley in deepest rural Styria.

Alma-Maria was content to stay with him, dance with him, sit with him, letting him talk on and on. She nodded sympathetically from time to time, paid sufficient attention to convince the poor old fellow that she was listening to him while devoting most of her mind to Gropius's miraculous appearance that afternoon, and the prospect of seeing him again the following day. She had been, she realized, drawn to the edge of feeling happy.

In the morning, however, she was beset with fears. Intimations of joy turned to apprehension and folly. Why had she been so utterly convinced that the day was going to be as golden as the previous day? When she peered out of the lounge windows overlooking the garden terraces, she could see, though the sun was shining, that there were puffy white clouds with inner edges of grey drifting between the rounded, glacial mountain summits at the head of the valley. And there was the question of time. Because the only timetable in the sanatorium was set by meals, baths, and outdoor exercise, she had not thought to set an exact hour for their meeting by the fountain. A dread came over her that they might miss each other.

By the time she descended into the infantile helplessness of the sulphur baths, she was in a state approaching panic. Perhaps he wouldn't come at all. Something might happen to prevent him – or her escaping from the grounds. Perhaps he had seen the state she was in, emotionally as in appearance, and had felt a need to play along with her in order to save himself embarrassment. At lunchtime, she was even less inclined to take her buttermilk, lettuce, and single slice of *Wurst* than usual; she had to fight back a rising nausea which, if she had yielded to it, would have prevented her from being allowed out at all. As she drew the shabby second-hand summer coat over her shift, she was already beginning to weep from disappointment.

She should have known better. From the moment she stepped out of the battered, neglected wooden gate behind the gardeners' shed into the sloping woodland a calmness of spirit enfolded her. She climbed upwards, the grass, still dew wet under the shadows of the trees, brushing her bare ankles. From the shadow, she moved into joyous warmth as she skirted the massive trunks of fallen trees.

He was there, waiting for her, sitting on the flat stone platform, his jacket spread under him, his collar and tie removed, his shirtsleeves rolled right up his arms to the sinewy thickness of his biceps. The hair on his chest, visible in the 'V' of his opened shirt, was bleached by the sun.

He stood up to greet her.

'If I had been blessed with your father's or even your stepfather's talent, I would remember how I saw you just now, coming up there – the white figure among the trees, the hair like spun gold as she moved from shadow into light.'

She had secured her hair in a single heavy plait. It fell forward over her shoulder. The heat beat off the rocks as she stood letting him look at her.

'But you do paint,' she said.

'I paint as an engineer should paint – to demonstrate, not interpret.

If I were to try to paint you, I wouldn't say what I wished to say.'

Alma-Maria was reminded of Mitzi Uchatius. She tried to dismiss her from her mind.

'I'd sit for you if I could,' she told him.

He shook his head. 'We must always stick to what we can do properly,' he said. 'I have run your errand for you, you see?'

He indicated the small brown paper parcel on the rock beside his jacket. She would have liked to have told him the truth: that in her excitement at the thought of seeing him again, she had forgotten her request. She was afraid he might not have believed her, so she kept silent. He reached for her hands, and she held them out for him to take. In looking at her, he was looking into the sun; his stare was that of a sailor scanning a far horizon, an explorer, or a visionary. His colouring was hers: golden and blue-eyed; they would have made a perfect match, like Eva and Walther von Stolzing whose love was endorsed and celebrated in the final act of *Die Meistersinger*. The great quintet sounded in her brain, in the heat from the rocks: its opening line – *Selig wir die Sonne meines Glückes lacht* – was so appropriate.

He drew her down onto his spread jacket. Her coat dropped from her shoulders. He squatted beside her.

'I don't believe you only design factories and electricity stations,' she said. 'Even if you do say they're twentieth-century cathedrals. You're an artist. I can tell you're an artist. Your eyes aren't those of an engineer.'

'You mean, you think I draw or paint imaginary cities and landscapes when nobody is watching?' he asked her.

She nodded, smiling.

'A secret vice?'

'A secret virtue,' she replied. 'I'm sure you have a poet's vision of the ideal, even if you won't admit it.'

'I have an ideal,' he said, 'But I don't think it would raise me in your estimation. You see, to me the machine is the ideal. The machine is my philosophy – even my God.' He sat down beside her, stretching his legs in front of him. 'As you perceived all those years ago,' he went on, 'I'm not in the least like Mahler. I feel no need to search for the great spiritual meaning of life – whatever that might mean. There is the machine. The machine proclaims a purpose, and it fulfils that purpose. A chair if it is a true chair is that object upon which a person may sit to greatest effect – to rest, to work, either with appropriate economy of action. At the same time, by looking at the chair, one may deduce its purpose and its right use. You may do the same with the world around you.'

'It sounds very cold and ruthless to me,' Alma-Maria said. 'Not at all what I expected.'

'I warned you, you wouldn't approve of me. I would say it was truth stripped of illusion.'

'Don't you ever feel there's something beyond that?' she asked. 'A longing for what is beautiful – a summons to paradise? Because that's what I think it is when people see something which is beautiful. It's a glimpse of paradise – of what lies beyond.'

She didn't feel she could express it very well. When Mahler had suggested to her that moments of great joy, of ecstasy, were as if the curtain dividing the mundane world and God's primal vision had been tweaked aside for an instant, she had felt as though he had presented her with a fundamental truth.

'The nearest we can ever know to paradise is the well organized state,' said Gropius. 'The social organization which endures to protect and benefit the race which forms it. Another machine, you see?'

Alma-Maria crossed her legs, hiding her feet under the grubby hem of her shift.

'I don't like that,' she said. 'It makes us all sound like animals.'

'You don't think nations survive by offering one another brotherly love, do you?' Gropius asked. 'I seem to remember that the last time we were together, your great philosophical hero was Nietzsche.'

'I believe in love,' she said quietly, staring into the brilliance of the pool.

'Why should you?' he asked. 'Have you ever really known it?'

The brutality of the question shocked her. She told him the truth: 'Yes. I knew it with my father.'

'But not with Mahler?'

'That is not a question you have any right to ask, Walter.'

'I always suspected Mahler of being one of those people who loves humanity but who hasn't the first idea of how to love an individual human being.'

'That is dreadfully unfair, Walter! You know nothing about him.'

'I know what everybody knows – that his orchestras admire him, respect him, and are afraid of him, but that not a single individual musician loves him!'

He took her silence for agreement.

'I know he regarded you as a possession. The Jew only knows he exists by turning everything into a possession he can count up as if it were a money bag.'

'I'm going back to Tobelberg,' said Alma-Maria.

She pulled herself to her feet. She would have to leave the brown paper parcel of cigarettes and Benedictine. Otherwise the gesture would lose its point.

He stared up at her without replying. For a terrible few moments, she thought he was letting her go. She had scrambled off the rock platform when he called after her,

'Alma! Listen to me!'

She turned. 'What?' she asked angrily.

'Forgive me – please! I'm still so jealous of Mahler! It's been eight years almost. Yet when I heard in Graz that you were here, without him, nothing could keep me from coming to search you out ... Please forgive me.'

'It doesn't matter,' she told him in a dull voice.

'It matters,' he urged. 'It matters terribly to me. I can't begin to tell you how disappointed I was feeling yesterday, when I thought I wasn't going to be able to find you. And then, when I came along here, quite by chance ... I tell you, Alma, you could have convinced me then about ecstasy, and glimpses of paradise! And now, by behaving stupidly, I've thrown it all away.'

'Not stupidly,' she said. 'The trouble is that there is some truth in what you're saying. It hasn't been all happiness by any means. I'm not even sure I'd have taken the road I did if I'd known what it was going to be like. But he's not how you described him, either. He's never treated me as a possession. He can be very gentle and kind. And I do love him ... What I mean is – things are not altogether his fault. I'd hate you to think that.'

Gropius nodded sympathetically.

Then she said,

'You don't need to feel jealous, Walter. Not in the way you mean ... My dear, I couldn't have walked off down there and left you.' She held out her arms to him.

'I suppose I felt angry at finding you here,' he said. 'As if he was responsible for putting you here.'

'That is unjust, you know,' she said.

'I do know.'

She leaned against him, cheek to cheek in his embrace, letting him feel against his body the nakedness of her breasts under her shift.

'I've been faithful to Mahler up to now,' she said. 'It is very important to me that you believe that. Do you promise that you believe it? ...'

The same night after dinner, she returned to the conservatory and allowed herself to be discovered there by the Quartermaster-Major of Uhlans once more. During the first waltz – a lady from the village was earning her ticket to salvation by playing the piano for the 'guests', simpering all the while a pretence that she was enjoying her own poor performance at what Dr Gessner had called 'the merrymaking' — the Quartermaster-Major asked conventional questions about the medical progress Alma-Maria was making. By the time they were seated once more among the potted ferns, she was dwelling in her own mind on Gropius and her own excitement, or even passion. There was, surely, no question of Mahler hearing about what had gone on between them. Gropius wasn't going to behave like some nineteen-year-old Cornet of Dragoons, boasting to his friends about the conquest he had made in Tobelbad, of all obscure places. In the meantime, the Quartermaster-Major's voice was droning on about how the German peoples were going to have to give the Serbs 'and all those damned South Slavs a hiding they won't forget in a hurry. They've got to be taught the hard way, the Balkans aren't their private playground, eh?'

Alma-Maria saw Dr Gessner standing by the piano. She excused herself from the Quartermaster-Major's side.

'Dr Gessner?'

'Frau Director?'

'I intend to tell Anneliese-Marie to bring my clothes – all my wardrobe – to my room tomorrow.'

Dr Gessner looked down at her with a thin, cheerless smile.

'Has our gallant Major of Uhlans been inspiring you with thoughts of mutiny, dear Frau Director?'

'Not in the least. Nor do I intend any mutiny – or even to run away. I would like, quite simply, to dress once I have had one of your loathsome baths so that I feel like a grown woman once more.'

Dr Gessner nodded at her. 'Well, Frau Director, I think I may say that when I next write a report to the esteemed Herr Director Gustav Mahler, I shall be able to say you are making great progress – very satisfactory progress ... You shall have your wardrobe, Frau Director, I promise.'

She was unable to stay in the pool for long. The water had stabbed into her like a knife; it must have fallen directly from the streaks of snow which, even in late August, lurked under the summit rocks out of the sunlight. Gasping, she clambered up onto the flat stone surface above the pool's edge. The rock platform was hot to the touch. She spread her petticoat out to lie on, the water from her wet hair falling in streams. A stream of water poured quite obscenely from her pubic thatch, and she was glad Walter could not see it. The sudden changes of temperature had raised her nipples stiff and erect, but the warmth of the sunlight was balm on her skin. She lay back feeling the hardness and the heat of the rock under the damp petticoat. Above her, a myriad pine needles shone in glory.

Walter was still in the water on the farther side of the pool. It had been his idea they should swim. She had allowed him to undress her, down to the sheerness of her Fifth Avenue lingerie which she had put on deliberately to provoke him. He came swimming across to join her, smoothly, powerfully, with scarcely any splash. He was like the old Mahler in his athletic disregard of the water's coldness. He differed from Mahler in that, instead of Mahler's wiry physique, he had the strength which came from a powerful build. In a way, he was the living embodiment of his Philosophy of the Machine – he was superb to watch in the exact economy of his movements. She sat up again, letting her legs dangle over the side of the platform as he approached. She lifted one knee and hugged it, knowing very well what she was revealing to his gaze by doing so. She smiled down at him to let him know that she knew. He pulled himself up out of the water by his arms, the water streaming off him, glittering in the sun. She couldn't help laughing.

'Oh Waltchen! You should be ashamed of yourself!'

It was the same, of course, as had happened to her with the hardening of her nipples.

'Waltchen!' she repeated as he stood before her.

She scrambled round into a kneeling position before him. She felt the extent of his tumescence, running her fingertips along it.

'You're so proud! You're proud of it! You've got no shame at all!'

She bent forward, letting his erection lie against her cheek as she kissed the gleaming mat of his hair. In the damp, there was the faintest hint of male sweat. She grasped him round his hips, holding his strength in her arms. She darted her tongue along the vein-ridge hardness. Hardly moving her lips from it, she said,

'Take me, Waltchen!'

She released him and lay back on her petticoat, opening her thighs to receive him. She reached up her arms to where he was standing. He came over her, obscuring the dazzlement which had been in her eyes. There was no clumsy weight on her as she lifted her legs and embraced his with them, only the strength of his penetration of her, and the clean warmth of his breath on her ear. He moved with that same controlled power, that efficiency with which he had driven himself through the water, bringing her excitement on in a single, smooth crescendo.

'Yes! Yes! Oh dear Christ, yes!'

Her body – that same body which could so afflict her during her periods – was now at one with her being, endeavouring to draw him in, to hold him. Framing its spasmodic clutching at him was a circle of the most intense pleasure she had ever experienced – more than with any of the others. It devoured all else in her and about her. It robbed her of the power of speech so that she couldn't even cry out, but had to make do with a noisy exhalation of squeezed breath. When the consummation came, it was only just in time to prevent her from being overwhelmed with panic lest she couldn't take breath fast enough. Her final, triumphant gasp or shout was at the very end of her lungs. She heard it separate from her, panting and gasping as it rose up into the branches above her, startling the birds who rustled and rattled away out of the cover of the pine needles.

Gropius rolled over, and lay down beside her. But he did not take his arms from round her. Beyond him was the sound of the mountain waters running and bubbling. They were caught up in the harmony of the world, she decided – one golden moment of Plato's notion of heaven. She was still panting for breath and, at the same moment, glorying in the wonder of her own physical release: it was as if everything that had needed to be healed had been healed. She turned her head to look at him, and he was all golden in the sunlight. He looked back at her. They kissed, and she could not have said who had kissed whom. She gazed into his face.

'I wish we could go back. Back and back,' she said.

'Do you think things might have been different?'

'If the me who is lying here now had been the me that was then – yes. I would have made different decisions ... If I had known how important some things were to me.' She gave a little laugh and reached her hand to fondle his groin where it was still sticky from lovemaking. 'I don't mean just this,' she said. It was wonderful to talk freely. 'You know Mahler did not want me to go on composing when we were married?'

'And you agreed to that condition?' Gropius asked.

'I didn't realize what it would mean to me. But it has hurt.' She raised her head, resting her chin in her hand. 'It was very foolish,' she said.

'He was so much older,' said Gropius. 'He should have had more understanding than that.'

'Love is the same isn't it? Music isn't music unless it's performed; I'm so hungry for love sometimes – just as I'm hungry to play my own music. Sometimes I feel I'm dragging myself around the world after Mahler in just the same way as I drag my music around.'

'Do you take your music about with you?' he asked.

'Oh yes. It goes with me everywhere. I suppose I felt I could deny myself when I married Mahler, for the sake of his genius – just like a nun denies herself for the sake of God's Holy Spirit. The trouble is – as one of our maids told me, at home, when I was quite a young girl – I was not born to be a nun.'

He placed his hand round her breast, stroking her nipple with the tip of his thumb.

'But it is true,' she said. 'Mahler *is* a genius. I didn't think so when we married, but I am sure of it now.'

Such an admission mitigated any residual feeling of disloyalty in what she had been saying and inferring.

She placed her own hand over his, retaining it on her breast.

'You see, I have to tell myself that really it was my fault, not his.'

'But you were young.'

'Oh yes! Terribly young ... I know I shouldn't say it, but just at this moment I'm so in love with you, my Walter. And the trouble is, I'm not young any more. It's a grown woman – one who has loved and suffered – telling you.'

He put his arms about her. He had risen up hard again.

'Oh Walter! Yes! I could die with you loving me. I could, my darling! I could!'

She was going insane in a new direction. What was going to happen? She didn't know Gropius: she hadn't dared even to ask him if he was married. All she knew about him was that he had been a very conceited, sulky young man, and he'd shown he was still capable of jealousy. And yet here she was, in his arms, pouring out confessions of love for him. But in the heat of lovemaking, she could not stop herself.

'I do so want to give you pleasure,' she managed to gasp in his ear as the tide of excitment rushed about her to possess her as before. 'I want to be so abandoned for you, my darling!"

There was no drug as effective as love, she was discovering. It was not only the boredom and humiliations of invalidism which were being swept away, nor the pent-up frustration of months and years, but all her fears and miseries and hatreds dwindled away like a complete relief from life's pain. The whole of existence was magically contained by the throbbing, perspiring, indescribable moment. Nor was it confined to the thrill of being physically possessed, the seconds in which she arched her back off the rock so that she might be attached to him more tightly, might feel his driving pressure inside her more acutely. When, once again, it was all over, with the pleasure of climax ebbing away like the fast withdrawal of a running tide, he continued to hold her closely in his powerful arms.

When he had helped her to dress, and she had tidied herself as best she could, she walked with him through the woods down to Tobelbad village. As long as they were in the cover of the trees and the path permitted, they walked with their arms round one another, stopping frequently to kiss greedily. Several times, they confessed their love for one another, she, for her part, thrillingly aware of detaching herself from both past and future.

They drank coffee and liqueurs in the garden of a village inn. In the gloaming, he walked her back to the Tobelberg Institute. Once again, they took a long, sheltered way round through the woods, stopping to embrace and kiss. She had never known lovemaking like it – so free from any sense of guilt or furtiveness or the demands of time. By now, with the light failing, she would be missed. She found herself testing herself to see whether she cared, or felt in any way responsible, and there was nothing.

'What will you do?' she asked. 'Will you be able to get back to Graz tonight?'

'I will find somewhere in the village, probably.'

'Then you'll be ready for me, tomorrow! Oh Waltchen! I shall think about you being so near. I shall wake up in the middle of the night and know that you're near me.'

'I shall wake and think of you, alone in your hospital bed,' he said.

'You'll behave yourself – won't you? When you're thinking about me? You'll keep yourself for tomorrow?'

He was walking on the narrow path behind her. She felt his arms round her, gathering her to him. As he kissed her neck under her hair, behind her ear, she pressed herself into his lap and moved her hips to and fro against him.

'How do you know I can wait until tomorrow?' he said.

'You have to use self-control,' she told him with a laugh. 'No you don't. You don't need to have any self-control with me.'

She scooped her skirt up over her arm. She felt the slight chill of the mountain evening air on her exposed parts between the tops of her stockings and the flounce of her petticoat bunched above her waist. She felt his hand spread over the curve of her rear. Just beyond them, a little below, through the trees was the wall and garden gate of the sanatorium. She pressed herself into his hand; the thought of lovemaking within a few metres of the sanatorium added to her sense of abandonment. He dropped his hand. For a moment, she did not know what he was doing. Then she realized he was kissing her – kissing her between the walls of her rear, his tongue exploring her.

'Walter! Walter! Walter!'

She quivered with the pleasure he was giving her.

'I don't think Herr Superintendent Doctor Foerster is going to be very pleased with you, Frau Director,' Sister Christiane informed her, catching her as she climbed the stairs to her room. Under the concealment of her skirts, Alma-Maria's legs were still trembling. They felt as if they might turn to water at any moment.

'I went for a walk on the mountain,' she replied. 'It was further than I'd intended. I'm quite tired now. But it was beautiful up there; I'm sure Dr Foerster will agree that it has done me a world of good.' She smiled her most dazzling smile. It was a piece of equipment she had not used for a long time. 'The problem is, dear Sister, I feel so well now, thanks to the excellent treatment, and particularly your kindness – the kindness of all of you who are looking after me – that I've been longing to go out and explore in the fresh air.'

It worked – thank God! Sister Christiane gave a coy smile as if somebody had given her an unexpected birthday bouquet.

'I'll see what we can do to explain to the Herr Superintendent, Frau Director,' she said very friendlily and conspiratorially.

'I know I shall sleep well, tonight,' Alma-Maria told her. 'Goodnight, Sister – and I am grateful for all you have done for me, believe me ...'

Three mornings later, the sun was still shining. Dr Gessner asked that she should call on him in his office after she had taken her bath. He was extremely affable.

'On Herr Superintendent Doctor Foerster's instructions, Frau Director Mahler, I wrote to your husband expressing our gratification at the alteration in your health and general disposition.' He smiled approvingly. Even before he spoke again, she knew what he was about to say. 'I fear that we shall not be having the pleasure of your presence among us as our guest for many more days, Frau Director. I know one gentleman at least who is going to be quite devastated ...'

She was seized with dread. Of course, they were bound to have found out about Gropius staying down in Tobelbad; in the confinement of this narrow mountain valley, the presence of a stranger would not remain a secret.

'I refer, as I'm sure you realize, *gnädige* Frau Director, to our honoured Quartermaster-Major of Uhlans, Franz Goerderer. You've won a heart there, I know. And I'm afraid you're going to break it.'

'Indeed I hope not, Dr Gessner!'

She managed to sound quite shocked and affronted at the suggestion she might have connived at a flirtation. She wondered how it was possible that a man as young as Dr Gessner could be so arch and priggish.

'I meant no offence, *gnädige* Frau!' he exclaimed hastily.

'I have taken none, I assure you, Dr Gessner.'

So that was all right. Dr Gessner opened the drawer of his desk.

'With the Frau Director's permission,' he said.

Was the show of formality the result of her being restored to health? she wondered – or because she had dared to offer the suggestion of a rebuke to the pompous young man?

He passed a letter to her across the desk. She recognized the familiar handwriting, and there was the postmark, Toblach-in-Altschluderbach. She felt a new sense of apprehension, of dread, coming over her.

'I dare say you will learn from that Herr Director Mahler's intentions regarding your return home,' he said.

She took the letter out into the garden to read it. As she stepped onto the terrace walk and smelled the fresh air and the woods, she had the sensation she had experienced sometimes when she was asleep: of slipping out of one dream and into another. She sat down and tore open the envelope. Had they found out about Gropius and herself? Had she been spied on in her walks up through the woods? Had they written to Mahler to warn him, or to hint at or suggest to him what had been going on? She felt her stomach tighten into a fist.

'My dearest Almscherl,' she forced herself to read:

You have been behaving splendidly. Dr Foerster has written to me in person to tell me all about it. I know how much you have suffered both mentally and physically ... You have borne all with such patience and fortitude – and with such a selfless concern for my well-being. If I were to remember nothing else through all eternity, I would remember your loving concern for me throughout our journey back from America; that you never did anything for your own comfort and everything for mine. Oh my brave little Almscherl ...

She found she had stopped breathing. She took a panicky gulp of breath.

Dear God! Did he really mean it? Of course he did. He might be utterly self-oriented but he never knowingly told an untruth. If anybody had been dishonest, it had been herself. She had played the dedicated nurse-secretary-companion, concealing from him the urgency of her own appetites and her festering resentment at their unfulfilment. That surely was what had brought her to this predicament. He had been taken in by her show of concern just as a child might be taken in by the nursemaid's show of affection in taking him to see the animals in the zoo when all her real desire is to meet there her soldier-sweetheart.

... And now Dr Foerster tells me with what stoicism you resigned yourself to his Spartan regimen. It gave me so much anxiety, knowing what a contrast it must be to everything you appreciate and enjoy, even if you understood that it all be of benefit in the long run. Oh my Almschililitzi! Now for the regrets and the apologies. Being here alone has given me time to think about what you wrote in your last letter. I wrote the things you complain of without thinking properly, because I believed you knew enough of me and my ways not to be wounded by me. I was so sure that you could see that I live only for you and our little Guckerl.

But now I realize how dreadfully smug and priggish my letters to you must have seemed. Your rebuke was so mild, yet I've felt like a husk, a shell which contains no living entity within. The emptiness without you is *hideous*. I haven't dared to venture down to the little composing house you obtained so thoughtfully for me. I'm afraid lest you left just so much of your spirit there to rebuke me for my stupidity.

My Luxerl! I'm so devoured by self I scarcely know which way to turn. All I long for is to have you at my side so that we can enjoy life together as the good comrades we have been in the past – living and loving together as the flowers of a tree growing ever higher, falling in season only to bud and burst forth in even greater splendour than before ...

She could have laughed if it hadn't all been so pitiful. His idea of apologizing was to appeal to her for sympathy. It was so, so typical of him.

I must be in Leipzig tomorrow (Saturday) for rehearsals – for the performance of the Sixth on Monday. I don't have to tell you that my mind will be filled with thoughts of you during the first movement and the *andante*. Then it's on to Munich for further discussion of arrangements for the first performance of our *Faust* symphony in September. I'll be returning to Vienna by train on Thursday after-noon. I shall be staying with your parents overnight. One word from you, and I'll come to fetch you on Friday and take you back home with me direct from Graz. I'll telephone for Anton to bring the car to meet us at Toblach station.

A thousand kisses from your Gustl.

PS The other day when I was staying on the Hohe Warte, who should arrive on your parents' doorstep but the Strausses. They insisted I should accompany them on a drive into the country. The object of the excursion was the castle of Pochlarn which is supposed to date back to the *Nibelungenlied*. It was a glorious setting, but utterly desolate, and defended by an impregnable outerwork of cow pats which had attracted every gnat and horsefly in Lower Austria. You won't be surprised when I tell you that Frau Pauline expressed her opinion of the object of our visit in her usual forthright manner, leaving Richard in an erotic ecstasy of cringeing self-humiliation.

What I meant to tell you, however, is that we returned to Vienna by way of Mautern and Göttweig, and through the Neulengbach region. That was how I realized all of a sudden that we were driving just below your old home, Plankenburg Castle in its lovely situation. I braved Frau Pauline's disapproval (you see how bold my love for you makes me, dearest Almscherl?) and insisted on walking up through the park to the moat pond. And all the time, unbeknownst to you, I felt I was wandering into some deep recess of your dear heart, and thought of you so hard that you must have felt a tingling – perhaps even a burning, though I hope not!

My very, very, very best love, G.

She closed her eyes. If she leaned her head over to one side of where she was sitting, there was a stone column which supported a pergola roof of pleached lindens. It was cool against her cheek.

She had been so sure that the sanatorium was an enclosed world, separated and removed from any other world. In some theoretic way, she had known that this would come about, that her stay here would come to an end. But it had not been a reality, any more than life outside was a reality. Here and now had become the reality, the other life, the dream.

Until this morning: for Mahler's letter had brought everything back into reality, the world of his music-making, the world of Mutti and Möll, and, most powerful and merciless of all, Plankenburg – dear, wonderful Plankenburg, with Pappi safe in his studio, and herself sitting with Sophie hulling peas by the moat while the maid told her things she ought not to have known.

Walter Gropius, who had possessed her with such passion and strength that she would willingly have given up her life at the moment of consummation, had no place in this world – did not touch on it at any point. It was so bewildering – how, at a single turn of events, and at an expected one at that, so much feeling, longing, expectation, uncontrollable physical desire, should be snatched away, leaving her with a sensation of trembling emptiness. It would be wonderful to be back safely in her own room in the Villa Möll, with Muttichen sitting beside her bed chatting to her about mundane household matters and social gossip, and of her own times past.

What if Gropius were to ask her to go away with him rather than with Mahler? How could she explain to him? How could she explain that Mahler, for all his defects as a husband, for all the fact that their marriage was no longer a marriage in the truest sense, was still Mahler – the greatest man she had ever known, the incomparable musician for whom she had sacrificed her own gift for composition? Her world, a world of friendships, the world of her lovers even, all idolized Mahler, from General Picquart to Alex von Zemlinsky. Klimt had consecrated her partnership with Mahler on the walls of the Sezession building. She *was* Alma Mahler – if not, who was she?

There was something else; something she had known from the beginning. Gropius was a superb, confident lover. But if he had the appearance of a Walther von Stolzing, he didn't have the impulsive, iconoclastic, romantic genius of the Renaissance poet-knight. That, as so often seemed to happen (God being a prankster like Richard Strauss), was to be found in the unsuitable form of Gustav Mahler.

She would have to make it seem as if their inevitable parting was an act of heroic self-abnegation on her part. Gropius was a true *Herr*. Knowing what had brought her to Tobelbad in the first place, and perceiving that it was the duty and loyalty to family, friends, and her little daughter and not wifely affection which compelled her to return to Mahler, surely he would not put any obstruction across her chosen path? She began to construct the scene in her mind – the sadness of it, tinged with erotic regret, yet filled with heroic resolution; the pain eased by the possibility that, since they were both still young, their paths might cross in some golden future.

That afternoon, as she strolled in a cautiously leisurely manner round the garden paths, the inclination came strongly upon her not to go up to the fountain pool. Perhaps, if Gropius were to wait for her in vain today, and perhaps again tomorrow, he would realize that the brief affair was over, and would return home to Westphalia. Perhaps, on the other hand, he would come straight down to the Institute, to search her out – a possibility which appalled her.

There was nothing for it but to go as usual, making her way further and further from the balustraded terraces until she reached the shade of the overhanging branches, and the gardeners' shed with its Doric temple façade. There was a dullness of spirit rather than anxiety clouding her brain as she went up through the woods, making her drowsy, as if she had taken a sedative. He had not yet arrived when she reached the pool.

She sat down on the edge of the rock platform which had become so peculiarly their own. There was the same sunlight sparkling the smooth surface of the water, the same dazzling edge to the pine needles overhead. Yet everything was changed, like a body from which the soul has departed.

Perhaps he would not come. Perhaps he had to return to Graz – or even home. Perhaps he had deserted her: that would be the most incredible joke; poor Walter, struggling back to Westphalia under the burden of a guilty conscience. Absurdity was heaped on absurdity as she realized how deeply wounded she would feel if that were indeed the case.

He was coming; she saw him from a distance, below where she was sitting. He was stepping over a fallen spruce. His jacket was slung over one shoulder; he had taken off his collar and tie. He waved, and she waved back. The moment was worse than she had anticipated. The feeling of sedation was gone. Here he was, climbing up between the trees, almost running in his eagerness to reach her. He knew nothing; she knew everything.

There was no need to tell him. It was nine days before Mahler would come to collect her. There was time for thought, time to see if matters would simply fall into place. The trouble was in her own feelings. As he dropped his jacket on the rock and took her in his arms, she knew she was incapable of the sort of pretence required.

'What's the matter, Alma?'

He let her go, so frozen had been her response.

'Nothing,' she said. She tried to smile up into his face. 'Nothing is the matter.'

'Alma?' He smiled at her. He put the tip of his forefinger on the edge of her chin. ' "Your mind is as a book where one may read strange matters." '

'It's Mahler,' she told him. 'He's written. He's coming here to take me home.'

He didn't answer immediately.

'That's why you don't feel passionate?' he asked.

But it was more like a statement. She shook her head, looking down at the ground.

'That's very understandable,' he said. He sat down on the rock, taking her hand to draw her down beside him. 'But no regrets?'

'No. Of course not.'

'We knew we'd come to it sooner or later, didn't we?' he asked her.

'I didn't think about it,' she replied. 'Not really.'

He reached into his jacket pocket and pulled out his cigarette case. He held it out to her. She took one.

'When is he arriving?' he said as he lit it for her.

She told the first lie. 'I don't know. He's going to telephone. Next week some time. Probably early next week. Everybody seems to have decided that I'm cured.'

She dazzled herself by looking directly into the light reflected in the pool.

'We have a little time left.' Gropius said.

She told the second lie.

'The trouble is, I can't give myself to you for the next few days.' The real sob in her throat lent conviction to the oldest of excuses. She raised her eyes to him again, and saw him in a blur of sunlight and tears. 'Oh Walter, I'm so sorry!'

'There's no need to be sorry on my behalf, *liebling*. I am so grateful for all you've given me.'

'I'm sorry for myself,' she said.

That was true enough. He gave her hand a gentle squeeze. Then silence – the relative silence of the woodland – came between them.

He said to her in a voice constricted by an unwonted lack of confidence, 'Do you want to go back to him?'

The moment of supreme challenge had come, she realized. She breathed deeply and thought out carefully what she should say; much more carefully now, on the moment, than she could have done walking up to the pool.

'No, Walter, I don't ... Dear Walter, I have to be absolutely honest with you, though I'm sure it's going to make it much harder for us, my dear ...'

'Duty?' he asked.

'I suppose that is part of it.'

She stared through her tears down at their hands clasped together, her wedding ring, his signet ring visible between one another's fingers. Dürer would have made a masterpiece of those hands, and future generations would have read a tragic meaning into them.

'I've always believed love to be the governing force of the world,' she said. 'I've always thought there was only one real sin – to offend against love ...' She would anticipate his reply: 'And I love you, Walter. And I know you love me.'

Once the terms and limits of the drama are set, it becomes easier for the participants to play out their necessary roles.

'But there was a time when I let Mahler believe that I loved him ... *I* believed that I loved him – never, never, never, as I've loved you. It was because I was a musician, as I was when you and I first met. He declared his love for me, as you know. And I, like everybody around me – like all my musical friends and half Vienna as well – hero-worshipped him. You see – I'm sure you understand – it was just the most incredible thing, that of all people, *der* Mahler should have fallen in love with a mere music student like myself. I know that you, like several wise heads, thought it was a terrible mistake. But Walter! I was so young and inexperienced – you can say my head was turned. And I'm afraid I thought you were just jealous – I was very conceited, you see ...'

'I was extremely jealous. I still am.'

'Darling Walter! You've no need to be. I promise ... And then the sort of remarks made about his being a Jew; they just made me all the more stubborn.'

'But it hasn't worked for you,' Gropius gently suggested. 'Finally it led you here, to a diet of lettuce and buttermilk – not a diet for a woman of your temperament, I think.'

The humour in his voice drew from what had seemed in her an emptiness of spirit a warm, sad tenderness towards him.

'Oh Walter!'

She sighed and breathed deeply. She closed her eyes but the sunlight danced between her shut lids.

'He seduced you,' said Gropius. 'Not like a dashing hussar seduces a laundrymaid perhaps – you would never have let yourself be seduced that way. He took advantage of you in his own, much more effective way.'

'He never stopped warning me about it, and worrying about it.'

'He knew what he was doing and he had the grace to feel guilty ... Alma, the truth is it hasn't worked. In your own manner of putting it, it has been an offence against love.'

His voice remained so calm and rational.

'Yes. I suppose that's true. And we're being punished for it.'

She began to choke once more with tears.

'It's been such a desert!' she exclaimed. She felt his arm going about her to comfort her. She laid her head on his shoulder. 'And suddenly, with you ... the living waters ... you know?'

'I know,' he said softly.

'Walter – I have to go back to him, at least for the time being. He doesn't understand the things we understand; he truly believes there is love between us, even if we no longer – behave like man and wife, you know? It's ridiculous, really. How God must laugh, sometimes! I shall be the loyal wife and go back to my husband. At the same time, I shall be completely faithful to you without giving anybody the least grounds for suspicion.'

'You make it seem a mockery,' said Gropius.

'I didn't mean to sound bitter, my darling. Please do try to understand. The reason I'm here – the true reason – is that I wore myself out looking after him returning from America. He is a sick man. He really does have a bad heart condition. And there's still a little of the hero-worshipper in me, if I'm honest with myself ... He is a very great musician. You can call it a weakness in myself if you like, but I could never let him know the truth about my feelings towards him – least of all now, in his present state of health.'

Her head was still resting on his shoulder. She raised it.

'Walter?' she asked in a small, anxious voice. 'Please tell me you do understand. I'm afraid what I'm saying goes against all your philosophy ... But I must know ...'

Tears prevented her from speaking for a moment or two. Gropius said,

'I've only one philosophy at the moment, Almschi. My concern for you.'

'Thank you, Waltchen,' she whispered.

Again they sat without speaking, and only the chatter and creak of the woods about them.

'I shall return to Vienna by the night train,' he said. 'It's selfish, perhaps, but I don't think I could bear to drag out our parting.'

'I'm sure you're right,' she told him.

Then she buried her face in her hands, letting tears spill between her fingers.

'Almschi! Almschi! Don't!'

He held her in a close embrace to comfort her.

'Waltchen,' she gulped. 'I want you to remember something. My body is yours. Only yours. If ever there's a time ... What I want to say is, I shall be keeping myself for you.'

She felt all the emotional excitement of a marriage commitment on the altar steps.

She watched him make his way down between the trees. He stopped to step over the fallen spruce, but he did not look back or send her a final wave. When he had disappeared, once again she rested her face in her hands, and gave herself up to the relief and luxury of uncontrolled weeping.

7 THE DEVIL IS DANCING OFF WITH ME: 1910-1911

IT WAS TWO O'CLOCK in the afternoon. A veil of cloud had rolled down the slopes of the Puster Valley, and a thin drizzle was falling across the meadows which spread between the farmhouse and the wood which concealed and protected the summerhouse. Alma-Maria looked out from the window of the music room. The meadow was empty. Even the cattle had moved to the edge of the wood to settle on the ground to protect their patch of dry earth.

When they had returned from Mahler's New York season she was determined to demonstrate her concern for his well-being. She had only to see the Trenkers' cattle moving towards the wood and immediately she would run down the slope to head them off lest they disturb him with the sound of their bells. Mahler had been amused and even remorseful when he discovered this. There was no need, he told her; hadn't she realized how he wove the sound of cow bells into his work?

A change had come over him over the past two years – a softening. The postman, who had been instructed to make a detour round the Maiernigg 'little composing house', now took Mahler's own correspondence down to the summerhouse, and was given a cup of freshly ground coffee and a milk roll for his pains. Children from the village of Old Toblach beat their way along the path across the fields for doles of sweets or spoonfuls of jam. Vagrants knew they could rely on a call there to obtain a schilling or a handful of hellers. Even mendicant nuns paid a regular call. It was as if the frailty of his physical condition made him want to take life into his arms.

Miss Turner complained that Gucki was positively encouraged by her father to wander down there whenever she pleased, in spite of the fact that the path led for a short way along the lake shore. On one such occasion, as Alma-Maria was leading Gucki back to the farm, Gucki said,

'You know that knife – that weeny teeny little knife – Pappi uses to scrape his music with?'

When he revised his scores in Indian ink, Mahler used a small nail-parer to scrape out mistakes.

'Yes, *liebchen*.'

'Muttichen, you remember you said Pappi's music was like children?'

'Yes.'

She had told Gucki in a moment of joking that writing a symphony was like giving birth.

'Pappi wouldn't ever want to scratch me out and blow me away, would he?' asked Gucki seriously.

'No, *liebchen!* Never!'

She had pretended to laugh. She had been taken by surprise at the effect on her of the child's question, as if it had contained implications which little Guckerl could never have dreamed of.

It had been to quieten her own anxieties that she had said, 'Your Pappi is the kindest, gentlest man I've ever known. And he loves you very much.'

'He is kind, isn't he?' Gucki had replied with the same seriousness.

Below the music room window, Marianna, the Trenkers' twelve-year-old daughter, came out of the kitchen door and crossed the yard towards one of the outhouses. She had a yoke across her shoulders, and a pair of empty buckets.

'Marianna?' Alma-Maria called. 'Have you seen the Herr Director?'

'No, Frau Director. My Mutti was just wondering if he didn't want any lunch today. He didn't say anything about it,' Marianna called up.

She was a pretty, sturdy girl, with grown-up manners, and Alma-Maria was delighted that Guckerl and she had become friends.

'Apologize to Frau Trenker for me, will you, Marianna? I shall have to go down to the summerhouse.'

Mahler was always so punctilious about time-keeping and in his consideration for his servants that something had to be wrong. Her first thought was, of course, for his heart.

She pulled rubber galoshes over her boots, and wrapped a shawl over her head and shoulders against the rain. She set off across the fields and through the trees. The front of the summerhouse was almost entirely made of wide panes of glass. The door itself was surrounded by more glass panes, to offer the maximum of light inside. So when she reached the well-beaten path which led to Old Toblach, and ran up it to the hut, she could see him sitting inside at his desk. He was quite motionless,

423

staring across the desk out of one of the side windows at the tall columns of the trees.

'Gustl!' she called.

But he did not move. As she mounted the wooden step she saw that drooping between his fingers was a letter, the torn envelope lying beside his hand. She opened the door.

'Gustl?'

He was old – so old. And his face was filled with pain as he turned to look at her.

'Almschi,' he said.

Everything was so precisely tidy, even by Gustav's meticulous standards. He had been there since six in the morning – now he was settled in the country for the time being, he no longer felt the need to spend half the morning in bed. Yet the manuscript of the new symphony on which he was working was stacked neatly beside him. Even the coffee pot was clean and cold.

He held the letter out to her. His lips moved as if he wished to speak. But no words came.

She took the single sheet. She saw the greeting

Highly-esteemed Herr Director Gustav Mahler...

She turned it over and saw the signature at the bottom of the page –

With best wishes, yours most sincerely, Walter Gropius.

The sense of shock enfolded her like a clammy blanket being wrapped round her.

She could guess the nature of the contents without reading it. There had been the thought – the fear – of it happening, but all that had faded from her mind months ago.

Mahler had turned his face away from her while she read the letter. She had to sit down. She pulled out the piano stool and settled on it before the fainting fit could engulf her. She read,

I had occasion to stay in Graz last August, and while there, learned that Alma was staying at the sanatorium at Tobelbad. Presuming on old acquaintance – you will recall, I dare say, that we have mutual friends in the Hofrat and Hofratin Emil Zuckerkandl – I travelled out to Tobelbad to call on Alma. As a result of that first call, during the subsequent days we met each afternoon.

To put the matter as briefly as possible, during our walks together in the woods above the Tobelberg, we made the discovery that we loved one another. I believe I may state in all honesty that during the course of those days, we became in as close communion one to another as a man and woman may achieve without the formalities prescribed by religious observance.

At the end of her period of convalescence, Alma came to the decision that duty and her obligations toward you as her legal husband required that, despite the profundity of her feelings for me, she return to you. The reason I am writing is because I have every reason to suppose that if you were willingly to offer her her freedom, she would feel absolved of her sense of duty and would be able to follow her own inclinations. I believe also that you would have no wish to hold on to her as a captive, when you know that her heart and spirit are committed to somebody else...

She had to struggle against the stifling sense of futility. Silence lapped around her. If Mahler had turned to look at her – had said something in accusation – it would have been easier.

'It's so stupid!' she managed to say at last. 'I can't imagine what could have given him the idea ... And it was almost a year ago!'

Her voice trailed off. The effort was too much for her. Nor was there any way of knowing whether Mahler was paying attention.

'I'm not going to deny I was pleased to see Herr Gropius at Tobelbad. I was glad to go for walks with him – to have the opportunity to talk to somebody intelligent. It was like being in prison, that place ...'

Again she broke off.

'He must have taken my being pleased to see him for something very much more. I think having somebody to talk to – a glimpse of the outside world – probably helped with my cure.'

'Why did you never tell me you were being visited by an old friend?' asked Mahler.

'Because he'd been a sort of rival, I suppose, in the old days. I was afraid of what you might have thought. I didn't want you troubled just when you were about to take over the New York Philharmonic Symphony.'

'Don't you think it's a great deal worse my finding out from a letter like this?'

'How did I know he was going to behave so stupidly? I mean, I didn't give him any grounds for supposing... And it was almost a year ago!' she repeated. The sense of injustice was stifling her.

'That's enough, Alma! I don't want to hear any more for the moment. I can't believe such a letter could have been written by somebody with whom you had nothing but polite conversation. You must have exchanged letters with him since.'

'No!' she cried out. 'No!'

He stood up. Still he didn't look at her. He patted the pockets of his frayed and shabby jacket as if he expected to find letters between herself and Gropius there.

'I prefer,' he said, 'that you should let me return to the house by myself.'

'Why don't you accuse me directly of being unfaithful to you?' she demanded.

But he said nothing. He closed the summerhouse door behind him, and she heard his footsteps treading last year's dead leaves on the path. She had not the will to do anything except sit where she was by the piano. Her first inclination was to remain there the rest of the day, and perhaps even the night, until he came back to fetch her. But after perching on the piano stool in the stillness of the hut, watching the rain gathering in drops on the branches outside for a quarter of an hour, she began to feel restless. Another thought occurred to her. If this was to prove to be the end of her marriage to Mahler, why should she not go with Gropius?

She got up. Gropius's letter was still in her hand. She had screwed it up as if, by so doing and by throwing it away, she could throw away the event itself. Now, she realized, she might need the address. She spread it out on the worktop of Mahler's desk, flattening it with the edge of her hand. Beside her was the manuscript score of the new symphony, the Tenth. She stared down at the address on the notepaper, the unfamiliar street name in an unfamiliar town in a part of Germany which was strange to her. Immediately she understood the impossibility of getting in touch with Gropius: that, once again, she could never bring herself to turn her back on her whole world, on her own identity even. She folded the letter neatly, and slipped it into her skirt pocket.

By accident she had brushed her hand against the score of the symphony. Several sheets of carefully scored manuscript had slid from the top of the pile. On one of the sheets thus exposed, there was a pencil inscription scrawled right across the meticulous Indian ink revision, as if written by somebody in physical pain: *Almschili, to live for you, to die for you!* And then, across the bottom of the same sheet: *Have mercy, O God! Why hast Thou forsaken me?*

Had he written it that same morning? she wondered. She turned page after page. One in every four or five was scrawled across in the same manic fashion: *Almschi, if you leave me, I shall go out like a torch deprived of air!* And: *My queen has sent me into deepest exile. O my dear God, what am I to do?* She continued turning pages. Surely he had not written all the ravings she found that same morning, since the postman had called. Under the heading to the third movement which, like the first, was in revised full score, he had scribbled: *Is this Purgatorio or Inferno? Alma! O my Almschi! Farewell my lyre!*

The third movement was very short. Only a few pages more and she came to the fourth movement – *allegro pesante*. It concluded with a single *fortissimo* beat on a funereal muffled drum. Beside it he had written: *Alma! Only you know what this means.* And then, along the bottom of the final page of the score: *The Devil is dancing off with me, madness is taking hold of me the accursed one ... All joy and singing withers and dies.*

Between two of the manuscript sheets, she found lying a sheet of notepaper. There was no way of knowing whether it was the draft of a letter, or an expression of uncontainable emotion like the scrawling across the score. She felt horrified yet entranced by the evidence of his suffering.

Life with all its everlasting switches of fortune has become for me a dreadful nightmare. Its people remind me of the dancers in a brilliantly lit ballroom into which one stares from outside in the dark, but at a distance so great that one cannot hear the music of their dance. Life seems so bereft of meaning, such a travesty of itself, that you might well wake from nightmare into death itself and still be screaming in horror and disgust...

As she read it and more, she was filled with pity. She also felt relieved and unexpectedly delivered. She replaced the score as she had originally found it, with the sheet of notepaper between the pages. She drew her shawl about her shoulders and up over her head, and stepped out into the drizzle. She made her way back through the woods and up the meadows to the farm. Across the yard, in the doorway leading up to the stairs, she was stopped by Frau Trenker.

'Frau Mahler! Herr Mahler has refused to take any lunch. Isn't he well?'

'It's all right, Frau Trenker. I know about it. I'm going up to him now.'

At the top of the stairs, Gucki was lying in wait for her.

'Muttichen? What's wrong with Pappi? He won't talk to me!'

'Never you mind, *liebchen*. It's nothing that you've done. You stay in there with Miss Turner, and we'll go for a nice walk across to the village afterwards ... Miss Turner, where is my husband?'

'He's in the drawing room, Frau Mahler.'

She hung up her shawl on a peg on the landing. She pulled her skirt straight and adjusted the flounces of her blouse before going into the drawing room. Mahler was in the deep, basket-framed armchair, his head sunk on his chest. He appeared to have shrunk even while he was sitting there. He was staring fixedly at the floor in front of him as if in a catatonic trance. She went to him and crouched down facing him. She put her hand on his. It was stone cold.

'Gustav?' she asked. When he did not reply, she said, 'I think you have to listen to me, you know, whether you want to or not. It's not just that that awful letter made you believe I've been unfaithful to you. I expect you were brooding about the possibility when I was away.'

'It would have been perfectly natural,' he replied in a harsh, dry voice. 'I was old and sick. You were young, beautiful, and very much alive. You still are. It's natural you should seek out your own kind.'

'That's so stupid, I don't know how to cope with it!' she told him. 'I expect you brooded yourself into a regular Othello, didn't you? Well let me tell you, Gustl, a diet of buttermilk and lettuce leaves, and daily sulphur baths at intolerable temperatures did nothing to stimulate physical passion, I assure you. And now this ridiculous letter is supposed to confirm all your worst fears.'

'You've read it, have you?'

'Yes. I've read it. It's the ravings of a man who still fancies he's in love with me.'

'You know what he's doing?' said Mahler. 'He's asking me for your hand in marriage. In effect, he's yet another man who has mistaken me for your father ... You slept with him, of course.'

The directness of the accusation caught her completely off guard.

'No, I most certainly did not!' Then she said, 'Oh Gustl! ... I may have encouraged him. I was ill – light-headed. And I was pleased to see him. To tell you the truth, I'd have been pleased to see anybody – Guido Adler, even Anna von Mildenburg. But I never gave him the least reason for – well – that letter ... Listen, Gustl! Let me tell you: I could never imagine life without you. Do you understand that? Least of all could I ever imagine life with another man. You are the hub of my entire existence. I am Alma Mahler – nobody else. How could I see myself as anybody else?'

He remained with his chin on his chest, staring at the floor immediately past where she was squatting. But she had noticed how he had blinked behind his spectacles.

She kept her hand on his, even if she did receive no response.

'I gave up everything for you, Gustav,' she said. 'I gave up my music. Maybe it wasn't the greatest music ever composed. Maybe it wasn't anything like as great as Gustav Mahler's, but it was there inside me, longing to be born, just as surely as it's inside you. I've accepted that I have to live like a nun, if that's what is best for you. I've accepted that I've got to be very quiet a lot of the time, and to keep myself a stranger from you almost, for the sake of your work. You know very well – I'm sure your heart tells you – that if you were to become seriously ill, I would be at your side looking after you. You *know* all these things, my Gustl. So why do you torture yourself with mistrust of me?'

She did not wait for an answer. There was no need, now; she was sure of it. She gave his hand a final pat, and stood up and left him still staring at the floor. Out on the landing, she called briskly,

'Guckerl? *Liebling?* Come to Mutti, and we'll go for a walk down into Old Toblach...'

Mahler did not speak to her, or anybody, all that evening. When she and Gucki returned from Old Toblach, it was to find that he had removed himself to the music room. Alma-Maria decided it was best to let him remain by himself; Anton took a tray into him with his evening meal, but he did not eat anything.

428

As night drew on, so her confidence began to ebb. The temptation grew within her to go in to him, though she was sure it was best to leave matters be and to remain patient. She dismissed Kathi for the night, and prepared for bed. Before settling down to sleep if she could, she went out onto the landing. She saw the lamplight shining under the door of the music room, but there was no sound from within. More strongly than ever, she was tempted to enter. There was the possibility, she told herself, that he was truly ill and needed her. She forced herself to creep back to the bedroom and go to bed.

He came in an hour later, a paraffin lamp held up in his hand. She pretended to be asleep, though the light glowed between her lids as he stood looking down at her. She heard him move back across the room. The latch of the door clicked shut. She opened her eyes again. It was dark. She rolled onto her back and stared up into the dark of the low ceiling. How long, she wondered, was this to continue? She heard the heavy thud on the landing, Mahler's cry, and the crash of broken glass and falling metal. She already had her bare feet on the floor when she saw the flamelight dancing beneath the door. She ran outside, pausing only to snatch up her shawl from a bedside chair. Mahler had fallen headlong, away from the bedroom. Burning paraffin was spilled from the brass body of the lamp; it ran in threads of flame across the floorboards in three directions, with the smashed glass funnel enveloped in flames at the centre. He was lying still. One arm was stretched into the flame – his jacket sleeve was already alight. In the second or two it had taken her to see what had happened, she noticed the blood from his face gleaming on the floorboard where it had spilled from his nose.

She dragged his arm back from the flame, throwing her shawl over it and beating out the burning sleeve.

'Gustl! Gustl!' she screamed, wondering for a moment whether he was lying so still only to frighten her.

Still screaming out for help, she grabbed at his legs and tried to pull him away from the rivulets of fire. The heat of the flames was growing intense, pricking sweat out of her like needle points all over her body. She should be trying to beat it out before the fire took hold of the landing itself and they all got killed. Instead she struggled more desperately to pull Mahler back – but his body was leaden.

There were people all about her – the grey, strong figure of the farmer, Jakob Trenker, a bucket of water in his arms which he kept ready filled downstairs. There was Frau Trenker, and Erich, the farm help, who grabbed Mahler's legs from her and heaved the unconscious body back towards the stairs as if it were no weight at all.

The fire was easily put out, leaving the landing filled with smoke which made them all cough. Alma-Maria sent Anton with the car to fetch Dr Martinelli from Altschluderbach, while Kathi with Frau Trenker went from room to room opening the windows. Jakob Trenker and Erich carried Mahler into the bedroom and stretched him out on the bed.

'I thought the gentleman was looking poorly, yesterday,' said Frau Trenker who, with Marianna, had opened the bedroom windows. Outside, the cattle had been disturbed by the unwonted noise. Bells chinked and clattered along the pasture fence.

Frau Trenker had made it sound like an accusation. Alma-Maria felt as much as saw her eyes and Marianna's, and Kathi's, and Guckerl's and Miss Turner's who were standing by the door looking in, all on her. How much did they all know about her own and Gustav's private life? How much did they guess? Of one thing she could be entirely sure: Mahler had never been held in such respect by the Viennese when he was Director of the Court Opera and the Vienna Philharmonic as he was now. Schoenberg had written to ask him when he would return to conduct in Vienna, adding that he would find himself 'so wrapped in honour that you would find it impossible to remember past calumnies or hold onto old and entirely justified resentments'. The Austrian musical press which, only two years ago, had been capable of dismissing his compositions as cacophony without structure or meaning now regarded him as the greatest living exponent of a tradition of symphonic writing which extended backwards via Schubert and Beethoven to Haydn, Mozart, and Gluck. If it ever became known that she was in any way responsible for harming *der* Mahler, her native city would never forgive her.

Jakob Trenker had felt Mahler's pulse and listened to his heart. Even before Dr Martinelli came, he was able to reassure Alma-Maria that he was not in mortal danger. Nevertheless, she administered sal volatile and raised his head and made him swallow two spoonfuls of the tincture of digitalis prescribed in New York by Dr Fraenkel. As he came to full consciousness, the others withdrew, leaving her sitting at his bedside.

When they were alone, he stared up at her.

'Alma?' he asked.

She took his hand lightly. 'I am here, Gustl. I'll always be here, you know.'

'You have always been for me the light – my fixed point.'

'Sh, Gustl! Rest. In my bed. I'll sit with you.'

'I came when you were asleep … I came to ask you …'

'Tomorrow, Gustl. Tomorrow will do.'

'No!' He struggled to sit up. She put her hand on his shoulder to insist he remain lying down. 'I came to ask you if I might dedicate our Eighth to you – formally, on the title page … before it is aired in Munich.'

'We'll talk about it tomorrow.'

'No, Almschi! Now. I must know whether I'm saved or damned, you see.'

It was the same note of unbalance as she had seen scrawled all over the manuscript of his Tenth, that afternoon. She tried to inject a hint of normality:

'You've never formally dedicated your work,' she told him in a low voice. 'I know the Fourth was for your mother. I know the movements of the Fifth and Sixth which were for me. I don't need a formal dedication.'

'But the Eighth is different, Almschi...' His face, near blind without his spectacles which had been broken in his fall, searched painfully for hers.

'Shall I fetch your other spectacles?' she asked.

'Not necessary,' he replied. 'Almschi – the Eighth, our *Faust* Symphony, is yours in a much more special way. It links up everything we've ever talked about. It reaches back to your days with your beloved father. It's about how you're the centre and salvation of my whole being...'

'Gustl, of course you must dedicate it to me if that's what you truly want to do.'

She stooped over him and kissed the cold, domed forehead. She was painfully aware that she was acknowledging the role in which he had placed her.

She had walked to Toblach to fetch the tablets which Dr Martinelli had prescribed from the apothecary near the railway station. She had taken Gucki with her. They were returning across the fields when they heard the sound of Mahler's Broadwood grand floating across from the open music room window.

'What's Pappi playing?' asked Gucki.

Already she was learning to recognize the work of several composers – Mozart, Haydn, Wagner, and Mussorgsky, a composer new to Mahler's repertoire, but one whose work he had begun eagerly to promote.

'Be quiet,' Alma-Maria told her.

She could not hear the voice at that distance, but she could supply the vocal line although she had not actually looked at the work for three years.

It was the third of her own '*Five Songs*' – *Der Erkennende:*

> Through no will of our own
> We burn for one another,
> Yet nothing and no one
> Will ever be mine.
> My tragedy is to know this ...

She grabbed Gucki's hand and hurried with her to the door. She left the child with Miss Turner, and ran straight to the music room without removing either her duster-coat or her wide-brimmed summer hat.

'Gustl! Where did you find them?'

He played to the end of the stanza, then lifted his skinny, tapering fingers off the keyboard.

'Almschi,' he said, blinking across at her. 'I've wronged you in so many ways.'

'You shouldn't have gone into ...'

She had long considered the description 'cardboard coffins' suitable for the folders in which she kept her own manuscripts.

'Forgive me, Almschili. . .' He gave her a look of dog-like penitence. 'I wanted to see what music you kept in your case. I wanted to spy on you, to find out what music would give you real pleasure for us to play together ... And so I found these. Almschili! What in God's name have I done? They are so good! I'm playing them over for the second time.'

He reached over for the stool from her piano and drew it over to beside his own.

'Sit down. We're going to go over them together. When we're sure they're ready, I'll see that Universal publish them. My God, I've been so blind!'

'Gustl! Let me take off my things! They've waited so long, I'm sure they can wait a few moments more.'

She went to her bedroom. She stood bareheaded at the open window staring out at the afternoon sunlight and the long shadows thrown by the haystooks in the meadow. Poor Gustav! It seemed she was only beginning to understand how terrified he had been at the possibility of losing her. It was his illness which had made him so terribly vulnerable – the fears he had always expressed about being too old for her had now multiplied tenfold. They were no longer neurotic but well-founded. And she had tasted the glory of youthful love with Gropius. That was to be her particular burden. As for her songs: she was not entirely sure she was interested now in reviving them from their moribund state. The fantasy of excellence, without which nobody would ever undertake the burden of artistic creation, had long since faded. She knew her *Lieder* for what they were – the work of an accomplished student. They had provided justifiable grounds for resentment against Mahler; but there was a suspicion lurking in her mind that if she had been possessed by the egotistic creative drive of a Mozart or Wagner, or even Mahler, no interdict would have prevented her from trying to give it utterance.

Supposing – just supposing – in a sunlit daydream of early evening an angel were to appear, to offer her the choice between composing, and a guilt-free, uninhibited affair with Walter Gropius. Which now, at this moment, would she choose? The answer made her smile, albeit a little regretfully.

As for Gustav: the truth was that he was understanding for the first time in his life that very thing which had inhibited her from following the dictates of passion – or so she assured herself – namely that there was such a thing as an inner obligation toward the person with whom one has solemnly and sacramentally been joined together. Her poor, hitherto-neglected *Lieder* were the outward and visible symbol of that part of her which he had cruelly neglected most of the time they had been together. If he wished to convince himself now of their excellence, she must not try to dissuade him.

They spent the remainder of the evening both before and after dinner playing them, with her singing them and patiently accepting his suggestions for small improvements and corrections. She was rewarded by catching the look of joy which occasionally transfigured the worn sadness of his sunken features.

From that night on, he began visiting her in the small hours of the morning – from the first, at Toblach, they had had separate rooms – to leave letters at her bedside:

> My breath of life!
> I've kissed your little slippers a thousand times and stood by your door with longing. This time you took pity on me, glorious one, but the demons come back with the dark to tear at me again for thinking always of myself and never of you, my dearest. I can scarcely tear myself from your door; I'd like to stand there all night listening to the sweet sound of your living and breathing. I bless you, my beloved – whatever fate awaits me at your hands. Every beat of my heart is *for you*.

And:

> My darling, my lyre,
> Come and exorcize the spirits of darkness, they claw hold of me, they throw me to the ground. Don't leave me, my rod of comfort, come to me soon today so that I may rise up. I lie here in the dark and ask myself whether my condition is past saving...

And again:

> Beloved,
> Tonight I have slept so well, and my feelings were not for a moment disturbed. A spirit visited me and spoke to my spirit; and now I believe there cannot be a moment when I do not feel the happiness of knowing: she loves me! That is the only meaning of my life. When I am unable to say that, I am dead!

Mahler's feelings might not have been for a moment disturbed. Alma-Maria's were. While, in many respects, things were working out better than she could have expected, the vehemence of his communications frightened her. He wanted her beside him as often as possible. As once before, at Maiernigg, he positively urged her to come down to the summerhouse to disturb him or to work with him – and when, on one or two occasions, she was delayed, she found him with his hands pushed under his spectacles, weeping, and once in a faint on the pinewood floor.

She telephoned Mutti from Toblach to come and join them. She drove with Anton to the mainline station at Lienz to meet her off the Vienna express. As they drove back with the communication window closed between them and Anton, she told Mutti of Mahler' terrible, self-torturing jealousy, and how it had been made worse because of Gropius's visits to her at Tobelbad.

'Did Gustav approve of Herr Walter's seeing you?' Mutti asked.

She was to be fooled only with difficulty; and she loved Mahler.

'Oh Muttichen! You know Gustl,' Alma-Maria replied. 'He would never express his disapproval – not, that is, until it's much too late. He can't bear to think of himself as being possessive. He bottles it up, and then – well – he hurts himself more than anybody. And just now . . . he isn't well enough to inflict that sort of strain on himself!'

She pulled out her handkerchief to dry her eyes.

'Perhaps you shouldn't have allowed Herr Walter to have visited you. After all, you know how he felt about you.

'That was nine years ago, Mutti! Besides, any friendly face would have been welcome in that place.'

'Any *man*'s friendly face is what you mean, isn't it Almschi?'

'Mutti! Dear God, you should try enduring sanatorium life for a few weeks!'

She turned her tear-stained face away from Mutti, and stared out at the passing scenery. Then suddenly, in anger at the way she felt Mutti was rejecting her plea for sympathy, she said,

'Is it such a terrible thing for a woman my age to want the sort of relations men and women are supposed to have when they're married? Go on, Mutti – you tell me! You should know!'

'That is entirely a matter, my dear Alma-Maria,' Mutti replied, 'between yourself and your husband.'

Reverend Mother at the Maria Theresia Institute could not have spoken more coldly.

When they arrived back at the farmhouse, the warmth with which Mutti embraced Mahler, and the care which she demonstrated for him from the first moment, seemed to Alma-Maria to be designed as compensation for some hypothetical neglect of him on her own part. But for the urgency of Mahler's own emotional need of her, she could have found herself excluded from the warmth of the domestic circle.

A few days after Mutti's arrival, Alma-Maria and Mahler were out for an afternoon's drive in the car – such drives had taken the place of the routine four-mile walks of earlier days – and were returning up the Puster Valley from Altschluderbach, not a quarter of a mile from the farm. As they passed over a narrow stone bridge across a fast-flowing hillside culvert, through the car window Alma-Maria saw, quite clearly and unmistakably, the figure of Walter Gropius in English plus fours with his Norfolk jacket slung over one shoulder in a familiar gesture, standing half concealed behind the parapet of the bridge.

She said nothing. She could not have spoken any more than she could have judged whether the intensity of feeling which had immediately possessed her was excitement or panic. Mahler had noticed nothing. She got out of the car in the yard. Marianna was driving cows into the sheds to be milked as if nothing untoward was about to happen.

The stupid thought was lodged in her head: how incredibly handsome he was, how perfectly Walther von Stolzing. If it had been possible to the least degree, she would have run back down the road and into his arms. She knew very well what he intended to do. He was coming to the farmhouse to seek a reply from Mahler to his letter. The idiot! Twice an idiot! If only he could have stayed in the village and communicated with her in some way. Now she realized that there was only one possible thing she could do. And because of Mutti and Mutti's priggish attitude, she had better do it straight away.

'Gustav, there's something I have to tell you – before we go inside.'

He looked at her. He had noticed her tone of voice and understood that what she was about to say was urgent and important. His expression was one almost of horror.

'Before I tell you,' she said. 'You have to know this – I shall never, ever leave you.'

He nodded and even tried to smile.

'Gropius is here … Not in the house. We passed him on the road. He was walking this way.' She reached up and put her hands on his shoulders. 'Do you understand, Gustl? Whatever happens, I'm never going to desert you.'

'Are you sure it was he, Almschi?' He was trembling.

'Quite certain,' she managed to reply in a calm voice. 'It is not a mistake I'm likely to make.'

She laughed. It sounded unpleasant, and she wished she hadn't.

Mahler returned to the car as Anton was about to park it at the end of the barn, under the roof. He took his walking stick out from the back seat. He buttoned his alpaca summer coat, and set off with a firm step toward the meadow path in the direction of Altschluderbach.

'Gustav!' she cried out in alarm.

When he did not hesitate, she ran after him to the gate. The fields, the trees, the lake water below were all absurdly still and calm in the early evening sunlight.

'Gustav!'

She followed him onto the beaten grass of the path, not caring what anyone watching might think.

'Gustav, what are you going to do?'

She was quite genuinely more frightened for him than on her own account.

'I'm going to bring him here. You may ask our Mutti if she would be so kind as to have dinner prepared for the four of us.'

'Why? To what purpose?' she pleaded.

Mahler at last stopped and turned. He stood leaning with both hands on his stick.

'The young man, as he claimed in his letter, is known to us – has been formally introduced to us in the past. It is therefore perfectly proper that I should extend the hospitality of our house to him.'

He was speaking calmly, though he was a little out of breath. She had become so convinced she had the upper hand. Yet he was showing all the old authority and determination.

'Gustav! You're mad!'

'Indeed! I'd be a great deal more mad if I were to let him come up here of his own volition, having worked up his emotions to make heaven knows what declarations and demands – and in front of Gucki and our Mutti and the servants ... and the Trenkers in all probability. No, my dear Alma. We shall observe the niceties of acceptable social intercourse.' He stared at her. He smiled wearily, and put his hand on her cheek. 'You will have an opportunity to speak to him alone,' he told her. 'I know that whatever you do shall be well done.'

She stood watching him as he descended the hill to the road. Then she turned back to the farmhouse.

Darkness had fallen before he returned, and with it old fears. Alma-Maria read apprehension in Mutti's face, where at first when she had told her what was happening there had been an 'I knew it would come to this in the end' disapproval. Too much time passed for Mutti to continue fussing around the dinner table over the napery and the silver. She finally sank into an armchair to sit and stare in front of her.

Alma-Maria heard them at the gate, and went to the window. They came across the yard: Mahler was in front carrying a lantern, Gropius following at a few paces distance. She could imagine them walking all the way in such a fashion, without exchanging a word. When they reached the top of the stairs, she kissed Mahler on the cheek and said,

'You took so long! We were quite worried.'

Gropius said in a strained attempt at normality:

'It was entirely my fault, Frau Alma. I had returned to the village. Herr Mahler had to find me out.'

Alma-Maria exchanged glances with Mahler. She tried to convey some suggestion of angry impatience.

'Well God be thanked you've both got back here safely at last!' Mutti said emolliently.

Gropius took her hand and bowed over it. He did not go through the charade of kissing Alma-Maria's hand. Mahler told her,

'Herr Gropius will be staying the night. Perhaps you'd be good enough to ask Frau Trenker to have the second guest room made ready.'

Her cry of protest died before it was uttered.

'Of course,' she said with as good grace as she could.

Was this some sort of refined punishment? she wondered.

Mutti struggled to keep some sort of conversation going over dinner, with gossip about Vienna and stories of the old days. It was a wonder, thought Alma-Maria, struggling with the nervous constriction of her own throat, that any of them was able to swallow a mouthful.

When they were at last finished – and they were spared nothing, Mahler insisting they linger over coffee, liqueurs, and *amoretti* – he said,

'I shall retire to the music room to work. Alma-Maria ...'

It was a form of address he had never, ever used before.

'... will you take Herr Gropius to the drawing room? Mutti, would you so very kindly oversee the preparation of the guestroom for Herr Gropius.'

'Yes. Certainly, Gustav,' Mutti replied, pointedly taking the message, though without approval.

Gropius followed Alma-Maria down the passage to the drawing room. She turned up the lamps and opened the windows onto the balcony. There was a strong scent of new-mown hay on the warm night air.

'It's from the other side of the valley,' she explained. 'The Trenkers cut theirs ages ago.'

'May I smoke?' asked Gropius.

'Please do.'

'Will you have one? Or doesn't Mahler approve of ladies smoking.'

'Mahler doesn't disapprove of my having the occasional cigarette.' She took one from him. 'In any case, we shall not be disturbed. He will see to that. He has to convince himself that he's putting no pressure on me.'

She lit her cigarette from his match.

'Which is, I imagine, the worst sort of pressure,' he suggested.

'Not quite, Walter. The worst sort of pressure is your coming here ... Do you know we'd even managed to get over your appalling letter? I meant every word I said when we last saw each other! I can't imagine anything more insane than your coming here like this. Did you really imagine I'd just pack a few things and come running after you? Apart from anything else, I have a child here whom I love.'

'I had no idea what would happen,' he said quite calmly. 'I only knew I had to come – that I couldn't stand the uncertainty.'

'What uncertainty?'

'The uncertainty of not knowing whether the feelings you expressed for me could only exist ... in Tobelbad. The words you spoke that afternoon are burned into my memory – when you said that you had to go back to him *for the time being*. I've been living on the hope those words gave me.'

She had forgotten she had ever said them. In fact, that last encounter had become a blur of sadness and self-abnegation in her mind in which all detail of what had been said was lost in confusion. Except that she had promised to keep herself physically for him.

'Didn't you know that writing that letter, and then coming here, would be so dreadfully unfair on me? Are you so selfish, so infantile, you never gave that a thought?' She put her hand on his sleeve. 'Walter, I will tell you this. I made a terrible mistake in marrying Mahler. I know that. But it's the sort of mistake that a great many women make, I should think. And we have to live with it . . .'

He was so much taller than Mahler, and so much stronger, she told herself. How was she going to bear a whole night with him sleeping only a few yards from her single room?

'I must go to him now,' she went on, as Gropius's fingers closed round hers. 'I have to be much more concerned for him than for you. He's had a fainting fit recently, and this situation you've landed us in can only have put even more strain on him.' She took her hand from his. 'I'm not coming back here. I shall go to my room, and you must go to yours. Tomorrow morning, as soon as you've had your coffee, the car will take you to Toblach station. If I can do it without causing Mahler any more pain and anxiety, I'll come with you to the station . . .' She drew nearer to him, unable, she felt, to help herself.

'What I do want to tell you, Walter,' she said, lowering her voice, 'is that I've never loved any man as deeply and passionately as I love you. And I can only beg you to behave yourself and be . . . merciful with me.'

She darted up her head and kissed his cheek, then turned away immediately and, without looking back, left him there.

The music room was lit only by the two candles on the brackets of Mahler's Broadwood grand. Mahler was sitting at the stool. She noticed straight away that her music was on the stand, though the folders were closed. She could imagine, if she had chosen to go away with Gropius, his sitting there alone, playing her sad little pieces as if they were, at least, a living part of her.

He stood up with painful slowness. There was a leather-bound book in his hand which he had been reading, or pretending or trying to read. It was Luther's Bible, the greatest masterpiece of German spiritual literature, but one which Catholics were not supposed to read, let alone prayerfully. Pappi would have shown the same gentle independence if he had ever sought the comfort of religion.

She went to him and took the Bible from him, laying it down on the piano. She took both his hands in hers. All the resolution which had driven him to walk to Toblach to bring Gropius back with him was now gone. The tears shone like stars, magnified by his spectacle lenses.

'Silly man!' she said quietly. 'Did you really believe I would have to make a choice? I've sent him to bed with a flea in his ear. I've said I'll take him in the car back to Toblach first thing in the morning, if you can spare Anton. And now you must promise me you will never worry about him again – ever!'

He sank down, back onto the piano stool. He struggled to smile. She drew her own piano stool close to him and sat holding his hands as the minutes passed. He kept on staring at her, trying to take her in, trying to imprint her face on his brain.

'My light,' he said. 'My inner light confirmed – unshadowed?'

She nodded.

'Oh Almschili! You'll never know the depths of my gratitude.'

She knew that he was watching, concealed behind the curtain edge of his bedroom window, as she got into the car with Gropius following her. The hood was down; there was no concealment, and no glass partition between Anton and his passengers.

There was nothing either of them could think of saying as they drove northwards out of the valley and through the small town. In the station yard, however, they had a few moments to themselves even if their behaviour had to be discreet, exposed as they were in so public and familiar a place. She sent Anton to buy Gropius's ticket through to Innsbruck and to see to the little baggage he possessed. Gropius had already stepped down, leaving her alone in the seat, when she beckoned to him to come close. He stepped up onto the running board, as close to her as the broad brim of her black straw sunhat permitted.

'Walter, I only thought of it this morning. Listen. Mahler is to give the first performance of his Eighth Symphony in Munich on the twelfth of September. He'll be away from here, organizing it and rehearsing it, from the last ten days in August onwards. I'll have to join him before the performance. But otherwise, for more than two weeks, I'm going to be here by myself. You wouldn't be able to come to the house, of course, and you mustn't stay here in Toblach because it's too small, and we're known. But if you stayed in Schluderbach, at the other end of the valley, we could see one another. It's within easy walking distance of the farm, across the fields ... Send me a letter to arrive *after* August the twenty-first, telling me where you are ...'

She looked into his eyes.

'I wish I could let you embrace me and kiss me – properly, I mean, like a lover – my Walther von Stolzing, my own and golden hero! ...'

Mahler broke off his rehearsal to meet her from the train. She had delayed the journey as long as she dared – there were only two days to the first performance of what he had been calling in his letters 'Your Symphony' rather than 'Our *Faust* Symphony' or, as Emil Gutmann, his Viennese impresario, more formally referred to it in the press, the 'Symphony of a Thousand'. She was shocked by his appearance. She had known, of course, of his septic sore throat, and that Bruno Walter had, until that very day, had to take rehearsals. But the figure that came limping briskly through the steam had shrunk inside its clothes to such a skeletal thinness that she did not recognize him on the instant. As he embraced her, his breath smelt ordurous, the breath of a man who has been starving through sickness. The voice with which he uttered a flood of endearments was hoarse.

Even so, she noticed that he glowed with happiness. Over the past week, the full resources required for his Eighth Symphony had assembled. They had been marshalled into their places in Munich's brand new Exhibition Hall (built in the English style, of prefabricated sections of steel and glass, and with perfect acoustics) on rostra planned and designed by Alfred Roller in conjunction with Bruno Walter. There was the Munich Concert Society Orchestra augmented for the occasion to 172 players, there was Adolf Hempel, organist of the Frauenkirche in Munich; there were 250 singers of the Leipzig Riedelverein, the finest choir, in Mahler's opinion, in Greater Germany; there were 250 veterans of Mahler's baton, the Vienna Singverein; there were the 350 children of the Munich Zentral Singschule; and there were the eight distinguished soloists – lead singers from the Vienna, Berlin, Hamburg, Frankfurt, and Munich Court Opera Houses. The very *ensemble* itself was Greater Germany's tribute to Mahler, not only as Europe's virtuoso conductor, but as one of its leading composers. And now Alma-Maria had arrived. His heart was overflowing with gratitude.

As they walked through the Hochbahnhof to the station concourse where Anton was waiting with the car, Mahler referred jokingly to his Barnum and Bailey Raree Show, but there was no concealing his boyish pleasure at the fuss which was being made over him, nor of his own achievement, and she was glad for him. He recited the names of fellow musicians who had already arrived in Munich and presented their compliments – the Schalks, Klemperer, Alfred Casella, Schoenberg, and Anton Webern; Richard Strauss had come from Berlin with Oskar Fried, Leopold Stokowski from London, and Siegfried Wagner from Bayreuth acting as his mother, Cosima's, personal representative for the occasion. The great theatre director and personal friend, Max Reinhardt, had arrived from Vienna bringing with him half the most famous names in Austrian contemporary literature, Hugo von Hofmannsthal, Arthur Schnitzler, and Stefan Zweig among others, while in Berta Zuckerkandl's party there were not only Paul and Sophie Clemenceau, but also Georges Clemenceau, albeit in an informal capacity.

'All it has needed is you to make the whole tableau come to life,' Mahler told her as he settled beside her in the car. 'Now that I'll be able to turn round on the podium and see my divinity there ... now I'll be able to brush your dearest face with a secret glance – one that nobody else would ever be able to guess at, eh? ... Now I shall know exactly what the whole circus is about, and why I'm standing there.'

'Do you really need me there to enjoy applause?' she asked.

Did he really have to be so dependent on her?

'I need to be able to place it at your feet, my darling Almscherl, or – I'm being absolutely serious – for me, it's no applause at all.'

'Oh Gustl', she said, 'that is so foolish. Don't you think there's a love between your music and those who love your music which has nothing to do with me?'

'But you are my music, Almschi. Don't you understand that? You were my music before ever I met you. It was only that I *recognized* you for what you were to me when I saw you that night at the Zuckerkandls'.'

'Gustl!' she repeated, shaking her head.

It was so long since she had last spoken to Berta Zuckerkandl. She felt very remote from her now. She knew she wouldn't be able to open her heart to her as she had done in earlier days.

They were driving down the Max-Josef Strasse. Soon they would have reached the Hotel Grand Continental where Mahler would put her down before driving off to the New Exhibition Hall to resume his rehearsals.

'Gustl – I must ask you a very particular favour. I know you of all people will understand.'

'What is it?'

'You've always said this is to be *my* symphony ...'

'But it is, Almscherl! It is yours wholly and entirely. It's about you, it's inspired by you, it's for you, every note. I can't speak for the words, of course – they're Goethe's.' He laughed. 'I'm sure they would have been, if he'd been lucky enough to have set eyes on you.'

'I don't want to come to any rehearsals, Gustl.' She blurted it out. 'Not today. Not tomorrow. Not even to the dress rehearsal tomorrow night.'

She saw his face fall.

'Please, Gustl,' she said. 'It's important to me. I want to hear it for the first time in its final form. When it's absolutely ready. As if you were giving me a present: you wouldn't give a present which wasn't quite made or wasn't quite wrapped, would you?'

'Of course I understand, my darling Almscherl.'

But his face, like his voice, was filled with pain. It made her feel resentful, so that even when he dropped her off at the hotel entrance, placing her in the care of the top-hatted and braided head commission-aire, and said, 'I can't tell you how wonderful it is to know that you're here at last, my darling,' she still felt angry at the weight of dependency he placed upon her.

Mahler had filled her private bedroom as well as the lounge with roses – they scented the whole place. An open window looked out over a quiet, sunlit old courtyard. On the table at the foot of her satin-quilted bed lay two volumes. Both of them were decorated and embellished with identical Grecian figures and entwining foliage. Framed in the decoration of the first was the legend.

Mein Lieben Frau
Alma-Maria
ACHTE SYMPHONIE
von
Gustav Mahler.

On the second volume was printed,

FÜNF LIEDER
komponiert von
ALMA-MARIA SCHINDLER-MAHLER.

On the cover of the latter was placed a small velvet-covered ring box. She opened it. Inside was a simple gold ring designed in the Wiener Werkstätte style. It was set with the most magnificent single blue-water diamond she had ever seen. There was a tiny scrap of paper folded under it. On it, in his neat, spinsterish hand, Mahler had written, '*For my Guardian Angel's birthday – late, but only a little late. A thousand birthday kisses. Your Gustl.*'

At first she was disinclined to remove the ring to try it on. So that was the explanation as to why he had insisted on taking her wedding ring away with him when he had left her at Toblach. She had assumed that it had been just another manifestation of the sentimentality which had become his current mode, and which, try though she may, she was finding increasingly cloying. And there was something so absurd, embarrassing even, about having her five little songs published in exactly the same format and typography as what was almost certain to prove to be his greatest masterpiece.

She called to Kathi to telephone for room service to bring up a bottle of Benedictine. She sat by the open window, still in her travelling clothes, holding the ring in its box, watching the changing colours of the diamond's facets as she turned it ever so slightly and the sharp poniard of light which dazzled her when it caught the sunlight. When Kathi had put down the receiver, she called to her to draw her a bath and then to unpack, describing the dress she wished to change into. Kathi had only just retired into the bathroom when the telephone rang. Calling to the girl to stay where she was, she went over to take up the receiver.

'Walter! You've arrived here already! . . . Not on the same train, surely? Now that was very naughty, even if you did take care . . . Of course I'm alone – Mahler's rehearsing at least until half-past seven . . . No.

Wait a moment. I've paper here, but I'll have to fetch a pencil from my purse . . .'

At first, after Mahler had left her, she had walked over to Alt-schluderbach nearly every day – fobbing Gucki off in the afternoons with ever more strained excuses. There had been several days of rain when she had not dared to go for fear of arousing suspicion – though she would have braved any weather, all else being equal. On the third consecutive rainy day, she spotted him standing on the far side of the meadows under the shelter of the trees. She had thrown on her coat and gone to him, the wet soaking through her stockings as she splashed across the grass.

'I would never have come up to the house, I give you my word,' he said as she led him away through the woods.

'They could have recognized you where you were,' she told him. 'You just can't help yourself, can you?'

She led him down to the summerhouse, now still and deserted. Why, she wondered, had she never thought of it before? They made love lying on the scented spruce planks of the bare floor, half under the case of Mahler's piano.

After that, they met at the summerhouse on several occasions. Once, in the late afternoon, when they were lying there in one another's arms. Alma-Maria heard Gucki's voice from outside in the woods, quite distinctly. Given her hearing, it meant the child could be very close indeed. In absolute panic, she scrambled up, crouching and stooping to keep under the level of the windows while she pulled down her skirts and pulled on and half buttoned her blouse. She dragged on her light summer coat over the dishevelment of her dress and, telling Gropius to remain lying where he was, stepped down onto the beaten track outside.

'What were you doing in Pappi's little house?' Gucki asked accusingly.

'Pappi wants me to send him something to Munich,' she replied.

Though why she should have to offer explanations to the child she did not understand, unless it was the effect of her own violent confusion.

'What?' Gucki demanded.

'Just a couple of papers, darling.'

She took her firmly by the hand.

'Can't I have a look inside?'

'Not when Pappi's not there.'

'But you're here.'

'That's different. I've just made everything tidy.'

'I won't untidy anything!'

'I've said no, and that is that! . . . Where is Miss Turner?'

'Miss Turner's asleep, and I didn't have anything to do. I wanted to be with you – you never play with me in the afternoon nowadays.'

'Come along,' said Alma-Maria.

She felt sick with the narrowness of her escape.

Never before had she abandoned herself to love as she had done during those past two and a half weeks. Never before had she been so greedy for fulfilment and so uninhibited in expressing her desire. She had kissed as she had never kissed before, following him in searching for untried means of expressing her passion. She had adopted postures intended to inflame him, and when he had taken her from behind, feeling her breasts and squeezing her nipples ever more tightly as her own sexual parts closed about and grasped his, not having him before her eyes she fantasized about being taken by giant African kings whose skin was black satin, whose members were the size of a stallion's, and cried out in triumph in the confusion of physical climax and her dream images. Only afterwards, as sensation drained away, had she noticed that Gropius's part in her rapture had increasingly become no more than mechanical. Even so, it was only when he had suggested that he would stop off in Munich on his way back to Westphalia that she felt reconciled to the thought of joining Mahler there.

She picked up the receiver once more.

'Now, I'm ready at last. What's the number ...?' She scribbled it down. 'The Hotel Drei Löwen, Schillerstrasse ... I shall have to come to you, my darling ...'

She glanced in the direction of the bathroom. There was steam pouring out of the door, but Kathi was still safely inside, her hearing no doubt impaired by the rush of water from the taps.

'I'll have to come heavily veiled, and call myself the *Grafin von* something-or-other ...' She giggled, then she said seriously, 'I can't this afternoon – honestly, Waltchen ... Oh darling! You know very well how I'm dying to! But there are bound to be people coming to call on me here. I've got to be available. The whole world will know I've arrived by this time. Tomorrow evening – I'm sure. Everybody will go off to the dress rehearsal – I've already explained to Mahler – and perhaps the day after in the late morning and early afternoon ... I'll have to be back here by three o'clock or so. My mother and Möll will be arriving with my little girl, and there will be a great fuss about dressing and making ready for the performance, so please be good and patient, my darling boy; wait for me to telephone you – I know it will be dreadful for you but you do know I'll do my very best don't you, my darling? And in the meantime, I kiss you *in a very special way* ... Sh, you bad thing! The maid is coming out of the bathroom ...'

She wasn't. But Alma-Maria put down the receiver. When all this was over, she and Mahler were going to spend a few days' holiday in the Bavarian Highlands. Then, it would be time to set off for New York once more. The affair would, therefore, end tidily.

'Almschi! Wherever have you been?' Mutti exclaimed. 'How are you going to be ready in time?'

'I was held up. I'm sorry. One can't move in Munich just now, not without running into acquaintances who insist on stopping to talk.'

'Frau Hofratin Zuckerkandl will be here with the Clemenceaus in half an hour! You can't keep the Prime Minister of the French Republic waiting.'

'I'll be ready! Where's Kathi? Please Muttichen! Ring for Kathi, and tell her to draw my bath straight away. I'm so hot and clammy. I'll just disappear into my room and make sure my clothes and jewellery are ready for me as soon as I get out of the bath.'

And also to give herself the opportunity to change her underwear before Mutti had the opportunity to see the state it was in.

She hadn't intended to be so late. It hadn't been at all like her reluctance to come to Munich. In fact, she had made up her mind to be back at the Continental before Mutti and the others arrived. At first, when she was in Gropius's hotel room, she had glanced at the clock in the corner every five or ten minutes, and had thanked God that the time seemed to be passing so wonderfully slowly. Then, after a period of tranquil drowsiness lying in his arms, when they had started lovemaking again knowing that there would not be another chance at least until the following summer, time had ceased to exist. She had been appalled when she had found out how late it was. Gropius had himself run out into Schillerstrasse in his shirtsleeves to summon the first cab he could find. There had scarcely been time for a farewell kiss. Perhaps that had been for the best: she was sure that he was going to find it a great deal more difficult than her. He was not, after all, attending the musical event of the year at which a single work dedicated to him was to be performed. Nor was he attending afterwards a private banquet to be held in his honour over which the Prime Minister of France would preside.

She had returned to her bedroom and was still wrapped in her towel, her shoulders steaming from the bath, when she heard voices in the lounge outside. She felt limp – the effect of energetic lovemaking and the heat of the bath. Now she began to panic with the idea that she could not possibly make herself ready in time.

There was a knock on the door. Berta Zuckerkandl's head appeared round it, as bird-like as ever, and more peppered with grey than Alma-Maria had remembered.

'I am allowed in, aren't I, darling?'

'Of course you are! ... Berta, let me present Kathi, who is quite wonderful – though not wonderful enough to have me dressed in time, I'm afraid.'

'Nonsense, Almschi. We'll be there with time to spare, with Hans driving.'

'Is Monsieur Georges Clemenceau here?' Alma-Maria asked.

'Georges is with Paul down in the lounge. Sophie is waiting in your lounge out there. Gustav's sister and Alfred Rosé have arrived with

445

Möll, I believe, and are taking charge of your mother. I'm taking charge of you, my darling.'

She picked up Alma-Maria's rose-pink slip from off the satin bed cover.

'Well!' she exclaimed.

Then she noticed the black, embroidered stockings and the Swedish suspender belt with its pink satin ribbons and tiny bows.

'Quite the coquette, eh?' she said. 'Is this the American influence.'

'It's Gustav's influence,' replied Alma-Maria. 'He chose them for me. He sometimes came with me on shopping expeditions along Fifth Avenue in New York or he shopped on his own. He likes Fifth Avenue.'

'I'd never have believed it!' Berta exclaimed. 'Mahler with an eye for ladies' underwear? Mahler going on shopping expeditions, if it comes to that. They'd never believe it in Vienna. You are quite a Circe, aren't you?'

'I don't let him choose my gowns,' said Alma-Maria.

'I didn't imagine this thaw in his puritanism extended to outer garments,' said Berta.

She drew up a chair close to the dressing table where Alma-Maria was sitting. Kathi was unwinding the Turkish towel which had been protecting Alma-Maria's hair.

'That is very beautiful!' said Berta.

She was looking at the diamond ring in its open case next to Alma-Maria's hair brushes.

'It is, isn't it? It's Gustav's birthday present. It was in here, waiting for me, when I arrived.'

'Has it something to do with tonight, as well?' Berta asked. 'You'll be wearing it, of course ... May I?' She reached over and picked it up. 'It is magnificent!' she said.

Alma-Maria had not intended wearing it. In some sense she was shy of it. Given all that had been happening, it seemed too heavy a symbol to accept easily. Yet now she heard herself saying,

'Yes, of course I shall wear it. It will be its first night out.'

The effect of Berta's presence was extraordinary. All of a sudden she was feeling secure, happy even, and filled with eager expectation. Berta sensed her mood.

'It is a wonderful evening, isn't it, Almschi? For both of you.'

Alma-Maria didn't answer straight away. She smiled at Berta in the mirror. Then she turned.

'What is wonderful is your being here, Berta! You always fill me with such reassurance – even at the darkest moments.'

Berta smiled back. 'I can't imagine why ...' She reached over and replaced the ring on the dressing table. 'But I'm deeply flattered, my darling.'

It was amazing, thought Alma-Maria, how far Gropius seemed to have floated from the centre of her present awareness.

They arrived in perfect time. From the passenger seat window of the Zuckerkandls' limousine, Alma-Maria was astonished to see crowds standing five deep behind the files of Bavarian Royal Guardsmen who lined the approach road to the New Exhibition Hall. The car drew up at the entrance; a bewigged and powdered footman came running down the carpeted steps, an unnecessary umbrella under his arm, to open the door. Emil Zuckerkandl stepped down first, followed by Paul Clemenceau. Georges Clemenceau went after, then turned to offer Alma-Maria his hand. He was smaller than his brother, white-haired and heavily moustached like a Napoleonic veteran, with the weather-beaten complexion of a Breton peasant, but also, belying his fierce stare, with the gentle, reassuring manners of the country physician he had once been. Alma-Maria took his hand and, managing her skirts with the other, stepped down into the glare of headlamps from other waiting cars, and the entrance lights on their wrought-iron brackets. She was conscious of eyes gleaming and staring from hundreds of faces, of the growl of recognition at the sight of the French Prime Minister, and then, in a warm swell of reassurance, the cries and murmurs of admiration at her own appearance.

As they mounted the steps, there were the hisses, popping, and blinding flashes of the photographers' light bars. Then, through the dazzlement and glare, she saw Mahler, immaculate on the edge of the white, diamond-studded celluloid of the shirt fronts and the bejewelled satins and ostrich sprays, in his English-tailored 'work clothes', with Bruno Walter on one side and Court Opera Conductor Felix Weingartner on the other. Amidst a scatter of applause from the throng who crowded between the gilded iron pillars of the foyer, he came forward to greet her. Clemenceau released her arm. Mahler held out his hands to take hers. She was conscious of Berta standing close to her train to ensure it remained free. She felt filled with pride in him.

'Almschi! You look so incredibly beautiful!' he exclaimed with a naturalness quite unlike the febrile compliments with which he had been showering her over the past few weeks.

She raised her hand to show him the diamond with its liquescent, multicoloured gleaming on the satin finger of her glove, and smiled.

'Gustl, I'm sure you shouldn't have come front-of-house before giving a performance,' she said. She turned to the two conductors who were with him. 'Isn't it supposed to bring bad luck?' she asked them.

'Not tonight, dear Frau Alma,' Bruno Walter told her. 'It will bring great good fortune.'

'I had to come to receive your blessing on the performance,' Mahler said. 'The benediction of the work's inspiration.'

It was a return of the floweriness which she had come to dislike.

'You know it has my blessing,' she replied with just the faintest hint of a rebuke.

But even as she said it, she sensed that in the midst of all this dazzlement, where the world had come to pay homage to the genius of this nervous, prematurely worn out little Jewish husband of hers, her impatience and resentment with him were shabby and misplaced.

'Gustl – I promise you, this is going to be the best and greatest of all,' she said to him, and kissed him on the lips.

There was a murmur of amused approval from the crowd about them. As Mahler went away, back to his musicians and his dressing room, she recognized faces gathered round her waiting to pay their regards to her: the playwright, Gerhard Hauptmann; Alfred Roller with Koloman Moser and their wives; Willem Mengelberg from Amsterdam, who had wanted to give the first performance of the Eighth himself at the Concertgebouw; Lilli Lehmann, legendary operatic soprano, now retired, on the arm of her younger sister, Riezl, also a distinguished singer; and towering above all others, the bluff Bavarian features of Richard Strauss.

The crowd parted. In front of her – like the bad Fairy Carabosse, was the thought which flashed through Alma-Maria's mind – stood Anna von Mildenburg, towering over her, with a complexion of Greek porphyry under her flowing, ragged chestnut curls, her large bosoms harbouring every note which Wagner ever conceived for soprano voice. She was wearing a white silk dress of the ancient Roman style, her waist enclosed with a silver belt. Over it, she wore a mantle of imperial purple which trailed behind her and was scooped up at the front to show her bare, silver-sandalled feet.

'Dear Frau Alma,' she said, smiling sweetly. She was holding in her arms an enormous bouquet held together by a small golden basket. 'Please,' she said coaxingly, 'Will you forgive me ...? On this night? This sacred night which we are all consecrating to Gustav – and his devotion to you, my dear. Say you forgive me for any ill-feeling I may have caused you in the past.' She held out the flowers. 'They're a tribute from someone who wishes to be counted a true friend, dear Frau Alma.'

Alma-Maria took them, and Mildenburg leant forward and quickly kissed her cheek. Despite the tiny voice inside her which told her that she was being fooled, Alma-Maria was touched. She felt as if she had taken some drug – or one glass too many of Benedictine – which had softened all her emotions. Clutching the flowers to her, she placed her disengaged arm round Mildenburg's neck, and returned her kiss. Mildenburg blinked. She whispered quickly, 'Thank you so much, dear Alma,' and returned to her husband's side.

Alma-Maria was in the midst of the crush, struggling to hear and to return the compliments which were being showered on her, when there was a sudden hush. Four trumpeters in evening dress – members of

Mahler's swollen orchestra, no doubt – had appeared at the rail of the first tier concourse above. The shrill blare of a fanfare resounded against the glass walls and the steel-ribbed vaulting. The crowd had fallen silent. Ushers with white wands formed a passageway to the foot of the steps. Accompanied by a small cloud of uniformed equerries in polished thigh-boots carrying swans'-feathered plumed helmets, and silver-satined ladies in waiting, Prince Ludwig-Ferdinand of Bavaria, with Princess Gisela, entered the foyer to be welcomed by the General Manager of the New Exhibition Buildings. Behind them came the Princess zu Thurn-und-Taxis and Princess Marietta von Hohenlohe.

The fanfare died on the stillness. The royal cortège moved through the crowd, bowing to left and to right. Members of the crowd bowed and curtsied. The procession stopped when it reached Alma-Maria and the Zuckerkandls' party. Prince Ludwig-Ferdinand was a tall, pale young man, prematurely encrusted in royal formality as stiff as his Uhlan uniform jacket. Princess Gisela, on the other hand, was childishly pretty and slightly awkward, as if not yet at ease with protocol.

Alma-Maria had expected the Prince to address Georges Clemenceau for all that the latter was, technically, incognito. To her surprise, she realized that His Highness's glassy stare was fixed on her. She curtsied deeply. He returned it with the slightest of nods.

'*Charmante! Charmante*, Frau Director Mahler!'

He might have been addressing something in the glass case of a museum, thought Alma-Maria.

'Your Highness is most kind,' she replied.

The little Princess Gisela said,

'You must be *so* proud of your husband, Frau Director!'

'Yes. I am, Your Highness,' Alma-Maria replied.

'This – er – symphony we are to hear tonight ... it's dedicated to you?' asked the Princess.

'Yes, Your Highness.'

'It would be so lovely,' the Princess explained with a slight lisp, 'if somebody would dedicate something to me – *and mean it*!'

She giggled, and tucked her arm into the Prince's. The two princesses behind the royal couple smiled at Alma-Maria, who curtsied once more. Prince Ludwig-Ferdinand addressed Berta Zuckerkandl,

'The Frau Hofratin is keeping well, I trust?'

'In the best of health, I thank Your Highness,' Berta replied.

The royal cortège moved on to the stairs. Neither word nor glance had been offered in the direction of Georges Clemenceau who was standing at Alma-Maria's side – surely the most distinguished person present in the hall that night. There was something so calculated about this omission, that it chilled her for a moment.

They followed the cortège up the stairs, and went round to the General Manager's box. As they took their places – a maid took Anna von

Mildenburg's bouquet from Alma-Maria, and placed it in the closet at the back – the audience was pouring in below, filling up the auditorium. Given that the symphony required a thousand performers, there was something entirely appropriate about its receiving its première in a hall as cavernous as a railway station. Even so, the platform, already huge, had been thrust further forward into the auditiorium to accommodate the army of musicians and singers, so that with the front stall seats gathered round it, an extraordinary sense of intimacy between performers and audience was already being established.

The orchestra was already out. Fragments of melody rose to hang above the general noise of instruments being tuned. A single violin sent soaring the melody Alma-Maria recognized as the song of the Young Angels; an oboe, unsuitably shrill, sounded the great summons to the Holy Spirit – *Veni, veni Creator Spiritus!* – which was the melodic foundation of the entire work.

Lined up below the adult choirs was a mass of gleaming brass – eight French horns, ten trumpets, seven trombones. To the left of them and below them was the dull gold of the four harps. Rearing above all was the gigantic concert organ in the glory of its Sezession-style casing. The audience was watching and pointing out to one another the assortment of instruments: the four mandolins, the contra-bassoons and bass clarinets, the celesta, glockenspiel, harmoniums, and tubular bells which augmented the large battery of percussion.

The score was already published and made available. There was a scattering of people through the audience who were examining the bulky volumes on their knees, inspecting Mahler's instrumentation. Perhaps they had not taken into account the fact that Mahler had entrusted the presentation of the performance to his old colleagues of the Vienna Court Opera. As the platform filled up, and the last of the audience squeezed through to their places, the auditorium lights dimmed, as in a theatre, and the platform lights came up. The two top doors, one on either side of the organ, opened, and the three hundred and fifty children of the Zentral Singschule came pouring down in their identical sailor suits to take their places on either wing of the adult choirs, to the delighted applause of their parents scattered around the hall. To another burst of applause, the organist and choirmaster of the Frauenkirche, Adolf Hempel, mounted the steps to the organ console. The eight soloists filed in through the first violins to further applause. Then the hall fell absolutely silent.

Mahler entered briskly, limping only slightly as he made his way through the violins to the podium. There was a ghostly flutter as the string players greeted him in the style reserved for those conductors whom they particulary admired or loved. Then quite suddenly a deafening roar of applause went up from audience and massed choirs alike. For a moment Mahler stood, a tiny figure on the podium, as if bewildered by what was happening. Alma-Maria saw him remove his glasses, a gesture she had never seen him make before on the podium, certainly not previous to a performance. He put his glasses back on and spread out his hands as if helpless to return such an extraordinary show of kindness.

The storm of applause roared on and on like the noise of a great waterfall. It clutched at Alma-Maria's throat, infecting her with a terrible sense of shame. The tiny figure turned in her direction and looked up. It was only for a moment – she could not be sure he had actually seen that she was smiling at him out of the gloom of the first tier. Then he turned again and picked up his stick. The applause died almost as rapidly as it had begun, fading into a hushed stillness.

Mahler turned to the children. In a clear resonant bass, as if his throat were returned to complete health, he said,

'Good evening, children.'

Amidst friendly laughter from the hall, three hundred and fifty children replied,

'Good evening, Herr Kapellmeister.'

The great hall was filled with a sense of ease and affection. What had happened to Gustav, Alma-Maria wondered? There had been admiration in Vienna and friendliness in New York. But he had never evoked an atmosphere like this – and she had seen enough to know that it was he, by his behaviour, who had inspired this prevailing mood of affection . . . Something of a saint – she remembered the suggestion.

He had raised his baton now. The stillness of the hall was palpable. Sophie Clemenceau's hand enclosed hers. The first great notes pealed forth *fortissimo* from the organ causing the ground under the vast auditorium to quiver. The all-embracing cry of soloists and massed choirs resounded from earth to heaven – *Veni! Veni Creator Spiritus!*

> Come! O come, Creator Spirit!
> Visit our souls.
> Fill us with thy Grace,
> Thou who didst create us!

Mahler was conducting the huge ensemble, holding it together as if it were a single instrument totally obedient to his will. There was an electricity generated by every wiry gesture, every movement of his stick; there was no hint of the tired, sick, prematurely old man. The forces assembled before him seem raised by him to a state of exaltation as they sang out their prayer to the Holy Spirit; adults and children alike were rejoicing in their willingness to submit themselves to his leadership. They rose to the enormous climaxes as one exhilarating voice, so intense that it seemed a miracle that iron frames and plate glass could contain the giant diapason. Then they dwindled into the awed, hushed diminuendo, as their opening prayer was answered, and the Holy Spirit led them to the wilderness of crags and deserts where their souls were to experience the vision of judgement.

The huge audience sat rapt, without the least movement, mesmerized by the ever-shifting currents and qualities of sound which poured around them. Even Alma-Maria had never seen Mahler so completely in command of his medium, as if the music in his head and the performers had become one single entity. When the chorus rang out, *Accende lumen sensibus* –

> Kindle our senses with Light.
> Pour They Love into our hearts! –

she seemed to find in herself that same fierce yearning which must have provoked such music. She was seared by its tenderness, so that she experienced compassion and fear simultaneously. When the voices of the soloists mingled with those of the children in singing in terrifying innocence of human love, she wanted to cry out to Gustav, to tell him of the intensity of feeling he was causing her; to cry out to him for forgiveness. Then the pure-toned voices of the Vienna Court Opera sopranos, Gertrud Foerstal and Martha Winternitz-Dorda, soared upwards:

> By the love that, on the feet
> of thy transfigured Son,
> The Penitent Woman let fall.

The voices wove and interwove mingling with the most ethereal sounds Alma-Maria had ever heard conjured from an orchestra. It was all tenderness and innocence – Gretchen washed free of sin by the intensity of the innocence surrounding her, then turning to reach out for Faust, to draw him ever upwards with her while the angelic, seraphic voices soared with them. Alma-Maria began to weep, unable to help herself. Mahler had realized in sound the feelings drawn from her deepest being, with which she had responded to Goethe's *Faust*. He had created in music that wonderful book which Pappi had given her and which had brought her childish soul alive. Now the child's tears were running down her cheeks, silently, like a grace bestowed, welcoming the return to her of the precious, gold-embossed volume which she had watched being consumed with her childhood innocence in the flames of the stove.

The tenor solo sang out with all the triumphant assurance of faith restored, the final summons of Goethe's poem. Solemnly, the great sound sweeping outwards to fill the hall, the massed choirs took up the summons;

'*Blicket auf!* ... Look upwards, up into the Redeemer's gaze, all creatures frail and contrite! ... Look upwards!'

The crescendo of sound increased in intensity, holding the vast audience in motionless attention. To Alma-Maria, in moments which were becoming so intense she did not know how she could bear it, it seemed as if she were truly standing before God. She heard herself inside her head whispering 'Gustl! Oh Gustl!' as if that would ease the awesome mingling of exaltation and vertigo.

The tide of sound receded. In an immense hush, the massed choirs and soloists calmly sang the last words of the poem:

> All that was past of us
> Was but reflected:
> All that was lost in us
> Here is corrected . . .

Choirs, soloists, organ and orchestra rose in one last crescendo while the augmented brass choir sounded a triumphant affirmation of the opening Creator Spirit *motif.*

Alma-Maria was unable to contain her feelings any longer. She turned round to Berta Zuckerkandl, reaching out for her and crying,

'Oh Berta! Berta!'

Berta took her in her arms to comfort her like a child, nodding reassuringly to those around them. She stroked Alma-Maria's hair and murmured comfortingly so that, in the midst of her tears, and not for the first time, Alma-Maria wondered whether Berta knew what was going on in her mind.

The ring of trumpets resounding, the peal of the organ, died on the stillness. The stillness remained. Her head against Berta's breast, her tears soaking Berta's taffeta frogging, Alma-Maria wondered if it was going to be like *Parsifal* at Bayreuth, an occasion too holy to be desecrated by applause. But the applause began – one single, full throated, stamping roar of approval, like the sound of a mighty sea. Alma-Maria raised her head. She took the handkerchief Berta offered her and mopped her eyes. On the floor below, the whole audience was on its feet. Some were streaming down the aisles towards the platform; at the head of one such column was the imposingly tall figure of Richard Strauss, half-running, clapping his hands above his head.

Mahler himself was off the podium. For a second, she wondered what had happened to him. Then she saw him: he had climbed up to the children and was shaking as many of them by the hand as he could reach, thanking them as gravely as if they had been the soloists, while they were standing, calling to him, each of them trying to attract his attention. Below and on either side, all the soloists, chorus, and the entire orchestra were on their feet, and had turned in his direction to applaud him. Everywhere there were smiles and laughter, despite the solemnity of the work itself.

At last Mahler turned away from the children. Now he had stepped down among the percussionists and was shaking their hands with both his own. There was more laughter from the audience and orchestra, who remembered criticism in the Viennese press about his addiction to percussion instruments, and the cartoons of orchestras equipped with hammers and anvils, klaxons, foghorns and strands of barbed wire.

Then, at last, he seemed to become conscious of the ovation which surged around him. He stood, a small, slight figure surrounded by so many who were taller and bigger than himself, one hand resting on the rim of one of the timpani. He bowed jerkily to left and to right. Then he looked up, staring towards the General Manager's box. The house lights had come up. Alma-Maria saw that he could see her. His face had broken into a broad, childlike smile of joy. Standing with the others, she reached out over the parapet, clapping her hands, speaking his name silently with her lips, and letting the tears of pride fall unchecked:

> All that was past of us
> Was but reflected;
> All that was lost in us
> Here is corrected . . .

She was filled with adoration and a sense of devotion.

That night – or next morning, for it was nearly dawn when finally they left the banquet held in their honour at the Hotel Vier Jahreszeiten – after she had undressed, she went unbidden to his room. She got under the quilt, beside him; she was small and he was so thin, there was room in the single bed for both of them if they lay close to one another. For the first time since their return from New York, they slept in one another's arms.

From then on, her devotion to Mahler was absolute. After his second performance of the Eighth Symphony she took him to the Zuckerkandls' summer home near Steinbach, which Berta had lent her. For the next three weeks they passed the happiest time they had ever spent together. Gustav was so relaxed in his manner that she wondered if at last the poor Jewish boy from Moravia had realized that the world acknowledged his genius, and that he had finally justified any sacrifices his family had made so that he might have a musical education. He no longer found it necessary to pour out extravagant declarations of his love for her, but accepted her care of him with simple gratitude. In the afternoons they walked arm in arm along the lake shore, while in the evenings, when the first autumn chill rolled down off the mountains, they would play together what he regarded as the greatest of all music – the final piano concertos of Mozart.

They returned to Vienna to pack for the voyage to New York, staying with Mutti and Möll on the Hohe Warte. Nearby the ground was being prepared for the building of a Haus Mahler; they would walk each day to the site to watch the foundations being laid, and to consult with the architect, Josef Hoffmann. Once, as they were walking back up Steindorfstrasse, Gustav said,

'You're going to be in great demand when I'm gone, you know. What with your youth and your looks.'

She felt stunned. She could think of nothing to say in reply.

'Who's it going to be, do you think?' he asked.

'Gustl! For God's sake don't say such things!'

And yet he had sounded perfectly collected – even amused at the prospect. He started reciting names, all of them so unlikely as to be quite absurd, and ended up by laughing and telling her,

'I think it'll be better if I stay with you for the time being.'

She had begun to cry. She hugged his arm and said reproachfully,

'Look Gustl. Now look what you've done!'

He went down to the Loew Institute for a check-up. Franz Chvostec decided that his tonsils should be cauterized to prevent a further inflammation like that he had suffered in Munich. After this minor operation, he was very pleased with himself, being convinced that he had nothing more to fear from his health. One sign of his transformation was that he was letting Anton dress him smartly in his English-made shirts and suits and shoes as much during daylight hours as at night. He remarked to Möll, who expressed surprise at how dapper was his appearance, that although Beethoven never took the least care either of his dress or of personal hygiene, 'spitting on the floor doesn't mean you're capable of composing *Fidelio*'.

But then, one night, he came to Alma-Maria when she was seated alone in Mutti's drawing room, bringing his manuscript scores containing his re-orchestrations of Schumann's four symphonies.

'I'm not yet to be counted among the world's greatest symphonists,' he told her. 'Not yet. But my time will come in the next forty years or so, you'll see.'

'*I'*ll see?' she laughed.

'Oh yes. So keep these carefully. One day they'll be valuable if only because people will want to see how I interpreted Schumann. And then you must have them published and sold.'

Two days before they left Vienna, when Alma-Maria and Kathi were in the midst of packing, a letter arrived from Thomas Mann:

Dear and honoured lady,

I have written to your husband telling him how deeply indebted I feel I am to him for the tremendous impression made on me by the performance of his sublime symphony on September 12th. I have enclosed a copy of my latest work – a poor return for what I have gained from him; a mere feather's weight indeed, but one which will, I trust, afford you both tolerable entertainment for an hour or two.

I hope you will not take it amiss if I beg you to take good care of this glorious man who, as I believe, expresses the art of his time in its most profound and sacred form ...

It was, of course, many years later that she heard from his son, Golo, that the universal approval in which Gustav had basked in Munich combined with his haggard and gaunt appearance had inspired Mann to create the character, Gustav von Aschenbach, protagonist of his most famous novel.

Throughout the voyage to New York, Gustav appeared more in love with life than he had ever been. There were none of the fears of the first voyage out on the SS *Augusta-Viktoria*. He had insisted they bring Gucki and the inevitable Miss Turner with them on this trip. When they were on the tender, sailing out of Cherbourg heading across a choppy sea to the huge bulk of the liner, Gucki cried out in delight and ran to the rail. Miss Turner ran after her and grabbed her by the hands.

'You're too excited!' she exclaimed. 'You're not to get excited!'

Gustav stooped and picked Gucki up. To Miss Turner's horror and Alma-Maria's trepidation, he sat the child on the rail with her legs hanging over the side and, holding her firmly, said,

'Now, my Guckerl, you be as excited as you like!'

'Really, Herr Mahler!' Miss Turner exclaimed indignantly.

They stayed at the Savoy Plaza Hotel, where their suite was larger than their previous rooms at the Majestic, but still overlooked the park. Their fellow guests included many of the stars of Metropolitan Opera – Caruso, Geraldine Farrar, Scotti, and Chaliapin, and also Toscanini who was sharing the conducting with Mahler for the season. Between rehearsals, Caruso and Chaliapin took it upon themselves to help Mahler take Gucki out for walks. Alma-Maria, watching from the lounge window, could see them as they snowballed, tobogganed, or skated, Chaliapin's six foot seven inches towering over Mahler's tiny figure and Caruso's small round one.

Mahler was contracted to conduct revivals of *Fidelio* and *Figaro*, and a new production of Tchaikovsky's *Queen of Spades*, a favourite of his. The latter he accomplished with such intensity that several of the women of the lady guarantors of the Metropolitan Opera fainted away during the performances. He also conducted the New York Philharmonic Symphony Orchestra in a series of concerts in Carnegie Hall. On 8 January, he gave a performance of his own Fourth Symphony, which was greeted with rapturous applause. He introduced several works which were new to New York audiences – Elgar's 'Enigma' Variations, Rachmaninov's Second Piano Concerto, with the composer playing the solo, and Busoni's 'Turandot' Suite. He caused a sensation by directing from the harpsichord – something which had not been done since the end of the eighteenth century – his own arrangement of movements from Bach's Suites in B minor and D major.

On 21 February, he was due to conduct the first performance of Busoni's 'Cradlesong at the Graveside of My Mother' at Carnegie Hall, in the presence of the composer, who was an old friend both of himself and of Alma-Maria. He woke up that morning with a sore throat and furred tongue; it was the first time he had suffered from a sore throat since he had had his tonsils cauterized. Alma-Maria insisted he stay in bed for the morning, and that he let Theodore Spiering, who was now leader of the New York Philharmonic, take the morning rehearsal. She called Dr Fraenkel, who found that Mahler was running a temperature. Dr Fraenkel tried to persuade him not to appear that night. Mahler, however, could not endure the thought of letting down Busoni. If he had never conducted when he was running a temperature, he told Dr Fraenkel, he would have missed half the concerts he had been booked to conduct during the past year and a half.

Outside his room, Alma-Maria told Dr Fraenkel,

'He's set his heart on conducting tonight ... You don't know his strength of will. He had tonsilitis in Munich. He had to miss several days of rehearsal because he had a sore throat and a temperature, but the moment he was up on the podium he'd recovered – and that was before he'd had his tonsils cauterized.'

'Cauterization isn't a wonder cure, you know,' Dr Fraenkel said. 'And your husband has a damaged heart.'

'Please, Dr Fraenkel. Trust me. I know Gustav.'

Dr Fraenkel shook his head doubtfully.

When Alma-Maria returned to the bedroom, Gustav was sitting bolt upright.

'Well?' he demanded.

She went and sat on the bed beside him. They held hands – his were burning hot. His eyes shone behind his spectacles.

'Dr Fraenkel says he won't keep you a prisoner here,' she told him.

'I knew I could trust my Almscherl!'

'There are conditions. You've got to let Dr Fraenkel go with you to Carnegie Hall. And he insists on bringing you back here. No after-concert dinners with the band!'

'And you? Are you going to take me?'

'Of course.'

'Then everything will be perfect.'

He lay back on the pillow and closed his eyes.

They took him to Carnegie Hall by car; he was wrapped in a travelling rug over his overcoat, for all that the journey was little more than a tour round the square. Dr Fraenkel remained with him backstage until it was time for the performance, then he came up and joined Alma-Maria and Busoni, who were with the Manager, Loudon Charlton, in his box.

During the first half of the concert, Mahler conducted Mendelssohn's 'Italian' Symphony and, as always, managed to invest one of the most

457

familiar pieces in the concert repertory with so much life that it sounded as though it had never before been performed as its composer had intended.

During the second half, Busoni went out onto the platform after the performance of 'Cradlesong' to take his bow and to shake Mahler's hand. He was greeted with sufficiently enthusiastic applause not to feel disappointed, and returned to the box well pleased. He whispered to Alma-Maria,

'Thank God it *was* Mahler! At least they heard it the way I wanted it.'

The concert concluded with a suite of dances by the Italian composer, Bossi, for comedies by Goldoni. It was the sort of lightweight *divertissement* designed to please the after-dinner audience in the tier *loges*, and they greeted it with great enthusiasm and demands for an encore. They continued to applaud loud and long in order to summon Mahler back to the podium, but he did not appear. The applause went on for at least another minute. Mahler could be stiff in front of audiences, almost to the point of rudeness, but never had he totally ignored an ovation. Alma-Maria felt a small, cold fist clench in her stomach. She glanced across at Busoni and saw the anxiety on his kindly face. Dr Fraenkel had already pulled himself to his feet.

The telephone in the back of the box buzzed and clattered. Loudon Charlton went up to answer it. He listened and then hung up the receiver. As the noise of clapping below diminished, turning to an angry muttering, he came back to Alma-Maria.

'I'm dreadfully sorry to have to tell you this, Frau Mahler, but Herr Mahler collapsed in a faint as he came off just now. The staff have carried him down to his dressing room and are sending for a doctor.'

'I'm Herr Mahler's medical adviser,' said Dr Fraenkel.

He indicated that Mr Charlton should show him the way. Alma-Maria followed. She glanced at Busoni.

'Will you come with me?' she asked.

'Certainly,' Busoni said.

There couldn't be anything really wrong, she told herself. Gustav had been in such good spirits when they left the hotel. Perhaps his constitution had been weakened by this infection in his throat. Perhaps Spiering would have to take over his assignments for a day or two – the concert with the New York Philharmonic on the twenty-fourth, for instance. Ever since Munich they had been so happy, there couldn't be anything serious ... And it didn't matter how he felt when he mounted the podium, he was always in a state of exhilaration when he stepped down; he'd always told her it was the best cure in the world, standing there waving a stick ...

She was sitting at Gustav's bedside feeding him from a dish of minced lamb, onion and carrots, spoonful by spoonful, when Dr Baehr arrived at the suite. Dr Baehr was a young man who had achieved distinction in his field remarkably quickly. He was neatly, expensively dressed, almost pretty, and wore the gravity of medical authority as if he had assumed it like a theatrical costume. The nurse retained by Alma-Maria brought him, escorted by Dr Fraenkel and Dr Libman, to the bedroom. They grouped themselves round the foot of the bed.

Gustav smiled at them. 'I hope, gentlemen,' he said in his throaty, catarrhal voice, 'you are all agreed on some lingering disease.'

Dr Fraenkel had called in Dr Libman, senior heart specialist at the Rockefeller Institute to confirm his original diagnosis. Dr Libman had called in Dr Baehr, senior bacteriologist at the Mount Sinai Hospital, to take blood samples to confirm their mutual opinion. Dr Baehr had now come back, five days after taking the samples, to return his verdict.

'Being fed like this,' Gustav added, 'is so nice, I would hate to have to give it up. In fact, I would recommend such treatment to anyone.'

The three doctors smiled politely, but their smiles could not conceal the gravity of their expressions. Dr Fraenkel said gently to Alma-Maria,

'Alma, my dear, I think it would be best if you left your patient to us for the moment.'

'Why?' she asked.

She was unable to conceal the anger which fear had provoked in her.

'Because, dearest Almschi,' croaked Gustav, 'Our friends might find it less difficult to talk to us one at a time.' He squeezed her hand weakly. 'Do go, my darling. But not too far away.'

She kissed his fingers, and went out into the lounge. She could scarcely believe what was happening. She crossed to the windows. She had asked Miss Turner to take Gucki out for a walk in the park when Dr Fraenkel had rung up to say that he and the others were driving over to the Savoy Plaza Hotel, although the light had begun to fail. Gucki had asked why they had to go out so late. Was Pappi composing something very special? she wanted to know.

There had been a procession of visitors through the suite ever since Gustav had had to take to his bed. Caruso had sat with him – had shown him his collection of cartoons of all the musicians and singers he had worked with, and had presented him with one of Gustav himself. Busoni had made him laugh by showing him ridiculously complicated exercises in counterpoint based on popular burlesque hall melodies. Chaliapin came and sang to him what he maintained were Russian songs of unparalleled bawdiness, but made both Alma-Maria and Gustav laugh by then translating them into a German so modest that they wouldn't have raised a blush on a convent girl's cheek. Throughout the passing of the days, there had been such a festive atmosphere maintained by their friends that it had been hard to grasp the gravity of Gustav's condition. But it was generally known, and it seemed as if he were as famous in

New York as in Vienna. The black hotel lift boy never failed to ask after him; the Irish policemen on duty on Plaza Square always asked if Maestro Mahler's condition was improving. Strangers on Fifth Avenue and 59th Street would stop her, asking after him and wishing them both well.

She stared out from the seventh floor, over the trees at the lines of gas lamps which lit the paths, and at the unwavering glow from West Manhattan. She wished Mutti would arrive. It was still less than a week since she had cabled Vienna. It took a day to reach Paris, and half a day to reach Cherbourg from Paris. The crossing took five days. She wouldn't arrive in New York until tomorrow morning at the very earliest . . .

'Alma?'

Dr Fraenkel had emerged from the bedroom. He was alone, she saw, looking at his reflection in the blackness of the window.

'You are going to tell me the truth, I hope, Dr Fraenkel.'

'I have to tell you that Dr Baehr's findings corroborate exactly the diagnosis made by Dr Libman and myself. Gustav is gravely ill, I'm afraid.'

He waited, but Alma-Maria simply told him,

'Go on.'

'Gustav is suffering a subacute bacterial endocarditis.'

'Which means in ordinary language?'

'It means there is a serious secondary infection of a heart which is already weakened by disease. Baehr has identified the presence of colonies of *Streptococcus viridans* in his bloodstream.'

She turned round to face him.

'Gustav knows. He asked to be told the exact truth about his condition – and the implications,' Dr Fraenkel continued. 'Libman has informed him.'

'What are . . . the implications?'

'Forgive me for being so abrupt, Alma – but he is dying. There's no escaping it.'

'So no more years of productive work?' she asked, echoing a conversation of some twenty-two months previously.

She saw the ghost of a smile on Dr Fraenkel's face. He too recalled their drive together under the ancient trees.

'No. I don't want to offer you any false hopes, my dear. You see, he doesn't have the stamina any more to fight so serious an infection. It is a matter of weeks rather than months – and possibly days rather than weeks. I can't tell you how sorry I am to have to be the bearer of such news.'

She nodded. The two other doctors came from the bedroom. The nurse closed the door after them. It was curious, thought Alma-Maria in a detached way, how the two distinguished older men seemed to defer to their young colleague.

Dr Baehr glanced in Dr Fraenkel's direction. Then he said to Alma-Maria,

'You may return to you husband's bedside, Frau Director. He is asking for you.'

Dr Libman checked her. He looked from Dr Fraenkel to Dr Baehr.

'Your husband, dear lady,' he said, 'has asked if it is possible for him, in his present state of health, to travel back to Vienna. Dr Baehr and I are agreed that there is no reason why his very natural wish to return home should not be granted.'

With clarity of mind, she realized immediately that they meant he was so sick that the rigours of the journey could not possibly do him any harm. Dr Fraenkel saw that she had understood.

'I shall cable Paris,' he told her. 'We shall ask Professor André Chantemesse of the Pasteur Institute to have a look at him. An examination after the sea voyage by one of the world's leading authorities on his condition won't do any harm, eh?'

He wasn't going to suggest it would do any good, either.

She went through to Gustav. With her back turned on the doctors and their grave self-control of manner, she was ready to run to him – to tell him that he wasn't to leave her, and that their real life together was just beginning. She wanted to tell him that her love for him was now so powerful that it could work miracles. But he prevented her. He was smiling so gently at her, and reaching out for her.

'Almscherl, when I'm better, will you go on being as loving to me as you've been these past weeks?'

'Oh Gustl! Why do you ask? Of course, of course, my darling! For ever and ever!'

One of the nurses had placed an armchair for Alma-Maria by the door of Gustav's private room. From end to end, the corridor was a mass of bouquets which had been brought in hourly since their arrival in Vienna.

Professor Chvostec, who had gone to Paris to meet them, to consult with Professor Chantemesse at the Pasteur Institute and to bring Gustav home, came out of the room with Carl Möll.

'Still here, Alma?' he asked in his robust voice. 'Better let your stepfather take you to your excellent mother. And get some rest, or you'll be on the same road as Mahler.'

He always talked loudly in the manner of some purple-faced cavalry colonel. She grabbed his hand.

'For God's sake keep your voice down!' she begged him. 'He might hear you.'

Professor Chvostec looked kindlily down at her. He patted her shoulder in the manner of all medical men who pride themselves on their avuncularity with attractive young women.

'He won't hear anything now, my dear,' he assured her. 'Except what's going on in his own head.'

'I'm staying here,' said Alma-Maria. She stared up at Möll and repeated herself. 'I'm staying here ... I promised him I wouldn't leave him.'

She felt it weakened rather than confirmed the impression of resolve. Still – they'd have to carry her away even though her head felt iron-clamped with fatigue, and the white of the hospital corridor in the bleak electric light burned her eyes.

The rail journey across Europe had been an extraordinary experience. News of Mahler's progress had been telegraphed ahead. At every station there had been newspaper reporters and small knots of well-wishers with bouquets of flowers. As they passed through Switzerland and the length of the Archduchy of Austria, the knots of well-wishers had become crowds, pushing and struggling to put flowers onto the train and to find out about the patient's condition, so that any innocent tourist might have thought that royalty was passing through.

During the sea voyage, Gustav had been well enough to have been dressed and taken up daily on deck. By the time he left the Pasteur Institute, his condition had so deteriorated that he could not be moved from his wheeled stretcher. Nevertheless, he remained conscious and awake through most of the journey to Vienna and the Loew Institute. He enjoyed the fuss made of him, insisting Alma-Maria tell him the names of the newspapers which were asking after him, and asking her to try to take the names and addresses of people who gave him flowers so that he could write personally to thank them when he was feeling better.

She had sat on an upturned suitcase beside his stretcher in the van, holding his poor limp hand. Several times he said to her,

'Do you know, Almschi, I never believed people could be so kind? Wasn't it stupid of me?'

When he did doze off it was never for long. Then he would start, and call out anxiously, 'Almscherl?' When she squeezed his hand to let him know she was still beside him, he would say, 'You're an angel.'

He talked about going to Egypt on several occasions.

'We're coming home in poor trim this time, my angel. But you'll see! We'll be on our feet again, and then we'll go to Egypt for a month or two and see nothing but blue sky.'

He had looked wonderfully beautiful with his pale, translucent skin, his quiff of jet black hair, and his burning dark eyes. She had kissed his hand from time to time, and rested her cheek against it, so that he would know even in his sleep that she was there with him.

The moment they had arrived in Vienna, Chvostec had had him trundled off the train and up into a motor-ambulance which had been drawn up on the platform of the Westbahnhof. They had driven directly to the Loew Institute. There, a large ground floor room had been prepared, with French windows looking out across a veranda to the gardens. Gustav had stared out from his bed, struggling to straighten his spectacles.

'It is so beautiful!' he had exclaimed. Then, again: 'People are so kind.'

From the multitude of flowers which arrived at the Institute that first day, one particularly enormous bouquet in an ivory white basket caught his attention. On the handle was an unusually large label.

'Read it,' he said to Alma-Maria.

There were some eighty signatures written around a bold inscription in old gothic script – 'From the Vienna Philharmonic'. When she told him, the tears began to run down his cheeks.

'*My* Philharmonic!' he had whispered over and over again. '*My* Philharmonic!'

During the forty-eight hours which had elapsed since then, his breathing had become laboured and he had had to be given oxygen. She had stayed with him, never leaving him, sleeping in the chair beside his bed. Sometimes he cried out like a child in fear, 'Almschi! Almschi!' She would press his fingers to her cheek, not knowing whether he was aware of her presence, and filled with guilt lest he be living some past agony of spirit.

Gucki had been brought to his bedside. He reached out his arms and held her.

'Stay good, my darling. As good as you have always been.'

Gucki replied obediently, 'Yes, Pappi,' then glanced at Alma-Maria to check that she had behaved correctly. Alma-Maria had eased her from Gustav's embrace, unsure of his fleeting consciousness, and returned her to Mutti's care.

Strauss had come from Munich to bid him farewell. Gustav was completely lucid. They held hands. Gustav asked, 'Will people always regard us as rivals?'

'My dear fellow! There are always going to be fools,' Strauss replied.

His sister, Justi, had come with her husband, Alfred Rosé, still leader of the Philharmonic. Gustav did not recognize them. He turned to Alma-Maria and asked,

'Who is the strange woman?'

For a moment, Alma-Maria thought it was a family joke, he had spoken so clearly. Then Justi burst into tears and Rosé had had to lead her away.

Swellings had appeared on his legs and abdomen. The bed quilt was thrown back and radium bags applied. Professor Chvostec was sent for. He examined him and shook his head.

'It will not be long now,' he told Alma-Maria. 'Uraemia has set in.'

Möll had appeared at nightfall, and had begged her to return with him to the Hohe Warte. She refused fiercely, telling him that near Gustav was the only place where she belonged.

Professor Chvostec reappeared in what had seemed to her the middle of the night. He had been attending a faculty dinner and was wearing white tie and tails. It seemed extraordinary to her that even among those who were looking after Gustav, ordinary life continued.

Gustav had been mumbling and reciting in a language wholly foreign to her. He started again in Chvostec's presence.

'Do you know what it is?' she asked him.

He smiled slightly and nodded.

'Memories of his early youth,' he said. 'Hebrew. He is reciting the passages of scripture he would have learnt in *shul*.'

She had felt as if a shaft had been shot through her breast: a spear-point intimation of the horrifying loneliness which was to come.

Another day had passed. Several times Gustav called out, 'Almschi! My angel!' as if from a darkness into which she could not follow. She had held his hand in both of hers, and had kissed his fingers hoping that she could evoke the least response that would tell her he knew she was there.

The darkness returned, and the flowers were removed from the room. The lights were dimmed. Thunder began to rumble over the hills, and there was a flicker of sheet lightning behind the trees out in the garden. A wind rose steadily, increasing in intensity until it was buffeting the trees and clattering the latches on the French windows. Gustav's breathing began to rattle – an absurd contribution to the general tempest noise, she thought. Then she saw that his eyes were wide open and staring brightly into the dark. She rang the bell to summon help. A male attendant answered immediately. He took one look at Gustav, and rang the bell three times. There was the sound of feet running in the corridor outside. Suddenly the room was filled with people – nurses in starched caps and aprons, registrars in white coats hastily pulled on. The oxygen trolley clattered on the wooden tiles of the floor as it was dragged across the room to the bedside. Somebody said something about telephoning for Professor Chvostec.

A registrar had led her gently from the bedside. Even she had realized that she could only be in the way if she had remained where she was. Then the nurse had brought the armchair and placed it among the flowers in the white corridor. Amidst the thunder and the sound of torrential rain, the corridor was filled with the scent of flowers.

She looked up at Möll standing beside Professor Chvostec.

'There's no point in your staying, Carl,' she told him. 'Go home to Mutti.'

'Almschi,' said Möll, 'won't you consider Professor Chvostec's advice? There's no point in damaging your own health.'

Ever since childhood, Möll's voice had always been that of restrained

464

common sense – restrained, passionless common sense.

'Please leave me, Carl. I know best where I belong.'

Möll looked to Professor Chvostec. Chvostec nodded.

'It won't be long,' he said.

'Very well,' Möll replied.

They moved away down the corridor. The electric light gleamed on Möll's scalp under the thin layer of hair.

'You will telephone me immediately ... ?'

The sound of Möll's voice was drowned in a deafening clap of thunder. Lightening flashed through the skylight windows of the corridor. Rain sluiced down the panes onto the roof and splashed down the gutter pipes. In the shortest of intervals in the noise, she heard Möll's voice say,

'... In the case of a death mask, it's absolutely necessary ...'

She stood up. 'I'm going to him!' she shouted.

The nightmare possibility that they might hasten Gustl's end in order to take his death mask had occurred to her. There was a sane person inside her who told her that it was nonsense – that Möll, though he might never have been her favourite person, would not have considered for one moment any such thing. But there was a panic terror threatening her which could at any moment overwhelm the sane Alma-Maria.

Professor Chvostec returned.

'One moment, Alma,' he said. 'Only a moment.'

He was perfectly calm and reasonable.

He went into Gustav's room. There was another thunder-crack and flash of lightning. She stood staring up at the skylight, waiting for another flash of lightning to show her the water cascading down the apex of the roof.

Professor Chvostec came up beside her and took her arm.

'You may go to him, Alma. We've done what we can do. He'll be in no discomfort, I promise you that.'

Two nurses brought the oxygen trolley out into the corridor. Chvostec took her to the door, and let her go in alone. A nurse replaced her chair by the bed. Gustav lay with his cheek on the pillow. The rattle in his breathing had stopped. He looked as if he were sleeping peacefully.

The thunder died away over the hills to the south. The rain stopped gradually. Lulled by the sound of Gustav's steady breathing, she too fell asleep for an hour or two. When she woke, she found it was already growing light. It was the presence of a nurse which had woken her – standing at the bedside feeling Gustav's pulse. Through the French windows, across the wet boards of the veranda, the garden gleamed with fallen rain.

Alma-Maria pulled herself up from the chair. She walked round the bed. Gustav had moved. He was now looking up from the pillows. The nurse laid his arm gently on the quilt and let it go. His face was so gaunt and pallid it seemed quite wrong his hair should be jet black and his eyes so bright. Then Alma-Maria noticed that his mouth and the creases at the corners of his eyes were shaping into a smile.

'Gustl?' she asked eagerly.

She glanced at the nurse, and saw that she too was watching. He was struggling to raise his head. He was breathing with difficulty, and there was a thread of spittle from the corner of his lips. But his face was radiant as if he had entered into a sudden great joy. He was staring not at her, but past her, as if somebody had come into the room behind her, some very dear friend whom he, not wearing his spectacles, had only just recognized. His mouth opened and closed several times in his effort to speak. Then, quite clearly, he said,

'Mozart! Dear Mozart!'

His head fell back and rolled sideways on the pillow. His eyes closed. The expression on his face was of happy peacefulness.

The nurse reached for his wrist once more. She turned to Alma-Maria. Loosing his hand, she said,

'It's all over. The Herr Director has passed from us.'

She made the sign of the Cross over the bib of her apron, and reached for the bell.

Alma-Maria stepped out of the front door of the Institute into the morning sunlight. Steam was rising from pavements still damp from the previous night's storm. Berta Zuckerkandl's car was parked against the opposite kerb. Hans, her chauffeur, was rubbing the brasswork round the radiator with a shammy leather. Berta stepped down from the passenger seat. She was in black from head to foot, with a light black veil over her face. She raised it in order to kiss Alma-Maria as Alma-Maria crossed the street to join her. How had she known to appear so promptly, and in mourning?

'Is it all over, darling?' Berta asked as she kissed her.

As she enfolded Alma-Maria in her arms, Alma-Maria remembered: Emil had died only a few weeks previously.

'All over,' she confirmed.

'Peacefully?'

'He looks so happy,' Alma-Maria replied.

Berta helped her up into the car.

'It'll be a little while before you feel anything,' Berta told her, speaking from recent experience.

But Alma-Maria did feel something. She felt as if Gustav had not said goodbye to her.

'Kovacs came round to see me last night. Chvostec had told him it would all be over by morning, so I thought I'd come and wait for you since I've all the time in the world.'

'I wish I'd gone with him,' said Alma-Maria in a matter-of-fact voice. She had scarcely managed to reach her room in the Villa Möll before

466

the bells started booming out – from St Stephen's, the Karlskirche, the Votivkirche, the Minoritenkirche, the Schottenkirche, the Franziskanerkirche, and all the other churches of Vienna – passing bell answering passing bell to toll the news of the death of one of Vienna's greatest citizens, until air and earth rocked with the sound of Gustav Mahler's departure from mortal life.

The *Neue Frei Presse* announced,

Mahler is dead, and Vienna mourns. 'One of the greatest sons of our city! ... One of the most charming of men ... The Director who raised our opera to unheard-of heights!' Vienna has always mourned thus. When the man lived, they found him ugly and bizarre. Now he has a noble, even a saintly, profile, and his music has the true originality of genius. One has to be dead to live comfortably in Vienna.

Truly, few can mourn as well as the Viennese

Alma-Maria devoured the obituary columns with possessive eagerness, column after column of unstinting praise and eulogy. Wryly she noted that not one newspaper in Vienna or Graz, or Innsbruck, or anywhere else in Austria, mentioned the solitary fact that they had invariably mentioned when he had been alive: that he was a Jew.

The bells were tolling again, today, across the city, to give notice that a solemn Requiem Mass was being offered in St Stephen's prior to the interment of Mahler's remains in the village graveyard in Grinzing. Driving in the first carriage (she was sure Gustav would have far preferred a cortège of motor-cars), as they turned off the Ring up the Kärntnerstrasse towards the Stephansplatz, she noticed the dense crowds thronging the pavements. There were shop assistants, waiters and waitresses standing on the steps, and secretaries, and young women clerks in sailor-collared blouses leaning out of first floor windows. As they approached the cathedral, the passing bell of St Stephen's boomed heavy and leaden into her brain. The carriage virtually ground to a standstill.

A police officer in a cocked hat with a short sword at his side came to the carriage window.

'Forgive me,' he began.

He saluted Alma-Maria, examining her face through her black veil, then glanced at Carl Möll, Gucki, Mutti, and twelve-year-old Marie in turn. He was not entirely sure which of the grown-ups to address, finally fixing on Möll as the solitary male.

'*Gnädige* Herr,' he saluted again. 'Forgive me. We had not expected such crowds. We are making a way through them now.'

Gucki, who had her hand in Mutti's lap, leaned forward to look out. The carriage lurched forward. So did Gucki. Marie took her arm and pulled her back.

'We are here to be seen, not to see, Guckerl,' she told her.

Alma-Maria wondered who had told her that; one of the maids in all probability. It had the sardonic ring of a Viennese kitchen area. But Gucki was full of wonder.

'Have they all come to say goodbye to Pappi?' she asked.

'Yes, *liebchen*. They have.'

There was a quavering in her voice she had not expected. Gucki searched her face through her veil.

'There must have been lots of people who liked him,' she said.

Alma-Maria did not attempt to reply. She reached across and gave Gucki's hand a squeeze.

The carriage finally drew up in front of the Great Gateway of the cathedral. There was a crowd of uniforms on the steps: silver and bronze helmets, and swan and ostrich plumes, and silver and gold braid. The carriage door was opened by a uniformed cathedral sidesman. Möll stepped down onto the pavement.

'Until afterwards, my dears,' he said, and the carriage door was closed behind him.

'Aren't we getting down here?' Gucki asked.

'Women and girls have to get down at the Bishop's Gate,' said Marie. 'That's the rule.'

Alma-Maria felt a sudden surge of panic. She was afraid she might faint on her way in.

'You'll stay close to me, won't you, Muttichen?' she whispered.

'Of course I will, my darling.'

Alma-Maria had the feeling Mutti was proud of her for being the widow of the great Gustav Mahler.

The carriage began its short passage round the Holy Cross Chapel to the Bishop's Gate on the north side of the cathedral. There were uniforms everywhere, and faces propped up by braided collars and polished leather stocks; veined, old men's cheeks half hidden under martinet whiskers, and smooth apple-pink cheeks of stripling boys with moustaches of soft down. How many of them could have borne listening to one of Gustav's symphonies? How many of them would have allowed him to set foot in one of their officers' clubs, knowing him to be a Moravian Jew? Yet the Kaiserlich-Königlich Chamberlain's office in the Hofburg had ordered them into their finery to bury him, and they had unquestioningly obeyed.

The carriage creaked to a halt once more. A group of cathedral wandsmen in blue and silver, with braided cocked hats under their arms, came to assist her down and to escort her over the threshold of the cathedral. The moment had come. Gustav had told her that for his sake she must remain beautiful after he had gone so that she should be a living key to his work. As she mounted the steps under the shadow of the cathedral porch, she lifted her veil, folding it onto the rim of her hat. Black satin and crêpe set off her blonde good looks – she knew it.

And so she dedicated herself to Gustav as she stepped out past the writhing marble of Prince Eugen's tomb into the broad beams of sunlight which struck down from the clear glass of the windows – dedicated herself as if she was approaching a nuptial rather than a funeral mass. The chief sacristan was waiting at the bottom of the centre aisle to guide her to her place. With Mutti and Gucki and Marie behind her, she set off. For once the expression 'sea of faces' was made real for her. As the great congregation turned to glance at her, the complexion of the mass of heads changed as the texture of the sea changes under the shifting pattern of cloud and sunlight and wind; and there was a steady, rising murmuring of voices which seemed to stretch away into crypts and invisible chantries. Above her, the passing bell struck once more, but this time its impact was muffled by the fabric of the cathedral and the sound was dissipated into the spaces outside.

There was a line of faldstools and prie-dieux at the foot of the sanctuary steps in front of the huge congregation. Justi and Arnold Rosé and other members of Mahler's family from Bohemia, and his cousin, Gustav Frank, from St Petersburg – in the full court uniform of a high ranking Imperial Russian ministerial officer – were already in place. They formed a scattered Jewish outpost hemmed in on three sides by the massed ranks of K-K officialdom with ribbons across its starched shirt fronts and jewelled orders pinned to its breasts, interspersed with the inevitable military splendour of glittering cuirasses and braided lanyards and epaulettes.

Before her, on the platform halfway up the steps, was the draped catafalque rising from a tidal surf of flowers and black-ribboned wreaths. At each corner stood the huge, gold-encrusted candlesticks which were brought out only for the funeral rites of Austria's greatest sons. Above the flowers, hidden, weighed down under the pall of stitched gold, was the small shrunken figure in its coffin – the object of all this formal adoration – the man whom they had never failed to carp at, insult, and mock during the years he had been making the Vienna Opera and the Vienna Philharmonic Orchestra the greatest and most famous musical enterprises in the world. And above it all, over the top of the catafalque, she could see, sitting against the Kaiser Friedrich Memorial, the Crown Prince, the Archduke Franz-Ferdinand, surrounded by his military equerries, his posture erect, stiff, his face vacant rather than bored.

The sense of déjà vu made her quite faint. It was all so precisely as it had been nearly twenty years before. The Cardinal-Archbishop moved forward through a cloud of incense to sprinkle the catafalque accompanied by a similar squadron of acolytes clutching at the lace of his cassock. From the Winter Chapel above the High Altar the Court Opera Chorus sang out the stately, decorous mourning of the opening of Mozart's D-minor Requiem. *Requiem aeternam dona eis ...*

As the first statement of the music ended, a solo soprano soared flawlessly upwards,

Te decet hymnus ... Unto Thee in Zion, O God, there shall be singing, and in Jerusalem prayer shall ascend unto Thee ...

It was Mildenburg, of course. There was no mistaking that rich, assured purity of voice.

Oh dear God! thought Alma-Maria. She lowered her veil over her face so that nobody should note her distress. She had let it happen again. She had let them take him from her, all the people who had never had a good word for him in life, and those who had exploited his genius for their own ends. She had let them kidnap him ... Pappi and Gustav: the only people in the whole world she had truly loved and who had truly loved her despite all her faults; they had taken them from her, stitched them up in a golden pall, surrounded them with military uniforms, smothered them in ceremony, and porphyrized them into public monuments – and all this to ensure that their daemon did not pop out of their coffins like Strauss's Till Eulenspiegel, and rush about the world pulling faces and proclaiming their lust for God's creation with indecent enthusiasm.

As the Liturgy for the Dead proceeded on its solemn and safe way, she sat at her prie-dieu increasingly unaware of her surroundings. She was possessed by the single thought: that they had leaded her little Gustl in so securely, with such a weight of ritual, that never again would she be able to put her arms about him, to warm his poor emaciated form, and to reassure him of her undying love ... and finally to draw him in her arms heavenwards.

A week after they had finally laid Gustav to rest in the quiet of the village churchyard at Grinzing, his succesor at the Vienna Court Opera, Felix Weingartner, came to the Villa Möll on the Hohe Warte. In the bottom drawer of the bureau in the Director's office, he had found, lying in a corner in a heap, the orders, ribbons and medals awarded to Mahler by Imperial and municipal authorities not only in Austria, but also in St Petersburg, Warsaw, Berlin, Hamburg, Paris, and Madrid. Clearly, Mahler had thrown them into the drawer and had never given them another thought. Weingartner had thought it appropriate that his widow should have them.

'I suppose they should have been placed on your husband's bier,' he remarked.

Poor Gustl couldn't have borne the weight of more ornamentation, thought Alma-Maria.

'Let the Opera keep them, Herr Director,' she told Weingartner. 'They'll serve to remind them of what they lost. For myself, I don't need any reminding.'

She picked up the framed photograph of him which she had brought down from her room when Weingartner had been announced, and carried it back upstairs. She carried it with her everywhere she went. When nobody was about, and in the long watches of the night, she talked to him so that he wouldn't be lonely.

'This is Anna Mahler speaking. Do you want to speak to my Mutti? . . .'

Alma-Maria looked across the room to the table by the window where Gucki was answering the telephone.

'Gucki, *liebchen*, who is it?'

She struggled to sit up. She had been lying on the sofa with her shoes off. She put down the liqueur glass she had been holding on the tray on the stool beside her, next to the half-empty Benedictine bottle. It stuck to her fingers, but she managed to loose hold of it without upsetting anything.

'No, she's not asleep, Grandpappi Carl,' Gucki said into the telephone. 'I think she's coming.'

There had been one time, last autumn, when she had first moved into the new Haus Mahler on the Wollergasse, when Gucki had answered the telephone and had told whoever was on the other end of the line that 'Mutti was busy upstairs talking to Pappi.' At least that wasn't going to happen again.

Her head wasn't in the least fuddled, but her movements were slightly unsteady – probably, if she were realistic, too slightly for Gucki to notice. Nevertheless, she was glad she kept an armchair by the table so that, having successfully navigated her course across the living room, she could sink into it as she took the telephone.

'Hello Carl?'

'Almschi? A young, poor, starving genius has just turned up on our doorstep, with a letter of introduction from Berta Zuckerkandl. He says he wants to paint you. In fact, he says it has been his ambition for several years now. You have seen some of his work with me, actually – at the Kunstschau Exhibition, last year. His name is Oskar Kokoschka.'

She remembered his work: a series of lithographic designs, disturbing and sensual, for what were supposed to be children's verses in the *Wunderhorn* style, but which were obviously his own nightmarish con-coctions; a huge, terrifying line drawing entitled, apparently after a play which he had written, *Murderer, The Hope of Women;* and in quite different mode, a lovely mountain scene in oils on canvas of the Dolomites, 'Winter Landscape'. She remembered she had thought when she had seen the latter how much she would have liked to have bought it for Gustav, and how much he would have appreciated it.

Somebody had pointed Kokoschka out to her, saying how impressed Klimt had been by his work. She recalled a young man in a frayed, shabby suit, his shirt collar and cuffs rimmed with dirt, and with the uppers of his shoes broken. He had had the most beautiful eyes; his lank dark hair had fallen at a slant across his brow, and his eyes had a wary slant about them to match. He had had a coarse, heavy lipped mouth and strong chin which had matched the roughness of his dress. He had excited her enough for her to have recalled his appearance in photographic detail.

'I don't know,' she replied down the telephone. 'I must have time to think.'

Möll said, 'If I were in your position, I'd let him paint me.' And he laughed.

'Very well, Carl. Let him come round here,' she replied.

She could always take one look at him and send him away.

Of course, Möll had his own reasons for encouraging a good-looking young artist to come round to the Wollergasse to ask if he could paint her – and not only because a portrait of Gustav Mahler's widow would attract attention to a struggling painter. Both Möll and Mutti were anxious to lure her away from Paul Kammerer.

It had been a strange year for her, since Gustav's death. First, there had been his will. She had found herself to be a great deal wealthier than she had expected. She was the inheritor of 179,000 kreutzers in securities, 19,000 in real estate, and Gustav's manuscripts were now reckoned to be worth the considerable sum of 10,000 kreutzers. She had her widow's pension from the Court Opera and the Philharmonic, her Privy Councillor's pension, and she was the possessor of four homes – the Haus Mahler on the Hohe Warte, a flat in the Elisabethstrasse in the centre of Vienna, the apartments at Toblach, and a new summer home at Semmering. On top of this, she was in receipt of pensions from the Metropolitan Opera, and the New York Philharmonic. She discovered, moreover, that though she had believed herself to have been managing Gustav's finances, unbeknown to her he had prudently invested more than a hundred thousand dollars in American securities in her name.

Joseph Fraenkel had come over from New York. Then, only two or three months after Gustav's death, she had still wished she could have died with him. Fraenkel had suggested that she should accompany him on a cruise of the Adriatic. It dawned on her through her bereavement that he was in love with her, and it had been that which had brought him to Vienna. Nevertheless, she agreed to go with him, inspired by the notion that they would revisit scenes she had first visited with Pappi. It was the first time for months she had been touched by the anticipation of a pleasurable experience. It was the first time she had felt the least inclination to go along with Mahler's wish, as expressed in his will, that she was not to wear mourning; that she was 'to see people and enjoy their company, and to go to concerts, the opera, the theatre, and to travel as much and as freely as she may desire'.

472

Fraenkel was an elderly man, already suffering from the cancer of the intestine which was to kill him. But he was an agreeable, gentle companion, who did not impose himself on her, but sought only to guide her back to life. At Durazzo, however, a second companion attached himself to her, who completed the work Dr Fraenkel had begun. This was a senior minister in the Albanian government who was sailing to Corfu. There was at the time one of those periodic crises in Balkan affairs which anybody like Alma-Maria found as tedious as they were incomprehensible, and which effectively prevented her from reading the centre pages of the newspapers. A dispute had broken out as to whether the port of Scutari should be administered by the Albanians or by Serbia's client kingdom of Montenegro. Standing leaning over the taff-rail, the Albanian minister, a handsome, bull-necked and broad-should-ered, swarthy mountain bandit, asked her for her opinion. Alma-Maria's mind wandered back to her stay at the sanatorium at Tobelbad, and the Quartermaster-Major of Uhlans. She remembered how his soldier servant had been murdered by a Serbian assassin. She repeated what the poor old fool had said.

'I think the important thing, Your Excellency, is that the Serbians be taught a lesson. Belgrade has to learn that the Balkans don't exist as its private playground.'

'My dear lady!' the Albanian minister exclaimed. 'We have here a beautiful woman who not only follows the development of foreign issues, but has the most perceptive views on the subject!'

During the latter part of the voyage, sickness kept Dr Fraenkel in his cabin. The Albanian minister became her regular dinner companion. He entranced her with his accounts of the semi-legendary history of the rugged coastline down which they were sailing, and the ruthless chivalry of the rival mountain tribes which inhabited it. He told her,

'You must always remember, dear lady, whenever there is discussion of the affairs of the western Balkan nations, that there is a saying common to all of us – 'Not the murderer, but the victim is the guilty party'. To let oneself become a victim – that is the greatest of all crimes. You should tell your Emperor and his ministers so when next they are faced with some trouble stirred up by the Serbians, eh?'

For some reason, the proverb echoed and re-echoed in her mind. *Not the murderer, but the victim is the guilty party.* She even wrote it into the travel journal she had begun to keep. It was so entirely opposed to the Jewish-inspired fatalism that one found in so much of Viennese art and letters.

Just two nights before they put into Corfu, the Albanian made the proposal which she had been expecting – that she should go down with him to his cabin. She agreed. But when she placed herself in his arms – she, so small against his powerful bulk – she told him,

'You must promise always to remember something, my dear. I am

473

giving myself to you freely. I'm not a victim of your seductive ways.'

He replied, 'Really, dear lady – you are the most remarkable woman I have ever met. I truly believe it.'

Returning to her own cabin afterwards, she knew that she had experienced pleasure. The fact that she was still a long way removed from knowing happiness somehow legitimized the adventure.

She and Dr Fraenkel had bidden the Albanian minister farewell after he had driven them to their hotel in Corfu from the harbour in his motor car. Bowing over her hand, and holding it with just the slightest hint of intimacy, he had reminded her,

Don't forget what you must tell the members of your government when you go home ... ?'

'Not the murderer, but the victim is the guilty party.'

'Quite correct. What a most remarkable lady you are, my dear! ... And your Emperor, if you should see him, eh?'

'What did he mean?' Dr Fraenkel had asked.

'It's an Albanian proverb,' she explained.

'It sounds an extremely dangerous one to me,' he said.

She had shrugged. Another proverb had come into her head as she watched the car drive away out of the gate and onto the dusty street beyond:

Amo – rather than *cogito – ergo sum*.

Mind you, the experience with him hadn't been love. But there had been enough regret in her at his going to be a pointer.

With her return to Vienna, loneliness had returned. Perhaps settling into the Haus Mahler instead of staying with Möll and Mutti had been a mistake. After his return to New York, Dr Fraenkel had written to her asking if he might return to Europe to see her again. But she had been afraid of encouraging him further. She wrote back:

> ... You are intellect, an embodied brain. I am earthy, and I know it. We must remain parted because of the divergence of our souls. When I am allowed to return to true life, it will be a physical life rooted in nature and the earth because they are the eternal source of all existence ...

She was too kind to tell him that what she longed for was a sense of youth and health and an affirmative view of creation which, she had always suspected, was denied to the members of the Jewish intelligentsia with whom she had constantly been surrounded in the past.

She sat one night on her bed with her safe-deposit box, and took from it the manuscript draft score of Gustav's uncompleted Tenth Symphony with its accompanying sketches and comments, and its scribbled cries of anguish about her and directed at her. On the bedside table under the electric lamp was the new bronze of Gustav's death mask, cast by Möll. The expression on the face was that of a smiling, peaceful resignation – no suggestion of a struggle to retain life.

The contrast between the two – the bitter outcry of the symphony compared to the gentle passivity of the bronze sleeping face awoke memories of old resentments. A thread of a suspicion ran through her mind that Gustav had allowed himself to slip away from her, and that the sufferings expressed across the manuscript scores, the terrible cries which had first inspired her to devote herself to him had been an illusion only of an appetite for love and living.

She had locked the symphony back in the safe-deposit box. She put it down on the floor beside the bed, and laid her head on the pillow, gazing into the bronze face on the table beside her.

'You know, Gustl?' she said aloud. 'I'm never going to allow anybody to perform that symphony. Ever!'

She had meant it as a punishment for his desertion of her.

During that autumn, she had attended the rehearsal of a concert piece by one of Gustav's young admirer-disciples, an erstwile pupil of Alex von Zemlinsky, Franz Schreker. Hearing that the widow Mahler was there in the darkened auditorium, the young composer had searched her out to pay homage to her. He was enjoying a brief period of success at the time – Gustav had been a strong advocate of his first opera, *Der Ferne Klang*. She invited him to come to visit her in her Elisabethstrasse flat. They spent a brief holiday together at Abbazia, rode to the top of Veprinaz Mountain and played four hand duets on the old, out of tune organ in the little church perched up on the summit.

On their return to Vienna, she had asked him to come up to the new house on the Wollergasse to play over a new opera in the presence of Otto Klemperer. Although he was no older than Alma-Maria herself, already Klemperer, by virtue of talent and success, had developed a magisterial presence. Schrecker had clearly been in awe of the famous conductor. His explanation of the new opera's plot was reduced to an incoherent recital of 'And there is ... and in comes ... and then there's this woman ...' Klemperer sat stiffly, a look of sarcastic wonderment on his face. Schrecker sat at Mahler's old Broadwood concert grand, and played through the first act. Klemperer sat behind him. Occasionally he cast a glance of ironic amusement in Alma-Maria's direction.

At the end of the first act, there was silence. Schrecker broke it.

'Well?' he said. 'What's the verdict?'

Klemperer gave a shrug. 'There's nothing there,' he said brutally.

'What do you mean?' Schrecker asked, his voice rising to a wail. 'There's this theme ... and this *motif* ...'

Klemperer smiled in Alma-Maria's direction.

'I don't hear them,' Klemperer told him. He went to the piano stool. 'My turn,' he said.

Schreker yielded his place to him. Klemperer played a piece of his own. He described it as a *ballade* but, in fact it was no more than a typical Viennese confection in three-four time.

'I *do* like that!' Schrecker had exclaimed. 'Herr Klemperer, would you allow me to play that in my next recital?'

Not the murderer, but the victim is guilty ...

Alma-Maria had felt nothing but contempt at the episode. She could not have borne having Schrecker spend another night in her arms.

In early December had come the greatest event since Gustav's passing. Bruno Walter had telephoned her, asking her to come as guest of honour to the first performance of Mahler's *Das Lied von der Erde*, to be given, like the first performance of the Eighth, in the New Exhibition Hall, Munich:

'We have chosen two young American artists to sing the solo parts – they both sang for Gustav in New York – Sarah-Jane Cahier and William Miller. The knowledge that you were in the audience would be more of an inspiration to them than I can possibly say ... And, of course, dear Alma, to me too ...'

She had made the eight-hour journey from Vienna to Munich in the company of Alban Berg and Anton Webern. Both clearly regarded the trip as a pilgrimage. Webern summed up their feelings:

'We're expecting to hear the most wonderful music there is ... Something of such magnificence as has never yet existed.'

She had stayed by herself in the Hotel Vier Jahreszeiten; she could not have borne staying at the Hotel Grand Continental again, with all its memory of rediscovering the full flood of her love for Gustl. In the suite next to hers were staying Thomas and Katia Mann who offered to accompany her to the concert, an offer she accepted eagerly.

Again, Munich was filling up with figures from the musical and literary world. But the atmosphere was entirely different, as if all were gathering to attend a great memorial service and to hear the last musical will and testament of the deceased. There were no princes and princesses in glittering uniforms and gowns or statesmen in ribbons and orders. But there was a procession of distinguished men and women to the Hotel Vier Jahreszeiten to pay their respects to Alma-Maria. Ferruccio Busoni came with his wife, Gerda. Alma-Maria felt peculiarly close to him because of his devotion to the dying Gustav those last days in New York.

'Now he's not with us, he seems to grow ever more beautiful. What purity there was in that soul!' he said to her.

One thing which surprised her about so many who spoke to her of Gustav as if he had been a saint (as, indeed, Möll had done) was that they were not themselves Jewish.

The huge audience in the Exhibition Hall listened intently to Bruno Walter's faithful interpretation of Mahler's score. There was a tension between the two young American singers and those listening such as occurs in the theatre when the actors in a great drama have brought the audience completely under their spell.

Alma knew the music. She had played it over with Gustav many times. And yet ... as with the Eighth, its immediate predecessor, she found that she had hardly known it. There was such a richness of creative imagination gone into the scoring. Nor had she realized that *Der Abschied* – the Farewell which constituted the last movement and a Mahlerian *adagio* to end all *adagios,* was as long as the rest of the entire work. Sarah-Jane Cahier's pure contralto poured out the liquid sound of Gustav's adieu to earthly life.

> I go wandering now in the mountains.
> I seek peace for my lonely heart.
> I wander to my homeland, my abode.

The great calm of the music, the gentleness of its message of reconciliation, was not what she had expected. Gustav had loved her, and because of her he had loved life. The sense of shock which came over her as she listened was in no way blunted by the fact that it confirmed all her suspicions regarding a Jewish quietism, a leaning towards surrender, which had lurked in his soul.

> Everywhere the good earth
> Once more grows green and blossoms into spring.
> Everywhere, for ever, distant spaces shine light blue.
> For ever ... For ever ... For ever ...

The voice died on the ever-fading repetition of the words, *for ever.*

Thomas and Katia Mann thought she had been overcome by the emotion which had seized the entire audience. In the same dramatic stillness with which the work had been heard, they assisted her from the box. As they supported her down the foyer stairs, the applause exploded behind them as if it would burst the doors asunder, and pealed on as they took her in the bitter early December night, across the concourse to their parked car.

When she was alone in her room, she wept and beat Gustav's bronze death mask until her knuckles started to bleed through the satin of her evening gloves.

She returned to Vienna the following day. Deliberately she avoided the company of Webern, Berg, the Schoenbergs, or anybody else who was likely to enthuse about what she knew to be one of Gustav's greatest works – if not *the* greatest. She drank as she did not usually drink, wilfully, deliberately, to kill pain. In the Pullman car she encountered – bumped into – Paul Kammerer, a distinguished and charming professor of biology at Vienna who had been to Munich to hear the concert. She had met him previously. She told him, as they sat together in the Pullman, that she had taken that particular train to avoid any fuss over the concert. To his intense gratification, she positively encouraged him

477

to talk about his work, bestowing on him the look of intense and concentrated interest which had not failed her since she was a young girl. As she observed, with a clarity which pushed aside the befuddlement of her drinking, the arousal in him of physical interest in her, she felt as though a warm breath of life was touching her cheek, as though the moon of Gustav's *Abschied*, 'floating like a silver ship on the night's blue sea', was gliding away from her ... far, far away.

She went, laughing, to Professor Kammerer's private berth. Before they stepped down onto the platform at the end of their journey, they had made arrangements to meet again. She had never seduced a married man before. It had been an entirely new adventure. She had even agreed to go to his laboratories disguised as a laboratory maid. It had seemed amusing at the time ...

'Frau Alma?' Kathi had come upstairs; she was wiping her hands on her blue kitchen apron.

Kathi had sacrificed a love left behind in New York for her mistress.

'There is a Herr Oskar ...'

She hesitated. Alma-Maria smiled affectionately at her.

'Kokoschka?' she suggested.

'That's him, Frau Alma. Thank you.'

He always signed his canvases, 'OK' which, since she had been in New York, always amused her. So let's see if he is OK, she thought, as she pulled herself up off the chair.

He was standing in the darkened hall, at the foot of the stairs. A shaft of light through the window from the street light immediately outside fell across his face and upper breast. He was exactly as she had remembered, she thought, as she clutched the banister to steady herself: a handsome figure, beautiful slanting eyes like those of an ancient Hunnish marauder, and a disturbingly coarse mouth. He was holding a shabby overcoat about him with fists dug into his pockets. Under his arm, she could see even in the semi-dark a board with sheets of cartridge paper. She pointed at it.

'My dear Herr Kokoschka! You don't waste any time, do you?'

'Not if I can help it, Frau Alma.'

'I have two living rooms, Herr Kokoschka. One, I have dedicated to poetry and the written word ...' She pointed vaguely upstairs behind her ... 'The other, I have dedicated to music.' She indicated the doorway leading off the hall. 'I think the Muses of painting and music are very close, don't you Herr Kokoschka?'

He nodded. He never took his eyes off her. She wondered if he were trying to hypnotize her.

'Katchen – bring coffee and liqueurs to the music room, would you?'

'Yes, Frau Alma.'

EPILOGUE
A PARTICULAR
JUDGEMENT: 1938

 GUCKI HAD BEEN before her; she had booked the hotel suite and had filled it with red roses. Alma-Maria was both touched and grateful. Even before she removed her coat and shoes, she rang for room service and ordered a bottle of Benedictine and of Moselwein to be brought up to her. She told herself that it would probably take more than a few drinks to eradicate the images of the train journey from Vienna to Prague from her fatigued brain.

She had been frightened all the way – conscious both physically and mentally of the gold and bank bills stitched in thick wads under the satin lining of her girdle, and of Mahler's autographed and annotated scores bearing the stamp of the Musikverein and the Vienna Philharmonic in her suitcases. At the Austro-Czechoslovakian frontier, everybody had been ordered off the train. Hundreds of people had stood huddled on the small wooden platform, their luggage heaped around them, in the cold, grey March afternoon. Women and children had given way to fear and had sat sobbing on their suitcases, clutching at each other for comfort.

There had been a second train, its engine pointing back in the direction of Vienna, standing at the platform opposite. German soldiers accompanied by docile Austrian police and customs men were pushing through the crowds shouting,

'Jews! Show your papers!'

A woman standing beside Alma-Maria watched the stream of men,

479

women, and children being directed across to the other train, wearily, forlornly humping their luggage with them.

'Fancy all those Jews,' she said, 'trying to smuggle their money out of Austria.'

The elderly man standing behind her said,

'That's what's been happening ever since the war. That's why we've had to let the Germans take us over. The Jews have been smuggling their money out of the country for years. Little Dollfuss tried to stop them, and look what happened to him – and then the Jew-press said the National Socialists had murdered him. Thank God I've lived long enough to see them get what they deserve, that's what I say!'

A black-uniformed German officer with two shabbily dressed Austrian policemen behind him rapped his cane on the woman's suitcase.

'Open! Immediately, if you please.'

'I'm not a Jew!' the woman exclaimed. 'I'm going to Prague to see my daughter – just for a few days.'

'Open, if you please.'

'That's what the Jews have brought down on our heads,' the elderly man said to Alma-Maria, glancing at the tiny party-member swastika badge she had pinned in the lapel of her coat.

The German officer, a smooth-cheeked, good-looking young man smiled slightly at her, as if suggesting that the protesting which was going on was all too typical of Austrian slovenliness. When he had finished his leisurely examination of the woman's luggage, he left her to sort out the confusion of toiletries, night attire and underwear, and smiled again mischievously in Alma-Maria's direction before passing on to his next victims. Alma-Maria had looked to her French maid, Ida, for support. She had thought she was about to black out.

Now, at last, she felt safe. Immediately outside the windows, the mists from the Moldau – or the Vltava, as the Czechs stupidly insisted on calling it – hung over the labyrinthine tangle of narrow streets, stairs, and courts of the old city. Beyond that lay the forests and mountains of the Sudetenland, and the famous defences manned by the Czech army, reputedly the best officered and best equipped army in Europe east of the Rhine. It was going to be a long and complicated journey back to her own and Werfel's apartment in Paris – avoiding Germany by travelling via Budapest, Zagreb, Trieste, and Milan – and she had telegraphed Werfel to meet her in Milan.

She asked Ida to open her overnight case. From it – always the first or second thing she did when staying somewhere – she took out the bronze of Mahler's death mask and placed it on the bedside table where she could talk to him if she felt lonely during the night. Then she pulled up her skirt and slip and, with Ida's help, at last divested herself of her heavy, cumbersome girdle. Ida just had time to drop it behind the bed – where it thumped like a deep-sea diver's leaded belt – before a waiter brought in the tray of drinks with some sandwiches. He stayed to open the wine. When he had gone, Alma-Maria poured a glass for Ida, and opened the Benedictine for herself. As she gave the maid the wine, she kissed her cheek and said in French,

'Thank you for sharing the danger with me. I could not have faced it alone. I'm so grateful, my dear.'

She lay back on the bed, kicked off her high-heeled shoes – a stupid vanity to compensate for her lack of height which had become a habit long ago – and watched Ida as she unpacked.

Gucki had prepared her way from Vienna with the same thoroughness as she herself had used to prepare Mahler's journeys. There was much in the girl – thirty-three-year-old woman – she had inherited from her father. For all her attractiveness – and though she was never beautiful as Alma-Maria had been, or her half-sister, Manon, she had no difficulty whatever in attracting people of both sexes – there was something in her features which reminded Alma-Maria of Mahler's solemnity and spiritual vision. It was, perhaps, because of that they had never succeeded in quarrelling to the point of detaching themselves from one another. Their lives had become a switchback of ferocious quarrelling and reconciliation.

It had started when, at the age of fifteen, Gucki had suddenly refused to play four hand versions of Wagner with Alma-Maria – she had inherited her mother's talent for sight-reading at the keyboard – stating her preference for Bach. It had reduced Alma-Maria to tears. Six months of continuous bickering later, Gucki flounced off to marry the first in a succession of wholly unsuitable husbands. When, fourteen years later, she finally succeeded in forming a stable relationship, it had been with a woman, a stiff-upper-lip Englishwoman. Alma-Maria finally gave vent to her long pent-up feelings, telling her that she only really existed between her waist and her knees. Gucki's earliest training in her life vocation to fine art had been sketching, from the age of seven, her mother's lovers, and watching Kokoschka paint his huge canvas ('Die Windsbraut'), depicting himself and her mother in post-coital repose. She laughed at her mother, but did not reply to her charge with the expected *tu quoque*. Instead, she pointed out with cruel accuracy that her mother was envious of her artistic success – Gucki had been commissioned to sculpt the official bust of the Chancellor of the Austrian Republic, Kurt von Schuschnigg, in 1935 and in 1937 had won the Paris World Exhibition Grand Prix for a larger than lifesize sculptured group, whereas her mother had made not the least attempt to pick up her career as a composer. That particular encounter had left Alma-Maria wondering from where Gucki had inherited such hardness and cruelty. Certainly not from her father, though in all probability she had inherited from him her obsessive creative drive.

During the past two years, Gucki had given Alma-Maria another cause for worry. She had begun openly proclaiming what most people were seeking to conceal – her Jewishness, or part-Jewishness. She was using her acquaintanceship with Chancellor Schuschnigg to warn the government of the Republic, and anybody else who would listen to her strident outpourings, of what was likely to happen to Austrian Jewry if the National Socialists ever succeeded in seizing control of the Hofburg. Fearful of offending the extreme right wing in Austria and Austria's northern neighbour alike, Schuschnigg had banned her from the environs of the Austrian Chancellery. When, on 11 March, Schuschnigg, as a result of a German ultimatum, cancelled the proposed referendum on whether the Austrian people would prefer independence to annexation into the Third Reich, Gucki had telephoned Alma-Maria to come to Vienna to rescue as many of Mahler's relics – his scores, letters, books – as she could, before the National Socialists obliterated them as they had tried to obliterate all memorials of Mendelssohn in Germany.

Alma-Maria had felt uneasy enough to have decided to visit Carl Möll, and the Eberstallers, her half-sister Marie and her husband, on the Hohe Warte. But there had lurked in her mind the thought that Gucki was simply giving way to typically Jewish hysteria. Despite having lived with a Jew, Franz Werfel, for the best part of twenty years, and been married to him for nine, and knowing what his family had been suffering for the past four years in Germany, she felt admiration for what Hitler had achieved:

'I see in him the embodiment of German idealism – something which Jews are incapable of understanding, alas!'

Conversations with a dear friend, Margherita Sarfatti, Mussolini's favourite mistress, at the apartment in Venice overlooking the Salute which she and Werfel had bought as their first shared love-nest, had convinced her of the truths embodied in Fascism. From that, it was only a short step to see the triumph of Mussolini in Italy and Hitler in Germany as the twentieth-century equivalent of the triumph of Elizabeth of England in Schiller's *Maria Stuart* – the triumph of the ruler who embodies a nation's sacred will. Hitler was the reincarnation of Wagner's Siegfried, who had reforged the broken sword of German national pride and had slain the dragon of a panic despair, and whom a lower order of humankind, motivated not by pride in race and nationhood, but by self-seeking acquisitiveness, would seek to pull down as surely as the evil Hagen had slain Siegfried.

There had been a confusion in her mind – a relationship in her own view – between the sufferings of the German peoples and her own emotional turmoil over a quarter of a century. So much had gone wrong since Mahler's death. When Kokoschka had come into her life, she gave up playing the laboratory maid and her affair with Paul Kammerer. Kammerer caused a public scandal by attempting to shoot himself over Mahler's grave in Grinzing churchyard. The relatively brief though passionate affair with Kokoschka ended when Gropius had come into her life again (she had started sleeping once more with Gropius even while little Gucki was standing in Kokoschka's studio watching him paint himself with her Mutti). The outbreak of war with Serbia and Russia in 1914 meant Kokoschka having to join the army, thus leaving the way open for her to marry Gropius. The fact that Gropius was a member of a distinguished non-Jewish German family had been a factor in her agreeing to marry him. More to the point was that she had been pregnant. During the early days of the marriage, when her pregnancy was not yet obvious, she met Franz Werfel, already a notable lyric poet. Gropius followed Kokoschka to the war. She fell in love with Werfel, whose poems to her were the finest artistic achievements inspired by her since Mahler's *adagietto* to his Fifth Symphony and his *Rückertlieder*. At that time she had not yet realized that he was a Jew.

Despite her desertion, Gropius maintained the pretence of their marriage in order to give Alma-Maria's baby, Manon, a name. However, she had convinced herself that Werfel represented her true destiny. Jew or no Jew, he represented German letters as surely as Mahler had represented German music. Then Kokoschka returned to Vienna, and the embers of an old passion flared up one more. She became pregnant yet again. Their baby was a boy, Martin.

Then the world ended. Vienna had always been far from the war. Until late in 1917, the Old Man had still presided over the Hofburg. Then he died, and it was all over. The musical and intellectual capital of Europe became a ruined, bankrupt provincial city. Plague and famine stalked the streets. Bodies of children, swollen with hunger, lay in the doorways. Entire families, struck down by the pandemic of Spanish influenza, lay neglected and decomposing in their homes. Over the corpses in the gutters, gangs of starving, demobilized soldiers fought each other in the name of monarchy, socialism, anarchy, or anything else which provided a soup kitchen and a label of identity. Alma-Maria had locked herself in her apartment on the Elisabethstrasse. There she sat behind closed shutters and watched her baby boy slowly die. She truly believed the days of the Apocalypse had come.

It was to Werfel she turned in those days of despair. At a time when she was drained of passion, he was unfailingly patient, kind and gentle. Kokoschka punished her for her desertion even more spectacularly than Paul Kammerer had done. He toured the nightmare streets of Vienna in an open *fiacre* drawn by a spavined skeleton of a horse. Beside him he had a life-size and realistic dummy representing the naked Alma-Maria, onto which he had painted her distinctive features, and had furnished with a wig of appropriately luxuriant hair both for her head and her crotch. In fact, the spectacle had not greatly shocked her; it seemed no more than a nightmare feature of an increasingly nightmarish world.

Gropius divorced her. She did not rush into another marriage. She lived openly with Werfel, but did not influence him deliberately into breaking with a family which was a deal more earnest in its Jewish observance than Mahler's family or relatives had ever been. She was fortunate in one respect at least. She was possessed of considerable securities in Rome, Paris, and above all in New York, so that she remained reasonably well off despite the monstrous inflation which afflicted all central Europe. Moreover, despite the scandals which her behaviour gave rise to, she retained the love and respect of a number of people whose opinion mattered to her – men like Schoenberg, Bruno Walter, Richard Strauss, Thomas Mann, Klemperer, Schnitzler, and Stefan Zweig.

Wherever she travelled, and she led a nomadic, restless life during the ensuing fifteen years, she attracted a salon of musical and literary talent about her. Werfel himself, who by the time they were married in 1929 had become recognized as a figure equal to none in German letters save Thomas Mann and was a candidate for a Nobel prize, was always a loyal, dependable, if not passionate husband who, unlike Mahler, took her infidelities in his stride without suggesting in any way that they disturbed his psychological balance. For her own part, she blunted the edges of her own emotional make-up more with Benedictine than sexual affairs. She was never really tipsy. Getting oneself tipsy was, in her opinion, a Jewish trait. None of the Jews she associated with, she had decided, had any head for drink. Werfel never became tipsy: he always vomited long before he had a chance to be drunk.

Werfel had another, considerable claim on her affections as well as his tolerance of her waywardness, and his gentleness. Alone among those with whom she had shared her bed since Mahler's death, he had raised no objection to the presence of Mahler's death mask by the lamp beside her. While she respected him for it, the thought had come to her that it was yet another proof of Jewish quietism.

In 1935, fate had struck her yet another terrible blow. Her adored and gloriously beautiful nineteen-year-old actress daughter, Manon, suffered an agonizing deterioration and death from poliomyelitis. During the last dreadful weeks of her life, a procession of those who had loved her passed through Haus Mahler on the Hohe Warte – the Strausses, the playwright Carl Zuckmayer who had been hoping to complete a play for her, the aged Gerhard Hauptmann, Werner Krauss and Franz Horch, both leading actors of the German stage, and, above all, Alban Berg who, although happily and devotedly married, had adored Manon since her earliest childhood, and who was already at work on the violin concerto ('To the Memory of an Angel') which was to prove her true epitaph.

As Manon had lain dying on Easter Day, 1935, staring out of her bedroom window at the garden, she said to Alma-Maria,

'Let me die in peace, Mutti. I know I'm never going to get better, so stop telling people to talk about me acting again ... You'll get over it quickly enough. You always get over everything.'

It was, thought Alma-Maria, the single most terrible thing that had ever been said to her. The words sounded in her head over and over again long after Manon's poor wasted body had been laid beside Mahler's in Grinzing churchyard. She couldn't understand why she had said it. It wasn't as if Manon had been Gucki. There had never been any real fights between them – and Manon had adored Werfel as he had adored her. It was then she had started to drink more heavily – Benedictine at breakfast, wine and beer all through the day, and then Benedictine again at night.

In her desperation, she had turned to the Church into which she had been baptized, but which she had barely known even in childhood. She went for instruction to Father Johannes Hollnsteiner, who had been her dinner companion at the state banquet presided over by Chancellor Schuschnigg in the Hofburg, in honour of Cardinal Innitzer's enthronement in St Stephen's Cathedral. Father Hollnsteiner was one of Vienna's most distinguished priests. Professor of Theology at the University, though only in his mid-thirties, tall, immensely handsome, with a true Viennese courtesy and charm, it was said that the only reason he was not occupying Cardinal Innitzer's place was his comparative youth, and that he would certainly prove to be Innitzer's successor as Cardinal-Archbishop of Vienna.

Father Hollnsteiner and Alma-Maria spent many hours together in her garden that summer while Werfel toured abroad giving readings of his poetry and promoting his latest novel, *The Forty Days of Musa Dagh*. She was formally received back into the bosom of the Church. But Father Hollnsteiner had fallen in love with her. She was, she discovered, the first woman he had ever slept with. But he was quite different from Mahler. Once instructed by her, it took him very little time to become as proficient a lover as the best she had known. On her account, he took rooms over a shop near the cathedral; they would go there after High Mass on Sundays, and spend the afternoons and most of the evenings together.

When the time came for Werfel's return from his travels, she knew she had to make a decision. Hollnsteiner was in his mid-thirties. She was approaching her fifty-seventh birthday. She wrote to him:

When you first took me in your arms, I knew you had to be either a scoundrel or an angel. Everything in me demanded that you should be an angel: and so you shall remain forever, in my heart. I know that compared to you, my dear, my husband is shallow – like all Jews, he likes only Italian music and cannot understand our German music and its philosophical profundity. But I can never leave him. Fifteen years cannot be erased from a woman's life, especially when a man has been as relentlessly good and noble to me as he has been. . . .

The moment she had sent the letter, an old desolation had closed around her. Then came to her the realization in her own mirror that the time for passionate, self-consuming physical love was over; the realization of the nonsense she had written, proclaimed by the austere intelligence in the bronze mask beside her; of the absurd and humiliating wreckage she had made of her return to religious observance. What was left to her?

Several nights later, she had taken down the Universal edition of her songs. She had selected three of them with the idea of working them up into a symphony. She had tried to improvise round them on the piano – Mahler's piano. But she had had too much to drink. She fumbled over chords and transitions which should have been child's play, and her fingers slipped from the keys. In her mind she could find nothing with which to create, as if all the great music which had once sounded in her imagination had withered and died from disuse....

There had lurked in her mind the hope that, instead of the fears expressed by Gucki over the telephone, she would find when she arrived in Vienna from Paris the emergence of a new, purified, purposeful Austro-Germany which would inspire in her own self a spiritual invigoration, a sense of meaningful identity.

She had expected to be met at the Westbahnhof, if not by Gucki, then by Möll or her half-sister Marie and her brilliant lawyer husband. In fact there was nobody; only a few people got off the train which had been almost empty, and the platform was all but deserted. As she stood waiting for a porter to come up, she noticed that across the tracks, on the platforms for outgoing trains, the scene was entirely different. There were dense crowds standing jam-packed between heaps of luggage, and so many children one would have supposed it was the school holidays.

She noticed that the porter who carried her suitcases to the cab rank was wearing a swastika badge in the lapel of his uniform. Near the ticket offices there was a choir, as at Christmas – a rough group of grinning faces, however, who were bawling out no Christmas carol but a song she had heard frequently in Germany:

> Storm, storm, storm towers and steeples,
> Ring out the bells!
> Judah has arisen to seize our Reich!
> Germany, awake to thunder out your revenge!

They directed their shouting at the grey-faced men and women who, clutching young children and luggage, hurried to join the crowds on the departure platforms.

She took a cab to her apartment on the Elisabethstrasse. As they drove down the Kärntnerstrasse, she noticed the plate glass window of the German Tourist Office. It contained a huge head-and-shoulders coloured photograph of Hitler. There were banks of flowers placed on the pavement in front of it so that it had become impassable. Around it, as if before some wayside calvary, women of the shopkeeping or respectable servant class were standing or kneeling as if at prayer. At the corner of the Kärntnerstrasse and the Opernring, people were shooting their hands up in the Nazi salute as they passed the policemen on point duty. She noticed that the policemen were all wearing crumpled swastika armbands. She wondered how many weeks they had been carrying them secretly in their pockets.

The cab turned down the Operngasse. They were only a few hundred metres from her apartment now, and she could see the familiar dome of the Sezession building, shabby and in need of a fresh gold coat. A car had been pulled up in front of them. A well-dressed man had jumped out and was running away down the pavement. Suddenly he was hemmed in by a small group of youths with a policeman. The youths were striking at him, aiming kicks at him, driving him up against the wall. The cab driver manoeuvred round the parked car as if nothing was happening. As they drove past, Alma-Maria saw the distinguished-looking, elderly man doubled up against the wall while the youths were kicking him without mercy. Her last impression was of the policeman grinning approvingly out into the street.

The cab driver said the one word, 'Jew', with a shrug of his shoulders.

Alma-Maria said,

'I can't believe it!' And she meant it.

'Never thought the day would come, eh?' said the cab driver.

She saw him smiling in the reflector above his head.

She found a note from Gucki in the apartment; Gucki had been warned by somebody at the Hofburg that her name was high on the Nazis' wanted list, and had decided to leave immediately to stay with a friend in Prague. She had put down the telephone number and address in Prague, and a strong suggestion that Alma-Maria should follow her as quickly as possible.

Alma-Maria's first move was to telephone Father Hollnsteiner at the University to ask his advice about the situation. He assured her that she had nothing to worry about – that there had been a great deal of unnecessary excitement stirred up by a hostile foreign press, largely under the control of world Jewry, of course. And if the Jews in Vienna had stayed quietly in their homes instead of trying to flee abroad, they would have been perfectly safe. Although she had been in Vienna no more than an hour, already Alma-Maria could not believe him.

She called another cab, and set off for the Hohe Warte. There she found her family in a state of triumph. Möll, Mutti, Marie, and her brother-in-law, Kurt Eberstaller, had all joined the National Socialist Movement two years previously. She could forgive Mutti, who looked very old and wasn't at all well, and was now completely under Möll's thumb. Eberstaller was slim, sleek and ambitious, and Marie had grown blonde and hard with the years, a suitable partner for her husband. For

Möll, Alma-Maria felt all the contempt of her adolescent years.

There was celebration that night. Hitler was entering Vienna the following morning to address the crowds in the Heldenplatz outside the Hofburg. Tonight he was in Linz. But more to the point, because of the dismissal of all Jews from government legal posts, Eberstaller was now promoted by Nazi Minister of Justice, Seyss-Inquart, to the position of a senior judge of the Viennese Criminal Court. That night they all drank just a little too much. Eberstaller even presented Alma-Maria – 'by virtue of my office, dearest sister', – with the swastika pin only worn by party members. She did not refuse it: in a flash of clear thinking, despite the wine, she saw that it might prove useful.

Quite amiably, with a tongue loosened by drink, Eberstaller had asked her,

'Tell me, dear Alma-Maria, how was it that the lovely daughter of our beloved Jakob-Emil Schindler came to marry not one but two Jews?'

The reply came straight to her tongue, almost without passing through her head.

'Perhaps, dear brother, you'll ask Carl here how he came to embrace so many Jews as friends?'

She began to recite the names of composers, artists, writers – a list she had not nearly completed when Eberstaller, who believed he could take a joke, laughed loudly, and begged her to stop. Then he noticed his aged father-in–law's embarrassment, nudged him with unseemly vigour, and said to him,

'We all make mistakes, eh Vathi? But some of us make more than others!'

The bully, thought Alma-Maria, was only just below the skin.

Later that night, as she was going up to bed, Möll called her into his studio. In the lamplight, she saw what a frail, pathetic old man he had become. At the same time, the moment he began speaking to her, she remembered another interview with him – in the empty library at Plankenburg, when he had told her that he intended to marry Mutti. There was the same patronizing look of benevolence on the now-sunken features.

'I have to tell you something, Almschi. The single greatest influence on my life was your dear father. The second was Gustav Mahler ... Yes. I know what you're thinking. That's why I wanted to talk to you. You know what St Paul says? "A Jew is not he who is outwardly a Jew, but he who is inwardly a Jew ..."'

She knew the quotation perfectly well. Gustl and she had often discussed it together. She knew also that it carried precisely the opposite burden to that which Möll was placing upon it. It was typical of Möll's shabbiness of mind.

'You see, if you think about it, our beloved Gustav may have been of Jewish parentage, but he didn't have a single Jewish characteristic. He had no false intellectual pretensions. He had no craving for financial gain. In a word, Almschi: I could never have gone along with what our son Eberstaller said just now because, quite simply, Mahler was not a Jew.'

He pulled out a cigar. His hand shook as he rolled it between his fingers and cut off the end.

'May I?' he asked.

She nodded. As he lit it, she said,

'Do you suppose, Carl, that they will allow the Philharmonic to play Gustav's music?'

He stared at her with moist, rheumy eyes. He had never sickened her so much as he groped in his weary old brain for some fresh casuistry.

'The Jews,' he replied carefully, 'have always crucified and stoned to death their own men of exception. We must think of such men in our own time similarly as martyrs to their race. Mahler is yet another victim of the worshippers of the Golden Calf. His reputation and his music will suffer temporarily in the noble cause of German nationhood. But when the Golden Calf has finally been extirpated and its worshippers scattered, there will be time to separate the wheat from the chaff. In the words of Mahler's own "Resurrection" Symphony: "Thou shalt rise up and live again!"'

'Goodnight, Carl,' she said coldly.

She turned on her heel, and went up to her room. She was just able to hear him call after her,

'Almschi! Almscherl!' But she ignored him.

She did not go out the next day. Marie and Eberstaller left for the Hofburg to join the crowd of ministers and high officials who would greet the Führer privately. She heard the bells ring out from the churches, and thought, as she stood on the balcony, that she could hear the shouting.

The following day, she went down into the centre of Vienna with her maid, Ida. She wore the small Party badge in her coat. Ida, being a French national, had nothing to fear. All round the Ring, the Kärntner-strasse, and the Graben, Jews had been dragged from their homes and places of work by uniformed National Socialists, and were being forced with kicks and blows to scrub from walls and pavements the slogans left from the aborted Referendum, 'Vote Yes for Austria', using their own coats, shirts, and petticoats as rags. The uniforms of the Austrian Nazis were shabby, creased, and ill-fitting in comparison with those of the German army officers and soldiers who stood by, observing with super-cilious smiles which were provoked as much by the persecutors as the persecuted.

There was one small group Alma-Maria saw by the Kapuzinerkirche surrounding an elderly, bearded Jew who was on his hands and knees scrubbing the pavement. The Nazis looked very young and fresh-faced under their peaked caps. Several of them carried leather dog whips with which they slapped their boots in a threatening manner. Three or four fluffy blonde shop girls were standing with the Nazi youths. One of them, greatly daring, stepped out in front of the others and kicked the Jew in the bottom with her high-heeled court shoe. When her companions started to laugh approvingly, she did it again, and smiled around for applause. Almost immediately, a helmeted German officer wearing a Hanoverian cuirasse about his collar stepped from nowhere, scattered the group, and addressed the girls. They teetered off down the pavement, glancing angrily over their shoulders. One of them stuck her tongue out at the German. The German watched them go. Once they had disappeared, he turned away leaving the Nazi youths to regroup around the elderly Jew who was still kneeling on the pavement.

Alma-Maria went first to the State Bank. She drew all her savings, and gave them to Ida to take back by cab to the Hohe Warte. She then returned to the Opera. There, she found herself far from welcome. The first thing she noticed was that Rodin's bust of Mahler was gone from the foyer. None of the staff was prepared, or able, to tell her where it had been placed. She became increasingly convinced that the officials she spoke to were actually afraid of her presence there. Ever since Mahler's death she had been accorded the freedom of the house, and she went through to the library. The chief music librarian looked positively sheepish at seeing her, though he greeted her with his customary courtesy. She demanded to the see the scores of *Fidelio, Tristan, Don Giovanni,* and *The Magic Flute* – Mahler's favourite four operas, which he had annotated, and which contained his production notes.

The librarian glanced over his shoulder. An erect, tall figure with the austere expression of a Savonarola, and wearing a suit of clerical black, came forward.

'Frau Mahler-Werfel?' he asked, with the slightest of bows.

She nodded.

'We no longer possess the scores prepared by Director Mahler,' he said.

He gave her a curious glance as he noticed the swastika pin in her coat.

'All scores of our great German music which have been desecrated with Jew-shit, have been destroyed ... Burned,' he added.

She swallowed back the surge of anger which threatened to overwhelm her. Quietly, she told the man,

'I wish to see State Opera Director Krauss.'

Three years ago, Clemens Krauss had conducted the Vienna Philharmonic in a superb performance of Mahler's Seventh Symphony – in her honour, he had told her.

The man smiled sympathetically.

'The Herr State Opera Director knows of your presence in Vienna, Frau Mahler–Werfel. He has given instructions that he is not available to see you.' He shrugged his shoulders. 'For fear of embarrassing you further, perhaps?' he suggested.

She left the Opera and walked the short distance to the Musik-vereingebäude, the home of the Philharmonic. There the orchestra's librarian was a dear old fellow who had been deputy librarian in Mahler's own time. When she was shown into his sanctum, he rose eagerly to greet her. Holding both her hands in his, and glancing about him to ensure there were no secretaries or office clerks to overhear, he said,

'Dear Frau Alma – I was afraid you'd come.'

'Do you have my late husband's annotated scores?' she asked.

He shook his head. 'All the scores annotated by Herr Director Mahler and State Opera Director Walter have been destroyed on orders from the Ministry ... I'm sorry, dear lady, that I'm the one to have to tell you. I had to take them down myself ...' He released her hands and displayed his own. 'Judas hands, Frau Alma – but I have a wife, you see.'

'I know,' she said.

'I've kept something for you,' he said in a voice so low she could hardly hear it.

He looked about him again. Then he took her to the small door which led to the stack in the cellars where aged scores were kept which fashion had passed into a state of disuse and neglect.

'Dear lady, take care on the steps,' he said. As they descended into the reek of dust, cobwebs, and old bindings, he told her, 'Only a week ago, Dr Walter conducted the Philharmonic in a wireless broadcast of Herr Director Mahler's Ninth Symphony. The National Socialists were so angry they waited outside for him. They knew it was his way of saying goodbye to the Philharmonic. They do say the Papal Nuncio in person drove Dr Walter away from here in his official car, straight over the frontier and down to Milan with Dr Walter still in his white tie and tails ...'

He stopped behind the third row of shelves. From under a heavy pile of musty sheet music – worn and ragged band parts – he drew out a wax-covered package.

'There, dear Frau Alma. Do you think you could manage that under your coat? It contains your late husband's scores of Schubert's Great C-major and the last three symphonies of Mozart. It's all I dared to hide away.'

Alma-Maria threw her arms around the old man's neck and wept.

'Oh my dear!' he kept saying to her. 'You mustn't weep. None of us is allowed to weep now. It is forbidden.'

Night and the river fog had closed round the hotel, and the bottle of Benedictine was half empty. She felt the effects of drinking more than usual, perhaps because she was tired from the journey and the emotional impact of the whole Vienna trip. In fact, she felt quite tipsy.

She was lying on the bed with her shoes off and the only light, that from a street lamp outside below the window which filtered through the fog. She should have gone down to the dining room and had something to eat. She had had nothing except the single round of sandwiches in the afternoon. The mixture of Benedictine, wine, and too many cigarettes had dried up her mouth and forged an iron band round her head. She felt like getting into bed fully dressed; she didn't think she was capable of managing on her own, and she didn't want even her long-suffering Ida to see her as she was.

She had stood her favourite photograph of Mahler beside the death mask. She could just make it out in the haunted foggy-yellow light from the window. It had been taken only a month or two before they were married, an enlargement of a snapshot of him standing on the concourse outside the Opera, one hand half in, half out of his jacket pocket, his bared head turned toward her as if he had only that second been made aware of her presence. In his face there was such a brightness, such a smile of joy at seeing her.

'Oh Gustl!' she whispered.

She wanted to tell him how wrong she had been about so many things; how lonely she was. He would understand.

'Dear Gustl!' she said aloud. 'I suppose I'm a Jew now, aren't I? You remember? ... A German in Bohemia? A Bohemian in Austria? A Jew everywhere? ... No home. No home anywhere ... You're not going to tell me I mustn't cry, are you? Of course not. You understood tears like nobody else in the whole wide world ...'

A warm consolation of self-pity was creeping over her. Even the sense of nausea from her drinking was drifting away to a safe distance.

The telephone tore at the stillness of the room and rent it. Gucki, she thought. It had to be Gucki; she was the only person in the world who knew where she was. She wondered whether she could be bothered to answer it. Then she thought of the roses in the room, and Gucki's concern for her. She rolled across the bed and picked up the receiver.

'Hallo? ... Yes?'

The voice – a man's – came from very far away.

'You'll have to speak up you know! I'm quite deaf,' she told whoever it was.

The thought came to her that it might be the police. But what could the Czech police have against her?

'Alma? ... Frau Alma?' the voice shouted at the other end. 'This is Wim Mengelberg! Is that you, Alma? Wim Mengelberg from Amsterdam.'

'Wim!' she exclaimed. 'Oh Wim, it can't be you!'

The sound of a friendly, affectionate voice was as welcome as it was completely unexpected.

'I've been in Vienna, Wim,' she said, as if that would explain the state she was in.

'I know,' he shouted back. 'I've tried every capital in Europe, I think. I managed to reach your daughter in Budapest. She told me where I might catch up with you ... Alma? The Concertgebouw here in Amsterdam is holding a Mahler Festival – yes? ... For a week – the first week in May. Our Concertgebouw President and his Committee, and I, of course, are all hoping you will be present for the week, if you can, as our honoured guest. Is that possible?'

She did not – she could not answer.

'Alma? Are you there?'

'Yes Wim. I'm here.'

'You will be very welcome. You will be very welcome to stay at my house in Wassenaar for as long as you wish. Would it please you?'

'Oh Wim! It would please me more than I can say!'

'That is good, then. You are coming here?'

'Yes. I shall be coming.'

After she had put down the receiver, she turned to look once more at Gustl. She reached out to touch his bronze face. The call had come so aptly, as if the good God had inspired Willem Mengelberg to reach her just at that precise moment, at her most need.

She rested her finger on the bronze lips.

'Gustl,' she said. 'Darling Gustl ... Isn't it wonderful? They shall see how proud – how wonderfully proud I am of my little Gustl!'

She turned onto her back and stared up at the ceiling.

Alma Mahler, she thought. Not Alma-Maria Schindler-Werfel. Not even Alma-Maria Schindler-Mahler-Werfel ... She was, she always would be, *in saecula saeculorum* ... Alma Mahler, amen.

AFTERWORD

ALMA MAHLER died in bed, in her New York apartment, on Friday, 11 December 1964 of pneumonia. She was eighty-five. She had outlived her lovers (Kokoschka excepted), her friends, and her enemies. Werfel, Strauss, von Zemlinsky, Schoenberg, Busoni, Webern and Alban Berg were all gone. Bruno Walter preceded her by a few months. Of her own family, Anna Möll died in Vienna very shortly after Alma had left for Prague. Carl Möll, his daughter and son-in-law, all committed suicide when the Russians were about to enter Vienna in 1945. Alma's other half-sister, Grete, was killed in a mental hospital, a victim of the Nazi euthanasia policy. Alma, who had put her from her mind for over forty years, made no reference to her either in conversation, or in her published reminiscences. Virtually all Mahler's family who were alive at the outbreak of the Second World War died in the Nazi death camps.

Following the German invasion of the Netherlands in the spring of 1940, Willem Mengelberg, whom both Mahler and Alma had always regarded as a particularly close friend, became an active collaborator with the Nazis, did nothing to hinder the despatching of seventeen Jewish members of the Amsterdam Concertgebouw Orchestra to their fate, and publicly declared that he had been wrong in his earlier estimation of Mahler's music. He died in well-deserved obscurity and disgrace in 1953.

Alma lived long enough to witness the resurgence in the 1950s and 1960s of interest in and love for Mahler's work, and to become the idol of a new generation of Mahlerians. She heard the golden recordings of the *Kindertotenlieder*, the *Rückertlieder*, and *Das Lied von der Erde*, made by Kathleen Ferrier with Mahler's own Vienna Philharmonic under Bruno Walter. Leonard Bernstein wrote to her every time he was going to conduct Mahler with the New York Philharmonic Symphony Orchestra; she attended every performance, and as many rehearsals as she could. Benjamin Britten, who had endeavoured to keep Mahler's reputation alive in England during years of neglect, dedicated to her his *Nocturne* op.60, for tenor and small orchestra, 'one of my very best and most personal works', he told her. Before embarking on a recording cycle of Mahler symphonies, Sir Georg Solti paid court to her, and found her blue-eyed gaze hypnotically beautiful (she was then eighty). Finally, she at last gave her consent to the first complete public performance of Deryck Cooke's masterly edition of the Tenth Symphony. She had always obstructed attempts to complete it – usually by greatly exaggerating the extent to which Mahler had left it incomplete (it was fully drafted, with copious indications as to orchestration), or by declaring that Mahler himself had told her he didn't want it performed – a statement for which there was no evidence save her own somewhat unreliable word. In all probability the truth lay in the fact that she associated the Tenth with a deeply painful period in their lives for which she held herself much to blame. It was given by the London Symphony Orchestra under Berthold Goldschmidt only four months before her death. BBC tapes were sent directly to her New York apartment; struggling against ever-increasing deafness, she listened, and was profoundly moved.

To the end, her relationship with Gucki remained a cycle of devotion, ferocious quarrels and reconciliation. She wrote two autobiographies, both of which are notable for their evasions, childish vanity, and downright lies. Her third book, a memoir of Mahler, is far more revealing about herself than about her subject, while being even more conspicuously evasive than her autobiographies.

It has rightly been pointed out that her autobiographical writing has done a great deal more damage to her memory than anything said about her by anybody else – including giving rise to the generally accepted view that the marriage between herself and Mahler was disastrous for both of them. It is highly improbable that either Mahler or Alma would have agreed with such a verdict.

She was never given to underselling herself – except in one vital sphere, her music. Her *Lieder* are rarely performed, and remain unrecorded even in Austria and Germany. Perhaps their limited survival is dependent on her notoriety in other fields. They are not works of genius, but there are a dozen or so of them – including the 'Five Songs' which Mahler had published – which are assured and accomplished examples of musical craftsmanship, the work of a very professional musician. In all probability, she let her talent as composer and musician wither not so much because of Mahler's insistence, but because of a more general prejudice (to which he undoubtedly subscribed) regarding women's role and women's place. The fact that she was a fashionable, flattered, and much sought-after beauty – a 'stunner', to use the late Victorian term – must have done a great deal to have sapped her resolve.

To the end of her life, she continued to drink – Benedictine, white wine, beer, Benedictine – through the day. Latterly, she was sometimes seen to be unsteady, partly, perhaps, on account of her deafness. She was never drunk ad nauseam, or even to the point of embarrassing others. She never wore knickers – and frequently and publicly expressed the opinion that if women had been intended by nature to cover their pudenda, they would have taken to wearing breeches from the beginning, rather than frocks.

To the end, she remained the creature of a battered Austro-German Romanticism; the child of Goethe, Schiller, and Novalis. On her death-bed, in her final delirium, she thought she was a young girl again with Plankenburg Castle as her home. She was climbing the Rofanspitze above the Achensee once more, as she had done so many years before with Max Burckhard. This time, it was Crown Prince Rudolf – the protagonist of the Mayerling tragedy – who was waiting for her on the summit. He was waiting to make love to her so that she might bear him an heir who would restore the Hapsburgs and Austria to their former glory.